The Nursery Rhyme
Murders

The Nursery Rhyme Murders

INCLUDING

A POCKET FULL OF RYE

HICKORY DICKORY DEATH

THE CROOKED HOUSE

By Agatha Christie

DODD, MEAD & COMPANY
New York

Library of Congress Catalog Card Number: 72-117622
Printed in the United States of America

Contents

A Pocket Full of Rye

CHAPTER 1

IT WAS MISS SOMERS' turn to make the tea. Miss Somers was the newest and the most inefficient of the typists. She was no longer young and had a mild worried face like a sheep. The kettle was not quite boiling when Miss Somers poured the water onto the tea, but poor Miss Somers was never quite sure when a kettle was boiling. It was one of the many worries that afflicted her in life.

She poured out the tea and took the cups round with a couple of limp sweet biscuits in each saucer.

Miss Griffith, the efficient head typist, a gray-haired martinet who had been with Consolidated Investments Trust for sixteen years, said sharply: "Water not boiling again, Somers!" and Miss Somers' worried meek face went pink and she said, "Oh dear, I did think it was boiling this time."

Miss Griffith thought to herself: "She'll last for another month, perhaps, just while we're so busy. . . . But really! The mess the silly idiot made of that letter to Eastern Developments—a perfectly straightforward job, and always so stupid over the tea. If it weren't so difficult to get hold of any intelligent typists—and the biscuit tin lid wasn't shut tightly last time, either. Really—"

Like so many of Miss Griffith's indignant inner communings, the sentence went unfinished.

At that moment Miss Grosvenor sailed in to make Mr. Fortescue's sacred tea. Mr. Fortescue had different tea, and different china and special biscuits. Only the kettle and the water from the cloakroom tap were the same. But on this occasion, being Mr. Fortescue's tea, the water boiled. Miss Grosvenor saw to that.

Miss Grosvenor was an incredibly glamorous blonde. She wore an expensively cut little black suit and her shapely legs were encased in the very best and most expensive black-market nylons.

She sailed back through the typists' room without deigning to give anyone a word or a glance. The typists might have been so many black beetles. Miss Grosvenor was Mr. Fortescue's own special personal secretary; unkind rumor always hinted that she was something more, but actually this was not true. Mr. Fortescue had recently married a second wife, both glamorous and expensive, and fully capable of absorbing all his attention. Miss Grosvenor was to Mr. Fortescue just a necessary part of the office décor, which was all very luxurious and very expensive.

Miss Grosvenor sailed back with the tray held out in front of her like a ritual offering. Through the inner office and through the waiting room, where the more important clients were allowed to sit, and through her own anteroom and finally with a light tap on the door she entered that holy of holies, Mr. Fortescue's office.

It was a large room with a gleaming expanse of parquet floor on which were dotted expensive oriental rugs. It was delicately paneled in pale wood and there were some enormous stuffed chairs upholstered in pale buff leather. Behind a colossal sycamore desk, the center and focus of the room, sat Mr. Fortescue himself.

Mr. Fortescue was less impressive than he should have been to match the room, but he did his best. He was a large flabby man with a gleaming bald head. It was his affectation to wear loosely-cut country tweeds in his city office. He was frowning down at some papers on his desk when Miss Grosvenor glided up to him in her swan-like manner. Placing the tray on the desk at his elbow, she murmured in a low impersonal voice, "Your tea, Mr. Fortescue," and withdrew.

Mr. Fortescue's contribution to the ritual was a grunt.

Seated at her own desk again, Miss Grosvenor proceeded with the business in hand. She made two telephone calls, corrected some letters that were lying there typed ready for Mr. Fortescue to sign, and took one incoming call.

"Ay'm afraid it's impossible just now," she said in haughty accents. "Mr. Fortescue is in conference."

As she laid down the receiver she glanced at the clock. It was ten minutes past eleven.

It was just then that an unusual sound penetrated through the almost soundproof door of Mr. Fortescue's office. Muffled, it was yet fully recognizable, a strangled, agonized cry. At the same moment the buzzer on Miss Grosvenor's desk sounded in a long-drawn, frenzied summons. Miss Grosvenor, startled for a moment into complete immobility, rose uncertainly to her feet. Confronted by the unexpected, her poise was shaken. However, she moved towards Mr. Fortescue's door in her usual statuesque fashion, tapped and entered.

What she saw upset her poise still further. Her employer behind his desk seemed contorted with agony. His convulsive movements were alarming to watch.

Miss Grosvenor said, "Oh dear, Mr. Fortescue, are you ill?" and was immediately conscious of the idiocy of the question. There was no doubt that Mr. Fortescue was very seriously ill. Even as she came up to him, his body was convulsed in a painful, spasmodic movement.

Words came out in jerky gasps.

"Tea—what the hell—you put in the tea—get help—quick, get a doctor—"

Miss Grosvenor fled from the room. She was no longer the supercilious blonde secretary. She was a thoroughly frightened woman who had lost her head.

She came running into the typists' office crying out,

"Mr. Fortescue's having a fit—he's dying—we must get a doctor—he looks awful—I'm sure he's dying."

Reactions were immediate, and varied a good deal.

Miss Bell, the youngest typist, said, "If it's epilepsy we ought to put a cork in his mouth. Who's got a cork?"

Nobody had a cork.

Miss Somers said, "At his age it's probably apoplexy."

Miss Griffith said, "We must get a doctor—at once."

But she was hampered in her usual efficiency because in all her sixteen years of service it had never been necessary to call a doctor to the city office. There was her own doctor but that was at Streatham Hill. Where was there a doctor near here?

Nobody knew. Miss Bell seized a telephone directory and began looking up Doctors under D. But it was not a classified directory, and doctors were not automatically listed like taxis. Someone suggested a hospital, but which hospital? "It has to be the right hospital," Miss Somers insisted, "or else they won't come. Because of the National Health, I mean. It's got to be in the area."

Someone suggested that she dial Emergency at 999 but Miss Griffith was shocked at that and said it would mean the police and that would never do. For citizens of a country which enjoyed the benefits of Medical Service for all, a group of quite reasonably intelligent women showed incredible ignorance of correct procedure. Miss Bell started looking up Ambulances under A. Miss Griffith said, "There's his own doctor—he must have a doctor." Someone rushed for the private address book. Miss Griffith instructed the office boy to go out and find a doctor—somehow, anywhere. In the private address book, Miss Griffith found Sir Edwin Sandeman with an address in Harley Street. Miss Grosvenor, collapsed in a chair, wailed in a voice whose accent was noticeably less Mayfair than usual, "I made the tea just as usual —reely I did—there couldn't have been anything wrong in it. . . ."

"Wrong in it?" Miss Griffith paused, her hand on the dial of the telephone. "Why do you say that?"

"He said it—Mr. Fortescue—he said it was the tea—"

Miss Griffith's hand hovered irresolutely between Welbeck and 999. Miss Bell, young and hopeful, said: "We ought to give him some mustard and water—now. Isn't there any mustard in the office?"

There was no mustard in the office.

Some short while later Dr. Isaacs of Bethnal Green, and Sir Edwin Sandeman met in the elevator just as two different ambulances drew up in front of the building. The telephone and the office boy had done their work.

CHAPTER 2

INSPECTOR NEELE SAT in Mr. Fortescue's sanctum behind Mr. Fortescue's vast sycamore desk. One of his underlings with a notebook sat unobtrusively against the wall near the door.

Inspector Neele had a smart, soldierly appearance with crisp brown hair growing back from a rather low forehead. When he uttered the phrase "just a matter of routine" those addressed were wont to think spitefully: "And routine is about all you're capable of!" They would have been quite wrong. Behind his unimaginative appearance, Inspector Neele was a highly imaginative thinker, and one of his methods of investigation was to propound to himself fantastic theories of guilt which he applied to such persons as he was interrogating at the time.

Miss Griffith, whom he had at once picked out with an unerring eye as being the most suitable person to give him a succinct account of the events which had led to his being seated where he was, had just left the room, having given him an admirable résumé of the morning's happenings. Inspector Neele propounded to himself three separate, highly colored reasons why the faithful *doyenne* of the typists' room should have poisoned her employer's midmorning cup of tea, and rejected them as unlikely.

He classified Miss Griffith as (a) not the type of a poisoner; (b) not in love with her employer; (c) no pronounced mental instability; (d) not a woman who cherished grudges. That really seemed to dispose of Miss Griffith except as a source of accurate information.

Inspector Neele glanced at the telephone. He was expecting a call from St. Jude's Hospital at any moment now.

It was possible, of course, that Mr. Fortescue's sudden illness was due to natural causes, but Dr. Isaacs of Bethnal Green had not thought so and Sir Edwin Sandeman of Harley Street had not thought so.

Inspector Neele pressed a buzzer conveniently situated at his left hand and demanded that Mr. Fortescue's personal secretary should be sent in to him.

Miss Grosvenor had recovered a little of her poise, but not much. She came in apprehensively, with nothing of the swan-like glide about her motions, and said at once defensively:

"I didn't do it!"

Inspector Neele murmured conversationally: "No?"

He indicated the chair where Miss Grosvenor was wont to place herself, pad in hand, when summoned to take down Mr. Fortescue's letters. She sat down now with reluctance and eyed Inspector Neele in alarm. Inspector Neele, his mind playing imaginatively on the themes—Seduction? Blackmail? Platinum Blonde in Court?, etc.,—looked reassuring and just a little stupid.

"There wasn't anything wrong with the tea," said Miss Grosvenor. "There couldn't have been."

"I see," said Inspector Neele. "Your name and address, please?

"Grosvenor. Irene Grosvenor."

"How do you spell it?"

"Oh. Like the Square."

"And your address?"

"14 Rushmoor Road, Muswell Hill."

Inspector Neele nodded in a satisfied fashion.

"No seduction," he said to himself. "No Love Nest. Respectable home with parents. No blackmail."

Another good set of speculative theories washed out.

"And so it was you who made the tea?" he said pleasantly.

"Well, I had to. I always do, I mean."

Unhurried, Inspector Neele took her closely through the morning ritual of Mr. Fortescue's Tea. The cup and saucer and teapot had already been packed up and dispatched to the appropriate quarter for analysis. Now Inspector Neele learned that Irene Grosvenor and only Irene Grosvenor had handled that cup and saucer and teapot. The kettle had been used for making the office tea and had been refilled from the cloakroom tap by Miss Grosvenor.

"And the tea itself?"

"It was Mr. Fortescue's own tea, special China tea. It's kept on the shelf in my room next door."

Inspector Neele nodded. He inquired about sugar and heard that Mr. Fortescue didn't take sugar.

The telephone rang. Inspector Neele picked up the receiver. His face changed a little.

"St. Jude's?"

He nodded to Miss Grosvenor in dismissal.

"That's all for now, thank you, Miss Grosvenor."

Miss Grosvenor sped out of the room hurriedly.

Inspector Neele listened carefully to the thin, unemotional tones speaking from St. Jude's Hospital. As the voice spoke he made a few cryptic signs with a pencil on the corner of the blotter in front of him.

"Died five minutes ago, you say?" he asked. His eye went to the watch on his wrist. Twelve forty-three, he wrote on the blotter.

The unemotional voice said that Doctor Bernsdorff himself would like to speak to Inspector Neele.

Inspector Neele said, "Right. Put him through," which rather scandalized the owner of the voice who had allowed a certain amount of reverence to seep into the official accents.

There were then various clicks, buzzes, and far-off ghostly murmurs. Inspector Neele sat patiently waiting.

Then without warning a deep bass roar caused him to shift the receiver an inch or two away from his ear.

"Hullo, Neele, you old vulture. At it again with your corpses?"

Inspector Neele and Professor Bernsdorff of St. Jude's had been brought together over a case of poisoning just over a year ago and had remained on friendly terms.

"Our man's dead, I hear, Doc."

"Yes. We couldn't do anything by the time he got here."

"And the cause of death?"

"There will have to be an autopsy, naturally. Very interesting case. Very interesting indeed. Glad I was able to be in on it."

The professional gusto in Bernsdorff's rich tones told Inspector Neele one thing, at least.

"I gather you don't think it was natural death," he said dryly.

"Not a dog's chance of it," said Dr. Bernsdorff robustly. "I'm speaking unofficially, of course," he added with belated caution.

"Of course. Of course. That's understood. He was poisoned?"

"Definitely. And what's more—this is quite unofficial, you understand—just between you and me—I'd be prepared to make a bet on what the poison was."

"In-deed?"

"Taxine, my boy. Taxine."

"Taxine? Never heard of it."

"I know. Most unusual. Really delightfully unusual! I don't say I'd have spotted it myself if I hadn't had a case only three or four weeks ago. Couple of kids playing dolls' tea-parties—pulled berries off a yew tree and used them for tea."

"Is that what it is? Yew berries?"

"Berries or leaves. Highly poisonous. Taxine, of course, is the alkaloid. Don't think I've heard of a case where it was used deliberately. Really most interesting and unusual. . . . You've no idea, Neele, how tired one gets of the inevitable weed-killer. Taxine is a real treat. Of course, I may be wrong—don't quote me, for Heaven's sake—but I don't think so. Interesting for you, too, I should think. Varies the routine!"

"A good time is to be had by all, is that the idea? With the exception of the victim."

"Yes, yes, poor fellow." Dr. Bernsdorff's tone was perfunctory. "Very bad luck on him."

"Did he say anything before he died?"

"Well, one of your fellows was sitting by him with a notebook. He'll have the exact details. He muttered something once about tea—that he'd been given something in his tea at the office—but that's nonsense, of course."

"Why is it nonsense?" Inspector Neele, who had been reviewing speculatively the picture of the glamorous Miss Grosvenor adding yew berries to a brew of tea, and finding it incongruous, spoke sharply.

"Because the stuff couldn't possibly have worked so soon. I understand the symptoms came on immediately he had drunk the tea?"

"That's what they say."

"Well, there are very few poisons that act as quickly as that, apart from the cyanides, of course—and possibly pure nicotine—"

"And it definitely wasn't cyanide or nicotine?"

"My dear fellow. He'd have been dead before the ambulance arrived. Oh no, there's no question of anything of that kind. I did suspect strychnine, but the convulsions were not at all typical. Still unofficial, of course, but I'll stake my reputation it's taxine."

"How long would that take to work?"

"Depends. An hour. Two hours, three hours. Deceased looked like a hearty eater. If he had a big breakfast, that would slow things up."

"Breakfast," said Inspector Neele thoughtfully. "Yes, it looks like breakfast."

"Breakfast with the Borgias." Dr. Bernsdorff laughed cheerfully. "Well, good hunting, my lad."

"Thanks, doctor. I'd like to speak to my sergeant before you ring off."

Again there were clicks and buzzes and far-off ghostly voices. And then the sound of heavy breathing came through, an inevitable prelude to Sergeant Hay's conversation.

"Sir," he said urgently. "Sir."

"Neele here. Did the deceased say anything I ought to know?"

"Said it was in the tea. The tea he had at the office. But the Medical Officer says not . . ."

"Yes, I know about that. Nothing else?"

"No, sir. But there's one thing that's odd. The suit he was wearing—I checked the contents of the pockets. The usual stuff—handkerchief, keys, change, wallet—but there was one thing that's downright peculiar. The right-hand pocket of his jacket. It had cereal in it."

"Cereal?"

"Yes, sir."

"What do you mean by cereal? Do you mean a breakfast food? Farmer's Glory or Wheatifax? Or do you mean corn or barley—"

"That's right, sir. Grain it was. Looked like rye to me. Quite a lot of it."

"I see. . . . Odd. . . . But it might have been a sample—something to do with a business deal."

"Quite so, sir—but I thought I'd better mention it."

"Quite right, Hay."

Inspector Neele sat staring ahead of him for a few moments after he had replaced the telephone receiver. His orderly mind was moving from Phase I to Phase II of the inquiry—from suspicion of poisoning to certainty of poisoning. Professor Bernsdorff's words may have been unofficial, but Professor Bernsdorff was not a man to be mistaken in his beliefs. Rex Fortescue had been poisoned and the poison had probably been administered one to three hours before the onset of the first symptoms. It seemed probable, therefore, that the office staff could be given a clean bill of health.

Neele got up and went into the outer office. A little desultory work was being done but the typewriters were not going at full speed.

"Miss Griffith? Can I have another word with you?"

"Certainly, Mr. Neele. Could some of the girls go out to lunch? It's long past their regular time. Or would you prefer that we get something sent in?"

"No. They can go to lunch. But they must return afterwards."

"Of course."

Miss Griffith followed Neele back into the private office. She sat down in her composed efficient way.

Without preamble, Inspector Neele said, "I have heard from St. Jude's Hospital. Mr. Fortescue died at 12:43."

17

Miss Griffith received the news without surprise, merely shook her head.

"I was afraid he was very ill," she said.

She was not, Neele noted, at all distressed.

"Will you please give me particulars of his home and family?"

"Certainly. I have already tried to get into communication with Mrs. Fortescue, but it seems she is out playing golf. She was not expected home to lunch. There is some uncertainty as to which course she is playing on." She added in an explanatory manner, "They live at Baydon Heath, you know, which is a center for three well-known golf courses."

Inspector Neele nodded. Baydon Heath was almost entirely inhabited by rich city men. It had an excellent train service, was only twenty miles from London and was comparatively easy to reach by car even in the rush of morning and evening traffic.

"The exact address, please, and the telephone number?"

"Baydon Heath 3400. The name of the house is Yewtree Lodge."

"*What?*" The sharp query slipped out before Inspector Neele could control it. "Did you say Yewtree Lodge?"

"Yes."

Miss Griffith looked faintly curious, but Inspector Neele had himself in hand again.

"Can you give me particulars of his family?"

"Mrs. Fortescue is his second wife. She is much younger than he is. They were married about two years ago. The first Mrs. Fortescue has been dead a long time. There are two sons and a daughter of the first marriage. The daughter lives at home and so does the elder son who is a partner in the firm. Unfortunately he is away in the North of England today on business. He is expected to return tomorrow."

"When did he go away?"

"The day before yesterday."

"Have you tried to get in touch with him?"

"Yes. After Mr. Fortescue was removed to hospital I rang up the Midland Hotel in Manchester where I thought he might be staying, but he had left early this morning. I believe he was also going to Sheffield and Leicester, but I am not sure about that. I can give you the names of certain firms in those cities which he might be visiting."

Certainly an efficient woman, thought the Inspector, and if she murdered a man she would probably murder him very efficiently, too. But he forced himself to abandon these speculations and concentrate once more on Mr. Fortescue's home front.

"There is a second son, you said?"

"Yes. But owing to a disagreement with his father he lives abroad."

"Are both sons married?"

"Yes. Mr. Percival has been married for three years. He and his wife occupy a self-contained flat in Yewtree Lodge, though they are moving into their own house at Baydon Heath very shortly."

"You were not able to get in touch with Mrs. Percival Fortescue when you rang up this morning?"

"She had gone to London for the day." Miss Griffith went on, "Mr. Lancelot got married less than a year ago. To the widow of Lord Frederick Anstice. I expect you've seen pictures of her. In the *Tatler*—with horses, you know. And at point to points."

Miss Griffith sounded a little breathless and her cheeks were faintly flushed. Neele, who was quick to catch the moods of human beings, realized that this marriage had thrilled the snob and the romantic in Miss Griffith. The aristocracy was the aristocracy to Miss Griffith, and the fact that the late Lord Frederick Anstice had had a somewhat unsavory reputation in sporting circles was almost certainly not known to her. Freddie Anstice had blown his brains out just before an inquiry by the Stewards into the running of one of his horses. Neele remembered something vaguely about his wife. She had been the daughter of an Irish peer and had been married before to an airman who had been killed in the Battle of Britain.

And now, it seemed, she was married to the black sheep of the Fortescue family, for Neele assumed that the disagreement with his father referred to primly by Miss Griffith, stood for some disgraceful incident in young Lancelot Fortescue's career.

Lancelot Fortescue! What a name! And what was the other son —Percival? He wondered what the first Mrs. Fortescue had been like? She'd had a curious taste in Christian names . . .

He drew the phone towards him and dialed TOL. He asked for Baydon Heath 3400.

Presently a man's voice said, "Baydon Heath 3400."

"I want to speak to Mrs. Fortescue or Miss Fortescue."

"Sorry. They aren't in, either of 'em."

19

The voice struck Inspector Neele as slightly alcoholic.

"Are you the butler?"

"That's right."

"Mr. Fortescue has been taken seriously ill."

"I know. They rung up and said so. But there's nothing I can do about it. Mr. Val's away up North and Mrs. Fortescue's out playing golf. Mrs. Val's gone up to London but she'll be back for dinner and Miss Elaine's out with her Brownies."

"Is there no one in the house I can speak to about Mr. Fortescue's illness? It's important."

"Well—I don't know." The man sounded doubtful. "There's Miss Ramsbottom—but she don't ever speak over the phone. Or there's Miss Dove—she's what you might call the 'ousekeeper."

"I'll speak to Miss Dove, please."

"I'll try and get hold of her."

His retreating footsteps were audible through the phone. Inspector Neele heard no approaching footsteps but a minute or two later a woman's voice spoke.

"This is Miss Dove speaking."

The voice was low and well poised, with clear-cut enunciation. Inspector Neele formed a favorable picture of Miss Dove.

"I am sorry to have to tell you, Miss Dove, that Mr. Fortescue died in St. Jude's Hospital a short time ago. He was taken suddenly ill in his office. I am anxious to get in touch with his relatives—"

"Of course. I had no idea—" She broke off. Her voice had held no agitation, but it was shocked. She went on: "It is all most unfortunate. The person you really want to get in touch with is Mr. Percival Fortescue. He would be the one to see to all the necessary arrangements. You might be able to get in touch with him at the Midland in Manchester or possibly at the Grand in Leicester. Or you might try Shearer and Bonds of Leicester. I don't know their telephone number, I'm afraid, but I know they are a firm on whom he was going to call and they might be able to inform you where he would be likely to be today. Mrs. Fortescue will certainly be in to dinner and she may be in to tea. It will be a great shock to her. It must have been very sudden? Mr. Fortescue was quite well when he left here this morning."

"You saw him before he left?"

"Oh yes. What was it? Heart?"

"Did he suffer from heart trouble?"

"No—no—I don't think so—but I thought as it was so sudden—" She broke off. "Are you speaking from St. Jude's Hospital? Are you a doctor?"

"No, Miss Dove, I'm not a doctor. I'm speaking from Mr. Fortescue's office in the city. I am Detective Inspector Neele of the C.I.D. and I shall be coming down to see you as soon as I can get there."

"Detective Inspector? Do you mean—what do you mean?"

"It was a case of sudden death, Miss Dove, and when there is a sudden death we get called to the scene, especially when the deceased man hasn't seen a doctor lately, which I gather was the case?"

It was only the faintest suspicion of a question mark, but the young woman responded.

"I know. Percival made an appointment twice for him, but he wouldn't keep it. He was quite unreasonable—they've all been worried—"

She broke off and then resumed in her former assured manner,

"If Mrs. Fortescue returns to the house before you arrive, what do you want me to tell her?"

Practical as they make 'em, thought Inspector Neele.

Aloud he said, "Just tell her that in a case of sudden death we have to make a few inquiries. Routine inquiries."

He hung up.

CHAPTER 3

NEELE PUSHED THE telephone away and looked sharply at Miss Griffith.

"So they've been worried about him lately," he said. "Wanted him to see a doctor. You didn't tell me that."

"I didn't think of it," said Miss Griffith, and added, "He never seemed to me really ill—"

"Not ill—but what?"

"Well, just odd. Unlike himself. Peculiar in his manner."

"Worried about something?"

"Oh no, not worried. It's we who were worried."

Inspector Neele waited patiently.

"It's difficult to say, really," said Miss Griffith. "He had moods, you know. Sometimes he was quite boisterous. Once or twice, frankly, I thought he had been drinking. . . . He boasted and told the most extraordinary stories which I'm sure couldn't possibly have been true. For most of the time I've been here he was always very close about his affairs—not giving anything away, you know. But lately he's been quite different, expansive, and positively—well, flinging money about. Most unlike his usual manner. Why, when the office boy had to go to his grandmother's funeral, Mr. Fortescue called him in and gave him a five-pound note and told him to put it on the second favorite and then roared with laughter. He wasn't—well, he just wasn't like himself. That's all I can say."

"As though, perhaps, he had something on his mind?"

"Not in the usual meaning of the term. It was as though he were looking forward to something pleasurable—exciting."

"Possibly a big deal that he was going to pull off?"

Miss Griffith agreed with more conviction. "Yes—yes, that's much more what I mean. As though everyday things didn't matter any more. He was excited. And some very odd-looking people came to see him on business. People who'd never been here before. It worried Mr. Percival dreadfully."

"Oh, it worried him, did it?"

"Yes. Mr. Percival's always been very much in his father's confidence, you see. His father relied on him. But lately—"

"Lately they weren't getting along so well?"

"Well, Mr. Fortescue was doing a lot of things that Mr. Percival thought unwise. Mr. Percival is always very careful and prudent. But suddenly his father didn't listen to him any more, and Mr. Percival was very upset."

"And they had a real row about it all?"

Inspector Neele was still probing.

"I don't know about a row. . . . Of course, I realize now Mr. Fortescue can't have been himself—shouting like that."

"Shouted, did he? What did he say?"

"He came right out in the typists' room—"

"So that you all heard?"

"Well—yes."

"And he called Percival names—abused him—swore at him . . . ? What did he say Percival had done?"

"It was more that he hadn't done anything . . . he called him a miserable, pettifogging little clerk. He said he had no large outlook, no conception of doing business in a big way. He said, 'I shall get Lance home again. He's worth ten of you—and he's married well. Lance has got guts even if he did risk a criminal prosecution once—' Oh dear, I oughtn't to have said that!" Miss Griffith, carried away as others before her had been under Inspector Neele's expert handling, was suddenly overcome with confusion.

"Don't worry," said Inspector Neele comfortingly. "What's past is past."

"Oh yes, it was a long time ago. Mr. Lance was just young and high-spirited and didn't really realize what he was doing."

Inspector Neele had heard that view before and didn't agree with it. But he passed on to fresh questions.

"Tell me a little more about the staff here."

Miss Griffith, hurrying to get away from her indiscretion, poured out information about the various personalities in the firm. Inspector Neele thanked her and then said he would like to see Miss Grosvenor again.

Detective Constable Waite sharpened his pencil. He remarked wistfully that this was a Ritzy joint. His glance wandered appreciatively over the huge chairs, the big desk and the indirect lighting.

"All these people have got Ritzy names, too," he said. "Grosvenor—that's something to do with a duke. And Fortescue—that's a classy name, too."

Inspector Neele smiled.

"His father's name wasn't Fortescue. Fontescu—and he came from somewhere in central Europe. I suppose this man thought Fortescue sounded better."

Detective Constable Waite looked at his superior officer with awe.

"So you know all about him?"

"I just looked up a few things before coming along on the call."

"Not got a record, had he?"

"Oh no. Mr. Fortescue was much too clever for that. He's had

23

certain connections with the Black Market and put through one or two deals that are questionable, to say the least of it, but they've always been just within the law."

"I see," said Waite. "Not a nice man."

"A twister," said Neele. "But we've got nothing on him. The Inland Revenue have been after him for a long time, but he's been too clever for them. Quite a financial genius, the late Mr. Fortescue."

"The sort of man," said Constable Waite, "who might have enemies?" He spoke hopefully.

"Oh yes, certainly enemies. But he was poisoned at home, remember. Or so it would seem. You know, Waite, I see a kind of pattern emerging. An old-fashioned, familiar kind of pattern. The good boy, Percival. The bad boy, Lance—attractive to women. The wife who's younger than her husband and who's vague about which course she's going to play golf on. It's all very, very familiar. But there's one thing that sticks out in a most incongruous way."

Constable Waite asked "What's that?" just as the door opened and Miss Grosvenor, her poise restored, and once more her glamorous self, inquired haughtily,

"You wished to see me?"

"I wanted to ask you a few questions about your employer—your late employer, perhaps I should say."

"Poor soul," said Miss Grosvenor unconvincingly.

"I want to know if you have noticed any difference in him lately."

"Well, yes. I did, as a matter of fact."

"In what way?"

"I couldn't really say. . . . He seemed to talk a lot of nonsense. I couldn't really believe half of what he said. And then he lost his temper very easily, especially with Mr. Percival. Not with me, because of course I never argue. I just say, 'Yes, Mr. Fortescue,' whatever peculiar thing he says—said, I mean."

"Did he ever—well, make any passes at you?"

Miss Grosvenor replied rather regretfully, "Well, no, I couldn't exactly say that."

"There's just one other thing, Miss Grosvenor. Was Mr. Fortescue in the habit of carrying grain about in his pocket?"

Miss Grosvenor displayed a lively surprise.

"Grain? In his pocket? Do you mean, to feed pigeons or something?"

"It could have been for that purpose."

"Oh, I'm sure he didn't. Mr. Fortescue? Feed pigeons? Oh no."

"Could he have had barley—or rye—in his pocket today for any special reason? A sample, perhaps? Some deal in grain?"

"Oh no. He was expecting the Asiatic Oil people this afternoon. And the President of the Atticus Building Society. . . . No one else."

"Oh well—" Neele dismissed the subject and Miss Grosvenor with a wave of the hand.

"Lovely legs she's got," said Constable Waite with a sigh. "And super nylons—"

"Legs are no help to me," said Inspector Neele. "I'm left with what I had before. A pocketful of rye—and no explanation of it."

CHAPTER 4

Mary Dove paused on her way downstairs and looked out through the big window on the stairs. A car had just driven up from which two men were alighting. The taller of the two stood for a moment with his back to the house surveying his surroundings. Mary Dove appraised the two men thoughtfully. Inspector Neele and presumably a subordinate.

She turned from the window and looked at herself in the full-length mirror that hung on the wall where the staircase turned. . . . She saw a small, demure figure with immaculate white collar and cuffs on a beige gray dress. Her dark hair was parted in the middle and drawn back in two shining waves to a knot in the back of the neck. . . . The lipstick she used was a pale rose color.

On the whole, Mary Dove was satisfied with her appearance. A very faint smile on her lips, she went on down the stairs.

Inspector Neele, surveying the house, was saying to himself:

Call it a lodge, indeed! Yewtree Lodge! The affectation of these rich people! The house was what he, Inspector Neele, would call a mansion. He knew what a lodge was. He'd been brought up in one! The lodge at the gates of Hartington Park, that vast, unwieldy Palladian house with its twenty-nine bedrooms which had now been taken over by the National Trust. The lodge had been small and attractive from the outside, and had been damp, uncomfortable and devoid of anything but the most primitive form of sanitation within. Fortunately these facts had been accepted as quite proper and fitting by Inspector Neele's parents. They had no rent to pay and nothing whatever to do except open and shut the gates when required, and there were always plenty of rabbits and an occasional pheasant or so for the pot. Mrs. Neele had never discovered the pleasures of electric irons, slow combustion stoves, airing cupboards, hot and cold water from taps, and the switching on of light by a mere flick of a finger. In winter the Neeles had an oil lamp, and in summer they went to bed when it got dark. They were a healthy family and a happy one, all thoroughly behind the times.

So when Inspector Neele heard the word Lodge, it was his childhood memories that stirred. But this place, this pretentiously named Yewtree Lodge was just the kind of mansion that rich people built themselves and then called it their "little place in the country." It wasn't in the country either, according to Inspector Neele's idea of the country. The house was a large, solid, red brick structure, sprawling lengthwise rather than upward, with rather too many gables, and a vast number of leaded paned windows. The gardens were highly artificial—all laid out in rose beds and pergolas and pools, and living up to the name of the house with large numbers of clipped yew hedges.

Plenty of yew here for anybody with a desire to obtain the raw material of taxine. Over on the right, behind the rose pergola, there was a bit of actual Nature left—a vast yew tree of the kind one associates with churchyards, its branches held up by stakes, like a kind of Moses of the forest world. That tree, the Inspector thought, had been there long before the rash of newly-built red brick houses had begun to spread over the countryside. It had been there before the golf courses had been laid out and the fashionable architects had walked round with their rich clients pointing out the advantages of the various sites. And since it was a valuable antique, the tree had been kept and incorporated in the new setup and had, perhaps, given its name to the new, desirable residence. Yewtree Lodge. And possibly the berries from that very tree—

Inspector Neele cut off these unprofitable speculations. Must get on with the job. He rang the bell.

It was opened promptly by a middle-aged man who fitted in quite accurately with the mental image Inspector Neele had formed of him over the phone. A man with a rather spurious air of smartness, a shifty eye and a rather unsteady hand.

Inspector Neele announced himself and his subordinate and had the pleasure of seeing an instant look of alarm come into the butler's eye. Neele did not attach too much importance to that. It might easily have nothing to do with the death of Rex Fortescue. It was quite possibly a purely automatic reaction.

"Has Mrs. Fortescue returned yet?"

"No, sir."

"Nor Mr. Percival Fortescue? Nor Miss Fortescue?"

"No, sir."

"Then I would like to see Miss Dove, please."

The man turned his head slightly. "Here's Miss Dove now—coming downstairs."

Inspector Neele took in Miss Dove as she came composedly down the wide staircase. This time the mental picture did not correspond with the reality. Unconsciously the word housekeeper had conjured up a vague impression of someone large and authoritative, dressed in black, with somewhere concealed about her a jingle of keys.

The Inspector was quite unprepared for the small, trim figure descending towards him. The soft dove-colored tones of her dress, the white collar and cuffs, the neat waves of hair, the faint Mona Lisa smile. It all seemed, somehow, just a little unreal, as though this young woman of under thirty was playing a part: not, he thought, the part of a housekeeper, but the part of Mary Dove. Her appearance was directed towards living up to her name.

She greeted him composedly. "Inspector Neele?"

"Yes. This is Sergeant Hay. Mr. Fortescue, as I told you through the phone, died in St. Jude's Hospital at 12:43. It seems likely that his death was the result of something he ate at breakfast this morning. I should be glad therefore if Sergeant Hay could be taken to the kitchen where he can make inquiries as to the food served."

Her eyes met his for a moment, thoughtfully; then she nodded. "Of course," she said. She turned to the uneasily hovering butler. "Crump, will you take Sergeant Hay out and show him whatever he wants to see."

The two men departed together. Mary Dove said to Neele, "Will you come in here?"

She opened the door of a room and preceded him into it. It was a characterless apartment, clearly labeled "Smoking Room," with paneling, rich upholstery, large stuffed chairs, and a suitable set of sporting prints on the walls.

"Please sit down."

He sat and Mary Dove sat opposite him. She chose, he noticed, to face the light. An unusual preference for a woman. Still more unusual if a woman had anything to hide. But perhaps Mary Dove had nothing to hide.

"It is very unfortunate," she said, "that none of the family is available. Mrs. Fortescue may return at any minute. And so may Mrs. Val. I have sent wires to Mr. Percival Fortescue at various places."

"Thank you, Miss Dove."

"You say that Mr. Fortescue's death was caused by something he may have eaten for breakfast? Food poisoning, you mean?"

"Possibly." He watched her.

She said composedly, "It seems unlikely. For breakfast this morning there were bacon and scrambled eggs, coffee, toast and marmalade. There was also a cold ham on the sideboard, but that had been cut yesterday, and no one felt any ill effects. No fish of any kind was served, no sausages—nothing like that."

"I see you know exactly what was served."

"Naturally. I order the meals. For dinner last night—"

"No." Inspector Neele interrupted her. "It would not be a question of dinner last night."

"I thought the onset of food poisoning could sometimes be delayed as much as twenty-four hours."

"Not in this case. . . . Will you tell me exactly what Mr. Fortescue ate and drank before leaving the house this morning?"

"He had early tea brought to his room at eight o'clock. Breakfast was at a quarter past nine. Mr. Fortescue, as I have told you, had scrambled eggs, bacon, coffee, toast and marmalade."

"Any cereal?"

"No, he doesn't like cereals."

"The sugar for the coffee—is it lump sugar or granulated?"

"Lump. But Mr. Fortescue does not take sugar in his coffee."

"Is he in the habit of taking any medicines in the morning? Salts? A tonic? Some digestive remedy?"

"No, nothing of that kind."

"Did you have breakfast with him also?"

"No. I do not take meals with the family."

"Who was at breakfast?"

"Mrs. Fortescue. Miss Fortescue. Mrs. Val Fortescue. Mr. Percival Fortescue, of course, was away."

"And Mrs. and Miss Fortescue ate the same things for breakfast?"

"Mrs. Fortescue has only coffee, orange juice and toast. Mrs. Val and Miss Fortescue always eat a hearty breakfast. Besides eating scrambled eggs and cold ham, they would probably have a cereal as well. Mrs. Val drinks tea, not coffee."

Inspector Neele reflected for a moment. The opportunities seemed at least to be narrowing down. Three people, and three people only, had had breakfast with the deceased: his wife, his daughter and his daughter-in-law. Either of them might have seized an opportunity to add taxine to his cup of coffee. The bitterness of the coffee would have masked the bitter taste of the taxine. There was the early morning tea, of course, but Bernsdorff had intimated that the taste would be noticeable in tea. But perhaps, first thing in the morning, before the senses were alert. . . . He looked up to find Mary Dove watching him.

"Your questions about tonic and medicines seem to me rather odd, Inspector," she said. "It seems to imply that either there was something wrong with a medicine, or that something had been added to it. Surely neither of those processes could be described as food poisoning."

Neele eyed her steadily.

"I did not say, definitely, that Mr. Fortescue died of food poisoning. But—some kind of poisoning. In fact, just poisoning."

She repeated softly, "Poisoning. . . ."

29

She appeared neither startled nor dismayed, merely interested. Her attitude was of one sampling a new experience.

In fact, she said as much, remarking after a moment's reflection: "I have never had anything to do with a poisoning case before."

"It's not very pleasant," Neele informed her dryly.

"No, I suppose not . . ."

She thought about it for a moment and then looked up at him with a sudden smile.

"I didn't do it," she said. "But I suppose everybody will tell you that!"

"Have you any idea who did do it, Miss Dove?"

She shrugged her shoulders. "Frankly, he was an odious man. Anybody might have done it."

"But people aren't poisoned just for being 'odious,' Miss Dove. There usually has to be a pretty solid motive."

"Yes, of course."

She was thoughtful.

"Do you care to tell me something about the household here?"

She looked up at him. He was a little startled to find her eyes cool and amused.

"This isn't exactly a statement you're asking me to make, is it? No, it couldn't be, because your Sergeant is busy upsetting the domestic staff. I shouldn't like to have what I say read out in court, but all the same I should rather like to say it—unofficially. Off the record, so to speak?"

"Go ahead then, Miss Dove. I've no witness, as you've already observed."

She leaned back, swinging one slim foot and narrowing her eyes.

"Let me start by saying that I've no feeling of loyalty to my employers. I work for them because it's a job that pays well and I insist that it should pay well."

"I was a little surprised to find you doing this type of job. It struck me that with your brains and education—"

"I ought to be confined in an office? Or compiling files in a Ministry? My dear Inspector Neele, this is the perfect racket. People will pay anything—anything—to be spared domestic worries. To find and engage a staff is a thoroughly tedious job. Writing to agencies, putting in advertisements, interviewing people, making arrangements for interviews, and finally keeping the whole thing running smoothly—it takes a certain capacity which most of these people haven't got."

"And suppose your staff when you've assembled it, runs out on you? I've heard of such things."

Mary smiled. "If necessary, I can make the beds, dust the rooms, cook a meal and serve it without anyone noticing the difference. Of course, I don't advertise that fact. It might give rise to ideas. But I can always be sure of tiding over any little gap. But there aren't often gaps. I work only for the extremely rich who will pay anything to be comfortable. I pay top prices and so I get the best of what's going."

"Such as the butler?"

She threw him an amused, appreciative glance.

"There's always that trouble with a couple. Crump stays because of Mrs. Crump, who is one of the best cooks I've ever come across. She's a jewel, and one would put up with a good deal to keep her. Our Mr. Fortescue likes his food—liked, I should say. In this household nobody has any scruples and they have plenty of money. Butter, eggs, cream, Mrs. Crump can command what she likes. As for Crump, he just makes the grade. His silver's all right, and his waiting at table is not too bad. I keep the key of the wine cellar and a sharp eye on the whisky and gin, and supervise his valeting."

Inspector Neele raised his eyebrows.

"The admirable Miss Crichton."

"I find one must know how to do everything oneself. Then—one need never do it. But you wanted to know my impressions of the family."

"If you don't mind."

"They are really all quite odious. The late Mr. Fortescue was the kind of crook who is always careful to play safe. He boasted a great deal of his various smart dealings. He was rude and overbearing in manner and was a definite bully. Mrs. Fortescue—Adele—is his second wife and about thirty years younger than he is. He came across her at Brighton. She was a manicurist on the lookout for big money. She is very good-looking—a real sexy piece, if you know what I mean."

Inspector Neele was shocked but managed not to show it. A girl like Mary Dove ought not to say such things, he felt.

The young lady was continuing composedly:

"Adele married him for his money, of course, and his son, Percival, and his daughter, Elaine, were simply livid about it. They're as nasty as they can be to her, but very wisely she doesn't care or even notice. She knows she's got the old man where she wants him. Oh dear, the wrong tense again. I haven't really grasped yet that he's dead . . ."

"Let's hear about the son."

"Dear Percival? Val, as his wife calls him. Percival is a mealy-mouthed hypocrite. He's prim and sly and cunning. He's terrified of his father and has always let himself be bullied, but he's quite clever at getting his own way. Unlike his father, he's mean about money. Economy is one of his passions. That's why he's been so long about finding a house of his own. Having a suite of rooms here saved his pocket."

"And his wife?"

"Jennifer's meek and seems very stupid. But I'm not so sure. She was a hospital nurse before her marriage—nursed Percival through pneumonia to a romantic conclusion. The old man was disappointed by the marriage. He's a snob and wanted Percival to make what he called a 'good marriage.' He despises poor Mrs. Val and snubs her. She dislikes—disliked him a good deal, I think. Her principal interests are shopping and the cinema; her principal grievance is that her husband keeps her short of money."

"What about the daughter?"

"Elaine? I'm rather sorry for Elaine. She's not a bad sort. One of those great schoolgirls who never grow up. She plays games quite well, and runs Girl Guides and Brownies and all that sort of thing. There was some sort of affair not long ago with a disgruntled young schoolmaster, but Father discovered the young man had communistic ideas and came down on the romance like a ton of bricks."

"She hadn't got the spirit to stand up to him?"

"*She* had. It was the young man who ratted. A question of money yet again, I fancy. Elaine is not particularly attractive, poor dear."

"And the other son?"

"I've never seen him. He's attractive, by all accounts, and a thoroughly bad lot. Some little matter of a forged check in the past. He lives in East Africa."

32

"And is estranged from his father."

"Yes, Mr. Fortescue couldn't cut him off with a shilling because he'd already made him a junior partner in the firm, but he's held no communication with him for years, and in fact if Lance was ever mentioned, he used to say, 'Don't talk to me of that rascal. He's no son of mine.' All the same—"

"Yes, Miss Dove?"

Mary said slowly, "All the same, I shouldn't be surprised if old Fortescue hadn't been planning to get him back here."

"What makes you think that?"

"Because, about a month ago, old Fortescue had a terrific row with Percival—he found out something that Percival had been doing behind his back—I don't know what it was—and he was absolutely furious. Percival suddenly stopped being the white-headed boy. He's been quite different lately, too."

"Mr. Fortescue was quite different?"

"No. I meant Percival. He's gone about looking worried to death."

"Now, what about servants? You've already described the Crumps. Who else is there?"

"Gladys Martin is the parlormaid or waitress, as they like to call themselves nowadays. She does the downstairs rooms, lays the table, clears away and helps Crump wait at table. Quite a decent sort of girl, but very nearly half-witted. The adenoidal type."

Neele nodded.

"The housemaid is Ellen Curtis. Elderly, very crabbed, and very cross, but has been in good service and is a first-class housemaid. The rest is outside help—odd women who come in."

"And those are the only people living here?"

"There's old Miss Ramsbottom."

"Who is she?"

"Mr. Fortescue's sister-in-law—his first wife's sister. His wife was a good deal older than he was and her sister again is a good deal older than she—which makes her well over seventy. She has a room of her own on the second floor—does her own cooking and all that, with just a woman coming in to clean. She's rather eccentric and she never liked her brother-in-law, but she came here while her sister was alive and stayed on when she died. Mr. Fortescue never bothered about her much. She's quite a character, though, is Aunt Effie."

"And that is all."

"That's all."

"So we come to you, Miss Dove."

"You want particulars? I'm an orphan. I took a secretarial course at the St. Alfred's Secretarial College. I took a job as shorthand typist, left it and took another, decided I was in the wrong racket, and started on my present career. I have been with three different employers. After about a year or eighteen months, I get tired of a particular place and move on. I have been at Yewtree Lodge just over a year. I will type out the names and addresses of my various employers and give them, with a copy of my references to Sergeant—Hay, is it? Will that be satisfactory?"

"Perfectly, Miss Dove." Neele was silent for a moment, enjoying a mental image of Miss Dove tampering with Mr. Fortescue's breakfast. His mind went back further, and he saw her methodically gathering yew berries in a little basket. With a sigh he returned to the present and reality. "Now, I would like to see the girl—er, Gladys—and then the housemaid, Ellen." He added as he rose, "By the way, Miss Dove, can you give me any idea why Mr. Fortescue would be carrying loose grain in his pocket?"

"Grain?" She stared at him with what appeared to be genuine surprise.

"Yes, grain. Does that suggest something to you, Miss Dove?"

"Nothing at all."

"Who looked after his clothes?"

"Crump."

"I see. Did Mr. Fortescue and Mrs. Fortescue occupy the same bedroom?"

"Yes. He had a dressing room and bath, of course, and so did she . . ." Mary glanced down at her wrist watch. "I really think that she ought to be back very soon now."

The Inspector had risen. He said in a pleasant voice:

"Do you know one thing, Miss Dove? It strikes me as very odd that even though there are three golf courses in the immediate neighborhood, it has yet not been possible to find Mrs. Fortescue on one of them before now?"

"It would not be so odd, Inspector, if she did not actually happen to be playing golf at all."

Mary's voice was dry. The Inspector said sharply:

"I was distinctly informed that she was playing golf."

"She took her golf clubs and announced her intention of doing so. She was driving her own car, of course."

He looked at her steadily, perceiving the inference.

"Whom was she playing with? Do you know?"

"I think it possible that it might be Mr. Vivian Dubois."

Neele contented himself by saying, "I see."

"I'll send Gladys in to you. She'll probably be scared to death." Mary paused for a moment by the door, then she said:

"I should hardly advise you to go too much by all I've told you. I'm a malicious creature."

She went out. Inspector Neele looked at the closed door and wondered. Whether actuated by malice or not, what she had told him could not fail to be suggestive. If Rex Fortescue had been deliberately poisoned, and it seemed almost certain that that was the case, then the setup at Yewtree Lodge seemed highly promising. Motives appeared to be lying thick on the ground.

CHAPTER 5

THE GIRL WHO entered the room with obvious unwillingness was an unattractive, frightened-looking girl, who managed to look faintly sluttish in spite of being tall and smartly dressed in a claret-colored uniform.

She said at once, fixing imploring eyes upon him:

"I didn't do anything. I didn't really. I don't know anything about it."

"That's all right," said Neele heartily. His voice had changed slightly. It sounded more cheerful and a good deal commoner in intonation. He wanted to put the frightened rabbit Gladys at her ease.

"Sit down here," he went on. "I just want to know about breakfast this morning."

"I didn't do anything at all."

"Well, you laid the breakfast, didn't you?"

"Yes, I did that." Even that admission came unwillingly. She looked both guilty and terrified, but Inspector Neele was used to witnesses who looked like that. He went on cheerfully, trying to put her at her ease, asking questions: Who had come down first? And who next?

Elaine Fortescue had been the first down to breakfast. She'd come in just as Crump was bringing in the coffeepot. Mrs. Fortescue was down next, and then Mrs. Val, and the master last. They waited on themselves. The tea and coffee and the hot dishes were all on hot plates on the sideboard.

He learnt little of importance from her that he did not know already. The food and drink were as Mary Dove had described them. The master and Mrs. Fortescue and Miss Elaine took coffee and Mrs. Val took tea. Everything had been quite as usual.

Neele questioned her about herself and here she answered more readily. She'd been in the NAAFI, a sort of USO called Navy, Army and Air Forces Institute, and after that in a café at Eastbourne. Then she thought she'd like to try private service and had come to Yewtree Lodge last September. She'd been there two months.

"And you like it?"

"Well, it's all right, I suppose." She added, "It's not so hard on your feet, but you don't get so much freedom . . ."

"Tell me about Mr. Fortescue's clothes—his suits. Who looked after them? Brushed them and all that?"

Gladys looked faintly resentful. "Mr. Crump's supposed to. But half the time he makes me do it."

"Who brushed and pressed the suit Mr. Fortescue had on today?"

"I don't remember which one he wore. He's got ever so many."

"Have you ever found grain in the pocket of one of his suits?"

"Grain?" She looked puzzled.

"Rye, to be exact."

"Rye? That's bread, isn't it? A sort of black bread—got a nasty taste, I always think."

"That's bread made from rye. Rye is the grain itself. There was some found in the pocket of your master's coat."

"In his coat pocket?"

"Yes. Do you know how it got there?"

"I couldn't say I'm sure. I never saw any."

He could get no more from her. For a moment or two he wondered if she knew more about the matter than she was willing to admit. She certainly seemed embarrassed and on the defensive, but on the whole he put it down to a natural fear of the police.

When he finally dismissed her, she asked:

"It's really true, is it? He's dead?"

"Yes, he's dead."

"Very sudden, wasn't it? They said when they rang up from the office that he'd had a kind of fit."

"Yes—it was a kind of fit."

Gladys said, "A girl I used to know had fits. Come on any time, they did. Used to scare me."

For the moment this reminiscence seemed to overcome her suspicions.

Inspector Neele made his way to the kitchen.

His reception was immediate and alarming. A woman of vast proportions, with a red face and armed with a rolling pin stepped towards him in a menacing fashion.

"Police, indeed," she said. "Coming here and saying my cooking's poisoned the master. Nothing of the kind, I'd have you know. Anything I've sent in to the dining-room has been just what it should be. Coming here and saying I poisoned the master. I'll have the law on you, police or no police. No bad food's ever been served in this house."

It was some time before Inspector Neele could appease the irate artist. Sergeant Hay looked in grinning from the pantry, and Inspector Neele gathered that he had already run the gantlet of Mrs. Crump's wrath.

The scene was terminated by the ringing of the telephone.

Neele went out into the hall to find Mary Dove taking the call. She was writing down a message on a pad. Turning her head over her shoulder, she said, "It's a telegram."

The call concluded, she replaced the receiver and handed the pad on which she had been writing to the Inspector. The place of origin was Paris and the message ran as follows:

Fortescue Yewtree Lodge Baydon Heath Surrey. Sorry your letter delayed. Will be with you tomorrow about teatime. Shall expect roast veal for dinner. Lance.

Inspector Neele raised his eyebrows.

"So the Prodigal Son had been summoned home," he said.

CHAPTER 6

AT THE MOMENT when Rex Fortescue had been drinking his last cup of tea, Lance Fortescue and his wife had been sitting under the trees on the Champs Elysées watching the people walking past.

"It's all very well to say 'describe him,' Pat. I'm a rotten hand at descriptions. What do you want to know? The Guvnor's a bit of an old crook, you know. But you won't mind that? You must be used to that more or less."

"Oh yes," said Pat. "Yes, as you say, I'm acclimatized."

She tried to keep a certain forlornness out of her voice. Perhaps, she reflected, the whole world was really crooked, or was it just that she herself had been unfortunate?

She was a tall, long-legged girl, not beautiful but with a charm that was made up of vitality and a warm-hearted personality. She moved well, and had lovely, gleaming chestnut-brown hair. Perhaps, from a long association with horses, she had acquired the look of a thoroughbred filly.

Crookedness in the racing world she knew about. Now, it seemed she was to encounter crookedness in the financial world. Though for all that, it seemed that her father-in-law whom she had not yet met, was, as far as the law was concerned, a pillar of rectitude. All these people who went about boasting of "smart work" were the same: technically they always managed to be within the law. Yet it seemed to her that her Lance, whom she loved, and who had admittedly strayed outside the ringed fence in earlier days, had an honesty that these successful practitioners of the crooked lacked.

"I don't mean," said Lance, "that he's a swindler, not anything like that. But he knows how to put over a fast one."

"Sometimes," said Pat, "I feel I hate people who put over fast ones." She added, "You're fond of him." It was a statement, not a question.

Lance considered it for a moment, and then said in a surprised kind of voice:

"Do you know, darling, I believe I am."

Pat laughed. He turned his head to look at her. His eyes narrowed. What a darling she was! He loved her. The whole thing was worth it for her sake.

"In a way, you know," he said, "it's hell going back. City life. Home on the 5:18. It's not my kind of life. I'm far more at home among the down-and-outs. But one's got to settle down sometime, I suppose. And with you to hold my hand, the process may even be quite a pleasant one. And since the old boy has come round, one ought to take advantage of it. I must say I was surprised when I got his letter. . . . Percival, of all people, blotting his copybook. Percival, the good little boy. Mind you, Percy was always sly. Yes, he was always sly."

"I don't think," said Patricia Fortescue, "that I'm going to like your brother Percival."

"Don't let me put you against him. Percy and I never got on—that's all there is to it. I blew my pocket money, he saved his. I had disreputable but entertaining friends, Percy made what's called 'worthwhile contacts.' Poles apart we were, he and I. I always thought him a poor fish, and he—sometimes, you know, I think he almost hated me. I don't know why, exactly . . ."

"I think I can see why."

"Can you, darling? You're so brainy. You know, I've always wondered—it's a fantastic thing to say—but—"

"Well? Say it."

"I've wondered if it wasn't Percival who was behind that check business—you know, when the old man kicked me out—and was mad that he'd given me a share in the firm and so couldn't disinherit me! Because the queer thing was that I never forged that check—though of course nobody would believe that after that time I swiped funds out of the till and put it on a horse. I was dead sure I could put it back, and anyway it was my own cash, in a manner of speaking. But that check business—no. I don't know why I've got the ridiculous idea that Percival did that, but I have, somehow."

39

"But it wouldn't have done him any good? It was paid into your account."

"I know. So it doesn't make sense, does it?"

Pat turned sharply towards him. "You mean, he did it to get you chucked out of the firm?"

"I wondered. Oh well, it's a rotten thing to say. Forget it. I wonder what old Percy will say when he sees the Prodigal returned. Those pale, boiled-gooseberry eyes of his will pop right out of his head!"

"Does he know you are coming?"

"I shouldn't be surprised if he didn't know a damned thing! The old man's got rather a funny sense of humor, you know."

"But what has your brother done to upset your father so much?"

"That's what I'd like to know. Something must have made the old man livid. Writing off to me the way he did."

"When was it you got his first letter?"

"Must be four—no, five months ago. A cagey letter, but a distinct holding out of the olive branch. 'Your elder brother has proved himself unsatisfactory in many ways.' 'You seem to have sown your wild oats and settled down.' 'I can promise you that it will be well worth your while financially.' 'Shall welcome you and your wife.' You know, darling, I think my marrying you had a lot to do with it. The old boy was impressed that I'd married into a class above me."

Pat laughed.

"What? Into the aristocratic riffraff?"

He grinned. "That's right. But riffraff didn't register and aristocracy did. You should see Percival's wife. She's the kind who says 'Pass the preserves, please' and talks about a postage stamp."

Pat did not laugh. She was considering the women of the family into which she had married. It was a point of view which Lance had not taken into account.

"And your sister?" she asked.

"Elaine? Oh, she's all right. She was pretty young when I left home. Sort of an earnest girl, but probably she's grown out of that. Very intense over things."

It did not sound very reassuring. Pat said, "She never wrote to you—after you went away?"

"I didn't leave an address. But she wouldn't have, anyway. We're not a devoted family."

40

"No."

He shot a quick look at her.

"Got the windup? About my family? You needn't. We're not going to live with them, or anything like that. We'll have our own little place somewhere. Horses, dogs, anything you like."

"But there will still be the 5:18."

"For me, yes. To and fro to the city all togged up. But don't worry, sweet—there are rural pockets, even round London. And lately I've felt the sap of financial affairs rising in me. After all it's in my blood, from both sides of the family."

"You hardly remember your mother, do you?"

"She always seemed to me incredibly old. She was old, of course. Nearly fifty when Elaine was born. She wore lots of clinking things and lay on the sofa and used to read me stories about knights and ladies which bored me stiff. Tennyson's *Idylls of the King*. I suppose I was fond of her. . . . She was very—colorless, you know. I realize that, looking back."

"You don't seem to have been particularly fond of anybody," said Pat disapprovingly.

Lance grasped and squeezed her arm.

"I'm fond of you," he said.

CHAPTER 7

INSPECTOR NEELE WAS still holding the telegraph message in his hand when he heard a car drive up to the front door and stop with a careless scrunching of brakes.

Mary Dove said, "That will be Mrs. Fortescue now."

Inspector Neele moved forwards to the front door. Out of the tail of his eye, he saw Mary Dove melt unobtrusively into the background and disappear. Clearly she intended to take no part in the forthcoming scene. A remarkable display of tact and discretion, and also a rather remarkable lack of curiosity. Most women, Inspector Neele decided, would have remained . . .

As he reached the front door he was aware of the butler, Crump, coming forward from the back of the hall. So he had heard the car.

The car was a Rolls Bentley sports model coupé. Two people got out of it and came towards the house. As they reached the door, it opened. Surprised, Adele Fortescue stared at Inspector Neele.

He realized at once that she was a very beautiful woman, and he realized too, the force of Mary Dove's comment which had so shocked him at the time. Adele Fortescue *was* a sexy piece. In figure and type she resembled the blonde Miss Grosvenor, but whereas Miss Grosvenor was all glamour without and all respectability within, Adele Fortescue was glamour all through. Her appeal was obvious, not subtle. It said simply to every man, "Here am I. I'm a woman." She spoke and moved and breathed sex, and yet, within it all, her eyes had a shrewd, appraising quality. Adele Fortescue, he thought, liked men, but she would always like money even better.

His eyes went on behind her to the figure who carried her golf clubs. He knew the type very well. It was the type that specialized in the young wives of rich and elderly men. Mr. Vivian Dubois, if this was he, had that rather forced masculinity which is, in reality, nothing of the kind. He was the type of man who "understands" women.

"Mrs. Fortescue?"

"Yes." It was a wide blue-eyed gaze. "But I don't know—"

"I am Inspector Neele. I'm afraid I have bad news for you."

"Do you mean—a burglary—something of that kind?"

"No, nothing of that kind. It is about your husband. He was taken seriously ill this morning."

"Rex? Ill?"

"We have been trying to get in touch with you since half past eleven this morning."

"Where is he? Here? Or in hospital?"

"He was taken to St. Jude's Hospital. I'm afraid you must prepare yourself for a shock."

"You don't mean—he isn't—dead."

She lurched forward a little and clutched his arm. Gravely, feeling like someone playing a part in a stage performance, the Inspector supported her into the hall. Crump was hovering eagerly.

"Brandy she'll be needing," he said.

The deep voice of Mr. Dubois said, "That's right, Crump. Get the brandy." To the Inspector he said, "In here."

He opened a door on the left. The procession filed in. The Inspector and Adele Fortescue, Vivian Dubois, and Crump with a decanter and two glasses.

Adele Fortescue sank onto an easy chair, her eyes covered with her hand. She accepted the glass that the Inspector offered and took a tiny sip, then pushed it away.

"I don't want it," she said. "I'm all right. But tell me, what was it? A stroke, I suppose? Poor Rex."

"It wasn't a stroke, Mrs. Fortescue."

"Did you say you were an Inspector?" It was Mr. Dubois who made the inquiry.

Neele turned to him. "That's right," he said pleasantly. "Inspector Neele of the C.I.D."

He saw the alarm grow in the dark eyes. Mr. Dubois did not like the appearance of an Inspector of the C.I.D. He didn't like it at all.

"What's up?" he said. "Something wrong, eh?"

Quite unconsciously he backed away a little towards the door. Inspector Neele noted the movement.

"I'm afraid," he said to Mrs. Fortescue, "that there will have to be an inquest."

"An inquest? Do you mean—what *do* you mean?"

"I'm afraid this is all very distressing for you, Mrs. Fortescue." The words came smoothly. "It seemed advisable to find out as soon as possible exactly what Mr. Fortescue had to eat or drink before leaving for the office this morning."

"Do you mean he might have been poisoned?"

"Well, yes, it would seem so."

"I can't believe it. Oh, you mean food poisoning." Her voice dropped half an octave on the last words.

His face wooden, his voice still smooth, Inspector Neele said, "Why, yes, madam, what did you think I meant?"

She ignored that question, hurrying on.

"But we've been all right—all of us."

"You can speak for all the members of the family?"

"Well, no—of course—I can't really."

Dubois said with a great show of consulting his watch, "I'll have to push off, Adele. Dreadfully sorry. You'll be all right, won't you? I mean, there are the maids, and the little Dove and all that—"

"Oh Vivian, don't. Don't go."

It was quite a wail, and it affected Mr. Dubois adversely. His retreat quickened.

"Awfully sorry, old girl. Important engagement. I'm putting up at the Dormy House, by the way, Inspector. If you—er, want me for anything."

Inspector Neele nodded. He had no wish to detain Mr. Dubois. But he recognized Mr. Dubois' departure for what it was. Mr. Dubois was running away from trouble.

Adele Fortescue said, in an attempt to carry off the situation, "It's such a shock, to come back and find the police in the house."

"I'm sure it must be. But you see, it was necessary to act promptly in order to obtain the necessary specimens of foodstuffs, coffee, tea, etc."

"Tea and coffee? But they're not poisonous? I expect it's the awful bacon we sometimes get. It's quite uneatable sometimes."

"We shall find out, Mrs. Fortescue. Don't worry. You'd be surprised at some of the things that can happen. We once had a case of digitalis poisoning. It turned out that foxglove leaves had been picked in mistake for horse-radish."

"You think something like that could happen here?"

"We shall know better after the autopsy, Mrs. Fortescue."

"The autop— Oh I see." She shivered.

The Inspector went on: "You've got a lot of yew round the house, haven't you, madam. There's no possibility, I suppose, of the berries or leaves having got—mixed up in anything?"

He was watching her closely. She stared at him.

"Yew berries? Are they poisonous?"

The wonder seemed a little too wide-eyed and innocent.

"Children have been known to eat them with unfortunate results."

Adele clasped her hands to her head.

"I can't bear to talk about it any more. Must I? I want to go and lie down. I can't stand any more. Mr. Percival Fortescue will arrange everything. I can't—I can't—it isn't fair to ask me."

"We are getting in touch with Mr. Percival Fortescue as soon

44

as possible. Unfortunately he is away in the North of England."

"Oh yes, I forgot."

"There's just one other thing, Mrs. Fortescue. There was a small quantity of grain in your husband's pocket. Could you give me some explanation of that?"

She shook her head. She appeared quite bewildered.

"Would anyone have slipped it in there as a joke?"

"I don't see why it would be a joke."

Inspector Neele did not see either. He said, "I won't trouble you any further at present, Mrs. Fortescue. Shall I send one of the maids to you? Or Miss Dove?"

"What?" The word came abstractedly. He wondered what she had been thinking about.

She fumbled with her bag and pulled out a handkerchief. Her voice trembled.

"It's so awful," she said unsteadily. "I'm only just beginning to take it in. I've really been numbed up to now. Poor Rex. Poor dear Rex."

She sobbed in a manner that was almost convincing.

Inspector Neele watched her respectfully for a moment or two.

"It's been very sudden, I know," he said. "I'll send someone to you."

He went towards the door, opened it and passed through. He paused for a moment before looking back into the room.

Adele Fortescue still held the handkerchief to her eyes. The ends of it hung down but did not quite obscure her mouth. On her lips was a very faint smile.

CHAPTER 8

"I'VE GOT WHAT I could, sir." So Sergeant Hay reporting. "The marmalade, bit of the ham. Samples of tea, coffee and sugar, for what they're worth. Actual brews have been thrown out by now, of course, but there's one point. There was a good lot of coffee left over and they had it in the servants' hall at elevenses. That's important, I should say."

"Yes, that's important. Shows that if he took it in his coffee, it must have been slipped into the actual cup."

"By one of those present. Exactly. I've inquired, cautious like, about this yew stuff—berries or leaves—there's been none of it seen about the house. Nobody seems to know anything about the cereal in his pocket, either. . . . It just seems daft to them. Seems daft to me, too. He doesn't seem to have been one of those food faddists who'll eat any mortal thing so long as it isn't cooked. My sister's husband's like that. Raw carrots, raw peas, raw turnips. But even he doesn't eat raw grain. Why, I should say it would swell up in your inside something awful."

The telephone rang, and on a nod from the Inspector Sergeant Hay sprinted off to answer it. Following him, Neele found that it was headquarters on the line. Contact had been made with Mr. Percival Fortescue, who was returning to London immediately.

As the Inspector replaced the telephone, a car drew up at the front door. Crump went to the door and opened it. The woman who stood there had her arms full of parcels. Crump took them from her.

"Thanks, Crump. Pay the taxi, will you? I'll have tea now. Is Mrs. Fortescue or Miss Elaine in?"

The butler hesitated, looking back over his shoulder.

"We've had bad news, ma'am," he said. "About the master."

"About Mr. Fortescue?"

Neele came forward. Crump said: "This is Mrs. Percival, sir."

"What is it? What's happened? An accident?"

The Inspector looked her over as he replied. Mrs. Percival Fortescue was a plump woman with a discontented mouth. Her age he judged to be about thirty. Her questions came with a kind of eagerness. The thought flashed across his mind that she must be very bored.

"I'm sorry to have to tell you that Mr. Fortescue was taken to St. Jude's Hospital this morning seriously ill and has since died."

"Died? You mean he's dead?" The news was clearly even more sensational than she had hoped for. "Dear me, this is a surprise. My husband's away. You'll have to get in touch with him. He's in the North somewhere. I daresay they'll know at the office.

He'll have to see to everything. Things always happen at the most awkward moment, don't they?"

She paused for a moment, turning things over in her mind.

"It all depends, I suppose," she said, "where they'll have the funeral. Down here, I suppose. Or will it be in London?"

"That will be for the family to say."

"Of course. I only just wondered." For the first time she took direct cognizance of the man who was speaking to her.

"Are you from the office?" she asked. "You're not a doctor, are you?"

"I'm a police officer. Mr. Fortescue's death was very sudden and—"

She interrupted him.

"Do you mean he was murdered?"

It was the first time that word had been spoken. Neele carefully surveyed her eager, questioning face.

"Now why should you think that, madam?"

"Well, people are, sometimes. You said 'sudden.' And you're police. Have you seen her about it? What did she say?"

"I don't quite understand to whom you are referring?"

"Adele, of course. I always told Val his father was crazy to go marrying a woman years younger than himself. There's no fool like an old fool. Besotted about that awful creature, he was. And now look what comes of it. . . . A nice mess we're all in. Pictures in the paper and reporters coming round."

She paused, obviously visualizing the future in a series of crude, highly-colored pictures. He thought that the prospect was still not wholly unpleasing. She turned back to him.

"What was it? Arsenic?"

In a repressive voice Inspector Neele said, "The cause of death has yet to be ascertained. There will be an autopsy and an inquest."

"But you know already, don't you? Or you wouldn't come down here."

There was a sudden shrewdness in her plump, rather foolish face.

"You've been asking about what he ate and drank, I suppose? Dinner last night. Breakfast this morning. And all the drinks, of course."

He could see her mind ranging vividly over all the possibilities.

47

He said, with caution, "It seems possible that Mr. Fortescue's illness resulted from something he ate at breakfast."

"Breakfast?" She seemed surprised. "That's difficult. I don't see how . . ."

She paused and shook her head.

"I don't see how she could have done it then . . . unless she slipped something into the coffee when Elaine and I weren't looking . . ."

A quiet voice spoke softly beside them:

"Your tea is all ready in the library, Mrs. Val."

Mrs. Val jumped.

"Oh thank you, Miss Dove. Yes, I could do with a cup of tea. Really, I feel quite bowled over. What about you, Mr.—Inspector—"

"Thank you, not just now."

The plump figure hesitated and then went slowly away.

As she disappeared through a doorway, Mary Dove murmured softly, "I don't think she's ever heard of the term slander."

Inspector Neele did not reply. Mary Dove went on: "Is there anything I can do for you?"

"Where can I find the housemaid, Ellen?"

"I will take you to her. She's just gone upstairs."

ii.

Ellen proved to be grim but unafraid. Her sour old face looked triumphantly at the Inspector.

"It's a shocking business, sir. And I never thought I'd live to find myself in a house where that sort of thing has been going on. But in a way I can't say that it surprises me. I ought to have given my notice in long ago and that's a fact. I don't like the language that's used in this house, and I don't like the amount of drink that's taken, and I don't approve of the goings-on there've been. I've nothing against Mrs. Crump, but Crump and that girl Gladys just don't know what proper service is. But it's the goings-on that I mind about most."

"What goings-on do you mean exactly?"

"You'll soon hear about them if you don't know already. It's common talk all over the place. They've been seen here, there and everywhere. All this pretending to play golf—or tennis. And I've seen things with my own eyes in this house. The library door was open and there they were, kissing and canoodling."

The venom of the spinster was deadly. Neele really felt it unnecessary to say "Whom do you mean?" but he said it nevertheless.

"Who should I mean? The mistress—and that man. No shame about it, they hadn't. But if you ask me, the master had got wise to it. Put someone on to watch them, he had. Divorce, that's what it would have come to. Instead, it's come to *this*."

"When you say this, you mean—"

"You've been asking questions, sir, about what the master ate and drank and who gave it to him. They're in it together, sir, that's what I'd say. He got the stuff from somewhere, and she gave it to the master, that was the way of it, I've no doubt."

"Have you ever seen any yew berries in the house, or thrown away anywhere?"

The small eyes glinted curiously.

"Yew? Nasty, poisonous stuff. Never you touch those berries, my mother said to me when I was a child. Was that what was used, sir?"

"We don't know yet what was used."

"I've never seen her fiddling about with yew." Ellen sounded disappointed. "No, I can't say I've seen anything of that kind."

Neele questioned her about the grain found in Fortescue's pocket, but here again he drew a blank.

"No, sir. I know nothing about that."

He went on to further questions, but with no gainful result. Finally, he asked if he could see Miss Ramsbottom.

Ellen looked doubtful.

"I could ask her, but it's not everyone she'll see. She's a very old lady, you know, and she's a bit odd."

The Inspector pressed his demand, and rather unwillingly Ellen led him along a passage and up a short flight of stairs to what he thought had probably been designed as a nursery suite.

He glanced out of a passage window as he followed her and saw Sergeant Hay standing by the yew tree talking to a man who was evidently a gardener.

Ellen tapped on a door, and when she received an answer, opened it and said, "There's a police gentleman here who would like to speak to you, miss."

The answer was apparently in the affirmative, for she drew back and motioned Neele to go in.

The room he entered was almost fantastically over-furnished. The Inspector felt rather as though he had taken a step backward into not merely Edwardian but Victorian times. At a table drawn up to a gas fire an old lady was sitting laying out a patience. She wore a maroon-colored dress and her sparse gray hair was slicked down each side of her face.

Without looking up or discontinuing her game, she said impatiently, "Well, come in, come in. Sit down if you like."

The invitation was not easy to accept as every chair appeared to be covered with tracts or publications of a religious nature.

As he moved them slightly aside on the sofa, Miss Ramsbottom asked sharply, "Interested in mission work?"

"Well, I'm afraid I'm not very, ma'am."

"Wrong. You should be. That's where the Christian spirit is nowadays. Darkest Africa. Had a young clergyman here last week. Black as your hat. But a true Christian."

Inspector Neele found it a little difficult to know what to say.

The old lady further disconcerted him by snapping, "I haven't got a wireless."

"I beg your pardon?"

"Oh, I thought perhaps you came about a wireless license. Or one of these silly forms. Well, man, what is it?"

"I'm sorry to have to tell you, Miss Ramsbottom, that your brother-in-law, Mr. Fortescue, was taken suddenly ill and died this morning."

Miss Ramsbottom continued with her patience without any sign of perturbation, merely remarking in a conversational way, "Struck down at last in his arrogance and sinful pride. Well, it had to come."

"I hope it's not a shock to you?"

It obviously wasn't, but the Inspector wanted to hear what she would say.

Miss Ramsbottom gave him a sharp glance over the top of her spectacles and said, "If you mean I am not distressed, that is quite right. Rex Fortescue was always a sinful man and I never liked him."

"His death was very sudden—"

"As befits the ungodly," said the old lady with satisfaction.

"It seems possible that he may have been poisoned—"

The Inspector paused to observe the effect he had made.

He did not seem to have made any. Miss Ramsbottom merely murmured, "Red seven on black eight. Now I can move up the king."

Struck apparently by the Inspector's silence, she stopped with a card poised in her hand and said sharply, "Well, what did you expect me to say? I didn't poison him if that's what you want to know."

"Have you any idea who might have done so?"

"That's a very improper question," said the old lady sharply. "Living in this house are two of my dead sister's children. I decline to believe that anybody with Ramsbottom blood in them could be guilty of murder. Because it's murder you're meaning, isn't it?"

"I didn't say so, madam."

"Of course it's murder. Plenty of people have wanted to murder Rex in their time. A very unscrupulous man. And old sins have long shadows, as the saying goes."

"Have you anyone in particular in mind?"

Miss Ramsbottom swept up the cards and rose to her feet. She was a tall woman.

"I think you'd better go now," she said.

She spoke without anger, but with a kind of cold finality.

"If you want my opinion," she went on, "it was probably one of the servants. That butler looks to me a bit of a rascal, and that parlormaid is definitely subnormal. Good evening."

Inspector Neele found himself meekly walking out. Certainly a remarkable old lady. Nothing to be got out of her.

He came down the stairs into the square hall to find himself suddenly face to face with a tall, dark girl. She was wearing a damp mackintosh and she stared into his face with a curious blankness.

"I've just come back," she said. "And they told me—about Father —that he's dead."

"I'm afraid that's true."

She pushed out a hand behind her as though blindly seeking for support. She touched an oak chest and slowly, stiffly, she sat down on it.

"Oh no," she said. "No . . ."

Slowly two tears rolled down her cheeks.

"It's awful," she said. "I didn't think that I even liked him. . . ."

51

I thought I hated him. . . . But that can't be so, or I wouldn't mind. I do mind."

She sat there, staring in front of her, and again tears forced themselves from her eyes and down her cheeks.

Presently she spoke again, rather breathlessly.

"The awful thing is that it makes everything come right. I mean, Gerald and I can get married now. I can do everything that I want to do. But I hate it happening this way. I don't want Father to be dead. . . . Oh, I don't. Oh Daddy—Daddy . . ."

For the first time since he had come to Yewtree Lodge, Inspector Neele was startled by what seemed to be genuine grief for the dead man.

CHAPTER 9

"Sounds like the wife to me," said the Assistant Commissioner. He had been listening attentively to Inspector Neele's report.

It had been an admirable précis of the case. Short, but with no relevant detail left out.

"Yes," said the A.C. "It looks like the wife. What do you think yourself, Neele, eh?"

Inspector Neele said that it looked like the wife to him, too. He reflected cynically that it usually was the wife—or the husband as the case might be.

"She had the opportunity all right. And motive?" The A.C. paused. "There is motive?"

"Oh, I think so, sir. This Mr. Dubois, you know."

"Think he was in it, too?"

"No, I shouldn't say that, sir." Inspector Neele weighed the idea. "A bit too fond of his own skin for that. He may have guessed what was in her mind, but I shouldn't imagine that he instigated it."

"No, too careful."

"Much too careful."

"Well, we mustn't jump to conclusions, but it seems a good working hypothesis. What about the other two who had opportunity?"

"That's the daughter and the daughter-in-law, sir. The daughter was mixed up with a young man whom her father didn't want her to marry. And he definitely wasn't marrying her unless she had the money. That gives her a motive. As to the daughter-in-law, I wouldn't like to say. Don't know enough about her yet. But any of the three of them could have poisoned him, and I don't see how anyone else could have done so. The parlormaid, the butler, the cook, they all handled the breakfast or brought it in, but I don't see how any of them could have been sure of Fortescue himself getting the taxine and nobody else. That is, if it was taxine."

The A.C. said, "It was taxine all right. I've just got the preliminary report."

"That settles that, then," said Inspector Neele. "We can go ahead."

"Servants seem all right?"

"The butler and the parlormaid both seem nervous. There's nothing uncommon about that. Often happens. The cook's fighting mad and the housemaid was grimly pleased. In fact, all quite natural and normal."

"There's nobody else whom you consider suspicious in any way?"

"No, I don't think so, sir." Involuntarily, Inspector Neele's mind went back to Mary Dove and her enigmatic smile. There had surely been a faint yet definite look of antagonism. Aloud, he said, "Now that we know it's taxine, there ought to be some evidence to be got as to how it was obtained or prepared."

"Just so. Well, go ahead, Neele. By the way, Mr. Percival Fortescue is here now. I've had a word or two with him and he's waiting to see you. We've located the other son, too. He's in Paris at the Bristol, leaving today. You'll have him met at the airport, I suppose."

"Yes, sir. That was my idea. . . ."

"Well, you'd better see Percival Fortescue now." The A.C. chuckled. "Percy Prim, that's what he is."

Mr. Percival Fortescue was a neat, fair man of thirty-odd with pale hair and eyelashes and a slightly pedantic way of speech.

"This has been a terrible shock to me, Inspector Neele, as you can well imagine."

"It must have been, Mr. Fortescue," said Inspector Neele.

"I can only say that my father was perfectly well when I left home the day before yesterday. This food poisoning, or whatever it was, must have been very sudden?"

"It was very sudden, yes. But it wasn't food poisoning, Mr. Fortescue."

Percival stared and frowned.

"No? So that's why—" he broke off.

"Your father," said Inspector Neele, "was poisoned by the administration of taxine."

"Taxine? I never heard of it."

"Very few people have, I should imagine. It is a poison that takes effect very suddenly and drastically."

The frown deepened.

"Are you telling me, Inspector, that my father was deliberately poisoned by someone?"

"It would seem so, yes, sir."

"That's terrible!"

"Yes indeed, Mr. Fortescue."

Percival murmured, "I understand now their attitude in the hospital—their referring me here." He broke off. After a pause he went on, "The funeral?" He spoke interrogatively.

"The inquest is fixed for tomorrow after the post-mortem. The proceedings at the inquest will be purely formal and the inquest will be adjourned."

"I understand. That is usually the case?"

"Yes, sir. Nowadays."

"May I ask have you formed any ideas, any suspicions of who could— Really, I—" Again he broke off.

"It's rather early days for that, Mr. Fortescue," murmured Neele.

"Yes, I suppose so."

"All the same it would be helpful to us, Mr. Fortescue, if you could give us some idea of your father's testamentary dispositions. Or perhaps you could put me in touch with his solicitor."

"His solicitors are Billingsley, Horsethorpe & Walters of Bedford Square. As far as his will goes I think I can more or less tell you its main dispositions."

"If you will be kind enough to do so, Mr. Fortescue. It's a routine that has to be gone through, I'm afraid."

"My father made a new will on the occasion of his marriage

two years ago," said Percival precisely. "My father left the sum of £100,000 to his wife absolutely and £50,000 to my sister, Elaine. I am his residuary legatee. I am already, of course, a partner in the firm."

"There was no bequest to your brother, Lancelot Fortescue?"

"No, there is an estrangement of long standing between my father and my brother."

Neele threw a sharp glance at him—but Percival seemed quite sure of his statement.

"So as the will stands," said Inspector Neele, "the three people who stand to gain are Mrs. Fortescue, Miss Elaine Fortescue and yourself?"

"I don't think I shall be much of a gainer." Percival sighed. "There are death duties, you know, Inspector. And of late my father has been—well, all I can say is, highly injudicious in some of his financial dealings."

"You and your father have not seen eye to eye lately about the conduct of the business?" Inspector Neele threw out the question in a genial manner.

"I put my point of view to him, but alas—" Percival shrugged his shoulders.

"Put it rather forcibly, didn't you?" Neele inquired. "In fact, not to put too fine a point on it, there was quite a row about it, wasn't there?"

"I should hardly say that, Inspector." A red flush of annoyance mounted to Percival's forehead.

"Perhaps the dispute you had was about some other matter then, Mr. Fortescue."

"There was no dispute, Inspector."

"Quite sure of that, Mr. Fortescue? Well, no matter. Did I understand that your father and brother are still estranged?"

"That is so."

"Then perhaps you can tell me what this means?"

Neele handed him the telephone message Mary Dove had jotted down.

Percival read it and uttered an exclamation of surprise and annoyance. He seemed both incredulous and angry.

"I can't understand it, I really can't. I can hardly believe it."

"It seems to be true, though, Mr. Fortescue. Your brother is arriving from Paris today."

"But it's extraordinary, quite extraordinary. No, I really can't understand it."

"Your father said nothing to you about it?"

"He certainly did not. How outrageous of him. To go behind my back and send for Lance."

"You've no idea, I suppose, why he did such a thing?"

"Of course I haven't. It's all on a par with his behavior lately —crazy!—unaccountable—it's got to be stopped—I—"

Percival came to an abrupt stop. The color ebbed away again from his pale face.

"I'd forgotten," he said. "For the moment I'd forgotten that my father was dead."

Inspector Neele shook his head sympathetically.

Percival Fortescue prepared to take his departure. As he picked up his hat he said, "Call upon me if there is anything I can do. But I suppose—" he paused—"you will be coming down to Yew-tree Lodge?"

"Yes, Mr. Fortescue. I've got a man in charge there now."

Percival shuddered in a fastidious way.

"It will all be most unpleasant. To think such a thing should happen to us—"

He sighed and moved towards the door.

"I shall be at the office most of the day. There is a lot to be seen to here. But I shall get down to Yewtree Lodge this evening."

"Quite so, sir."

Percival Fortescue went out.

"Percy Prim," murmured Neele.

Sergeant Hay, who was sitting unobtrusively by the wall, looked up and said "Sir?" interrogatively.

Then, as Neele did not reply, he asked, "What do you make of it all, sir?"

"I don't know," said Neele. He quoted softly, " 'They're all very unpleasant people.' "

Sergeant Hay looked somewhat puzzled.

"Alice in Wonderland," said Neele. "Don't you know your Alice, Hay?"

"It's a classic, isn't it, sir?" said Hay. "Third Program stuff. I don't listen to the Third Program."

56

CHAPTER 10

It was about five minutes after leaving Le Bourget that Lance Fortescue opened his copy of the continental *Daily Mail*. A minute or two later he uttered a startled exclamation. Pat, in the seat beside him, turned her head inquiringly.

"It's the old man," said Lance. "He's dead."

"Dead! Your father?"

"Yes, he seems to have been taken suddenly ill at the office, was taken to St. Jude's Hospital and died there soon after arrival."

"Darling, I'm so sorry. What was it, a stroke?"

"I suppose so. Sounds like it."

"Did he ever have a stroke before?"

"No. Not that I know of."

"I thought people never died from a first one."

"Poor old boy," said Lance. "I never thought I was particularly fond of him, but somehow, now that he's dead . . ."

"Of course you were fond of him."

"We haven't all got your nice nature, Pat. Oh well, it looks as though my luck's out again, doesn't it."

"Yes. It's odd that it should happen just now. Just when you were on the point of coming home."

He turned his head sharply towards her.

"Odd? What do you mean by odd, Pat?"

She looked at him with slight surprise.

"Well, a sort of coincidence."

"You mean that whatever I set out to do goes wrong?"

"No, darling, I didn't mean that. But there is such a thing as a run of bad luck."

"Yes, I suppose there is."

Pat said again, "I'm so sorry."

When they arrived at Heath Row and were waiting to disem-

57

bark from the plane, an official of the air company called out in a clear voice:

"Is Mr. Lancelot Fortescue aboard?"

"Here," said Lance.

"Would you just step this way, Mr. Fortescue."

Lance and Pat followed him out of the plane, preceding the other passengers. As they passed a couple in the last seat, they heard the man whisper to his wife,

"Well-known smugglers, I expect. Caught in the act."

ii.

"It's fantastic," said Lance. "Quite fantastic." He stared across the table at Detective Inspector Neele.

Inspector Neele nodded his head sympathetically.

"Taxine—yewberries—the whole thing seems like some kind of melodrama. I daresay this sort of thing seems ordinary enough to you, Inspector. All in the day's work. But poisoning, in our family, seems wildly farfetched."

"You've no idea then at all," asked Inspector Neele, "who might have poisoned your father?"

"Good Lord, no. I expect the old man's made a lot of enemies in business, lots of people who'd like to skin him alive, do him down financially—all that sort of thing. But poisoning? Anyway, I wouldn't be in the know. I've been abroad for a good many years and have known very little of what's going on at home."

"That's really what I wanted to ask you about, Mr. Fortescue. I understand from your brother that there was an estrangement between you and your father which had lasted for many years. Would you like to tell me the circumstances that led to your coming home at this time?"

"Certainly, Inspector. I heard from my father, let me see, it must be about—yes, six months ago now. It was soon after my marriage. My father wrote and hinted that he would like to let bygones be bygones. He suggested that I should come home and enter the firm. He was rather vague in his terms and I wasn't really sure that I wanted to do what he asked. Anyway, the upshot was that I came over to England last—yes, last August, just about three months ago. I went down to see him at Yewtree Lodge and he made me, I must say, a very advantageous offer. I told him that

I'd have to think about it and I'd have to consult my wife. He quite understood that. I flew back to East Africa, talked it over with Pat. The upshot was that I decided to accept the old boy's offer. I had to wind up my affairs there, but I agreed to do so before the end of last month. I told him I would wire to him the date of my actual arrival in England."

Inspector Neele coughed.

"Your arrival back seems to have caused your brother some surprise."

Lance gave a sudden grin. His rather attractive face lit up with the spirit of pure mischief.

"Don't believe old Percy knew a thing about it," he said. "He was away on his holiday in Norway at the time. If you ask me, the old man picked that particular time on purpose. He was going behind Percy's back. In fact, I've a very shrewd suspicion that my father's offer to me was actuated by the fact that he had a blazing row with poor old Percy—or Val as he prefers to be called. Val, I think, had been more or less trying to run the old man. Well, the old man would never stand for anything of that kind. What the exact row was about I don't know, but he was furious. And I think he thought it a jolly good idea to get me there and thereby spike poor old Val. For one thing he never liked Percy's wife much and he was rather pleased, in a snobbish kind of way, with my marriage. It would be just his idea of a good joke to get me home and suddenly confront Percy with the accomplished fact."

"How long were you at Yewtree Lodge on this occasion?"

"Oh, not more than an hour or two. He didn't ask me to stay the night. The whole idea, I'm sure, was a kind of secret offensive behind Percy's back. I don't think he even wanted the servants to report upon it. As I say, things were left that I'd think it over, talk about it to Pat and then write him my decision, which I did. I wrote giving him the approximate date of my arrival, and I finally sent him a telegram yesterday from Paris."

Inspector Neele nodded.

"A telegram which surprised your brother very much."

"I bet it did. However, as usual, Percy wins. I've arrived too late."

"Yes," said Inspector Neele thoughtfully, "you've arrived too late." He went on briskly, "On the occasion of your visit last August, did you meet any other members of the family?"

"My stepmother was there at tea."

59

"You had not met her previously?"

"No." He grinned suddenly. "The old boy certainly knew how to pick them. She must be thirty years younger than he, at least."

"You will excuse my asking, but did you resent your father's remarriage, or did your brother do so?"

Lance looked surprised.

"I certainly didn't, and I shouldn't think Percy did either. After all, our own mother died when we were about—oh, ten, twelve years old. What I'm really surprised at is that the old man didn't marry again before."

Inspector Neele murmured, "It may be considered taking rather a risk to marry a woman very much younger than yourself."

"Did my dear brother say that to you? It sounds rather like him. Percy is a great master of the art of insinuation. Is that the setup, Inspector? Is my stepmother suspected of poisoning my father?"

Inspector Neele's face became blank.

"It's early days to have any definite ideas about anything, Mr. Fortescue," he said pleasantly. "Now, may I ask you what your plans are?"

"Plans?" Lance considered. "I shall have to make new plans, I suppose. Where is the family? All down at Yewtree Lodge?"

"Yes."

"I'd better go down there straightaway." He turned to his wife. "You'd better go to a hotel, Pat."

She protested quickly. "No, no, Lance, I'll come with you."

"No, darling."

"But I want to."

"Really, I'd rather you didn't. Go and stay at the—oh, it's so long since I stayed in London—Barnes'. Barnes' Hotel used to be a nice, quiet sort of place. That's still going, I suppose?"

"Oh, yes, Mr. Fortescue."

"Right, Pat, I'll settle you in there if they've got a room, then I'll go on down to Yewtree Lodge."

"But why can't I come with you, Lance?"

Lance's face took suddenly a rather grim line.

"Frankly, Pat, I'm not sure of my welcome. It was Father who invited me there, but Father's dead. I don't know whom the place belongs to now. Percy, I suppose, or perhaps Adele. Anyway, I'd like to see what reception I get before I bring you there. Besides—"

"Besides what?"

"I don't want to take you to a house where there's a poisoner at large."

"Oh, what nonsense."

Lance said firmly, "Where you're concerned, Pat, I'm taking no risks."

CHAPTER 11

MR. DUBOIS WAS annoyed. He tore Adele Fortescue's letter angrily across and threw it into the wastepaper basket. Then, with a sudden caution, he fished out the various pieces, struck a match and watched them burn to ashes. He muttered under his breath, "Why have women got to be such damned fools? Surely common prudence. . . ."

But then, Mr. Dubois reflected gloomily, women never had any prudence. Though he had profited by this lack many a time, it annoyed him now. He himself had taken every precaution. If Mrs. Fortescue rang up, they had instructions to say that he was out. Already Adele Fortescue had rung him up three times, and now she had written. On the whole, writing was far worse. He reflected for a moment or two, then went to the telephone.

"Can I speak to Mrs. Fortescue, please? Yes, Mr. Dubois." A minute or two later he heard her voice.

"Vivian, at last."

"Yes, yes, Adele, but be careful. Where are you speaking from?"

"From the library."

"Sure nobody's listening in, in the hall?"

"Why should they?"

"Well, you never know. Are the police still about the house?"

"No, they've gone for the moment, anyhow. Oh, Vivian dear, it's been awful."

"Yes, yes, it must have, I'm sure. But look here, Adele, we've got to be careful."

"Oh, of course, darling."

61

"Don't call me darling through the phone. It isn't safe."

"Aren't you being a little bit panicky, Vivian? After all, everybody says darling nowadays."

"Yes, yes, that's true enough. But listen. Don't telephone to me, and don't write."

"But Vivian——"

"It's just for the present, you understand. We must be careful."

"Oh. All right." Her voice sounded offended.

"Adele, listen. My letters to you. You did burn them, didn't you?"

There was a momentary hesitation before Adele Fortescue said, "Of course. I told you I was going to do so."

"That's all right, then. Well, I'll ring off now. Don't phone and don't write. You'll hear from me in good time."

He put the receiver back on its hook. He stroked his cheek thoughtfully. He didn't like that moment's hesitation. Had Adele burnt his letters? Women were all the same. They promised to burn things and then didn't.

Letters, Mr. Dubois thought to himself. Women always wanted you to write them letters. He himself tried to be careful, but sometimes one could not get out of it. What had he said exactly in the few letters he had written to Adele Fortescue? It was the usual sort of gup, he thought, gloomily. But were there any special words—special phrases that the police could twist to make them say what they wanted them to say? He remembered the Edith Thompson case. His letters were innocent enough, he thought, but he could not be sure. His uneasiness grew. Even if Adele had not already burnt his letters, would she have the sense to burn them now? Or had the police already got hold of them? Where did she keep them, he wondered. Probably in that sitting-room of hers upstairs. That gimcrack little desk, probably. Sham antique Louis xiv. She had said something to him once about there being a secret drawer in it. Secret drawer! That would not fool the police long. But there were no police about the house now. She had said so. They had been there that morning, and now they had all gone away.

Up to now they had probably been busy looking for possible sources of poison in the food. They would not, he hoped, have got round to a room-by-room search of the house. Perhaps they would have to ask permission or get a search warrant to do that. It was possible that if he acted now, at once——

He visualized the house clearly in his mind's eye. It would be getting towards dusk. Tea would be brought in, either into the library or into the drawing-room. Everyone would be assembled downstairs and the servants would be having tea in the servants' hall. There would be no one upstairs on the first floor. Easy to walk up through the garden, skirting the yew hedges that provided such admirable cover. Then there was the little door at the side onto the terrace. That was never locked until just before bedtime. One could slip through there and, choosing one's moment, slip upstairs.

Vivian Dubois considered very carefully what it behooved him to do next. If Fortescue's death had been put down to a seizure or to a stroke, as surely it ought to have been, the position would be very different. As it was—Dubois murmured under his breath, "Better be safe than sorry."

ii.

Mary Dove came slowly down the big staircase. She paused a moment at the window on the half landing, from which she had seen Inspector Neele arrive on the preceding day. Now, as she looked out in the half-light, she noticed a man's figure just disappearing round the yew hedge. She wondered if it was Lancelot Fortescue, the prodigal son. He had, perhaps, dismissed his car at the gate and was wandering round the garden, recollecting old times there before tackling a possibly hostile family. Mary Dove felt rather sympathetic towards Lance. A half smile on her lips, she went on downstairs. In the hall she encountered Gladys, the maid, who jumped nervously at the sight of her.

"Was that the telephone I heard just now?" Mary asked. "Who was it?"

"Oh, that was a wrong number. Thought we were the laundry." Gladys sounded breathless and rather hurried. "And before that, it was Mr. Dubois. He wanted to speak to the mistress."

"I see."

Mary went on across the hall. Turning her head, she said, "It's teatime, I think. Haven't you brought it in yet?"

Gladys said, "I don't think it's half-past four yet, is it, miss?"

"It's twenty minutes to five. Bring it in now, will you?"

Mary Dove went on into the library where Adele Fortescue, sitting on the sofa, was staring at the fire, picking with her fingers at a small lace handkerchief. Adele said fretfully, "Where's tea?"

Mary Dove said, "It's just coming in."

A log had fallen out of the fireplace, and Mary Dove knelt down at the grate and replaced it with the tongs, adding another piece of wood and a little coal.

Gladys went out into the kitchen where Mrs. Crump raised a red and wrathful face from the kitchen table where she was mixing pastry in a large bowl.

"The library bell's been ringing and ringing. Time you took in the tea, my girl."

"All right, all right, Mrs. Crump."

"What I'll say to Crump tonight," muttered Mrs. Crump. "I'll tell him off."

Gladys went on into the pantry. She had not cut any sandwiches. Well, she jolly well wasn't going to cut sandwiches. They'd got plenty to eat without that, hadn't they? Two cakes, biscuits, and scones and honey. Fresh, black-market farm butter. Plenty without her bothering to cut tomato or *foie gras* sandwiches. She'd got other things to think about. Fair temper Mrs. Crump was in, all because Mr. Crump had gone out this afternoon. Well, it was his day out, wasn't it? Quite right of him, Gladys thought.

Mrs. Crump called out from the kitchen, "The kettle's boiling its head off. Aren't you ever going to make that tea?"

"Coming."

She jerked some tea without measuring it into the big silver pot, carried the pot into the kitchen and poured the boiling water into it. She added the teapot and the kettle to the big silver tray and carried the whole thing through to the library where she set it on the small table near the sofa. She went back hurriedly for the other tray with the eatables on it. She carried the latter as far as the hall when the sudden jarring noise of the grandfather clock preparing itself to strike made her jump.

In the library, Adele Fortescue said querulously to Mary Dove, "Where is everybody this afternoon?"

"I really don't know, Mrs. Fortescue. Miss Fortescue came in some time ago. I think Mrs. Percival's writing letters in her room."

Adele said pettishly, "Writing letters, writing letters. That woman never stops writing letters. She's like all people of her class. She takes an absolute delight in death and misfortune. Ghoulish, that's what I call it. Absolutely ghoulish."

Mary murmured tactfully, "I'll tell her that tea is ready."

Going towards the door, she drew back a little in the doorway as Elaine Fortescue came into the room.

Elaine said, "It's cold," and dropped down by the fireplace, rubbing her hands before the blaze.

Mary stood for a moment in the hall. A large tray with cakes on it was standing on one of the hall chests. Since it was getting dark in the hall, Mary switched on the light. As she did so, she thought she heard Jennifer Fortescue walking along the passage upstairs. Nobody, however, came down the stairs, and Mary went up the staircase and along the corridor.

Percival Fortescue and his wife occupied a self-contained suite in one wing of the house. Mary tapped on the sitting-room door. Mrs. Percival liked you to tap on doors, a fact which always roused Crump's scorn of her. Her voice said briskly, "Come in."

Mary opened the door and murmured, "Tea is just coming in, Mrs. Percival."

She was rather surprised to see Jennifer Fortescue with her outdoor clothes on. She was just divesting herself of a long, camel-hair coat.

"I didn't know you'd been out," said Mary.

Mrs. Percival sounded slightly out of breath.

"Oh, I was just in the garden, that's all. Just getting a little air. Really, though, it was too cold. I shall be glad to get down to the fire. The central heating here isn't as good as it might be. Somebody must speak to the gardeners about it, Miss Dove."

"I'll do so," Mary promised.

Jennifer Fortescue dropped her coat on a chair and followed Mary out of the room. She went down the stairs ahead of Mary, who drew back a little to give her precedence. In the hall, rather to Mary's surprise, she noticed the tray of eatables was still there. She was about to go out to the pantry and call to Gladys when Adele Fortescue appeared in the door of the library, saying in an irritable voice, "Aren't we ever going to have anything to eat for tea?"

Quickly Mary picked up the tray and took it into the library, disposing the various things on low tables near the fireplace. She

65

was carrying the empty tray out to the hall again when the front doorbell rang. Setting down the tray, Mary went to the door herself. If this was the prodigal son, at last she was rather curious to see him. How unlike the rest of the Fortescues, Mary thought, as she opened the door and looked up into the dark, lean face and the faintly quizzical twist of the mouth. She said quietly, "Mr. Lancelot Fortescue?"

"Himself."

Mary peered beyond him.

"Your luggage?"

"I've paid off the taxi. This is all I've got."

He picked up a medium-sized zip bag. Some faint feeling of surprise in her mind, Mary said, "Oh, you did come in a taxi. I thought perhaps you'd walked up. And your wife?"

His face set in a rather grim line, Lance said, "My wife won't be coming. At least, not just yet."

"I see. Come this way, will you, Mr. Fortescue? Everyone is in the library, having tea."

She took him to the library door and left him there. She thought to herself that Lancelot Fortescue was a very attractive person. A second thought followed the first. Probably a great many other women thought so, too.

iii.

"Lance!"

Elaine came hurrying forward towards him. She flung her arms round his neck and hugged him with a schoolgirl abandon that Lance found quite surprising.

"Hullo. Here I am."

He disengaged himself gently.

"This is Jennifer?"

Jennifer Fortescue looked at him with eager curiosity.

"I'm afraid Val's been detained in town," she said. "There's so much to see to, you know. All the arrangements to make and everything. Of course it all comes on Val. He has to see to everything. You can really have no idea what we're all going through."

"It must be terrible for you," said Lance gravely.

He turned to the woman on the sofa, who was sitting with a piece of scone and honey in her hand, quietly appraising him.

"Of course," cried Jennifer, "you don't know Adele, do you?"

Lance murmured "Oh yes, I do" as he took Adele Fortescue's hand in his. As he looked down at her, her eyelids fluttered. She set down the scone she was eating with her left hand and just touched the arrangement of her hair. It was a feminine gesture. It marked her recognition of the entry to the room of a personable man. She said in her thick, soft voice, "Sit down here on the sofa beside me, Lance." She poured out a cup of tea for him. "I'm so glad you've come," she went on. "We badly need another man in the house."

Lance said, "You must let me do everything I can to help."

"You know—but perhaps you don't know—we've had the police here. They think—they think—" she broke off and cried out passionately, "Oh, it's awful! Awful!"

"I know." Lance was grave and sympathetic. "As a matter of fact, they met me at London Airport."

"The police met you?"

"Yes."

"What did they say?"

"Well," Lance was deprecating. "They told me what had happened."

"He was poisoned," said Adele, "that's what they think, what they say. Not food poisoning. Real poisoning, by someone. I believe, I really do believe they think it's one of us."

Lance gave her a sudden, quick smile.

"That's their pigeon," he said consolingly. "It's no good our worrying. What a scrumptious tea! It's a long time since I've seen a good English tea."

The others fell in with his mood soon enough. Adele said suddenly, "But your wife—haven't you got a wife, Lance?"

"I've got a wife, yes. She's in London."

"But aren't you—hadn't you better bring her down here?"

"Plenty of time to make plans," said Lance. "Pat—oh, Pat's quite all right where she is."

Elaine said sharply,

"You don't mean—you don't think—"

Lance said quickly, "What a wonderful-looking chocolate cake. I must have some." Cutting himself a slice, he asked, "Is Aunt Effie alive still?"

"Oh, yes, Lance. She won't come down and have meals with

us or anything, but she's quite well. Only, she's getting very peculiar."

"She always was peculiar," said Lance. "I must go up and see her after tea."

Jennifer Fortescue murmured, "At her age one does really feel that she ought to be in some kind of a home. I mean somewhere where she will be properly looked after."

"Heaven help any old ladies' home that got Aunt Effie in their midst," said Lance. He added, "Who's the demure piece of goods who let me in?"

Adele looked surprised.

"Didn't Crump let you in? The butler? Oh no, I forgot. It's his day out today. But surely Gladys——"

Lance gave a description. "Blue eyes, hair parted in the middle, soft voice, butter wouldn't melt in the mouth. What goes on behind it all, I wouldn't like to say."

"That," said Jennifer, "would be Mary Dove."

Elaine said, "She sort of runs things for us."

"Does she, now."

Adele said, "She's really very useful."

"Yes," said Lance thoughtfully, "I should think she might be."

"But what is so nice is," said Jennifer, "that she knows her place. She never presumes, if you know what I mean."

"Clever Mary Dove," said Lance, and helped himself to another piece of chocolate cake.

CHAPTER 12

"So you've turned up again like a bad penny," said Miss Ramsbottom.

Lance grinned at her. "Just as you say, Aunt Effie."

"Humph!" Miss Ramsbottom sniffed disapprovingly. "You've chosen a nice time to do it. Your father got himself murdered

68

yesterday, the house is full of police poking about everywhere, grubbing in the dustbins, even. I've seen them out of the window." She paused, sniffed again, and asked, "Got your wife with you?"

"No. I left Pat in London."

"That shows some sense. I shouldn't bring her here if I were you. You never know what might happen."

"To her? To Pat?"

"To anybody," said Miss Ramsbottom.

Lance Fortescue looked at her thoughtfully.

"Got any ideas about it all, Aunt Effie?" he asked.

Miss Ramsbottom did not reply directly. "I had an Inspector here yesterday asking me questions. He didn't get much change out of me. But he wasn't such a fool as he looked, not by a long way." She added with some indignation, "What your grandfather would feel if he knew we had the police in the house—it's enough to make him turn in his grave. A strict Plymouth Brother he was all his life. The fuss there was when he found out I'd been attending Church of England services in the evening! And I'm sure that was harmless enough compared to murder."

Normally Lance would have smiled at this, but his long, dark face remained serious. He said, "D'you know, I'm quite in the dark after having been away so long. What's been going on here of late?"

Miss Ramsbottom raised her eyes to heaven.

"Godless doings," she said firmly.

"Yes, yes, Aunt Effie, you would say that anyway. But what gives the police the idea that Dad was killed here, in this house?"

"Adultery is one thing and murder is another," said Miss Ramsbottom. "I shouldn't like to think it of her, I shouldn't, indeed."

Lance looked alert. "Adele?" he asked.

"My lips are sealed," said Miss Ramsbottom.

"Come on, old dear," said Lance. "It's a lovely phrase, but it doesn't mean a thing. Adele had a boy friend? Adele and the boy friend fed him henbane in the morning tea. Is that the setup?"

"I'll trouble you not to joke about it."

"I wasn't really joking, you know."

"I'll tell you one thing," said Miss Ramsbottom suddenly. "I believe that girl knows something about it."

"Which girl?" Lance looked surprised.

"The one that sniffs," said Miss Ramsbottom. "The one that ought to have brought me up my tea this afternoon, but didn't. Gone out without leave, so they say. Well, shouldn't wonder if she had gone to the police. Who let you in?"

"Someone called Mary Dove, I understand. Very meek and mild, but not really. Is she the one who's gone to the police?"

"She wouldn't go to the police," said Miss Ramsbottom. "No—I mean that silly little parlormaid. She's been twitching and jumping like a rabbit all day. 'What's the matter with you?' I said. 'Have you got a guilty conscience?' She said, 'I never did anything—I wouldn't do a thing like that.' 'I hope you wouldn't,' I said to her, 'but there's something worrying you now, isn't there?' Then she began to sniff and said she didn't want to get anybody into trouble, she was sure it must be all a mistake. I said to her, I said, 'Now, my girl, you speak the truth and shame the devil.' That's what I said. 'You go to the police,' I said, 'and tell them anything you know, because no good ever came,' I said, 'of hushing up the truth, however unpleasant it is.' Then she talked a lot of nonsense about she couldn't go to the police, they'd never believe her and what on earth should she say? She ended up by saying anyway she didn't know anything at all."

"You don't think," Lance hesitated, "that she was just making herself important?"

"No, I don't. I think she was scared. I think she saw something or heard something that's given her some idea about the whole thing. It may be important, or it mayn't be of the least consequence."

"You don't think she herself could've had a grudge against Father and—" Lance hesitated.

Miss Ramsbottom was shaking her head decidedly.

"She's not the kind of girl your father would have taken the least notice of. No man ever will take much notice of her, poor girl. Ah, well, it's all the better for her soul, that, I dare say."

Lance took no interest in Gladys's soul. He asked, "You think she may have run along to the police station?"

Aunt Effie nodded vigorously.

"Yes. I think she mayn't like to've said anything to them in this house, in case somebody overheard her."

Lance asked, "Do you think she may have seen someone tampering with the food?"

Aunt Effie threw him a sharp glance.

"It's possible, isn't it?" she said.

"Yes, I suppose so." Then he added apologetically, "The whole thing still seems so wildly improbable. Like a detective story."

"Percival's wife is a hospital nurse," said Miss Ramsbottom.

The remark seemed so unconnected with what had gone before that Lance looked at her in a puzzled fashion.

"Hospital nurses are used to handling drugs," said Miss Ramsbottom.

Lance looked doubtful.

"This stuff—taxine—is it ever used in medicine?"

"They get it from yewberries, I gather. Children eat yewberries sometimes," said Miss Ramsbottom. "Makes them very ill, too. I remember a case when I was a child. It made a great impression on me. I never forgot it. Things you remember come in useful sometimes."

Lance raised his head sharply and stared at her.

"Natural affection is one thing," said Miss Ramsbottom, "and I hope I've got as much of it as anyone. But I won't stand for wickedness. Wickedness has to be destroyed."

ii.

"Went off without a word to me," said Mrs. Crump, raising her red, wrathful face from the pastry she was now rolling out on the board. "Slipped out without a word to anybody. Sly, that's what it is. Sly! Afraid she'd be stopped, and I would have stopped her if I'd caught her! The idea! There's the master dead, Mr. Lance coming home that hasn't been home for years, and I said to Crump, I said, 'Day out or no day out, I know my duty. There's not going to be cold supper tonight as is usual on a Thursday, but a proper dinner. A gentleman coming home from abroad with his wife, what was formerly married in the aristocracy, things must be properly done.' You know me, miss, you know I take a pride in my work."

Mary Dove, the recipient of these confidences, nodded her head gently.

"And what does Crump say?" Mrs. Crump's voice rose angrily. " 'It's my day off and I'm goin' off,' that's what he says. 'And a fig for the aristocracy,' he says. No pride in his work, Crump

71

hasn't. So off he goes and I tell Gladys she'll have to manage alone tonight. She just says, 'All right, Mrs. Crump,' then, when my back's turned out she sneaks. It wasn't her day out, anyway. Friday's her day. How we're going to manage now, I don't know! Thank goodness, Mr. Lance hasn't brought his wife here with him today."

"We shall manage, Mrs. Crump," Mary's voice was both soothing and authoritative, "if we just simplify the menu a little." She outlined a few suggestions. Mrs. Crump nodded unwilling acquiescence. "I shall be able to serve that quite easily," Mary concluded.

"You mean you'll wait at table yourself, miss?" Mrs. Crump sounded doubtful.

"If Gladys doesn't come back in time."

"She won't come back," said Mrs. Crump. "Gallivanting off, wasting her money somewhere in the shops. She's got a young man, you know, miss, though you wouldn't think it to look at her. Albert his name is. Going to get married next spring, so she tells me. Don't know what the married state's like, these girls don't. What I've been through with Crump." She sighed, then said in an ordinary voice, "What about tea, miss? Who's going to clear it away and wash it up?"

"I'll do that," said Mary. "I'll go and do it now."

The lights had not been turned on in the drawing-room, though Adele Fortescue was still sitting on the sofa behind the tea tray.

"Shall I switch the lights on, Mrs. Fortescue?" Mary asked. Adele did not answer.

Mary switched on the lights and went across to the window where she pulled the curtains across. It was only then that she turned her head and saw the face of the woman who had sagged back against the cushions. A half-eaten scone spread with honey was beside her and her tea cup was still half-full. Death had come to Adele Fortescue suddenly and swiftly.

iii.

"Well?" demanded Inspector Neele impatiently.

The doctor said promptly,

"Cyanide—potassium cyanide probably—in the tea."

72

"Cyanide," muttered Neele.

The doctor looked at him with slight curiosity.

"You're taking this hard. Any special reason?"

"She was cast as a murderess," said Neele.

"And she turns out to be a victim. Hm. You'll have to think again, won't you?"

Neele nodded. His face was bitter and his jaw was grimly set.

Poisoned! Right under his nose. Taxine in Rex Fortescue's breakfast coffee, cyanide in Adele Fortescue's tea. Still an intimate family affair. Or so it seemed.

Adele Fortescue, Jennifer Fortescue, Elaine Fortescue and the newly arrived Lance Fortescue had had tea together in the library. Lance had gone up to see Miss Ramsbottom, Jennifer had gone to her own sitting-room to write letters, Elaine had been the last to leave the library. According to her, Adele had then been in perfect health and had just been pouring herself out a last cup of tea.

A last cup of tea! Yes, it had indeed been her last cup of tea.

And after that a blank twenty minutes, perhaps, until Mary Dove had come into the room and discovered the body.

And during that twenty minutes——

Inspector Neele swore to himself and went out into the kitchen.

Sitting in a chair by the kitchen table, the vast figure of Mrs. Crump, her belligerence pricked like a balloon, hardly stirred as he came in.

"Where's that girl? Has she come back yet?"

"Gladys? No, she's not back. Won't be, I suspect, until eleven o'clock."

"She made the tea, you say, and took it in."

"I didn't touch it, sir, as God's my witness. And what's more, I don't believe Gladys did anything she shouldn't. She wouldn't do a thing like that—not Gladys. She's a good enough girl, sir—a bit foolish like, that's all—not wicked."

No, Neele did not think that Gladys was wicked. He did not think that Gladys was a poisoner. And in any case the cyanide had not been in the teapot.

"But what made her go off suddenly—like this? It wasn't her day out, you say."

"No, sir, tomorrow's her day out."

"Does Crump—"

Mrs. Crump's belligerence suddenly revived. Her voice rose wrathfully.

"Don't you go fastening anything on Crump. Crump's out of it. He went off at three o'clock—and thankful I am now that he did. He's as much out of it as Mr. Percival himself."

Percival Fortescue had only just returned from London—to be greeted by the astounding news of this second tragedy.

"I wasn't accusing Crump," said Neele mildly. "I just wondered if he knew anything about Gladys's plans."

"She had her best nylons on," said Mrs. Crump. "She was up to something. Don't tell me! Didn't cut any sandwiches for tea, either. Oh yes, she was up to something. I'll give her a piece of my mind when she comes back."

When she comes back——

A faint uneasiness possessed Neele. To shake it off, he went upstairs to Adele Fortescue's bedroom. A lavish apartment—all rose brocade hangings and a vast gilt bed. On one side of the room was a door into a mirror-lined bathroom with a sunken, orchid-pink porcelain bath. Beyond the bathroom, reached by a communicating door, was Rex Fortescue's room. Neele went back into Adele's bedroom, and through the door on the farther side of the room into her sitting-room.

The room was furnished in Empire style with a rose pile carpet. Neele only gave it a cursory glance, for that particular room had had his close attention on the preceding day—with special attention paid to the small, elegant desk.

Now, however, he stiffened to sudden attention. On the center of the rose pile carpet was a small piece of caked mud.

Neele went over to it and picked it up. The mud was still damp.

He looked round—there were no footprints visible—only this one, isolated fragment of wet earth.

iv.

Inspector Neele looked round the bedroom that belonged to Gladys Martin. It was past eleven o'clock. Crump had come in half an hour ago, but there was still no sign of Gladys. Inspector Neele looked round him. Whatever Gladys's training had been, her own natural instincts were slovenly. The bed, Inspector Neele judged, was seldom made, the windows seldom opened. Gladys's personal habits, however, were not his immediate concern. Instead, he went carefully through her possessions.

They consisted, for the most part, of cheap and rather pathetic finery. There was little that was durable or of good quality. The elderly Ellen, whom he had called upon to assist him, had not been helpful. She didn't know what clothes Gladys had or hadn't. She couldn't say what, if anything, was missing. He turned from the clothes and the underclothes to the contents of the chest of drawers. There Gladys kept her treasures. There were picture post cards and newspaper cuttings, knitting patterns, hints on beauty culture, dressmaking and fashion advice.

Inspector Neele sorted them neatly into various categories. The picture post cards consisted mainly of views of various places where he presumed Gladys had spent her holidays. Among them were three picture post cards signed "Bert." Bert he took to be the "young man" referred to by Mrs. Crump. The first post card said, in an illiterate hand, "All the best. Missing you a lot. Yours ever, Bert." The second said, "Lots of nice-looking girls here but not one that's a patch on you. Be seeing you soon. Don't forget our date. And remember after that—it's thumbs up and living happy ever after." The third said merely, "Don't forget. I'm trusting you. Love, B."

Next, Neele looked through the newspaper cuttings and sorted them into three piles. There were the dressmaking and beauty hints, there were items about cinema stars to which Gladys had appeared greatly addicted, and she had also, it appeared, been attracted by the latest marvels of science. There were cuttings about flying saucers, about secret weapons, about truth drugs used by Russians, and claims for fantastic drugs discovered by American doctors. All the witchcraft, so Neele thought, of our twentieth century. But in all the contents of the room there was nothing to give him a clue to her disappearance. She had kept no diary, not that he had expected that. It was a remote possibility. There was no unfinished letter, no record at all of anything she might have seen in the house which could have had a bearing on Rex Fortescue's death. Whatever Gladys had seen, whatever Gladys had known, there was no record of it. It would still have to be guesswork why the second tea tray had been left in the hall, and Gladys herself had so suddenly vanished.

Sighing, Neele left the room, shutting the door behind him.

As he prepared to descend the small, winding stairs he heard a noise of running feet coming along the landing below.

The agitated face of Sergeant Hay looked up at him from the bottom of the stairs. Sergeant Hay was panting a little.

"Sir," he said urgently, "Sir! We've found her."

"Found her?"

"It was the housemaid, sir—Ellen—remembered as she hadn't brought the clothes in from where they were hanging on the line—just round the corner from the back door. So she went out with a torch to take them in and she almost fell over the body— the girl's body—strangled, she was, with a stocking round her throat—been dead for hours, I'd say. And, sir, it's a wicked kind of joke—there was a clothes peg clipped on her nose——"

CHAPTER 13

AN ELDERLY LADY traveling by train had bought three morning papers, and each of them, as she finished it, folded it and laid it aside, showed the same headline. It was no longer a question now of a small paragraph hidden away in the corner of the papers. There were headlines with flaring announcements of Triple Tragedy at Yewtree Lodge.

The old lady sat very upright, looking out of the window of the train, her lips pursed together, an expression of distress and disapproval on her pink and white wrinkled face. Miss Marple had left St. Mary Meade by the early train, changing at the junction and going on to London where she took a Circle train to another London terminus and thence on to Baydon Heath.

At the station she signaled a taxi and asked to be taken to Yewtree Lodge. So charming, so innocent, such a fluffy and pink and white old lady was Miss Marple that she gained admittance to what was now practically a fortress in a state of siege far more easily than could have been believed possible. Though an army of reporters and photographers was being kept at bay by the police, Miss Marple was allowed to drive in without question, so impossible would it have been to believe that she was anyone but an elderly relative of the family.

Miss Marple paid off the taxi in a careful assortment of small change, and rang the front doorbell. Crump opened it and Miss Marple summed him up with an experienced glance. A shifty eye, she said to herself. Scared to death, too.

Crump saw a tall, elderly lady wearing an old-fashioned tweed coat and skirt, a couple of scarves and a small felt hat with a bird's wing. The old lady carried a capacious handbag, and an aged but good quality suitcase reposed by her feet.

Crump recognized a lady when he saw one and said, "Yes, madam?" in his best and most respectful voice.

"Could I see the mistress of the house, please?" said Miss Marple.

Crump drew back to let her in. He picked up the suitcase and put it carefully down in the hall.

"Well, madam," he said rather dubiously, "I don't know who exactly——"

Miss Marple helped him out.

"I have come," she said, "to speak about the poor girl who was killed. Gladys Martin."

"Oh, I see, madam. Well, in that case—" he broke off, and looked towards the library door from which a tall young woman had just emerged. "This is Mrs. Lance Fortescue, madam," he said.

Pat came forward, and she and Miss Marple looked at each other. Miss Marple was aware of a faint feeling of surprise. She had not expected to see someone like Patricia Fortescue in this particular house. Its interior was much as she had pictured it, but Pat did not somehow match with that interior.

"It's about Gladys, madam," said Crump helpfully.

Pat said rather hesitatingly, "Will you come in here? We shall be quite alone."

She led the way into the library and Miss Marple followed her.

"There wasn't anyone specially you wanted to see, was there?" said Pat, "because perhaps I shan't be much good. You see, my husband and I only came back from Africa a few days ago. We don't really know anything much about the household. But I can fetch my sister-in-law or my brother-in-law's wife."

Miss Marple looked at the girl and liked her. She liked her gravity and her simplicity. For some strange reason she felt sorry for her. A background of shabby chintz and horses and dogs, Miss Marple felt vaguely, would have been much more suitable than this richly furnished interior décor. At the pony show and gymkhanas held locally round St. Mary Meade, Miss Marple had met many Pats and knew them well. She felt at home with this rather unhappy-looking girl.

"It's very simple, really," said Miss Marple, taking off her gloves carefully and smoothing out the fingers of them. "I read in the paper, you see, about Gladys Martin having been killed. And of course I know all about her. She comes from my part of the country. I trained her, in fact, for domestic service. And since this terrible thing has happened to her, I felt—well, I felt that I ought to come and see if there was anything I could do about it."

"Yes," said Pat. "Of course. I see."

And she did see. Miss Marple's action appeared to her natural and inevitable.

"I think it's a very good thing you have come," said Pat. "Nobody seems to know very much about her. I mean relations and all that."

"No," said Miss Marple, "of course not. She hadn't got any relations. She came to me from the orphanage. St. Faith's. A very well-run place, though sadly short of funds. We do our best for the girls there, try to give them a good training and all that. Gladys came to me when she was seventeen, and I taught her how to wait at table and keep the silver and everything like that. Of course, she didn't stay long. They never do. As soon as she got a little experience, she went and took a job in a café. The girls nearly always want to do that. They think it's freer, you know, and a gayer life. Perhaps it may be. I really don't know."

"I never even saw her," said Pat. "Was she a pretty girl?"

"Oh, no," said Miss Marple, "not at all. Adenoids, and a good many spots. She was rather pathetically stupid, too. I don't suppose," went on Miss Marple thoughtfully, "that she ever made many friends anywhere. She was very keen on men, poor girl. But men didn't take much notice of her, and other girls rather made use of her."

"It sounds rather cruel," said Pat.

"Yes, my dear," said Miss Marple, "life is cruel, I'm afraid. One doesn't really know what to do with the Gladyses. They enjoy going to the pictures and all that, but they're always thinking of impossible things that can't possibly happen to them. Perhaps that's happiness of a kind. But they get disappointed. I think Gladys was disappointed in café and restaurant life. Nothing very glamorous or interesting happened to her and it was just hard on the feet. Probably that's why she came back into private service. Do you know how long she'd been here?"

Pat shook her head.

"Not very long, I should think. Only a month or two." Pat paused and then went on, "It seems so horrible and futile that she should have been caught up in this thing. I suppose she'd seen something or noticed something."

"It was the clothes peg that really worried me," said Miss Marple in her gentle voice.

"The clothes peg?"

"Yes. I read about it in the papers. I suppose it is true? That when she was found there was a clothes peg clipped onto her nose."

Pat nodded. The color rose to Miss Marple's pink cheeks.

"That's what made me so very angry, if you can understand, my dear. It was such a cruel, contemptuous gesture. It gave me a kind of picture of the murderer. To do a thing like that! It's very wicked, you know, to affront human dignity. Particularly if you've already killed."

Pat said slowly,

"I think I see what you mean." She got up. "I think you'd better come and see Inspector Neele. He's in charge of the case, and he's here now. You'll like him, I think. He's a very human person." She gave a sudden, quick shiver. "The whole thing is such a horrible nightmare. Pointless. Mad. Without rhyme or reason in it."

"I wouldn't say that, you know," said Miss Marple. "No, I wouldn't say that."

Inspector Neele was looking tired and haggard. Three deaths, and the press of the whole country whooping down the trail. A case that seemed to be shaping in well-known fashion had gone suddenly haywire. Adele Fortescue, that appropriate suspect, was now the second victim of an incomprehensible murder case. At the close of that fatal day the Assistant Commissioner had sent for Neele, and the two men had talked far into the night.

In spite of his dismay, or rather behind it, Inspector Neele had felt a faint inward satisfaction. That pattern of the wife and the lover. It had been too slick, too easy. He had always mistrusted it. And now that mistrust of his was justified.

"The whole thing takes on an entirely different aspect," the A.C. had said, striding up and down his room and frowning. "It looks to me, Neele, as though we'd got someone mentally unhinged to deal with. First the husband, then the wife. But the very circumstances of the case seem to show that it's an inside job. It's all there, in the family. Someone who sat down to breakfast with Fortescue put taxine in his coffee or on his food. Someone who had tea with the family that day put potassium cyanide in Adele Fortescue's cup of tea. Someone trusted, unnoticed, one of the family. Which of 'em, Neele?"

Neele said drily,

"Percival wasn't there, so that lets him out again. That lets him out again," Inspector Neele repeated.

The A.C. looked at him sharply. Something in the repetition had attracted his attention.

"What's the idea, Neele? Out with it, man."

Inspector Neele looked stolid.

"Nothing, sir. Not so much as an idea. All I say is it was very convenient for him."

"A bit too convenient, eh?" The A.C. reflected and shook his head. "You think he might have managed it somehow? Can't see how, Neele. No, I can't see how."

He added, "And he's a cautious type, too."

"But quite intelligent, sir."

"You don't fancy the women. Is that it? Yet the women are indicated. Elaine Fortescue and Percival's wife. They were at breakfast and they were at tea that day. Either of them could have done it. No signs of anything abnormal about them? Well, it doesn't always show. There might be something in their past medical record."

Inspector Neele did not answer. He was thinking of Mary Dove. He had no definite reason for suspecting her, but that was the way his thoughts lay. There was something unexplained about her, unsatisfactory. A faint, amused antagonism. That had been her attitude after the death of Rex Fortescue. What was her attitude now? Her behavior and manner were, as always, exemplary. There was no longer, he thought, amusement. Perhaps not even antagonism, but he wondered whether, once or twice, he had not seen a trace of fear. He had been to blame, culpably to blame, in the matter of Gladys Martin. That slight, guilty confusion of hers he had put down to no more than a natural nervousness of the police. He had come across that guilty nervousness so often. In this case it had been something more. Gladys had seen or heard something which had aroused her suspicions. It was probably, he thought, some quite small thing, something so vague and indefinite that she had hardly liked to speak about it. And now, poor little rabbit, she would never speak.

Inspector Neele looked with some interest at the mild, earnest face of the old lady who confronted him now at Yewtree Lodge. He had been in two minds at first how to treat her, but he quickly made up his mind. Miss Marple would be useful to him. She was upright, of unimpeachable rectitude and she had, like most old ladies, time on her hands and an old maid's nose for scenting bits of gossip. She'd get things out of servants and out of the women of the Fortescue family perhaps, that he and his policemen would never get. Talk, conjecture, reminiscences, repetitions of things said and done, out of them all she would pick the salient facts. So Inspector Neele was gracious.

"It's uncommonly good of you to have come here, Miss Marple," he said.

"It was my duty, Inspector Neele. The girl had lived in my house. I feel, in a sense, responsible for her. She was a very silly girl, you know."

Inspector Neele looked at her appreciatively.

"Yes," he said, "just so."

She had gone, he felt, to the heart of the matter.

"She wouldn't know," said Miss Marple, "what she ought to do. If, I mean, something came up. Oh, dear, I'm expressing myself very badly."

Inspector Neele said that he understood.

"She hadn't got good judgment as to what was important or not, that's what you mean, isn't it?"

"Oh yes, exactly, Inspector."

81

"When you say that she was silly—" Inspector Neele broke off. Miss Marple took up the theme.

"She was the credulous type. She was the sort of girl who would have given her savings to a swindler, if she'd had any savings. Of course, she never did have any savings because she always spent her money on most unsuitable clothes."

"What about men?" asked the Inspector.

"She wanted a young man badly," said Miss Marple. "In fact, that's really, I think, why she left St. Mary Meade. The competition there is very keen. So few men. She did have hopes of the young man who delivered the fish. Young Fred had a pleasant word for all the girls, but of course he didn't mean anything by it. That upset poor Gladys quite a lot. Still, I gather she did get herself a young man in the end?"

Inspector Neele nodded.

"It seems so. Albert Evans, I gather, his name was. She seems to have met him at some holiday camp. He didn't give her a ring or anything, so maybe she made it all up. He was a mining engineer, so she told the cook."

"That seems most unlikely," said Miss Marple, "but I dare say it's what he told her. As I say, she'd believe anything. You don't connect him with this business at all?"

Inspector Neele shook his head.

"No. I don't think there are any complications of that kind. He never seems to have visited her. He sent her a post card from time to time, usually from a seaport. Probably Fourth Engineer on a boat on the Baltic run."

"Well," said Miss Marple, "I'm glad she had her little romance. Since her life has been cut short in this way——" She tightened her lips. "You know, Inspector, it makes me very, very angry." And she added, as she had said to Pat Fortescue, "Especially the clothes peg. That, Inspector, was really wicked."

Inspector Neele looked at her with interest.

"I know just what you mean, Miss Marple," he said.

Miss Marple coughed apologetically.

"I wonder—I suppose it would be great presumption on my part—if only I could assist you in my very humble and, I'm afraid, very feminine way. This is a wicked murderer, Inspector Neele, and the wicked should not go unpunished."

"That's an unfashionable belief nowadays, Miss Marple," Inspector Neele said rather grimly. "Not that I don't agree with you."

"There is a hotel near the station, or there's the Golf Hotel," said Miss Marple tentatively, "and I believe there's a Miss Ramsbottom in this house who is interested in foreign missions."

Inspector Neele looked at Miss Marple appraisingly.

"Yes," he said. "You've got something there, maybe. I can't say that I've had great success with the lady."

"It's really very kind of you, Inspector Neele," said Miss Marple. "I'm so glad you don't think I'm just a sensation hunter."

Inspector Neele gave a sudden, rather unexpected smile. He was thinking to himself that Miss Marple was very unlike the popular idea of an avenging fury. And yet, he thought, that was perhaps exactly what she was.

"Newspapers," said Miss Marple, "are often so sensational in their accounts. But hardly, I fear, as accurate as one might wish." She looked inquiringly at Inspector Neele. "If one could be sure of having just the sober facts."

"They're not particularly sober," said Neele. "Shorn of undue sensation, they're as follows. Mr. Fortescue died in his office as a result of taxine poisoning. Taxine is obtained from the berries and leaves of yew trees."

"Very convenient," Miss Marple said.

"Possibly," said Inspector Neele, "but we've no evidence as to that. As yet, that is." He stressed the point because it was here that he thought Miss Marple might be useful. If any brew or concoction of yewberries had been made in the house, Miss Marple was quite likely to come upon traces of it. She was the sort of old pussy who would make home-made liquors, cordials and herb teas herself. She would know methods of making and methods of disposal.

"And Mrs. Fortescue?"

"Mrs. Fortescue had tea with the family in the library. The last person to leave the room and the tea table was Miss Elaine Fortescue, her stepdaughter. She states that as she left the room Mrs. Fortescue was pouring herself out another cup of tea. Some twenty minutes or half-hour later Miss Dove, who acts as housekeeper, went in to remove the tea tray. Mrs. Fortescue was still sitting on the sofa, dead. Beside her was a tea cup a quarter full, and in the dregs of it was potassium cyanide."

"Which is almost immediate in its action, I believe," said Miss Marple.

"Exactly."

"Such dangerous stuff," murmured Miss Marple. "One has it to take wasps' nests but I'm always very, very careful."

"You're quite right," said Inspector Neele. "There was a packet of it in the gardener's shed here."

"Again very convenient," said Miss Marple. She added, "Was Mrs. Fortescue eating anything?"

"Oh, yes. They'd had tea."

"Cake, I suppose? Bread and butter? Scones, perhaps? Jam? Honey?"

"Yes, there were honey and scones, chocolate cake and swiss roll and various other plates of things." He looked at her curiously. "The potassium cyanide was in the tea, Miss Marple."

"Oh, yes, yes. I quite understand that. I was just getting the whole picture, so to speak. Rather significant, don't you think?"

He looked at her in a slightly puzzled fashion. Her cheeks were pink, her eyes were bright.

"And the third death, Inspector Neele?"

"Well, the facts there seem clear enough, too. The girl, Gladys, took in the tea tray, then she brought the next tray into the hall, but left it there. She'd been rather absent-minded all the day, apparently. After that no one saw her. The cook, Mrs. Crump, jumped to the conclusion that the girl had gone out without telling anybody. She based her belief, I think, on the fact that the girl was wearing a good pair of nylon stockings and her best shoes. There, however, she was proved quite wrong. The girl had obviously remembered suddenly that she had not taken in some clothes that were drying outside on the clothes line. She ran out to fetch them in, had taken down half of them apparently, when somebody took her unawares by slipping a stocking round her neck and—well, that was that."

"Someone from outside?" said Miss Marple.

"Perhaps," said Inspector Neele. "But perhaps someone from inside. Someone who'd been waiting his or her opportunity to get the girl alone. The girl was upset, nervous, when we first questioned her, but I'm afraid we didn't quite appreciate the importance of that."

"Oh, but how could you?" cried Miss Marple. "People so often do look guilty and embarrassed when they are questioned by the police."

"That's just it. But this time, Miss Marple, it was rather more than that. I think the girl Gladys had seen someone performing some action that seemed to her needed explanation. It can't, I think, have been anything very definite. Otherwise she would have spoken out. But I think she did betray the fact to the person in question. That person realized that Gladys was a danger."

"And so Gladys was strangled and a clothes peg clipped on her nose," murmured Miss Marple to herself.

"Yes, that's a nasty touch. A nasty, sneering sort of touch. Just a nasty bit of unnecessary bravado."

Miss Marple shook her head.

"Hardly unnecessary. It does all make a pattern, doesn't it?"

Inspector Neele looked at her curiously.

"I don't quite follow you, Miss Marple. What do you mean by a pattern?"

Miss Marple immediately became flustered.

"Well, I mean it does seem—I mean, regarded as a sequence, if you understand—well, one can't get away from facts, can one?"

"I don't think I quite understand."

"Well, I mean—first we have Mr. Fortescue. Rex Fortescue. Killed in his office in the city. And then we have Mrs. Fortescue, sitting here in the library and having tea. There were scones and honey. And then poor Gladys with the clothes peg on her nose. Just to point the whole thing. That very charming Mrs. Lance Fortescue said to me that there didn't seem to be any rhyme or reason in it, but I couldn't agree with her, because it's the rhyme that strikes one, isn't it?"

Inspector Neele said slowly, "I don't think——"

Miss Marple went on quickly, "I expect you're about thirty-five or thirty-six, aren't you, Inspector Neele? I think there was rather a reaction just then, when you were a little boy, I mean, against nursery rhymes. But if one has been brought up on Mother Goose—I mean it is really highly significant, isn't it? What I wondered was," Miss Marple paused, then appearing to take her courage in her hands, went on bravely, "Of course, it is great impertinence I know, on my part, saying this sort of thing to you."

"Please say anything you like, Miss Marple."

"Well, that's very kind of you. I shall. Though, as I say, I do it with the utmost diffidence because I know I am very old and rather muddle-headed, and I dare say my idea is of no value at all. But what I mean to say is: have you gone into the question of blackbirds?"

CHAPTER 14

FOR ABOUT TEN seconds Inspector Neele stared at Miss Marple with the utmost bewilderment. His first idea was that the old lady had gone off her head.

"Blackbirds?" he repeated.

Miss Marple nodded her head vigorously.

"Yes," she said, and forthwith recited,

"Sing a song of sixpence, a pocketful of rye,
Four and twenty blackbirds baked in a pie.
When the pie was opened the birds began to sing.
Wasn't that a dainty dish to set before the king?

The king was in his counting house, counting out his money,
The queen was in the parlour eating bread and honey,
The maid was in the garden hanging out the clothes,
When there came a little dickey bird and nipped off her nose."

"Good Lord," Inspector Neele said.

"I mean, it does fit," said Miss Marple. "It was rye in his pocket, wasn't it? One newspaper said so. The others just said cereal, which might mean anything. Farmer's Glory or Cornflakes—or even maize—but it was rye?"

Inspector Neele nodded.

"There you are," said Miss Marple, triumphantly. "Rex Fortescue. Rex means King. In his Counting House. And Mrs. Fortescue, the Queen in the parlor, eating bread and honey. And so,

86

of course, the murderer had to put that clothes peg on poor Gladys's nose."

Inspector Neele said, "You mean the whole set up is crazy?"

"Well, one mustn't jump to conclusions, but it is certainly very odd. But you really must make inquiries about blackbirds. Because there must be blackbirds!"

It was at this point that Sergeant Hay came into the room, saying urgently, "Sir."

He broke off at sight of Miss Marple.

Inspector Neele, recovering himself, said, "Thank you, Miss Marple. I'll look into the matter. Since you are interested in the girl, perhaps you would care to look over the things from her room. Sergeant Hay will show you them presently."

Miss Marple, accepting her dismissal, twittered her way out.

"Blackbirds!" murmured Inspector Neele to himself.

Sergeant Hay stared.

"Yes, Hay, what is it?"

"Sir," said Sergeant Hay urgently again. "Look at this."

He produced an article wrapped in a somewhat grubby handkerchief.

"Found it in the shrubbery," said Sergeant Hay. "Could have been chucked there from one of the back windows."

He tipped the object down on the desk in front of the Inspector, who leaned forward and inspected it with rising excitement. The exhibit was a nearly full pot of marmalade.

The Inspector stared at it without speech. His face assumed a peculiarly wooden and stupid appearance. In actual fact, this meant that Inspector Neele's mind was racing once more round an imaginary track. A moving picture was enacting itself before the eyes of his mind. He saw a new pot of marmalade, he saw hands carefully removing its cover, he saw a small quantity of marmalade removed, mixed with a preparation of taxine and replaced in the pot, the top smoothed over and the lid carefully replaced.

He broke off at this point to ask Sergeant Hay, "They don't take marmalade out of the pot and put it in fancy pots?"

"No, sir. Got into the way of serving it in its own pot during the war when things were scarce, and it's gone on like that ever since."

Neele murmured, "That made it easier, of course."

"What's more," said Sergeant Hay, "Mr. Fortescue was the only one that took marmalade for breakfast (and Mr. Percival when he was at home). The others had jam or honey."

Neele nodded.

"Yes," he said. "That made it very simple, didn't it?"

After a slight gap the moving picture went on in his mind. It was the breakfast table now. Rex Fortescue stretching out his hand for the marmalade pot, taking out a spoonful of marmalade and spreading it on his toast and butter. Easier, far easier that way than the risk and difficulty of insinuating it into his coffee cup. A foolproof method of administering the poison! And afterwards? Another gap and a picture that was not quite so clear. The replacing of that pot of marmalade by another with exactly the same amount taken from it. And then an open window. A hand and an arm flinging out that pot into the shrubbery. Whose hand and arm?

Whoever had tampered with that pot of marmalade need not have been present at the breakfast table . . .

Inspector Neele said in a business-like voice,

"Well, we'll have of course to get this analyzed. See if there are any traces of taxine. We can't jump to conclusions."

"No, sir. There may be fingerprints, too."

"Probably not the ones we want," said Inspector Neele gloomily. "There'll be Gladys's, of course, and Crump's and Fortescue's own. Then probably Mrs. Crump's, the grocer's assistant and a few others! If anyone put taxine in here, they'd take care not to go playing about with their own fingers all over the pot. Anyway, as I say, we mustn't jump to conclusions. How do they order marmalade and where is it kept?"

The industrious Sergeant Hay had his answer pat for all these questions.

"Marmalade and jams comes in in batches of six at a time. A new pot would be taken into the pantry when the old one was getting low."

"That means," said Neele, "that it could have been tampered with several days before it was actually brought onto the breakfast table. And anyone who was in the house or had access to the house could have tampered with it."

The term "access to the house" puzzled Sergeant Hay slightly. He did not see in what way his superior's mind was working.

But Neele was postulating what seemed to him a logical assumption.

If the marmalade had been tampered with beforehand, then surely that ruled out those persons who were actually at the breakfast table on the fatal morning.

Which opened up some interesting new possibilities.

He planned in his mind interviews with various people—this time with rather a different angle of approach.

He'd keep an open mind. . . .

He'd even consider seriously that old Miss What's-her-name's suggestions about the nursery rhyme. Because there was no doubt that that nursery rhyme fitted in a rather startling way. It fitted with a point that had worried him from the beginning. The pocketful of rye.

"Blackbirds?" murmured Inspector Neele to himself.

Sergeant Hay stared.

"It's not blackberry jelly, sir," he said. "It's marmalade."

ii.

Inspector Neele went in search of Mary Dove.

He found her in one of the bedrooms on the first floor, superintending Ellen, who was denuding the bed of what seemed to be clean sheets. A little pile of clean towels lay on a chair.

Inspector Neele looked puzzled.

"Somebody coming to stay?" he asked.

Mary Dove smiled at him. In contrast to Ellen, who looked grim and truculent, Mary was her usual imperturbable self.

"Actually," she said, "the opposite is the case."

Neele looked inquiringly at her.

"This is the guest room we had prepared for Mr. Gerald Wright."

"Gerald Wright? Who is he?"

"He's a friend of Miss Elaine Fortescue's." Mary's voice was carefully devoid of inflection.

"He was coming here—when?"

"I believe he arrived at the Golf Hotel the day after Mr. Fortescue's death."

"The day after."

"So Miss Fortescue said." Mary's voice was still impersonal.

"She told me she wanted him to come and stay in the house, so I had a room prepared. Now, after these other two—tragedies—it seems more suitable that he should remain at the hotel."

"The Golf Hotel?"

"Yes."

"Quite," said Inspector Neele.

Ellen gathered up the sheets and towels and went out of the room.

Mary Dove looked inquiringly at Neele.

"You wanted to see me about something?"

Neele said pleasantly, "It's becoming important to get exact times very clearly stated. Members of the family all seem a little vague about time—perhaps understandably. You, on the other hand, Miss Dove, I have found extremely accurate in your statements as to times."

"Again understandably!"

"Yes—perhaps—I must certainly congratulate you on the way you have kept this house going in spite of the—well, panic—these last deaths must have caused." He paused and then asked curiously: "How did you do it?"

He had realized, astutely, that the one chink in the armor of Mary Dove's inscrutability was her pleasure in her own efficiency. She unbent slightly now as she answered.

"The Crumps wanted to leave at once, of course."

"We couldn't have allowed that."

"I know. But I also told them that Mr. Percival Fortescue would be more likely to be—well—generous—to those who had spared him inconvenience."

"And Ellen?"

"Ellen does not wish to leave."

"Ellen does not wish to leave," Neele repeated. "She has good nerves."

"She enjoys disasters," said Mary Dove. "Like Mrs. Percival, she finds in disaster a kind of pleasurable drama."

"Interesting—do you think Mrs. Percival has—enjoyed the tragedies?"

"No—of course not. That is going too far. I would merely say that it has enabled her to—well—stand up to them."

"And how have you yourself been affected, Miss Dove?"

Mary Dove shrugged her shoulders.

"It has not been a pleasant experience," she said drily.

Inspector Neele felt again a longing to break down this cool young woman's defenses—to find out what was really going on behind the careful and efficient understatement of her whole attitude.

He merely said brusquely, "Now, to recapitulate times and places: the last time you saw Gladys Martin was in the hall before tea, and that was at twenty minutes to five?"

"Yes, I told her to bring in tea."

"You yourself were coming from where?"

"From upstairs. I thought I had heard the telephone a few minutes before."

"Gladys, presumably, had answered the telephone?"

"Yes. It was a wrong number. Some one who wanted the Baydon Heath Laundry."

"And that was the last time you saw her?"

"She brought the tea tray into the library about ten minutes or so later."

"After that Miss Elaine Fortescue came in?"

"Yes, about three or four minutes later. Then I went up to tell Mrs. Percival tea was ready."

"Did you usually do that?"

"Oh, no. People came in to tea when they pleased, but Mrs. Fortescue asked where everybody was. I thought I heard Mrs. Percival coming down, but that was a mistake——"

Neele interrupted. Here was something new.

"You mean you heard someone upstairs moving about?"

"Yes, at the head of the stairs, I thought. But no one came down so I went up. Mrs. Percival was in her bedroom. She had just come in. She had been out for a walk."

"Out for a walk—I see. The time being then—"

"Oh, nearly five o'clock, I think."

"And Mr. Lancelot Fortescue arrived—when?"

"A few minutes after I came downstairs again. I thought he had arrived earlier, but—"

Inspector Neele interrupted:

"Why did you think he had arrived earlier?"

"Because I thought I had caught sight of him through the landing window."

"In the garden, you mean?"

"Yes, I caught a glimpse of someone through the yew hedge, and I thought it would probably be he."

"This was when you were coming down, after telling Mrs. Percival Fortescue tea was ready?"

Mary corrected him.

"No, not then. It was earlier—when I came down the first time."

Inspector Neele stared.

"Are you sure about that, Miss Dove?"

"Yes, I'm perfectly sure. That's why I was surprised to see him —when he actually did ring the bell."

Inspector Neele shook his head. He kept his inner excitement out of his voice as he said, "It couldn't have been Lancelot Fortescue you saw. His train—which was due at 4:28—was nine minutes late. He arrived at Baydon Heath Station at 4:37. He had to wait a few minutes for a taxi—that train is always very full. It was actually nearly a quarter to five (five minutes after you had seen the man in the garden) when he left the station and it is a ten minutes' drive. He paid off the taxi at the gate here at about five minutes to five at the earliest. No, it wasn't Lancelot Fortescue you saw."

"I'm sure I did see someone."

"Yes, you saw someone. It was getting dark. You couldn't have seen the man clearly?"

"Oh no, I couldn't see his face or anything like that—just his build—tall and slender. We were expecting Lancelot Fortescue, so I jumped to the conclusion that that's who it was."

"He was going—which way?"

"Along behind the yew hedge towards the east side of the house."

"There is a side door there. Is it kept locked?"

"Not until the house is locked up for the night."

"Anyone could have come in by that side door without being observed by any of the household."

Mary Dove considered.

"I think so. Yes." She added quickly, "You mean, the person I heard later upstairs could have come in that way? Could have been hiding—upstairs?"

"Something of the kind."

"But who—?"

"That remains to be seen. Thank you, Miss Dove."

As she turned to go away Inspector Neele said in a casual voice, "By the way, you can't tell me anything about blackbirds, I suppose?"

For the first time, so it seemed, Mary Dove was taken aback. She turned back sharply.

"I—what did you say?"

"I was just asking you about blackbirds."

"Do you mean——"

"Blackbirds," said Inspector Neele.

He had on his most stupid expression.

"You mean that silly business last summer? But surely that can't . . ." She broke off.

Inspector Neele said pleasantly, "There's been a bit of talk about it, but I was sure I'd get a clear account from you."

Mary Dove was her calm, practical self again.

"It must, I think, have been some silly, spiteful joke," she said. "Four dead blackbirds were on Mr. Fortescue's desk in his study here. It was summer and the windows were open, and we rather thought it must have been the gardener's boy, though he insisted he'd never done anything of the kind. But they were actually blackbirds the gardener had shot, which had been hanging up by the fruit bushes."

"And somebody had cut them down and put them on Mr. Fortescue's desk?"

"Yes."

"Any sort of reason behind it—any association with blackbirds?"

Mary shook her head.

"I don't think so."

"How did Mr. Fortescue take it? Was he annoyed?"

"Naturally he was annoyed."

"But not upset in any way?"

"I really can't remember."

"I see," said Inspector Neele.

He said no more. Mary Dove once more turned away, but this time, he thought, she went rather unwillingly, as though she would have liked to know more of what was in his mind. Ungratefully, all that Inspector Neele felt was annoyance with Miss Marple. She had suggested to him that there would be blackbirds and sure enough, there the blackbirds were! Not four and twenty of them, that was true. What might be called a token consignment.

That had been as long ago as last summer, and where it fitted in Inspector Neele could not imagine. He was not going to let this blackbird bogy divert him from the logical and sober investigation of murder by a sane murderer for a sane reason, but he would be forced from now on to keep the crazier possibilities of the case in mind.

CHAPTER 15

"I'M SORRY, MISS FORTESCUE, to bother you again, but I want to be quite, quite clear about this. As far as we know you were the last person—or rather the last person but one—to see Mrs. Fortescue alive. It was about twenty past five when you left the drawing-room?"

"About then," said Elaine, "I can't say exactly." She added defensively, "One doesn't look at clocks the whole time."

"No, of course not. During the time that you were alone with Mrs. Fortescue after the others had left, what did you talk about?"

"Does it matter what we talked about?"

"Probably not," said Inspector Neele, "but it might give me some clue as to what was in Mrs. Fortescue's mind."

"You mean—you think she might have done it herself?"

Inspector Neele noticed the brightening of her face. It would certainly be a very convenient solution as far as the family was concerned. Inspector Neele did not think it was true for a moment. Adele Fortescue was not, to his mind, a suicidal type. Even if she had poisoned her husband and was convinced the crime was about to be brought home to her, she would not, he thought, have ever thought of killing herself. She would have been optimistically sure that even if she were tried for murder she would be sure to be acquitted. He was not, however, averse to Elaine

94

Fortescue's entertaining the hypothesis. He said, therefore, quite truthfully,

"There's a possibility of it, at least, Miss Fortescue. Now perhaps you'll tell me just what your conversation was about."

"Well, it was really about my affairs." Elaine hesitated.

"Your affairs being . . . ?" He paused questioningly with a genial expression.

"I—a friend of mine had just arrived in the neighborhood, and I was asking Adele if she would have any objection to—to my asking him to stay here at the house."

"Ah. And who is this friend?"

"It's a Mr. Gerald Wright. He's a schoolmaster. He—he's staying at the Golf Hotel."

"A very close friend, perhaps?"

Inspector Neele gave an avuncular beam which added at least fifteen years to his age.

"We may expect an interesting announcement shortly, perhaps?"

He felt almost compunction as he saw the awkward gesture of the girl's hand and the flush on her face. She was in love with the fellow all right.

"We—we're not actually engaged and of course we couldn't have it announced just now, but—well, yes I think we do—— I mean we are going to get married."

"Congratulations," said Inspector Neele pleasantly. "Mr. Wright is staying at the Golf Hotel, isn't he? How long has he been there?"

"I wired him when Father died."

"And he came at once. I see," said Inspector Neele.

He used this favorite phrase of his in a friendly and reassuring way.

"What did Mrs. Fortescue say when you asked her about his coming here?"

"Oh, she said, all right, I could have anybody I pleased."

"She was nice about it then?"

"Not exactly nice. I mean, she said——"

"Yes, what else did she say?"

Again Elaine flushed.

"Oh, something stupid about my being able to do a lot better for myself now. It was the sort of thing Adele would say."

95

"Ah, well," said Inspector Neele soothingly, "relations say these sort of things."

"Yes, yes, they do. But people often find it difficult to—to appreciate Gerald properly. He's an intellectual, you see, and he's got a lot of unconventional and progressive ideas that people don't like."

"That's why he didn't get on with your father?"

Elaine flushed hotly.

"Father was very prejudiced and unjust. He hurt Gerald's feelings. In fact, Gerald was so upset by my father's attitude that he went off and I didn't hear from him for weeks."

And probably wouldn't have heard from him now if your father hadn't died and left you a packet of money, Inspector Neele thought. Aloud he said, "Was there any more conversation between you and Mrs. Fortescue?"

"No. No, I don't think so."

"And that was about twenty-five past five, and Mrs. Fortescue was found dead at five minutes to six. You didn't return to the room during that half hour?"

"No."

"What were you doing?"

"I—I went out for a short walk."

"To the Golf Hotel?"

"I—well, yes, but Gerald wasn't in."

Inspector Neele said "I see" again, but this time with a rather dismissive effect.

Elaine Fortescue got up and said, "Is that all?"

"That's all, thank you, Miss Fortescue."

As she got up to go, Neele said casually, "You can't tell me anything about blackbirds, can you?"

She stared at him.

"Blackbirds? You mean the ones in the pie?"

They would be in the pie, the Inspector thought to himself. He merely said, "When was this?"

"Oh! Three or four months ago—and there were some on Father's desk, too. He was furious."

"Furious, was he? Did he ask a lot of questions?"

"Yes, of course. But we couldn't find out who put them there."

"Have you any idea why he was so angry?"

"Well, it was rather a horrid thing to do, wasn't it?"

Neele looked thoughtfully at her, but he did not see any signs of evasion in her face. He said, "Oh, just one more thing, Miss Fortescue. Do you know if your stepmother made a will at any time?"

Elaine shook her head.

"I've no idea. I suppose so. People usually do, don't they?"

"They should do, but it doesn't always follow. Have you made a will yourself, Miss Fortescue?"

"No—no—I haven't—up to now I haven't had anything to leave. Now, of course—"

He saw the realization of the changed position come into her eyes.

"Yes," he said. "Fifty thousand pounds is quite a responsibility. It changes a lot of things, Miss Fortescue."

ii.

For some minutes after Elaine Fortescue left the room, Inspector Neele sat staring in front of him thoughtfully. He had, indeed, new food for thought. Mary Dove's statement that she had seen a man in the garden at approximately 4:35 opened up certain new possibilities. That is, of course, if Mary Dove was speaking the truth. It was never Inspector Neele's habit to assume that anyone was speaking the truth. But, examine her statement as he might, he could see no real reason why she should have lied. He was inclined to think that Mary Dove was speaking the truth when she spoke of having seen a man in the garden. It was quite clear that that man could not have been Lancelot Fortescue, although her reason for assuming that it was he was quite natural under the circumstances. It had not been Lancelot Fortescue, but it had been a man about the height and build of Lancelot Fortescue, and if there had been a man in the garden at that particular time, moreover a man moving furtively, as it seemed, to judge from the way he had crept behind the yew hedges, then that certainly opened up a line of thought.

Added to this statement of hers, there had been the further statement that she had heard someone moving about upstairs. That, in its turn, tied up with something else. The small piece of mud he had found on the floor of Adele Fortescue's boudoir. Inspector Neele's mind dwelt on the small, dainty desk in that

97

room. Pretty little sham antique with a rather obvious secret drawer in it. There had been three letters in that drawer, letters written by Vivian Dubois to Adele Fortescue. A great many love letters of one kind or another had passed through Inspector Neele's hands in the course of his career. He was acquainted with passionate letters, foolish letters, sentimental letters and nagging letters. There had also been cautious letters. Inspector Neele was inclined to classify these three as of the latter kind. Even if read in the divorce court, they could pass as inspired by a merely platonic friendship. Though in this case—"Platonic friendship, my foot!" thought the Inspector inelegantly.

Neele, when he had found the letters, had sent them up at once to the Yard since, at that time, the main question was whether the Public Prosecutor's office thought that there was sufficient evidence to proceed with the case against Adele Fortescue or Adele Fortescue and Vivian Dubois together. Everything had pointed towards Rex Fortescue having been poisoned by his wife with or without her lover's connivance. These letters, though cautious, made it fairly clear that Vivian Dubois was her lover, but there had not been in the wording, so far as Inspector Neele could see, any signs of incitement to crime. There might have been incitement of a spoken kind, but Vivian Dubois would be far too cautious to put anything of that kind down on paper.

Inspector Neele surmised accurately that Vivian Dubois had asked Adele Fortescue to destroy his letters and that Adele Fortescue had told him she had done so.

Well, now they had two more deaths on their hands. And that meant, or should mean, that Adele Fortescue had not killed her husband.

Unless, that is—Inspector Neele considered a new hypothesis. Adele Fortescue had wanted to marry Vivian Dubois and Vivian Dubois had wanted, not Adele Fortescue, but Adele Fortescue's hundred thousand pounds which would come to her on the death of her husband. He had assumed, perhaps, that Rex Fortescue's death would be put down to natural causes. Some kind of seizure or stroke. After all, everybody seemed to be worried over Rex Fortescue's health during the last year. (Parenthetically, Inspector Neele said to himself that he must look into that question. He had a subconscious feeling that it might be important in some way.) To continue: Rex Fortescue's death had not gone according to plan. It had been diagnosed, without loss of time, as poisoning and the correct poison named.

Supposing that Adele Fortescue and Vivian Dubois had been guilty, what state would they be in then? Vivian Dubois would have been scared and Adele Fortescue would have lost her head. She might have done or said foolish things. She might have rung up Dubois on the telephone, talking indiscreetly in a way that he would have realized might have been overheard in Yewtree Lodge. What would Vivian Dubois have done next?

It was early as yet to try and answer that question, but Inspector Neele proposed very shortly to make inquiries at the Golf Hotel as to whether Dubois had been in or out of the hotel between the hours of 4:15 and 6 o'clock. Vivian Dubois was tall and dark like Lance Fortescue. He might have slipped through the garden to the side door, made his way upstairs, and then what? Looked for the letters and found them gone? Waited there, perhaps, till the coast was clear, then come down into the library when tea was over and Adele Fortescue was alone?

But all this was going too fast——

Neele had questioned Mary Dove and Elaine Fortescue; he must see now what Percival Fortescue's wife had to say.

CHAPTER 16

INSPECTOR NEELE FOUND Mrs. Percival in her own sitting-room upstairs, writing letters. She got up rather nervously when he came in.

"Is there anything—what—are there——"

"Please sit down, Mrs. Fortescue. There are only just a few more questions I would like to ask you."

"Oh, yes. Yes, of course, Inspector. It's all so dreadful, isn't it? So very dreadful."

She sat down rather nervously in an armchair. Inspector Neele sat down in the small, straight chair near her. He studied her rather more carefully than he had done heretofore. In some ways a mediocre type of woman, he thought—and thought also that she was not very happy. Restless, unsatisfied, limited in mental outlook, yet he thought she might have been efficient and skilled in her own profession of hospital nurse. Though she had achieved leisure by her marriage with a well-to-do man, leisure had not satisfied her. She bought clothes, read novels and ate sweets, but he remembered her avid excitement on the night of Rex Fortescue's death, and he saw in it not so much a ghoulish satisfaction but rather a revelation of the arid deserts of boredom which encompassed her life. Her eyelids fluttered and fell before his searching glance. They gave her the appearance of being both nervous and guilty, but he could not be sure that that was really the case.

"I'm afraid," he said soothingly, "we have to ask people questions again and again. It must be very tiresome for you all. I do appreciate that, but so much hangs, you understand, on the exact timing of events. You came down to tea rather late, I understand? In fact, Miss Dove came up and fetched you."

"Yes. Yes, she did. She came and said tea was in. I had no idea it was so late. I'd been writing letters."

Inspector Neele just glanced over at the writing desk.

"I see," he said. "Somehow, or other, I thought you'd been out for a walk."

"Did she say so? Yes, now I believe you're right. I had been writing letters; then it was so stuffy and my head ached so I went out and—er—went for a walk. Only round the garden."

"I see. You didn't meet anyone?"

"Meet anyone?" She stared at him. "What do you mean?"

"I just wondered if you'd seen anybody or anybody had seen you during this walk of yours."

"I saw the gardener in the distance, that's all." She was looking at him suspiciously.

"Then you came in, came up here to your room and you were just taking your things off when Miss Dove came to tell you that tea was ready?"

"Yes. Yes, and so I came down."

"And who was there?"

"Adele and Elaine, and a minute or two later Lance arrived.

My brother-in-law, you know. The one who's come back from Kenya."

"And then you all had tea?"

"Yes, we had tea. Then Lance went up to see Aunt Effie and I came up here to finish my letters. I left Elaine there with Adele."

He nodded reassuringly.

"Yes. Miss Fortescue seems to have been with Mrs. Fortescue for quite five or ten minutes after you left. Your husband hadn't come home yet?"

"Oh no. Percy—Val—didn't get home until about half-past six or seven. He'd been kept up in town."

"He came back by train?"

"Yes. He took a taxi from the station."

"Was it unusual for him to come back by train?"

"He does sometimes. Not very often. I think he'd been to places in the city where it's rather difficult to park the car. It was easier for him to take a train home from Cannon Street."

"I see," said Inspector Neele. He went on, "I asked your husband if Mrs. Fortescue had made a will before she died. He said he thought not. I suppose you don't happen to have any idea?"

To his surprise Jennifer Fortescue nodded vigorously.

"Oh, yes," she said. "Adele made a will. She told me so."

"Indeed! When was this?"

"Oh, it wasn't very long ago. About a month ago, I think."

"That's very interesting," said Inspector Neele.

Mrs. Percival leant forward eagerly. Her face now was all animation. She clearly enjoyed exhibiting her superior knowledge.

"Val didn't know about it," she said. "Nobody knew. It just happened that I found out about it. I was in the street. I had just come out of the stationer's; then I saw Adele coming out of the solicitor's office. Ansell and Worrall's, you know. In the High Street."

"Ah," said Neele, "the local solicitors?"

"Yes. And I said to Adele, 'Whatever have you been doing there?' And she laughed and said, 'Wouldn't you like to know?' And then as we walked along together she said, 'I'll tell you, Jennifer. I've been making my will.' 'Well,' I said, 'why are you doing that, Adele? You're not ill or anything, are you?' And she said no, of course she wasn't ill. She'd never felt better. But everyone ought to make a will. She said she wasn't going to those

101

stuck-up family solicitors in London, Mr. Billingsley. She said the old sneak would go round and tell the family. 'No,' she said, 'My will's my own business, Jennifer, and I'll make it my own way and nobody's going to know about it.' 'Well, Adele,' I said, 'I shan't tell anybody.' She said, 'It doesn't matter if you do. You won't know what's in it.' But I didn't tell anyone. No, not even Percy. I do think women ought to stick together, don't you, Inspector Neele?"

"I'm sure that's a very nice feeling on your part, Mrs. Fortescue," said Inspector Neele diplomatically.

"I'm sure I'm never ill-natured," said Jennifer. "I didn't particularly care for Adele, if you know what I mean. I always thought she was the kind of woman who would stick at nothing in order to get what she wanted. Now she's dead, perhaps I misjudged her, poor soul."

"Well, thank you very much, Mrs. Fortescue, for being so helpful to me."

"You're welcome, I'm sure. I'm only too glad to do anything I can. It's all so very terrible, isn't it? Who is the old lady who's arrived this morning?"

"She's a Miss Marple. She very kindly came here to give us what information she could about the girl Gladys. It seems Gladys Martin was once in service with her."

"Really? How interesting?"

"There's one other thing, Mrs. Percival. Do you know anything about blackbirds?"

Jennifer Fortescue started violently. She dropped her handbag on the floor and bent to pick it up.

"Blackbirds, Inspector? Blackbirds? What kind of blackbirds?" Her voice was rather breathless.

Smiling a little, Inspector Neele said, "Just blackbirds. Alive or dead or even, shall we say, symbolical?"

Jennifer Fortescue said sharply, "I don't know what you mean. I don't know what you're talking about."

"You don't know anything about blackbirds, then, Mrs. Fortescue?"

She said slowly, "I suppose you mean the ones last summer in the pie. All very silly."

"There were some left on the library table, too, weren't there?"

"It was all a very silly practical joke. I don't know who's been talking to you about it. Mr. Fortescue, my father-in-law, was very much annoyed by it."

"Just annoyed? Nothing more?"

"Oh. I see what you mean. Yes, I suppose—yes, it's true. He asked us if there were any strangers about the place."

"Strangers!" Inspector Neele raised his eyebrows.

"Well, that's what he said," said Mrs. Percival defensively.

"Strangers," repeated Inspector Neele thoughtfully. Then he asked, "Did he seem afraid in any way?"

"Afraid? I don't know what you mean."

"Nervous. About strangers, I mean."

"Yes. Yes, he did, rather. Of course, I don't remember very well. It was several months ago, you know. I don't think it was anything except a silly practical joke. Crump perhaps. I really do think that Crump is a very unbalanced man, and I'm perfectly certain that he drinks. He's really very insolent in his manner sometimes. I've sometimes wondered if he could have had a grudge against Mr. Fortescue. Do you think that's possible, Inspector?"

"Anything's possible," said Inspector Neele and went away.

ii.

Percival Fortescue was in London, but Inspector Neele found Lancelot sitting with his wife in the library. They were playing chess together.

"I don't want to interrupt you," said Neele apologetically.

"We're only killing time, Inspector, aren't we, Pat?"

Pat nodded.

"I expect you'll think it's rather a foolish question I'm asking you," said Neele. "Do you know anything about blackbirds, Mr. Fortescue?"

"Blackbirds?" Lance looked amused. "What kind of blackbirds? Do you mean genuine birds, or the slave trade?"

Inspector Neele said with a sudden, disarming smile, "I'm not sure what I mean, Mr. Fortescue. It's just that a mention of blackbirds has turned up."

"Good Lord." Lancelot looked suddenly alert, "Not the old Blackbird Mine, I suppose?"

Inspector Neele said sharply,

"The Blackbird Mine? What was that?"

Lance frowned in a puzzled fashion.

"The trouble is, Inspector, that I can't really remember much myself. I just have a vague idea about some shady transaction in my papa's past. Something on the West Coast of Africa. Aunt Effie, I believe, once threw it in his teeth, but I can't remember anything definite about it."

"Aunt Effie? That will be Miss Ramsbottom, won't it?"

"Yes."

"I'll go and ask her about it," said Inspector Neele. He added ruefully, "She's rather a formidable old lady, Mr. Fortescue. Always makes me feel quite nervous."

Lance laughed.

"Yes. Aunt Effie is certainly a character, but she may be helpful to you, Inspector, if you get on the right side of her. Especially if you're delving into the past. She's got an excellent memory; she takes a positive pleasure in remembering anything that's detrimental in any way." He added thoughtfully, "There's something else. I went up to see her, you know, soon after I got back here. Immediately after tea that day, as a matter of fact. And she was talking about Gladys. The maid who got killed. Not that we knew she was dead then, of course. But Aunt Effie was saying she was quite convinced that Gladys knew something that she hadn't told the police."

"That seems fairly certain," said Inspector Neele. "She'll never tell it now, poor girl."

"No. It seems Aunt Effie had given her good advice as to spilling anything she knew. Pity the girl didn't take it."

Inspector Neele nodded. Bracing himself for the encounter, he penetrated to Miss Ramsbottom's fortress. Rather to his surprise, he found Miss Marple there. The two ladies appeared to be discussing foreign missions.

"I'll go away, Inspector." Miss Marple rose hurriedly to her feet.

"No need, madam," said Inspector Neele.

"I've asked Miss Marple to come and stay in the house," said Miss Ramsbottom. "No sense in spending money in that ridiculous Golf Hotel. A wicked nest of profiteers, that is. Drinking and card-playing all the evening. She'd better come and stay in a decent Christian household. There's a room next door to mine. Dr. Mary Peters, the missionary, had it last."

"It's very, very kind of you," said Miss Marple, "but I really think I mustn't intrude in a house of mourning."

"Mourning? Fiddlesticks," said Miss Ramsbottom. "Who'll weep for Rex in this house? Or Adele either? Or is it the police you're worried about? Any objections, Inspector?"

"None from me, madam."

"There you are," said Miss Ramsbottom.

"It's very kind of you," said Miss Marple gratefully. "I'll go and telephone to the hotel to cancel my booking." She left the room.

Miss Ramsbottom said sharply to the Inspector, "Well, and what do you want?"

"I wondered if you could tell me anything about the Blackbird Mine, ma'am."

Miss Ramsbottom uttered a sudden, shrill cackle of laughter.

"Ha. You've got on to that, have you! Took the hint I gave you the other day. Well, what do you want to know about it?"

"Anything you can tell me, madam."

"I can't tell you much. It's a long time ago now—oh, twenty to twenty-five years, maybe. Some concession or other in East Africa. My brother-in-law went into it with a man called MacKenzie. They went out there to investigate the mine together, and MacKenzie died out there of fever. Rex came home and said the claim or the concession or whatever you call it was worthless. That's all I know."

"I think you know a little more than that, ma'am," said Neele persuasively.

"Anything else is hearsay. You don't like hearsay in the law, so I've been told."

"We're not in court yet, ma'am."

"Well, I can't tell you anything. The MacKenzies kicked up a fuss. That's all I know. They insisted that Rex had swindled MacKenzie. I daresay he did. He was a clever, unscrupulous fellow, but I've no doubt whatever he did it was all legal. They couldn't prove anything. Mrs. MacKenzie was an unbalanced sort of woman. She came here and made a lot of threats of revenge. Said Rex had murdered her husband. Silly, melodramatic fuss! I think she was a bit off her head—in fact, I believe she went into an asylum not long after. Came here dragging along a couple of young children who looked scared to death. Said she'd bring up her children to have revenge. Something like that. Tomfoolery, all of it. Well, that's all I can tell you. And mind you, the Blackbird Mine wasn't the only swindle that Rex put over in his lifetime. You'll find a good many more if you look for them. What put you on to the Blackbird? Did you come across some trail leading to the MacKenzies?"

"You don't know what became of the family, ma'am?"

"No idea," said Miss Ramsbottom. "Mind you, I don't think Rex would have actually murdered MacKenzie, but he might have left him to die. The same thing before the Lord, but not the same thing before the law. If he did, retribution's caught up with him. The mills of God grind slowly, but they grind exceeding small. You'd better go away now. I can't tell you any more and it's no good your asking."

"Thank you very much for what you have told me," said Inspector Neele.

"Send that Marple woman back," Miss Ramsbottom called after him. "She's frivolous, like all Church of England people, but she knows how to run a charity in a sensible way."

Inspector Neele made a couple of telephone calls, the first to Ansell and Worrall and the second to the Golf Hotel. Then he summoned Sergeant Hay and told him that he was leaving the house for a short period.

"I've a short call to pay at a solicitor's office; after that, you can get me at the Golf Hotel if anything urgent turns up."

"Yes, sir."

"And find out anything you can about blackbirds," added Neele over his shoulder.

"Blackbirds, sir?" Sergeant Hay repeated, thoroughly mystified.

"That's what I said—not blackberry jelly—blackbirds."

"Very good sir," said Sergeant Hay bewilderedly.

CHAPTER 17

INSPECTOR NEELE FOUND Mr. Ansell the type of solicitor who was more easily intimidated than intimidating. A member of a small and not very prosperous firm, he was anxious not to stand upon his rights but instead to assist the police in every way possible.

Yes, he said, he had made a will for the late Mrs. Adele Fortescue. She had called at his office about five weeks previously. It had seemed to him rather a peculiar business, but naturally he had not said anything. Peculiar things did happen in a solicitor's business, and of course the Inspector would understand that discretion, etc., etc. The Inspector nodded to show he understood. He had already discovered Mr. Ansell had not transacted any legal business previously for Mrs. Fortescue or for any of the Fortescue family.

"Naturally," said Mr. Ansell, "she didn't want to go to her husband's firm of lawyers about this."

Shorn of verbiage, the facts were simple. Adele Fortescue had made a will leaving everything of which she died possessed to Vivian Dubois.

"But I gathered," said Mr. Ansell, looking at Neele in an interrogating manner, "that she hadn't actually much to leave."

Inspector Neele nodded. At the time Adele Fortescue made her will that was true enough. But since then Rex Fortescue had died, and Adele Fortescue had inherited £100,000 and presumably that £100,000 (less death duties) now belonged to Vivian Edward Dubois.

ii.

At the Golf Hotel, Inspector Neele found Vivian Dubois nervously awaiting his arrival. Dubois had been on the point of leaving, indeed his bags were packed, when he had received over the telephone a civil request from Inspector Neele to remain. Inspector Neele had been very pleasant about it, quite apologetic. But behind the conventional words the request had been an order. Vivian Dubois had demurred, but not too much.

He said now, "I do hope you realize, Inspector Neele, that it is very inconvenient for me to have to stay on. I really have urgent business that needs attending to."

"I didn't know you were in business, Mr. Dubois," said Inspector Neele genially.

"I'm afraid none of us can be as leisured as we would like to appear to be nowadays."

"Mrs. Fortescue's death must have been a great shock to you, Mr. Dubois. You were great friends, were you not?"

"Yes," said Dubois. "She was a charming woman. We played golf quite often together."

"I expect you'll miss her very much."

"Yes, indeed." Dubois sighed. "The whole thing is really quite, quite terrible."

"You actually telephoned her, I believe, on the afternoon of her death?"

"Did I? I really cannot remember now."

"About four o'clock, I understand."

"Yes, I believe I did."

"Don't you remember what your conversation was about, Mr. Dubois?"

"It wasn't of any significance. I think I asked her how she was feeling and if there was any further news about her husband's death——a more or less conventional inquiry."

"I see," said Inspector Neele. He added, "And then you went out for a walk?"

"Er—yes—yes, I—I did, I think. At least, not a walk, I played a few holes of golf."

Inspector Neele said gently, "I think not, Mr. Dubois. . . . Not that particular day. . . . The porter here noticed you walking down the road towards Yewtree Lodge."

Dubois' eyes met his, then shied away again nervously.

"I'm afraid I can't remember, Inspector."

"Perhaps you actually went to call upon Mrs. Fortescue?"

Dubois said sharply, "No. No, I didn't do that. I never went near the house."

"Where did you go, then?"

"Oh, I—went on down the road, down as far as the Three Pigeons and then I turned around and came back by the links."

"You're quite sure you didn't go to Yewtree Lodge?"

"Quite sure, Inspector."

The Inspector shook his head.

"Come, now, Mr. Dubois," he said, "it's much better to be frank with us, you know. You may have had some quite innocent reason for going there."

"I tell you I never went to see Mrs. Fortescue that day."

The Inspector stood up.

"You know, Mr. Dubois," he said pleasantly, "I think we'll have to ask you for a statement and you'll be well advised and quite within your rights in having a solicitor present when you are making that statement."

The color fled from Mr. Dubois' face, leaving it a sickly greenish color.

"You're threatening me," he said. "You're threatening me."

"No, no, nothing of the kind." Inspector Neele spoke in a shocked voice. "We're not allowed to do anything of that sort. Quite the contrary. I'm actually pointing out to you that you have certain rights."

"I had nothing to do with it all, I tell you! Nothing to do with it."

"Come now, Mr. Dubois, you were at Yewtree Lodge round about half-past four on that day. Somebody looked out of the window, you know, and saw you."

"I was only in the garden. I didn't go into the house."

"Didn't you?" said Inspector Neele. "Are you sure? Didn't you go in by the side door, and up the stairs to Mrs. Fortescue's sitting-room on the first floor? You were looking for something, weren't you, in the desk there?"

"You've got them, I suppose," said Dubois sullenly. "That fool Adele kept them, then she swore she burnt them. But they don't mean what you think they mean."

"You're not denying, are you, Mr. Dubois, that you were a very close friend of Mrs. Fortescue's?"

"No, of course I'm not. How can I when you've got the letters? All I say is, there's no need to go reading any sinister meaning into them. Don't think for a moment that we—that she—ever thought of getting rid of Rex Fortescue. Good God, I'm not that kind of man!"

"But perhaps she was that kind of woman?"

"Nonsense," cried Vivian Dubois, "wasn't she killed, too?"

"Oh yes, yes."

"Well, isn't it natural to believe that the same person who killed her husband killed her?"

"It might be. It certainly might be. But there are other solutions. For instance (this is quite a hypothetical case, Mr. Dubois), it's possible that Mrs. Fortescue got rid of her husband, and that after his death she became somewhat of a danger to someone else. Someone who had, perhaps, not helped her in what she had done but who had at least encouraged her and provided, shall we say, the motive for the deed. She might be, you know, a danger to that particular person."

Dubois stammered, "You c-c-can't build up a case against me. You can't."

"She made a will, you know," said Inspector Neele. "She left all her money to you. Everything she possessed."

"I don't want the money. I don't want a penny of it."

"Of course, it isn't very much really," said Inspector Neele. "There's jewelery and some furs, but I imagine very little actual cash."

Dubois stared at him, his jaw dropping.

"But I thought her husband—"

He stopped dead.

"Did you, Mr. Dubois?" said Inspector Neele, and there was steel now in his voice. "That's very interesting. I wondered if you knew the terms of Rex Fortescue's will."

iii.

Inspector Neele's second interview at the Golf Hotel was with Mr. Gerald Wright. Mr. Gerald Wright was a thin, intellectual and very superior young man. He was, Inspector Neele noted, not unlike Vivian Dubois in build.

"What can I do for you, Inspector Neele?" he asked.

"I thought you might be able to help us with a little information, Mr. Wright."

"Information? Really? It seems very unlikely."

"It's in connection with the recent events at Yewtree Lodge. You've heard of them, of course?"

Inspector Neele put a little irony into the question. Mr. Wright smiled patronizingly.

"Heard of them," he said, "is hardly the right word. The newspapers appear to be full of nothing else. How incredibly bloodthirsty our public press is! What an age we live in! On one side the manufacture of atom bombs, on the other our newspapers delight in reporting brutal murders! But you said you had some questions to ask. Really, I cannot see what they can be. I know nothing about this Yewtree Lodge affair. I was actually in the Isle of Man when Mr. Rex Fortescue was killed."

"You arrived here very shortly afterwards, didn't you, Mr. Wright? You had a telegram, I believe, from Miss Elaine Fortescue."

"Our police know everything, do they not? Yes, Elaine sent for me. I came, of course, at once."

"And you are, I understand, shortly to be married?"

"Quite right, Inspector Neele. You have no objections, I hope."

"It is entirely Miss Fortescue's business. I understand the attachment between you dates from some time back? Six or seven months ago, in fact?"

"Quite correct."

"You and Miss Fortescue became engaged to be married, but Mr. Fortescue refused to give his consent and informed you that if his daughter married against his wishes he did not propose to give her an income of any kind. Whereupon, I understand, you broke off the engagement and departed."

Gerald Wright smiled rather pityingly.

"A very crude way of putting things, Inspector Neele. Actually, I was victimized for my political opinions. Rex Fortescue was the worst type of capitalist. Naturally, I could not sacrifice my political beliefs and convictions for money."

"But you have no objections to marrying a wife who has just inherited £50,000?"

Gerald Wright gave a thin, satisfied smile.

"Not at all, Inspector Neele. The money will be used for the benefit of the community. But surely you did not come here to discuss with me either my financial circumstances—or my political convictions?"

"No, Mr. Wright. I wanted to talk to you about a simple question of fact. As you are aware, Mrs. Adele Fortescue died as a result of cyanide poisoning on the afternoon of November first. Since you were in the neighborhood of Yewtree Lodge on that afternoon I thought it possible that you might have seen or heard something that had a bearing on the case."

"And what leads you to believe that I was, as you call it, in the neighborhood of Yewtree Lodge at the time?"

"You left this hotel at a quarter-past four on that particular afternoon, Mr. Wright. On leaving the hotel you walked down the road in the direction of Yewtree Lodge. It seems natural to suppose that you were going there."

"I thought of it," said Gerald Wright, "but I considered that it would be a rather pointless thing to do. I already had an arrangement to meet Miss Fortescue—Elaine—at the hotel at six o'clock. I went for a walk along a lane that branches off from the main road and returned to the Golf Hotel just before six o'clock. Elaine did not keep her appointment. Quite naturally, under the circumstances."

"Anybody see you on this walk of yours, Mr. Wright?"

"A few cars passed me, I think, on the road. I did not see anyone I knew, if that's what you mean. The lane was little more than a cart track and too muddy for cars."

"So, between the time you left the hotel at a quarter-past four until six o'clock when you arrived back again, I've only your words for it as to where you were?"

Gerald Wright continued to smile in a superior fashion.

"Very distressing for us both, Inspector, but there it is."

Inspector Neele said softly, "Then if someone said they looked out of a landing window and saw you in the garden of Yewtree Lodge at about 4:35—" He paused and left the sentence unfinished.

Gerald Wright raised his eyebrows and shook his head.

"Visibility must have been very bad by then," he said. "I think it would be difficult for anyone to be sure."

"Are you acquainted with Mr. Vivian Dubois, who is also staying here?"

"Dubois. Dubois? No, I don't think so. Is that the tall, dark man with a pretty taste in suede shoes?"

"Yes. He also was out for a walk that afternoon, and he also left the hotel and walked past Yewtree Lodge. You did not notice him in the road by any chance?"

"No. No. I can't say I did."

Gerald Wright looked for the first time faintly worried.

Inspector Neele said thoughtfully, "It wasn't really a very nice afternoon for walking, especially after dark in a muddy lane. Curious how energetic everyone seems to have felt."

iv.

On Inspector Neele's return to the house he was greeted by Sergeant Hay with an air of satisfaction.

"I've found out about the blackbirds for you, sir," he said.

"You have, have you?"

"Yes, sir, in a pie they were. Cold pie was left out for Sunday night's supper. Somebody got at that pie in the larder or somewhere. They'd taken off the crust and they'd taken out the veal and 'am what was inside it, and what d'you think they put in, instead? Some stinkin' blackbirds they got out of the gardener's shed. Nasty sort of trick to play, wasn't it?"

"'*Wasn't that a dainty dish to set before the king'?*" said Inspector Neele.

He left Sergeant Hay staring after him.

CHAPTER 18

"JUST WAIT A minute," said Miss Ramsbottom. "This patience is going to come out."

She transferred a king and his various impedimenta into an empty space, put a red seven on a black eight, built up the four, five and six of spades on her foundation heap, made a few more rapid transfers of cards and then leaned back with a sigh of satisfaction.

"That's the double jester," she said. "It doesn't often come out."

She leaned back in a satisfied fashion, then raised her eyes at the girl standing by the fireplace.

"So you're Lance's wife," she said.

Pat, who had been summoned upstairs to Miss Ramsbottom's presence, nodded her head.

"Yes," she said.

"You're a tall girl," said Miss Ramsbottom, "and you look healthy."

"I'm very healthy."

Miss Ramsbottom nodded in a satisfied manner.

"Percival's wife is pasty," she said. "Eats too many sweets and doesn't take enough exercise. Well, sit down, child, sit down. Where did you meet my nephew?"

"I met him out in Kenya when I was staying there with some friends."

"You've been married before, I understand."

"Yes. Twice."

Miss Ramsbottom gave a profound sniff.

"Divorce, I suppose."

"No," said Pat. Her voice trembled a little. "They both—died. My first husband was a fighter pilot. He was killed in the war."

"And your second husband? Let me see—somebody told me. Shot himself, didn't he?"

Pat nodded.

"Your fault?"

"No," said Pat. "It wasn't my fault."

"Racing man, wasn't he?"

"Yes."

"I've never been on a race course in my life," said Miss Ramsbottom. "Betting and card-playing—all devices of the devil!"

Pat did not reply.

"I wouldn't go inside a theater or a cinema," said Miss Ramsbottom. "Ah, well, it's a wicked world nowadays. A lot of wickedness was going on in this house, but the Lord struck them down."

Pat still found it difficult to say anything. She wondered if Lance's Aunt Effie was really quite all there. She was, however, a trifle disconcerted by the old lady's shrewd glance at her.

114

"How much," demanded Aunt Effie, "do you know about the family you've married into?"

"I suppose," said Pat, "as much as one ever knows of the family one marries into."

"H'm, something in that, something in that. Well, I'll tell you this. My sister was a fool, my brother-in-law was a rogue, Percival is a sneak, and your Lance was always the bad boy of the family."

"I think that's all nonsense," said Pat robustly.

"Maybe you're right," said Miss Ramsbottom unexpectedly. "You can't just stick labels on people. But don't underestimate Percival. There's a tendency to believe that those who are labeled good are also stupid. Percival isn't the least bit stupid. He's quite clever in a sanctimonious kind of way. I've never cared for him. Mind you, I don't trust Lance and I don't approve of him, but I can't help being fond of him. . . . He's a reckless sort of fellow—always has been. You've got to look after him and see he doesn't go too far. Tell him not to underestimate Percival, my dear. Tell him not to believe everything that Percival says. They're all liars in this house." The old lady added with satisfaction, "Fire and brimstone shall be their portion."

ii.

Inspector Neele was finishing a telephone conversation with Scotland Yard.

The Assistant Commissioner at the other end said, "We ought to be able to get that information for you—by circularizing the various private sanatoriums. Of course, she may be dead."

"Probably is. It's a long time ago."

Old sins cast long shadows. Miss Ramsbottom had said that—said it with significance, too, as though she was giving him a hint.

"It's a fantastic theory," said the A.C.

"Don't I know it, sir. But I don't feel we can ignore it altogether. Too much fits in."

"Yes—yes—rye—blackbirds—the man's Christian name."

Neele said, "I'm concentrating on the other lines too. Dubois is a possibility. So is Wright. The girl Gladys could have caught sight of either of them outside the side door. She could have left the tea tray in the hall and gone out to see who it was and what they were doing. Whoever it was could have strangled her then and there and carried her body round to the clothes line and put the peg on her nose—"

"A crazy thing to do in all conscience! A nasty one, too."

"Yes, sir. That's what upset the old lady—Miss Marple, I mean. Nice old lady—and very shrewd. She's moved into the house to be near old Miss Ramsbottom, and I've no doubt she'll get to hear anything that's going."

"What's your next move, Neele?"

"I've an appointment with the London solicitors. I want to find out a little more about Rex Fortescue's affairs. And though it's old history, I want to hear a little more about the Blackbird Mine."

iii.

Mr. Billingsley, of Billingsley, Horsethorpe & Walters, was an urbane man whose discretion was concealed habitually by a misleadingly forthcoming manner. It was the second interview that Inspector Neele had had with him, and on this occasion Mr. Billingsley's discretion was less noticeable than it had been on the former one. The triple tragedy at Yewtree Lodge had shaken Mr. Billingsley out of his professional reserve. He was now only too anxious to put all the facts he could before the police.

"Most extraordinary business, this whole thing," he said. "A most extraordinary business. I don't remember anything like it in all my professional career."

"Frankly, Mr. Billingsley," said Inspector Neele, "we need all the help we can get."

"You can count on me, my dear sir. I shall be only too happy to assist you in every way I can."

"First let me ask you how well you knew the late Mr. Fortescue, and how well do you know the affairs of his firm?"

"I knew Rex Fortescue fairly well. That is to say I've known him for a period of, well, sixteen years, I should say. Mind you, we are not the only firm of solicitors he employed, not by a long way."

Inspector Neele nodded. He knew that. Billingsley, Horsethorpe & Walters were what one might describe as Rex Fortescue's reputable solicitors. For his less reputable dealings he had employed several different and slightly less scrupulous firms.

"Now what do you want to know?" continued Mr. Billingsley.

"I've told you about his will. Percival Fortescue is the residuary legatee."

"I'm interested now," said Inspector Neele, "in the will of his widow. On Mr. Fortescue's death she came into the sum of one hundred thousand pounds, I understand?"

Billingsley nodded his head.

"A considerable sum of money," he said, "and I may tell you in confidence, Inspector, that it is one the firm could ill have afforded to pay out."

"The firm, then, is not prosperous?"

"Frankly," said Mr. Billingsley, "and strictly between ourselves, it's drifting on to the rocks and has been for the last year and a half."

"For any particular reason?"

"Why, yes. I should say the reason was Rex Fortescue himself. For the last year Rex Fortescue's been acting like a madman. Selling good stock here, buying speculative stuff there, talking big about it all the time in the most extraordinary way. Wouldn't listen to advice. Percival—the son, you know—he came here urging me to use my influence with his father. He'd tried, apparently, and been swept aside. Well, I did what I could, but Fortescue wouldn't listen to reason. Really, he seems to have been a changed man."

"But not, I gather, a depressed man," said Inspector Neele.

"No, no. Quite the contrary. Flamboyant, bombastic."

Inspector Neele nodded. An idea which had already taken form in his mind was strengthened. He thought he was beginning to understand some of the causes of friction between Percival and his father. Mr. Billingsley was continuing.

"But it's no good asking me about the wife's will. I didn't make any will for her."

"No. I know that," said Neele. "I'm merely verifying that she had something to leave. In short, a hundred thousand pounds."

Mr. Billingsley was shaking his head violently.

"No, no, my dear sir. You're wrong there."

"Do you mean the hundred thousand pounds was only left to her for her lifetime?"

"No—no—it was left to her outright. But there was a clause in the will governing that bequest. That is to say, Fortescue's wife did not inherit the sum unless she survived him for one month.

That, I may say, is a clause fairly common nowadays. It has come into operation owing to the uncertainties of air travel. If two people are killed in an air accident, it becomes exceedingly difficult to say who was the survivor and a lot of very curious problems arise."

Inspector Neele was staring at him.

"Then Adele Fortescue had not got a hundred thousand pounds to leave. What happened to that money?"

"It goes back into the firm. Or rather, I should say, it goes to the residuary legatee."

"And the residuary legatee is Mr. Percival Fortescue."

"That's right," said Billingsley, "it goes to Percival Fortescue. And with the state the firm's affairs are in," he added unguardedly, "I should say that he'll need it!"

iv.

"The things you policemen want to know," said Inspector Neele's doctor friend.

"Come on, Bob, spill it."

"Well, as we're alone together you can't quote me, fortunately! But I should say, you know, that your idea's dead right. General Paralysis of the Insane, by the sound of it all. The family suspected it and wanted to get him to see a doctor. He wouldn't. It acts just in the way you describe. Loss of judgment, megalomania, violent fits of irritation and anger, boastfulness, delusions of grandeur— of being a great financial genius. Anyone suffering from that would soon put a solvent firm on the rocks, unless he could be restrained, and that's not so easy to do, especially if the man himself has an idea of what you're after. Yes, I should say it was a bit of luck for your friends that he died."

"They're no friends of mine," said Neele. He repeated what he had once said before:

"They're all very unpleasant people. . . ."

CHAPTER 19

IN THE DRAWING-ROOM at Yewtree Lodge, the whole Fortescue family was assembled. Percival Fortescue, leaning against the mantelpiece, was addressing the meeting.

"It's all very well," said Percival. "But the whole position is most unsatisfactory. The police come and go and don't tell us anything. One supposes they're pursuing some line of research. In the meantime, everything's at a standstill. One can't make plans, one can't arrange things for the future."

"It's all so inconsiderate," said Jennifer. "And so stupid."

"There still seems to be this ban against anyone leaving the house," went on Percival. "Still, I think among ourselves we might discuss future plans. What about you, Elaine? I gather you're going to marry—what's-his-name—Gerald Wright? Have you any idea when?"

"As soon as possible," said Elaine.

Percival frowned.

"You mean, in about six months' time?"

"No, I don't. Why should we wait six months?"

"I think it would be more decent," said Percival.

"Rubbish," said Elaine. "A month. That's the longest we'll wait."

"Well, it's for you to say," said Percival. "And what are your plans when you are married, if you have any?"

"We're thinking of starting a school."

Percival shook his head.

"That's a very risky speculation in these times. What with the shortage of domestic labor, the difficulty of getting an adequate teaching staff—really, Elaine, it sounds all right. But I should think twice about it if I were you."

"We have thought. Gerald feels that the whole future of this country lies in right education."

"I am seeing Mr. Billingsley the day after tomorrow," said Percival. "We've got to go into various questions of finance. He was suggesting that you might like to make this money that's been left to you by Father, into a trust for yourself and your children. It's a very sound thing to do nowadays."

"I don't want to do that," said Elaine. "We shall need the money to start up our school. There's a very suitable house we've heard of for sale. It's in Cornwall. Beautiful grounds and quite a good house. It would have to be built onto a good deal—several wings added."

"You mean—you mean you're going to take all your money out of the business? Really, Elaine, I don't think you're wise."

"Much wiser to take it out than leave it in, I should say," said Elaine. "Businesses are going phut all over the place. You said yourself, Val, before father died, that things were getting into a pretty bad state."

"One says that sort of thing," said Percival vaguely, "but I must say, Elaine, to take out all your capital and sink it in the buying, equipping and running of a school is crazy. If it's not a success, look what happens? You're left without a penny."

"It will be a success," said Elaine doggedly.

"I'm with you." Lance, lying sprawled out in a chair, spoke up encouragingly. "Have a crack at it, Elaine. In my opinion it'll be a damned odd sort of school, but it's what you want to do—you and Gerald. If you do lose your money you'll at any rate have had the satisfaction of doing what you wanted to do."

"Just what one might have expected you to say, Lance," said Percival acidly.

"I know, I know," said Lance. "I'm the spendthrift prodigal son. But I still think I've had more fun out of life than you have, Percy, old boy."

"It depends on what you call fun," said Percival acidly. "Which brings us to your own plans, Lance. I suppose you'll be off again back to Kenya—or Canada—or climbing Mount Everest or something fairly fantastic?"

"Now what makes you think that?" said Lance.

"Well, you've never had much use for a stay-at-home life in England, have you?"

"One changes as one gets older," said Lance. "One settles down. D'you know, Percy my boy, I'm quite looking forward to having a crack at being a sober business man."

"Do you mean . . . ?"

"I mean I'm coming into the firm with you, old boy." Lance grinned. "Oh, you're the senior partner, of course. You've got the lion's share. I'm only a very junior partner. But I have got a holding in it that gives me the right to be in on things, doesn't it?"

"Well—yes—of course, if you put it that way. But I can assure you, my dear boy, you'll be very, very bored."

"I wonder now. I don't believe I shall be bored."

Percival frowned.

"You don't seriously mean, Lance, that you're coming into the business?"

"Having a finger in the pie? Yes, that's exactly what I am doing."

Percival shook his head.

"Things are in a very bad way, you know. You'll find that out. It's going to be about all we can do to pay out Elaine her share, if she insists on having it paid out."

"There you are, Elaine," said Lance. "You see how wise you were to insist on grabbing your money while it's there to grab."

"Really, Lance," Percival spoke angrily, "these jokes of yours are in very bad taste."

"I do think, Lance, you might be more careful what you say," said Jennifer.

Sitting a little way away near the window, Pat studied them one by one. If this was what Lance had meant by twisting Percival's tail, she could see that he was achieving his object. Percival's neat impassivity was quite ruffled. He snapped again, angrily:

"Are you serious, Lance?"

"Dead serious."

"It won't work, you know. You'll soon get fed up."

"Not me. Think what a lovely change it'll be for me. A city office, typists running and going. I shall have a blonde secretary like Miss Grosvenor—is it Grosvenor? I suppose you've snaffled her. But I shall get one just the same. 'Yes, Mr. Lancelot, no, Mr. Lancelot. Your tea, Mr. Lancelot.' "

"Oh, don't play the fool," snapped Percival.

"Why are you so angry, my dear brother? Don't you look forward to having me sharing your city cares?"

"You haven't the least conception of the mess everything's in."

"No. You'll have to put me wise to all that."

"First, you've got to understand that for the last six months—

no, more, a year—father's not been himself. He's done the most incredibly foolish things, financially. Sold out good stock, acquired various wildcat holdings. Sometimes he's really thrown away money hand over fist. Just, one might say, for the fun of spending it."

"In fact," said Lance, "it's just as well for the family that he had taxine in his tea."

"That's a very ugly way of putting it, but in essence you're quite right. It's about the only thing that saved us from bankruptcy. But we shall have to be extremely conservative and go very cautiously for a bit."

Lance shook his head.

"I don't agree with you. Caution never does anyone any good. You must take a few risks, strike out. You must go for something big."

"I don't agree," said Percy. "Caution and economy. Those are our watchwords."

"Not mine," said Lance.

"You're only the junior partner, remember," said Percival.

"All right, all right. But I've got a little say-so all the same."

Percival walked up and down the room agitatedly.

"It's no good, Lance. I'm fond of you and all that—"

"Are you?" Lance interpolated. Percival did not appear to hear him.

". . . But I really don't think we're going to pull together at all. Our outlooks are totally different."

"That may be an advantage," said Lance.

"The only sensible thing," said Percival, "is to dissolve the partnership."

"You're going to buy me out—is that the idea?"

"My dear boy, it's the only sensible thing to do, with our ideas so different."

"If you find it hard to pay Elaine out her legacy, how are you going to manage to pay me my share?"

"Well, I didn't mean in cash," said Percival. "We could—er—divide up the holdings."

"With you keeping the gilt-edged and me taking the worst of the speculative off you, I suppose?"

"They seem to be what you prefer," said Percival.

Lance grinned suddenly.

"You're right in a way, Percy, old boy. But I can't indulge my own taste entirely. I've got Pat here to think of."

Both men looked towards her. Pat opened her mouth, then shut it again. Whatever game Lance was playing, it was best that she should not interfere. That Lance was driving at something special, she was quite sure, but she was still a little uncertain as to what his actual object was.

"Line 'em up, Percy," said Lance, laughing. "Bogus Diamond Mines, Inaccessible Rubies, the Oil Concessions where no oil is. Do you think I'm quite as big a fool as I look?"

Percival said:

"Of course, some of these holdings are highly speculative, but remember, they may turn out immensely valuable."

"Changed your tune, haven't you?" said Lance, grinning. "Going to offer me Father's latest wildcat acquisitions as well as the old Blackbird Mine and things of that kind. By the way, has the Inspector been asking you about this Blackbird Mine?"

Percival frowned.

"Yes, he did. I can't imagine what he wanted to know about it. I couldn't tell him much. You and I were children at the time. I just remember vaguely that Father went out there and came back saying the whole thing was no good."

"What was it—a gold mine?"

"I believe so. Father came back pretty certain that there was no gold there. And, mind you, he wasn't the sort of man to be mistaken."

"Who got him into it? A man called MacKenzie, wasn't it?"

"Yes. MacKenzie died out there."

"MacKenzie died out there," said Lance thoughtfully. "Wasn't there a terrific scene? I seem to remember. . . . Mrs. MacKenzie, wasn't it? Came here. Ranted and stormed at Father. Hurled down curses on his head. She accused him, if I remember rightly, of murdering her husband."

"Really," said Percival repressively. "I can't recollect anything of the kind."

"I remember it, though," said Lance. "I was a good bit younger than you, of course. Perhaps that's why it appealed to me. As a child it struck me as full of drama. Where was Blackbird? West Africa, wasn't it?"

"Yes, I think so."

"I must look up the concession sometime," said Lance, "when I'm at the office."

"You can be quite sure," said Percival, "that Father made no mistake. If he came back saying there was no gold, there was no gold."

"You're probably right there," said Lance. "Poor Mrs. MacKenzie. I wonder what happened to her and to those two kids she brought along. Funny—they must be grown up by now."

CHAPTER 20

AT THE PINEWOOD Private Sanatorium, Inspector Neele, sitting in the visitors' parlor, was facing a gray-haired, elderly lady. Helen MacKenzie was sixty-three, though she looked younger. She had pale blue, rather vacant-looking eyes, and a weak, indeterminate chin. She had a long upper lip which occasionally twitched. She held a large book in her lap and was looking down at it as Inspector Neele talked to her. In Inspector Neele's mind was the conversation he had just had with Doctor Crosbie, the head of the establishment.

"She's a voluntary patient, of course," said Doctor Crosbie, "not certified."

"She's not dangerous, then?"

"Oh, no. Most of the time she's as sane to talk to as you or I. It's one of her good periods now so that you'll be able to have a perfectly normal conversation with her."

Bearing this in mind, Inspector Neele started his first conversational essay.

"It's very kind of you to see me, madam," he said. "My name is Neele. I've come to see you about a Mr. Fortescue who has recently died. A Mr. Rex Fortescue. I expect you know the name."

Mrs. MacKenzie's eyes were fixed on her book. She said: "I don't know what you're talking about."

"Mr. Fortescue, madam. Mr. Rex Fortescue."

"No," said Mrs. MacKenzie. "No. Certainly not."

Inspector Neele was slightly taken aback. He wondered whether this was what Doctor Crosbie called being completely normal.

"I think, Mrs. MacKenzie, you knew him a good many years ago."

"Not really," said Mrs. MacKenzie. "It was yesterday."

"I see," said Inspector Neele, falling back upon his formula rather uncertainly. "I believe," he went on, "that you paid him a visit many years ago at his residence, Yewtree Lodge."

"A very ostentatious house," said Mrs. MacKenzie.

"Yes. Yes, you might call it that. He had been connected with your husband, I believe, over a certain mine in Africa. The Blackbird Mine, I believe it was called."

"I have to read my book," said Mrs. MacKenzie. "There's not much time and I have to read my book."

"Yes, madam. Yes, I quite see that." There was a pause, then Inspector Neele went on, "Mr. MacKenzie and Mr. Fortescue went out together to Africa to survey the mine."

"It was my husband's mine," said Mrs. MacKenzie. "He found it and staked a claim to it. He wanted money to capitalize it. He went to Rex Fortescue. If I'd been wiser, if I'd known more, I wouldn't have let him do it."

"No, I see that. As it was, they went out together to Africa, and there your husband died of fever."

"I must read my book," said Mrs. MacKenzie.

"Do you think Mr. Fortescue swindled your husband over the Blackbird Mine, Mrs. MacKenzie?"

Without raising her eyes from the book, Mrs. MacKenzie said, "How stupid you are."

"Yes, yes, I dare say. . . . But you see, it's all a long time ago and making inquiries about a thing that is over a long time ago is rather difficult."

"Who said it was over?"

"I see. You don't think it is over?"

"*No question is ever settled until it is settled right.* Kipling said that. Nobody reads Kipling nowadays, but he was a great man."

"Do you think the question will be settled right one of these days?"

"Rex Fortescue is dead, isn't he? You said so."

"He was poisoned," said Inspector Neele.

Rather disconcertingly, Mrs. MacKenzie laughed.

"What nonsense," she said, "he died of fever."

"I'm talking about Mr. Rex Fortescue."

"So am I." She looked up suddenly and her pale blue eyes fixed his. "Come now," she said, "he died in his bed, didn't he? He died in his bed?"

"He died in St. Jude's Hospital," said Inspector Neele.

"Nobody knows where my husband died," said Mrs. MacKenzie. "Nobody knows how he died or where he was buried. . . . All anyone knows is what Rex Fortescue said. And Rex Fortescue was a liar!"

"Do you think there may have been foul play?"

"Foul play, foul play, fowls lay eggs, don't they?"

"You think that Rex Fortescue was responsible for your husband's death?"

"I had an egg for breakfast this morning," said Mrs. MacKenzie. "Quite fresh, too. Surprising, isn't it, when one thinks that it was thirty years ago?"

Neele drew a deep breath. It seemed unlikely that he was ever going to get anywhere at this rate, but he persevered.

"Somebody put dead blackbirds on Rex Fortescue's desk about a month or two before he died."

"That's interesting. That's very, very interesting."

"Have you any idea, madam, who might have done that?"

"Ideas aren't any help to one. One has to have action. I brought them up for that, you know, to take action."

"You're talking about your children?"

She nodded her head rapidly.

"Yes. Donald and Ruby. They were nine and seven and left without a father. I told them. I told them every day. I made them swear it every night."

Inspector Neele leant forward.

"What did you make them swear?"

"That they'd kill him, of course."

"I see."

Inspector Neele spoke as though it was the most reasonable remark in the world.

"Did they?"

"Donald went to Dunkirk. He never came back. They sent me a wire saying he was dead. 'Deeply regret killed in action.' Action, you see, the wrong kind of action."

"I'm sorry to hear that, madam. What about your daughter?"

"I haven't got a daughter," said Mrs. MacKenzie.

"You spoke of her just now," said Neele. "Your daughter, Ruby."

"Ruby. Yes, Ruby." She leaned forward. "Do you know what I've done to Ruby?"

"No, madam. What have you done to her?"

She whispered suddenly,

"Look here at the Book."

He saw then that what she was holding in her lap was a Bible. It was a very old Bible and as she opened it, on the front page, Inspector Neele saw that various names had been written. It was obviously a family Bible in which the old-fashioned custom had been continued of entering each new birth. Mrs. MacKenzie's thin forefinger pointed to the two last names. "Donald MacKenzie" with the date of his birth, and "Ruby MacKenzie" with the date of hers. But a thick line was drawn through Ruby MacKenzie's name.

"You see?" said Mrs. MacKenzie. "I struck her out of the Book. I cut her off forever! The Recording Angel won't find her name there."

"You cut her name out of the Book? Now, why, madam?"

Mrs. MacKenzie looked at him cunningly.

"You know why," she said.

"But I don't. Really, madam, I don't."

"She didn't keep faith. You know she didn't keep faith."

"Where is your daughter now, madam?"

"I've told you. I have no daughter. There isn't such a person as Ruby MacKenzie any longer."

"You mean she's dead?"

"Dead?" The woman laughed suddenly. "It would be better for her if she were dead. Much better. Much, much better." She sighed and turned restlessly in her seat. Then, her manner reverting to a kind of formal courtesy, she said, "I'm so sorry, but really I'm afraid I can't talk to you any longer. You see, the time is getting very short, and I must read my book."

To Inspector Neele's further remarks Mrs. MacKenzie returned no reply. She merely made a faint gesture of annoyance and continued to read her Bible with her finger following the line of the verse she was reading.

Neele got up and left. He had another brief interview with the Superintendent.

"Do any of her relations come to see her?" he asked. "A daughter, for instance?"

"I believe a daughter did come to see her in my predecessor's time, but her visit agitated the patient so much that he advised her not to come again. Since then everything is arranged through solicitors."

"And you've no idea where this Ruby MacKenzie is now?"

The Superintendent shook his head.

"No idea whatsoever."

"You've no idea whether she's married, for instance?"

"I don't know. All I can do is to give you the address of the solicitors who deal with us."

Inspector Neele had already tracked down those solicitors. They were unable, or said they were unable, to tell him anything. A trust fund had been established for Mrs. MacKenzie, which they managed. These arrangements had been made some years previously, and they had not seen Miss MacKenzie since.

Inspector Neele tried to get a description of Ruby MacKenzie, but the results were not encouraging. So many relations came to visit patients that after a lapse of years they were bound to be remembered dimly, with the appearance of one mixed up with the appearance of another. The Matron, who had been there for many years, seemed to remember that Miss MacKenzie was small and dark. The only other nurse who had been there for any length of time recalled that she was heavily built and fair.

"So there we are, sir," said Inspector Neele as he reported to the Assistant Commissioner. "There's a whole crazy setup and it fits together. It must mean something."

The A.C. nodded thoughtfully.

"The blackbirds in the pie tying up with the Blackbird Mine, rye in the dead man's pocket, bread and honey with Adele Fortescue's tea (not that that is conclusive. After all, anyone might have had bread and honey for tea!). The third murder, that girl strangled with a stocking and a clothes peg nipped onto her nose. Yes, crazy as the setup is, it certainly can't be ignored."

"Half a minute, sir," said Inspector Neele.

"What is it?"

Neele was frowning.

"You know, what you've just said. It didn't ring true. It was wrong somewhere." He shook his head and sighed. "No. I can't place it."

CHAPTER 21

Lance and Pat wandered round the well-kept grounds surrounding Yewtree Lodge.

"I hope I'm not hurting your feelings, Lance," Pat murmured, "if I say this is quite the nastiest garden I've ever been in."

"It won't hurt my feelings," said Lance. "Is it? Really I don't know. It seems to have three gardeners working on it very industriously."

Pat said, "Probably that's what's wrong with it. No expense spared, no signs of any individual taste. All the right rhododendrons and all the right bedding out, done in the proper season, I expect."

"Well, what would you put in an English garden, Pat, if you had one?"

"My garden," said Pat, "would have hollyhocks, larkspurs and Canterbury bells, no bedding out and none of these horrible yews."

She glanced up at the dark yew hedges disparagingly.

"Association of ideas," said Lance easily.

"There's something awfully frightening about a poisoner," said Pat. "I mean, it must be a horrid, brooding revengeful mind."

"So that's how you see it? Funny! I just think of it as businesslike and cold-blooded."

"I suppose one could look at it that way." She resumed, with a slight shiver, "All the same, to do three murders. . . . Whoever did it must be mad."

"Yes," said Lance, in a low voice. "I'm afraid so." Then, breaking out sharply, he said, "For God's sake, Pat, do go away from here. Go back to London. Go down to Devonshire or up to the

Lakes. Go to Stratford on Avon or go and look at the Norfolk Broads. The police wouldn't mind your going—you had nothing to do with all this. You were in Paris when the old man was killed and in London when the other two died. I tell you it worries me to death to have you here."

Pat paused a moment before saying quietly:

"You know who it is, don't you?"

"No, I don't."

"But you think you know. . . . That's why you're frightened for me. I wish you'd tell me."

"I can't tell you. I don't know anything. But I wish to God you'd go away from here."

"Darling," said Pat, "I'm not going. I'm staying here. For better, for worse. That's how I feel about it." She added, with a sudden catch in her voice, "Only with me it's always for worse."

"What on earth do you mean, Pat?"

"I bring bad luck. That's what I mean. I bring bad luck to anybody I come in contact with."

"My dear, adorable nitwit, you haven't brought bad luck to me. Look how after I married you the old man sent for me to come home and make friends with him."

"Yes, and what happened when you did come home? I tell you, I'm unlucky to people."

"Look here, my sweet, you've got a thing about all this. It's superstition, pure and simple."

"I can't help it. Some people do bring bad luck. I'm one of them."

Lance took her by the shoulders and shook her violently. "You're my Pat and to be married to you is the greatest luck in the world. So get that into your silly head." Then, calming down, he said in a more sober voice, "But, seriously, Pat, do be very careful. If there is someone unhinged round here, I don't want you to be the one who stops the bullet or drinks the henbane."

"Or drinks the henbane, as you say."

"When I'm not around, stick to that old lady. What's-her-name Marple. Why do you think Aunt Effie asked her to stay here?"

"Goodness knows why Aunt Effie does anything. Lance, how long are we going to stay here?"

Lance shrugged his shoulders.

"Difficult to say."

"I don't think," said Pat, "that we're really awfully welcome." She hesitated as she spoke the words. "The house belongs to your brother now, I suppose? He doesn't really want us here, does he?"

Lance chuckled suddenly.

"Not he, but he's got to stick us for the present, at any rate."

"And afterwards? What are we going to do, Lance? Are we going back to East Africa, or what?"

"Is that what you'd like to do, Pat?"

She nodded vigorously.

"That's lucky," said Lance, "because it's what I'd like to do, too. I don't take much to this country nowadays."

Pat's face brightened.

"How lovely. From what you said the other day, I was afraid you might want to stop here."

A devilish glint appeared in Lance's eyes.

"You're to hold your tongue about our plans, Pat," he said. "I have it in my mind to twist dear brother Percival's tail a bit."

"Oh, Lance, do be careful."

"I'll be careful, my sweet, but I don't see why old Percy should get away with everything."

ii.

With her head a little on one side, looking like an amiable cockatoo, Miss Marple sat in the large drawing-room listening to Mrs. Percival Fortescue. Miss Marple looked particularly incongruous in the drawing-room. Her light, spare figure was alien to the vast, brocaded sofa in which she sat, with its many-hued cushions strewn round her. Miss Marple sat very upright because she had been taught to use a back-board as a girl, and not to loll. In a large armchair beside her, dressed in elaborate black, was Mrs. Percival, talking away volubly at nineteen to the dozen. "Exactly," thought Miss Marple, "like poor Mrs. Emmett, the bank manager's wife." She remembered how one day Mrs. Emmett had come to call and talk about the selling arrangements for Poppy Day, and how after the preliminary business had been settled, Mrs. Emmett had suddenly begun to talk and talk and talk. Mrs. Emmett occupied rather a difficult position in St. Mary Meade. She did not belong to the old guard of ladies in reduced circumstances who lived in neat houses round the church, and who knew intimately all the ramifications of the County families, even though they might not be strictly County themselves. Mr. Emmett, the bank manager, had undeniably married beneath him and the result was that his wife was in a position of great loneliness since she could not, of course, associate with the wives of the trades people. Snobbery here raised its hideous head and marooned Mrs. Emmett on a permanent island of loneliness.

The necessity to talk grew upon Mrs. Emmett, and on that particular day it had burst its bounds, and Miss Marple had received the full flood of the torrent. She had been sorry for Mrs. Emmett then, and today she was rather sorry for Mrs. Percival Fortescue.

Mrs. Percival had had a lot of grievances to bear and the relief of airing them to a more or less total stranger was enormous.

"Of course, I never want to complain," said Mrs. Percival. "I've never been of the complaining kind. What I always say is that one must put up with things. What can't be cured must be endured and I'm sure I've never said a word to anyone. It's really difficult to know whom I could have spoken to. In some ways one is very isolated here—very isolated. It's very convenient, of course, and a great saving of expense to have our own set of rooms in this house. But, of course, it's not at all like having a place of your own. I'm sure you agree."

Miss Marple said she agreed.

"Fortunately, our new house is almost ready to move into. It is a question really of getting the painters and decorators out. These men are so slow. My husband, of course, has been quite satisfied living here. But then it's different for a man. That's what I always say—it's so different for a man. Don't you agree?"

Miss Marple agreed that it was very different for a man. She could say this without a qualm as it was what she really believed. "The gentlemen" were, in Miss Marple's mind, in a totally different category from her own sex. They required two eggs plus bacon for breakfast, three good nourishing meals a day, and were never to be contradicted or argued with before dinner. Mrs. Percival went on:

"My husband, you see, is away all day in the city. When he comes home he's just tired and wants to sit down and read. But I, on the contrary, am alone here all day with no congenial company at all. I've been perfectly comfortable and all that. Excellent food. But what I do feel one needs is a really pleasant social circle. The people round here are really not my kind. Part of them are what I call a flashy, bridge-playing lot. Not nice bridge. I like a hand at bridge myself as well as anyone, but of course they're all very rich down here. They play for enormously high stakes, and there's a great deal of drinking. In fact, the sort of life that I call really fast society. Then, of course, there's a sprinkling of— well, you can only call them old pussies who love to potter round with a trowel and do gardening."

Miss Marple looked slightly guilty, since she was herself an inveterate gardener.

"I don't want to say anything against the dead," resumed Mrs. Percy rapidly, "but there's no doubt about it, Mr. Fortescue, my father-in-law, I mean, made a very foolish second marriage. My —well, I can't call her my mother-in-law, she was the same age as I am. The real truth of it is she was man-mad. Absolutely man-mad. And the way she spent money! My father-in-law was an absolute fool about her. Didn't care what bills she ran up. It vexed Percy very much, very much indeed. Percy is always so careful about money matters. He hates waste. And then what with Mr. Fortescue being so peculiar and so bad-tempered, flashing out in these terrible rages, spending money like water, backing wildcat schemes. Well—it wasn't at all nice."

Miss Marple ventured upon making a remark.

"That must have worried your husband, too?"

"Oh yes, it did. For the last year Percy's been very worried, indeed. It's really made him quite different. His manner, you know, changed even towards me. Sometimes when I talked to him he used not to answer." Mrs. Percy sighed, then went on, "Then Elaine, my sister-in-law, you know, she's a very odd sort of girl. Very out-of-doors and all that. Not exactly unfriendly, but not sympathetic, you know. She never wanted to go up to London and shop, or go to a matinée or anything of that kind. She wasn't even interested in clothes." Mrs. Percival sighed again and murmured, "But, of course, I don't want to complain in any way." A qualm of compunction came over her. She said, hurriedly: "You must think it most odd, talking to you like this when you are a comparative stranger. But really, what with all the strain and shock—I think really it's the shock that matters most. Delayed shock. I feel so nervous, you know, that I really—well, I really must speak to someone. You remind me so much of a dear old lady, Miss Trefusis James. She fractured her femur when she was seventy-five. It was a very long business nursing her, and we became great friends. She gave me a fox fur cape when I left and I did think it was kind of her."

"I know just how you feel," said Miss Marple.

And this again was true. Mrs. Percival's husband was obviously bored by her and paid very little attention to her, and the poor woman had managed to make no local friends. Running up to London and shopping, matinées and a luxurious house to live in did not make up for the lack of humanity in her relations with her husband's family.

"I hope it's not rude of me to say so," said Miss Marple in a gentle, old lady's voice, "but I really feel that the late Mr. Fortescue cannot have been a very nice man."

"He wasn't," said his daughter-in-law. "Quite frankly, my dear, between you and me, he was a detestable old man. I don't wonder —I really don't—that someone put him out of the way."

"You've no idea at all who—" began Miss Marple and broke off. "Oh dear, perhaps this is a question I should not ask—not even an idea who—who—well, who it might have been?"

"Oh, I think it was that horrible man, Crump," said Mrs. Percival. "I've always disliked him very much. He's got a manner, not really rude, you know, but yet it is rude. Impertinent, that's more it."

"Still, there would have to be a motive, I suppose."

"I really don't know that that sort of person requires much motive. I daresay Mr. Fortescue ticked him off about something, and I rather suspect that sometimes he drinks too much. But what I really think is that he's a bit unbalanced, you know. Like that footman, or butler, whoever it was, who went round the house shooting everybody. Of course, to be quite honest with you, I did suspect that it was Adele who poisoned Mr. Fortescue. But now, of course, one can't suspect that since she's been poisoned herself. She may have accused Crump, you know. And then he lost his head and perhaps managed to put something in the sandwiches and Gladys saw him do it and so he killed her too. I think it's really dangerous having him in the house at all. Oh dear, I wish I could get away, but I suppose these horrible policemen won't let one do anything of the kind." She leant forward impulsively and put a plump hand on Miss Marple's arm. "Sometimes I feel I must get away—that if it doesn't all stop soon I shall —I shall actually run away—"

She leant back studying Miss Marple's face.

"But perhaps—that wouldn't be wise?"

"No, I don't think it would be very wise. The police could soon find you, you know."

"Could they? Could they really? You think they're clever enough for that?"

"It is very foolish to underestimate the police. Inspector Neele strikes me as a particularly intelligent man."

"Oh! I thought he was rather stupid."

Miss Marple shook her head.

"I can't help feeling—" Jennifer Fortescue hesitated—"that it's dangerous to stay here."

"Dangerous for you, you mean?"

"Ye-es—well, yes—"

"Because of something you—know?"

Mrs. Percival seemed to take breath.

"Oh no, of course, I don't know anything. What should I know? It's just—just that I'm nervous. That man Crump—"

But it was not, Miss Marple thought, of Crump that Mrs. Percival Fortescue was thinking, watching the clenching and unclenching of Jennifer's hands. Miss Marple thought that for some reason Jennifer Fortescue was very badly frightened indeed.

CHAPTER 22

IT WAS GROWING dark. Miss Marple had taken her knitting over to the window in the library. Looking out of the glass pane, she saw Pat Fortescue walking up and down the terrace outside. Miss Marple unlatched the window and called through it.

"Come in, my dear. Do come in. I'm sure it's much too cold and damp for you to be out there without a coat on."

Pat obeyed the summons. She came in and shut the window and turned on two of the lamps.

"Yes," she said, "it's not a very nice afternoon." She sat down on the sofa by Miss Marple. "What are you knitting?"

"Oh, just a little matinée coat, dear. For a baby, you know. I always say young mothers can't have too many matinée coats for their babies. It's the second size. I always knit the second size. Babies so soon grow out of the first size."

Pat stretched out long legs towards the fire.

"It's nice in here today," she said. "With the fire and the lamps and you knitting things for babies. It all seems cozy and homely and as England ought to be."

"It's as England is," said Miss Marple. "There are not so many Yewtree Lodges, my dear."

"I think that's a good thing," said Pat. "I don't believe this was ever a happy house. I don't believe anybody was ever happy in it, in spite of all the money they spent and the things they had."

"No," Miss Marple agreed. "I shouldn't say it had been a happy house."

"I suppose Adele may have been happy," said Pat. "I never met her, of course, so I don't know, but Jennifer is pretty miserable and Elaine's been eating her heart out over a young man who she probably knows in her heart of hearts doesn't care for her. Oh, how I want to get away from here!" She looked at Miss Marple and smiled suddenly. "D'you know," she said, "that Lance told me to stick as close to you as I could? He seemed to think I should be safe that way."

"Your husband's no fool," said Miss Marple.

"No. Lance isn't a fool. At least, he is in some ways. But I wish he'd tell me exactly what he's afraid of. One thing seems clear enough. Somebody in this house is mad, and madness is always frightening because you don't know how mad people's minds will work. You don't know what they'll do next."

"My poor child," said Miss Marple.

"Oh, I'm all right, really. I ought to be tough enough by now."

Miss Marple said gently, "You've had a good deal of unhappiness, haven't you, my dear?"

"Oh, I've had some very good times, too. I had a lovely childhood in Ireland, riding, hunting, and a great big, bare, draughty house with lots and lots of sun in it. If you've had a happy childhood, nobody can take that away from you, can they? It was afterwards—when I grew up—that things seemed always to go wrong. To begin with, I suppose, it was the war."

"Your husband was a fighter pilot, wasn't he?"

"Yes. We'd only been married about a month when Don was shot down." She stared ahead of her into the fire. "I thought at first I wanted to die, too. It seemed so unfair, so cruel. And yet—in the end—I almost began to see that it had been the best thing. Don was wonderful in the war. Brave and reckless and gay. He had all the qualities that are needed, wanted in a war. But I don't believe, somehow, peace would have suited him. He had a kind of—oh, how shall I put it?—arrogant insubordination. He wouldn't have fitted in or settled down. He'd have fought against things. He was, well, antisocial in a way. No, he wouldn't have fitted in."

"It's wise of you to see that, my dear." Miss Marple bent over her knitting, picked up a stitch, counted under her breath, "Three plain, two purl, slip one, knit two together," and then said, aloud, "And your second husband, my dear?"

"Freddy? Freddy shot himself."

"Oh dear. How very sad. What a tragedy."

"We were very happy together," said Pat. "I began to realize, about two years ago after we were married, that Freddy wasn't —well, wasn't always straight. I began to find out the sort of things that were going on. But it didn't seem to matter, between us two, that is. Because, you see, Freddy loved me and I loved him. I tried not to know what was going on. That was cowardly of me, I suppose, but I couldn't have changed him, you know. You can't change people."

"No," said Miss Marple, "you can't change people."

"I'd taken him and loved him and married him for what he was, and I sort of felt that I just had to—put up with it. Then things went wrong and he couldn't face it, and he shot himself. After he died I went out to Kenya to stay with some friends there. I couldn't stop on in England and go on meeting all—all the old crowd that knew about it all. And out in Kenya I met Lance." Her face changed and softened. She went on looking into the fire, and Miss Marple looked at her. Presently Pat turned her

137

head and said, "Tell me, Miss Marple, what do you really think of Percival?"

"Well, I've not seen very much of him. Just at breakfast, usually. That's all. I don't think he very much likes my being here."

Pat laughed suddenly.

"He's mean, you know. Terribly mean about money. Lance says he always was. Jennifer complains of it, too. Goes over the housekeeping accounts with Miss Dove. Complaining of every item. But Miss Dove manages to hold her own. She's really rather a wonderful person. Don't you think so?"

"Yes, indeed. She reminds me of Mrs. Latimer in my own village, St. Mary Meade. She ran the Women's Voluntary Services, you know, and the Girl Guides, and indeed, she ran practically everything there. It wasn't for quite five years that we discovered that—oh, but I mustn't gossip. Nothing is more boring than people talking to you about places and people whom you've never seen and know nothing about. You must forgive me, my dear."

"Is St. Mary Meade a very nice village?"

"Well, I don't know what you would call a nice village, my dear. It's quite a pretty village. There are some nice people living in it and some extremely unpleasant people as well. Very curious things go on there just as in any other village. Human nature is much the same everywhere, is it not?"

"You go up and see Miss Ramsbottom a good deal, don't you?" said Pat. "Now, she really frightens me."

"Frightens you? Why?"

"Because I think she's crazy. I think she's got religious mania. You don't think she could be—really—mad, do you?"

"In what way, mad?"

"Oh, you know what I mean, Miss Marple, well enough. She sits up there and never goes out, and broods about sin. Well, she might have felt in the end that it was her mission in life to execute judgment."

"Is that what your husband thinks?"

"I don't know what Lance thinks. He won't tell me. But I'm quite sure of one thing—that he believes that it's someone who's mad, and it's someone in the family. Well, Percival's sane enough, I should say. Jennifer's just stupid and rather pathetic. She's a bit nervy, but that's all, and Elaine is one of those queer, tempestuous, tense girls. She's desperately in love with this young man of hers and she'll never admit to herself for a moment that he's marrying her for her money."

"You think he is marrying her for money?"

"Yes, I do. Don't you think so?"

"I should say quite certainly," said Miss Marple. "Like young Ellis who married Marion Bates, the rich ironmonger's daughter. She was a very plain girl and absolutely besotted about him. However, it turned out quite well. People like young Ellis and this Gerald Wright are only really disagreeable when they've married a poor girl for love. They are so annoyed with themselves for doing it that they take it out of the girl. But if they marry a rich girl they continue to respect her."

"I don't see," went on Pat, frowning, "how it can be anybody from outside. And so—and so that accounts for the atmosphere that is here. Everyone watching everybody else. Only something's got to happen soon—"

"There won't be any more deaths," said Miss Marple. "At least, I shouldn't think so."

"You can't be sure of that."

"Well, as a matter of fact, I am fairly sure. The murderer's accomplished his purpose, you see."

"His?"

"Well, his or her. One says his for convenience."

"You say his or her purpose. What sort of purpose?"

Miss Marple shook her head—she was not yet quite sure herself.

CHAPTER 23

ONCE AGAIN MISS SOMERS had just made tea in the typists' room, and once again the kettle had not been boiling when Miss Somers poured the water on to the tea. History repeats itself. Miss Griffith, accepting her cup, thought to herself, I really must speak to Mr. Percival about Somers. I'm sure we can do better. But with all this terrible business going on, one doesn't like to bother him over office details.

As so often before, Miss Griffith said sharply, "Water not boiling again, Somers."

Miss Somers, going pink, replied in her usual formula, "Oh, dear, I was sure it was boiling this time."

Further developments on the same line were interrupted by the entrance of Lance Fortescue. He looked round him somewhat vaguely, and Miss Griffith, jumping up, came forward to meet him.

"Mr. Lance!" she exclaimed.

He swung round towards her and his face lit up in a smile.

"Hullo. Why, it's Miss Griffith."

Miss Griffith was delighted. Eleven years since he had seen her and he knew her name. She said in a confused voice, "Fancy your remembering."

And Lance said easily, with all his charm to the fore, "Of course I remember."

A flicker of excitement was running round the typists' room. Miss Somers' troubles over the tea were forgotten. She was gaping at Lance with her mouth slightly open. Miss Bell gazed eagerly over the top of her typewriter and Miss Chase unobtrusively drew out her compact and powdered her nose. Lance Fortescue looked round him.

"So everything's still going on just the same here," he said.

"Not many changes, Mr. Lance. How brown you look and how well! I suppose you must have had a very interesting life abroad."

"You could call it that," said Lance, "but perhaps I am now going to try and have an interesting life in London."

"You're coming back here to the office?"

"Maybe."

"Oh, but how delightful."

"You'll find me very rusty," said Lance. "You'll have to show me all the ropes, Miss Griffith."

Miss Griffith laughed delightedly.

"It will be very nice to have you back, Mr. Lance. Very nice indeed."

Lance threw her an appreciative glance.

"That's sweet of you," he said, "that's very sweet of you."

"We never believed—none of us thought. . . ." Miss Griffith broke off and flushed.

Lance patted her on the arm.

"You didn't believe the devil was as black as he was painted? Well, perhaps he wasn't. But that's all old history now. There's no good going back over it. The future's the thing." He added, "Is my brother here?"

"He's in the inner office, I think."

Lance nodded easily and passed on. In the anteroom to the inner sanctum a hard-faced woman of middle age rose behind a desk and said forbiddingly, "Your name and business, please?"

Lance looked at her doubtfully.

"Are you—Miss Grosvenor?" he asked.

Miss Grosvenor had been described to him as a glamorous blonde. She had, indeed, appeared so in the pictures that had been published in the newspapers reporting the inquest on Rex Fortescue. This, surely, could not be Miss Grosvenor.

"Miss Grosvenor left last week. I am Mrs. Hardcastle, Mr. Percival Fortescue's personal secretary."

How like old Percy, thought Lance. To get rid of a glamorous blonde and take on a Gorgon instead. I wonder why? Was it safety or was it because this one comes cheaper? Aloud he said easily, "I'm Lancelot Fortescue. You haven't met me yet."

"Oh, I'm so sorry, Mr. Lancelot," Mrs. Hardcastle apologized. "This is the first time, I think, you've been to the office?"

"The first time but not the last," said Lance, smiling.

He crossed the room and opened the door of what had been his father's private office. Somewhat to his surprise, it was not Percival who was sitting behind the desk there, but Inspector Neele. Inspector Neele looked up from a large wad of papers which he was sorting, and nodded his head.

"Good morning, Mr. Fortescue, you've come to take up your duties, I suppose."

"So you've heard I decided to come into the firm?"

"Your brother told me so."

"He did, did he? With enthusiasm?"

Inspector Neele endeavored to conceal a smile.

"The enthusiasm was not marked," he said gravely.

"Poor Percy," commented Lance.

Inspector Neele looked at him curiously.

"Are you really going to become a City man?"

"You don't think it's likely, Inspector Neele?"

"It doesn't seem quite in character, Mr. Fortescue."

"Why not? I'm my father's son."

"And your mother's."

Lance shook his head.

"You haven't got anything there, Inspector. My mother was a Victorian romantic. Her favorite reading was the *Idylls of the King,* as indeed you may have deduced from our curious Christian names. She was an invalid and always, I should imagine, out of touch with reality. I'm not like that at all. I have no sentiment, very little sense of romance and I'm a realist first and last."

"People aren't always what they think themselves to be," Inspector Neele pointed out.

"No, I suppose that's true," said Lance.

He sat down in a chair and stretched his long legs out in his own characteristic fashion. He was smiling to himself. Then he said unexpectedly, "You're shrewder than my brother, Inspector."

"In what way, Mr. Fortescue?"

"I've put the wind up Percy, all right. He thinks I'm all set for the City life. He thinks he's going to have my fingers fiddling about in his pie. He thinks I'll launch out and spend the firm's money and try and embroil him in wildcat schemes. It would be almost worth doing just for the fun of it! Almost, but not quite. I couldn't really stand an office life, Inspector. I like the open air and some possibilities of adventure. I'd stifle in a place like this." He added quickly, "This is off the record, mind. Don't give me away to Percy, will you?"

"I don't suppose the subject will arise, Mr. Fortescue."

"I must have my bit of fun with Percy," said Lance. "I want to make him sweat a bit. I've got to get a bit of my own back."

"That's rather a curious phrase, Mr. Fortescue," said Neele. "Your own back—for what?"

Lance shrugged his shoulders.

"Oh, it's old history now. Not worth going back over."

"There was a little matter of a check, I understand, in the past. Would that be what you're referring to?"

"How much you know, Inspector!"

"There was no question of prosecution, I understand," said Neele. "Your father wouldn't have done that."

"No. He just kicked me out, that's all."

Inspector Neele eyed him speculatively, but it was not Lance Fortescue of whom he was thinking, but of Percival. The honest, industrious, parsimonious Percival. It seemed to him that wherever he got in the case he was always coming up against the enigma of Percival Fortescue, a man of whom everybody knew the outer aspects, but whose inner personality was much harder to gauge. One would have said from observing him, a somewhat colorless and insignificant character, a man who had been very much under his father's thumb. Percy Prim, in fact, as the A.C. had once said. Neele was trying now, through Lance, to get at a closer appreciation of Percival's personality. He murmured in a tentative manner:

"Your brother seems always to have been very much—well, how shall I put it—under your father's thumb."

"I wonder." Lance seemed definitely to be considering the point. "I wonder. Yes, that would be the effect, I think, given. But I'm not sure that it was really the truth. It's astonishing, you know, when I look back through life, to see how Percy always got his own way without seeming to do so, if you know what I mean."

Yes, Inspector Neele thought, it was indeed astonishing. He sorted through the papers in front of him, fished out a letter and shoved it across the desk towards Lance.

"This is a letter you wrote last August, isn't it, Mr. Fortescue?"

Lance took it, glanced at it and returned it.

"Yes," he said, "I wrote it after I got back to Kenya last summer. Dad kept it, did he? Where was it—here in the office?"

"No, Mr. Fortescue, it was among your father's papers in Yewtree Lodge."

The Inspector considered it speculatively as it lay on the desk in front of him. It was not a long letter.

"Dear Dad, I've talked things over with Pat and I agree to your proposition. It will take me a little time to get things fixed up here, say about the end of October or beginning of November. I'll let you know nearer the time. I hope we'll pull together better than we used to do. Anyway, I'll do my best. I can't say more. Look after yourself. Yours, Lance."

"Where did you address this letter, Mr. Fortescue? To the office or Yewtree Lodge?"

Lance frowned in an effort of recollection.

"It's difficult. I can't remember. You see, it's almost three months now. The office, I think. Yes, I'm almost sure. Here to the office." He paused a moment before asking with frank curiosity, "Why?"

"I wondered," said Inspector Neele. "Your father did not put it on the file here among his private papers. He took it back with him to Yewtree Lodge, and I found it in his desk there. I wondered why he should have done that."

Lance laughed.

"To keep it out of Percy's way, I suppose."

"Yes," said Inspector Neele, "it would seem so. Your brother, then, had access to your father's private papers here?"

"Well," Lance hesitated and frowned, "not exactly. I mean, I suppose he could have looked through them at any time if he liked, but he wouldn't be. . . ."

Inspector Neele finished the sentence for him.

"Wouldn't be supposed to do so?"

Lance grinned broadly. "That's right. Frankly, it would have been snooping. But Percy, I should imagine, always did snoop."

Inspector Neele nodded. He, also, thought it probable that Percival Fortescue snooped. It would be in keeping with what the Inspector was beginning to learn of his character.

"And talk of the devil," murmured Lance, as at that moment the door opened and Percival Fortescue came in. About to speak to the Inspector, he stopped, frowning, as he saw Lance.

"Hallo," he said. "You here? You didn't tell me you were coming here today."

"I felt a kind of zeal for work coming over me," said Lance, "so here I am ready to make myself useful. What do you want me to do?"

Percival said testily, "Nothing at present. Nothing at all. We shall have to come to some kind of arrangement as to what side of the business you're going to look after. We shall have to arrange for an office for you."

Lance inquired with a grin:

"By the way, why did you get rid of glamorous Grosvenor, old boy, and replace her by Horse-faced Hetty out there?"

"Really, Lance," Percival protested sharply.

"Definitely a change for the worse," said Lance. "I've been

looking forward to the glamorous Grosvenor. Why did you sack her? Thought she knew a bit too much?"

"Of course not. What an idea!" Percy spoke angrily, a flush mounting his pale face. He turned to the Inspector. "You mustn't pay any attention to my brother," he said coldly. "He has a rather peculiar sense of humor." He added, "I never had a very high opinion of Miss Grosvenor's intelligence. Mrs. Hardcastle has excellent references and is most capable, besides being very moderate in her terms."

"Very moderate in her terms," murmured Lance, casting his eyes towards the ceiling. "You know, Percy, I don't really approve of skimping over the office personnel. By the way, considering how loyally the staff has stood by us during these last tragic weeks, don't you think we ought to raise their salaries all round?"

"Certainly not," snapped Percival Fortescue. "Quite uncalled for and unnecessary."

Inspector Neele noticed the gleam of devilry in Lance's eyes. Percival, however, was far too much upset to notice it.

"You always had the most extraordinarily extravagant ideas," he stuttered. "In the state in which this firm has been left, economy is our only hope."

Inspector Neele coughed apologetically.

"That's one of the things I wanted to talk to you about, Mr. Fortescue," he said to Percival.

"Yes, Inspector?" Percival switched his attention to Neele.

"I want to put certain suggestions before you, Mr. Fortescue. I understand that for the past six months or longer, possibly a year, your father's general behavior and conduct have been a source of increasing anxiety to you."

"He wasn't well," said Percival with finality. "He certainly wasn't at all well."

"You tried to induce him to see a doctor but you failed. He refused categorically?"

"That is so."

"May I ask you if you suspected that your father was suffering from what is familiarly referred to as G.P.I., General Paralysis of the Insane, a condition with signs of megalomania and irritability, which terminates sooner or later in hopeless insanity?"

Percival looked surprised. "It is remarkably astute of you, Inspector. That is exactly what I did fear. That is why I was so anxious for my father to submit to medical treatment."

Neele went on:

"In the meantime, until you could persuade your father to do that, he was capable of causing a great deal of havoc to the business?"

"He certainly was," Percival agreed.

"A very unfortunate state of affairs," said the Inspector.

"Quite terrible. No one knows the anxiety I have been through."

Neele said gently, "From the business point of view, your father's death was an extremely fortunate circumstance."

Percival said sharply, "You can hardly think I would regard my father's death in that light."

"It is not a question of how you regard it, Mr. Fortescue. I'm speaking merely of a question of fact. Your father died before his finances were completely on the rocks."

Percival said impatiently, "Yes, yes. As a matter of actual fact, you are right."

"It was a fortunate occurrence for your whole family, since they are dependent on this business."

"Yes. But really, Inspector, I don't see what you're driving at. . . ." Percival broke off.

"Oh, I'm not driving at anything, Mr. Fortescue," said Neele. "I just like getting my facts straight. Now, there's another thing. I understood you to say that you'd had no communication of any kind with your brother here since he left England many years ago."

"Quite so," said Percival.

"Yes, but it isn't quite so, is it, Mr. Fortescue? I mean that last summer when you were so worried about your father's health, you actually wrote to your brother in Africa, told him of your anxiety about your father's behavior. You wanted, I think, your brother to combine with you in getting your father medically examined and put under restraint, if necessary."

"I—I—really, I don't see. . . ."

Percival was badly shaken.

"That is so, isn't it, Mr. Fortescue?"

"Well, actually, I thought it only right. After all, Lancelot was a junior partner."

146

Inspector Neele transferred his gaze to Lance. Lance was grinning.

"You received that letter?" Inspector Neele asked.

Lance Fortescue nodded.

"What did you reply to it?"

Lance's grin widened.

"I told Percy to go and boil his head and to let the old man alone. I said the old man probably knew what he was doing quite well."

Inspector Neele's gaze went back again to Percival.

"Were those the terms of your brother's answer?"

"I—I—well, I suppose roughly, yes. Far more offensively couched, however."

"I thought the Inspector had better have a bowdlerized version," said Lance. He went on, "Frankly, Inspector Neele, that is one of the reasons why, when I got a letter from my father, I came home to see for myself what I thought. In the short interview I had with my father, frankly, I couldn't see anything much wrong with him. He was slightly excitable, that was all. He appeared to me perfectly capable of managing his own affairs. Anyway, after I got back to Africa and had talked things over with Pat, I decided that I'd come home and—what shall we say?—see fair play."

He shot a glance at Percival as he spoke.

"I object," said Percival Fortescue. "I object strongly to what you are suggesting. I was not intending to victimize my father. I was concerned for his health. I admit that I was also concerned. . . ." he paused.

Lance filled the pause quickly.

"You were also concerned for your pocket, eh? For Percy's little pocket." He got up and all of a sudden his manner changed. "All right, Percy, I'm through. I was going to string you along a bit by pretending to work here. I wasn't going to let you have things all your own sweet way, but I'm damned if I'm going on with it. Frankly, it makes me sick to be in the same room with you. You've always been a dirty, mean little skunk all your life. Prying and snooping and lying and making trouble. I'll tell you another thing. I can't prove it, but I've always believed it was you who forged that check there was all the row about, that got me shot out of here. For one thing, it was a damn bad forgery, a forgery that

147

drew attention to itself in letters a foot high. My record was too bad for me to be able to protest effectively, but I often wondered that the old boy didn't realize that if I had forged his name I could have made a much better job of it than that."

Lance swept on, his voice rising, "Well, Percy, I'm not going on with the silly game. I'm sick of this country, and of the City. I'm sick of little men like you with their pin-stripe trousers and their black coats and their mincing voices and their mean, shoddy, financial deals. We'll share out as you suggested, and I'll get back with Pat to a different country—a country where there's room to breathe and move about. You can make your own list of securities. Keep the gilt-edged and the conservative ones, keep the safe 2 per cent and 3 per cent and 3½ per cent. Give me father's latest wildcat speculations, as you call them. Most of them are probably duds. But I'll bet that one or two of them will pay better in the end than all your playing safe with 3 per cent Trustee stocks will do. Father was a shrewd old devil. He took chances, plenty of them. Some of those chances paid five and six and 700 per cent. I'll back his judgment and his luck. As for you, you little worm. . . ."

Lance advanced towards his brother, who retreated rapidly round the end of the desk towards Inspector Neele. "All right," said Lance, "I'm not going to touch you. You wanted me out of here, you're getting me out of here. You ought to be satisfied." He added as he strode towards the door, "You can throw in the old Blackbird Mine concession too, if you like. If you've got the murdering MacKenzies on our trail, I'll draw them off to Africa." He added, as he swung through the doorway, "Revenge—after all these years—scarcely seems credible. But Inspector Neele seems to take it seriously, don't you, Inspector?"

"Nonsense," said Percival. "Such a thing is impossible!"

"Ask him," said Lance. "Ask him why he's making all these inquiries into blackbirds and rye in father's pocket."

Gently stroking his upper lip, Inspector Neele said, "You remember the blackbirds last summer, Mr. Fortescue. There are certain grounds for inquiry."

"Nonsense," said Percival again. "Nobody's heard of the Mac-Kenzies for years."

"And yet," said Lance, "I'd almost dare to swear that there's

148

a MacKenzie in our midst. I rather imagine the Inspector thinks so, too."

ii.

Inspector Neele caught up Lancelot Fortescue as the latter emerged into the street below.

Lance grinned at him rather sheepishly.

"I didn't mean to do that," he said. "But I suddenly lost my temper. Oh, well, it would have come to the same before long. I'm meeting Pat at the Savoy. Are you coming my way, Inspector?"

"No, I'm returning to Baydon Heath. But there's just something I'd like to ask you, Mr. Fortescue."

"Yes?"

"When you came into the inner office and saw me there, you were surprised. Why?"

"Because I didn't expect to see you, I suppose. I thought I'd find Percy there."

"You weren't told that he'd gone out?"

Lance looked at him curiously.

"No. They said he was in his office."

"I see. Nobody knew he'd gone out. There's no second door out of the inner office, but there is a door leading straight into the corridor from the little antechamber. I suppose your brother went out that way, but I'm surprised Mrs. Hardcastle didn't tell you so."

Lance laughed.

"She'd probably been to collect her cup of tea."

"Yes, yes—quite so."

Lance looked at him.

"What's the idea, Inspector?"

"Just puzzling over a few little things, that's all, Mr. Fortescue."

IN THE TRAIN on the way down to Baydon Heath, Inspector Neele had singularly little success doing the *Times* crossword. His mind was distracted by various possibilities. In the same way, he read the news with only half his brain taking it in. He read of an earthquake in Japan, of the discovery of uranium deposits in Tanganyika, of the body of a merchant seaman washed up near Southampton, and of the imminent strike among the dockers. He read of the latest victims of the cosh and of a new drug that had achieved wonders in advanced cases of tuberculosis.

All these items made a queer kind of pattern in the back of his mind. Presently he returned to the crossword puzzle and was able to put down three clues in rapid succession.

When he reached Yewtree Lodge he had come to a certain decision. He said to Sergeant Hay, "Where's that old lady? Is she still here?"

"Miss Marple? Oh, yes, she's here still. Great buddies with the old lady upstairs."

"I see." Neele paused for a moment and then said, "Where is she now? I'd like to see her."

Miss Marple arrived in a few minutes' time, looking rather flushed, and breathing fast.

"You want to see me, Inspector Neele? I do hope I haven't kept you waiting. Sergeant Hay couldn't find me at first. I was in the kitchen, talking to Mrs. Crump. I was congratulating her on her pastry and how light her hand is, and telling her how delicious the soufflé was last night. I always think, you know, it's better to approach a subject gradually, don't you? At least, I suppose it isn't so easy for you. You more or less have to come almost straightaway to the questions you want to ask. But, of course, for an old lady like me who has all the time in the world, as you might say, it's really expected of her that there should be a great deal of unnecessary talk. And the way to a cook's heart, as they say, is through her pastry."

"What you really wanted to talk to her about," said Inspector Neele, "was Gladys Martin."

Miss Marple nodded.

"Yes. Gladys. You see, Mrs. Crump could really tell me a lot about the girl. Not in connection with the murder. I don't mean that. But about her spirits lately and the odd things she said. I don't mean odd in the sense of peculiar. I mean just the odds and ends of conversation."

"Did you find it helpful?" asked Inspector Neele.

"Yes," said Miss Marple. "I found it very helpful indeed. I really think, you know, that things are becoming very much clearer, don't you?"

"I do and I don't," said Inspector Neele.

Sergeant Hay, he noticed, had left the room. He was glad of it because what he was about to do and say now was, to say the least of it, slightly unorthodox.

"Look here, Miss Marple," he said, "I want to talk to you seriously."

"Yes, Inspector Neele?"

"In a way," said Inspector Neele, "you and I represent different points of view. I admit, Miss Marple, that I've heard something about you at the Yard." He said, "It seems you're fairly well known there."

"I don't know how it is," fluttered Miss Marple, "but I so often seem to get mixed up in things that are really no concern of mine. Crimes, I mean, and peculiar happenings."

"You've got a reputation," said Inspector Neele.

"Sir Henry Clithering, of course," said Miss Marple, "is a very old friend of mine."

"As I said before," Neele went on, "you and I represent opposite points of view. One might almost call them sanity and insanity."

Miss Marple put her head a little on one side.

"Now what exactly do you mean by that, I wonder, Inspector?"

"Well, Miss Marple, there's a sane way of looking at things. This murder benefits certain people. One person, I may say, in particular. The second murder benefits the same person. The third murder one might call a murder for safety."

"But which do you call the third murder?" Miss Marple asked.

Her eyes, a very bright china blue, looked shrewdly at the Inspector. He nodded.

"Yes. You've got something there, perhaps. You know, the other day when the A.C. was speaking to me of these murders, something that he said seemed to me to be wrong. That was it. I was thinking, of course, of the nursery rhyme. The king in his counting house, the queen in the parlor and the maid hanging out the clothes."

"Exactly," said Miss Marple. "A sequence in that order, but actually Gladys must have been murdered before Mrs. Fortescue, mustn't she?"

"I think so," said Neele. "I take it it's quite certainly so. Her body wasn't discovered till late that night, and of course it was difficult then to say exactly how long she'd been dead. But I think myself that she must almost certainly have been murdered round about five o'clock, because otherwise. . . ."

Miss Marple cut in. "Because otherwise she would certainly have taken the second tray into the drawing-room?"

"Quite so. She took one tray in with the tea on it, she brought the second tray into the hall, and then something happened. She saw something or she heard something. The question is what that something was. It might have been Dubois coming down the stairs from Mrs. Fortescue's room. It might have been Elaine Fortescue's young man, Gerald Wright, coming in at the side door. Whoever it was lured her away from the tea tray and out into the garden. And once that had happened, I don't see any possibility of her death being long delayed. It was cold out and she was wearing only her thin uniform."

"Of course you're quite right," said Miss Marple. "I mean it was never a case of 'the maid was in the garden hanging up the clothes.' She wouldn't be hanging up clothes at that time of the evening and she wouldn't go out to the clothes line without putting a coat on. That was all camouflage, like the clothes peg, to make the thing fit in with the rhyme."

"Exactly," said Inspector Neele, "crazy. That's where I can't yet see eye to eye with you. I can't—I simply can't swallow this nursery rhyme business."

"But it fits, Inspector. You must agree it fits."

"It fits," said Neele heavily, "but all the same the sequence is wrong. I mean the rhyme definitely suggests that the maid was the third murder. But we know that the Queen was the third murder. Adele Fortescue was not killed until between twenty-five past five and five minutes to six. By then Gladys must already have been dead."

"And that's all wrong, isn't it?" said Miss Marple. "All wrong for the nursery rhyme—that's very significant, isn't it?"

Inspector Neele shrugged his shoulders.

"It's probably splitting hairs. The deaths fulfill the conditions of the rhyme, and I suppose that's all that was needed. But I'm talking now as though I were on your side. I'm going to outline my side of the case now, Miss Marple. I'm washing out the blackbirds and the rye and all the rest of it. I'm going by sober facts and common sense and the reasons for which sane people do murders. First, the death of Rex Fortescue, and whom his death benefits. Well, it benefits quite a lot of people, but most of all it benefits his son, Percival. His son Percival wasn't at Yewtree Lodge that morning. He couldn't have put poison in his father's coffee or in anything that he ate for breakfast. Or that's what we thought at first."

"Ah," Miss Marple's eyes brightened. "So there was a method, was there? I've been thinking about it, you know, a good deal, and I've had several ideas. But, of course, no evidence or proof."

"There's no harm in my letting you know," said Inspector Neele. "Taxine was added to a new jar of marmalade. That jar of marmalade was placed on the breakfast table and the top layer of it was eaten by Mr. Fortescue at breakfast. Later that jar of marmalade was thrown out into the bushes and a similar jar with a similar amount taken out of it was placed in the pantry. The jar in the bushes was found, and I've just had the result of the analysis. It shows definite evidence of taxine."

"So that was it," murmured Miss Marple. "So simple and easy to do."

"Consolidated Investments," Neele went on, "was in a bad way. If the firm had had to pay out a hundred thousand pounds to Adele Fortescue under her husband's will, it would, I think, have crashed. If Mrs. Fortescue had survived her husband for a month, that money would have had to be paid out to her. She would have had no feeling for the firm or its difficulties. But she didn't survive her husband for a month. She died, and as a result of her death the gainer was the residuary legatee of Rex Fortescue's will. In other words, Percival Fortescue again.

"Always Percival Fortescue," the Inspector continued bitterly. "And though he could have tampered with the marmalade, he couldn't have poisoned his stepmother or strangled Gladys. According to his secretary, he was in his city office at five o'clock that afternoon, and he didn't arrive back here until nearly seven."

"That makes it very difficult, doesn't it?" said Miss Marple.

"It makes it impossible," said Inspector Neele gloomily. "In other words, Percival is out." Abandoning restraint and prudence, he spoke with some bitterness, almost unaware of his listener. "Wherever I go, wherever I turn, I always come up against the same person. Percival Fortescue! Yet it can't be Percival Fortescue." Calming himself a little he said, "Oh, there are other possibilities, other people who had a perfectly good motive."

"Mr. Dubois, of course," said Miss Marple sharply. "And that young Mr. Wright. I do so agree with you, Inspector. Wherever there is a question of gain, one has to be very suspicious. The great thing to avoid is having in any way a trustful mind."

In spite of himself, Neele smiled.

"Always think the worst, eh?" he asked.

It seemed a curious doctrine to be proceeding from this charming and fragile-looking old lady.

"Oh yes," said Miss Marple fervently. "I always believe the worst. What is so sad is that one is usually justified in doing so."

"All right," said Neele, "let's think the worst. Dubois could have done it, Gerald Wright could have done it (that is to say, if he'd been acting in collusion with Elaine Fortescue and she tampered with the marmalade), Mrs. Percival could have done it, I suppose. She was on the spot. But none of the people I have mentioned tie up with the crazy angle. They don't tie up with blackbirds and pockets full of rye. That's your theory and it may be that you're right. If so, it boils down to one person, doesn't it? Mrs. Mackenzie's in a mental home and has been for a good number of years. She hasn't been messing about with marmalade pots or putting cyanide in the drawing-room afternoon tea. Her son Donald was killed at Dunkirk. That leaves the daughter, Ruby Mackenzie. And if your theory is correct, if this whole series of murders arises out of the old Blackbird Mine business, then Ruby

Mackenzie must be here in this house, and there's only one person that Ruby Mackenzie could be."

"I think, you know," said Miss Marple, "that you're being a little too dogmatic."

Inspector Neele paid no attention.

"Just one person," he said grimly.

He got up and went out of the room.

ii.

Mary Dove was in her own sitting room. It was a small, rather austerely furnished room, but comfortable. When Inspector Neele tapped at the door, Mary Dove raised her head, which had been bent over a pile of tradesmen's books, and said in her clear voice:

"Come in."

The Inspector entered.

"Do sit down, Inspector." Miss Dove indicated a chair. "Could you wait just one moment? The total of the fishmonger's account does not seem to be correct, and I must check it."

Inspector Neele sat in silence, watching her as she totted up the column. How wonderfully calm and self-possessed the girl was, he thought. He was intrigued, as so often before, by the personality that underlay that self-assured manner. He tried to trace in her features any resemblance to those of the woman he had talked to at the Pinewood Sanatorium. The coloring was not unlike, but he could detect no real facial rememblance. Presently Mary Dove raised her head from her accounts and said:

"Yes, Inspector? What can I do for you?"

Inspector Neele said quietly, "You know, Miss Dove, there are certain very peculiar features about this case."

"Yes?"

"To begin with, there is the odd circumstance of the rye found in Mr. Fortescue's pocket."

"That was very extraordinary," Mary Dove agreed. "You know, I really cannot think of any explanation for that."

"Then there is the curious circumstance of the blackbirds. Those four blackbirds on Mr. Fortescue's desk last summer, and also the incident of the blackbirds being substituted for the veal and ham in the pie. You were here, I think, Miss Dove, at the time of both those occurrences?"

155

"Yes, I was. I remember now. It was most upsetting. It seemed such a very purposeless, spiteful thing to do, especially at the time."

"Perhaps not entirely purposeless. What do you know, Miss Dove, about the Blackbird Mine?"

"I don't think I've ever heard of the Blackbird Mine?"

"Your name, you told me, is Mary Dove. Is that your real name, Miss Dove?"

Mary Dove raised her eyebrows. Inspector Neele was almost sure that a wary expression had come into her blue eyes.

"What an extraordinary question, Inspector. Are you suggesting that my name is not Mary Dove?"

"That is exactly what I am suggesting. I'm suggesting," said Neele pleasantly, "that your name is Ruby Mackenzie."

She stared at him. For a moment her face was entirely blank, with neither protest on it nor surprise. There was, Inspector Neele thought, a very definite effect of calculation. After a minute or two she said in a quiet, colorless voice, "What do you expect me to say?"

"Please answer me. Is your name Ruby Mackenzie?"

"I have told you my name is Mary Dove."

"Yes, but have you proof of that, Miss Dove?"

"What do you want to see? My birth certificate?"

"That might be helpful or it might not. You might, I mean, be in possession of the birth certificate of a Mary Dove. That Mary Dove might be a friend of yours or might be someone who had died."

"Yes, there are a lot of possibilities, aren't there?" Amusement had crept back into Mary Dove's voice. "It's really quite a dilemma for you, isn't it, Inspector?"

"They might possibly be able to recognize you at Pinewood Sanatorium," said Neele.

"Pinewood Sanatorium!" Mary raised her eyebrows. "What or where is Pinewood Sanatorium?"

"I think you know very well, Miss Dove."

"I assure you I am quite in the dark."

"And you deny categorically that you are Ruby Mackenzie?"

"I shouldn't really like to deny anything. I think, you know, Inspector, that it's up to you to prove I am this Ruby Mackenzie, whoever she is." There was definite amusement now in her blue eyes, amusement and challenge. Looking him straight in the eyes, Mary Dove said, "Yes, it's up to you, Inspector. Prove that I'm Ruby Mackenzie, if you can."

CHAPTER 25

"THE OLD TABBY's looking for you, sir," said Sergeant Hay in a conspiratorial whisper, as Inspector Neele descended the stairs. "It appears as how she's got a lot more to say to you."

"Hell and damnation," said Inspector Neele.

"Yes, sir," said Sergeant Hay, not a muscle of his face moving. He was about to move away when Neele called him back.

"Go over those notes given us by Miss Dove, Hay, notes as to her former employment and situations. Check up on them—and, yes, there are just one or two other things that I would like to know. Put these inquiries in hand, will you?"

He jotted down a few lines on a sheet of paper and gave them to Sergeant Hay who said, "I'll get on to it at once, sir."

Hearing a murmur of voices in the library as he passed, Inspector Neele looked in. Whether Miss Marple had been looking for him or not, she was now fully engaged talking to Mrs. Percival Fortescue while her knitting needles clicked busily. The middle of the sentence which Inspector Neele caught was:

". . . . . I have really always thought it was a vocation you needed for nursing. It certainly is very noble work."

Inspector Neele withdrew quietly. Miss Marple had noticed him, he thought, but she had taken no notice of his presence.

She went on in her gentle, soft voice:

"I had such a charming nurse looking after me when I once broke my wrist. She went on from me to nurse Mrs. Sparrow's son, a very nice young naval officer. Quite a romance, really, because they became engaged. So romantic I thought it. They were married and were very happy and had two dear little children." Miss Marple sighed sentimentally. "It was pneumonia, you know. So much depends on nursing in pneumonia, does it not?"

"Oh, yes," said Jennifer Fortescue, "nursing is nearly everything in pneumonia, though, of course, nowadays M and B Sulfa works wonders, and it's not the long, protracted battle it used to be."

"I'm sure you must have been an excellent nurse, my dear," said Miss Marple. "That was the beginning of your romance, was it not? I mean, you came here to nurse Mr. Percival Fortescue, did you not?"

"Yes," said Jennifer, "yes, yes—that's how it did happen."

Her voice was not encouraging, but Miss Marple seemed to take no notice.

"I understand. One should not listen to servants' gossip, of course, but I'm afraid an old lady like myself is always interested to hear about the people in the house. Now, what was I saying? Oh, yes. There was another nurse at first, was there not? and she got sent away—something like that. Carelessness, I believe."

"I don't think it was carelessness," said Jennifer. "I believe her father or something was desperately ill, and so I came to replace her."

"I see," said Miss Marple. "And you fell in love and that was that. Yes, very nice indeed, very nice."

"I'm not so sure about that," said Jennifer Fortescue. "I often wish," her voice trembled, "I often wish I was back in the wards again."

"Yes, yes, I understand. You were keen on your profession."

"I wasn't so much at the time, but now when I think of it— life's so monotonous, you know. Day after day with nothing to do, and Val so absorbed in business."

Miss Marple shook her head.

"Gentlemen have to work so hard nowadays," she said. "There really doesn't seem any leisure, no matter how much money there is."

"Yes, it makes it very lonely and dull for a wife sometimes. I often wish I'd never come here," said Jennifer. "Oh, well, I dare say it serves me right. I ought never to have done it."

"Ought never to have done what, my dear?"

"I ought never to have married Val. Oh, well—" she sighed abruptly. "Don't let's talk of it any more."

Obligingly, Miss Marple began to talk about the new skirts that were being worn in Paris.

"So kind of you not to interrupt just now," said Miss Marple when, having tapped at the door of the study, Inspector Neele had told her to come in. "There were just one or two little points, you know, that I wanted to verify." She added reproachfully, "We didn't really finish our talk just now."

"I'm so sorry, Miss Marple." Inspector Neele summoned up a charming smile. "I'm afraid I was rather rude. I summoned you to a consultation and did all the talking myself."

"Oh, that's quite all right," said Miss Marple immediately, "because, you see, I wasn't really quite ready then to put all my cards on the table. I mean, I wouldn't like to make any accusation unless I was absolutely sure about it. Sure, that is, in my own mind. And I am sure, now."

"You're sure about what, Miss Marple?"

"Well, certainly about who killed Mr. Fortescue. What you told me about the marmalade, I mean, just clinches the matter. Showing how, I mean, as well as who, and well within the mental capacity."

Inspector Neele blinked a little.

"I'm so sorry," said Miss Marple, perceiving this reaction on his part, "I'm afraid I find it difficult sometimes to make myself perfectly clear."

"I'm not quite sure yet, Miss Marple, what we're talking about."

"Well, perhaps," said Miss Marple, "we'd better begin all over again. I mean, if you could spare the time. I would rather like to put my own point of view before you. You see, I've talked a good deal to people, to old Miss Ramsbottom and to Mrs. Crump and to her husband. He, of course, is a liar, but that doesn't really matter because if you know liars are liars, it comes to the same thing. But I did want to get the telephone calls clear and the nylon stockings and all that."

Inspector Neele blinked again and wondered what he had let himself in for and why he had ever thought that Miss Marple might be a desirable and clear-headed colleague. Still, he thought to himself, however muddle-headed she was, she might have picked up some useful bits of information. All Inspector Neele's successes in his profession had come from listening well. He was prepared to listen now.

"Please tell me all about it, Miss Marple," he said, "but start at the beginning, won't you?"

"Yes, of course," said Miss Marple, "and the beginning is Gladys. I mean I came here because of Gladys. And you very kindly let me look through all her things. And what with that and the nylon stocking and the telephone calls and one thing and another, it did come out perfectly clear. I mean about Mr. Fortescue and the taxine."

"You have a theory?" asked Inspector Neele, "as to who put the taxine into Mr. Fortescue's marmalade."

"It isn't a theory," said Miss Marple. "I know."

For the third time Inspector Neele blinked.

"It was Gladys, of course," said Miss Marple.

CHAPTER **26**

INSPECTOR NEELE STARED at Miss Marple and slowly shook his head.

"Are you saying," he said incredulously, "that Gladys Martin deliberately murdered Rex Fortescue? I'm sorry, Miss Marple, but I simply don't believe it."

"No, of course she didn't mean to murder him," said Miss Marple, "but she did it all the same! You said yourself that she was nervous and upset when you questioned her. And that she looked guilty."

"Yes, but not guilty of murder."

"Oh, no, I agree. As I say, she didn't mean to murder anybody, but she put the taxine in the marmalade. She didn't think it was poison, of course."

"What did she think it was?" Inspector Neele's voice still sounded incredulous.

"I rather imagine she thought it was a truth drug," said Miss

Marple. "It's very interesting, you know, and very instructive—the things these girls cut out of papers and keep. It's always been the same, you know, all through the ages. Recipes for beauty, for attracting the man you love. And witchcraft and charms and marvellous happenings. Nowadays they're mostly lumped together under the heading of Science. Nobody believes in magicians any more, nobody believes that anyone can come along and wave a wand and turn you into a frog. But if you read in the paper that by injecting certain glands scientists can alter your vital tissues and you'll develop froglike characteristics, well, everybody would believe that. And having read in the papers about truth drugs, of course Gladys would believe it absolutely when he told her that that's what it was."

"When who told her?" asked Inspector Neele.

"Albert Evans," said Miss Marple. "Not, of course, that that is really his name. But, anyway, he met her last summer at a holiday camp, and he flattered her up and made love to her, and I should imagine, told her some story of injustice or persecution, or something like that. Anyway, the point was that Rex Fortescue had to be made to confess what he had done and make restitution. I don't know this, of course, Inspector Neele, but I'm pretty sure about it. He got her to take a post here, and it's really very easy nowadays, with the shortage of domestic staff, to obtain a post where you want one. Staffs are changing the whole time. Then they arranged a date together. You remember on that last post card he said, 'Remember our date.' That was to be the great day they were working for. Gladys would put the drug that he gave her into the top of the marmalade, so that Mr. Fortescue would eat it at breakfast, and she would also put the rye in his pocket. I don't know what story he told her to account for the rye, but as I told you from the beginning, Inspector Neele, Gladys Martin was a very credulous girl. In fact, there's hardly anything she wouldn't believe if a personable young man put it to her the right way."

"Go on," said Inspector Neele in a dazed voice.

"The idea probably was," continued Miss Marple, "that Albert was going to call upon him at the office that day, and that by that time the truth drug would have worked, and that Mr. Fortescue would have confessed everything and so on and so on. You can imagine the poor girl's feelings when she hears that Mr. Fortescue is dead."

"But, surely," Inspector Neele objected, "she would have told?"

Miss Marple asked sharply, "What was the first thing she said to you when you questioned her?"

"She said 'I didn't do it,'" Inspector Neele said.

"Exactly," said Miss Marple triumphantly. "Don't you see that's exactly what she would say? If she broke an ornament, you know, Gladys would always say, 'I didn't do it, Miss Marple. I can't think how it happened.' They can't help it, poor dears. They're very upset at what they've done and their great idea is to avoid blame. You don't think that a nervous young woman who had murdered someone when she didn't mean to murder him, is going to admit it, do you? That would have been quite out of character."

"Yes," Neele said, "I suppose it would."

He ran his mind back over his interview with Gladys. Nervous, upset, guilty, shifty-eyed, all those things. They might have had small significance or a big one. He could not really blame himself for having failed to come to the right conclusion.

"Her first idea, as I say," went on Miss Marple, "would be to deny it all. Then, in a confused way, she would try to sort it all out in her mind. Perhaps Albert hadn't known how strong the stuff was, or he'd made a mistake and given her too much of it. She'd think of excuses for him and explanations. She'd hope he'd get in touch with her, which, of course, he did. By telephone."

"Do you know that?" asked Neele sharply.

Miss Marple shook her head.

"No. I admit I'm assuming it. But there were calls that day. That is to say, people rang up, and when Crump, or Mrs. Crump answered, the phone was hung up. That's what he'd do, you know. Ring up and wait until Gladys answered the phone, and then he'd make an appointment with her to meet him."

"I see," said Neele. "You mean she had an appointment to meet him on the day she died."

Miss Marple nodded vigorously.

"Yes, that was indicated. Mrs. Crump was right about one thing. The girl had on her best nylon stockings and her good shoes. She was going to meet someone. Only, she wasn't going out to meet him. He was coming to Yewtree Lodge. That's why she was on the lookout that day and flustered and late with tea. Then, as she brought the second tray into the hall, I think she looked along the passage to the side door, and saw him there, beckoning to her. She put the tray down and went out to meet him."

"And then he strangled her," said Neele.

Miss Marple pursed her lips together. "It would only take a minute," she said, "but he couldn't risk her talking. She had to die, poor, silly, credulous girl. And then—he put a clothes peg on her nose!" Stern anger vibrated the old lady's voice. "To make it fit in with the rhyme. The rye, the blackbirds, the counting house, the bread and honey, and the clothes peg—the nearest he could get to a little dickey bird that nipped off her nose."

"And I suppose at the end of it all he'll go to Broadmoor, and we shan't be able to hang him because he's crazy!" said Neele slowly.

"I think you'll hang him all right," said Miss Marple. "And he's not crazy, Inspector, not for a moment!"

Inspector Neele looked hard at her.

"Now see here, Miss Marple, you've outlined a theory to me. Yes, yes—although you say you know, it's only a theory. You're saying that a man is responsible for these crimes, who called himself Albert Evans, who picked up the girl Gladys at a holiday camp and used her for his own purposes. This Albert Evans was someone who wanted revenge for the old Blackbird Mine business. You're suggesting, aren't you, that Mrs. MacKenzie's son, Don MacKenzie, didn't die at Dunkirk. That he's still alive, that he's behind all this?"

But to Inspector Neele's surprise, Miss Marple was shaking her head violently.

"Oh no!" she said, "oh no! I'm not suggesting that at all. Don't you see, Inspector Neele, all this blackbird business is really a complete fake? It was used, that was all, used by somebody who heard about the blackbirds—the ones in the library and in the pie. The blackbirds were genuine enough. They were put there by someone who knew about the old business, who wanted revenge for it. But only the revenge of trying to frighten Mr. Fortescue or to make him uncomfortable. I don't believe, you know, Inspector Neele, that children can really be brought up and taught to wait and brood and carry out revenge. Children, after all, have got a lot of sense. But anyone whose father had been swindled and perhaps left to die, might be willing to play a malicious trick on the person who was supposed to have done it. That's what happened, I think. And the killer used it."

"The killer," said Inspector Neele. "Come now, Miss Marple, let's have your ideas about the killer. Who was he?"

"You won't be surprised," said Miss Marple. "Not really. Because you'll see, as soon as I tell you who he is or rather who I think he is, for one must be accurate, must one not? You'll see that he's just the type of person who would commit these murders. He's sane, brilliant and quite unscrupulous. And he did it, of course, for money, probably for a good deal of money."

"Percival Fortescue?" Inspector Neele spoke almost imploringly, but he knew as he spoke that he was wrong. The picture of the man that Miss Marple had built up for him had no resemblance to Percival Fortescue.

"Oh, no," said Miss Marple. "Not Percival. Lance."

CHAPTER 27

"IT'S IMPOSSIBLE," SAID Inspector Neele.

He leaned back in his chair and watched Miss Marple with fascinated eyes. As Miss Marple had said, he was not surprised. His words were a denial not of probability, but of possibility. Lance Fortescue fitted the description: Miss Marple had outlined it well enough. But Inspector Neele simply could not see how Lance could be the answer.

Miss Marple leaned forward in her chair and gently, persuasively, and rather in the manner of someone explaining the simple facts of arithmetic to a small child, outlined her theory.

"He's always been like that, you see. I mean, he's always been bad. Bad all through, although with it he's always been attractive. Especially attractive to women. He's got a brilliant mind and he'll take risks. He's always taken risks, and because of his charm people have always believed the best and not the worst about him. He came home in the summer to see his father. I don't believe for a moment that his father wrote to him or sent for him—unless, of course, you've got actual evidence to that effect." She paused inquiringly.

Neele shook his head. "No," he said, "I've no evidence of his father sending for him. I've got a letter that Lance is supposed to have written to him. But Lance could quite easily have slipped that among his father's papers in the study here the day he arrived."

"Sharp of him," said Miss Marple, nodding her head. "Well, as I say, he probably flew over here and attempted a reconciliation with his father, but Mr. Fortescue wouldn't have it. You see, Lance had recently got married, and the small pittance he was living on and which he had doubtless been supplementing in various dishonest ways, was not enough for him any more. He was very much in love with Pat (who is a dear, sweet girl) and he wanted a respectable, settled life with her—nothing shifty. And that, from his point of view, meant having a lot of money. When he was at Yewtree Lodge, he must have heard about these blackbirds. Perhaps his father mentioned them. Perhaps Adele did. He jumped to the conclusion that MacKenzie's daughter was established in the house, and it occurred to him that she would make a very good scapegoat for murder. Because, you see, when he realized that he couldn't get his father to do what he wanted, he must have cold-bloodedly decided that murder it would have to be. He may have realized that his father wasn't—er—very well—and have feared that by the time his father died there would have been a complete crash."

"He knew about his father's health all right," said the Inspector.

"Ah—that explains a good deal. Perhaps the coincidence of his father's Christian name being Rex together with the blackbird incident suggested the idea of the nursery rhyme. Make a crazy business of the whole thing—and tie it up with that old revenge threat of the MacKenzies. Then, you see, he could dispose of Adele, too, and that hundred thousand pounds going out of the firm. But there would have to be a third character, the 'maid in the garden hanging up the clothes'—and I suppose that suggested the whole wicked plan to him. An innocent accomplice whom he could silence before she could talk. And that would give him what he wanted—a genuine alibi for the first murder."

"The rest was easy. He arrived here from the station just before five o'clock, which was the time when Gladys brought the second tray into the hall. He came to the side door, saw her and beckoned to her. Strangling her and carrying her body round the house to where the clothes lines were would only have taken three or four minutes. Then he rang the front doorbell, was admitted to the house, and joined the family for tea. After tea he went up to see Miss Ramsbottom. When he came down, he slipped into the drawing-room, found Adele alone there drinking a last cup of tea and sat down by her on the sofa, and while he was talking to her, he managed to slip the cyanide into her tea. It wouldn't be difficult, you know. A little piece of white stuff, like sugar. He might have stretched out his hand to the sugar basin and taken a lump and apparently dropped it into her cup. He'd laugh and say 'Look, I've dropped more sugar into your tea.' She'd say she didn't mind, stir it and drink it. It would be as easy and audacious as that. Yes, he's an audacious fellow."

Inspector Neele said slowly, "It's actually possible—yes. But I cannot see—really, Miss Marple, I cannot see—what he stood to gain by it. Granted that unless old Fortescue died the business would soon be on the rocks, is Lance's share big enough to cause him to plan three murders? I don't think so. I really don't think so."

"That is a little difficult," admitted Miss Marple. "Yes, I agree with you. That does present difficulties. I suppose. . . ." She hesitated, looking at the Inspector. "I suppose—I am so very ignorant in financial matters—but I suppose it is really true that the Blackbird Mine is worthless?"

Neele reflected. Various scraps fitted together in his mind. Lance's willingness to take the various speculative or worthless shares off Percival's hands. His parting words today in London that Percival had better get rid of the Blackbird and its hoodoo. A gold mine. A worthless gold mine. But perhaps the mine had not been worthless. And yet, somehow, that seemed unlikely. Old Rex Fortescue was hardly likely to have made a mistake on that point, although of course there might have been soundings recently. Where was the mine? West Africa, Lance had said. Yes, but somebody else—was it Miss Ramsbottom—had said it was in East Africa. Had Lance been deliberately misleading when he said West instead of East? Miss Ramsbottom was old and forgetful, and yet she might have been right and not Lance. East Africa. Lance had just come from East Africa. Had he perhaps some recent knowledge?

Suddenly with a click another piece fitted into the Inspector's puzzle. Sitting in the train, reading the *Times. Uranium deposits found in Tanganyika.* Supposing that the uranium deposits were on the site of the old Blackbird? That would explain everything. Lance had come to have knowledge of that, being on the spot, and with uranium deposits there, there was a fortune to be grasped. An enormous fortune! He sighed. He looked at Miss Marple.

"How do you think," he asked reproachfully, "that I'm ever going to be able to prove all this?"

Miss Marple nodded at him encouragingly as an aunt might have encouraged a bright nephew who was going in for a scholarship exam.

"You'll prove it," she said. "You're a very, very clever man, Inspector Neele. I've seen that from the first. Now you know who it is, you ought to be able to get the evidence. At that holiday camp, for instance, they'll recognize his photograph. He'll find it hard to explain why he stayed there for a week calling himself Albert Evans."

Yes, Inspector Neele thought, Lance Fortescue was brilliant and unscrupulous, but he was foolhardy, too. The risks he took were just a little too great.

Neele thought to himself, "I'll get him!" Then, doubt sweeping over him, he looked at Miss Marple.

"It's all pure assumption, you know," he said.

"Yes—but you are sure, aren't you?"

"I suppose so. After all, I've known his kind before."

The old lady nodded.

"Yes—that matters so much—that's really why I'm sure."

Neele looked at her playfully.

"Because of your knowledge of criminals."

"Oh, no, of course not. Because of Pat—a dear girl—and the kind that always marries a bad lot. That's really what drew my attention to him at the start."

"I may be sure—in my own mind," said the Inspector, "but there's a lot that needs explaining—the Ruby MacKenzie business for instance. I could swear that—"

Miss Marple interrupted, "And you're quite right. But you've been thinking of the wrong person. Go and talk to Mrs. Percy."

ii.

"Mrs. Fortescue," said Inspector Neele, "do you mind telling me your name before you were married."

"Oh!" Jennifer gasped. She looked frightened.

"You needn't be nervous, madam," said Inspector Neele, "but it's much better to come out with the truth. I'm right, I think, in saying that your name before you were married was Ruby Mac-Kenzie?"

"My—well, oh well—oh dear—well, why shouldn't it be?" said Mrs. Percival Fortescue.

"No reason at all," said Inspector Neele gently, and added, "I was talking to your mother a few days ago at Pinewood Sanatorium."

"She's very angry with me," said Jennifer. "I never go and see her now because it only upsets her. Poor Mumsy, she was so devoted to Dad, you know."

"And she brought you up to have very melodramatic ideas of revenge?"

"Yes," said Jennifer. "She kept making us swear on the Bible that we'd never forget and that we'd kill him one day. Of course, once I'd gone into hospital and started my training, I began to realize that her mental balance wasn't what it should be."

"You yourself must have felt revengeful though, Mrs. Fortescue?"

"Well, of course I did. Rex Fortescue practically murdered my father! I don't mean he actually shot him, or knifed him or anything like that. But I'm quite certain that he did leave Father to die. That's the same thing, isn't it?"

"It's the same thing morally—yes."

"So I did want to pay him back," said Jennifer. "When a friend of mine came to nurse his son I got her to leave and to propose my replacing her. I don't know exactly what I meant to do. . . . I didn't, really I didn't, Inspector, I never meant to kill Mr. Fortescue. I had some idea, I think, of nursing his son so badly that the son would die. But, of course, if you are a nurse by profession, you can't do that sort of thing. Actually, I had quite a job pulling Val through. And then he got fond of me and asked me to marry

168

him and I thought, Well, really, that's a far more sensible revenge than anything else. I mean, to marry Mr. Fortescue's eldest son and get the money he swindled Father out of back that way. I think it was a far more sensible way."

"Yes, indeed," said Inspector Neele, "far more sensible." He added, "It was you, I suppose, who put the blackbirds on the desk and in the pie?"

Mrs. Percival flushed.

"Yes. I suppose it was silly of me really. . . . But Mr. Fortescue had been talking about suckers one day and boasting of how he'd swindled people—got the best of them. Oh, in quite a legal way. And I thought I'd just like to give him—well, a kind of fright. And it did give him a fright! He was awfully upset." She added anxiously, "But I didn't do anything else! I didn't really, Inspector. You don't—you don't honestly think I would murder anyone, do you?"

Inspector Neele smiled.

"No," he said, "I don't." He added, "By the way, have you given Miss Dove any money lately?"

Jennifer's jaw dropped.

"How did you know?"

"We know a lot of things," said Inspector Neele and added to himself, "And guess a good many, too."

Jennifer continued, speaking rapidly.

"She came to me and said that you'd accused her of being Ruby MacKenzie. She said if I'd get hold of five hundred pounds she'd let you go on thinking so. She said if you knew that I was Ruby MacKenzie, I'd be suspected of murdering Mr. Fortescue and my stepmother. I had an awful job getting the money because, of course, I couldn't tell Percival. He doesn't know about me. I had to sell my diamond engagement ring and a very beautiful necklace Mr. Fortescue gave me."

"Don't worry, Mrs. Percival," said Inspector Neele, "I think we can get your money back for you."

iii.

It was on the following day that Inspector Neele had another interview with Miss Mary Dove.

169

"I wonder, Miss Dove," he said, "if you'd give me a check for five hundred pounds payable to Mrs. Percival Fortescue."

He had the pleasure of seeing Mary Dove lose countenance for once.

"The silly fool told you, I suppose," she said.

"Yes. Blackmail, Miss Dove, is rather a serious charge."

"It wasn't exactly blackmail, Inspector. I think you'd find it hard to make out a case of blackmail against me. I was just doing Mrs. Percival a special service to oblige her."

"Well, if you'll give me that check, Miss Dove, we'll leave it like that."

Mary Dove got her checkbook and took out her fountain pen.

"It's very annoying," she said with a sigh. "I'm particularly hard up at the moment."

"You'll be looking for another job soon, I suppose?"

"Yes. This one hasn't turned out quite according to plan. It's all been very unfortunate from my point of view."

Inspector Neele agreed.

"Yes, it put you in rather a difficult position, didn't it? I mean, it was quite likely that at any moment we might have to look into your antecedents."

Mary Dove, cool once more, allowed her eyebrows to rise.

"Really, Inspector, my past is quite blameless, I assure you."

"Yes, it is," Inspector Neele agreed cheerfully. "We've nothing against you at all, Miss Dove. It's a curious coincidence, though, that in the last three places which you have filled so admirably, there have happened to be robberies about three months after you left. The thieves have seemed remarkably well informed as to where mink coats, jewels, et cetera, were kept. Curious coincidence, isn't it?"

"Coincidences do happen, Inspector."

"Oh, yes," said Neele. "They happen. But they mustn't happen too often, Miss Dove. I dare say," he added, "that we may meet again in the future."

"I hope," said Mary Dove, "I don't mean to be rude, Inspector Neele—but I hope we don't."

CHAPTER 28

Miss Marple smoothed over the top of her suitcase, tucked in an end of woolly shawl and shut the lid down. She looked round her bedroom. No, she had left nothing behind. Crump came in to fetch down her luggage. Miss Marple went into the next room to say good-by to Miss Ramsbottom.

"I'm afraid," said Miss Marple, "that I've made a very poor return for your hospitality. I hope you will be able to forgive me some day."

"Hah," said Miss Ramsbottom.

She was as usual playing patience.

"Black knave, red queen," she observed, then she darted a shrewd, sideways glance at Miss Marple. "You found out what you wanted to, I suppose," she said.

"Yes."

"And I suppose you've told that police inspector all about it? Will he be able to prove a case?"

"I'm almost sure he will," said Miss Marple. "It may take a little time."

"I'm not asking you any questions," said Miss Ramsbottom. "You're a shrewd woman. I knew that as soon as I saw you. I don't blame you for what you've done. Wickedness is wickedness and has got to be punished. There's a bad streak in this family. It didn't come from our side, I'm thankful to say. Elvira, my sister, was a fool. Nothing worse.

"Black knave," repeated Miss Ramsbottom, fingering the card. "Handsome, but a black heart. Yes, I was afraid of it. Ah, well, you can't always help loving a sinner. The boy always had a way with him. Even got round me. . . . Told a lie about the time he left me that day. I didn't contradict him, but I wondered. . . . I've wondered ever since. But he was Elvira's boy—I couldn't bring myself to say anything. Ah, well, you're a righteous woman, Jane Marple, and right must prevail. I'm sorry for his wife, though."

"So am I," said Miss Marple.

In the hall Pat Fortescue was waiting to say good-by.

"I wish you weren't going," she said. "I shall miss you."

"It's time for me to go," said Miss Marple. "I've finished what I came here to do. It hasn't been—altogether pleasant. But it's important, you know, that wickedness shouldn't triumph."

Pat looked puzzled.

"I don't understand."

"No, my dear. But perhaps you will someday. If I might venture to advise, if anything ever—goes wrong in your life—I think the happiest thing for you would be to go back to where you were happy as a child. Go back to Ireland, my dear. Horses and dogs. All that."

Pat nodded.

"Sometimes I wish I'd done just that when Freddy died. But if I had" her voice changed and softened "I'd never have met Lance."

Miss Marple sighed.

"We're not staying here, you know," said Pat. "We're going back to East Africa as soon as everything's cleared up. I'm so glad."

"God bless you, dear child," said Miss Marple. "One needs a great deal of courage to get through life. I think you have it."

She patted the girl's hand and, releasing it, went through the front door to the waiting taxi.

ii.

Miss Marple reached home late that evening.

Kitty, the latest graduate from St. Faith's Home, let her in and greeted her with a beaming face.

"I've got a herring for your supper, miss. I'm so glad to see you home. You'll find everything very nice in the house. Regular spring cleaning I've had."

"That's very nice, Kitty. I'm glad to be home."

Six spider webs on the cornice, Miss Marple noted. These girls never raised their heads! She was none the less too kind to say so.

"Your letters is on the hall table, miss. And there's one as went to Daisymead by mistake. Always doing that, aren't they? Does look a bit alike, Dane and Daisy, and the writing's so bad I don't wonder this time. They've been away there and the house shut up. They only got back and sent it round today. Said as how they hoped it wasn't important."

Miss Marple picked up her correspondence. The letter to which Kitty had referred was on top of the others. A faint chord of remembrance stirred in Miss Marple's mind at the sight of the blotted scrawled handwriting. She tore it open.

Dear Madam,

I hope as you'll forgive me writing this but I really don't know what to do indeed I don't and I never meant no harm. Dear madam, you'll have seen the newspapers it was murder they say but it wasn't me that did it, not really because I would never do anything wicked like that and I know as how he woun't either. Albert, I mean. I'm telling this badly, but you see we met last summer and was going to be married only Bert hadn't got his rights, he'd been done out of them, swindled by this Mr. Fortescue who's dead. And Mr. Fortescue he just denied everything and of course everybody believed him and not Bert because he was rich and Bert was poor. But Bert had a friend who works in a place where they make these new drugs and there's what they call a truth drug you've read about it perhaps in the paper and it makes people speak the truth whether they want to or not. Bert was going to see Mr. Fortescue in his office on Oct. 31st, and taking a lawyer with him and I was to be sure to give him the drug at breakfast that morning and then it would work just right for when they came and he'd admit as all what Bert said was quite true. Well, madam, I put it in the marmalade but now he's dead and I think as how it must have been too strong but it wasn't Bert's fault because Bert would never do a thing like that but I can't tell the police because maybe they'd think Bert did it on purpose which I know he didn't. Oh, madam, I don't know what to do or what to say and the police are here in the house and it's awful and they ask you questions and look at you so stern and I don't know what to do and I haven't heard from Bert. Oh, madam, I don't like to ask it of you but if you could only come here and help me they'd listen to you and you were always so kind to me and, I didn't mean anything wrong and Bert didn't either. If you could only help us.

Yours respectfully,
Gladys Martin

P.S. I'm enclosing a snap of Bert and me. One of the boys took it at the camp and give it me. Bert doesn't know I've got it—he hates being snapped. But you can see, madam, what a nice boy he is.

Miss Marple, her lips pursed together, stared down at the photograph. The pair pictured there were looking at each other. Miss Marple's eyes went from Gladys's pathetic, adoring face, the mouth slightly open, to the other face—the dark, handsome, smiling face of Lance Fortescue.

The last words of the pathetic letter echoed in her mind:

You can see what a nice boy he is.

The tears rose in Miss Marple's eyes. Succeeding pity, there came anger—anger against a heartless killer.

And then, displacing both these emotions, there came a surge of triumph—the triumph some specialist might feel who has successfully reconstructed an extinct animal from a fragment of jawbone and a couple of teeth.

Hickory Dickory Death

CHAPTER 1

Hercule Poirot frowned.

"Miss Lemon," he said.

"Yes, M. Poirot?"

"There are three mistakes in this letter."

His voice held incredulity. For Miss Lemon, that hideous and efficient woman, never made mistakes. She was never ill, never tired, never upset, never inaccurate. For all practical purposes, that is to say, she was not a woman at all. She was a machine—the perfect secretary. She knew everything, she coped with everything. She ran Hercule Poirot's life for him, so that it, too, functioned like a machine. Order and method had been Hercule Poirot's watchwords from many years ago. With George, his perfect manservant, and Miss Lemon, his perfect secretary, order and method ruled supreme in his life. Now that crumpets were baked square as well as round, he had nothing about which to complain.

And yet, this morning Miss Lemon had made three mistakes in typing a perfectly simple letter, and moreover, had not even noticed those mistakes. The stars stood still in their courses!

Hercule Poirot held out the offending document. He was not annoyed, he was merely bewildered. This was one of the things that could not happen—but it had happened!

Miss Lemon took the letter. She looked at it. For the first time in his life, Poirot saw her blush; a deep ugly unbecoming flush that dyed her face right up to the roots of her strong grizzled hair.

"Oh, dear," she said. "I can't think how—at least, I can. It's because of my sister."

"Your sister?"

Another shock. Poirot had never conceived of Miss Lemon's

177

having a sister. Or, for that matter, having a father, mother or even grandparents. Miss Lemon, somehow, was so completely machine made—a precision instrument, so to speak—that to think of her having affections, or anxieties, or family worries, seemed quite ludicrous. It was well known that the whole of Miss Lemon's heart and mind was given, when she was not on duty, to the perfection of a new filing system which was to be patented and bear her name.

"Your sister?" Hercule Poirot repeated, therefore, with an incredulous note in his voice.

Miss Lemon nodded a vigorous assent.

"Yes," she said. "I don't think I've ever mentioned her to you. Practically all her life has been spent in Singapore. Her husband was in the rubber business there."

Hercule Poirot nodded understandingly. It seemed to him appropriate that Miss Lemon's sister should have spent most of her life in Singapore. That was what places like Singapore were for. The sisters of women like Miss Lemon married men in business in Singapore, so that the Miss Lemons of this world could devote themselves with machine-like efficiency to their employers' affairs (and of course to the invention of filing systems in their moments of relaxation).

"I comprehend," he said. "Proceed."

Miss Lemon proceeded.

"She was left a widow four years ago. No children. I managed to get her fixed up in a very nice little flat at quite a reasonable rent—"

(Of course Miss Lemon would manage to do just that almost impossible thing.)

"She is reasonably off—though money doesn't go as far as it did, but her tastes aren't expensive and she has enough to be quite comfortable if she is careful."

Miss Lemon paused and then continued:

"But the truth is, of course, she was lonely. She had never lived in England and she'd got no old friends or cronies and of course she had a lot of time on her hands. Anyway, she told me about six months ago that she was thinking of taking up this job."

"Job?"

"Warden, I think they call it—or Matron of a Hostel for Students. It was owned by a woman who was partly Greek and she

178

wanted someone to run it for her. Manage the catering and see that things went smoothly. It's an old fashioned roomy house—in Hickory Road, if you know where that is—" Poirot did not—"It used to be quite a superior neighbourhood once, and the houses are well built. My sister was to have very nice accommodation, bedroom and sitting room and a tiny bath kitchenette of her own—"

Miss Lemon paused. Poirot made an encouraging noise. So far this did not seem at all like a tale of disaster.

"I wasn't any too sure about it myself, but I saw the force of my sister's arguments. She's never been one to sit with her hands crossed all day long and she's a very practical woman and good at running things—and of course it wasn't as though she were thinking of putting money into it or anything like that. It was purely a salaried position—not a high salary, but she didn't need that, and there was no hard physical work. She's always been fond of young people and good with them, and having lived in the East so long she understands racial differences and people's susceptibilities. Because these students at the hostel were of all nationalities; mostly English, but some of them actually black, I believe."

"Naturally," said Hercule Poirot.

"Half the nurses in our hospitals seem to be black nowadays," said Miss Lemon, doubtfully, "and I understand much pleasanter and more attentive than the English ones. But that's neither here nor there. We talked the scheme over and finally my sister moved in. Neither she nor I cared very much for the proprietress, Mrs. Nikoletis, a woman of very uncertain temper, sometimes charming and sometimes, I'm sorry to say, quite the reverse—and both cheese-paring and impractical. Still, naturally, if she'd been a thoroughly competent woman, she wouldn't have needed any assistance. My sister is not one to let people's tantrums and vagaries worry her. She can hold her own with anyone and she never stands any nonsense."

Poirot nodded. He felt a vague resemblance to Miss Lemon showing in this account of Miss Lemon's sister—a Miss Lemon softened as it were, by marriage and the climate of Singapore, but a woman with the same hard core of sense.

"So your sister took the job?" he asked.

"Yes, she moved into 26 Hickory Road about six months ago. On the whole, she liked her work there and found it interesting."

Hercule Poirot listened. So far the adventures of Miss Lemon's sister had been disappointingly tame.

"But for some time now she's been badly worried. Very badly worried."

"Why?"

"Well, you see, M. Poirot, she doesn't like the things that are going on."

"There are students there of both sexes?" Poirot inquired delicately.

"Oh no, M. Poirot, I don't mean *that!* One is always prepared for difficulties of *that* kind, one *expects* them! No, you see, things have been disappearing."

"Disappearing?"

"Yes. And such odd things . . . And all in rather an unnatural way."

"When you say things have been disappearing, you mean things have been stolen?"

"Yes."

"Have the police been called in?"

"No. Not yet. My sister hopes that it may not be necessary. She is fond of these young people—of some of them, that is—and she would very much prefer to straighten things out by herself."

"Yes," said Poirot thoughtfully. "I can quite see that. But that does not explain, if I may say so, your own anxiety which I take to be a reflex of your sister's anxiety."

"I don't like the situation, M. Poirot. I don't like it at all. I cannot help feeling that something is going on which I do not understand. No ordinary explanation seems quite to cover the facts—and I really cannot imagine what other explanation there can be."

Poirot nodded thoughtfully.

Miss Lemon's Heel of Achilles had always been her imagination. She had none. On questions of fact she was invincible. On questions of surmise, she was lost. Not for her the state of mind of Cortex' men upon the peak of Darien.

"Not ordinary petty thieving? A kleptomaniac, perhaps?"

"I do not think so. I read up the subject," said the conscientious

Miss Lemon, "in the Encyclopaedia Britannica and in a medical work. But I was not convinced."

Hercule Poirot was silent for a minute and a half.

Did he wish to embroil himself in the troubles of Miss Lemon's sister and the passions and grievances of a polyglot Hostel? But it was very annoying and inconvenient to have Miss Lemon making mistakes in typing his letters. He told himself that *if* he were to embroil himself in the matter, that would be the reason. He did not admit to himself that he had been rather bored of late and that the very triviality of the business attracted him.

" 'The parsley sinking into the butter on a hot day,' " he murmured to himself.

"Parsley? Butter?" Miss Lemon looked startled.

"A quotation from one of your classics," he said. "You are acquainted, no doubt, with the Adventures, to say nothing of the Exploits, of Sherlock Holmes."

"You mean these Baker Street societies and all that," said Miss Lemon. "Grown men being so silly! But there, that's men all over. Like the model railways they go on playing with. I can't say I've ever had time to read any of the stories. When I do get time for reading which isn't often, I prefer an improving book."

Hercule Poirot bowed his head gracefully.

"How would it be, Miss Lemon, if you were to invite your sister here for some suitable refreshment—afternoon tea, perhaps? I might be able to be of some slight assistance to her."

"That's very kind of you, M. Poirot. Really very kind indeed. My sister is always free in the afternoons."

"Then shall we say tomorrow, if you can arrange it?"

And in due course, the faithful George was instructed to provide a meal of square crumpets richly buttered, symmetrical sandwiches, and other suitable components of a lavish English afternoon tea.

CHAPTER 2

MISS LEMON'S SISTER whose name was Mrs. Hubbard had a definite resemblance to her sister. She was a good deal yellower of skin, she was plumper, her hair was more frivolously done, and she was less brisk in manner, but the eyes that looked out of a round and amiable countenance were the same shrewd eyes that gleamed through Miss Lemon's pince nez.

"This is very kind of you, I'm sure, M. Poirot," she said. "Very kind. And such a delicious tea, too. I'm sure I've eaten far more than I should—well perhaps just one more sandwich—tea? Well, just half a cup."

"First," said Poirot, "we make the repast—afterwards we get down to business."

He smiled at her amiably and twirled his moustaches, and Mrs. Hubbard said:

"You know, you're exactly like I pictured you from Felicity's description."

After a moment's startled realization that Felicity was the severe Miss Lemon's Christian name, Poirot replied that he should have expected no less, given Miss Lemon's efficiency.

"Of course," said Mrs. Hubbard absently taking a second sandwich, "Felicity has never cared for people. I do. That's why I'm so worried."

"Can you explain to me exactly what does worry you?"

"Yes, I can. It would be natural enough for money to be taken —small sums here and there. And if it were jewellery that's quite straightforward too—at least, I don't mean straightforward, quite the opposite—but it would fit in—with kleptomania or dishonesty. But I'll just read you a list of the things that have been taken, that I've put down on paper."

Mrs. Hubbard opened her bag and took out a small notebook.

Evening shoe (one of a new pair)
Bracelet (costume jewellery)
Diamond ring (found in plate of soup)
Powder compact
Lipstick
Stethoscope
Ear-rings
Cigarette lighter
Old flannel trousers
Electric light bulbs
Box of chocolates
Silk scarf (found cut to pieces)
Rucksack (ditto)
Boracic powder
Bath salts
Cookery book

Hercule Poirot drew in a long deep breath.

"Remarkable," he said, "and quite—quite fascinating."

He was entranced. He looked from the severe disapproving face of Miss Lemon to the kindly, distressed face of Mrs. Hubbard.

"I congratulate you," he said, warmly, to the latter.

She looked startled.

"But why, M. Poirot?"

"I congratulate you on having such a unique and beautiful problem."

"Well, perhaps it makes sense to you, M. Poirot, but—"

"It does not make sense at all. It reminds me of nothing so much as a round game I was recently persuaded to play by some young friends during the Christmas season. It was called, I understand, the Three Horned Lady. Each person in turn uttered the following phrase, 'I went to Paris and bought—' adding some article. The next person repeated that and added a further article and the object of the game was to memorise in their proper order the articles thus enumerated, some of them I may say, of a most monstrous and ridiculous nature. A piece of soap, a white elephant, a gate-legged table and a Muscovy duck were, I remember, some of the items. The difficulty of the memorisation lay, of course, in the totally unrelated nature of the objects—the lack of sequence, so to speak. As in the list you have just shown me. By the time that, say, twelve objects had been mentioned, to enumerate them in their proper order became almost impossible. A failure to do so resulted in a paper horn being handed to the competitor and he or she had to continue the recitation next time in the terms, 'I, a one horned lady, went to Paris,' etc. After three horns had been acquired, retirement was compulsory, the last left in was the winner."

"I'm sure you were the winner, M. Poirot," said Miss Lemon with the faith of a loyal employee.

Poirot beamed.

"That was, in fact, so," he said. "To even the most haphazard assembly of objects one can bring order, and with a little ingenuity, sequence, so to speak. That is: one says to oneself mentally 'With a piece of soap I wash the dirt from a large white marble elephant which stands on a gate-legged table'—and so on."

Mrs. Hubbard said respectfully: "Perhaps you could do the same thing with the list of things I've given you."

"Undoubtedly I could. A lady with her right shoe on, puts a bracelet on her left arm. She then puts on powder and lipstick and goes down to dinner and drops her ring in the soup, and so on—I could thus commit your list to memory—but it is not that that we are seeking. Why was such a haphazard collection of things stolen? Is there any system behind it? Some fixed idea of any kind? We have here primarily a process of analysis. The first thing to do is to study the list of objects very carefully."

There was a silence whilst Poirot applied himself to study. Mrs. Hubbard watched him with the rapt attention of a small boy watching a conjuror, waiting hopefully for a rabbit or at least streams of coloured ribbons to appear. Miss Lemon, unimpressed, withdrew into consideration of the finer points of her filing system.

When Poirot finally spoke, Mrs. Hubbard jumped.

"The first thing that strikes me is this," said Poirot. "Of all these things that disappeared, most of them were of small value (some quite negligible) with the exception of two—a stethoscope and a diamond ring. Leaving the stethoscope aside for a moment, I should like to concentrate on the ring. You say a valuable ring —how valuable?"

"Well, I couldn't say exactly, M. Poirot. It was a solitaire diamond, with a cluster of small diamonds top and bottom. It had been Miss Lane's mother's engagement ring, I understand. She was most upset when it was missing, and we were all relieved when it turned up the same evening in Miss Hobhouse's plate of soup. Just a nasty practical joke, we thought."

"And so it may have been. But I myself consider that its theft and return are significant. If a lipstick, or a powder compact or a book are missing—it is not sufficient to make you call in the police. But a valuable diamond ring is different. There is every chance that the police will be called in. So the ring is returned."

"But why take it if you're going to return it?" said Miss Lemon, frowning.

"Why indeed," said Poirot. "But for the moment we will leave the questions. I am engaged now on classifying these thefts, and I am taking the ring first. Who is this Miss Lane from whom it was stolen?"

"Patricia Lane? She's a very nice girl. Going in for a what-do-you-call-it, a diploma in history or archaeology or something."

"Well off?"

"Oh no. She's got a little money of her own, but she's very careful always. The ring, as I say, belonged to her mother. She has one or two nice bits of jewellery but she doesn't have many new clothes, and she's given up smoking lately."

"What is she like? Describe her to me in your own words."

"Well, she's sort of betwixt and between in colouring. Rather washed out looking. Quiet and ladylike, but not much spirits or life to her. What you'd call rather a—well, an earnest type of girl."

"And the ring turned up again in Miss Hobhouse's plate of soup. Who is Miss Hobhouse?"

"Valerie Hobhouse? She's a clever dark girl with rather a sarcastic way of talking. She works in a beauty parlour. Sabrina Fair —I suppose you have heard of it."

"Are these two girls friendly?"

Mrs. Hubbard considered.

"I should say so—yes. They don't have much to do with each other. Patricia gets on well with everybody, I should say, without being particularly popular or anything like that. Valerie Hobhouse has her enemies, her tongue being what it is—but she's got quite a following too, if you know what I mean."

"I think I know," said Poirot.

So Patricia Lane was nice but dull, and Valerie Hobhouse had personality. He resumed his study of the list of thefts.

"What is so intriguing is all the different categories represented here. There are the small trifles that would tempt a girl who was both vain and hard up, the lipstick, the costume jewellery, a powder compact—bath salts—the box of chocolates, perhaps. Then we have the stethoscope, a more likely theft for a man who would know just where to sell it or pawn it. Who did it belong to?"

"It belonged to Mr. Bateson—he's a big friendly young man."

"A medical student?"

"Yes."

"Was he very angry?"

"He was absolutely livid, M. Poirot. He's got one of those flaring up tempers—say anything at the time, but it's soon over. He's not the sort who'd take kindly to having his things pinched."

"Does anyone?"

"Well, there's Mr. Gopal Ram, one of our Indian students. He smiles at everything. He waves his hand and says material possessions do not matter—"

"Has anything been stolen from him?"

"No."

"Ah! Who did the flannel trousers belong to?"

"Mr. McNabb. Very old they were, and anyone else would say they were done for, but Mr. McNabb is very attached to his old clothes and he never throws anything away."

"So we have come to the things that it would seem were not worth stealing—old flannel trousers, electric light bulbs, boracic powder, bath salts—a cookery book. They may be important, more likely they are not. The boracic was probably removed by error, someone may have removed a dead bulb and intended to replace it, but forgot—the cookery book may have been borrowed and not returned. Some charwoman may have taken away the trousers."

"We employ two very reliable cleaning women. I'm sure they would neither of them have done such a thing without asking first."

"You may be right. Then there is the evening shoe, one of a new pair, I understand? Who do they belong to?"

"Sally Finch. She's an American girl studying over here on a Fulbright scholarship."

"Are you sure that the shoe has not simply been mislaid? I cannot conceive what use one shoe could be to anyone."

"It wasn't mislaid, M. Poirot. We all had a terrific hunt. You see Miss Finch was going out to a party in what she calls 'formal dress'—evening dress to us—and the shoes were really vital—they were her only evening ones."

"It caused her inconvenience—and annoyance—yes . . . yes, I wonder. Perhaps there is something there . . ."

He was silent for a moment or two and then went on.

"And there are two more items—a rucksack cut to pieces and a silk scarf in the same state. Here we have something that is neither vanity, nor profit—instead we have something that is deliberately vindictive. Who did the rucksack belong to?"

"Nearly all the students have rucksacks—they all hitch-hike a lot, you know. And a great many of the rucksacks are the same—bought at the same place, so it's hard to identify one from the other. But it seems fairly certain that this one belonged to Leonard Bateson or Colin McNabb."

"And the silk scarf that was also cut about. To whom did that belong?"

"To Valerie Hobhouse. She had it as a Christmas present—it was emerald green and really good quality."

"Miss Hobhouse . . . I see."

Poirot closed his eyes. What he perceived mentally was a kaleidoscope, no more, no less. Pieces of cut up scarves and rucksacks, cookery books, lipsticks, bath salts; names and thumb nail sketches of odd students. Nowhere was there cohesion or form. Unrelated incidents and people whirled round in space. But Poirot knew quite well that somehow and somewhere there must be a pattern. Possibly several patterns. Possibly each time one shook the kaleidoscope one got a different pattern. . . . But one of the patterns would be the right pattern. . . . The question was where to start. . . .

He opened his eyes.

"This is a matter that needs some reflection. A good deal of reflection."

"Oh, I'm sure it does, M. Poirot," assented Mrs. Hubbard eagerly. "And I'm sure I didn't want to trouble you—"

"You are not troubling me. I am intrigued. But whilst I am reflecting, we might make a start on the practical side. A start . . . The shoe, the evening shoe . . . yes, we might make a start there. Miss Lemon."

"Yes, M. Poirot?" Miss Lemon banished filing from her thoughts, sat even more upright, and reached automatically for pad and pencil.

"Mrs. Hubbard will obtain for you, perhaps, the remaining shoe. Then go to Baker Street station, to the lost property department. The loss occurred—when?"

Mrs. Hubbard considered.

"Well, I can't remember exactly now, M. Poirot. Perhaps two months ago. I can't get nearer than that. But I could find out from Sally Finch the date of the party."

"Yes. Well—" He turned once more to Miss Lemon. "You can be a little vague. You will say you left a shoe in an Inner Circle train—that is the most likely—or you may have left it in some other train. Or possibly a bus. How many buses serve the neighbourhood of Hickory Road?"

"Two only, M. Poirot."

"Good. If you get no results from Baker Street, try Scotland Yard and say it was left in a taxi."

"Lambeth," corrected Miss Lemon efficiently.

Poirot waved a hand.

"You always know these things."

"But why do you think—" began Mrs. Hubbard.

Poirot interrupted her.

"Let us see first what results we get. Then, if they are negative or positive, you and I, Mrs. Hubbard, must consult again. You will tell me then those things which it is necessary that I should know."

"I really think I've told you everything I can."

"No, no. I disagree. Here we have young people herded together, of varying temperaments, of different sexes. A loves B, but B loves C, and D and E are at daggers drawn because of A perhaps. It is all that that I need to know. The interplay of human emotions. The quarrels, the jealousies, the friendships, the malice and all uncharitableness."

"I'm sure," said Mrs. Hubbard, uncomfortably, "I don't know anything about that sort of thing. I don't mix at all. I just run the place and see to the catering and all that."

"But you are interested in people. You have told me so. You like young people. You took this post, not because it was of much interest financially, but because it would bring you in contact with human problems. There will be those of the students that you like and some that you do not like so well, or indeed at all, perhaps. You will tell me—yes, you will tell me! Because you are worried—not about what has been happening—you could go to the police about that—"

"Mrs. Nicoletis wouldn't like to have the police in, I assure you."

Poirot swept on, disregarding the interruption.

"No, you are worried about someone—someone who you think may have been responsible or at least mixed up in this. Someone, therefore, that you like."

"Really, M. Poirot."

"Yes, really. And I think you are right to be worried. For that silk scarf cut to pieces, it is not nice. And the slashed rucksack, that also is not nice. For the rest it seems childishness—and yet —I am not sure. No, I am not sure at all!"

CHAPTER *3*

Hurrying a little as she went up the steps, Mrs. Hubbard inserted her latch key into the door of 26 Hickory Road. Just as the door opened, a big young man with fiery red hair ran up the steps behind her.

"Hullo, Ma," he said, for in such fashion did Len Bateson usually address her. He was a friendly soul, with a cockney accent and mercifully free from any kind of inferiority complex. "Been out gallivanting?"

"I've been out to tea, Mr. Bateson. Don't delay me now, I'm late."

"I cut up a lovely corpse today," said Len. "Smashing!"

"Don't be so horrid, you nasty boy. A lovely corpse, indeed! The idea. You make me feel quite squeamish."

Len Bateson laughed, and the hall echoed the sound in a great Ha ha.

"Nothing to Celia," he said. "I went along to the Dispensary. 'Come to tell you about a corpse,' I said. She went as white as a sheet and I thought she was going to pass out. What do you think of that, Mother Hubbard?"

"I don't wonder at it," said Mrs. Hubbard. "The idea! Celia probably thought you meant a real one."

"What do you mean—a real one? What do you think our corpses are? Synthetic?"

A thin young man with long untidy hair strolled out of a room on the right, said in a waspish way:

"Oh, it's only you. I thought it was at least a *posse* of strong men. The voice is but the voice of one man, but the volume is as the volume of ten."

"Hope it doesn't get on your nerves, I'm sure."

"Not more than usual," said Nigel Chapman and went back again.

"Our delicate flower," said Len.

"Now don't you two scrap," said Mrs. Hubbard. "Good temper, that's what I like, and a bit of give and take."

The big young man grinned down at her affectionately.

"I don't mind our Nigel, Ma," he said.

A girl coming down the stairs at that moment said:

"Oh, Mrs. Hubbard, Mrs. Nicoletis is in her room and said she would like to see you as soon as you got back."

Mrs. Hubbard sighed and started up the stairs. The tall dark girl who had given the message stood against the wall to let her pass.

Len Bateson, divesting himself of his mackintosh, said,

"What's up, Valerie? Complaints of our behaviour to be passed on by Mother Hubbard in due course?"

The girl shrugged her thin elegant shoulders. She came down the stairs and across the hall.

"This place gets more like a madhouse every day," she said over her shoulder.

She went through the door at the right as she spoke. She moved with that insolent effortless grace that is common to those who have been professional mannequins.

26 Hickory Road was in reality two houses, 24 and 26 semi-detached. They had been thrown into one on the ground floor, so that there was both a communal sitting room and a large dining room on the ground floor, as well as two cloak-rooms and a small office towards the back of the house. Two separate staircases led to the floors above which remained detached. The girls occupied bedrooms in the right hand side of the house, and the men on the other, the original No. 24.

Mrs. Hubbard went upstairs loosening the collar of her coat. She sighed as she turned in the direction of Mrs. Nicoletis's room.

"In one of her states again, I suppose," she muttered.

She tapped on the door and entered.

Mrs. Nicoletis's sitting room was kept very hot. The big electric fire had all its bars turned on and the window was tightly shut. Mrs. Nicoletis was sitting smoking on a sofa surrounded by a lot of rather dirty silk and velvet sofa cushions. She was a big dark woman, still good looking, with a bad tempered mouth and enormous brown eyes.

"Ah! So there you are," Mrs. Nicoletis made it sound like an accusation.

Mrs. Hubbard, true to her Lemon blood, was unperturbed.

"Yes," she said tartly, "I'm here. I was told you wanted to see me specially."

"Yes, indeed I do. It is monstrous, no less, monstrous!"

"What's monstrous?"

"These bills! Your accounts!" Mrs. Nicoletis produced a sheaf of papers from beneath a cushion in the manner of a successful conjuror. "What are we feeding these miserable students on? *Foie gras* and quails? Is this the Ritz? Who do they think they are, these students?"

"Young people with a healthy appetite," said Mrs. Hubbard. "They get a good breakfast and a decent evening meal—plain food but nourishing. It all works out very economically."

"Economically? Economically? You dare to say that to me? When I am being ruined?"

"You make a very substantial profit, Mrs. Nicoletis, out of this place. For students, the rates are on the high side."

"But am I not always full? Do I ever have a vacancy that is not applied for three times over? Am I not sent students by the British Council, by London University Lodging Board—by the Embassies—by the French Lycée? Are not there always three applications for every vacancy?"

"That's very largely because the meals here are appetizing and sufficient. Young people must be properly fed."

"Bah! These totals are scandalous. It is that Italian cook and her husband. They swindle you over the food."

"Oh no, they don't, Mrs. Nicoletis. I can assure you that no foreigner is going to put anything over on *me*."

"Then it is you yourself—you who are robbing me."

Mrs. Hubbard remained unperturbed.

"I can't allow you to say things like that," she said in the voice an old fashioned Nanny might have used to a particularly truculent charge. "It isn't a nice thing to do, and one of these days it will land you in trouble."

"Ah!" Mrs. Nicoletis threw the sheaf of bills dramatically up in the air whence they fluttered to the ground in all directions. Mrs. Hubbard bent and picked them up, pursing her lips. "You enrage me," shouted her employer.

"I daresay," said Mrs. Hubbard, "but it's bad for you, you know, getting all worked up. Tempers are bad for the blood pressure."

"You admit that these totals are higher than those of last week?"

"Of course they are. There's been some very good cut price stuff going at Lampson's Stores. I've taken advantage of it. Next week's totals will be below average."

Mrs. Nicoletis looked sulky.

"You explain everything so plausibly."

"There," Mrs. Hubbard put the bills in a neat pile on the table. "Anything else?"

"The American girl, Sally Finch, she talks of leaving—I do not want her to go. She is a Fulbright scholar. She will bring here other Fulbright scholars. She must not leave."

"What's her reason for leaving?"

Mrs. Nicoletis humped monumental shoulders.

"How can I remember? It was not genuine. I could tell *that*. I always know."

Mrs. Hubbard nodded thoughtfully. She was inclined to believe Mrs. Nicoletis on that point.

"Sally hasn't said anything to me," she said.

"But you will talk to her?"

"Yes, of course."

"And if it is these coloured students, these Indians, these Negresses—then they can all go, you understand? The colour bar, it means everything to these Americans—and for me it is the Americans that matter—as for these coloured ones— Scram!"

She made a dramatic gesture.

"Not while I'm in charge," said Mrs. Hubbard coldly. "And anyway, you're wrong. There's no feeling of that sort here amongst the students, and Sally certainly isn't like that. She and Mr. Akibombo have lunch together quite often, and nobody could be blacker than he is."

"Then it is Communists—you know what the Americans are about Communists. Nigel Chapman now—he is a Communist."

"I doubt it."

"Yes, yes. You should have heard what he was saying the other evening."

"Nigel will say anything to annoy people. He is very tiresome that way."

"You know them all so well. Dear Mrs. Hubbard, you are wonderful! I say to myself again and again—what should I do without Mrs. Hubbard? I rely on you *utterly*. You are a wonderful wonderful woman."

"After the powder, the jam," said Mrs. Hubbard.

"What is that?"

"Don't worry. I'll do what I can."

She left the room cutting short a gushing speech of thanks.

Muttering to herself "Wasting my time—what a maddening woman she is!" she hurried along the passage and into her own sitting room.

But there was to be no peace for Mrs. Hubbard as yet. A tall figure rose to her feet as Mrs. Hubbard entered and said,

"I should be glad to speak to you for a few minutes, please."

"Of course, Elizabeth."

Mrs. Hubbard was rather surprised. Elizabeth Johnston was a

girl from the West Indies who was studying law. She was a hard worker, ambitious, who kept very much to herself. She had always seemed particularly well balanced and competent, and Mrs. Hubbard had always regarded her as one of the most satisfactory students in the Hostel.

She was perfectly controlled now, but Mrs. Hubbard caught the slight tremor in her voice although the dark features were quite impassive.

"Is something the matter?"

"Yes. Will you come with me to my room, please?"

"Just a moment." Mrs. Hubbard threw off her coat and gloves and then followed the girl out of the room and up the next flight of stairs. The girl had a room on the top floor. She opened the door and went across to a table near the window.

"Here are the notes of my work," she said. "This represents several months of hard study. You see what has been done?"

Mrs. Hubbard caught her breath with a slight gasp.

Ink had been spilled on the table. It had run all over the papers, soaking them through. Mrs. Hubbard touched it with her finger tip. It was still wet.

She said, knowing the question to be foolish as she asked it, "You didn't spill the ink yourself?"

"No. It was done whilst I was out."

"Mrs. Biggs, do you think—"

Mrs. Biggs was the cleaning woman who looked after the top floor bedrooms.

"It was not Mrs. Biggs. It was not even my own ink. That is here on the shelf by my bed. It has not been touched. It was done by someone who brought ink here and did it deliberately."

Mrs. Hubbard was shocked.

"What a very wicked—and cruel thing to do."

"Yes, it is a bad thing."

The girl spoke quite quietly, but Mrs. Hubbard did not make the mistake of underrating her feelings.

"Well, Elizabeth, I hardly know what to say. I am shocked, badly shocked, and I shall do my utmost to find out who did this wicked malicious thing. You've no ideas yourself as to that?"

The girl replied at once.

"This is green ink, you saw that."

"Yes, I noticed that."

"It is not very common, this green ink. I know one person here who uses it. Nigel Chapman."

"Nigel? Do you think Nigel would do a thing like that?"

"I should not have thought so—no. But he writes his letters and his notes with green ink."

"I shall have to ask a lot of questions. I'm very sorry, Elizabeth, that such a thing should happen in this house and I can only tell you that I shall do my best to get to the bottom of it."

"Thank you, Mrs. Hubbard. There have been—other things, have there not?"

"Yes—er—yes."

Mrs. Hubbard left the room and started towards the stairs. But she stopped suddenly before proceeding down and instead went along the passage to a door at the end of the corridor. She knocked and the voice of Miss Sally Finch bid her enter.

The room was a pleasant one and Sally Finch herself, a cheerful redhead, was a pleasant person.

She was writing on a pad and looked up with a bulging cheek. She held out an open box of sweets and said indistinctly,

"Candy from home. Have some."

"Thank you, Sally. Not just now. I'm rather upset." She paused. "Have you heard what's happened to Elizabeth Johnston?"

"What's happened to Black Bess?"

The nickname was an affectionate one and had been accepted as such by the girl herself.

Mrs. Hubbard described what had happened. Sally showed every sign of sympathetic anger.

"I'll say that's a mean thing to do. I wouldn't believe anyone would do a thing like that to our Bess. Everybody likes her. She's quiet and doesn't get around much, or join in, but I'm sure there's no one who dislikes her."

"That's what I should have said."

"Well—it's all of a piece, isn't it, with the other things. That's why—"

"That's why what?" Mrs. Hubbard asked as the girl stopped abruptly.

Sally said slowly,

"That's why I'm getting out of here. Did Mrs. Nick tell you?"

"Yes. She was very upset about it. Seemed to think you hadn't given her the real reason."

"Well, I didn't. No point in making her go up in smoke. You know what she's like. But that's the reason, right enough. I just don't like what's going on here. It was odd losing my shoe, and then Valerie's scarf being all cut to bits—and Len's rucksack . . . it wasn't so much things being pinched—after all, that may happen any time—it's not nice but it's roughly normal—but this other isn't." She paused for a moment, smiling, and then suddenly grinned. "Akibombo's scared," she said. "He's always very superior and civilised—but there's a good old West African belief in Magic very close to the surface."

"Tchah!" said Mrs. Hubbard crossly. "I've no patience with superstitious nonsense. Just some ordinary human being making a nuisance of themselves. That's all there is to it."

Sally's mouth curved up in a wide cat-like grin.

"The emphasis," she said, "is on *ordinary*. I've a sort of feeling that there's a person in this house who isn't ordinary!"

Mrs. Hubbard went on down the stairs. She turned into the students' common room on the ground floor. There were four people in the room. Valerie Hobhouse, prone on a sofa with her narrow, elegant feet stuck up over the arm of it; Nigel Chapman sitting at a table with a heavy book open in front of him; Patricia Lane leaning against the mantelpiece and a girl in a mackintosh who had just come in and who was pulling off a woolly cap as Mrs. Hubbard entered. She was a stocky, fair girl with brown eyes set wide apart and a mouth that was usually just a little open so that she seemed perpetually startled.

Valerie, removing a cigarette from her mouth, said in a lazy drawling voice:

"Hullo, Ma, have you administered soothing syrup to the old devil, our revered proprietress?"

Patricia Lane said:

"Has she been on the war path?"

"And how!" said Valerie and chuckled.

"Something very unpleasant has happened," said Mrs. Hubbard. "Nigel, I want you to help me."

"Me, Ma'am?" Nigel looked up at her and shut his book. His thin, malicious face was suddenly illumined by a mischievous but surprisingly sweet smile. "What have I done?"

"Nothing, I hope," said Mrs. Hubbard. "But ink has been deliberately and maliciously spilt all over Elizabeth Johnston's notes and it's green ink. You write with green ink, Nigel."

He stared at her, his smile disappearing.

"Yes, I use green ink."

"Horrid stuff," said Patricia. "I wish you wouldn't, Nigel. I've always told you I think it's horribly affected of you."

"I like being affected," said Nigel. "Lilac ink would be even better, I think. I must try and get some. But are you serious, Mum? About the sabotage, I mean?"

"Yes, I am serious. Was it your doing, Nigel?"

"No, of course not. I like annoying people, as you know, but I'd never do a filthy trick like that—and certainly not to Black Bess who minds her own business in a way that's an example to some people I could mention. Where is that ink of mine? I filled my pen yesterday evening, I remember. I usually keep it on the shelf over there." He sprang up and went across the room. "Here it is." He picked the bottle up, then whistled. "You're right. The bottle's nearly empty. It should be practically full."

The girl in the mackintosh gave a little gasp.

"Oh dear," she said. "Oh dear. I don't like it—"

Nigel wheeled at her accusingly.

"Have you got an alibi, Celia?" he said menacingly.

The girl gave a gasp.

"I didn't do it. I really didn't do it. Anyway, I've been at the Hospital all day. I couldn't—"

"Now, Nigel," said Mrs. Hubbard. "Don't tease Celia."

Patricia Lane said angrily,

"I don't see why Nigel should be suspected. Just because *his* ink was taken—"

Valerie said cattishly,

"That's right, darling, defend your young."

"But it's so unfair—"

"But really I didn't have anything to do with it," Celia protested earnestly.

"Nobody thinks you did, infant," said Valerie impatiently. "All the same, you know," her eyes met Mrs. Hubbard's and exchanged a glance, "all this is getting beyond a joke. Something will have to be done about it."

"Something is going to be done," said Mrs. Hubbard grimly.

CHAPTER 4

"HERE YOU ARE, M. Poirot."

Miss Lemon laid a small brown paper parcel before Poirot. He removed the paper and looked appraisingly at a well cut silver evening shoe.

"It was at Baker Street just as you said."

"That has saved us trouble," said Poirot. "Also it confirms my ideas."

"Quite," said Miss Lemon who was sublimely incurious by nature.

She was, however, susceptible to the claims of family affection. She said:

"If it is not troubling you too much, M. Poirot, I received a letter from my sister. There have been some new developments."

"You permit that I read it?"

She handed it to him and after reading it, he directed Miss Lemon to get her sister on the telephone. Presently Miss Lemon indicated that the connection had been obtained. Poirot took the receiver.

"Mrs. Hubbard?"

"Oh yes, M. Poirot. So kind of you to ring me up so promptly. I was really very—"

Poirot interrupted her.

"Where are you speaking from?"

"Why—from 26 Hickory Road, of course. Oh I see what you mean. I am in my own sitting room."

"There is an extension?"

"This is the extension. The main phone is downstairs in the hall."

"Who is in the house who might listen in?"

"All the students are out at this time of day. The cook is out marketing. Geronimo, her husband, understands very little English. There is a cleaning woman, but she is deaf and I'm quite sure wouldn't bother to listen in."

"Very good, then. I can speak freely. Do you occasionally have lectures in the evening, or films? Entertainments of some kind?"

"We do have lectures occasionally. Miss Baltrout, the explorer, came not long ago, with her coloured transparencies. And we had an appeal for Far Eastern Missions, though I am afraid quite a lot of the students went out that night."

"Ah. Then this evening you will have prevailed on M. Hercule Poirot, the employer of your sister, to come and discourse to your students on the more interesting of my cases."

"That will be very nice, I'm sure, but do you think—"

"It is not a question of thinking. I am sure!"

That evening, students entering the Common Room found a notice tacked up on the Board which stood just inside the door.

M. Hercule Poirot, the celebrated private detective, has kindly consented to give a talk this evening on the theory and practice of successful detection, with an account of certain celebrated criminal cases.

Returning students made varied comments on this.

"Who's this private Eye?" "Never heard of him." "Oh, I have. There was a man who was condemned to death for the murder of a charwoman and this detective got him off at the last moment by finding the real person." "Sounds crumby to me." "I think it might be rather fun." "Colin ought to enjoy it. He's mad on criminal psychology." "I would not put it precisely like that, but I'll not deny that a man who has been closely acquainted with criminals might be interesting to interrogate."

Dinner was at seven thirty and most of the students were already seated when Mrs. Hubbard came down from her sitting room (where sherry had been served to the distinguished guest) followed by a small elderly man with suspiciously black hair and a moustache of ferocious proportions which he twirled contentedly.

"These are some of our students, M. Poirot. This is M. Hercule Poirot who is kindly going to talk to us after dinner."

Salutations were exchanged and Poirot sat down by Mrs. Hubbard and busied himself with keeping his moustaches out of the excellent *minestrone* which was served by a small active Italian manservant from a big tureen.

This was followed by a piping hot dish of spaghetti and meat balls and it was then that a girl sitting on Poirot's right spoke shyly to him.

"Does Mrs. Hubbard's sister really work for you?"

Poirot turned to her.

"But yes indeed. Miss Lemon has been my secretary for many years. She is the most efficient woman that ever lived. I am sometimes afraid of her."

"Oh I see. I wondered—"

"Now what did you wonder, Mademoiselle?"

He smiled upon her in paternal fashion, making a mental note as he did so.

"*Pretty, worried, not too quick mentally, frightened . . .*" He said:

"May I know your name and what it is you are studying?"

"Celia Austin. I don't study. I'm a dispenser at St. Catherine's Hospital."

"Ah, that is interesting work?"

"Well, I don't know—perhaps it is." She sounded rather uncertain.

"And these others? Can you tell me something about them, perhaps? I understood this was a Home for Foreign Students, but these seem mostly to be English."

"Some of the foreign ones are out. Mr. Chandra Lal and Mr. Gopal Ram—they're Indians—and Miss Reinjeer who's Dutch—and Mr. Achmed Ali who's Egyptian and frightfully political!"

"And those who are here? Tell me about these."

"Well, sitting on Mrs. Hubbard's left is Nigel Chapman. He's studying Mediaeval History and Italian at London University. Then there's Patricia Lane, next to him, with the spectacles. She's taking a diploma in Archaeology. The big red-headed boy is Len Bateson, he's a medical and the dark girl is Valerie Hobhouse, she's in a Beauty shop. Next to her is Colin McNabb—he's doing a post graduate course in psychiatry."

There was a faint change in her voice as she described Colin. Poirot glanced keenly at her and saw that the colour had come up in her face.

He said to himself:

"So—she is in love and she cannot easily conceal the fact."

He noticed that young McNabb never seemed to look at her

across the table, being far too much taken up with his conversation with a laughing red-headed girl beside him.

"That's Sally Finch. She's American—over here on a Fulbright. Then there's Genevieve Maricaud. She's doing English, and so is René Halle who sits next to her. The small fair girl is Jean Tomlinson—she's at St. Catherine's too. She's a physio-therapist. The black man is Akibombo—he comes from West Africa and he's frightfully nice. Then there's Elizabeth Johnston, she's from Jamaica and she's studying law. Next to us on my right are two Turkish students who came about a week ago. They know hardly any English."

"Thank you. And do you all get on well together? Or do you have quarrels?"

The lightness of his tone robbed the words of seriousness.

Celia said,

"Oh, we're all too busy really to have fights, although—"

"Although what, Miss Austin?"

"Well—Nigel—next to Mrs. Hubbard. He likes stirring people up and making them angry. And Len Bateson *gets* angry. He gets wild with rage sometimes. But he's very sweet really."

"And Colin McNabb—does he too get annoyed?"

"Oh no. Colin just raises his eyebrows and looks amused."

"I see. And the young ladies, do you have your quarrels?"

"Oh no, we all get on very well. Genevieve has feelings sometimes. I think French people are inclined to be touchy—oh I mean —I'm sorry—"

Celia was the picture of confusion.

"Me, I am Belgian," said Poirot solemnly. He went on quickly, before Celia could recover control of herself,

"What did you mean just now, Miss Austin, when you said that you wondered. You wondered—what?"

She crumbled her bread nervously.

"Oh that—nothing—nothing really—just, there have been some silly practical jokes lately—I thought Mrs. Hubbard— But really, it was silly of me. I didn't mean anything."

Poirot did not press her. He turned away to Mrs. Hubbard and was presently engaged in a three cornered conversation with her and with Nigel Chapman who introduced the controversial challenge that crime was a form of creative art—and that the misfits of society were really the police who only entered that profession because of their secret sadism. Poirot was amused to note that the anxious looking young woman in spectacles of about thirty-five who sat beside him tried desperately to explain away his remarks as fast as he made them. Nigel, however, took absolutely no notice of her.

Mrs. Hubbard looked benignantly amused.

"All you young people nowadays think of nothing but politics and psychology," she said. "When I was a girl we were much more lighthearted. We danced. If you rolled back the carpet in the Common Room there's quite a good floor, and you could dance to the wireless, but you never do."

Celia laughed and said with a tinge of malice,

"But you used to dance, Nigel. I've danced with you myself once, though I don't expect you remember."

"You've danced with *me*," said Nigel incredulously. "Where?"

"At Cambridge—in May Week."

"Oh, May Week!" Nigel waved away the follies of youth. "One goes through that adolescent phase. Mercifully it soon passes."

Nigel was clearly not much more than twenty-five now. Poirot concealed a smile in his moustache.

Patricia Lane said earnestly,

"You see, Mrs. Hubbard, there is so much study to be done. With lectures to attend and one's notes to write up, there's really no time for anything but what is really worth while."

"Well, my dear, one's only young once," said Mrs. Hubbard.

A chocolate pudding succeeded the spaghetti and afterwards they all went into the Common Room, and helped themselves to coffee from an urn that stood on a table. Poirot was then invited to begin his discourse. The two Turks politely excused themselves. The rest seated themselves and looked expectant.

Poirot rose to his feet and spoke with his usual aplomb. The sound of his own voice was always pleasant to him, and he spoke for three quarters of an hour in a light and amusing fashion, recalling those of his experiences that lent themselves to an agreeable exaggeration. If he managed to suggest, in a subtle fashion, that he was, perhaps, something of a mountebank, it was not too obviously contrived.

"And so, you see," he finished, "I say to this City gentleman that I am reminded of a soap manufacturer I knew in Liége who poisoned his wife in order to marry a beautiful blonde secretary.

I say it very lightly, but at once I get a reaction. He presses upon me the stolen money I had just recovered for him. He goes pale and there is fear in his eyes. 'I will give this money,' I say, 'to a deserving charity.' 'Do anything you like with it,' he says. And I say to him then, and I say it very significantly, 'It will be advisable, Monsieur, to be *very* careful.' He nods, speechless, and as I go out, I see that he wipes his forehead. He has had the big fright, and I—I have saved his life. For though he is infatuated with his blonde secretary he will not now try and poison his stupid and disagreeable wife. Prevention, always, is better than cure. We want to prevent murders—not wait until they have been committed."

He bowed and spread out his hands.

"There, I have wearied you long enough."

The students clapped him vigorously. Poirot bowed. And then, as he was about to sit down, Colin McNabb took his pipe from between his teeth and observed:

"And now, perhaps, you'll talk about what you're really here for!"

There was a momentary silence and then Patricia said reproachfully, "Colin."

"Well, we can all guess, can't we?" He looked round scornfully. "M. Poirot's given us a very amusing little talk, but that's not what he came for. He's on the job. You don't really think, M. Poirot, that we're not wise to that?"

"You speak for yourself, Colin," said Sally.

"It's true, isn't it?" said Colin.

Again Poirot spread out his hands in a graceful acknowledging gesture.

"I will admit," he said, "that my kind hostess has confided to me that certain events have caused her—worry."

Len Bateson got up, his face heavy and truculent.

"Look here," he said, "what's all this? Has this been planted on us?"

"Have you really only just tumbled to that, Bateson?" asked Nigel sweetly.

Celia gave a frightened gasp and said: "Then I was right!"

Mrs. Hubbard spoke with decisive authority.

"I asked M. Poirot to give us a talk, but I also wanted to ask him his advice about various things that have happened lately.

Something's got to be done and it seemed to me that the only other alternative is—the police."

At once a violent altercation broke out. Genevieve burst into heated French. "It was a disgrace, shameful, to go to the police!" Other voices chimed in, for or against. In a final lull Leonard Bateson's voice was raised with decision.

"Let's hear what M. Poirot has to say about our trouble."

Mrs. Hubbard said,

"I've given M. Poirot all the facts. If he wants to ask any questions, I'm sure none of you will object."

Poirot bowed to her.

"Thank you." With the air of a conjuror he brought out a pair of evening shoes and handed them to Sally Finch.

"Your shoes, Mademoiselle?"

"Why—yes—both of them? Where did the missing one come from?"

"From the Lost Property Office at Baker Street Station."

"But what made you think it might be there, M. Poirot?"

"A very simple process of deduction. Someone takes a shoe from your room. Why? Not to wear and not to sell. And since the house will be searched by everyone to try and find it, then the shoe must be got out of the house, or destroyed. But it is not so easy to destroy a shoe. The easiest way is to take it in a bus or train in a parcel in the rush hour and leave it thrust down under a seat. That was my first guess and it proved right—so I knew that I was on safe ground—the shoe was taken, as your poet says, 'to annoy, because he knows it teases.'"

Valerie gave a short laugh.

"That points to you, Nigel, my love, with an unerring finger."

Nigel said, smirking a little, "If the shoe fits, wear it."

"Nonsense," said Sally. "Nigel didn't take my shoe."

"Of course he didn't," said Patricia angrily. "It's the most absurd idea."

"I don't know about absurd," said Nigel. "Actually I didn't do anything of the kind—as no doubt we shall all say."

It was as though Poirot had been waiting for just those words as an actor waits for his cue. His eyes rested thoughtfully on Len Bateson's flushed face, then they swept inquiringly over the rest of the students.

He said, using his hands in a deliberately foreign gesture,

"My position is delicate. I am a guest here. I have come at the invitation of Mrs. Hubbard—to spend a pleasant evening, that is all. And also, of course, to return a very charming pair of evening shoes to Mademoiselle. For anything further—" he paused. "Monsieur—Bateson? yes, Bateson—has asked me to say what I myself think of this—trouble. But it would be an impertinence for me to speak unless I were invited so to do not by one person alone, but by you all."

Mr. Akibombo was seen to nod his black curled head in vigorous asseveration.

"That is very correct procedure, yes," he said. "True democratic proceeding is to put matter to the voting of all present."

The voice of Sally Finch rose impatiently.

"Oh, shucks," she said. "This is a kind of party, all friends together. Let's hear what M. Poirot advises without any more fuss."

"I couldn't agree with you more, Sally," said Nigel.

Poirot bowed his head.

"Very well," he said. "Since you all ask me this question, I reply that my advice is quite simple. Mrs. Hubbard—or Mrs. Nicoletis rather—should call in the police at once. No time should be lost."

CHAPTER 5

THERE WAS NO DOUBT that Poirot's statement was unexpected. It caused not a ripple of protest or comment, but a sudden and uncomfortable silence.

Under cover of that momentary paralysis, Poirot was taken by Mrs. Hubbard up to her own sitting room, with only a quick polite "Good night to you all," to herald his departure.

Mrs. Hubbard switched on the light, closed the door, and begged M. Poirot to take the arm chair by the fireplace. Her nice good humoured face was puckered with doubt and anxiety. She offered her guest a cigarette, but Poirot refused politely, explaining that he preferred his own. He offered her one, but she refused, saying in an abstracted tone: "I don't smoke, M. Poirot."

Then, as she sat down opposite him, she said, after a momentary hesitation:

"I daresay you're right, M. Poirot. Perhaps we *should* get the police in on this—especially after this malicious ink business. But I rather wish you hadn't said so—right out like that."

"Ah," said Poirot, as he lit one of his tiny cigarettes and watched the smoke ascend. "You think I should have dissembled?"

"Well, I suppose it's nice to be fair and above board about things—but it seems to me it might have been better to keep quiet, and just ask an officer to come round and explain things privately to him. What I mean is, whoever's been doing these stupid things —well, that person's warned now."

"Perhaps, yes."

"I should say quite certainly," said Mrs. Hubbard rather sharply. "No perhaps about it! Even if it's one of the servants or a student who wasn't here this evening, the word will get around. It always does."

"So true. It always does."

"And there's Mrs. Nicoletis, too. I really don't know what attitude she'll take up. One never does know with her."

"It will be interesting to find out."

"Naturally we can't call in the police unless she agrees— Oh, who's that now?"

There had been a sharp authoritative tap on the door. It was repeated and almost before Mrs. Hubbard had called an irritable "Come in" the door opened and Colin McNabb, his pipe clenched firmly between his teeth and a scowl on his forehead, entered the room.

Removing the pipe, and closing the door behind him, he said:

"You'll excuse me, but I was anxious to just have a word with M. Poirot here."

"With me?" Poirot turned his head in innocent surprise.

"Ay, with you." Colin spoke grimly.

He drew up a rather uncomfortable chair and sat squarely on it facing Hercule Poirot.

"You've given us an amusing talk tonight," he said indulgently. "And I'll not deny that you're a man who's had a varied and lengthy experience, but if you'll excuse me for saying so, your methods and your ideas are both equally antiquated."

"Really, Colin," said Mrs. Hubbard, colouring. "You're extremely rude."

"I'm not meaning to give offence, but I've got to make things clear. Crime and Punishment, M. Poirot—that's as far as your horizon stretches."

"They seem to me a natural sequence," said Poirot.

"You take the narrow view of the Law—and what's more of the Law at its most old-fashioned. Nowadays, even the Law has to keep itself cognizant of the newest and most up to date theories of what causes crime. It is the *causes* that are important, M. Poirot."

"But there," cried Poirot, "to speak in your new fashioned phrase, I could not agree with you more!"

"Then you've got to consider the *cause* of what has been happening in this house—you've got to find out *why* these things have been done."

"But I am still agreeing with you—yes, that is most important."

"Because there always is a reason, and it may be, to the person concerned, a very good reason."

At this point, Mrs. Hubbard, unable to contain herself, interjected sharply, "Rubbish."

"That's where you're wrong," said Colin, turning slightly towards her. "You've got to take into account the psychological background."

"Psychological balderdash," said Mrs. Hubbard. "I've no patience with all that sort of talk!"

"That's because you know precisely nothing about it," said Colin in a gravely rebuking fashion. He returned his gaze to Poirot.

"I'm interested in these subjects. I am at present taking a post graduate course in psychiatry and psychology. We come across the most involved and astounding cases, and what I'm pointing out to you, M. Poirot, is that you can't just dismiss the criminal with a doctrine of original sin, or wilful disregard of the laws of the land. You've got to have an understanding of the root of the trouble if you're ever to effect a cure of the young delinquent. These ideas were not known or thought of in your day and I've no doubt you find them hard to accept—"

"Stealing's stealing," put in Mrs. Hubbard stubbornly.

Colin frowned impatiently.

Poirot said meekly,

"My ideas are doubtless old fashioned, but I am perfectly prepared to listen to you, Mr. McNabb."

Colin looked agreeably surprised.

"That's very fairly said, M. Poirot. Now I'll try to make this matter clear to you, using very simple terms."

"Thank you," said Poirot meekly.

"For convenience's sake, I'll start with the pair of shoes you brought with you tonight and returned to Sally Finch. If you remember, one shoe was stolen. Only one."

"I remember being struck by the fact," said Poirot.

Colin McNabb leaned forward, his dour but handsome features were lit up by eagerness.

"Ah, but you didn't see the *significance* of it. It's one of the prettiest and most satisfying examples anyone could wish to come across. We have here, very definitely, a Cinderella complex. You are maybe acquainted with the Cinderella fairy story."

"Of French origin—*mais oui.*"

"Cinderella, the unpaid drudge, sits by the fire, her sisters dressed in their finery, go to the Prince's ball. A Fairy Godmother sends Cinderella too, to that ball. At the stroke of midnight, her finery turns back to rags—she escapes hurriedly, leaving behind her one slipper. So here we have a mind that compares itself to Cinderella (unconsciously, of course). Here we have frustration, envy, the sense of inferiority. The girl steals a slipper. Why?"

"A girl?"

"But naturally, a girl. That," said Colin reprovingly, "should be clear to the meanest intelligence."

"Really, Colin!" said Mrs. Hubbard.

"Pray continue," said Poirot, courteously.

"Probably she herself does not know why she does it—but the inner wish is clear. She wants to be the Princess, to be identified by the Prince and claimed by him. Another significant fact, the slipper is stolen from an attractive girl who is going to a Ball."

Colin's pipe had long since gone out. He waved it now with mounting enthusiasm.

"And now we'll take a few of the other happenings. A magpie acquiring of pretty things—all things associated with attractive femininity. A powder compact, lipsticks, earrings, a bracelet, a ring—there is a twofold significance here. The girl wants to be noticed. She wants, even, to be punished—as is frequently the case with very young juvenile delinquents. These things are none of them what you would call ordinary criminal thefts. It is not the value of these things that is wanted. In just such a way do well-to-do women go into department stores and steal things they could perfectly well afford to pay for."

"Nonsense," said Mrs. Hubbard belligerently. "Some people are just plain dishonest, that's all there is to it."

"Yet a diamond ring of some value was amongst the things stolen," said Poirot, ignoring Mrs. Hubbard's interpolation.

"That was returned."

"And surely, M. McNabb, you would not say that a stethoscope is a feminine pretty pretty?"

"That had a deeper significance. Women who feel they are deficient in feminine attraction can find sublimation in the pursuit of a career."

"And the cookery book?"

"A symbol of home life, husband and family."

"And boracic powder?"

Colin said irritably,

"My dear M. Poirot. *Nobody* would steal boracic powder! Why should they?"

"That is what I have asked myself. I must admit, M. McNabb, that you seem to have an answer for everything. Explain to me, then, the significance of the disappearance of an old pair of flannel trousers—your flannel trousers, I understand."

For the first time, Colin appeared ill at ease. He blushed and cleared his throat.

"I could explain that—but it would be somewhat involved, and perhaps—er well, rather embarrassing."

"Ah, you spare my blushes."

Suddenly Poirot leaned forward and tapped the young man on the knee.

"And the ink that is spilt over another student's papers, the silk scarf that is cut and slashed. Do these things cause you no disquietude?"

The complacence and superiority of Colin's manner underwent a sudden and not unlikeable change.

"They do," he said. "Believe me, they do. It's serious. She ought to have treatment—at once. But medical treatment, that's the point. It's not a case for the police. The poor little devil doesn't even know what it's all about. She's all tied up in knots. If I . . ."

Poirot interrupted him.

"You know then who she is?"

"Well, I have a very strong suspicion."

Poirot murmured with the air of one who is recapitulating.

"A girl who is not outstandingly successful with the other sex. A shy girl. An affectionate girl. A girl whose brain is inclined to be slow in its reactions. A girl who feels frustrated and lonely. A girl . . ."

There was a tap on the door. Poirot broke off. The tap was repeated.

"Come in," said Mrs. Hubbard.

The door opened and Celia Austin came in.

"Ah," said Poirot, nodding his head. "Exactly. Miss Celia Austin."

Celia looked at Colin with agonised eyes.

"I didn't know you were here," she said breathlessly. "I came —I came . . ."

She took a deep breath and rushed to Mrs. Hubbard.

"Please, please don't send for the police. It's me. I've been taking those things. I don't know why. I can't imagine. I didn't want to. It just—it just came over me." She whirled round on Colin. "So now you know what I'm like . . . and I suppose you'll never speak to me again. I know I'm awful . . ."

"Och! not a bit of it," said Colin. His rich voice was warm and friendly. "You're just a bit mixed up, that's all. It's just a kind of illness you've had, from not looking at things clearly. If you'll trust me, Celia, I'll soon be able to put you right."

"Oh, Colin—really?"

Celia looked at him with unconcealed adoration.

"I've been so dreadfully worried."

He took her hand in a slightly avuncular manner.

"Well, there's no need to worry any more." Rising to his feet he drew Celia's hand through his arm and looked sternly at Mrs. Hubbard.

"I hope now," he said, "that there'll be no more foolish talk of calling in the police. Nothing's been stolen of any real worth and what has been taken, Celia will return."

"I can't return the bracelet and the powder compact," said Celia anxiously. "I pushed them down a gutter. But I'll buy new ones."

"And the stethoscope?" said Poirot. "Where did you put that?"

Celia flushed.

"I never took any stethoscope. What should I want with a silly old stethoscope?" Her flush deepened. "And it wasn't me who spilt ink all over Elizabeth's papers. I'd never do a—a malicious thing like that."

"Yet you cut and slashed Miss Hobhouse's scarf, Mademoiselle."

Celia looked uncomfortable. She said rather uncertainly,

"That was different. I mean—Valerie didn't mind."

"And the rucksack?"

"Oh, I didn't cut that up. That was just temper."

Poirot took out the list he had copied from Mrs. Hubbard's little book.

"Tell me," he said, "and this time it must be the truth. What are you or are you not responsible for of these happenings?"

Celia glanced down the list and her answer came at once.

"I don't know anything about the rucksack, or the electric light bulbs, or boracic or bath salts, and the ring was just a mistake. When I realised it was valuable I returned it."

"I see."

"Because really I didn't mean to be dishonest. It was only—"

"Only what?"

A faintly wary look came into Celia's eyes.

"I don't know—really I don't. I'm all mixed up."

Colin cut in in a peremptory manner.

"I'll be thankful if you'll not catechise her. I can promise you that there will be no recurrence of this business. From now on I'll definitely make myself responsible for her."

"Oh Colin, you *are* good to me."

"I'd like you to tell me a great deal about yourself, Celia. Your early home life, for instance. Did your father and mother get on well together."

"Oh no, it was awful—at home—"

"Precisely. And—"

Mrs. Hubbard cut in. She spoke with the voice of authority.

"That will do now, both of you. I'm glad, Celia, that you've come and owned up. You've caused a great deal of worry and anxiety though, and you ought to be ashamed of yourself. But I'll say this. I accept your word that you didn't spill ink deliberately on Elizabeth's notes. I don't believe you'd do a thing like that. Now take yourselves off, you and Colin. I've had enough of you both for this evening."

As the door closed behind them, Mrs. Hubbard drew a deep breath.

"Well," she said. "What do you think of that?"

There was a twinkle in Hercule Poirot's eye. He said, "I think —that we have assisted at a love scene—modern style."

Mrs. Hubbard made an ejaculation of disapproval.

"*Autres temps, autres moeurs*," murmured Poirot. "In my young day the young men lent the girls books on Theosophy or discussed Maeterlinck's Bluebird. All was sentiment and high ideals. Nowadays it is the maladjusted lives and the complexes which bring a boy and girl together."

"All such nonsense," said Mrs. Hubbard.

Poirot dissented.

"No, it is not all nonsense. The underlying principles are sound enough—but when one is an earnest young researcher like Colin one sees nothing *but* complexes and the victim's unhappy home life."

"Celia's father died when she was four years old," said Mrs. Hubbard. "And she's had a very agreeable childhood with a nice but stupid mother."

"Ah, but she is wise enough not to say so to the young Mc-Nabb! She will say what he wants to hear. She is very much in love."

"Do you believe all this hooey, M. Poirot?"

"I do not believe that Celia had a Cinderella complex or that she stole things without knowing what she was doing. I think she took the risk of stealing unimportant trifles with the object of attracting the attention of the earnest Colin McNabb—in which object she has been successful. Had she remained a pretty shy ordinary girl he might never have looked at her. In my opinion," said Poirot, "a girl is entitled to attempt desperate measures to get her man."

"I shouldn't have thought she had the brains to think it up," said Mrs. Hubbard.

Poirot did not reply. He frowned. Mrs. Hubbard went on.

"So the whole thing's been a mare's nest! I really do apologise,

M. Poirot, for taking up your time over such a trivial business. Anyway, all's well that ends well."

"No, no." Poirot shook his head. "I do not think we are at the end yet. We have cleared out of the way something rather trivial that was at the front of the picture. But there are things still that are not explained and me, I have the impression that we have here something serious—really serious."

Mrs. Hubbard's face clouded over again.

"Oh, M. Poirot, do you really think so?"

"It is my impression. . . . I wonder, Madame, if I could speak to Miss Patricia Lane. I would like to examine the ring that was stolen."

"Why, of course, M. Poirot. I'll go down and send her up to you. I want to speak to Len Bateson about something."

Patricia Lane came in shortly afterwards with an inquiring look on her face.

"I am so sorry to disturb you, Miss Lane."

"Oh, that's all right. I wasn't busy. Mrs. Hubbard said you wanted to see my ring."

She slipped it off her finger and held it out to him.

"It's quite a large diamond really, but of course it's an old fashioned setting. It was my mother's engagement ring."

Poirot, who was examining the ring, nodded his head.

"She is alive still, your mother?"

"No. Both my parents are dead."

"That is sad."

"Yes. They were both very nice people but somehow I was never quite so close to them as I ought to have been. One regrets that afterwards. My mother wanted a frivolous pretty daughter, a daughter who was fond of clothes and social things. She was very disappointed when I took up archaeology."

"You have always been of a serious turn of mind?"

"I think so, really. One feels life is so short one ought really to be doing something worth while."

Poirot looked at her thoughtfully.

Patricia Lane was, he guessed, in her early thirties. Apart from a smear of lipstick, carelessly applied, she wore no make-up. Her mouse coloured hair was combed back from her face and arranged without artifice. Her quite pleasant blue eyes looked at you seriously through glasses.

"No allure, *bon Dieu*," said Poirot to himself with feeling. "And her clothes! What is it they say? Dragged through a hedge backwards? *Ma foi*, that expresses it exactly!"

He was disapproving. He found Patricia's well bred unaccented tones wearisome to the ear. "She is intelligent and cultured, this girl," he said to himself, "and, alas, every year she will grow more boring! In old age—" His mind darted for a fleeting moment to the memory of the Countess Vera Rossakoff. What exotic splendour there, even in decay! These girls of nowadays—

"But that is because I grow old," said Poirot to himself. "Even this excellent girl may appear a veritable Venus to some man." But he doubted that.

Patricia was saying,

"I'm really very shocked about what happened to Bess—to Miss Johnston. Using that green ink seems to me to be a deliberate attempt to make it look as though it was Nigel's doing. But I do assure you, M. Poirot, Nigel would never do a thing like that."

"Ah." Poirot looked at her with more interest. She had become flushed and quite eager.

"Nigel's not easy to understand," she said earnestly. "You see, he had a very difficult home life as a child."

"*Mon Dieu*, another of them!"

"I beg your pardon?"

"Nothing. You were saying—"

"About Nigel. His being difficult. He's always had the tendency to go against authority of any kind. He's very clever—brilliant really, but I must admit that he sometimes has a very unfortunate manner. Sneering—you know. And he's much too scornful ever to explain or defend himself. Even if everybody in this place thinks he did that trick with the ink, he won't go out of his way to say he didn't. He'll just say 'Let them think it if they want to.' And that attitude is really so utterly foolish."

"It can be misunderstood, certainly."

"It's a kind of pride, I think. Because he's been so much misunderstood always."

"You have known him many years?"

"No, only for about a year. We met on a tour of the Chateaux of the Loire. He went down with flu which turned to pneumonia and I nursed him through it. He's very delicate and he takes absolutely no care of his own health. In some ways, in spite of his being so independent, he needs looking after like a child. He really needs someone to look after him."

Poirot sighed. He felt, suddenly, very tired of love. . . . First there had been Celia, with the adoring eyes of a spaniel. And now here was Patricia looking like an earnest Madonna. Admittedly there must be love, young people must meet and pair off, but he, Poirot, was mercifully past all that. He rose to his feet.

"Will you permit me, Mademoiselle, to retain your ring? It shall be returned to you tomorrow without fail."

"Certainly, if you like," said Patricia, rather surprised.

"You are very kind. And please, Mademoiselle, be careful."

"Careful? Careful of what?"

"I wish I knew," said Hercule Poirot, still worried.

CHAPTER 6

The following day Mrs. Hubbard found exasperating in every particular. She had wakened with a considerable sense of relief. The nagging doubt about recent occurrences was at last relieved. A silly girl, behaving in that silly modern fashion (with which Mrs. Hubbard had no patience), had been responsible. And from now on, order would reign.

Descending to breakfast in this comfortable assurance, Mrs. Hubbard found her newly attained ease menaced. The students chose this particular morning to be particularly trying, each in his or her way.

Mr. Chandra Lal who had heard of the *sabotage* to Elizabeth's papers became excited and voluble. "Oppression," he spluttered, "deliberate oppression of native races. Contempt and prejudice, colour prejudice. It is here well authenticated example."

"Now, Mr. Chandra Lal," said Mrs. Hubbard sharply. "You've no call to say anything of that kind. Nobody knows who did it or why it was done."

"Oh but, Mrs. Hubbard, I thought Celia had come to you herself and really faced up," said Jean Tomlinson. "I thought it splendid of her. We must all be very kind to her."

"Must you be so revoltingly pi, Jean?" demanded Valerie Hobhouse angrily.

"I think that's a very unkind thing to say."

"Faced up," said Nigel with a shudder. "Such an utterly revolting term."

"I don't see why. The Oxford Group use it and—"

"Oh, for Heaven's sake, have we got to have the Oxford Group for breakfast?"

"What's all this, Ma? Is it Celia who's been pinching those things, do you say? Is that why she's not down to breakfast?"

"I do not understand, please," said Mr. Akibombo.

Nobody enlightened him. They were all too anxious to say their own piece.

"Poor kid," Len Bateson went on. "Was she hard up or something?"

"I'm not really surprised, you know," said Sally slowly—"I always had a sort of idea . . ."

"You are saying that it was Celia who spilt ink on my notes?" Elizabeth Johnston looked incredulous. "That seems to me surprising and hardly credible."

"Celia did not throw ink on your work," said Mrs. Hubbard. "And I wish you would all stop discussing this. I meant to tell you all quietly later but—"

"But Jean was listening outside the door last night," said Valerie.

"I was not listening. I just happened to go—"

"Come now, Bess," said Nigel. "You know quite well who spilt the ink. I, said bad Nigel, with my little green phial. _I_ spilt the ink."

"He didn't. He's only pretending! Oh, Nigel, how can you be so stupid?"

"I'm being noble and shielding you, Pat. Who borrowed my ink yesterday morning? You did."

"I do not understand, please," said Mr. Akibombo.

"You don't want to," Sally told him. "I'd keep right out of it if I were you."

Mr. Chandra Lal rose to his feet.

"You ask why is the Mau Mau? You ask why does Egypt resent the Suez Canal?"

"Oh, hell!" said Nigel violently, and crashed his cup down on his saucer. "First the Oxford Group and now politics! At breakfast! I'm going."

He pushed back his chair violently and left the room.

"There's a cold wind. Do take your coat." Patricia rushed after him.

"Cluck, cluck, cluck," said Valerie unkindly. "She'll grow feathers and flap her wings soon."

The French girl, Genevieve, whose English was as yet not equal to following rapid exchanges had been listening to explanations hissed into her ear by René. She now burst into rapid French, her voice rising to a scream.

"Comment donc? C'est cette petite qui m'a vole mon compact? Ah, par example! J'irais à la police. Je ne supporterais pas une pareille . . ."

Colin McNabb had been attempting to make himself heard for some time, but his deep superior drawl had been drowned by the higher pitched voices. Abandoning his superior attitude he now brought down his fist with a heavy crash on the table and startled everyone into silence. The marmalade pot skidded off the table and broke.

"Will you hold your tongues, all of you, and hear me speak. I've never heard more crass ignorance and unkindness! Don't any of you have even a nodding acquaintance with psychology? The girl's not to be blamed, I tell you. She's been going through a severe emotional crisis and she needs treating with the utmost sympathy and care—or she may remain unstable for life. I'm warning you. The utmost care—that's what she needs."

"But after all," said Jean, in a clear, priggish voice, "although I quite agree about being kind—we oughtn't to condone that sort of thing, ought we? Stealing, I mean."

"Stealing," said Colin. "This wasn't stealing. Och! You make me sick—all of you."

"Interesting case, is she, Colin?" said Valerie and grinned at him.

"If you're interested in the workings of the mind, yes."

"Of course, she didn't take anything of mine—" began Jean, "but I do think—"

"No, she didn't take anything of yours," said Colin, turning to scowl at her. "And if you knew in the least what that meant you'd maybe not be too pleased about it."

"Really, I don't see—"

"Oh, come on, Jean," said Len Bateson. "Let's stop nagging and nattering. I'm going to be late and so are you."

They went out together. "Tell Celia to buck up," he said over his shoulder.

"I should like to make formal protest," said Mr. Chandra Lal. "Boracic powder, very necessary for my eyes which much inflamed by study, was removed."

"And you'll be late too, Mr. Chandra Lal," said Mrs. Hubbard firmly.

"My Professor is often unpunctual," said Mr. Chandra Lal gloomily, but moving towards the door. "Also, he is irritable and unreasonable when I ask many questions of searching nature—"

"*Mais il faut qu'elle me la rende, cette compacte,*" said Genevieve.

"You must speak English, Genevieve—you'll never learn English if you go back into French whenever you're excited. And you had Sunday dinner in this week and you haven't paid me for it."

"Ah, I have not my purse just now. Tonight—*Viens, Rene, nous serons en retard.*"

"Please," said Mr. Akibombo, looking round him beseechingly. "I do not understand."

"Come along, Akibombo," said Sally. "I'll tell you all about it on the way to the Institute."

She nodded reassuringly to Mrs. Hubbard and steered the bewildered Akibombo out of the room.

"Oh dear," said Mrs. Hubbard, drawing a deep breath. "Why in the world I ever took this job on!"

Valerie, who was the only person left, grinned in a friendly fashion.

"Don't worry, Ma," she said. "It's a good thing it's all come out! Everyone was getting on the jumpy side."

"I must say I was very surprised."

"That it turned out to be Celia?"

"Yes. Weren't you?"

Valerie said in a rather absent voice,

"Rather obvious, really, I should have thought."

"Have you been thinking so all along?"

"Well, one or two things made me wonder. At any rate she's got Colin where she wants him."

"Yes. I can't help feeling that it's wrong."

"You can't get a man with a gun," Valerie laughed. "But a spot of kleptomania does the trick? Don't worry, Mum. And for God's sake make Celia give Genevieve back her *compacte*, otherwise we shall never have any peace at meals."

Mrs. Hubbard said with a sigh,

"Nigel has cracked his saucer and the marmalade pot is broken."

"Hell of a morning, isn't it?" said Valerie. She went out. Mrs. Hubbard heard her voice in the hall saying cheerfully,

"Good morning, Celia. The coast's clear. All is known and all is going to be forgiven—by order of Pious Jean. As for Colin, he's been roaring like a lion on your behalf."

Celia came into the dining room. Her eyes were reddened with crying.

"Oh, Mrs. Hubbard."

"You're very late, Celia. The coffee's cold and there's not much left to eat."

"I didn't want to meet the others."

"So I gather. But you've got to meet them sooner or later."

"Oh, yes, I know. But I thought—by this evening—it would be easier. And of course I shan't stop on here. I'll go at the end of the week."

Mrs. Hubbard frowned.

"I don't think there's any need for that. You must expect a little unpleasantness—that's only fair—but they're generous minded young people on the whole. Of course you'll have to make reparation as far as possible—"

Celia interrupted her eagerly.

"Oh yes. I've got my cheque book here. That's one of the things I wanted to say to you." She looked down. She was holding a cheque book and an envelope in her hand. "I'd written to you in case you weren't about when I got down, to say how sorry I was and I meant to put in a cheque, so that you could square up with people—but my pen ran out of ink."

"We'll have to make a list."

"I have—as far as possible. But I don't know whether to try and buy new things or just to give the money."

"I'll think it over. It's difficult to say offhand."

"Oh, but do let me give you a cheque now. I'd feel so much better."

About to say uncompromisingly "Really? And why should you be allowed to make yourself feel better?" Mrs. Hubbard reflected that since the students were always short of ready cash, the whole affair would be more easily settled that way. It would also placate Genevieve who otherwise might make trouble with Mrs. Nicoletis. (There would be trouble enough there anyway.)

"All right," she said. She ran her eye down the list of objects. "It's difficult to say how much offhand—"

Celia said eagerly, "Let me give you a cheque for what you think roughly and then you find out from people and I can take some back or give you more."

"Very well." Mrs. Hubbard tentatively mentioned a sum which gave, she considered, ample margin, and Celia agreed at once. She opened the cheque book.

"Oh bother my pen." She went over to the shelves where odds and ends were kept belonging to various students. "There doesn't seem to be any ink here except Nigel's awful green. Oh, I'll use that. Nigel won't mind. I must remember to get a new bottle of Quink when I go out."

She filled the pen and came back and wrote out the cheque.

Giving it to Mrs. Hubbard, she glanced at her watch.

"I shall be late. I'd better not stop for breakfast."

"Now you'd better have something, Celia—even if it's only a bit of bread and butter—no good going out on an empty stomach. Yes, what is it?"

Geronimo, the Italian manservant, had come into the room and was making emphatic gestures with his hands, his wizened monkey-like face screwed up in a comical grimace.

"The Padrona, she just come in. She want to see you." He added, with a final gesture, "She plenty mad."

"I'm coming."

Mrs. Hubbard left the room while Celia hurriedly began hacking a piece off the loaf.

Mrs. Nicoletis was walking up and down her room in a fairly good imitation of a tiger at the Zoo near feeding time.

"What is this I hear?" she burst out. "You send for the police? Without a word to me? Who do you think you are? My God, who does the woman think she is?"

"I did not send for the police."

"You are a liar."

"Now then, Mrs. Nicoletis, you can't talk to me like that."

"Oh no. Certainly not! It is *I* who am wrong, not *you*. Always *me*. Everything *you* do is perfect. Police in my respectable Hostel."

"It wouldn't be the first time," said Mrs. Hubbard, recalling various unpleasant incidents. "There was that West Indian student who was wanted for living on immoral earnings and the notorious young communist agitator who came here under a false name—and—"

"Ah! You throw that in my teeth? Is it my fault that people come here and lie to me and have forged papers and are wanted to assist the police in murder cases? And you reproach me for what I have suffered!"

"I'm doing nothing of the kind. I only point out that it wouldn't be exactly a novelty to have the police here—I daresay it's inevitable with a mixed lot of students. But the fact is that no one has 'called in the police.' A private detective with a big reputation happened to dine here as my guest last night. He gave a very interesting talk on criminology to the students."

"As if there were any need to talk about criminology to our students! They know quite enough already. Enough to steal and destroy and sabotage as they like! And nothing is done about it —nothing!"

"I have done something about it."

"Yes, you have told this friend of yours all about our most intimate affairs. That is a gross breach of confidence."

"Not at all. I'm responsible for running this place. I'm glad to tell you the matter is now cleared up. One of the students has confessed that she has been responsible for most of these happenings."

"Dirty little cat," said Mrs. Nicoletis. "Throw her into the street."

"She is ready to leave of her own accord and she is making full reparation."

"What is the good of that? My beautiful Students' Home will now have a bad name. No one will come." Mrs. Nicoletis sat down on the sofa and burst into tears. "Nobody thinks of my feelings," she sobbed. "It is abominable, the way I am treated. Ignored! Thrust aside! If I were to die tomorrow, who would care?"

Wisely leaving this question unanswered, Mrs. Hubbard left the room.

"May the Almighty give me patience," said Mrs. Hubbard to herself and went down to the kitchen to interview Maria.

Maria was sullen and unco-operative. The word 'police' hovered unspoken in the air.

"It is I who will be accused. I and Geronimo—the *povero*. What justice can you expect in a foreign land? No, I cannot cook the risotto as you suggest—they send the wrong rice. I make you instead the spaghetti."

"We had spaghetti last night."

"It does not matter. In my country we eat the spaghetti every day—every single day. The pasta, it is good all the time."

"Yes, but you're in England now."

"Very well then, I make the stew. The English stew. You will not like it but I make it—pale—pale—with the onions boiled in much water instead of cooked in the oil—and pale meat on cracked bones."

Maria spoke so menacingly that Mrs. Hubbard felt she was listening to an account of a murder.

"Oh, cook what you like," she said angrily and left the kitchen.

By six o'clock that evening, Mrs. Hubbard was once more her efficient self again. She had put notes in all the students' rooms asking them to come and see her before dinner, and when the various summonses were obeyed, she explained that Celia had asked her to arrange matters. They were all, she thought, very nice about it. Even Genevieve, softened by a generous estimate of the value of her compact, said cheerfully that all would be *sans rancune* and added with a wise air, "One knows that these crises of the nerves occur. She is rich, this Celia, she does not need to steal. No, it is a storm in her head. M. McNabb is right there."

Len Bateson drew Mrs. Hubbard aside as she came down when the dinner bell rang.

"I'll wait for Celia out in the hall," he said, "and bring her in. So that she sees it's all right."

"That's very nice of you, Len."

"That's O.K., Ma."

In due course, as soup was being passed round, Len's voice was heard booming from the hall.

"Come along in, Celia. All friends here."

Nigel remarked waspishly to his soup plate,

"Done his good deed for the day!" but otherwise controlled his tongue and waved a hand of greeting to Celia as she came in with Len's large arm passed round her shoulders.

There was a general outburst of cheerful conversation on various topics and Celia was appealed to by one and the other.

Almost inevitably this manifestation of goodwill died away into a doubtful silence. It was then that Mr. Akibombo turned a beaming face towards Celia and leaning across the table, said:

"They have explained me good now all that I did not understand. You very clever at steal things. Long time nobody know. Very clever."

At this point Sally Finch, gasping out, "Akibombo, you'll be the death of me," had such a severe choke that she had to go out in the hall to recover. And the laughter broke out in a thoroughly natural fashion.

Colin McNabb came in late. He seemed reserved and even more uncommunicative than usual. At the close of the meal and before the others had finished he got up and said in an embarrassed mumble,

"Got to go out and see someone. Like to tell you all first Celia and I—hope to get married next year when I've done my course."

The picture of blushing misery, he received the congratulations and jeering cat-calls of his friends and finally escaped, looking terribly sheepish. Celia, on the other side, was pink and composed.

"Another good man gone West," sighed Len Bateson.

"I'm so glad, Celia," said Patricia. "I hope you'll be very happy."

"Everything in the garden is now perfect," said Nigel. "Tomorrow we'll bring some *chianti* in and drink your health. Why is our dear Jean looking so grave? Do you disapprove of marriage, Jean?"

"Of course not, Nigel."

"I always think it's so much better than Free Love, don't you? Nicer for the children. Looks better on their passports."

"But the mother should not be too young," said Genevieve. "They tell one that in the Physiology classes."

"Really, dear," said Nigel, "you're not suggesting that Celia's below the age of consent or anything like that, are you? She's free, white, and twenty-one."

"That," said Mr. Chandra Lal, "is a most offensive remark."

"No, no, Mr. Chandra Lal," said Patricia. "It's just a—a kind of idiom. It doesn't mean anything."

"I do not understand," said Mr. Akibombo. "If a thing does not mean anything, why should it be said?"

Elizabeth Johnston said suddenly, raising her voice a little,

"Things are sometimes said that do not seem to mean anything but they may mean a good deal. No, it is not your American quotation I mean. I am talking of something else." She looked round the table. "I am talking of what happened yesterday."

Valerie said sharply,

"What's up, Bess?"

"Oh, please," said Celia. "I think—I really do—that by tomorrow everything will be cleared up. I really mean it. The ink on your papers, and that silly business of the rucksack. And if—if the person owns up, like I've done, then everything will be cleared up."

She spoke earnestly, with a flushed face, and one or two people looked at her curiously.

Valerie said with a short laugh,

"And we'll all live happy ever afterwards."

Then they got up and went into the Common Room. There was quite a little competition to give Celia her coffee. Then the wireless was turned on, some students left to keep appointments or to work and finally the inhabitants of 24 and 26 Hickory Road got to bed.

It had been, Mrs. Hubbard reflected, as she climbed gratefully between the sheets, a long wearying day.

"But thank goodness," she said to herself. "It's all over now."

CHAPTER 7

MISS LEMON WAS SELDOM, if ever, unpunctual. Fog, storm, epidemics of flu, transport breakdowns—none of these things seemed to affect that remarkable woman. But this morning Miss Lemon arrived, breathless, at five minutes past ten instead of on the stroke of ten o'clock. She was profusely apologetic and for her, quite ruffled.

"I'm extremely sorry, M. Poirot—really extremely sorry. I was just about to leave the flat when my sister rang up."

"Ah, she is in good health and spirits, I trust?"

"Well, frankly no." Poirot looked inquiring. "In fact, she's very distressed. One of the students has committed suicide."

Poirot stared at her. He muttered something softly under his breath.

"I beg your pardon, M. Poirot?"

"What is the name of the student?"

"A girl called Celia Austin."

"How?"

"They think she took morphia."

"Could it have been an accident?"

"Oh no. She left a note, it seems."

Poirot said softly, "It was not this I expected, no, it was not this . . . and yet it is true, I expected something."

He looked up to find Miss Lemon at attention, waiting with pencil poised above her pad. He sighed and shook his head.

"No, I will hand you here this morning's mail. File them, please, and answer what you can. Me, I shall go round to Hickory Road."

Geronimo let Poirot in and recognising him as the honoured guest of two nights before became at once voluble in a sibilant conspiratorial whisper.

"Ah, Signor, it is you. We have here the trouble—the big trouble. The little Signorina, she is dead in her bed this morning. First the doctor come. He shake his head. Now comes an Inspector of the Police. He is upstairs with the Signora and the Padrona. Why should she wish to kill herself, the *poverina?* When last night all is so gay and the betrothment is made?"

"Betrothment?"

"*Si, si.* To Mr. Colin—you know—big, dark, always smoke the pipe."

"I know."

Geronimo opened the door of the Common Room and introduced Poirot into it with a redoublement of the conspiratorial manner.

"You stay here, yes? Presently, when the police go, I tell the Signora you are here. That is good, yes?"

Poirot said that it was good and Geronimo withdrew. Left to himself, Poirot who had no scruples of delicacy, made as minute an examination as possible of everything in the room with special attention to everything belonging to the students. His rewards were mediocre. The students kept most of their belongings and personal papers in their bedrooms.

Upstairs, Mrs. Hubbard was sitting facing Inspector Sharpe who was asking questions in a soft apologetic voice. He was a big comfortable looking man with a deceptively mild manner.

"It's very awkward and distressing for you, I know," he said soothingly. "But you see, as Dr. Coles has already told you, there will have to be an inquest, and we have just to get the picture right, so to speak. Now this girl had been distressed and unhappy lately, you say?"

"Yes."

"Love affair?"

"Not exactly." Mrs. Hubbard hesitated.

"You'd better tell me, you know," said Inspector Sharpe, persuasively. "As I say, we've got to get the picture. There was a reason, or she thought there was, for taking her own life? Any possibility that she might have been pregnant?"

"It wasn't that kind of thing at all. I hesitated, Inspector Sharpe, simply because the child had done some very foolish things and I hoped it needn't be necessary to bring them out in the open."

Inspector Sharpe coughed.

"We have a good deal of discretion, and the Coroner is a man of wide experience. But we have to know."

"Yes, of course. I was being foolish. The truth is that for some time past, three months or more, things have been disappearing —small things, I mean—nothing very important."

"Trinkets, you mean, finery, nylon stockings and all that? Money, too?"

"No money as far as I know."

"Ah. And this girl was responsible?"

"Yes."

"You'd caught her at it?"

"Not exactly. The night before last a—er—a friend of mine came to dine. A M. Hercule Poirot—I don't know if you know the name."

Inspector Sharpe had looked up from his notebook. His eyes had opened rather wide. It happened that he did know that name.

"M. Hercule Poirot?" he said. "Indeed? Now that's very interesting."

"He gave us a little talk after dinner and the subject of these thefts came up. He advised me, in front of them all, to go to the police."

"He did, did he?"

"Afterwards, Celia came along to my room and owned up. She was very distressed."

"Any question of prosecution?"

"No. She was going to make good the losses, and everyone was very nice to her about it."

"Had she been hard up?"

"No. She has an adequately paid job as dispenser at St. Catherine's Hospital and has a little money of her own, I believe. She's rather better off than most of our students."

"So she'd no need to steal—but did," said the Inspector, writing it down.

"It's kleptomania, I suppose," said Mrs. Hubbard.

"That's the label that's used. I just mean one of the people that don't need to take things, but nevertheless do take them."

"I wonder if you're being a little unfair to her. You see, there was a young man."

"And he ratted on her?"

227

"Oh no. Quite the reverse. He spoke very strongly in her defence and as a matter of fact last night, after supper, he announced that they'd become engaged."

Inspector Sharpe's eyebrows mounted his forehead in a surprised fashion.

"And then she goes up to bed and takes morphia? That's rather surprising, isn't it?"

"It is. I can't understand it."

Mrs. Hubbard's face was creased with perplexity and distress.

"And yet the facts are clear enough." Sharpe nodded to the small torn piece of paper that lay on the table between them.

Dear Mrs. Hubbard, (it ran) *I really am sorry and this is the best thing I can do.*

"It's not signed, but you've no doubt it's her handwriting?"

"No."

Mrs. Hubbard spoke rather uncertainly and frowned as she looked at the torn scrap of paper. Why did she feel so strongly that there was something wrong about it—?

"There's one clear fingerprint on it which is definitely hers," said the Inspector. "The morphia was in a small bottle with the label of St. Catherine's Hospital on it and you tell me that she works as a dispenser in St. Catherine's. She'd have access to the poison cupboard and that's where she probably got it. Presumably she brought it home with her yesterday with suicide in mind."

"I really can't believe it. It doesn't seem right somehow. She was so happy last night."

"Then we must suppose that a reaction set in when she went up to bed. Perhaps there's more in her past than you know about. Perhaps she was afraid of that coming out. You think she was very much in love with this young man—what's his name, by the way?"

"Colin McNabb. He's doing a post graduate course at St. Catherine's."

"A doctor? Hm. And at St. Catherine's?"

"Celia was very much in love with him, more I should say, than he with her. He's a rather self-centred young man."

"Then that's probably the explanation. She didn't feel worthy of him, or hadn't told him all she ought to tell him. She was quite young, wasn't she?"

"Twenty-three."

"They're idealistic at that age and they take love affairs hard. Yes, that's it, I'm afraid. Pity."

He rose to his feet. "I'm afraid the actual facts will have to come out, but we'll do all we can to gloss things over. Thank you, Mrs. Hubbard. I've got all the information I need now. Her mother died two years ago and the only relative you know of is this elderly aunt in Yorkshire—we'll communicate with her."

He picked up the small torn fragment with Celia's agitated writing on it.

"There's something wrong about that," said Mrs. Hubbard suddenly.

"Wrong? In what way?"

"I don't know—but I feel I ought to know. Oh dear."

"You're quite sure it's her handwriting?"

"Oh yes. It's not that." Mrs. Hubbard pressed her hands to her eyeballs.

"I feel so dreadfully stupid this morning," she said apologetically.

"It's all been very trying for you, I know," said the Inspector with gentle sympathy. "I don't think we'll need to trouble you further at the moment, Mrs. Hubbard."

Inspector Sharpe opened the door and immediately fell over Geronimo who was pressed against the door outside.

"Hullo," said Inspector Sharpe pleasantly. "Listening at doors, eh?"

"No, no," Geronimo answered with an air of virtuous indignation. "I do not listen—never, never! I am just coming in with message."

"I see. What message?"

Geronimo said sulkily,

"Only that there is gentleman downstairs to see *la Signora Hubbard*."

"All right. Go along in, sonny, and tell her."

He walked past Geronimo down the passage and then, taking a leaf out of the Italian's book, turned sharply, and tip-toed noiselessly back. Might as well know if little monkey face had been telling the truth.

He arrived in time to hear Geronimo say,

"The gentleman who came to supper the other night, the gentleman with the moustaches, he is downstairs waiting to see you."

229

"Eh? What?" Mrs. Hubbard sounded abstracted. "Oh, thank you, Geronimo. I'll be down in a minute or two."

"Gentleman with the moustaches, eh," said Sharpe to himself, grinning. "I bet I know who that is."

He went downstairs and into the Common Room.

"Hullo, M. Poirot," he said. "It's a long time since we met."

Poirot rose without visible discomposure from a kneeling position by the bottom shelf near the fireplace.

"Aha," he said. "But surely—yes, it is Inspector Sharpe, is it not? But you were not formerly in this division?"

"Transferred two years ago. Remember that business down at Crays Hill?"

"Ah yes. That is a long time ago now. You are still a young man, Inspector—"

"Getting on, getting on."

"—and I am an old one. Alas!" Poirot sighed.

"But still active, eh, M. Poirot. Active in certain ways, shall we say?"

"Now what do you mean by that?"

"I mean that I'd like to know why you came along here the other night to give a talk on criminology to students."

Poirot smiled.

"But there is such a simple explanation. Mrs. Hubbard here is the sister of my much valued secretary, Miss Lemon. So when she asked me—"

"When she asked you to look into what had been going on here, you came along. That's it really, isn't it?"

"You are quite correct."

"But why? That's what I want to know. What was there in it for you?"

"To interest me, you mean?"

"That's what I mean. Here's a silly kid who's been pinching a few things here and there. Happens all the time. Rather small beer for you, M. Poirot, isn't it?"

Poirot shook his head.

"It is not so simple as that."

"Why not? What isn't simple about it?"

Poirot sat down on a chair. With a slight frown he dusted the knees of his trousers.

"I wish I knew," he said simply.

Sharpe frowned.

"I don't understand," he said.

"No, and I do not understand. The things that were taken—" he shook his head. "They did not make a pattern—they did not make sense. It is like seeing a trail of footprints and they are not all made by the same feet. There is, quite clearly, the print of what you have called 'a silly kid'—but there is more than that. Other things happened that were meant to fit in with the pattern of Celia Austin—but they did not fit in. They were meaningless, apparently purposeless. There was evidence, too, of malice. And Celia was not malicious."

"She was a kleptomaniac?"

"I should very much doubt it."

"Just an ordinary petty thief, then?"

"Not in the way you mean. I give it you as my opinion that all this pilfering of petty objects was done to attract the attention of a certain young man."

"Colin McNabb?"

"Yes. She was desperately in love with Colin McNabb. Colin never noticed her. Instead of a nice, pretty, well behaved young girl, she displayed herself as an interesting young criminal. The result was successful. Colin McNabb immediately fell for her, as they say, in a big way."

"He must be a complete fool, then."

"Not at all. He is a keen psychologist."

"Oh," Inspector Sharpe groaned. "One of those! I understand now." A faint grin showed on his face. "Pretty smart of the girl."

"Surprisingly so."

Poirot repeated, musingly, "Yes, surprisingly so."

Inspector Sharpe looked alert.

"Meaning by that, M. Poirot?"

"That I wondered—I still wonder—if the idea had been suggested to her by someone else?"

"For what reason?"

"How do I know? Altruism? Some ulterior motive? One is in the dark."

"Any idea as to who it might have been who gave her the tip?"

"No—unless—but no—"

"All the same," said Sharpe, pondering, "I don't quite get it.

If she's been simply trying this kleptomania business on, and it's succeeded, why the hell go and commit suicide?"

"The answer is that she should not have committed suicide."

The two men looked at each other.

Poirot murmured:

"You are quite sure that she did?"

"It's clear as day, M. Poirot. There's no reason to believe otherwise and—"

The door opened and Mrs. Hubbard came in. She looked flushed and triumphant. Her chin stuck out aggressively.

"I've got it," she said, triumphantly. "Good morning, M. Poirot. I've got it, Inspector Sharpe. It came to me quite suddenly. Why that suicide note looked wrong, I mean. Celia couldn't possibly have written it."

"Why not, Mrs. Hubbard?"

"Because it's written in ordinary blue black ink. And Celia filled her pen with green ink—that ink over there," Mrs. Hubbard nodded towards the shelf, "at breakfast time yesterday morning."

Inspector Sharpe, a somewhat different Inspector Sharpe, came back into the room which he had left abruptly after Mrs. Hubbard's statement.

"Quite right," he said. "I've checked up. The only pen in the girl's room, the one that was by her bed, has green ink in it. Now that green ink—"

Mrs. Hubbard held up the nearly empty bottle.

Then she explained, clearly and concisely, the scene at the breakfast table.

"I feel sure," she ended, "that the scrap of paper was torn out of the letter she had written to me yesterday—and which I never opened."

"What did she do with it? Can you remember?"

Mrs. Hubbard shook her head.

"I left her alone in here and went to do my housekeeping. She must, I think, have left it lying somewhere in here, and forgotten about it."

"And somebody found it . . . and opened it . . . somebody—"

He broke off.

"You realise," he said, "what this means? I haven't been very happy about this torn bit of paper all along. There was quite a pile of lecture notepaper in her room—much more natural to write a suicide note on one of them. This means that somebody saw the possibility of using the opening phrase of her letter to you—to suggest something very different. To suggest suicide—"

He paused and then said slowly,

"This means—"

"Murder," said Hercule Poirot.

CHAPTER 8

Though personally deprecating *le five o'clock* as inhibiting the proper appreciation of the supreme meal of the day, dinner, Poirot was now getting quite accustomed to serving it.

The resourceful George had on this occasion produced large cups, a pot of really strong Indian tea and, in addition to the hot and buttery square crumpets, bread and jam and a large square of rich plum cake.

All this for the delectation of Inspector Sharpe who was leaning back contentedly sipping his third cup of tea.

"You don't mind my coming along like this, M. Poirot? I've got an hour to spare until the time when the students will be getting back. I shall want to question them all—and, frankly, it's not a business I'm looking forward to. You met some of them the other night and I wondered if you could give me any useful dope—on the foreigners, anyway."

"You think I am a good judge of foreigners? But, *mon cher*, there were no Belgians amongst them."

"No Belg— Oh, I see what you mean! You mean that as you're a Belgian, all the other nationalities are as foreign to you as they are to me. But that's not quite true, is it? I mean you probably know more about the Continental types than I do—though not the Indians and the West Africans and that lot."

"Your best assistance will probably be from Mrs. Hubbard. She has been there for some months in intimate association with these young people and she is quite a good judge of human nature."

"Yes, thoroughly competent woman. I'm relying on her. I shall have to see the proprietress of the place, too. She wasn't there this morning. Owns several of these places, I understand, as well as some of the student clubs. Doesn't seem to be much liked."

Poirot said nothing for a moment or two, then he asked,

"You have been to St. Catherine's?"

"Yes. The Chief Pharmacist was most helpful. He was much shocked and distressed by the news."

"What did he say of the girl?"

"She'd worked there for just over a year and was well liked. He described her as rather slow, but very conscientious." He paused and then added, "The morphia came from there all right."

"It did? That is interesting—and rather puzzling."

"It was morphine tartrate. Kept in the poison cupboard in the Dispensary. Upper shelf—among drugs that were not often used. The hypodermic tablets, of course, are what are in general use, and it appears that morphine hydrochloride is more often used than the tartrate. There seems to be a kind of fashion in drugs like everything else. Doctors seem to follow one another in prescribing like a lot of sheep. He didn't say that. It was my own thought. There are some drugs in the upper shelf of that cupboard that were once popular, but haven't been prescribed for years."

"So the absence of one small dusty phial would not immediately be noticed?"

"That's right. Stock-taking is only done at regular intervals. Nobody remembers any prescription with morphine tartrate in it for a long time. The absence of the bottle wouldn't be noticed until it was wanted—or until they went over stock. The three dispensers all had keys of the poison cupboard and the Dangerous Drug cupboard. The cupboards are opened as needed, and as on a busy day (which is practically every day) someone is going to the cupboard every few minutes, the cupboard is unlocked and remains unlocked till the end of work."

"Who had access to it, other than Celia herself?"

"The two other women Dispensers, but they have no connection of any kind with Hickory Road. One has been there for four years, the other only came a few weeks ago, was formerly at a Hospital in Devon. Good record. Then there are the three senior pharmacists who have all been at St. Catherine's for years. Those are the people who have what you might call rightful and normal access to the cupboard. Then there's an old woman who scrubs the floors. She's there between nine and ten in the morning and she could have grabbed a bottle out of the cupboard if the girls were busy at the outpatients' hatches, or attending to the ward baskets, but she's been working for the Hospital for years and it seems very unlikely. The lab attendant comes through with stock bottles and he, too, could help himself to a bottle if he watched his opportunity—but none of these suggestions seem at all probable."

"What outsiders come into the Dispensary?"

"Quite a lot, one way or another. They'd pass through the Dispensary to go to the Chief Pharmacist's office, for instance—or travellers from the big wholesale drug houses would go through it to the manufacturing departments. Then, of course, friends come in occasionally to see one of the dispensers—not a usual thing, but it happens."

"That is better. Who came in recently to see Celia Austin?" Sharpe consulted his notebook.

"A girl called Patricia Lane came in on Tuesday of last week. She wanted Celia to come to meet her at the pictures after the Dispensary closed."

"Patricia Lane," said Poirot thoughtfully.

"She was only there about five minutes and she did not go near the poison cupboard but remained near the Outpatients windows talking to Celia and another girl. They also remember a coloured girl coming—about two weeks ago—a very superior girl, they said. She was interested in the work and asked questions about it and made notes. Spoke perfect English."

"That would be Elizabeth Johnston. She was interested, was she?"

"It was a Welfare Clinic afternoon. She was interested in the organisation of such things and also in what was prescribed for such ailments as infant diarrhoea and skin infections."

Poirot nodded.

"Anyone else?"

"Not that can be remembered."

"Do doctors come to the Dispensary?"

Sharpe grinned.

"All the time. Officially and unofficially. Sometimes to ask about a particular formula, or to see what is kept in stock."

"To see what is kept in stock?"

"Yes, I thought of that. Sometimes they ask advice—about a substitute for some preparation that seems to irritate a patient's skin or interfere with digestion unduly. Sometimes a physician just strolls in for a chat—slack moment. A good many of the young chaps come in for veganin or aspirin when they've got a hangover —and occasionally, I'd say, for a flirtatious word or two with one of the girls if the opportunity arises. Human nature is always human nature. You see how it is. Pretty hopeless."

Poirot said, "And if I recollect rightly, one or more of the students at Hickory Road is attached to St. Catherine's—a big red-haired boy—Bates—Bateman—"

"Leonard Bateson. That's right. And Colin McNabb is doing a post graduate course there. Then there's a girl, Jean Tomlinson, who works in the physiotherapy department."

"And all of these have probably been quite often in the Dispensary?"

"Yes, and what's more, nobody remembers when because they're used to seeing them and know them by sight. Jean Tomlinson was by way of being a friend of the senior Dispenser—"

"It is not easy," said Poirot.

"I'll say it's not! You see, anyone who was on the staff could take a look in the poison cupboard, say, 'Why on earth do you have so much Liquor Arsenicalis' or something like that. 'Didn't know anybody used it nowadays.' And nobody would think twice about it or remember it."

Sharpe paused and then said:

"What we are postulating is that someone gave Celia Austin morphia and afterwards put the morphia bottle and the torn out fragment of letter in her room to make it look like suicide. But why, M. Poirot, why?"

Poirot shook his head. Sharpe went on:

"You hinted this morning that someone might have suggested the kleptomania idea to Celia Austin."

Poirot moved uneasily.

"That was only a vague idea of mine. It was just that it seemed doubtful if she would have had the wits to think of it herself."

"Then who?"

"As far as I know, only three of the students would have been capable of thinking out such an idea. Leonard Bateson would have

236

had the requisite knowledge. He is aware of Colin's enthusiasm for "maladjusted personalities." He might have suggested something of the kind to Celia more or less as a joke and coached her in her part. But I cannot really see him conniving at such a thing for month after month—unless, that is, he had an ulterior motive, or is a very different person from what he appears to be. (That is always a thing one must take into account.) Nigel Chapman has a mischievous and slightly malicious turn of mind. He'd think it good fun, and I should imagine, would have no scruples whatever. He is a kind of grown up *'enfant terrible.'* The third person I have in mind is a young woman called Valerie Hobhouse. She has brains, is modern in outlook and education, and has probably read enough psychology to judge Colin's probable reaction. If she were fond of Celia, she might think it legitimate fun to make a fool of Colin."

"Leonard Bateson, Nigel Chapman, Valerie Hobhouse," said Sharpe, writing down the names. "Thanks for the tip. I'll remember when I'm questioning them. What about the Indians? One of them is a medical student, too."

"His mind is entirely occupied with politics and persecution mania," said Poirot. "I don't think he would be interested enough to suggest kleptomania to Celia Austin and I don't think she would have accepted such advice from him."

"And that's all the help you can give me, M. Poirot?" said Sharpe, rising to his feet and buttoning away his notebook.

"I fear so. But I consider myself personally interested—that is if you do not object, my friend?"

"Not in the least. Why should I?"

"In my own amateurish way I shall do what I can. For me, there is, I think, only one line of action."

"And that is?"

Poirot sighed.

"Conversation, my friend. Conversation and again conversation! All the murderers I have ever come across enjoyed talking. In my opinion the strong silent man seldom commits a crime—and if he does it is simple, violent, and perfectly obvious. But our clever subtle murderer—he is so pleased with himself that sooner or later he says something unfortunate and trips himself up. Talk to these people, *mon cher*, do not confine yourself to simple interrogation. Encourage their views, demand their help, inquire about their hunches—but, *bon Dieu!* I do not need to teach you your business. I remember your abilities well enough."

Sharpe smiled gently.

"Yes," he said, "I've always found—well—amiability—a great help."

The two men smiled at each other in mutual accord.

Sharpe rose to depart.

"I suppose every single one of them is a possible murderer," he said slowly.

"I should think so," said Poirot nonchalantly. "Leonard Bateson, for instance, has a temper. He could lose control. Valerie Hobhouse has brains and could plan cleverly. Nigel Chapman is the childish type that lacks proportion. There is a French girl there who might kill if enough money were involved. Patricia Lane is a maternal type and maternal types are always ruthless. The American girl, Sally Finch, is cheerful and gay, but she could play an assumed part better than most. Jean Tomlinson is very full of sweetness and righteousness, but we have all known killers who attended Sunday school with sincere devotion. The West Indian girl Elizabeth Johnston has probably the best brains of anyone in the Hostel. She has subordinated her emotional life to her brain—that is dangerous. There is a charming young African who might have motives for killing about which we could never guess. We have Colin McNabb, the psychologist. How many psychologists does one know to whom it might be said *Physician, heal thyself?*"

"For heaven's sake, Poirot. You are making my head spin! Is nobody incapable of murder?"

"I have often wondered," said Hercule Poirot.

CHAPTER 9

INSPECTOR SHARPE SIGHED, leaned back in his chair and rubbed his forehead with a handkerchief. He had interviewed an indignant and tearful French girl, a supercilious and unco-operative young Frenchman, a stolid and suspicious Dutchman, a voluble and aggressive Egyptian. He had exchanged a few brief remarks with two nervous young Turkish students who did not really understand what he was saying and the same went for a charming young Iraqi. None of these, he was pretty certain, had had anything to do, or could help him in any way, with the death of Celia Austin. He had dismissed them one by one with a few reassuring words and was now preparing to do the same to Mr. Akibombo.

The young West African looked at him with smiling white teeth and childlike rather plaintive eyes.

"I should like to help—yes—please," he said. "She is very nice to me, this Miss Celia. She give me once a box of Edinburgh rock— very nice confection which I do not know before. It seems very sad she should be killed. Is it blood feud, perhaps? Or is it perhaps fathers or uncles who come and kill her because they have heard false stories that she do wrong things."

Inspector Sharpe assured him that none of these things were remotely possible. The young man shook his head sadly.

"Then I do not know why it happened," he said. "I do not see why anybody here should want to do harm to her. But you give me piece of her hair and nail clippings," he continued, "and I see if I find out by old method. Not scientific, not modern, but very much in use where I come from."

"Well, thank you, Mr. Akibombo, but I don't think that will be necessary. We—er—don't do things that way over here."

"No, sir, I quite understand. Not modern. Not Atomic Age. Not

239

done at home now by new policemen—only old men from bush. I am sure all new methods very superior and sure to achieve complete success." Mr. Akibombo bowed politely and removed himself. Inspector Sharpe murmured to himself,

"I sincerely hope we do meet with success—if only to maintain prestige."

His next interview was with Nigel Chapman, who was inclined to take the conduct of the conversation into his own hands.

"This is an absolutely extraordinary business, isn't it?" he said. "Mind you, I had an idea that you were barking up the wrong tree when you insisted on suicide. I must say, it's rather gratifying to me to think that the whole thing hinges, really, on her having filled her fountain pen with my green ink. Just the one thing the murderer couldn't possibly foresee. I suppose you've given due consideration as to what can possibly be the motive for this crime?"

"I'm asking the questions, Mr. Chapman," said Inspector Sharpe drily.

"Oh, of course, of course," said Nigel, airily waving a hand. "I was trying to make a bit of a short cut of it, that was all. But I suppose we've got to go through with all the red tape as usual. Name, Nigel Chapman. Age, twenty-five. Born, I believe, in Nagasaki—it really seems a most ridiculous place. What my father and mother were doing there at the time I can't imagine. On a world tour, I suppose. However, it doesn't make me necessarily a Japanese, I understand. I'm taking a diploma at London University in Bronze Age and Mediaeval History. Anything else you want to know?"

"What is your home address, Mr. Chapman?"

"No home address, my dear sir. I have a papa, but he and I have quarrelled, and his address is therefore no longer mine. So 26 Hickory Road and Coutts Bank, Leadenhall Street Branch, will always find me as one says to travelling acquaintances whom you hope you will never meet again."

Inspector Sharpe displayed no reaction towards Nigel's airy impertinence. He had met 'Nigels' before and shrewdly suspected that Nigel's impertinence masked a natural nervousness of being questioned in connection with murder.

"How well did you know Celia Austin?" he asked.

"That's really quite a difficult question. I knew her very well in the sense of seeing her practically every day, and being on quite cheerful terms with her, but actually I didn't know her at all. Of course, I wasn't in the least bit interested in her and I think she probably disapproved of me, if anything."

"Did she disapprove of you for any particular reason?"

"Well, she didn't like my sense of humour very much. Then, of course, I wasn't one of those brooding, rude young men like Colin McNabb. That kind of rudeness is really the perfect technique for attracting women."

"When was the last time you saw Celia Austin?"

"At dinner yesterday evening. We'd all given her the big hand, you know. Colin had got up and hemmed and hahed and finally admitted, in a coy and bashful way, that they were engaged. Then we all ragged him a bit, and that was that."

"Was that at dinner or in the Common Room?"

"Oh, at dinner. Afterwards, when we went into the Common Room, Colin went off somewhere."

"And the rest of you had coffee in the Common Room."

"If you call the fluid they serve coffee—yes," said Nigel.

"Did Celia Austin have coffee?"

"Well, I suppose so. I mean, I didn't actually notice her having coffee, but she must have had it."

"You did not personally hand her her coffee, for instance?"

"How horribly suggestive all this is! When you said that and looked at me in that searching way, d'you know I felt quite certain that I had handed Celia her coffee and had filled it up with strychnine, or whatever it was. Hypnotic suggestion, I suppose, but actually, Mr. Sharpe, I didn't go near her—and to be frank, I didn't even notice her drinking coffee, and I can assure you, whether you believe me or not, that I have never had any passion for Celia myself and that the announcement of her engagement to Colin McNabb aroused no feelings of murderous revenge in me."

"I'm not really suggesting anything of the kind, Mr. Chapman," said Sharpe mildly. "Unless I'm very much mistaken, there's no particular love angle to this, but somebody wanted Celia Austin out of the way. Why?"

"I simply can't imagine why, Inspector. It's really most intriguing because Celia was really a most harmless kind of girl, if you know what I mean. Slow on the uptake; a bit of a bore; thoroughly nice; and absolutely, I should say, not the kind of girl to get herself murdered."

"Were you surprised when you found that it was Celia Austin who had been responsible for the various disappearances, thefts, et cetera, in this place?"

"My dear man, you could have knocked me over with a feather! Most uncharacteristic, that's what I thought."

"You didn't, perhaps, put her up to doing these things?"

Nigel's stare of surprise seemed quite genuine.

"I? Put her up to it? Why should I?"

"Well, that would be rather the question, wouldn't it? Some people have a funny sense of humour."

"Well, really, I may be dense, but I can't see anything amusing about all this silly pilfering that's been going on."

"Not your idea of a joke?"

"It never occurred to me it was meant to be funny. Surely, Inspector, the thefts were purely psychological?"

"You definitely consider that Celia Austin was a kleptomaniac?"

"But surely there can't be any other explanation, Inspector?"

"Perhaps you don't know as much about kleptomaniacs as I do, Mr. Chapman."

"Well, I really can't think of any other explanation."

"You don't think it's possible that someone might have put Miss Austin up to all this as a means of—say—arousing Mr. McNabb's interest in her?"

Nigel's eyes glistened with appreciative malice.

"Now that really is a most diverting explanation, Inspector," he said. "You know, when I think of it, it's perfectly possible and of course old Colin would swallow it, line, hook and sinker." Nigel savoured this with much glee for a second or two. Then he shook his head sadly.

"But Celia wouldn't have played," he said. "She was a serious girl. She'd never have made fun of Colin. She was soppy about him."

"You've no theory of your own, Mr. Chapman, about the things that have been going on in this house? About, for instance, the spilling of ink over Miss Johnston's papers?"

"If you're thinking I did it, Inspector Sharpe, that's quite untrue. Of course, it looks like me because of the green ink, but if you ask me, that was just spite."

"What was spite?"

"Using my ink. Somebody deliberately used my ink to make it look like me. There's a lot of spite about here, Inspector."

The Inspector looked at him sharply.

"Now what exactly do you mean by a lot of spite about?"

But Nigel immediately drew back into his shell and became non-committal.

"I didn't mean anything really—just that when a lot of people are cooped up together, they get rather petty."

The next person on Inspector Sharpe's list was Leonard Bateson. Len Bateson was even less at his ease than Nigel, though it showed in a different way. He was suspicious and truculent.

"All right!" he burst out, after the first routine enquiries were concluded. "I poured out Celia's coffee and gave it to her. So what?"

"You gave her her after-dinner coffee—is that what you're saying, Mr. Bateson?"

"Yes. At least, I filled the cup up from the urn and put it down beside her and you can believe it or not, but there was no morphia in it."

"You saw her drink it?"

"No, I didn't actually see her drink it. We were all moving around and I got into an argument with someone just after that. I didn't notice when she drank it. There were other people round her."

"I see. In fact, what you are saying is that anybody could have dropped morphia into her coffee cup?"

"You try and put anything in anyone's cup! Everybody would see you."

"Not necessarily," said Sharpe.

Len burst out aggressively,

"What the hell do you think I wanted to poison the kid for? I'd nothing against her."

"I've not suggested that you did want to poison her."

"She took the stuff herself. She must have taken it herself. There's no other explanation."

"We might think so, if it weren't for that faked suicide note."

"Faked my hat! She wrote it, didn't she?"

"She wrote it as part of a letter, early that morning."

"Well—she could have torn a bit out and used it as a suicide note."

"Come now, Mr. Bateson. If you wanted to write a suicide note you'd write one. You wouldn't take a letter you'd written to somebody else and carefully tear out one particular phrase."

"I might do. People do all sorts of funny things."

"In that case, where is the rest of the letter?"

"How should I know? That's your business, not mine."

"I'm making it my business. You'd be well advised, Mr. Bateson, to answer my questions civilly."

"Well, what do you want to know? I didn't kill the girl, and I'd no motive for killing her."

"You liked her?"

Len said less agressively:

"I liked her very much. She was a nice kid. A bit dumb, but nice."

"You believed her when she owned up to having committed the thefts which had been worrying everyone for some time past?"

"Well, I believed her, of course, since she said so. But I must say it seemed odd."

"You didn't think it was a likely thing for her to do?"

"Well, no. Not really."

Leonard's truculence had subsided now that he was no longer on the defensive and was giving his mind to a problem which obviously intrigued him.

"She didn't seem to be the type of a kleptomaniac, if you know what I mean," he said. "Nor a thief either."

"And you can't think of any other reason for her having done what she did?"

"Other reason? What other reason could there be?"

"Well, she might have wanted to arouse the interest of Mr. Colin McNabb."

"That's a bit far-fetched, isn't it?"

"But it did arouse his interest."

"Yes, of course it did. Old Colin's absolutely dead keen on any kind of psychological abnormality."

"Well, then. If Celia Austin knew that . . ."

Len shook his head.

"You're wrong there. She wouldn't have been capable of thinking a thing like that out. Of planning it, I mean. She hadn't got the knowledge."

"You've got the knowledge, though, haven't you?"

"What do you mean?"

"I mean that, out of a purely kindly intention, you might have suggested something of the kind to her."

Len gave a short laugh.

"Think I'd do a damfool thing like that? You're crazy."

The Inspector shifted his ground.

"Do you think that Celia Austin spilled the ink over Elizabeth Johnston's papers or do you think someone else did it?"

"Someone else. Celia said she didn't do that and I believe her. Celia never got riled by Bess; not like some other people did."

"Who got riled by her—and why?"

"She ticked people off, you know." Len thought about it for a moment or two. "Anyone who made a rash statement. She'd look across the table and she'd say, in that precise way of hers, 'I'm afraid that is not borne out by the facts. It has been well established by statistics that . . .' Something of that kind. Well, it was riling, you know—especially to people who like making rash statements, like Nigel Chapman for instance."

"Ah yes. Nigel Chapman."

"And it was green ink, too."

"So you think it was Nigel who did it?"

"Well, it's possible, at least. He's a spiteful sort of cove, you know, and I think he might have a bit of racial feeling. About the only one of us who has."

"Can you think of anybody else who Miss Johnston annoyed with her exactitude and her habit of correction?"

"Well, Colin McNabb wasn't too pleased, now and again, and she got Jean Tomlinson's goat once or twice."

Sharpe asked a few more desultory questions but Len Bateson had nothing useful to add. Next Sharpe saw Valerie Hobhouse.

Valerie was cool, elegant and wary. She displayed much less nervousness than either of the men had done. She had been fond of Celia, she said. Celia was not particularly bright and it was rather pathetic the way she had set her heart on Colin McNabb.

"Do you think she was a kleptomaniac, Miss Hobhouse?"

"Well, I suppose so. I don't really know much about the subject."

"Do you think anyone had put her up to doing what she did?"

Valerie shrugged her shoulders.

"You mean in order to attract that pompous ass Colin?"

"You're very quick on the point, Miss Hobhouse. Yes, that's what I mean. You didn't suggest it to her yourself, I suppose?"

Valerie looked amused.

"Well, hardly, my dear man, considering that a particularly favourite scarf of mine was cut to ribbons. I'm not so altruistic as that."

"Do you think anybody else suggested it to her?"

"I should hardly think so. I should say it was just natural on her part."

"What do you mean by natural?"

"Well, I first had a suspicion that it was Celia when all the fuss happened about Sally's shoe. Celia was jealous of Sally. Sally Finch, I'm talking about. She's far and away the most attractive girl here and Colin paid her a fair amount of attention. So on the night of this party Sally's shoe disappears and she has to go in an old black dress and black shoes. There was Celia looking as smug as a cat that's swallowed cream about it. Mind you, I didn't suspect her of all these petty thievings of bracelets and compacts."

"Who did you think was responsible for those?"

Valerie shrugged her shoulders.

"Oh, I don't know. One of the cleaning women, I thought."

"And the slashed rucksack?"

"Was there a slashed rucksack? I'd forgotten. That seems very pointless."

"You've been here a good long time, haven't you, Miss Hobhouse?"

"Well, yes. I should say I'm probably the oldest inhabitant. That is to say, I've been here two years and a half, now."

"So you probably know more about this hostel than anybody else?"

"I should say so, yes."

"Have you any ideas of your own about Celia Austin's death? Any idea of the motive that underlay it?"

Valerie shook her head. Her face was serious now.

"No," she said. "It was a horrible thing to happen. I can't see anybody who could possibly have wanted Celia to die. She was a nice, harmless child, and she'd just got engaged to be married, and . . ."

"Yes. And?" the Inspector prompted.

"I wondered if that was why," said Valerie slowly. "Because

she'd got engaged. Because she was going to be happy. But that means, doesn't it, somebody—well—mad."

She said the word with a little shiver, and Inspector Sharpe looked at her thoughtfully.

"Yes," he said. "We can't quite rule out madness." He went on, "Have you any theory about the damage done to Elizabeth Johnston's notes and papers?"

"No. That was a spiteful thing, too. I don't believe for a moment that Celia would do a thing like that."

"Any idea who it could have been?"

"Well . . . Not a reasonable idea."

"But an unreasonable one?"

"You don't want to hear something that's just a hunch, do you, Inspector?"

"I'd like to hear a hunch very much. I'll accept it as such, and it'll only be between ourselves."

"Well, I may probably be quite wrong, but I've got a sort of idea that it was Patricia Lane's work."

"Indeed! Now you do surprise me, Miss Hobhouse. I shouldn't have thought of Patricia Lane. She seems a very well balanced, amiable young lady."

"I don't say she did do it. I just had a sort of idea she might have done."

"For what reason in particular?"

"Well, Patricia disliked Black Bess. Black Bess was always ticking off Patricia's beloved Nigel, putting him right, you know, when he made silly statements in the way he does sometimes."

"You think it was more likely to have been Patricia Lane than Nigel himself?"

"Oh, yes. I don't think Nigel would bother, and he'd certainly not go using his own pet brand of ink. He's got plenty of brains. But it's just the sort of stupid thing that Patricia would do without thinking that it might involve her precious Nigel as a suspect."

"Or again, it might be somebody who had a down on Nigel Chapman and wanted to suggest that it was his doing?"

"Yes, that's another possibility."

"Who dislikes Nigel Chapman?"

"Oh, well, Jean Tomlinson for one. And he and Len Bateson are always scrapping a good deal."

"Have you any ideas, Miss Hobhouse, how morphia could have been administered to Celia Austin?"

"I've been thinking and thinking. Of course, I suppose the coffee is the most obvious way. We were all milling around in the Common Room. Celia's coffee was on a small table near her and she always waited until her coffee was nearly cold before she drank it. I suppose anybody who had sufficient nerve could have dropped a tablet or something into her cup without being seen, but it would be rather a risk to take. I mean, it's the sort of thing that might be noticed quite easily."

"The morphia," said Inspector Sharpe, "was not in tablet form."

"What was it? Powder?"

"Yes."

Valerie frowned.

"That would be rather more difficult, wouldn't it?"

"Anything else besides coffee you can think of?"

"She sometimes had a glass of hot milk before she went to bed. I don't think she did that night, though."

"Can you describe to me exactly what happened that evening in the Common Room?"

"Well, as I say, we all sat about, talked; somebody turned the wireless on. Most of the boys, I think, went out. Celia went up to bed fairly early and so did Jean Tomlinson. Sally and I sat on there fairly late. I was writing letters and Sally was mugging over some notes. I rather think I was the last to go up to bed."

"It was just a usual evening, in fact?"

"Absolutely, Inspector."

"Thank you, Miss Hobhouse. Will you send Miss Lane to me now?"

Patricia Lane looked worried, but not apprehensive. Questions and answers elicited nothing very new. Asked about the damage to Elizabeth Johnston's papers Patricia said that she had no doubt that Celia had been responsible.

"But she denied it, Miss Lane, very vehemently."

"Well, of course," said Patricia. "She would. I think she was ashamed of having done it. But it fits in, doesn't it, with all the other things?"

"Do you know what I find about this case, Miss Lane? That nothing fits in very well."

"I suppose," said Patricia, flushing, "that you think it was Nigel

248

who messed up Bess's papers. Because of the ink. That's such absolute nonsense. I mean, Nigel wouldn't have used his own ink if he'd done a thing like that. He wouldn't be such a fool. But anyway, he wouldn't do it."

"He didn't always get on very well with Miss Johnston, did he?"

"Oh, she had an annoying manner sometimes, but he didn't really mind." Patricia Lane leaned forward earnestly. "I would like to try and make you understand one or two things, Inspector. About Nigel Chapman, I mean. You see, Nigel is really very much his own worst enemy. I'm the first to admit that he's got a very difficult manner. It prejudices people against him. He's rude and sarcastic and makes fun of people, and so he puts people's backs up and they think the worst of him. But really he's quite different from what he seems. He's one of those shy, rather unhappy people who really want to be liked but who, from a kind of spirit of contradiction, find themselves saying and doing the opposite to what they mean to say and do."

"Ah," said Inspector Sharpe. "Rather unfortunate for them, that."

"Yes, but they really can't help it, you know. It comes from having had an unfortunate childhood. Nigel had a very unhappy home life. His father was very harsh and severe and never understood him. And his father treated his mother very badly. After she died they had the most terrific quarrel and Nigel flung out of the house and his father said that he'd never give him a penny and he must get on as well as he could without any help from him. Nigel said he didn't want any help from his father; and wouldn't take it if it was offered. A small amount of money came to him under his mother's will, and he never wrote to his father or went near him again. Of course, I think that was a pity in a way, but there's no doubt that his father is a very unpleasant man. I don't wonder that that's made Nigel bitter and difficult to get on with. Since his mother died, he's never had anyone to care for him and look after him. His health's not been good though his mind is brilliant. He is handicapped in life and he just can't show himself as he really is."

Patricia Lane stopped. She was flushed and a little breathless as the result of her long earnest speech. Inspector Sharpe looked at her thoughtfully. He had come across many Patricia Lanes before. 'In love with the chap,' he thought to himself. 'Don't suppose he cares twopence for her, but probably accepts being mothered.

Father certainly sounds a cantankerous old cuss, but I daresay the mother was a foolish woman who spoilt her son and by doting on him, widened the breach between him and his father. I've seen enough of that kind of thing.' He wondered if Nigel Chapman had been attracted at all to Celia Austin. It seemed unlikely, but it might be so. 'And if so,' he thought, 'Patricia Lane might have bitterly resented the fact.' Resented it enough to wish to do Celia an injury? Resented it enough to do murder? Surely not—and in any case, the fact that Celia had got engaged to Colin McNabb would surely wash that out as a possible motive for murder. He dismissed Patricia Lane and asked for Jean Tomlinson.

CHAPTER 10

MISS TOMLINSON WAS a severe-looking young woman of twenty-seven with fair hair, regular features and a rather pursed-up mouth. She sat down and said primly,

"Yes, Inspector? What can I do for you?"

"I wonder if you can help us at all, Miss Tomlinson, about this very tragic matter."

"It's shocking. Really quite shocking," said Jean. "It was bad enough when we thought Celia had committed suicide, but now that it's supposed to be murder . . ." She stopped and shook her head, sadly.

"We are fairly sure that she did not poison herself," said Sharpe. "You know where the poison came from?"

Jean nodded.

"I gather it came from St. Catherine's Hospital, where she works. But surely that makes it seem more like suicide?"

"It was intended to, no doubt," said the Inspector.

"But who else could possibly have got that poison except Celia?"

"Quite a lot of people," said Inspector Sharpe, "if they were determined to do so. Even you, yourself, Miss Tomlinson," he said, "might have managed to help yourself to it if you had wished to do so."

"Really, Inspector Sharpe!" Jean's tones were sharp with indignation.

"Well, you visited the Dispensary fairly often, didn't you, Miss Tomlinson?"

"I went in there to see Mildred Carey, yes. But naturally I would never have dreamed of tampering with the poison cupboard."

"But you could have done so?"

"I certainly couldn't have done anything of the kind!"

"Oh, come now, Miss Tomlinson. Say that your friend was busy packing up the ward baskets and the other girl was at the Outpatients window. There are frequent times when there are only two dispensers in the front room. You could have wandered casually round the back of the shelves of bottles that run across the middle of the floor. You could have nipped a bottle out of the cupboard and into your pocket, and neither of the two dispensers would have dreamed of what you had done."

"I resent what you say very much, Inspector Sharpe. It's—it's a—disgraceful accusation."

"But it's not an accusation, Miss Tomlinson. It's nothing of the kind. You mustn't misunderstand me. You said to me that it wasn't possible for you to do such a thing, and I'm trying to show you that it was possible. I'm not suggesting for a moment that you did do so. After all," he added, "why should you?"

"Quite so. You don't seem to realise, Inspector Sharpe, that I was a friend of Celia's."

"Quite a lot of people get poisoned by their friends. There's a certain question we have to ask ourselves sometimes. 'When is a friend not a friend?'"

"There was no disagreement between me and Celia; nothing of the kind. I liked her very much."

"Had you any reason to suspect it was she who had been responsible for these thefts in the house?"

"No, indeed. I was never so surprised in my life. I always thought Celia had high principles. I wouldn't have dreamed of her doing such a thing."

"Of course," said Sharpe, watching her carefully, "kleptomaniacs can't really help themselves, can they?"

Jean Tomlinson's lips pursed themselves together even more closely. Then she opened them and spoke.

"I can't say I can quite subscribe to that idea, Inspector Sharpe. I'm old-fashioned in my views and believe that stealing is stealing."

"You think that Celia stole things because, frankly, she wanted to take them?"

"Certainly I do."

"Plain dishonest, in fact?"

"I'm afraid so."

"Ah!" said Inspector Sharpe, shaking his head. "That's bad."

"Yes, it's always upsetting when you feel you're disappointed in anyone."

"There was a question, I understand, of our being called in— the police, I mean."

"Yes. That would have been the right thing to do, in my opinion."

"Perhaps you think it ought to have been done anyway?"

"I think it would have been the right thing. Yes, I don't think, you know, people ought to be allowed to get away with these things."

"With calling oneself a kleptomaniac when one is really a thief, do you mean?"

"Well, more or less, yes—that is what I mean."

"Instead of which everything was ending happily and Miss Austin had wedding bells ahead."

"Of course, one isn't surprised at anything Colin McNabb does," said Jean Tomlinson viciously. "I'm sure he's an atheist and a most disbelieving, mocking, unpleasant young man. He's rude to everybody. It's my opinion that he's a Communist!"

"Ah!" said Inspector Sharpe. "Bad!" He shook his head.

"He backed up Celia, I think, because he hasn't got any proper feeling about property. He probably thinks everyone should help themselves to everything they want."

"Still, at any rate," said Inspector Sharpe, "Miss Austin did own up."

"After she was found out. Yes," said Jean, sharply.

"Who found her out?"

"That Mr—what-was-his-name . . . Poirot, who came."

"But why do you think he found her out, Miss Tomlinson? He didn't say so. He just advised calling in the police."

"He must have shown her that he knew. She obviously knew the game was up and rushed off to confess."

"What about the ink on Elizabeth Johnston's papers? Did she confess to that?"

"I really don't know. I suppose so."

"You suppose wrong," said Sharpe. "She denied most vehemently that she had anything to do with that."

"Well, perhaps that may be so. I must say it doesn't seem very likely."

"You think it is more likely that it was Nigel Chapman?"

"No, I don't think Nigel would do that either. I think it's much more likely to be Mr. Akibombo."

"Really? Why should he do it?"

"Jealousy. All these coloured people are very jealous of each other and very hysterical."

"That's interesting, Miss Tomlinson. When was the last time you saw Celia Austin?"

"After dinner on Friday night."

"Who went up to bed first? Did she or did you?"

"I did."

"You did not go to her room or see her after you'd left the Common Room?"

"No."

"And you've no idea who could have introduced morphia into her coffee?—if it was given that way?"

"No idea at all."

"You never saw this morphia lying about the house or in anyone's room?"

"No. No, I don't think so."

"You don't think so? What do you mean by that, Miss Tomlinson?"

"Well, I just wondered. There was that silly bet, you know."

"What bet?"

"One—oh, two or three of the boys were arguing—"

"What were they arguing about?"

"Murder, and ways of doing it. Poisoning in particular."

"Who was concerned in the discussion?"

"Well, I think Colin and Nigel started it, and then Len Bateson chipped in and Patricia was there too—"

"Can you remember, as closely as possible, what was said on that occasion—how the argument went?"

Jean Tomlinson reflected a few moments.

"Well, it started, I think, with a discussion on murdering by poisoning, saying that the difficulty was to get hold of the poison, that the murderer was usually traced by either the sale of the poison or having an opportunity to get it, and Nigel said that wasn't at all necessary. He said that he could think of three distinct ways by which anyone could get hold of poison, and nobody would ever know they had it. Len Bateson said then that he was talking through his hat. Nigel said no he wasn't, and he was quite prepared to prove it. Pat said that of course Nigel was quite right. She said that either Len or Colin could probably help themselves to poison any time they liked from a hospital, and so could Celia, she said. And Nigel said that wasn't what he meant at all. He said it would be noticed if Celia took anything from the Dispensary. Sooner or later they'd look for it and find it gone. And Pat said no, not if she took the bottle and emptied some stuff out and filled it up with something else. Colin laughed then and said there'd be very serious complaints from the patients one of these days, in that case. But Nigel said of course he didn't mean special opportunities. He said that he himself, who hadn't got any particular access, either as a doctor or dispenser, could jolly well get three different kinds of poison by three different methods. Len Bateson said, 'All right, then, but what are your methods?' and Nigel said, 'I shan't tell you, now, but I'm prepared to bet you that within three weeks I can produce samples of three deadly poisons here,' and Len Bateson said he'd bet him a fiver he couldn't do it."

"Well?" said Inspector Sharpe, when Jean stopped.

"Well, nothing more came of it, I think, for some time and then, one evening, in the Common Room, Nigel said, 'Now then, chaps, look here—I'm as good as my word,' and he threw down three things on the table. He had a tube of hyoscine tablets, and a bottle of tincture digitalin and a tiny bottle of morphine tartrate."

The Inspector said sharply,

"Morphine tartrate. Any label on it?"

"Yes, it had St. Catherine's Hospital on it. I do remember that because, naturally, it caught my eye."

"And the others?"

"I didn't notice. They were not hospital stores, I should say."

"What happened next?"

"Well, of course, there was a lot of talk and jawing, and Len Bateson said, 'Come now, if you'd done a murder this would be traced to you soon enough,' and Nigel said, 'Not a bit of it. I'm a layman. I've no connection with any clinic or hospital and nobody will connect me for one moment with these. I didn't buy them over the counter,' and Colin McNabb took his pipe out of his teeth and said, 'No, you'd certainly not be able to do that. There's no chemist would sell you those three things without a doctor's prescription.' Anyway, they argued a bit but in the end Len said he'd pay up. He said, 'I can't do it now, because I'm a bit short of cash, but there's no doubt about it; Nigel's proved his point,' and then he said, 'What are we going to do with the guilty spoils?' Nigel grinned and said we'd better get rid of them before any accidents occurred, so they emptied out the tube and threw the tablets on the fire and emptied out the powder from the morphine tartrate and threw that on the fire too. The tincture of digitalis they poured down the lavatory."

"And the bottles?"

"I don't know what happened to the bottles . . . I should think they probably were just thrown into the waste paper basket."

"But the poison itself was destroyed?"

"Yes. I'm sure of that. I saw it."

"And that was—when?"

"About, oh just over a fortnight ago I think."

"I see. Thank you, Miss Tomlinson."

Jean lingered, clearly wanting to be told more.

"D'you think it might be important?"

"It might be. One can't tell."

Inspector Sharpe remained brooding for a few moments. Then he had Nigel Chapman in again.

"I've just had a rather interesting statement from Miss Jean Tomlinson," he said.

"Ah! Who's dear Jean been poisoning your mind against? Me?"

"She's been talking about poison, and in connection with you, Mr. Chapman."

255

"Poison and me? What on earth?"

"Do you deny that some weeks ago you had a wager with Mr. Bateson about methods of obtaining poison in some way that could not be traced to you?"

"Oh, that!" Nigel was suddenly enlightened. "Yes, of course! Funny I never thought of that. I don't even remember Jean being there. But you don't think it could have any possible significance, do you?"

"Well, one doesn't know. You admit the fact, then?"

"Oh yes, we were arguing on the subject. Colin and Len were being very superior and high-handed about it so I told them that with a little ingenuity anyone could get hold of a suitable supply of poison—in fact I said I could think of three distinct ways of doing it, and I'd prove my point, I said, by putting them into practice."

"Which you then proceeded to do?"

"Which I then proceeded to do, Inspector."

"And what were those three methods, Mr. Chapman?"

Nigel put his head a little on one side.

"Aren't you asking me to incriminate myself?" he said. "Surely you ought to warn me?"

"It hasn't come to warning you yet, Mr. Chapman, but, of course, there's no need for you to incriminate yourself, as you put it. In fact you're perfectly entitled to refuse my questions if you like to do so."

"I don't know that I want to refuse." Nigel considered for a moment or two, a slight smile playing round his lips.

"Of course," he said, "what I did was, no doubt, against the law. You could haul me in for it if you liked. On the other hand, this is a murder case and if it's got any bearing on poor little Celia's death I suppose I ought to tell you."

"That would certainly be the sensible point of view to take."

"All right then. I'll talk."

"What were these three methods?"

"Well." Nigel leant back in his chair. "One's always reading in the papers, isn't one, about doctors losing dangerous drugs from a car? People are being warned about it?"

"Yes."

"Well, it occurred to me that one very simple method would be to go down to the country, follow a G.P. about on his rounds,

256

when occasion offered—just open the car, look in the doctor's case, and extract what you wanted. You see, in these country districts, the doctor doesn't always take his case into the house. It depends what sort of patient he's going to see."

"Well?"

"Well, that's all. That's to say that's all for method number one. I had to sleuth three doctors until I had found a suitably careless one. When I did, it was simplicity itself. The car was left outside a farmhouse in a rather lonely spot. I opened the door, looked at the case, took out a tube of hyoscine hydrobromide, and that was that."

"Ah! And method number two?"

"That entailed just a little pumping of dear Celia, as a matter of fact. She was quite unsuspicious. I told you she was a stupid girl, she had no idea what I was doing. I simply talked a bit about the mumbo jumbo Latin of doctors' prescriptions, and asked her to write me out a prescription in the way a doctor writes it, for tincture digitalin. She obliged quite unsuspecting. All I had to do after that was to find a doctor in the classified directory, living in a far off district of London, add his initials or slightly illegible signature. I then took it to a chemist in a busy part of London, who would not be likely to be familiar with that particular doctor's signature, and I received the prescription made up without any difficulty at all. Digitalin is prescribed in quite large quantities for heart cases and I had written out the prescription on hotel notepaper."

"Very ingenious," said Inspector Sharpe, drily.

"I am incriminating myself! I can hear it in your voice."

"And the third method?"

Nigel did not reply at once. Then he said,

"Look here. What exactly am I letting myself in for?"

"The theft of drugs from an unlocked car is larceny," said Inspector Sharpe. "Forging a prescription . . ."

Nigel interrupted him.

"Not exactly forging, is it? I mean, I didn't obtain money by it, and it wasn't actually an imitation of any doctor's signature. I mean, if I write a prescription and write H. R. James on it, you can't say I'm forging any particular Dr. James's name, can you?" He went on with rather a wry smile. "You see what I mean? I'm sticking my neck out. If you like to turn nasty over this—well—I'm obviously for it. On the other hand, if . . ."

"Yes, Mr. Chapman, on the other hand?"

Nigel said with a sudden passion,

"I don't like murder. It's a beastly, horrible thing. Celia, poor little devil, didn't deserve to be murdered. I want to help. But does it help? I can't see that it does. Telling you my peccadilloes, I mean."

"The police have a good deal of latitude, Mr. Chapman. It's up to them to look upon certain happenings as a lighthearted prank of an irresponsible nature. I accept your assurance that you want to help in the solving of this girl's murder. Now please go on, and tell me about your third method."

"Well," said Nigel, "we're coming fairly near the bone now. It was a bit more risky than the other two, but at the same time it was a great deal more fun. You see, I'd been to visit Celia once or twice in her Dispensary. I knew the lay of the land there . . ."

"So you were able to pinch the bottle out of the cupboard?"

"No, no, nothing as simple as that. That wouldn't have been fair from my point of view. And, incidentally, if it had been a real murder—that is, if I had been stealing the poison for the purpose of murder—it would probably be remembered that I had been there. Actually, I hadn't been in Celia's Dispensary for about six months. No, I knew that Celia always went into the back room at eleven fifteen for what you might call 'elevenses,' that is, a cup of coffee and a biscuit. The girls went in turn, two at a time. There was a new girl there who had only just come and she certainly wouldn't know me by sight. So what I did was this. I strolled into the Dispensary with a white coat on and a stethoscope round my neck. There was only the new girl there and she was busy at the Outpatients' hatch. I strolled in, went along to the poison cupboard, took out a bottle, strolled round the end of the partition, said to the girl, 'What strength adrenalin do you keep?' She told me and I nodded, then I asked her if she had a couple of veganin as I had a terrific hangover. I swallowed them down and strolled out again. She never had the least suspicion that I wasn't somebody's houseman or a medical student. It was child's play. Celia never even knew I'd been there."

"A stethoscope," said Inspector Sharpe curiously. "Where did you get a stethoscope?"

258

Nigel grinned suddenly.

"It was Len Bateson's," he said. "I pinched it."

"From this house?"

"Yes."

"So that explains the theft of the stethoscope. That was not Celia's doing."

"Good Lord no! Can't see a kleptomaniac stealing a stethoscope, can you?"

"What did you do with it afterwards?"

"Well, I had to pawn it," said Nigel apologetically.

"Wasn't that a little hard on Bateson?"

"Very hard on him. But without explaining my methods, which I didn't mean to do, I couldn't tell him about it. However," added Nigel cheerfully, "I took him out not long after and gave him a hell of a party one evening."

"You're a very irresponsible young man," said Inspector Sharpe.

"You should have seen their faces," said Nigel, his grin widening, "when I threw down those three lethal preparations on the table and told them I had managed to pinch them without anybody being wise as to who took them."

"What you're telling me is," said the Inspector, "that you had three means of poisoning someone by three different poisons and that in each case the poison could not have been traced to you."

Nigel nodded.

"That's fair enough," he said. "And given the circumstances it's not a very pleasant thing to admit. But the point is, that the poisons were all disposed of at least a fortnight ago or longer."

"That is what you think, Mr. Chapman, but it may not really be so."

Nigel stared at him.

"What do you mean?"

"You had these things in your possession, how long?"

Nigel considered.

"Well, the tube of hyoscine about ten days, I suppose. The morphine tartrate, about four days. The tincture digitalin I'd only got that very afternoon."

"And where did you keep these things—the hyoscine hydrobromide and the morphine tartrate, that is to say?"

"In the drawer of my chest-of-drawers, pushed to the back under my socks."

"Did anyone know you had it there?"

"No. No, I'm sure they didn't."

There had been, however, a faint hesitation in his voice which Inspector Sharpe noticed, but for the moment he did not press the point.

"Did you tell anyone what you were doing? Your methods? The way you were going about these things?"

"No. At least—no, I didn't."

"You said 'at least,' Mr. Chapman."

"Well, I didn't actually. As a matter of fact, I was going to tell Pat, then I thought she wouldn't approve. She's very strict, Pat is, so I fobbed her off."

"You didn't tell her about stealing the stuff from the doctor's car, or the prescription, or the morphia from the hospital?"

"Actually, I told her afterwards about the digitalin; that I'd written a prescription and got a bottle from the chemist, and about masquerading as a doctor at the hospital. I'm sorry to say Pat wasn't amused. I didn't tell her about pinching things from a car. I thought she'd go up in smoke."

"Did you tell her you were going to destroy this stuff after you'd won the bet?"

"Yes. She was all worried and het up about it. Started to insist I take the things back or something like that."

"That course of action never occurred to you yourself?"

"Good Lord no! That would have been fatal; it would have landed me in no end of a row. No, we three just chucked the stuff on the fire and poured it down the Lou and that was that. No harm done."

"You say that, Mr. Chapman, but it's quite possible that harm was done."

"How can it have been, if the stuff was chucked away as I tell you?"

"Has it ever occurred to you, Mr. Chapman, that someone might have seen where you put those things, or found them perhaps, and that someone might have emptied morphia out of the bottle and replaced it with something else?"

"Good Lord no!" Nigel stared at him. "I never thought of anything of that kind. I don't believe it."

"But it's a possibility, Mr. Chapman."

"But nobody could possibly have known."

"I should say," said the Inspector, drily, "that in a place of this kind a great deal more is known than you yourself might believe possible."

"Snooping, you mean?"

"Yes."

"Perhaps you're right there."

"Which of the students might normally, at any time, be in your room?"

"Well, I share it with Len Bateson. Most of the men here have been in it now and again. Not the girls, of course. The girls aren't supposed to come to the bedroom floors on our side of the house. Propriety. Pure living."

"They're not supposed to, but they might do so, I suppose?"

"Anyone might," said Nigel. "In the daytime. The afternoon, for instance, there's nobody about."

"Does Miss Lane ever come to your room?"

"I hope you don't mean that the way it sounds, Inspector. Pat comes to my room sometimes to replace some socks she's been darning. Nothing more than that."

Leaning forward Inspector Sharpe said,

"You do realise, Mr. Chapman, that the person who could most easily have taken some of that poison out of the bottle and substituted something else for it, was yourself?"

Nigel looked at him, his face suddenly hard and haggard.

"Yes," he said. "I've seen that just a minute and a half ago. I could have done just exactly that. But I'd no reason on earth for putting that girl out of the way, Inspector, and I didn't do it. Still, there it is—I quite realise that you've only got my word for it."

CHAPTER 11

THE STORY of the bet and the disposal of the poison was confirmed by Len Bateson and by Colin McNabb. Sharpe retained Colin McNabb after the others had gone.

"I don't want to cause you more pain than I can help, Mr. McNabb," he said. "I can realise what it means to you for your fiancée to have been poisoned on the very night of your engagement."

"There'll be no need to go into that aspect of it," said Colin McNabb, his face immovable. "You'll not need to concern yourself with my feelings. Just ask me any questions you like which you think may be useful to you."

"It was your considered opinion that Celia Austin's behaviour had a psychological origin?"

"There's no doubt about it at all," said Colin McNabb. "If you'd like me to go into the theory of the thing . . ."

"No, no," said Inspector Sharpe, hastily. "I'm taking your word for it as a student of psychology."

"Her childhood had been particularly unfortunate. It had set up an emotional block. . . ."

"Quite so, quite so." Inspector Sharpe was desperately anxious to avoid hearing the story of yet another unhappy childhood. Nigel's had been quite enough.

"You had been attracted to her for some time?"

"I would not say precisely that," said Colin, considering the matter conscientiously. "These things sometimes surprise you by the way they dawn upon you suddenly, like. Subconsciously no doubt, I had been attracted, but I was not aware of the fact. Since it was not my intention to marry young, I had no doubt set up a considerable resistance to the idea in my conscious mind."

"Yes. Just so. Celia Austin was happy in her engagement to

you? I mean, she expressed no doubts? Uncertainties? There was nothing she felt she ought to tell you?"

"She made a very full confession of all she'd been doing. There was nothing more in her mind to worry her."

"And you were planning to get married—when?"

"Not for a considerable time. I'm not in a position, at the moment, to support a wife."

"Had Celia any enemy here? Anyone who did not like her?"

"I can hardly believe so. I've given that point of view a great deal of thought, Inspector. Celia was well liked here. I'd say, myself, it was not a personal matter at all which brought about her end."

"What do you mean by 'not a personal matter'?"

"I do not wish to be very precise at the moment. It's only a vague kind of idea I have and I'm not clear about it myself."

From that position the Inspector could not budge him.

The last two students to be interviewed were Sally Finch and Elizabeth Johnston. The Inspector took Sally Finch first.

Sally was an attractive girl with a mop of red hair and eyes that were bright and intelligent. After routine enquiries Sally Finch suddenly took the initiative.

"D'you know what I'd like to do, Inspector? I'd like to tell you just what I think. I personally. There's something all wrong about this house, something very wrong indeed. I'm sure of that."

"You mean because Celia Austin was poisoned?"

"No, I mean before that. I've been feeling it for some time. I didn't like the things that were going on here. I didn't like that rucksack which was slashed about and I didn't like Valerie's scarf being cut to pieces. I didn't like Black Bess's notes being covered with ink. I was going to get out of here and get out quick. That's what I still mean to do, as soon, that is, as you let us go."

"You mean you're afraid of something, Miss Finch?"

Sally nodded her head.

"Yes. I'm afraid. There's something or someone here who's pretty ruthless. The whole place isn't—well, how shall I put it? —it isn't what it seems. No, no, Inspector, I don't mean Communists. I can see that just trembling on your lips. It's not Communists I mean. Perhaps it isn't even criminal. I don't know. But I'll bet you anything you like that awful old woman knows about it all."

"What old woman? You don't mean Mrs. Hubbard?"

"No. Not Ma Hubbard. She's a dear. I mean old Nicoletis. That old she-wolf."

"That's interesting, Miss Finch. Can you be more definite? About Mrs. Nicoletis, I mean."

Sally shook her head.

"No. That's just what I can't be. All I can tell you is she gives me the creeps every time I pass her. Something queer is going on here, Inspector."

"I wish you could be a little more definite."

"So do I. You'll be thinking I'm fanciful. Well, perhaps I am, but other people feel it too. Akibombo does. He's scared. I believe Black Bess does, too, but she wouldn't let on. And I think, Inspector, that Celia knew something about it."

"Knew something about what?"

"That's just it. What? But there were things she said. Said that last day. About clearing everything up. She had owned up to her part in what was going on, but she sort of hinted that there were other things she knew about and she wanted to get them cleared up too. I think she knew something, Inspector, about someone. That's the reason I think she was killed."

"But if it was something as serious as that . . ."

Sally interrupted him.

"I'd say that she had no idea how serious it was. She wasn't bright, you know. She was pretty dumb. She got hold of something but she'd no idea that the something she'd got hold of was dangerous. Anyway, that's my hunch for what it's worth."

"I see. Thank you. . . . Now the last time you saw Celia Austin was in the Common Room after dinner last night, is that right?"

"That's right. At least, actually, I saw her after that."

"You saw her after that? Where? In her room?"

"No. When I went up to bed she was going out of the front door just as I came out of the Common Room."

"Going out of the front door? Out of the house, do you mean?"

"Yes."

"That's rather surprising. Nobody else has suggested that."

"I daresay they didn't know. She certainly said good night and that she was going up to bed, and if I hadn't seen her I would have assumed that she had gone up to bed."

"Whereas actually, she went upstairs, put on some outdoor things and then left the house. Is that right?"

Sally nodded.

"And I think she was going out to meet someone."

"I see. Someone from outside. Or could it have been one of the students?"

"Well it's my hunch that it would be one of the students. You see, if she wanted to speak to somebody privately, there was nowhere very well she could do it in the house. Someone might have suggested that she come out and meet them somewhere outside."

"Have you any idea when she got in again?"

"No idea whatever."

"Would Geronimo know, the manservant?"

"He'd know if she came in after eleven o'clock because that's the time he bolts and chains the door. Up to that time anyone can get in with their own key."

"Do you know exactly what time it was when you saw her going out of the house?"

"I'd say it was about—ten. Perhaps a little past ten, but not much."

"I see. Thank you, Miss Finch, for what you've told me."

Last of all the Inspector talked to Elizabeth Johnston. He was at once impressed with the quiet capability of the girl. She answered his questions with intelligent decision and then waited for him to proceed.

"Celia Austin," he said, "protested vehemently that it was not she who damaged your papers, Miss Johnston. Do you believe her?"

"I do not think Celia did that. No."

"You don't know who did?"

"The obvious answer is Nigel Chapman. But it seems to me a little too obvious. Nigel is intelligent. He would not use his own ink."

"And if not Nigel, who then?"

"That is more difficult. But I think Celia knew who it was— or at least guessed."

"Did she tell you so?"

"Not in so many words; but she came to my room on the evening of the day she died, before going down to dinner. She came to tell me that though she was responsible for the thefts she had not sabotaged my work. I told her that I accepted that assurance. I asked her if she knew who had done so?"

"And what did she say?"

"She said," Elizabeth paused a moment, as though to be sure of the accuracy of what she was about to say. "She said, '*I can't really be sure, because I don't see why. . . . It might have been a mistake or an accident. . . . I'm sure whoever did it is very unhappy about it, and would really like to own up.*' Celia went on, '*There are some things I don't understand, like the electric light bulbs the day the police came.*'"

Sharpe interrupted.

"What's this about the police and electric light bulbs?"

"I don't know. All Celia said was: 'I didn't take them out.' And then she said: 'I wondered if it had anything to do with the passport?' I said, 'What passport are you talking about?' And she said: 'I think someone might have a forged passport.'"

The Inspector was silent for a moment or two.

Here at last some vague pattern seemed to be taking shape. A passport. . . .

He asked, "What more did she say?"

"Nothing more. She just said: 'Anyway I shall know more about it tomorrow.'"

"She said that, did she? 'I shall know more about it tomorrow.' That's a very significant remark, Miss Johnston."

"Yes."

The Inspector was again silent as he reflected.

Something about a passport—and a visit from the police. . . . Before coming to Hickory Road, he had carefully looked up the files. A fairly close eye was kept on hostels which housed foreign students. 26 Hickory Road had a good record. Such details as there were, were meagre and unsuggestive. A West African student wanted by the Sheffield police for living on a woman's earnings; the student in question had been at Hickory Road for a few days and had then gone elsewhere, and had in due course been gathered in and since deported. There had been a routine check of all hostels and boarding houses for a Eurasian 'wanted to assist the police' in the murder of a publican's wife near Cambridge. That had been cleared up when the young man in question had walked into the police station at Hull and had given himself up for the crime. There had been an inquiry into a student's distribution of subversive pamphlets. All these occurrences had taken place some time ago and could not possibly have any connection with the death of Celia Austin.

He sighed and looked up to find Elizabeth Johnston's dark intelligent eyes watching him.

On an impulse, he said, "Tell me, Miss Johnston, have you ever had a feeling—an impression—of something wrong about this place?"

She looked surprised.

"In what way—wrong?"

"I couldn't really say. I'm thinking of something Miss Sally Finch said to me."

"Oh—Sally Finch!"

There was an intonation in her voice which he found hard to place. He felt interested and went on:

"Miss Finch seemed to me a good observer, both shrewd and practical. She was very insistent on there being something—odd about this place—though she found it difficult to define just what it was."

Elizabeth said sharply,

"That is her American way of thought. They are all the same, these Americans, nervous, apprehensive, suspecting every kind of foolish thing! Look at the fools they make of themselves with their witch hunts, their hysterical spy mania, their obsession over communism. Sally Finch is typical."

The Inspector's interest grew. So Elizabeth disliked Sally Finch. Why? Because Sally was an American? Or did Elizabeth dislike Americans merely because Sally Finch was an American, and had she some reason of her own for disliking the attractive red-head? Perhaps it was just simple female jealousy.

He resolved to try a line of approach that he had sometimes found useful. He said smoothly,

"As you may appreciate, Miss Johnston, in an establishment like this, the level of intelligence varies a great deal. Some people —most people, we just ask for facts. But when we come across someone with a high level of intelligence—"

He paused. The inference was flattering. Would she respond?

After a brief pause, she did.

"I think I understand what you mean, Inspector. The intellectual level here is not, as you say, very high. Nigel Chapman has a certain quickness of intellect, but his mind is shallow. Leonard Bateson is a plodder—no more. Valerie Hobhouse has a good quality of mind, but her outlook is commercial, and she's too lazy to use her brains on anything worth while. What you want is the detachment of a trained mind."

"Such as yours, Miss Johnston."

She accepted the tribute without a protest. He realised, with some interest, that behind her modest pleasant manner, here was a young woman who was positively arrogant in her appraisement of her own qualities.

"I'm inclined to agree with your estimate of your fellow students, Miss Johnston. Chapman is clever but childish. Valerie Hobhouse has brains but a *blasé* attitude to life. You, as you say, have a trained mind. That's why I'd value your views—the views of a powerful detached intellect."

For a moment he was afraid he had overdone it, but he need have had no fears.

"There is nothing wrong about this place, Inspector. Pay no attention to Sally Finch. This is a decent well run hostel. I am certain that you will find no trace here of any subversive activities."

Inspector Sharpe felt a little surprised.

"It wasn't really subversive activities I was thinking about."

"Oh—I see—" She was a little taken aback. "I was linking up what Celia said about a passport. But looking at it impartially and weighing up all the evidence, it seems quite certain to me that the reason for Celia's death was what I should express as a private one—some sex complication, perhaps. I'm sure it had nothing to do with what I might call the hostel as a hostel, or anything 'going on' here. Nothing, I am sure, is going on. I should be aware of the fact if it were so, my perceptions are very keen."

"I see. Well, thank you, Miss Johnston. You've been very kind and helpful."

Elizabeth Johnston went out. Inspector Sharpe sat staring at the closed door and Sergeant Cobb had to speak to him twice before he roused himself.

"Eh?"

"I said that's the lot, sir."

"Yes, and what have we got? Precious little. But I'll tell you one thing, Cobb. I'm coming back here tomorrow with a search warrant. We'll go away talking pretty now and they'll think it's all over. But there's something going on in this place. Tomorrow I'll turn it upside down—not so easy when you don't know what you're looking for, but there's a chance that I'll find something to give me a clue. That's a very interesting girl who just went out. She's got the ego of a Napoleon, and I strongly suspect that she knows something."

CHAPTER **12**

HERCULE POIROT, at work upon his correspondence, paused in the middle of a sentence that he was dictating. Miss Lemon looked up questioningly.

"Yes, M. Poirot?"

"My mind wanders!" Poirot waved a hand. "After all, this letter is not important. Be so kind, Miss Lemon, as to get me your sister upon the telephone."

"Yes, M. Poirot."

A few moments later Poirot crossed the room and took the receiver from his secretary's hand.

"'Allo!" he said.

"Yes, M. Poirot?"

Mrs. Hubbard sounded rather breathless.

"I trust, Mrs. Hubbard, that I am not disturbing you?"

"I'm past being disturbed," said Mrs. Hubbard.

"There have been agitations, yes?" Poirot asked delicately.

"That's a very nice way of putting it, M. Poirot. That's exactly what they have been. Inspector Sharpe finished questioning all the students yesterday, and then he came back with a search warrant today and I've got Mrs. Nicoletis on my hands with raving hysterics."

Poirot clucked his tongue sympathetically.

Then he said, "It is just a little question I have to ask. You sent me a list of those things that had disappeared—and other queer happenings—what I have to ask is this, did you write that list in chronological order?"

"You mean?"

"I mean, were the things written down exactly in the order of their disappearance?"

"No, they weren't. I'm sorry—I just put them down as I thought of them. I'm so sorry if I've misled you."

"I should have asked you before," said Poirot. "But it did not strike me then as important. I have your list here. It begins, one evening shoe, bracelet, powder compact, diamond ring, cigarette lighter, stethoscope, and so on. But you say that that was not the order of disappearance?"

"No."

"Can you remember now, or would it be too difficult for you, what was the proper order?"

"Well, I'm not sure if I could now, M. Poirot. You see it's all some time ago. I should have to think it out. Actually, after I had talked with my sister and knew I was coming to see you, I made a list, and I should say that I put it down in the order of the things as I remembered them. I mean, the evening shoe because it was so peculiar; and then the bracelet and the powder compact and the cigarette lighter and the diamond ring because they were all rather important things and looked as though we had a genuine thief at work; and then I remembered the other more unimportant things later and added them. I mean the boracic and the electric light bulbs and the rucksack. They weren't really important and I only really thought of them as a kind of afterthought."

"I see," said Poirot. "Yes, I see . . . Now what I would ask of you, Madame, is to sit down now, when you have the leisure, that is . . ."

"I daresay when I've got Mrs. Nicoletis to bed with a sedative and calmed down Geronimo and Maria, I shall have a little time. What is it you want me to do?"

"Sit down and try to put down, as nearly as you can, the chronological order in which the various incidents occurred."

"Certainly, M. Poirot. The rucksack, I believe, was the first and the electric light bulbs—which I really didn't think had any connection with the other things—and then the bracelet and the compact, no—the evening shoe. But there, you don't want to hear me speculate about it. I'll put them down as best I can."

"Thank you, Madame. I shall be much obliged to you."

Poirot hung up the phone.

"I am vexed with myself," he said to Miss Lemon. "I have departed from the principles of order and method. I should have made quite sure from the start, the exact order in which these thefts occurred."

"Dear, dear," said Miss Lemon, mechanically. "Are you going to finish these letters now, M. Poirot?"

But once again Poirot waved her impatiently away.

ii

On arrival back at Hickory Road with a search warrant on Saturday morning, Inspector Sharpe had demanded an interview with Mrs. Nicoletis who always came on Saturdays to do accounts with Mrs. Hubbard. He had explained what he was about to do.

Mrs. Nicoletis protested with vigour.

"But it is an insult, that!—My students they will leave—they will all leave. I shall be ruined . . ."

"No, no, Madame. I'm sure they will be sensible— After all, this is a case of murder."

"It is not murder—it is suicide."

"And I'm sure once I've explained, no one will object . . ."

Mrs. Hubbard put in a soothing word.

"I'm sure," she said, "everyone will be sensible—except," she added thoughtfully, "perhaps Mr. Ahmed Ali and Mr. Chandra Lal."

"Pah!" said Mrs. Nicoletis. "Who cares about them?"

"Thank you, Madame," said the Inspector. "Then I'll make a start here, in your sitting room."

An immediate and violent protest came from Mrs. Nicoletis at the suggestion.

"You search where you please," she said, "but here, no! I refuse."

"I'm sorry, Mrs. Nicoletis, but I have to go through the house from top to bottom."

"That is right, yes, but not in my room. I am above the law."

"No one's above the law. I'm afraid I shall have to ask you to stand aside."

"It is an outrage," Mrs. Nicoletis screamed with fury. "You are officious busybodies. I will write to everyone. I will write to my Member of Parliament. I will write to the papers."

"Write to anyone you please, Madame," said Inspector Sharpe, "I'm going to search this room."

He started straight away upon the bureau. A large carton of confectionery, a mass of papers, and a large variety of assorted junk rewarded his search. He moved from there to a cupboard in the corner of the room.

"This is locked. Can I have the key, please?"

"Never!" screamed Mrs. Nicoletis. "Never, never, never shall you have the key! Beast and pig of a policeman, I spit at you. I spit! I spit! I spit!"

"You might just as well give me the key," said Inspector Sharpe. "If not, I shall simply prise the door open."

"I will not give you the key! You will have to tear my clothes off me before you get the key! And that—that will be a scandal."

"Get a chisel, Cobb," said Inspector Sharpe resignedly.

Mrs. Nicoletis uttered a scream of fury. Inspector Sharpe paid no attention. The chisel was brought. Two sharp cracks and the door of the cupboard came open. As it swung forward a large consignment of empty brandy bottles poured out of the cupboard.

"Beast! Pig! Devil!" screamed Mrs. Nicoletis.

"Thank you, Madame," said the Inspector politely. "We've finished in here."

Mrs. Hubbard tactfully replaced the bottles while Mrs. Nicoletis had hysterics.

One mystery, the mystery of Mrs. Nicoletis's tempers, was now cleared up.

iii

Poirot's telephone call came through just as Mrs. Hubbard was pouring out an appropriate dose of sedative from the private medicine cupboard in her sitting room. After replacing the receiver she went back to Mrs. Nicoletis whom she had left screaming and kicking her heels on the sofa in her own sitting room.

"Now you drink this," said Mrs. Hubbard. "And you'll feel better."

"Gestapo!" said Mrs. Nicoletis who was now quiet but sullen.

"I shouldn't think any more about it if I were you," said Mrs. Hubbard soothingly.

"Gestapo!" said Mrs. Nicoletis again. "Gestapo! That is what they are!"

"They have to do their duty, you know," said Mrs. Hubbard.

"Is it their duty to pry into my private cupboards? I say to them, 'That is not for you.' I lock it. I put the key down my bosom. If you had not been there as a witness they would have torn my clothes off me without shame."

"Oh no, I don't think they would have done that," said Mrs. Hubbard.

"That is what you say! Instead they get a chisel and they force my door. That is structural damage to the house for which I shall be responsible."

"Well, you see, if you wouldn't give them the key . . ."

"Why should I give them the key? It is my key. My private key. And this is my private room. My private room and I say to the police, 'Keep out' and they do not keep out."

"Well, after all, Mrs. Nicoletis, there has been a murder, remember. And after a murder one has to put up with certain things which might not be very pleasant at ordinary times."

"I spit upon the murder!" said Mrs. Nicoletis. "That little Celia she commits suicide. She has a silly love affair and she takes poison. It is the sort of thing that is always happening. They are so stupid about love, these girls—as though love mattered! One year, two years and it is all finished, the grand passion! The man is the same as any other man! But these silly girls they do not know that. They take the sleeping draught and the disinfectant and they turn on gas taps and then it is too late."

"Well," said Mrs. Hubbard, returning full circle, as it were, to where the conversation had started, "I shouldn't worry any more about it all now."

"That is all very well for you. Me, I have to worry. It is not safe for me any longer."

"Safe?" Mrs. Hubbard looked at her, startled.

"It was my private cupboard," Mrs. Nicoletis insisted. "Nobody knows what was in my private cupboard. I did not want them to

273

know. And now they do know. I am very uneasy. They may think —what will they think?"

"Who do you mean by they?"

Mrs. Nicoletis shrugged her large, handsome shoulders and looked sulky.

"You do not understand," she said, "but it makes me uneasy. Very uneasy."

"You'd better tell me," said Mrs. Hubbard. "Then perhaps I can help you."

"Thank goodness I do not sleep here," said Mrs. Nicoletis. "These locks on the doors here they are all alike; one key fits any other. No, thanks to heaven, I do not sleep here."

Mrs. Hubbard said,

"Mrs. Nicoletis, if you are afraid of something, hadn't you better tell me just what it is?"

Mrs. Nicoletis gave her a flickering look from her dark eyes and then looked away again.

"You have said it yourself," she said evasively. "You have said there has been murder in this house, so naturally one is uneasy. Who may be next? One does not even know who the murderer is. That is because the police are so stupid, or perhaps they have been bribed."

"That's all nonsense and you know it," said Mrs. Hubbard. "But tell me, have you got any cause for real anxiety . . ."

Mrs. Nicoletis flew into one of her tempers.

"Ah, you do not think I have any cause for anxiety? You know best as usual! You know everything! You are so wonderful; you cater, you manage, you spend money like water on food so that the students are fond of you, and now you want to manage my affairs! But that, no! I keep my affairs to myself and nobody shall pry into them, do you hear? No, Mrs. What-do-you-call-it Paul Pry."

"Please yourself," said Mrs. Hubbard, exasperated.

"You are a spy—I always knew it."

"A spy on what?"

"Nothing," said Mrs. Nicoletis. "There is nothing here to spy upon. If you think there is it is because you made it up. If lies are told about me I shall know who told them."

"If you wish me to leave," said Mrs. Hubbard, "you've only got to say so."

"No, you are not to leave. I forbid it. Not at this moment. Not when I have all the cares of the police, of murder, of everything else on my hands. I shall not allow you to abandon me."

"Oh, all right," said Mrs. Hubbard helplessly. "But really, it's very difficult to know what you do want. Sometimes I don't think you know yourself. You'd better lie down on my bed and have a sleep—"

CHAPTER 13

HERCULE POIROT ALIGHTED from a taxi at 26 Hickory Road.

The door was opened to him by Geronimo who welcomed him as an old friend. There was a constable standing in the hall and Geronimo drew Poirot into the dining room and closed the door.

"It is terrible," he whispered, as he assisted Poirot off with his overcoat. "We have police here all time! Ask questions, go here, go there, look in cupboards, look in drawers, come into Maria's kitchen even. Maria very angry. She say she like to hit policeman with rolling pin but I say better not. I say policeman not like being hit by rolling pins and they make us more embarrassments if Maria do that."

"You have the good sense," said Poirot, approvingly. "Is Mrs. Hubbard at liberty?"

"I take you upstairs to her."

"A little moment." Poirot stopped him. "Do you remember the day when certain electric light bulbs disappeared?"

"Oh yes, I remember. But that long time ago now. One—two—three month ago."

"Exactly what electric light bulbs were taken?"

"The one in the hall and I think in the Common Room. Someone make joke. Take all the bulbs out."

"You don't remember the exact date?"

Geronimo struck an attitude as he thought.

"I do not remember," he said. "But I think it was on day when policeman come, some time in February—"

"A policeman? What did a policeman come here for?"

"He come here to see Mrs. Nicoletis about a student. Very bad student, come from Africa. Not do work. Go to labour exchange, get National Assistance, then have woman and she go out with men for him. Very bad that. Police not like that. All this in Manchester, I think, or Sheffield so he ran away from there and he come here, but police come after him and they talk to Mrs. Hubbard about him. Yes. And she say he not stop here because she no like him and she send him away."

"I see. They were trying to trace him."

"Scusi?"

"They were trying to find him?"

"Yes, yes, that is right. They find him and then they put him in prison because he live on woman, and live on woman must not do. This is nice house here. Nothing like that here."

"And that was the day the bulbs were missing?"

"Yes. Because I turn switch and nothing happen. And I go into Common Room and no bulb there, and I look in drawer here for spares and I see bulbs have been taken away. So I go down to kitchen and ask Maria if she know where spare bulbs—but she angry because she not like police come and she say spare bulbs not her business, so I bring just candles."

Poirot digested this story as he followed Geronimo up the stairs to Mrs. Hubbard's room.

Poirot was welcomed warmly by Mrs. Hubbard, who was looking tired and harassed. She held out, at once, a piece of paper to him.

"I've done my best, M. Poirot, to write down these things in the proper order but I wouldn't like to say that it's a hundred per cent accurate now. You see, it's very difficult when you look back over a period of months to remember just when this, that or the other happened."

"I am deeply grateful to you, Madame. And how is Mrs. Nicoletis?"

"I've given her a sedative and I hope she's asleep now. She made a terrible fuss over the search warrant. She refused to open the cupboard in her room and the Inspector broke it open and quantities of empty brandy bottles tumbled out."

"Ah!" said Poirot, making a tactful sound.

"Which really explains quite a lot of things," said Mrs. Hubbard. "I really can't imagine why I didn't think of that before, having seen as much of drink as I have out in Singapore. But all that, I'm sure, isn't what interests you."

"Everything interests me," said Poirot.

He sat down and studied the piece of paper that Mrs. Hubbard had handed to him.

"Ah!" he said, after a moment or two. "I see that now the rucksack heads the list."

"Yes. It wasn't a very important thing, but I do remember now, definitely, that it happened before the jewellery and those sort of things began to disappear. It was all rather mixed up with some trouble we had about one of the coloured students. He'd left a day or two before this happened and I remember thinking that it might have been a revengeful act on his part before he went. There'd been—well—a little trouble."

"Ah! Geronimo has recounted to me something like that. You had, I believe, the police here? Is that right?"

"Yes. It seems they had an enquiry from Sheffield or Birmingham or somewhere. It had all been rather a scandal. Immoral earnings and all that sort of thing. He was had up about it in court later. Actually, he'd only stayed here about three or four days. Then I didn't like his behaviour, the way he was carrying on, so I told him that his room was engaged and that he'd have to go. I wasn't really at all surprised when the police called. Of course, I couldn't tell them where he'd gone to, but they got on his track all right."

"And it was after that that you found the rucksack?"

"Yes, I think so—it's hard to remember. You see, Len Bateson was going off on a hitch-hike and he couldn't find his rucksack anywhere and he created a terrible fuss about it and everyone did a lot of searching and at last Geronimo found it shoved behind the boiler all cut to ribbons. Such an odd thing to happen. So curious; and pointless, M. Poirot."

"Yes," Poirot agreed. "Curious and pointless."

He remained thoughtful for a moment.

"And it was on that same day, the day that the police came to enquire about this African student, that some electric bulbs disappeared—or so Geronimo tells me. Was it that day?"

"Well, I really can't remember. Yes, yes, I think you're right, because I remember coming downstairs with the police inspector and going into the Common Room with him and there were candles there. We wanted to ask Akibombo whether this other young man had spoken to him at all or told him where he was going to stay."

"Who else was in the Common Room?"

"Oh, I think most of the students had come back by that time. It was in the evening, you know, just about six o'clock. I asked Geronimo about the bulbs and he said they'd been taken out. I asked him why he hadn't replaced them and he said we were right out of electric bulbs. I was rather annoyed as it seemed such a silly pointless joke. I thought of it as a joke, not as stealing, but I was surprised that we had no more electric bulbs because we usually keep quite a good supply in stock. Still, I didn't take it seriously, M. Poirot, not at that time."

"The bulbs and the rucksack," said Poirot thoughtfully.

"But it still seems to me possible," said Mrs. Hubbard, "that those two things have no connection with poor little Celia's peccadilloes. You remember she denied very earnestly that she'd ever touched the rucksack at all."

"Yes, yes, that is true. How soon after this did the thefts begin?"

"Oh dear, M. Poirot, you've no idea how difficult all this is to remember. Let me see—that was March, no, February—the end of February. Yes, yes, I think Genevieve said she'd missed her bracelet about a week after that. Yes, between the 20th and 25th of February."

"And after that the thefts went on fairly continuously?"

"Yes."

"And this rucksack was Len Bateson's?"

"Yes."

"And he was very annoyed about it?"

"Well, you mustn't go by that, M. Poirot," said Mrs. Hubbard, smiling a little. "Len Bateson is that kind of boy, you know. Warm-hearted, generous, kind to a fault, but one of those fiery, outspoken tempers."

"What was it, this rucksack—something special?"

"Oh no, it was just the ordinary kind."

"Could you show me one like it?"

"Well, yes, of course. Colin's got one, I think, just like it. So has Nigel—in fact Len's got one again now because he had to go and buy another. The students usually buy them at the shop at the end of the road. It's a very good place for all kinds of camping equipment and hikers' outfits. Shorts, sleeping bags, all that sort of thing. And very cheap—much cheaper than any of the big stores."

"If I could just see one of these rucksacks, Madame?"

Mrs. Hubbard obligingly led him to Colin McNabb's room. Colin himself was not there, but Mrs. Hubbard opened the wardrobe, stooped, and picked up a rucksack which she held out to Poirot.

"There you are, M. Poirot. That's exactly like the one that was missing and that we found all cut up."

"It would take some cutting," murmured Poirot, as he fingered the rucksack appreciatively. "One could not snip at this with a little pair of embroidery scissors."

"Oh no, it wasn't what you'd expect a—well, a girl to do, for instance. There must have been a certain amount of strength involved, I should say. Strength and—well—malice, you know."

"I know, yes, I know. It is not pleasant. Not pleasant to think about."

"Then, when later that scarf of Valerie's was found, also slashed to pieces, well, it did look—what shall I say—unbalanced."

"Ah," said Poirot. "But I think there you are wrong, Madame. I do not think there is anything unbalanced about this business. I think it has aim and purpose and shall we say, method."

"Well, I daresay you know more about these things, M. Poirot, than I do," said Mrs. Hubbard. "All I can say is, I don't like it. As far as I can judge we've got a very nice lot of students here and it would distress me very much to think that one of them is—well, not what I'd like to think he or she is."

Poirot had wandered over to the window. He opened it and stepped out on to the old-fashioned balcony.

The room looked out over the back of the house. Below was a small, sooty garden.

"It is more quiet here than at the front, I expect?" he said.

"In a way. But Hickory Road isn't really a noisy road. And facing this way you get all the cats at night. Yowling, you know, and knocking the lids off the dust bins."

Poirot looked down at four large battered ash cans and other assorted back yard junk.

"Where is the boiler house?"

"That's the door to it, down there next to the coal house."

"I see."

He gazed down speculatively.

"Who else has rooms facing this way?"

"Nigel Chapman and Len Bateson have the next room to this."

"And beyond them?"

"Then it's the next house—and the girls' rooms. First the room Celia had and beyond it Elizabeth Johnston's and then Patricia Lane's. Valerie and Jean Tomlinson look out to the front."

Poirot nodded and came back into the room.

"He is neat, this young man," he murmured, looking round him appreciatively.

"Yes. Colin's room is always very tidy. Some of the boys live in a terrible mess," said Mrs. Hubbard. "You should see Len Bateson's room." She added indulgently, "But he is a nice boy, M. Poirot."

"You say that these rucksacks are bought at the shop at the end of the road?"

"Yes."

"What is the name of that shop?"

"Now really, M. Poirot, when you ask me like that I can't remember. Mabberley, I think. Or else Kelso. No, I know they don't sound the same kind of name but they're the same sort of name in my mind. Really, of course, because I knew some people once called Kelso and some other ones called Mabberley, and they were very alike."

"Ah," said Poirot. "That is one of the reasons for things that always fascinate me. The unseen link."

He looked once more out of the window and down into the garden, then took his leave of Mrs. Hubbard and left the house.

He walked down Hickory Road until he came to the corner and turned into the main road. He had no difficulty in recognising the shop of Mrs. Hubbard's description. It displayed in great profusion picnic baskets, rucksacks, thermos flasks, sports equipment of all kinds, shorts, bush shirts, topees, tents, swimming suits, bicycle lamps and torches; in fact all possible needs of young and athletic youth. The name above the shop, he noted, was neither Mabberley nor Kelso but Hicks. After a careful study of the goods displayed in the window, Poirot entered and represented himself as desirous of purchasing a rucksack for a hypothetical nephew.

"He makes 'le camping,' you understand," said Poirot at his most foreign. "He goes with other students upon the feet and all he needs he takes with him on his back, and the cars and the lorries that pass, they give him a lift."

The proprietor, who was a small, obliging man with sandy hair, replied promptly.

"Ah, hitch-hiking," he said. "They all do it nowadays. Must lose the buses and the railways a lot of money, though. Hitch-hike themselves all over Europe some of these young people do. Now it's a rucksack you're wanting, sir. Just an ordinary rucksack?"

"I understand so. Yes. You have a variety then?"

"Well, we have one or two extra light ones for ladies, but this is the general article we sell. Good, stout, stand a lot of wear, and really very cheap though I say it myself."

He produced a stout canvas affair which was, as far as Poirot could judge, an exact replica of the one he had been shown in Colin's room. Poirot examined it, asked a few more exotic and unnecessary questions and ended by paying for it then and there.

"Ah yes, we sell a lot of these," said the man as he made it up into a parcel.

"A good many students lodge round here, do they not?"

"Yes. This is a neighbourhood with a lot of students."

"There is one hostel, I believe, in Hickory Road?"

"Oh yes, I've sold several to the young gentlemen there. And the young ladies. They usually come here for any equipment they want before they go off. My prices are cheaper than the big stores, and so I tell them. There you are, sir, and I'm sure your nephew will be delighted with the service he gets out of this."

Poirot thanked him and went out with his parcel.

He had only gone a step or two when a hand fell on his shoulder.

It was Inspector Sharpe.

"Just the man I want to see," said Sharpe.

"You have accomplished your search of the house?"

"I've searched the house, but I don't know that I've accomplished very much. There's a place along here where you can get a very decent sandwich and a cup of coffee. Come along with me if you're not busy. I'd like to talk to you."

The sandwich bar was almost empty. The two men carried their plates and cups to a small table in a corner.

Here Sharpe recounted the results of his questioning of the students.

"The only person we've got any evidence against is young Chapman," he said. "And there we've got too much. Three lots of poison through his hands. But there's no reason to believe he'd any animus against Celia Austin, and I doubt if he'd have been as frank about his activities if he was really guilty."

"It opens out other possibilities, though."

"Yes—all that stuff knocking about in a drawer. Silly young ass!"

He went on to Elizabeth Johnston and her account of what Celia had said to her.

"If what she said is true, it's significant."

"Very significant," Poirot agreed.

The Inspector quoted,

"'I shall know more about it tomorrow.'"

"And so—tomorrow never came for that poor girl! Your search of the house—did it accomplish anything?"

"There were one or two things that were—what shall I say? Unexpected, perhaps."

"Such as?"

"Elizabeth Johnston is a member of the Communist party. We found her Party card."

"Yes," said Poirot, thoughtfully. "That is interesting."

"You wouldn't have expected it," said Inspector Sharpe. "I didn't until I questioned her yesterday. She's got a lot of personality, that girl."

"I should think she was a valuable recruit to the Party," said Hercule Poirot. "She is a young woman of quite unusual intelligence, I should say."

"It was interesting to me," said Inspector Sharpe, "because she has never paraded those sympathies, apparently. She's kept very quiet about it at Hickory Road. I don't see that it has any significance in connection with the case of Celia Austin, I mean —but it's a thing to bear in mind."

"What else did you find?"

Inspector Sharpe shrugged his shoulders.

"Miss Patricia Lane, in her drawer, had a handkerchief rather extensively stained with green ink."

Poirot's eyebrows rose.

"Green ink? Patricia Lane! So it may have been she who took the ink and spilled it over Elizabeth Johnston's papers and then wiped her hands afterwards. But surely . . ."

"Surely she wouldn't want her dear Nigel to be suspected," Sharpe finished for him.

"One would not have thought so. Of course, someone else might have put the handkerchief in her drawer."

"Likely enough."

"Anything else?"

"Well," Sharpe reflected for a moment. "It seems Leonard Bateson's father is in Longwith Vale Mental Hospital, a certified patient. I don't suppose it's of any particular interest, but . . ."

"But Len Bateson's father is insane. Probably without significance, as you say, but it is a fact to be stored away in the memory. It would even be interesting to know what particular form his mania takes."

"Bateson's a nice young fellow," said Sharpe, "but of course his temper is a bit, well, uncontrolled."

Poirot nodded. Suddenly, vividly, he remembered Celia Austin saying 'Of course, I wouldn't cut up a rucksack. That's just silly. Anyway, that was only temper.' How did she know it was temper? Had she seen Len Bateson hacking at that rucksack? He came back to the present to hear Sharpe say, with a grin,

". . . and Mr. Ahmed Ali has some extremely pornographic literature and postcards which explains why *he* went up in the air over the search."

"There were many protests, no doubt?"

"I should say there were. A French girl practically had hysterics and an Indian, Mr. Chandra Lal, threatened to make an international incident of it. There were a few subversive pamphlets amongst his belongings—the usual half baked stuff—and one of the West Africans had some rather fearsome souvenirs and fetishes. Yes, a search warrant certainly shows you the peculiar side of human nature. You heard about Mrs. Nicoletis and her private cupboard?"

"Yes, I heard about that."

Inspector Sharpe grinned.

"Never seen so many empty brandy bottles in my life! And was she mad at us!"

He laughed, and then, abruptly, became serious.

"But we didn't find what we went after," he said. "No passports except strictly legitimate ones."

"You can hardly expect such a thing as a false passport to be left about for you to find, *mon ami.* You never had occasion, did you, to make an official visit to 26 Hickory Road in connection with a passport? Say, in the last six months?"

"No. I'll tell you the only occasions on which we did call round —within the times you mention."

He detailed them carefully.

Poirot listened with a frown.

"All that, it does not make sense," he said.

He shook his head.

"Things will only make sense if we begin at the beginning."

"What do you call the beginning, Poirot?"

"The rucksack, my friend," said Poirot softly. "The rucksack. All this began with a rucksack."

CHAPTER 14

MRS. NICOLETIS CAME up the stairs from the basement where she had just succeeded in thoroughly infuriating both Geronimo and the temperamental Maria.

"Liars and thieves," said Mrs. Nicoletis in a loud triumphant voice. "All Italians are liars and thieves!"

Mrs. Hubbard who was just descending the stairs gave a short vexed sigh.

"It's a pity," she said, "to upset them just while they're cooking the supper."

"What do I care?" said Mrs. Nicoletis. "I shall not be here for supper."

Mrs. Hubbard suppressed the retort that rose to her lips.

"I shall come in as usual on Monday," said Mrs. Nicoletis.

"Yes, Mrs. Nicoletis."

"And please get someone to repair my cupboard door first thing Monday morning. The bill for repairing it will go to the police, do you understand? To the police."

Mrs. Hubbard looked dubious.

"And I want fresh electric light bulbs put in the dark passages —stronger ones. The passages are too dark."

"You said especially that you wanted low power bulbs in the passages—for economy."

"That was last week," snapped Mrs. Nicoletis. "Now—it is different. Now I look over my shoulder—and I wonder, 'Who is following me?' "

Was her employer dramatising herself, Mrs. Hubbard wondered, or was she really afraid of something or someone? Mrs. Nicoletis had such a habit of exaggerating everything that it was always hard to know how much reliance to place on her statements.

Mrs. Hubbard said doubtfully,

"Are you sure you ought to go home by yourself? Would you like me to come with you?"

"I shall be safer there than here, I can tell you!"

"But what is it you are afraid of? If I knew, perhaps I could—"

"It is not your business. I tell you nothing. I find it insupportable the way you continually ask me questions."

"I'm sorry, I'm sure—"

"Now you are offended." Mrs. Nicoletis gave her a beaming smile. "I am bad tempered and rude—yes. But I have much to worry me. And remember I trust you and rely on you. What I should do without you, dear Mrs. Hubbard, I really do not know. See, I kiss my hand to you. Have a pleasant weekend. Good night."

Mrs. Hubbard watched her as she went out through the front door and pulled it to behind her. Relieving her feelings with a rather inadequate "Well, really!" Mrs. Hubbard turned towards the kitchen stairs.

Mrs. Nicoletis went down the front steps, out through the gate and turned to the left. Hickory Road was a fairly broad road. The houses in it were set back a little in their gardens. At the end of the road, a few minutes' walk from number 26, was one of London's main thoroughfares, down which buses were roaring. There were trafficlights at the end of the road and a public house, The Queen's Necklace, at the corner. Mrs. Nicoletis walked in the middle of the pavement and from time to time sent a nervous glance over her shoulder, but there was no one in sight. Hickory Road appeared to be unusually deserted this evening. She quickened her steps a little as she drew near The Queen's Necklace. Taking another hasty glance round she slipped rather guiltily through into the Saloon Bar.

Sipping the double brandy that she had asked for, her spirits revived. She no longer looked the frightened and uneasy woman that she had a short time previously. Her animosity against the police, however, was not lessened. She murmured under her breath, "Gestapo! I shall make them pay. Yes, they shall pay!" and finished off her drink. She ordered another and brooded over recent happenings. Unfortunate, extremely unfortunate, that the police should have been so tactless as to discover her secret hoard, and too much to hope that word would not get around amongst the students and the rest of them. Mrs. Hubbard would be discreet, perhaps, or again perhaps not, because really, could one trust anyone? These things always did get round. Geronimo knew. He had probably already told his wife, and she would tell the cleaning women and so it would go on until—she started violently as a voice behind her said,

"Why, Mrs. Nick, I didn't know this was a haunt of yours?"

She wheeled round sharply and then gave a sigh of relief.

"Oh, it's you," she said. "I thought . . ."

"Who did you think it was? The big bad wolf? What are you drinking? Have another on me."

"It is all the worry," Mrs. Nicoletis explained with dignity. "These policemen searching my house, upsetting everyone. My poor heart. I have to be very careful with my heart. I do not care for drink, but really I felt quite faint outside. I thought a little brandy . . ."

"Nothing like brandy. Here you are."

Mrs. Nicoletis left The Queen's Necklace a short while later feeling revived and positively happy. She would not take a bus, she decided. It was such a fine night and the air would be good for her. Yes, definitely the air would be good for her. She felt not exactly unsteady on her feet but just a little bit uncertain. One brandy less, perhaps, would have been wise, but the air would soon clear her head. After all, why shouldn't a lady have a quiet drink in her own room from time to time? What was there wrong with it? It was not as though she had ever allowed herself to be seen intoxicated. Intoxicated? Of course, she was never intoxicated. And anyway, if they didn't like it; if they ticked her off, she'd soon tell them where they got off! She knew a thing or two, didn't she? If she liked to shoot off her mouth! Mrs. Nicoletis tossed her head in a bellicose manner and swerved abruptly to avoid a pillar-box which had advanced upon her in a menacing manner. No doubt, her head was swimming a little. Perhaps if she just leant against the wall here for a little? If she closed her eyes for a moment or two . . .

*   *   *

Police Constable Bott, swinging magnificently down on his beat, was accosted by a timid-looking clerk.

"There's a woman here, officer. I really—she seems to have been taken ill or something. She's lying in a heap."

Police Constable Bott bent his energetic steps that way, and stooped over the recumbent form. A strong aroma of brandy confirmed his suspicions.

"Passed out," he said. "Drunk. Ah well, don't worry, sir, we'll see to it."

ii

Hercule Poirot, having finished his Sunday breakfast, wiped his moustaches carefully free from all traces of his breakfast cup of chocolate and passed into his sitting room.

Neatly arranged on the table were four rucksacks, each with its bill attached—the result of instructions given to George the day before. Poirot took the rucksack he had purchased the day before from its wrapping, and added it to the others. The result was interesting. The rucksack he had bought from Mr. Hicks did not seem inferior in any way that he could see, to the articles purchased by George from various other establishments. But it was very decidedly cheaper.

"Interesting," said Hercule Poirot.

He stared at the rucksacks.

Then he examined them in detail. Inside and outside, turning them upside down, feeling the seams, the pockets, the handles. Then he rose, went into the bathroom and came back with a small sharp corn-knife. Turning the rucksack he had bought at Mr. Hicks' store inside out, he attacked the bottom of it with the knife. Between the inner lining and the bottom there was a heavy piece of corrugated stiffening, rather resembling in appearance corrugated paper. Poirot looked at the dismembered rucksack with a great deal of interest.

Then he proceeded to attack the other rucksacks.

He sat back finally and surveyed the amount of destruction he had just accomplished.

Then he drew the telephone towards him and after a short delay managed to get through to Inspector Sharpe.

"*Ecoutez, mon cher,*" he said. "I want to know just two things."

Something in the nature of a guffaw from Inspector Sharpe.

"*I know two things about the horse,*
And one of them is rather coarse," he observed.

"I beg your pardon," said Hercule Poirot, surprised.

"Nothing. Nothing. Just a rhyme I used to know. What are the two things you want to know?"

"You mentioned yesterday certain police inquiries at Hickory Road made during the last three months. Can you tell me the dates of them and also the time of day they were made?"

"Yes—well—that should be easy. It'll be in the files. Just wait and I'll look it up."

It was not long before the Inspector returned to the phone. "First inquiry as to Indian student disseminating subversive propaganda, 18th December last—3.30 P. M."

"That is too long ago."

"Inquiry re Montagu Jones, Eurasian, wanted in connection with murder of Mrs. Alice Combe of Cambridge—February 24th —5.30 P. M. Inquiry re William Robinson—native West Africa, wanted by Sheffield police—March 6th, 11 A. M."

"Ah! I thank you."

"But if you think that either of those cases could have any connection with—"

Poirot interrupted him.

"No, they have no connection. I am interested only in the time of day they were made."

"What are you up to, Poirot?"

"I dissect rucksacks, my friend. It is very interesting."

Gently he replaced the receiver.

He took from his pocket book the amended list that Mrs. Hubbard had handed him the day before. It ran as follows:

Rucksack (Len Bateson's)
Electric light bulbs
Bracelet (Miss Rysdorff's)
Diamond Ring (Patricia's)
Powder Compact (Genevieve's)
Evening shoe (Sally's)
Lipstick (Elizabeth Johnston's)
Earrings (Valerie's)
Stethoscope (Len Bateson's)
Bathsalts (?)
Scarf cut in pieces (Valerie's)
Trousers (Colin's)
Cookery Book (?)
Boracic (Chandra Lal's)
Costume brooch (Sally's)
Ink spilled on Elizabeth's notes.

    (This is the best I can do. It's not absolutely accurate.
    L. Hubbard.)

Poirot looked at it a long time.

He sighed and murmured to himself, "Yes . . . decidedly . . . we have to eliminate the things that do not matter. . . ."

He had an idea as to who could help him to do that. It was Sunday. Most of the students would probably be at home.

He dialled the number of 26 Hickory Road and asked to speak to Miss Valerie Hobhouse. A thick rather guttural voice seemed rather doubtful as to whether she was up yet, but said it would go and see.

Presently he heard a low husky voice,

"Valerie Hobhouse speaking."

"It is Hercule Poirot here. You remember me?"

"Of course, M. Poirot. What can I do for you?"

"I would like, if I may, to have a short conversation with you?"

"Certainly."

"I may come round, then, to Hickory Road?"

"Yes. I'll be expecting you. I'll tell Geronimo to bring you up to my room. There's not much privacy here on a Sunday."

"Thank you, Miss Hobhouse. I am most grateful."

Geronimo opened the door to Poirot with a flourish, then bending forward he spoke with his usual conspiratorial air.

"I take you up to Miss Valerie very quietly. Hush sh sh."

Placing his finger on his lips, he led the way upstairs and into a good sized room overlooking Hickory Road. It was furnished with taste and a reasonable amount of luxury as a bed sitting room. The divan bed was covered with a worn but beautiful Persian rug, and there was an attractive Queen Anne walnut bureau which Poirot judged hardly likely to be one of the original furnishings of 26 Hickory Road.

Valerie Hobhouse was standing ready to greet him. She looked tired, he thought, and there were dark circles round her eyes.

"Mais vous êtes très bien ici," said Poirot as he greeted her. "It is *chic*. It has an air."

Valerie smiled.

"I've been here a good time," she said. "Two and a half years. Nearly three. I've dug myself in more or less and I've got some of my own things."

"You are not a student, are you, Mademoiselle?"

"Oh no. Purely commercial. I've got a job."

"In a—cosmetic firm, was it?"

"Yes. I'm one of the buyers for Sabrina Fair—it's a Beauty Salon. Actually I have a small share in the business. We run a certain amount of side-lines besides beauty treatment. Accessories, that type of thing. Small Parisian novelties. And that's my department."

"You go over then fairly often to Paris and to the Continent?"

"Oh yes, about once a month, sometimes oftener."

"You must forgive me," said Poirot, "if I seem to be displaying curiosity. . . ."

"Why not?" She cut him short. "In the circumstances in which we find ourselves we must all put up with curiosity. I've answered a good many questions yesterday from Inspector Sharpe. You look as though you would like an upright chair, Monsieur Poirot, rather than a low armchair."

"You display the perspicacity, Mademoiselle." Poirot sat down carefully and squarely in a high-backed chair with arms to it.

Valerie sat down on the divan. She offered him a cigarette and took one herself and lighted it. He studied her with some attention. She had a nervous, rather haggard elegance that appealed to him more than mere conventional good looks would have done. An intelligent and attractive young woman, he thought. He wondered if her nervousness was the result of the recent inquiry or whether it was a natural component of her manner. He remembered that he had thought much the same about her on the evening when he had come to supper.

"Inspector Sharpe has been making inquiries of you?" he asked.

"Yes, indeed."

"And you have told him all that you know?"

"Of course."

"I wonder," said Poirot, "if that is true."

She looked at him with an ironic expression.

"Since you did not hear my answers to Inspector Sharpe you can hardly be a judge," she said.

"Ah no. It is merely one of my little ideas. I have them, you know—the little ideas. They are here." He tapped his head.

It could be noticed that Poirot, as he sometimes did, was deliberately playing the mountebank. Valerie, however, did not smile. She looked at him in a straightforward manner. When she spoke it was with a certain abruptness.

"Shall we come to the point, M. Poirot?" she asked. "I really don't know what you're driving at."

"But certainly, Miss Hobhouse."

He took from his pocket a little package.

"You can guess, perhaps, what I have here?"

"I'm not clairvoyant, M. Poirot. I can't see through paper and wrappings."

"I have here," said Poirot, "the ring that was stolen from Miss Patricia Lane."

"Patricia's engagement ring? I mean, her mother's engagement ring? But why should you have it?"

"I asked her to lend it to me for a day or two."

Again Valerie's rather surprised eyebrows mounted her forehead.

"Indeed," she observed.

"I was interested in the ring," said Poirot. "Interested in its disappearance, in its return and in something else about it. So I asked Miss Lane to lend it to me. She agreed readily. I took it straight away to a jeweller friend of mine."

"Yes?"

"I asked him to report on the diamond in it. A fairly large stone, if you remember, flanked at either side by a little cluster of small stones. You remember—Mademoiselle?"

"I think so. I don't really remember it very well."

"But you handled it, didn't you? It was in your soup plate."

"That was how it was returned! Oh yes, I remember that. I nearly swallowed it." Valerie gave a short laugh.

"As I say, I took the ring to my jeweller friend and I asked him his opinion on the diamond. Do you know what his answer was?"

"How could I?"

"His answer was that the stone was not a diamond. It was merely a zircon. A white zircon."

"Oh!" She stared at him. Then she went on, her tone a little uncertain, "D'you mean that—Patricia thought it was a diamond but it was only a zircon or . . ."

Poirot was shaking his head.

"No, I do not mean that. It was the engagement ring, so I understand, of this Patricia Lane's mother. Miss Patricia Lane is a young lady of good family and her people, I should say, certainly before recent taxation, were in comfortable circumstances. In those circles, Mademoiselle, money is spent upon an engagement ring. An engagement ring must be a handsome ring—a diamond ring or a ring containing some other precious stone. I am quite certain that the papa of Miss Lane would not have given her mamma anything but a valuable engagement ring."

"As to that," said Valerie, "I couldn't agree with you more. Patricia's father was a small country squire, I believe."

"Therefore," said Poirot, "it would seem that the stone in the ring must have been replaced by another stone later."

"I suppose," said Valerie slowly, "that Pat might have lost the stone out of it, couldn't afford to replace it with a diamond, and had a zircon put in instead."

"That is possible," said Hercule Poirot, "but I do not think it is what happened."

"Well, Monsieur Poirot, if we're guessing, what do you think happened?"

"I think," said Poirot, "that the ring was taken by Mademoiselle Celia and that the diamond was deliberately removed and the zircon substituted before the ring was returned."

Valerie sat up very straight.

"You think Celia stole that diamond deliberately?"

Poirot shook his head.

"No," he said. "I think you stole it, Mademoiselle."

Valerie Hobhouse caught her breath sharply.

"Well, really!" she exclaimed. "That seems to me pretty thick. You've no earthly evidence of any kind."

"But yes," Poirot interrupted her. "I have evidence. The ring was returned in a plate of soup. Now me, I dined here one evening. I noticed the way the soup was served. It was served from a tureen on the side table. Therefore, if anyone found a ring in their soup plate it could only have been placed there either by the person who was serving the soup (in this case Geronimo) or by the person whose soup plate it was. You! I do not think it was Geronimo. I think that you staged the return of the ring in the soup in that way because it amused you. You have, if I may make the criticism, rather too humourous a sense of the dramatic. To hold up the ring! To exclaim! I think you indulged your sense of humour there, Mademoiselle, and did not realise that you betrayed yourself in so doing."

"Is that all?" Valerie spoke scornfully.

"Oh, no, it is by no means all. You see, when Celia confessed that evening to having been responsible for the thefts here, I noticed several small points. For instance, in speaking of this ring she said, 'I didn't realise how valuable it was. As soon as I knew, I managed to return it.' How did she know, Miss Valerie? Who told her how valuable the ring was? And then again in speaking of the cut scarf, little Miss Celia said something like, 'That didn't matter. Valerie didn't mind. . . .' Why did you not mind if a good quality silk scarf belonging to you was cut to shreds? I formed the impression then and there that the whole campaign of stealing things, of making herself out to be a kleptomaniac, and so attracting the attention of Colin McNabb had been thought out for Celia by someone else. Someone with far more intelligence than Celia Austin had and with a good working knowledge of psychology. You told her the ring was valuable; you took it from her and arranged for its return. In the same way it was at your suggestion that she slashed a scarf of yours to pieces."

"These are all theories," said Valerie, "and rather far-fetched theories at that. The Inspector has already suggested to me that I put Celia up to doing these tricks."

"And what did you say to him?"

"I said it was nonsense," said Valerie.

"And what do you say to me?"

Valerie looked at him searchingly for a moment or two. Then she gave a short laugh, stubbed out her cigarette, leaned back thrusting a cushion behind her back and said:

"You're quite right. I put her up to it."

"May I ask you why?"

Valerie said impatiently,

"Oh, sheer foolish good nature. Benevolent interfering. There Celia was, mooning about like a little ghost, yearning over Colin who never looked at her. It all seemed so silly. Colin's one of those conceited, opinionated young men wrapped up in psychology and complexes and emotional blocks and all the rest of it, and I thought really it would be rather fun to egg him on and make a fool of him. Anyway I hated to see Celia look so miserable, so I got hold of her, gave her a talking-to, explained in outline the whole scheme, and urged her on to it. She was a bit nervous, I think, about it all, but rather thrilled at the same time. Then, of course, one of the first things the little idiot does is to find Pat's ring left in the bathroom and pinch that—a really valuable piece of jewellery about which there'd be a lot of hoo-ha and the police would be called in and the whole thing might take a serious turn. So I grabbed the ring off her, told her I'd return it somehow, and urged her in future to stick to costume jewellery and cosmetics and a little wilful damage to something of mine which wouldn't land her in trouble."

Poirot drew a deep breath.

"That was exactly what I thought," he said.

"I wish that I hadn't done it now," said Valerie sombrely. "But I really did mean well. That's an atrocious thing to say and just like Jean Tomlinson, but there it is."

"And now," said Poirot, "we come to this business of Patricia's ring. Celia gave it to you. You were to find it somewhere and return it to Patricia. But before returning it to Patricia," he paused. "What happened?"

He watched her fingers nervously plaiting and unplaiting the end of a fringed scarf that she was wearing round her neck. He went on, in an even more persuasive voice,

"You were hard up, eh, was that it?"

Without looking up at him she gave a short nod of the head.

"I said I'd come clean," she said and there was bitterness in her voice. "The trouble with me is, Monsieur Poirot, I'm a gambler. That's one of the things that's born in you and you can't do anything much about it. I belong to a little club in Mayfair—oh, I shan't tell you just where—I don't want to be responsible for getting it raided by the police or anything of that kind. We'll just let it go at the fact that I belong to it. There's roulette there, baccarat, all the rest of it. I've taken a nasty series of losses one after the other. I had this ring of Pat's. I happened to be passing a shop where there was a zircon ring. I thought to myself, 'If this diamond was replaced with a white zircon Pat would never know the difference!' You never do look at a ring you know really well. If the diamond seems a bit duller than usual you just think it needs cleaning or something like that. All right, I had an impulse. I fell. I prised out the diamond and sold it. Replaced it with a zircon and that night I pretended to find it in my soup. That was a damn silly thing to do, too, I agree. There! Now you know it all. But honestly, I never meant Celia to be blamed for that."

"No, no, I understand." Poirot nodded his head. "It was just an opportunity that came your way. It seemed easy and you took it. But you made there a great mistake, Mademoiselle."

"I realise that," said Valerie drily. Then she broke out unhappily, "But what the hell! Does that matter now? Oh, turn me in if you like. Tell Pat. Tell the Inspector. Tell the world! But what good is it going to do? How's it going to help us with finding out who killed Celia?"

Poirot rose to his feet.

"One never knows," he said, "what may help and what may not. One has to clear out of the way so many things that do not matter and that confuse the issue. It was important for me to know who had inspired the little Celia to play the part she did. I know that now. As to the ring, I suggest that you go yourself to Miss Patricia Lane and that you tell her what you did and express the customary sentiments."

Valerie made a grimace.

"I daresay that's pretty good advice on the whole," she said. "All right, I'll go to Pat and I'll eat humble pie. Pat's a very decent sort. I'll tell her that when I can afford it again I'll replace the diamond. Is that what you want, M. Poirot?"

"It is not what I want, it is what is advisable."

The door opened suddenly and Mrs. Hubbard came in.

She was breathing hard and the expression on her face made Valerie exclaim,

"What's the matter, Mum? What's happened?"

Mrs. Hubbard dropped into a chair.

"It's Mrs. Nicoletis."

"Mrs. Nick? What about her?"

"Oh, my dear. She's dead."

"Dead?" Valerie's voice came harshly. "How? When?"

"It seems she was picked up in the street last night—they took her to the police station. They thought she was—was—"

"Drunk? I suppose . . ."

"Yes—she had been drinking. But anyway—she died—"

"Poor old Mrs. Nick," said Valerie. There was a tremor in her husky voice.

Poirot said gently,

"You were fond of her, Mademoiselle?"

"It's odd in a way—she could be a proper old devil—but yes—I was. . . . When I first came here—three years ago, she wasn't nearly as—as temperamental as she became later— She was good company—amusing—warm-hearted— She's changed a lot in the last year—"

Valerie looked at Mrs. Hubbard.

"I suppose that's because she'd taken to drinking on the quiet —they found a lot of bottles and things in her room, didn't they?"

"Yes," Mrs. Hubbard hesitated, then burst out,

"I do blame myself—letting her go off home alone last night —she was afraid of something, you know."

"Afraid?"

Poirot and Valerie said it in unison.

Mrs. Hubbard nodded unhappily. Her mild round face was troubled.

"Yes. She kept saying she wasn't safe. I asked her to tell me what she was afraid of—and she snubbed me. And one never knew with her, of course, how much was exaggeration— But now—I wonder—"

Valerie said,

"You don't think that she—that she, too—that she was—"

She broke off with a look of horror in her eyes.

Poirot asked,

"What did they say was the cause of death?"

Mrs. Hubbard said unhappily,

"They—they didn't say— There's to be an inquest—on Tuesday—"

CHAPTER 15

IN A QUIET ROOM at New Scotland Yard, four men were sitting round a table.

Presiding over the conference was Superintendent Wilding of the Narcotics squad. Next to him was Sergeant Bell, a young man of great energy and optimism who looked rather like an eager greyhound. Leaning back in his chair, quiet and alert, was Inspector Sharpe. The fourth man was Hercule Poirot. On the table was a rucksack.

Superintendent Wilding stroked his chin thoughtfully.

"It's an interesting idea, M. Poirot," he said cautiously. "Yes, it's an interesting idea."

"It is, as I say, simply an idea," said Poirot.

Wilding nodded.

"We've outlined the general position," he said. "Smuggling goes on all the time, of course, in one form or another. We clear up one lot of operators and after a due interval, things start again somewhere else. Speaking for my own branch, there's been a good lot of the stuff coming into this country in the last year and a half. Heroin mostly—a fair amount of coke. There are various depots dotted here and there on the continent. The French police have got a lead or two as to how it comes into France—they're less certain how it goes out again."

"Would I be right in saying," Poirot asked, "that your problem could be divided roughly under three heads. There is the problem of distribution, there is the problem of how the consignments enter the country, and there is the problem of who really runs the business and takes the main profits?"

"Roughly I'd say that's quite right. We know a fair amount about the small distributors and how the stuff is distributed. Some of the distributors we pull in, some we leave alone hoping that they may lead us to the big fish. It's distributed in a lot of different ways, night clubs, pubs, drugstores, an odd doctor or so, fashionable women's dressmakers and hairdressers. It's handed over on race courses, and in antique dealers', sometimes in a crowded multiple store. But I needn't tell you all this. It's not that side of it that's important. We can keep pace with all that fairly well. And we've got certain very shrewd suspicions as to what I've called the big fish. One or two very respectable wealthy gentlemen against whom there's never a breath of suspicion. Very careful they are; they never handle the stuff themselves, and the little fry don't even know who they are. But every now and again, one of them makes a slip—and then—we get him."

"That is all very much as I supposed. The line in which I am interested is the third line—how do the consignments come into the country?"

"Ah. We're an island. The most usual way is the good old fashioned way of the sea. Running a cargo. Quiet landing somewhere on the East coast, or a little cove down South, by a motor boat that's slipped quietly across the Channel. That succeeds for a bit but sooner or later we get a line on the particular fellow who owns the boat and once he's under suspicion his opportunity's gone. Once or twice lately the stuff's come in on one of the air liners. There's big money offered, and occasionally one of the stewards or one of the crew proves to be only too human. And then there are the commercial importers. Respectable firms that import grand pianos or what have you! They have quite a good run for a bit, but we usually get wise to them in the end."

"You would agree that it is one of the chief difficulties when you are running an illicit trade—the entry from abroad into this country?"

"Decidedly. And I'll say more. For some time now, we've been worried. More stuff is coming in than we can keep pace with."

"And what about other things, such as gems?"

Sergeant Bell spoke.

298

"There's a good deal of it going on, sir. Illicit diamonds and other stones are coming out of South Africa and Australia, some from the Far East. They're coming into this country in a steady stream, and we don't know how. The other day a young woman, an ordinary tourist, in France, was asked by a casual acquaintance if she'd take a pair of shoes across the Channel. Not new ones, nothing dutiable, just some shoes someone had left behind. She agreed quite unsuspiciously. We happened to be on to that. The heels of the shoes turned out to be hollow and packed with uncut diamonds."

Superintendent Wilding said,

"But look here, M. Poirot, what is it you're on the track of, dope or smuggled gems?"

"Either. Anything, in fact, of high value and small bulk. There is an opening, it seems to me, for what you might call a freight service, conveying goods such as I have described to and fro across the Channel. Stolen jewellery, the stones removed from their settings, could be taken out of England, illicit stones and drugs brought in. It could be a small independent agency, unconnected with distribution, that carried stuff on a commission basis. And the profits might be high."

"I'll say you're right there! You can pack ten or twenty thousand pounds' worth of heroin in a very small space and the same goes for uncut stones of high quality."

"You see," said Poirot, "the weakness of the smuggler is always the human element. Sooner or later you suspect a *person*, an air liner steward, a yachting enthusiast with a small cabin cruiser, the woman who travels to and fro to France too often, the importer who seems to be making more money than is reasonable, the man who lives well without visible means of support. But if the stuff is brought into this country by an innocent person, and what is more, by a different person each time, then the difficulties of spotting the cargoes are enormously increased."

Wilding pushed a finger towards the rucksack. "And that's your suggestion?"

"Yes. Who is the person who is least vulnerable to suspicion these days? The student. The earnest, hardworking student. Badly off, travelling about with no more luggage than what he can carry on his back. Hitchhiking his way across Europe. If one particular student were to bring the stuff in all the time, no doubt you'd get wise to him or her, but the whole essence of the arrangement is that the carriers are innocent and that there are a lot of them."

Wilding rubbed his jaw.

"Just how exactly do you think it's managed, M. Poirot?" he asked.

Hercule Poirot shrugged his shoulders.

"As to that it is my guess only. No doubt I am wrong in many details, but I should say that it worked roughly like this: First, a line of rucksacks are placed on the market. They are of the ordinary, conventional type, just like any other rucksack, well and strongly made and suitable for their purpose. When I say 'just like any other rucksack' that is not so. The lining at the base is slightly different. As you see, it is quite easily removable and is of a thickness and composition to allow of rouleaux of gems or powder concealed in the corrugations. You would never suspect it unless you were looking for it. Pure heroin or pure cocaine would take up very little room."

"Too true," said Wilding. "Why," he measured with rapid fingers, "you could bring in stuff worth five or six thousand pounds each time without anyone being the wiser."

"Exactly," said Hercule Poirot. "Alors! The rucksacks are made, put on the market, are on sale—probably in more than one shop. The proprietor of the shop may be in the racket or he may not. It may be that he has just been sold a cheap line which he finds profitable, since his prices will compare favourably with that charged by other camping-outfit sellers. There is, of course, a definite organisation in the background; a carefully kept list of students at the medical schools, at London University and at other places. Someone who is himself a student, or posing as a student is probably at the head of the racket. Students go abroad. At some point in the return journey a duplicate rucksack is exchanged. The student returns to England; customs investigations will be perfunctory. The student arrives back at his or her hostel, unpacks, and the empty rucksack is tossed into a cupboard or into a corner of the room. At this point there will be again an exchange of rucksacks or possibly the false bottom will be neatly extracted and an innocent one replace it."

"And you think that's what happened at Hickory Road?"

Poirot nodded.

"That is my suspicion. Yes."

"But what put you on to it, M. Poirot—assuming you're right, that is?"

"A rucksack was cut to pieces," said Poirot. "Why? Since the reason is not plain, one has to imagine a reason. There is something queer about the rucksacks that come to Hickory Road. They are too cheap. There have been a series of peculiar happenings at Hickory Road, but the girl responsible for them swore that the destruction of the rucksack was not her doing. Since she has confessed to the other things why should she deny that unless she was speaking the truth? So there must be another reason for the destruction of the rucksack—and to destroy a rucksack, I may say, is not an easy thing. It was hard work and someone must have been pretty desperate to undertake it. I got my clue when I found that roughly—(only roughly, alas, because people's memories after a period of some months are not too certain) but roughly—that that rucksack was destroyed at about the date when a police officer called to see the person in charge of the Hostel. The actual reason that the police officer called had to do with another matter, but I will put it to you like this: You are someone concerned in this smuggling racket. You go home to the house that evening and you are informed that the police have called and are at the moment upstairs with Mrs. Hubbard. Immediately you assume that the police are on to the smuggling racket, that they have come to make an investigation; and let us say that at that moment there is in the house a rucksack just brought back from abroad containing —or which has recently contained—contraband. Now, if the police have a line on what has been going on, they will have come to Hickory Road for the express purpose of examining the rucksacks of the students. You dare not walk out of the house with the rucksack in question because, for all you know, somebody may have been left outside by the police to watch the house with just that object in view, and a rucksack is not an easy thing to conceal or disguise. The only thing you can think of is to rip up the rucksack, and cram the pieces away among the junk in the boiler-house. If there is dope—or gems on the premises, they can be concealed in bath salts as a temporary measure. But even an empty rucksack, if it had held dope, might yield traces of heroin or cocaine on closer examination or analysis. So the rucksack must be destroyed. You agree that that is possible?"

"It's an idea, as I said before," said Superintendent Wilding.

"It also seems possible that a small incident not hitherto regarded as important may be connected with the rucksack. According to the Italian servant, Geronimo, on the day, or one of the days, when the police called the light in the hall had gone. He went to look for a bulb to replace it; found the spare bulbs, too, were missing. He was quite sure that a day or two previously there had been spare bulbs in the drawer. It seems to me a possibility—this is far-fetched and I would not say that I am sure of it, you understand, it is a mere possibility—that there was someone with a guilty conscience who had been mixed up with a smuggling racket before and who feared that his face might be known to the police if they saw him in a bright light. So he quietly removed the bulb from the hall light and took away the new ones so that it should not be replaced. As a result the hall was illuminated by a candle only. This, as I say, is merely a supposition."

"It's an ingenious idea," said Wilding.

"It's possible, sir," said Sergeant Bell eagerly. "The more I think of it the more possible I think it is."

"But if so," went on Wilding, "there's more to it than just Hickory Road?"

Poirot nodded.

"Oh yes. The organisation must cover a wide range of students' clubs and so on."

"You have to find a connecting link between them," said Wilding.

Inspector Sharpe spoke for the first time.

"There is such a link, sir," he said, "or there was. A woman who ran several student clubs and organisations. A woman who was right on the spot at Hickory Road. Mrs. Nicoletis."

Wilding flicked a quick glance at Poirot.

"Yes," said Poirot. "Mrs. Nicoletis fits the bill. She had a financial interest in all these places though she didn't run them herself. Her method was to get someone of unimpeachable integrity and antecedents to run the place. My friend Mrs. Hubbard is such a person. The financial backing was supplied by Mrs. Nicoletis—but there again I suspect her of being only a figurehead."

"Hm," said Wilding. "I think it would be interesting to know a little more about Mrs. Nicoletis."

Sharpe nodded.

"We're investigating her," he said. "Her background and where she came from. It has to be done carefully. We don't want to alarm our birds too soon. We're looking into her financial background, too. My word, that woman was a tartar if there ever was one."

He described his experiences with Mrs. Nicoletis when confronted with a search warrant.

"Brandy bottles, eh?" said Wilding. "So she drank? Well, that ought to make it easier. What's happened to her? Hooked it—?"

"No, sir. She's dead."

"Dead?" Wilding raised his eyebrows. "Monkey business, do you mean?"

"We think so—yes. We'll know for certain after the autopsy. I think myself she'd begun to crack. Maybe she didn't bargain for murder."

"You're talking about the Celia Austin case. Did the girl know something?"

"She knew something," said Poirot, "but if I may so put it, I do not think she knew what it was she knew!"

"You mean she knew something but didn't appreciate the implications of it?"

"Yes. Just that. She was not a clever girl. She would be quite likely to fail to grasp an inference. But having seen something, or heard something; she may have mentioned the fact quite unsuspiciously."

"You've no idea what she saw or heard, M. Poirot?"

"I make guesses," said Poirot. "I cannot do more. There has been mention of a passport. Did someone in the house have a false passport allowing them to go to and fro to the Continent under another name? Would the revelation of that fact be a serious danger to that person? Did she see the rucksack being tampered with or did she, perhaps, one day see someone removing the false bottom from the rucksack without realising what it was that that person was doing? Did she perhaps see the person who removed the light bulbs? And mention the fact to him or her, not realising that it was of any importance? Ah, *mon Dieu!*" said Hercule Poirot with irritation. "Guesses! guesses! guesses! One must know more. Always one must know more!"

"Well," said Sharpe, "we can make a start on Mrs. Nicoletis' antecedents. Something may come up."

"She was put out of the way because they thought she might talk? Would she have talked?"

"She'd been drinking secretly for some time . . . and that means her nerves were shot to pieces," said Sharpe. "She might have broken down and spilled the whole thing. Turned Queen's Evidence."

"She didn't really run the racket, I suppose?"

Poirot shook his head.

"I should not think so, no. She was out in the open, you see. She knew what was going on, of course, but I should not say she was the brains behind it. No."

"Any idea who is the brains behind it?"

"I could make a guess—I might be wrong. Yes—I might be wrong!"

CHAPTER 16

"HICKORY, DICKORY, DOCK," said Nigel, "the mouse ran up the clock. The police said 'Boo,' I wonder who, Will eventually stand in the Dock?"

He added,

"To tell or not to tell? That is the question!"

He poured himself out a fresh cup of coffee and brought it back to the breakfast table.

"Tell what?" asked Len Bateson.

"Anything one knows," said Nigel, with an airy wave of the hand.

Jean Tomlinson said disapprovingly,

"But of course! If we have any information that may be of use, of course we must tell the police. That would be only right."

"And there speaks our bonny Jean," said Nigel.

"*Moi, je n'aime pas les flics*," said René, offering his contribution to the discussion.

"Tell what?" Leonard Bateson asked again.

"The things we know," said Nigel. "About each other, I mean," he added helpfully. His glance swept round the breakfast room table with a malicious gleam.

"After all," he said, cheerfully, "we all do know lots of things about each other, don't we? I mean, one's bound to, living in the same house."

"But who is to decide what is important or not? There are many things no business of the police at all," said Mr. Ahmed Ali. He spoke hotly, with an injured remembrance of the Inspector's sharp remarks about his collection of postcards.

"I hear," said Nigel, turning towards Mr. Akibombo, "that they found some very interesting things in your room."

Owing to his colour, Mr. Akibombo was not able to blush, but his eyelids blinked in a discomfited manner.

"Very much superstition in my country," he said. "My grandfather give me things to bring here. I keep out of feeling of piety and respect. I, myself, am modern and scientific; not believe in voodoo, but owing to imperfect command of language I find very difficult to explain to policeman."

"Even dear little Jean has her secrets, I expect," said Nigel, turning his gaze back to Miss Tomlinson.

Jean said hotly that she wasn't going to be insulted.

"I shall leave this place and go to the Y.W.C.A.," she said.

"Come now, Jean," said Nigel. "Give us another chance."

"Oh, cut it out, Nigel!" said Valerie wearily. "The police have to snoop, I suppose, under the circumstances."

Colin McNabb cleared his throat, preparatory to making a remark.

"In my opinion," he said judicially, "the present position ought to be made clear to us. What exactly was the cause of Mrs. Nick's death?"

"We'll hear at the inquest, I suppose," said Valerie, impatiently.

"I very much doubt it," said Colin. "In my opinion they'll adjourn the inquest."

"I suppose it was her heart, wasn't it?" said Patricia. "She fell down in the street."

"Drunk and incapable," said Len Bateson. "That's how she got taken to the police station."

"So she did drink," said Jean. "You know, I always thought so.

"When the police searched the house they found cupboards full of empty brandy bottles in her room, I believe," she added.

"Trust our Jean to know all the dirt," said Nigel, approvingly.

"Well, that does explain why she was sometimes so odd in her manner," said Patricia.

Colin cleared his throat again.

"Ah! hem," he said. "I happened to observe her going into The Queen's Necklace on Saturday evening, when I was on my way home."

"That's where she got tanked up, I suppose," said Nigel.

"I suppose she just died of drink, then?" said Jean.

Len Bateson shook his head.

"Cerebral haemorrhage? I rather doubt it."

"For goodness' sake, you don't think she was murdered, too, do you?" said Jean.

"I bet she was," said Sally Finch. "Nothing would surprise me less."

"Please," said Mr. Akibombo. "It is thought someone killed her? Is that right?"

He looked from face to face.

"We've no reason to suppose anything of the sort yet," said Colin.

"But who would want to kill her?" demanded Genevieve. "Had she much money to leave? If she was rich it is possible, I suppose."

"She was a maddening woman, my dear," said Nigel. "I'm sure everybody wanted to kill her. I often did," he added, helping himself happily to marmalade.

ii

"Please, Miss Sally, may I ask you a question? It is after what was said at breakfast. I have been thinking very much."

"Well, I shouldn't think too much if I were you, Akibombo," said Sally. "It isn't healthy."

Sally and Akibombo were partaking of an open air lunch in Regent's Park. Summer was officially supposed to have come and the restaurant was open.

"All this morning," said Akibombo mournfully, "I have been much disturbed. I cannot answer my professor's questions good at all. He is not pleased at me. He says to me that I copy large bits

306

out of books and do not think for myself. But I am here to acquire wisdom from much books and it seems to me that they say better in the books than the way I put it, because I have not good command of the English. And besides, this morning I find it very hard to think at all except of what goes on at Hickory Road and difficulties there."

"I'll say you're right about that," said Sally. "I just couldn't concentrate myself, this morning."

"So that is why I ask you please to tell me certain things, because as I say, I have been thinking very much."

"Well, let's hear what you've been thinking about, then."

"Well, it is this bor—ass—sic."

"Bor-ass-sic? Oh, boracic! Yes. What about it?"

"Well, I do not understand very well. It is an acid, they say? An acid like sulphuric acid?"

"Not like sulphuric acid, no," said Sally.

"It is not something for laboratory experiment only?"

"I shouldn't imagine they ever did any experiments in laboratories with it. It's something quite mild and harmless."

"You mean, even, you could put it in your eyes?"

"That's right. That's just what one does use it for."

"Ah, that explains that then. Mr. Chandra Lal, he have little white bottle with white powder, and he puts powder in hot water and bathes his eyes with it. He keeps it in bathroom and then it is not there one day and he is very angry. That would be the bor-ac-ic, yes?"

"What is all this about boracic?"

"I tell you by and by. Please not now. I think some more."

"Well, don't go sticking your neck out," said Sally. "I don't want yours to be the next corpse, Akibombo."

iii

"Valerie, do you think you could give me some advice?"

"Of course I could give you advice, Jean, though I don't know why anyone ever wants advice. They never take it."

"It's really a matter of conscience," said Jean.

"Then I'm the last person you ought to ask. I haven't got any conscience, to speak of."

"Oh, Valerie, don't say things like that!"

"Well, it's quite true," said Valerie. She stubbed out a cigarette as she spoke. "I smuggle clothes in from Paris and tell the most frightful lies about their faces to the hideous women who come to the *salon*. I even travel on buses without paying my fare when I'm hard up. But come on, tell me. What's it all about?"

"It's what Nigel said at breakfast. If one knows something about someone else, do you think one ought to tell?"

"What an idiotic question! You can't put a thing like that in general terms. What is it you want to tell, or don't want to tell?"

"It's about a passport."

"A passport?" Valerie sat up, surprised. "Whose passport?"

"Nigel's. He's got a false passport."

"Nigel?" Valerie sounded disbelieving. "I don't believe it. It seems most improbable."

"But he has. And you know, Valerie, I believe there's some question—I think I heard the police saying that Celia had said something about a passport. Supposing she'd found out about it and he killed her?"

"Sounds very melodramatic," said Valerie. "But frankly, I don't believe a word of it. What is this story about a passport?"

"I saw it."

"How did you see it?"

"Well, it was absolutely an accident," said Jean. "I was looking for something in my despatch case a week or two ago, and by mistake I must have looked in Nigel's attache case instead. They were both on the shelf in the Common Room."

Valerie laughed rather disagreeably.

"Tell that to the marines!" she said. "What were you really doing? Snooping?"

"No, of course not!" Jean sounded justly indignant. "The one thing I'd never do is to look among anybody's private papers. I'm not that sort of person. It was just that I was feeling rather absent-minded, so I opened the case and I was just sorting through it . . ."

"Look here, Jean, you can't get away with that. Nigel's attache case is a good deal larger than yours and it's an entirely different colour. While you're admitting things you might just as well admit that you are that sort of person. All right. You found a chance to go through some of Nigel's things and you took it."

Jean rose.

"Of course, Valerie, if you're going to be so unpleasant and so very unfair and unkind, I shall . . ."

"Oh, come back, child!" said Valerie. "Get on with it. I'm getting interested now. I want to know."

"Well, there was this passport," said Jean. "It was down at the bottom and it had a name on it. Stanford or Stanley or some name like that, and I thought, 'How odd that Nigel should have somebody else's passport here.' I opened it and the photograph inside was Nigel! So don't you see, he must be leading a double life? What I wonder is, ought I to tell the police? Do you think it's my duty?"

Valerie laughed.

"Bad luck, Jean," she said. "As a matter of fact, I believe there's a quite simple explanation. Pat told me. Nigel came into some money, or something, on condition that he changed his name. He did it perfectly properly by deed poll or whatever it is, but that's all it is. I believe his original name was Stanfield or Stanley, or something like that."

"Oh!" Jean looked thoroughly chagrined.

"Ask Pat about it if you don't believe me," said Valerie.

"Oh—no—well, if it's as you say, I must have made a mistake."

"Better luck next time," said Valerie.

"I don't know what you mean, Valerie."

"You'd like to get your knife into Nigel, wouldn't you? And get him in wrong with the police?"

Jean drew herself up.

"You may not believe me, Valerie," she said, "but all I wanted to do was my duty."

She left the room.

"Oh, hell!" said Valerie.

There was a tap at the door and Sally entered.

"What's the matter, Valerie? You're looking a bit down in the mouth."

"It's that disgusting Jean. She really is too awful! You don't think, do you, that there's the remotest chance it was Jean that bumped off poor Celia? I should rejoice madly if I ever saw Jean in the dock."

"I'm with you there," said Sally. "But I don't think it's particularly likely. I don't think Jean would ever stick her neck out enough to murder anybody."

"What do you think about Mrs. Nick?"

"I just don't know what to think. I suppose we shall hear soon."

"I'd say ten to one she was bumped off, too," said Valerie.

"But why? What's going on here?" said Sally.

"I wish I knew. Sally, do you ever find yourself looking at people?"

"What do you mean, Val, looking at people?"

"Well, looking and wondering, 'Is it you?' I've got a feeling, Sally, that there's someone here who's mad. Really mad. Bad mad, I mean—not just thinking they're a cucumber."

"That may well be," said Sally. She shivered.

"Ouch!" she said. "Somebody's walking over my grave."

iv

"Nigel, I've got something I must tell you."

"Well, what is it, Pat?" Nigel was burrowing frantically in his chest of drawers. "What the hell I did with those notes of mine I can't imagine. I shoved them in here, I thought."

"Oh, Nigel, don't scrabble like that! You leave everything in such a frightful mess and I've just tidied it."

"Well, what the hell, I've got to find my notes, haven't I?"

"Nigel, you must listen!"

"O.K., Pat, don't look so desperate. What is it?"

"It's something I've got to confess."

"Not murder, I hope?" said Nigel with his usual flippancy.

"No, of course not!"

"Good. Well, what lesser sin?"

"It was one day when I mended your socks and I brought them along here to your room and was putting them away in your drawer . . ."

"Yes?"

"And the bottle of morphia was there. The one you told me about, that you got from the hospital."

"Yes, and you made such a fuss about it!"

"But Nigel, it was there in your drawer among your socks, where anybody could have found it."

"Why should they? Nobody else goes routing about among my socks except you."

"Well, it seemed to me dreadful to leave it about like that, and

I know you'd said you were going to get rid of it after you'd won your bet, but in the meantime there it was, still there."

"Of course. I hadn't got the third thing yet."

"Well, I thought it was very wrong, and so I took the bottle out of the drawer and I emptied the poison out of it, and I replaced it with some ordinary bicarbonate of soda. It looked almost exactly the same."

Nigel paused in his scramble for his lost notes.

"Good Lord!" he said. "Did you really? You mean that when I was swearing to Len and old Colin that the stuff was morphine sulphate or tartrate or whatever it was, it was merely bicarbonate of soda all the time?"

"Yes. You see . . ."

Nigel interrupted her. He was frowning.

"I'm not sure, you know, that that doesn't invalidate the bet. Of course, I'd no idea—"

"But Nigel, it was really dangerous keeping it there."

"Oh, Lord, Pat, must you always fuss so? What did you do with the actual stuff?"

"I put it in the Sodi Bic bottle and I hid it at the back of my handkerchief drawer."

Nigel looked at her in mild surprise.

"Really, Pat, your logical thought processes beggar description! What was the point?"

"I felt it was safer there."

"My dear girl, either the morphia should have been under lock and key, or if it wasn't, it couldn't really matter whether it was among my socks or your handkerchiefs."

"Well, it did matter. For one thing, I have a room to myself and you share yours."

"Why, you don't think poor old Len was going to pinch the morphia off me, do you?"

"I wasn't going to tell you about it, ever, but I must now. Because, you see, it's *gone*."

"You mean the police have swiped it?"

"No. It disappeared before that."

"Do you mean . . . ?" Nigel gazed at her in consternation. "Let's get this straight. There's a bottle labelled 'Sodi Bic,' containing morphine sulphate, which is knocking about the place somewhere, and at any time someone may take a heaping teaspoonful of it if they've got a pain in their middle? Good God, Pat! You have done it! Why the hell didn't you throw the stuff away if you were so upset about it?"

"Because I thought it was valuable and ought to go back to the hospital instead of being just thrown away. As soon as you'd won your bet, I meant to give it to Celia and ask her to put it back."

"You're sure you didn't give it to her?"

"No, of course not. You mean I gave it to her, and she took it and it was suicide, and it was all my fault?"

"Calm down. When did it disappear?"

"I don't know exactly. I looked for it the day before Celia died. I couldn't find it, but I just thought I'd perhaps put it somewhere else."

"It was gone the day before she died?"

"I suppose," said Patricia, her face white, "that I've been very stupid."

"That's putting it mildly," said Nigel. "To what lengths can a muddled mind and an active conscience go!"

"Nigel. D'you think I ought to tell the police?"

"Oh, hell!" said Nigel. "I suppose so, yes. And it's going to be all my fault."

"Oh, no, Nigel darling, it's me. I—"

"I pinched the damned stuff in the first place," said Nigel. "It all seemed to be a very amusing stunt at the time. But now—I can already hear the vitriolic remarks from the bench."

"I am sorry. When I took it I really meant it for—"

"You meant it for the best. I know. I know! Look here, Pat, I simply can't believe the stuff has disappeared. You've forgotten just where you put it. You do mislay things sometimes, you know."

"Yes, but—"

She hesitated, a shade of doubt appearing on her frowning face.

Nigel rose briskly.

"Let's go along to your room and have a thorough search."

v

"Nigel, those are my underclothes."

"Really, Pat, you can't go all prudish on me at this stage. Down

312

among the panties is just where you would hide a bottle, now, isn't it?"

"Yes, but I'm sure I—"

"We can't be sure of anything until we've looked everywhere. And I'm jolly well going to do it."

There was a perfunctory tap on the door and Sally Finch entered. Her eyes widened with surprise. Pat, clasping a handful of Nigel's socks, was sitting on the bed, and Nigel, the bureau drawers all pulled out, was burrowing like an excited terrier into a heap of pullovers whilst about him was strewn panties, brassières, stockings and other component parts of female attire.

"For land's sake," said Sally, "what goes on?"

"Looking for bicarbonate," said Nigel briefly.

"Bicarbonate? Why?"

"I've got a pain," said Nigel grinning. "A pain in my tum-tum-tum—and nothing but bicarbonate will assuage it."

"I've got some somewhere, I believe."

"No good, Sally, it's got to be Pat's. Hers is the only brand that will ease my particular ailment."

"You're crazy," said Sally. "What's he up to, Pat?"

Patricia shook her head miserably.

"You haven't seen my Sodi Bic, have you, Sally?" she asked. "Just a little in the bottom of the bottle."

"No." Sally looked at her curiously. Then she frowned. "Let me see. Somebody around here—no, I can't remember— Have you got a stamp, Pat? I want to mail a letter and I've run out."

"In the drawer there."

Sally opened the shallow drawer of the writing table, took out a book of stamps, extracted one, affixed it to the letter she held in her hand, dropped the stamp book back in the drawer, and put two pence halfpenny on the desk.

"Thanks. Shall I mail this letter of yours at the same time?"

"Yes—no— No, I think I'll wait."

Sally nodded and left the room.

Pat dropped the socks she had been holding, and twisted her fingers nervously together.

"Nigel?"

"Yes?" Nigel had transferred his attention to the wardrobe and was looking in the pockets of a coat.

"There's something else I've got to confess."

313

"Good Lord, Pat, what else have you been doing?"

"I'm afraid you'll be angry."

"I'm past being angry. I'm just plain scared. If Celia was poisoned with the stuff that I pinched, I shall probably go to prison for years and years, even if they don't hang me."

"It's nothing to do with that. It's about your father."

"What?" Nigel spun round, an expression of incredulous astonishment on his face.

"You do know he's very ill, don't you?"

"I don't care how ill he is."

"It said so on the wireless last night. 'Sir Arthur Stanley, the famous research chemist, is lying in a very critical condition.'"

"So nice to be a V.I.P. All the world gets the news when you're ill."

"Nigel, if he's dying, you ought to be reconciled to him."

"Like hell, I will!"

"But if he's dying."

"He's the same swine dying as he was when he was in the pink of condition!"

"You mustn't be like that, Nigel. So bitter and unforgiving."

"Listen, Pat—I told you once: he killed my mother."

"I know you said so, and I know you adored her. But I do think, Nigel, that you sometimes exaggerate. Lots of husbands are unkind and unfeeling and their wives resent it and it makes them very unhappy. But to say your father killed your mother is an extravagant statement and isn't really true."

"You know so much about it, don't you?"

"I know that some day you'll regret not having made it up with your father before he died. That's why—" Pat paused and braced herself. "That's why I—I've written to your father—telling him—"

"You've written to him? Is that the letter Sally wanted to post?" He strode over to the writing table. "I see."

He picked up the letter lying addressed and stamped, and with quick nervous fingers, he tore it into small pieces and threw it into the waste paper basket.

"That's that! And don't you dare do anything of that kind again."

"Really, Nigel, you are absolutely childish. You can tear the letter up, but you can't stop me writing another, and I shall."

"You're so incurably sentimental. Did it never occur to you

that when I said my father killed my mother, I was stating just a plain unvarnished fact? My mother died of an overdose of veronal. Took it by mistake, they said at the inquest. But she didn't take it by mistake. It was given to her, deliberately, by my father. He wanted to marry another woman, you see, and my mother wouldn't give him a divorce. It's a plain sordid murder story. What would you have done in my place? Denounced him to the police? My mother wouldn't have wanted that. . . . So I did the only thing I could do—told the swine I knew—and cleared out—for ever. I even changed my name."

"Nigel—I'm sorry . . . I never dreamed . . ."

"Well, you know now. . . . The respected and famous Arthur Stanley with his researches and his antibiotics. Flourishing like the green bay tree! But his fancy piece didn't marry him after all. She sheered off. I think she guessed what he'd done—"

"Nigel dear, how awful—I am sorry . . ."

"All right. We won't talk of it again. Let's get back to this blasted bicarbonate business. Now think back carefully to exactly what you did with the stuff— Put your head in your hands and think, Pat."

vi

Genevieve entered the Common Room in a state of great excitement. She spoke to the assembled students in a low thrilled voice.

"I am sure now, but absolutely sure I know who killed the little Celia."

"Who was it, Genevieve?" demanded René. "What has arrived to make you so positive?"

Genevieve looked cautiously round to make sure the door of the Common Room was closed. She lowered her voice.

"It is Nigel Chapman."

"Nigel Chapman, but why?"

"Listen. I pass along the corridor to go down the stairs just now and I hear voices in Patricia's room. It is Nigel who speaks."

"Nigel? In Patricia's room?" Jean spoke in a disapproving voice. But Genevieve swept on.

"And he is saying to her that his father killed his mother, and that, *pour ça*, he has changed his name. So it is clear, is it not?

315

His father was a convicted murderer, and Nigel he has the hereditary taint . . ."

"It is possible," said Mr. Chandra Lal, dwelling pleasurably on
the possibility. "It is certainly possible. He is so violent, Nigel,
so unbalanced. No self control. You agree?" He turned conde-
scendingly to Akibombo who nodded an enthusiastic black woolly
head and showed his white teeth in a pleased smile.

"I've always felt very strongly," said Jean, "that Nigel has *no*
moral sense. . . . A thoroughly degenerate character."

"It is sex murder, yes," said Mr. Ahmed Ali. "He sleeps with
this girl, then he kills her. Because she is nice girl, respectable,
she will expect marriage. . . ."

"Rot," said Leonard Bateson explosively.

"What did you say?"

"I said ROT!" roared Len.

CHAPTER 17

SEATED IN A ROOM at the police station, Nigel looked nervously
into the stern eyes of Inspector Sharpe. Stammering slightly, he
had just brought his narrative to a close.

"You realise, Mr. Chapman, that what you have just told us is
very serious? Very serious indeed."

"Of course I realise it. I wouldn't have come here to tell you
about it unless I'd felt that it was urgent."

"And you say Miss Lane can't remember exactly when she last
saw this bicarbonate bottle containing morphine?"

"She's got herself all muddled up. The more she tries to think
the more uncertain she gets. She said I flustered her. She's trying
to think it out quietly while I came round to you."

"We'd better go round to Hickory Road right away."

As the Inspector spoke the telephone on the table rang and

the constable who had been taking notes of Nigel's story, stretched out his hand and lifted the receiver.

"It's Miss Lane now," he said as he listened. "Wanting to speak to Mr. Chapman."

Nigel leaned across the table and took the receiver from him.

"Pat? Nigel here."

The girl's voice came, breathless, eager, the words tumbling over each other.

"Nigel. I think I've got it! I mean, I think I know now who must have taken—you know—taken it from my handkerchief drawer, I mean—you see, there's only one person who—"

The voice broke off.

"Pat. Hullo? Are you there? Who was it?"

"I can't tell you now. Later. You'll be coming round?"

The receiver was near enough for the constable and the Inspector to have heard the conversation clearly, and the latter nodded in answer to Nigel's questioning look.

"Tell her 'at once,' " he said.

"We're coming round at once," said Nigel. "On our way this minute."

"Oh! Good. I'll be in my room."

"So long, Pat."

Hardly a word was spoken during the brief ride to Hickory Road. Sharpe wondered to himself whether this was a break at last. Would Patricia Lane have any definite evidence to offer, or would it be pure surmise on her part? Clearly she had remembered something that had seemed to her important. He supposed that she had been telephoning from the hall, and that therefore she had had to be guarded in her language. At this time in the evening so many people would have been passing through.

Nigel opened the front door of 26 Hickory Road with his key and they passed inside. Through the open door of the Common Room, Sharpe could see the rumpled red head of Leonard Bateson bent over some books.

Nigel led the way upstairs and along the passage to Pat's room. He gave a short tap on the door and entered.

"Hallo, Pat. Here we—"

His voice stopped, dying away in a long choking gasp. He stood motionless. Over his shoulder, Sharpe saw also what there was to see.

Patricia Lane lay slumped on the floor.

The Inspector pushed Nigel gently aside. He went forward and knelt down by the girl's huddled body. He raised her head, felt for the pulse, then delicately let the head resume its former position. He rose to his feet, his face grim and set.

"No?" said Nigel, his voice high and unnatural. "No. No. No."

"Yes, Mr. Chapman. She's dead."

"No, no. Not Pat! Dear stupid Pat. How—"

"With this."

It was a simple, quickly improvised weapon. A marble paper-weight slipped into a woollen sock.

"Struck on the back of the head. A very efficacious weapon. If it's any consolation to you, Mr. Chapman, I don't think she even knew what happened to her."

Nigel sat down shakily on the bed. He said:

"That's one of my socks. . . . She was going to mend it. . . . Oh, God, she was going to mend it . . ."

Suddenly he began to cry. He cried like a child—with abandon and without self-consciousness.

Sharpe was continuing his reconstruction.

"It was someone she knew quite well. Someone who picked up a sock and just slipped the paper-weight into it. Do you recognise the paper-weight, Mr. Chapman?"

He rolled the sock back so as to display it.

Nigel, still weeping, looked.

"Pat always had it on her desk. A Lion of Lucerne."

He buried his face in his hands.

"Pat—oh, Pat! What shall I do without you!"

Suddenly he sat upright, flinging back his untidy fair hair.

"I'll kill whoever did this! I'll kill him! Murdering swine!"

"Gently, Mr. Chapman. Yes, yes, I know how you feel. A brutal piece of work."

"Pat never harmed anybody . . ."

Speaking soothingly, Inspector Sharpe got him out of the room. Then he went back himself into the bedroom. He stooped over the dead girl. Very gently he detached something from between her fingers.

Geronimo, perspiration running down his forehead, turned frightened dark eyes from one face to the other.

"I see nothing. I hear nothing, I tell you. I do not know anything at all. I am with Maria in kitchen. I put the *minestrone* on, I grate the cheese—"

Sharpe interrupted the catalogue.

"Nobody's accusing you. We just want to get some times quite clear. Who was in and out of the house the last hour?"

"I do not know. How should I know?"

"But you can see very clearly from the kitchen window who goes in and out, can't you?"

"Perhaps, yes."

"Then just tell us."

"They come in and out all the time at this hour of the day."

"Who was in the house from six o'clock until six thirty-five when we arrived?"

"Everybody except Mr. Nigel and Mrs. Hubbard and Miss Hobhouse."

"When did they go out?"

"Mrs. Hubbard she go out before teatime, she has not come back yet."

"Go on."

"Mr. Nigel goes out about half an hour ago, just before six—look very upset. He come back with you just now—"

"That's right, yes."

"Miss Valerie, she goes out just at six o'clock. Time signal, pip, pip, pip. Dressed for cocktails, very smart. She still out."

"And everybody else is here?"

"Yes, sir. All here."

Sharpe looked down at his notebook. The time of Patricia's call was noted there. Eight minutes past six, exactly.

"Everybody else was here, in the house? Nobody came back during that time?"

"Only Miss Sally. She been down to pillar box with letter and come back in—"

"Do you know what time she came in?"

Geronimo frowned.

"She came back while the news was going on."

"After six, then?"

"Yes, sir."

"What part of the news was it?"

"I don't remember, sir. But before the sport. Because when sport come we switch off."

Sharpe smiled grimly. It was a wide field. Only Nigel Chapman, Valerie Hobhouse and Mrs. Hubbard could be excluded. It would mean long and exhaustive questioning. Who had been in the Common Room, who had left it? And when? Who could vouch for whom? Add to that, that many of the students, especially the Asiatic and African ones, were constitutionally vague about times, and the task was no enviable one.

But it would have to be done.

iii

In Mrs. Hubbard's room the atmosphere was unhappy. Mrs. Hubbard herself, still in her outdoor things, her nice round face strained and anxious, sat on the sofa. Sharpe and Sergeant Cobb at a small table.

"I think she telephoned from in here," said Sharpe. "Around about 6.8 several people left or entered the Common Room, or so they say—and nobody saw or noticed or heard the hall telephone being used. Of course, their times aren't reliable, half these people never seem to look at a clock. But I think that anyway she'd come in here if she wanted to telephone the police station. You were out, Mrs. Hubbard, but I don't suppose you lock your door?"

Mrs. Hubbard shook her head.

"Mrs. Nicoletis always did, but I never do—"

"Well then, Patricia Lane comes in here to telephone, all agog with what she's remembered. Then, whilst she was talking, the door opened and somebody looked in or came in. Patricia stalled and hung up. Was that because she recognised the intruder as the person whose name she was just about to say? Or was it just a general precaution? Might be either. I incline myself to the first supposition."

Mrs. Hubbard nodded emphatically.

"Whoever it was may have followed her here, perhaps listened outside the door. Then came in to stop Pat from going on."

"And then—"

Sharpe's face darkened. "That person went back to Patricia's room with her, talking quite normally and easily. Perhaps Patricia taxed her with removing the bicarbonate, and perhaps the other gave a plausible explanation."

Mrs. Hubbard said sharply,

"Why do you say 'her'?"

"Funny thing—a pronoun! When we found the body, Nigel Chapman said, 'I'll kill whoever did this. I'll kill him.' 'Him,' you notice. Nigel Chapman clearly believed the murder was done by a man. It may be because he associated the idea of violence with a man. It may be that he's got some particular suspicion pointing to a man, to some particular man. If the latter, we must find out his reasons for thinking so. But speaking for myself, I plump for a woman."

"Why?"

"Just this. Somebody went into Patricia's room with her— someone with whom she felt quite at home. That points to another girl. The men don't go to the girls' bedroom floors unless it's for some special reason. That's right, isn't it, Mrs. Hubbard?"

"Yes. It's not exactly a hard and fast rule, but it's fairly generally observed."

"The other side of the house is cut off from this side, except on the ground floor. Taking it that the conversation earlier between Nigel and Pat was overheard, it would in all probability be a woman who overheard it."

"Yes, I see what you mean. And some of the girls seem to spend half their time here listening at keyholes."

She flushed and added apologetically,

"That's rather too harsh. Actually, although these houses are solidly built, they've been cut up and partitioned, and all the new work is flimsy as anything, like paper. You can't help hearing through it. Jean, I must admit, does do a good deal of snooping. She's the type. And of course, when Genevieve heard Nigel telling Pat his father had murdered his mother, she stopped and listened for all she was worth."

The Inspector nodded. He had listened to the evidence of Sally Finch and Jean Tomlinson and Genevieve. He said:

"Who occupies the rooms on either side of Patricia's?"

"Genevieve's is beyond it—but that's a good original wall. Elizabeth Johnston's is on the other side, nearer the stairs. That's only a partition wall."

"That narrows it down a bit," said the Inspector.

"The French girl heard the end of the conversation, Sally Finch was present earlier on, before she went out to post her letter. But the fact that those two girls were there automatically excludes anybody else having been able to snoop, except for a very short period. Always with the exception of Elizabeth Johnston who could have heard everything through the partition wall if she'd been in her bedroom, but it seems to be fairly clear that she was already in the Common Room when Sally Finch went out to the post.

"She did not remain in the Common Room all the time?"

"No, she went upstairs again at some period to fetch a book she had forgotten. As usual, nobody can say when."

"It might have been any of them," said Mrs. Hubbard helplessly.

"As far as their statements go, yes—but we've got a little extra evidence."

He took a small folded paper packet out of his pocket.

"What's that?" demanded Mrs. Hubbard.

Sharpe smiled.

"A couple of hairs—I took them from between Patricia Lane's fingers."

"You mean that—"

There was a tap on the door.

"Come in," said the Inspector.

The door opened to admit Mr. Akibombo. He was smiling broadly, all over his black face.

"Please," he said.

Inspector Sharpe said impatiently,

"Yes, Mr.—er—um, what is it?"

"I think, please, I have statement to make. Of first class importance to elucidation of sad and tragic occurrence."

"Now, Mr. Akibombo," said Inspector Sharpe resignedly, "let's hear, please, what all this is about."

Mr. Akibombo had been provided with a chair. He sat facing the others who were all looking at him with keen attention.

"Thank you. I begin now?"

"Yes, please."

"Well, it is, you see, that sometimes I have the disquieting sensations in my stomach."

"Oh."

"Sick to my stomach. That is what Miss Sally calls it. But I am not, you see, actually sick. I do not, that is, vomit."

Inspector Sharpe restrained himself with difficulty while these medical details were elaborated.

"Yes, yes," he said. "Very sorry, I'm sure. But you want to tell us—"

"It is, perhaps, unaccustomed food. I feel very full here." Mr. Akibombo indicated exactly where. "I think myself, not enough meat, and too much what you call cardohydrates."

"Carbohydrates," the Inspector corrected him mechanically. "But I don't see—"

"Sometimes I take small pill, soda mint; and sometimes stomach powder. It does not matter very much what it is—so that a great pouf comes and much air—like this." Mr. Akibombo gave a most realistic and gigantic belch. "After that," he smiled seraphically, "I feel much better, much better."

The Inspector's face was becoming a congested purple. Mrs. Hubbard said authoritatively,

"We understand all about that. Now get on to the next part."

"Yes. Certainly. Well, as I say, this happens to me early last week—I do not remember exactly which day. Very good macaroni and I eat a lot, and afterwards feel very bad. I try to do work for my Professor but difficult to think with fulness here." (Again Akibombo indicated the spot.) "It is after supper in the Common Room and only Elizabeth there and I say to her, 'Have you bicarbonate or stomach powder? I have finished mine.' And she says, 'No. But,' she says, 'I saw some in Pat's drawer when I was putting back a handkerchief I borrowed from her. I will get it for you,' she says. 'Pat will not mind.' So she goes upstairs and comes back with sodi bicarbonate bottle. Very little left, at bottom of bottle, almost empty. I thank her and go with it to the bathroom, and I put nearly all of it, about a teaspoonful in water and stir it up and drink it."

"A teaspoonful? A teaspoonful! My God!"

The Inspector gazed at him fascinated. Sergeant Cobb leaned forward with an astonished face. Mrs. Hubbard said obscurely, "Rasputin!"

"You swallowed a teaspoonful of morphia?"

"Naturally, I think it is bicarbonate."

"Yes, yes, what I can't understand is why you're sitting here now!"

"And then, afterwards, I was ill, but really ill. Not just the fulness. Pain, bad pain in my stomach."

"I can't make out why you're not dead!"

"Rasputin," said Mrs. Hubbard. "They used to give him poison again and again, lots of it, and it didn't kill him!"

Mr. Akibombo was continuing.

"So then, next day, when I am better, I take the bottle and the tiny bit of powder that is left in it to a chemist and I say please tell me, what is this I have taken, that has made me feel so bad?"

"Yes?"

"And he says come back later, and when I do, he says, 'No wonder! This is not the bicarbonate. It is the Borass—eek. The Acid Borasseek. You can put it in the eyes, yes, but if you swallow a teaspoonful it makes you ill."

"Boracic?" The Inspector stared at him stupefied. "But how did Boracic get into that bottle? What happened to the morphia?" He groaned, "Of all the haywire cases!"

"And I have been thinking, please," went on Akibombo.

The Inspector groaned again.

"You have been thinking," he said. "And what have you been thinking?"

"I have been thinking of Miss Celia and how she died, and that someone, after she was dead, must have come into her room and left there the empty morphia bottle and the little piece of paper that say she killed herself—"

Akibombo paused and the Inspector nodded.

"And so I say—who could have done that? And I think if it is one of the girls it will be easy, but if a man not so easy, because he would have to go downstairs in our house and up the other stairs and someone might wake up and hear him or see him. So I think again, and I say, suppose it is someone in our house, but in the next room to Miss Celia's—only she is in this house, you understand? Outside his window is a balcony and outside hers is a balcony, too, and she will sleep with her window open because that is hygienic practice. So if he is big and strong and athletic he could jump across."

"The room next to Celia's in the other house," said Mrs. Hubbard. "Let me see, that's Nigel's and—and . . ."

"Len Bateson's," said the Inspector. His finger touched the folded paper in his hand. "Len Bateson."

"He is very nice, yes," said Mr. Akibombo sadly. "And to me most pleasant, but psychologically one does not know what goes on below top surface. That is so, is it not? That is modern theory. Mr. Chandra Lal very angry when his boracic for the eyes disappears and later, when I ask, he says he has been told that it was taken by Len Bateson. . . ."

"The morphia was taken from Nigel's drawer and boracic was substituted for it, and then Patricia Lane came along and substituted sodi bicarbonate for what she thought was morphia but which was really boracic powder. . . . Yes. . . . I see . . ."

"I have helped you, yes?" Mr. Akibombo asked politely.

"Yes, indeed, we're most grateful to you. Don't—er—repeat any of this."

"No, sir. I will be most careful."

Mr. Akibombo bowed politely to all and left the room.

"Len Bateson," said Mrs. Hubbard in a distressed voice. "Oh! No."

Sharpe looked at her.

"You don't want it to be Len Bateson?"

"I've got fond of that boy. He's got a temper, I know, but he's always seemed so nice."

"That's been said about a lot of criminals," said Sharpe.

Gently he unfolded his little paper packet. Mrs. Hubbard obeyed his gesture and leaned forward to look.

On the white paper were two red short curly hairs. . . .

"Oh! dear," said Mrs. Hubbard.

"Yes," said Sharpe reflectively. "In my experience a murderer usually makes at least one mistake."

CHAPTER **19**

"BUT IT IS BEAUTIFUL, my friend," said Hercule Poirot with admiration. "So clear—so beautifully clear."

"You sound as if you were talking about soup," grumbled the Inspector. "It may be consommé to you—but to me there's a good deal of thick mock turtle about it, still."

"Not now. Everything fits in in its appointed place."

"Even these?"

As he had done to Mrs. Hubbard, Inspector Sharpe produced his exhibit of two red hairs.

Poirot's answer was almost in the same words as Sharpe had used.

"Ah—yes," he said. "What do you call it on the radio? The one deliberate mistake."

The eyes of the two men met.

"No one," said Hercule Poirot, "is as clever as they think they are."

Inspector Sharpe was greatly tempted to say:

"Not even Hercule Poirot?" but he restrained himself.

"For the other, my friend, it is all fixed?"

"Yes, the balloon goes up tomorrow."

"You go yourself?"

"No, I'm scheduled to appear at 26 Hickory Road. Cobb will be in charge."

"We will wish him good luck."

Gravely, Hercule Poirot raised his glass. It contained crème de menthe.

Inspector Sharpe raised his whisky glass.

"Here's hoping," he said.

ii

"They do think up things, these places," said Sergeant Cobb.

He was looking with grudging admiration at the display window of SABRINA FAIR. Framed and enclosed in an expensive illustration of the glassmaker's art—the "glassy green translucent wave"—Sabrina was displayed recumbent, clad in brief and exquisite panties and happily surrounded with every variety of deliciously packaged cosmetics. Besides the panties she wore various examples of barbaric costume jewellery.

Detective Constable McCrae gave a snort of deep disapproval. "Blasphemy, I call it. Sabrina Fair, that's Milton, that is."

"Well, Milton isn't the Bible, my lad."

"You'll not deny that Paradise Lost is about Adam and Eve and the Garden of Eden and all the devils of Hell and if that's not religion, what is?"

Sergeant Cobb did not enter on these controversial matters. He marched boldly into the establishment, the dour constable at his heels. In the shell pink interior of Sabrina Fair the Sergeant and his satellite looked as out of place as the traditional bull in a china shop.

An exquisite creature in delicate salmon pink swam up to them, her feet hardly seeming to touch the floor.

Sergeant Cobb said, "Good morning, Madam," and produced his credentials. The lovely creature withdrew in a flutter. An equally lovely but slightly older creature appeared. She in turn gave way to a superb and resplendent Duchess whose blue-grey hair and smooth cheeks set age and wrinkles at nought. Appraising steel grey eyes met the steady gaze of Sergeant Cobb.

"This is most unusual," said the Duchess severely. "Please come this way."

She led him through a square salon with a centre table where magazines and periodicals were heaped carelessly. All round the walls were curtained recesses where glimpses could be obtained of recumbent women supine under the ministrant hands of pink robed priestesses.

The Duchess led the police officers into a small business-like apartment with a big roll top desk, severe chairs, and no softening of the harsh Northern light.

"I am Mrs. Lucas, the proprietress of this establishment," she said. "My partner, Miss Hobhouse, is not here today."

"No, Madam," said Sergeant Cobb, to whom this was no news.

"This search warrant of yours seems to be most high-handed," said Mrs. Lucas. "This is Miss Hobhouse's private office. I sincerely hope that it will not be necessary for you to—er—upset our clients in any way."

"I don't think you need to worry unduly on that score," said Cobb. "What we're after isn't likely to be in the public rooms."

He waited politely until she unwillingly withdrew. Then he looked round Valerie Hobhouse's office. The narrow window gave a view of the back premises of other Mayfair firms. The walls were panelled in pale grey and there were two good Persian rugs on the floor. His eyes went from the small wall safe to the big desk.

"Won't be in the safe," said Cobb. "Too obvious."

A quarter of an hour later, the safe and the drawers of the desk had yielded up their secrets.

"Looks like it's maybe a mare's nest," said McCrae who was by nature both gloomy and disapproving.

"We're only beginning," said Cobb.

Having emptied the drawers of their contents and arranged the latter neatly in piles, he now proceeded to take the drawers out and turn them upside down.

He uttered an ejaculation of pleasure.

"Here we are, my lad," he said.

Fastened to the underneath side of the bottom drawer with adhesive tape were a half dozen small dark blue books with gilt lettering.

"Passports," said Sergeant Cobb. "Issued by Her Majesty's Secretary of State for Foreign Affairs, God bless his trusting heart."

McCrae bent over with interest as Cobb opened the passports and compared the affixed photographs.

"Hardly think it was the same woman, would you?" said McCrae.

The passports were those of Mrs. da Silva, Miss Irene French, Mrs. Olga Kohn, Miss Nina Le Mesurier, Mrs. Gladwys Thomas, and Miss Moira O'Neele. They represented a dark young woman whose age varied between twenty-five and forty.

"It's the different hair-do every time that does it," said Cobb. "Pompadour, curls, straight out, page boy bob, etc. She's done something to her nose for Olga Kohn, plumpers in her cheeks for Mrs. Thomas. Here are two more—foreign passports—Madame Mahmoudi, Algerian. Sheila Donovan, Eire. I'll say she's got bank accounts in all these different names."

"Bit complicated, isn't that?"

"It has to be complicated, my lad. Inland Revenue. Always snooping round asking embarrassing questions. It's not so difficult to make money by smuggling goods—but it's hell and all to account for money when you've got it! I bet this little gambling club in Mayfair was started by the lady for just that reason. Winning money by gambling is about the only thing an Income Tax Inspector can't check up on. A good part of the loot, I should say, is cached around in Algerian and French banks and in Eire. The whole thing's a thoroughly well thought out business-like set-up. And then, one day, she must have had one of these fake passports lying about at Hickory Road and that poor little devil Celia saw it."

CHAPTER 20

"IT WAS A CLEVER IDEA of Miss Hobhouse's," said Inspector Sharpe. His voice was indulgent, almost fatherly.

He shuffled the passports from one hand to the other like a man dealing cards.

"Complicated thing, finance," he said. "We've had a busy time hareing round from one Bank to the other. She covered her tracks well—her financial tracks, I mean. I'd say that in a couple of years' time she could have cleared out, gone abroad and lived happily ever after, as they say, on ill-gotten gains. It wasn't a big show—illicit diamonds, sapphires, etc., coming in—stolen stuff going out—and narcotics on the side, as you might say. Thoroughly well organised. She went abroad under her own and under different names, but never too often, and the actual smuggling was always done, unknowingly, by someone else. She had agents abroad who saw to the exchange of rucksacks at the right moment. Yes, it was a clever idea. And we've got M. Poirot here to thank for putting us on to it. It was smart of her, too, to suggest that psychological stealing stunt to poor little Miss Austin. You were wise to that almost at once, weren't you, M. Poirot?"

Poirot smiled in a deprecating manner and Mrs. Hubbard looked admiringly at him. The conversation was strictly off the record in Mrs. Hubbard's sitting room.

"Greed was her undoing," said Poirot. "She was tempted by that fine diamond in Patricia Lane's ring. It was foolish of her because it suggested at once that she was used to handling precious stones—that business of prising the diamond out and replacing it with a zircon. Yes, that certainly gave me ideas about Valerie Hobhouse. She was clever, though, when I taxed her with inspiring Celia, she admitted it and explained it in a thoroughly sympathetic way."

"But murder!" said Mrs. Hubbard. "Cold-blooded murder. I can't really believe it even now."

Inspector Sharpe looked gloomy.

"We aren't in a position to charge her with the murder of Celia Austin yet," he said. "We've got her cold on the smuggling, of course. No difficulties about that. But the murder charge is more tricky. The public prosecutor doesn't see his way. There's motive, of course, and opportunity. She probably knew all about the bet and Nigel's possession of morphia, but there's no real evidence, and there are the two other deaths to take into account. She could have poisoned Mrs. Nicoletis all right—but on the other hand, she definitely did not kill Patricia Lane. Actually she's about the only person who's completely in the clear. Geronimo says positively that she left the house at six o'clock. He sticks to that. I don't know whether she bribed him—"

"No," said Poirot, shaking his head. "She did not bribe him."

"And we've the evidence of the chemist at the corner of the road. He knows her quite well and he sticks to it that she came in at five minutes past six and bought face powder and aspirin and used the telephone. She left his shop at quarter past six and took a taxi from the rank outside."

Poirot sat up in his chair.

"But that," he said, "is magnificent! It is just what we want!"

"What on earth do you mean?"

"I mean that she actually telephoned from the box at the chemist's shop."

Inspector Sharpe looked at him in an exasperated fashion.

"Now, see here, M. Poirot. Let's take the known facts. At eight minutes past six, Patricia Lane is alive and telephoning to the police station from this room. You agree to that?"

"I do not think she was telephoning from this room."

"Well then, from the hall downstairs."

"Not from the hall either."

Inspector Sharpe sighed.

"I suppose you don't deny that a call was put through to the police station? You don't think that I and my Sergeant and Police Constable Nye, and Nigel Chapman were the victims of mass hallucination?"

"Assuredly not. A call was put through to you. I should say at a guess that it was put through from the public call box at the chemist's on the corner."

Inspector Sharpe's jaw dropped for a moment.

"You mean that Valerie Hobhouse put through that call? That she pretended to speak as Patricia Lane, and that Patricia Lane was already dead?"

"That is what I mean, yes."

The Inspector was silent for a moment, then he brought down his fist with a crash on the table.

"I don't believe it. The voice—I heard it myself—"

"You heard it, yes. A girl's voice—breathless, agitated. But you didn't know Patricia Lane's voice well enough to say definitely that it was her voice."

331

"I didn't, perhaps. But it was Nigel Chapman who actually took the call. You can't tell me that Nigel Chapman could be deceived. It isn't so easy to disguise a voice over the telephone, or to counterfeit somebody else's voice. Nigel Chapman would have known if it wasn't Pat's voice speaking."

"Yes," said Poirot. "Nigel Chapman would have known. Nigel Chapman knew quite well that it wasn't Patricia. Who should know better than he, since he had killed her with a blow on the back of the head only a short while before."

It was a moment or two before the Inspector recovered his voice.

"Nigel Chapman? Nigel Chapman? But when we found her dead—he cried—cried like a child."

"I daresay," said Poirot. "I think he was as fond of that girl as he could be of anybody—but that wouldn't save her—not if she represented a menace to his interests. All along, Nigel Chapman has stood out as the obvious probability. Who had morphia in his possession? Nigel Chapman. Who has the shallow brilliant intellect to plan, and the audacity to carry out fraud and murder? Nigel Chapman. Who do we know to be both ruthless and vain? Nigel Chapman. He has all the hallmarks of the killer; the overweening vanity, the spitefulness, the growing recklessness that led him to draw attention to himself in every conceivable way—using the green ink in a stupendous double bluff, and finally overreaching himself by the silly deliberate mistake of putting Len Bateson's hairs in Patricia's fingers, oblivious of the fact that as Patricia was struck down from behind, she could not possibly have grasped her assailant by the hair. They are like that, these murderers—carried away by their own egoism, by their admiration of their own cleverness, relying on their charm—for he has charm, this Nigel—he has all the charm of a spoiled child who has never grown up, who never will grow up—who sees only one thing, Himself, and what he wants!"

"But why, M. Poirot? Why murder? Celia Austin, perhaps, but why Patricia Lane?"

"That," said Poirot, "we have got to find out."

CHAPTER 21

"I HAVEN'T SEEN YOU for a long time," said old Mr. Endicott to Hercule Poirot. He peered at the other keenly. "It's very nice of you to drop in."

"Not really," said Hercule Poirot. "I want something."

"Well, as you know, I'm deeply in your debt. You cleared up that nasty Abernethy business for me."

"I am surprised really to find you here. I thought you had retired."

The old lawyer smiled grimly. His firm was a most respectable and old established one.

"I came in specially today to see a very old client. I still attend to the affairs of one or two old friends."

"Sir Arthur Stanley was an old friend and client, was he not?"

"Yes. We've undertaken all his legal work since he was quite a young man. A very brilliant man, Poirot—quite an exceptional brain."

"His death was announced on the six o'clock news yesterday, I believe."

"Yes. The funeral's on Friday. He's been ailing some time. A malignant growth, I understand."

"Lady Stanley died some years ago?"

"Two and a half years ago, roughly."

The keen eyes below the bushy brows looked sharply at Poirot. "How did she die?"

The lawyer replied promptly.

"Overdose of sleeping stuff. Medinal as far as I remember."

"There was an inquest?"

"Yes. The verdict was that she took it accidentally."

"Did she?"

333

Mr. Endicott was silent for a moment.

"I won't insult you," he said. "I've no doubt you've got a good reason for asking. Medinal's a rather dangerous drug, I understand, because there's not a big margin between an effective dose and a lethal one. If the patient gets drowsy and forgets she's taken a dose and takes another—well, it can have a fatal result."

Poirot nodded.

"Is that what she did?"

"Presumably. There was no suggestion of suicide, or suicidal tendencies."

"And no suggestion of—anything else?"

Again that keen glance was shot at him.

"Her husband gave evidence."

"And what did he say?"

"He made it clear that she did sometimes get confused after taking her nightly dose and ask for another."

"Was he lying?"

"Really, Poirot, what an outrageous question. Why should you suppose for a minute that I should know?"

Poirot smiled. The attempt at bluster did not deceive him.

"I suggest, my friend, that you know very well. But for the moment I will not embarrass you by asking you what you know. Instead I will ask you for an opinion. The opinion of one man about another. Was Arthur Stanley the kind of man who would do away with his wife if he wanted to marry another woman?"

Mr. Endicott jumped as though he had been stung by a wasp.

"Preposterous," he said angrily. "Quite preposterous. And there was no other woman. Stanley was devoted to his wife."

"Yes," said Poirot. "I thought so. And now—I will come to the purpose of my call upon you. You are the solicitors who drew up Arthur Stanley's will. You are, perhaps, his executor."

"That is so."

"Arthur Stanley had a son. The son quarrelled with his father at the time of his mother's death. Quarrelled with him and left home. He even went so far as to change his name."

"That I did not know. What's he calling himself?"

"We shall come to that. Before we do I am going to make an assumption. If I am right, perhaps you will admit the fact. I think that Arthur Stanley left a sealed letter with you, a letter to be opened under certain circumstances or after his death."

"Really, Poirot! In the Middle Ages you would certainly have been burnt at the stake. How you can possibly know the things you do!"

"I am right then? I think there was an alternative in the letter. Its contents were either to be destroyed—or you were to take a certain course of action."

He paused. The other did not speak.

"*Bon Dieu!*" said Poirot, with alarm. "You have not already destroyed—"

He broke off in relief as Mr. Endicott slowly shook his head in negation.

"We never act in haste," he said reprovingly. "I have to make full enquiries—to satisfy myself absolutely—"

He paused. "This matter," he said severely, "is highly confidential. Even to you, Poirot—" He shook his head.

"And if I show you good cause why you should speak?"

"That is up to you. I cannot conceive how you can possibly know anything at all that is relevant to the matter we are discussing."

"I do not know—so I have to guess. If I guess correctly—"

"Highly unlikely," said Mr. Endicott with a wave of his hand.

Poirot drew a deep breath.

"Very well then. It is in my mind that your instructions are as follows. In the event of Sir Arthur's death, you are to trace his son Nigel, to ascertain where he is living and how he is living and particularly whether he is or has been engaged in any criminal activity whatsoever."

This time Mr. Endicott's impregnable legal calm was really shattered. He uttered an exclamation such as few had ever heard from his lips.

"Since you appear to be in full possession of the facts," he said, "I'll tell you anything you want to know. I gather you've come across young Nigel in the course of your professional activities. What's the young devil been up to?"

"I think the story goes as follows. After he left home he changed his name, telling anyone who was interested that he had to do so as a condition of a legacy. He then fell in with some people who were running a smuggling racket—drugs and jewels. I think it was due to him that the racket assumed its final form—an exceedingly clever one involving the using of innocent *bona fide* students. The whole thing was operated by two people, Nigel Chapman, as he now called himself, and a young woman called Valerie Hobhouse who, I think, originally introduced him to the smuggling trade. It was a small private concern and they worked it on a commission basis—but it was immensely profitable. The goods had to be of small bulk, but thousands of pounds' worth of gems and narcotics occupy a very small space. Everything went well until one of those unforeseen chances occurred. A police officer came one day to a students' hostel to make inquiries in connection with a murder near Cambridge. I think you know the reason why that particular piece of information should cause Nigel to panic. He thought the police were after him. He removed certain electric light bulbs so that the light should be dim and he also, in a panic, took a certain rucksack out into the back yard, hacked it to pieces and threw it behind the boiler since he feared traces of narcotic might be found in its false bottom.

"His panic was quite unfounded—the police had merely come to ask questions about a certain Eurasian student—but one of the girls living in the Hostel had happened to look out of her window and had seen him destroying the rucksack. That did not immediately sign her death warrant. Instead, a clever scheme was thought up by which she herself was induced to commit certain foolish actions which would place her in a very invidious position. But they carried that scheme too far. I was called in. I advised going to the police. The girl lost her head and confessed. She confessed, that is, to the things that *she* had done. But she went, I think, to Nigel, and urged him to confess also to the rucksack business and to spilling ink over a fellow student's work. Neither Nigel nor his accomplice could consider attention being called to the rucksack—their whole plan of campaign would be ruined. Moreover Celia, the girl in question, had another dangerous piece of knowledge which she revealed, as it happened, the night I dined there. She knew who Nigel really was."

"But surely—" Mr. Endicott frowned.

"Nigel had moved from one world to another. Any former friends he met, might know that he now called himself Chapman, but they knew nothing of what he was doing. In the Hostel nobody knew that his real name was Stanley—but Celia suddenly revealed that she knew him in both capacities. She also knew that Valerie Hobhouse, on one occasion at least, had travelled abroad on a false passport. She knew too much. The next evening she went out to meet him by appointment somewhere. He gave her a drink of coffee and in it was morphia. She died in her sleep with everything arranged to look like suicide."

Mr. Endicott stirred. An expression of deep distress crossed his face. He murmured something under his breath.

"But that was not the end," said Poirot. "The woman who owned the chain of hostels and students' clubs died soon after in suspicious circumstances and then, finally, there came the last most cruel and heartless crime. Patricia Lane, a girl who was devoted to Nigel and of whom he himself was really fond, meddled unwittingly in his affairs, and moreover insisted that he should be reconciled to his father before the latter died. He told her a string of lies, but he realised that her obstinacy might urge her actually to write a second letter after the first was destroyed. I think, my friend, that you can tell me why, from his point of view, that would have been such a fatal thing to happen."

Mr. Endicott rose. He went across the room to a safe, unlocked it, and came back with a long envelope in his hand. It had a broken red seal on the back of it. He drew out two enclosures and laid them before Poirot.

"Dear Endicott. You will open this after I am dead. I wish you to trace my son Nigel and find out if he has been guilty of any criminal actions whatsoever.

"The facts I am about to tell you are known to me only. Nigel has always been profoundly unsatisfactory in his character. He has twice been guilty of forging my name to a cheque. On each occasion I acknowledged the signature as mine, but warned him that I would not do so again. On the third occasion it was his mother's name he forged. She charged him with it. He begged her to keep silence. She refused. She and I had discussed him, and she made it clear she was going to tell me. It was then that, in handing her her evening sleeping mixture, he administered an overdose. Before it took effect, however, she had come to my room and told me all about matters. When, the next morning, she was found dead, I knew who had done it.

"I accused Nigel and told him that I intended to make a clean breast of all the facts to the police. He pleaded desperately with me. What would you have done, Endicott? I have no illusions about my son, I know him for what he is, one of those dangerous misfits who have neither conscience nor pity. I had no cause to save him. But it was the thought of my beloved wife that swayed me. Would she wish me to execute justice? I thought that I knew the answer—she would have wanted her son saved from the scaffold. She would have shrunk, as I shrank, from the dragging down of our name. But there was another consideration. I firmly believe that once a killer, always a killer. There might be, in the future, other victims. I made a bargain with my son, and whether I did right or wrong, I do not know. He was to write out a confession of his crime which I should keep. He was to leave my house and never return, but make a new life for himself. I would give him a second chance. Money belonging to his mother would come to him automatically. He had had a good education. He had every chance of making good.

"But—if he were convicted of any criminal activity whatsoever the confession he had left with me should go to the police. I safeguarded myself by explaining that my own death would not solve the problem.

"You are my oldest friend. I am placing a burden on your shoulders, but I ask it in the name of a dead woman who was also your friend. Find Nigel. If his record is clean, destroy this letter and the enclosed confession. If not—then justice must be done.

"Your affectionate friend,

Arthur Stanley."

"Ah!" Poirot breathed a long sigh.

He unfolded the enclosure.

"I hereby confess that I murdered my mother by giving her an overdose of medinal on November 18, 195–.

Nigel Stanley."

CHAPTER 22

"You QUITE UNDERSTAND your position, Miss Hobhouse. I have already warned you—"

Valerie Hobhouse cut him short.

"I know what I'm doing. You've warned me that what I say

will be used in evidence. I'm prepared for that. You've got me on the smuggling charge. I haven't got a hope. That means a long term of imprisonment. This other means that I'll be charged as an accessory to murder."

"Your being willing to make a statement may help you, but I can't make any promise or hold out any inducement."

"I don't know that I care. Just as well end it all as languish in prison for years. I want to make a statement. I may be what you call an accessory, but I'm not a killer. I never intended murder or wanted it. I'm not such a fool. What I do want is that there should be a clear case against Nigel . . .

"Celia knew far too much, but I could have dealt with that somehow. Nigel didn't give me time. He got her to come out and meet him, told her that he was going to own up to the rucksack and the ink business and then slipped her the morphia in a cup of coffee. He'd got hold of her letter to Mrs. Hubbard earlier on and had torn out a useful 'suicide' phrase. He put that and the empty morphia phial (which he had retrieved after pretending to throw it away) by her bed. I see now that he'd been contemplating murder for quite a little time. Then he came and told me what he'd done. For my own sake I had to stand in with him.

"The same thing must have happened with Mrs. Nick. He'd found out that she drank, that she was getting unreliable—he managed to meet her somewhere on her way home, and poisoned her drink. He denied it to me—but I know that that's what he did. Then came Pat. He came up to my room and told me what had happened. He told me what I'd got to do—so that both he and I would have an unbreakable alibi. I was in the net by then, there was no way out. . . . I suppose, if you hadn't caught me, I'd have got away abroad somewhere, and made a new life for myself. But you did catch me. . . . And now I only care about one thing—to make sure that that cruel smiling devil gets hanged."

Inspector Sharpe drew a deep breath. All this was eminently satisfactory, it was an unbelievable piece of luck; but he was puzzled.

The Constable licked his pencil.

"I'm not sure that I quite understand," began Sharpe.

She cut him short.

"You don't need to understand. I've got my reasons."

Hercule Poirot spoke very gently.

"Mrs. Nicoletis?" he asked.

He heard the sharp intake of her breath.

"She was—your mother, was she not?"

"Yes," said Valerie Hobhouse. "She was my mother. . . ."

CHAPTER 23

"I DO NOT UNDERSTAND," said Mr. Akibombo plaintively.

He looked anxiously from one red head to the other.

Sally Finch and Len Bateson were conducting a conversation which Mr. Akibombo found it hard to follow.

"Do you think," asked Sally, "that Nigel meant *me* to be suspected, or you?"

"Either, I should say," replied Len. "I believe he actually took the hairs from my brush."

"I do not understand, please," said Mr. Akibombo. "Was it then Mr. Nigel who jumped the balcony?"

"Nigel can jump like a cat. I couldn't have jumped across that space. I'm far too heavy."

"I want to apologise very deeply and humbly for wholly unjustifiable suspicions."

"That's all right," said Len.

"Actually, you helped a lot," said Sally. "All your thinking—about the boracic."

Mr. Akibombo brightened up.

"One ought to have realised all along," said Len, "that Nigel was a thoroughly maladjusted type and—"

"Oh, for heaven's sake—you sound just like Colin. Frankly, Nigel always gave me the creeps—and at last I see why. Do you realise, Len, that if poor Sir Arthur Stanley hadn't been sentimental and had turned Nigel straight over to the police, three other people would be alive today? It's a solemn thought."

"Still, one can understand what he felt about it—"

"Please, Miss Sally."

"Yes, Akibombo?"

"If you meet my Professor at University party tonight will you tell him, please, that I have done some good thinking? My Professor he says often that I have a muddled thought process."

"I'll tell him," said Sally.

Len Bateson was looking the picture of gloom.

"In a week's time you'll be back in America," he said.

There was a momentary silence.

"I shall come back," said Sally. "Or you might come and do a course over there."

"What's the use?"

"Akibombo," said Sally, "would you like, one day, to be Best Man at a wedding?"

"What is Best Man, please?"

"The bridegroom, Len here for instance, gives you a ring to keep for him, and he and you go to church very smartly dressed and at the right moment he asks you for the ring and you give it to him, and he puts it on my finger, and the organ plays the wedding march and everybody cries. And there we are."

"You mean that you and Mr. Len are to be married?"

"That's the idea."

"Sally!"

"Unless, of course, Len doesn't care for the idea."

"Sally! But you don't know—about my father—"

"So what? Of course I know. So your father's nuts. All right, so are lots of people's fathers."

"It isn't a hereditary type of mania. I can assure you of that, Sally, if you only knew how desperately unhappy I've been about you."

"I did just have a tiny suspicion."

"In Africa," said Mr. Akibombo, "in old days, before Atomic Age and scientific thought had come, marriage customs very curious and interesting. I tell you—"

"You'd better not," said Sally. "I have an idea they might make both Len and me blush, and when you've got red hair it's very noticeable when you blush."

Hercule Poirot signed the last of the letters that Miss Lemon had laid before him.

"*Très bien*," he said gravely. "Not a single mistake."

Miss Lemon looked slightly affronted.

"I don't often make mistakes, I hope," she said.

"Not often. But it has happened. How is your sister, by the way?"

"She is thinking of going on a cruise, M. Poirot. To the Northern capitals."

"Ah," said Hercule Poirot.

He wondered if—possibly—on a cruise—?

Not that he himself would undertake a sea voyage—not for any inducement. . . .

The clock behind him struck one.

> "*The clock struck one,*
> *The mouse ran down,*
> *Hickory dickory dock,*"

declared Hercule Poirot.

"I beg your pardon, M. Poirot?"

"Nothing," said Hercule Poirot.

The Crooked House

CHAPTER 1

I FIRST CAME to know Sophia Leonides in Egypt towards the end of the war. She held a fairly high administrative post in one of the Foreign Office departments out there. I knew her first in an official capacity, and I soon appreciated the efficiency that had brought her to the position she held, in spite of her youth (she was at that time just twenty two).

Besides being extremely easy to look at, she had a clear mind and a dry sense of humour that I found very delightful. We became friends. She was a person whom it was extraordinarily easy to talk to and we enjoyed our dinners and occasional dances very much.

All this I knew; it was not until I was ordered East at the close of the European war that I knew something else—that I loved Sophia and that I wanted to marry her.

We were dining at Shepheard's when I made this discovery. It did not come to me with any shock of surprise, but more as the recognition of a fact with which I had been long familiar. I looked at her with new eyes—but I saw what I had already known for a long time. I liked everything I saw. The dark crisp hair that sprang up proudly from her forehead, the vivid blue eyes, the small square fighting chin, and the straight nose. I liked the well cut light grey tailormade, and the crisp white shirt. She looked refreshingly English and that appealed to me strongly after three years without seeing my native land. Nobody, I thought, could be more English —and even as I was thinking exactly that, I suddenly wondered if, in fact, she was, or indeed could be, as English as she looked. Does the real thing ever have the perfection of a stage performance?

I realised that much and freely as we had talked together, discussing ideas, our likes and dislikes, the future, our immediate friends and acquaintances—Sophia had never mentioned her home or her family. She knew all about me (she was, as I have indicated, a good listener) but about her I knew nothing. She had, I supposed, the usual background, but she had never talked about it. And until this moment I had never realised the fact.

Sophia asked me what I was thinking about.

I replied truthfully: "You."

"I see," she said. And she sounded as though she did see.

"We may not meet again for a couple of years," I said. "I don't know when I shall get back to England. But as soon as I do get back, the first thing I shall do will be to come and see you and ask you to marry me."

She took it without batting an eyelash. She sat there, smoking, not looking at me.

For a moment or two I was nervous that she might not understand.

"Listen," I said. "The one thing I'm determined not to do, is to ask you to marry me now. That wouldn't work out anyway. First you might turn me down, and then I'd go off miserable and probably tie up with some ghastly woman just to restore my vanity. And if you didn't turn me down what could we do about it? Get married and part at once? Get engaged and settle down to a long waiting period. I couldn't stand your doing that. You might meet someone else and feel bound to be 'loyal' to me. We've been living in a queer hectic get-on-with-it-quickly atmosphere. Marriages and love affairs making and breaking all round us. I'd like to feel you'd gone home, free and independent, to look round you and size up the new post-war world and decide what you want out of it. What is between you and me, Sophia, has got to be permanent. I've no use for any other kind of marriage."

"No more have I," said Sophia.

"On the other hand," I said, "I think I'm entitled to let you know how I—well—how I feel."

"But without undue lyrical expression?" murmured Sophia.

"Darling—don't you understand? I've tried not to say I love you—"

She stopped me.

"I do understand, Charles. And I like your funny way of doing things. And you may come and see me when you come back—if you still want to—"

It was my turn to interrupt.

"There's no doubt about that."

"There's always a doubt about everything, Charles. There may always be some incalculable factor that upsets the apple cart. For one thing, you don't know much about me, do you?"

"I don't even know where you live in England."

"I live at Swinly Dean."

I nodded at the mention of the well-known outer suburb of London which boasts three excellent golf courses for the city financier.

She added softly in a musing voice: "In a little crooked house . . ."

I must have looked slightly startled, for she seemed amused, and explained by elaborating the quotation "'*And they all lived together in a little crooked house.*' That's us. Not really such a little house either. But definitely crooked—running to gables and half-timbering!"

"Are you one of a large family? Brothers and sisters?"

"One brother, one sister, a mother, a father, an uncle, an aunt by marriage, a grandfather, a great aunt and a step grandmother."

"Good gracious!" I exclaimed, slightly overwhelmed.

She laughed.

"Of course we don't normally all live together. The war and blitzes have brought that about—but I don't know—" she frowned reflectively—"perhaps spiritually the family has always lived together—under my grandfather's eye and protection. He's rather a Person, my grandfather. He's over eighty, about four foot ten, and everybody else looks rather dim beside him."

"He sounds interesting," I said.

"He is interesting. He's a Greek from Smyrna. Aristide Leonides." She added, with a twinkle, "He's extremely rich."

"Will anybody be rich after this is over?"

"My grandfather will," said Sophia with assurance. "No Soak-the-rich tactics would have any effect on him. He'd just soak the soakers.

"I wonder," she added, "if you'll like him?"

"Do you?" I asked.

"Better than anyone in the world," said Sophia.

CHAPTER 2

IT WAS over two years before I returned to England. They were not easy years. I wrote to Sophia and heard from her fairly frequently. Her letters, like mine, were not love letters. They were letters written to each other by close friends—they dealt with ideas and thoughts and with comments on the daily trend of life. Yet I know that as far as I was concerned, and I believed as far as Sophia was concerned too, our feeling for each other grew and strengthened.

I returned to England on a soft grey day in September. The leaves on the trees were golden in the evening light. There were playful gusts of wind. From the airfield I sent a telegram to Sophia.

"Just arrived back. Will you dine this evening Mario's nine o'clock Charles."

A couple of hours later I was sitting reading the Times; and scanning the Births Marriages and Death column my eye was caught by the name Leonides:

On Sept. 19th, at Three Gables, Swinly Dean, Aristide Leonides, beloved husband of Brenda Leonides, in his eighty fifth year. Deeply regretted.

There was another announcement immediately below:

Leonides. Suddenly, at his residence Three Gables, Swinly Dean, Aristide Leonides. Deeply mourned by his loving children and grandchildren. Flowers to St. Eldred's Church, Swinly Dean.

I found the two announcements rather curious. There seemed to have been some faulty staff work resulting in overlapping. But my main preoccupation was Sophia. I hastily sent her a second telegram:

"Just seen news of your grandfather's death. Very sorry. Let me know when I can see you. Charles."

A telegram from Sophia reached me at six o'clock at my father's house. It said:

"Will be at Mario's nine o'clock. Sophia."

The thought of meeting Sophia again made me both nervous and excited. The time crept by with maddening slowness. I was at Mario's waiting twenty minutes too early. Sophia herself was only five minutes late.

It is always a shock to meet again someone whom you have not seen for a long time but who has been very much present in your mind during that period. When at last Sophia came through the swing doors our meeting seemed completely unreal. She was wearing black, and that, in some curious way, startled me! Most other women were wearing black, but I got it into my head that it was definitely mourning—and it surprised me that Sophia should be the kind of person who did wear black—even for a near relative.

We had cocktails—then went and found our table. We talked rather fast and feverishly—asking after old friends of the Cairo days. It was artificial conversation but it tided us over the first awkwardness. I expressed commiseration for her grandfather's death and Sophia said quietly that it had been "very sudden." Then we started off again reminiscing. I began to feel, uneasily, that something was the matter—something, I mean, other than the first natural awkwardnesses of meeting again. There was something wrong, definitely wrong, with Sophia herself. Was she, perhaps, going to tell me that she had found some other man whom she cared for more than she did for me? That her feeling for me had been "all a mistake"?

Somehow I didn't think it was that—I didn't know what it was. Meanwhile we continued our artificial talk.

Then, quite suddenly, as the waiter placed coffee on the table and retired bowing, everything swung into focus. Here were Sophia and I sitting together as so often before at a small table in a restaurant. The years of our separation might never have been.

"Sophia," I said.

And immediately she said, "Charles!"

I drew a deep breath of relief.

"Thank goodness that's over," I said. "What's been the matter with us?"

"Probably my fault. I was stupid."

"But it's all right now?"

"Yes, it's all right now."

We smiled at each other.

"Darling!" I said. And then: "How soon will you marry me?"

Her smile died. The something, whatever it was, was back.

"I don't know," she said. "I'm not sure, Charles, that I can ever marry you."

"But, Sophia! Why not? Is it because you feel I'm a stranger? Do you want time to get used to me again? Is there someone else? No—" I broke off. "I'm a fool. It's none of those things."

"No, it isn't." She shook her head. I waited. She said in a low voice:

"It's my grandfather's death."

"Your grandfather's death? But why? What earthly difference can that make? You don't mean—surely you can't imagine—is it money? Hasn't he left any? But surely, dearest—"

"It isn't money." She gave a fleeting smile. "I think you'd be quite willing to 'take me in my shift' as the old saying goes. And grandfather never lost any money in his life."

"Then what is it?"

"It's just his death—you see, I think, Charles, that he didn't just—die. I think he may have been—killed . . ."

I stared at her.

"But—what a fantastic idea. What made you think of it?"

"I didn't think of it. The doctor was queer to begin with. He wouldn't sign a certificate. They're going to have a post mortem. It's quite clear that they suspect something is wrong."

I didn't dispute that with her. Sophia had plenty of brains; any conclusions she had drawn could be relied upon.

Instead I said earnestly:

"Their suspicions may be quite unjustified. But putting that aside, supposing that they are justified, how does that affect you and me?"

"It might under certain circumstances. You're in the Diplomatic Service. They're rather particular about wives. No—please don't say all the things that you're just bursting to say. You're bound to say them—and I believe you really think them—and theoretically

I quite agree with them. But I'm proud—I'm devilishly proud. I want our marriage to be a good thing for everyone—I don't want to represent one half of a sacrifice for love! And, as I say, it may be all right . . ."

"You mean the doctor—may have made a mistake?"

"Even if he hasn't made a mistake, it won't matter—so long as the right person killed him."

"What do you mean, Sophia?"

"It was a beastly thing to say. But, after all, one might as well be honest."

She forestalled my next words.

"No, Charles, I'm not going to say any more. I've probably said too much already. But I was determined to come and meet you tonight—to see you myself and make you understand. We can't settle anything until this is cleared up."

"At least tell me about it."

She shook her head.

"I don't want to."

"But—Sophia—"

"No, Charles. I don't want you to see us from my angle. I want you to see us unbiassed from the outside point of view."

"And how am I to do that?"

She looked at me, a queer light in her brilliant blue eyes.

"You'll get that from your father," she said.

I had told Sophia in Cairo that my father was Assistant Commissioner of Scotland Yard. He still held that office. At her words, I felt a cold weight settling down on me.

"It's as bad as that, then?"

"I think so. Do you see a man sitting at a table by the door all alone—rather a nice-looking stolid ex-Army type?"

"Yes."

"He was on Swinly Dean platform this evening when I got into the train."

"You mean he's followed you here?"

"Yes. I think we're all—how does one put it?—under observation. They more or less hinted that we'd all better not leave the house. But I was determined to see you." Her small square chin shot out pugnaciously. "I got out of the bathroom window and shinned down the water pipe."

"Darling!"

351

"But the police are very efficient. And of course there was the telegram I sent you. Well—never mind—we're here—together . . . But from now on, we've both got to play a lone hand."

She paused and then added:

"Unfortunately—there's no doubt—about our loving each other."

"No doubt at all," I said. "And don't say unfortunately. You and I have survived a world war, we've had plenty of near escapes from sudden death—and I don't see why the sudden death of just one old man—how old was he, by the way?"

"Eighty five."

"Of course. It was in the Times. If you ask me, he just died of old age, and any self-respecting G.P. would accept the fact."

"If you'd known my grandfather," said Sophia, "you'd have been surprised at his dying of anything!"

CHAPTER 3

I'D ALWAYS taken a certain amount of interest in my father's police work, but nothing had prepared me for the moment when I should come to take a direct and personal interest in it.

I had not yet seen the Old Man. He had been out when I arrived, and after a bath, a shave and a change I had gone out to meet Sophia. When I returned to the house, however, Glover told me that he was in his study.

He was at his desk, frowning over a lot of papers. He jumped up when I came in.

"Charles! Well, well, it's been a long time."

Our meeting, after five years of war, would have disappointed a Frenchman. Actually all the emotion of reunion was there all right. The Old Man and I are very fond of each other, and we understand each other pretty well.

"I've got some whisky," he said. "Say when. Sorry I was out

when you got here. I'm up to the ears in work. Hell of a case just unfolding."

I leaned back in my chair and lit a cigarette.

"Aristide Leonides?" I asked.

His brows came down quickly over his eyes. He shot me a quick appraising glance. His voice was polite and steely.

"Now what makes you say that, Charles?"

"I'm right then?"

"How did you know about this?"

"Information received."

The Old Man waited.

"My information," I said, "came from the stable itself."

"Come on, Charles, let's have it."

"You mayn't like it," I said. "I met Sophia Leonides out in Cairo. I fell in love with her. I'm going to marry her. I met her tonight. She dined with me."

"Dined with you? In London? I wonder just how she managed to do that? The family were asked—oh, quite politely, to stay put."

"Quite so. She shinned down a pipe from the bathroom window."

The Old Man's lips twitched for a moment into a smile.

"She seems," he said, "to be a young lady of some resource."

"But your police force is fully efficient," I said. "A nice Army type tracked her to Mario's. I shall figure in the reports you get. Five foot eleven, brown hair, brown eyes, dark blue pinstripe suit etc."

The Old Man looked at me hard.

"Is this—serious?" he asked.

"Yes," I said. "It's serious, dad."

There was a moment's silence.

"Do you mind?" I asked.

"I shouldn't have minded—a week ago. They're a well established family—the girl will have money—and I know you. You don't lose your head easily. As it is—"

"Yes, dad?"

"It may be all right, if—"

"If what?"

"If the right person did it."

It was the second time that night I had heard that phrase. I began to be interested.

353

"Just who is the right person?"

He threw a sharp glance at me.

"How much do you know about it all?"

"Nothing."

"Nothing?" He looked surprised. "Didn't the girl tell you?"

"No . . . She said she'd rather I saw it all—from an outside point of view."

"Now I wonder why that was?"

"Isn't it rather obvious?"

"No, Charles. I don't think it is."

He walked up and down frowning. He had lit a cigar and the cigar had gone out. That showed me just how disturbed the old boy was.

"How much do you know about the family?" he shot at me.

"Damnall! I know there was the old man and a lot of sons and grandchildren and in-laws. I haven't got the ramifications clear." I paused and then said, "You'd better put me in the picture, dad."

"Yes." He sat down. "Very well then—I'll begin at the beginning —with Aristide Leonides. He arrived in England when he was twenty four."

"A Greek from Smyrna."

"You do know that much?"

"Yes, but it's about all I do know."

The door opened and Glover came in to say that Chief Inspector Taverner was here.

"He's in charge of the case," said my father. "We'd better have him in. He's been checking up on the family. Knows more about them than I do."

I asked if the local police had called in the Yard.

"It's in our jurisdiction. Swinly Dean is Greater London."

I nodded as Chief Inspector Taverner came into the room. I knew Taverner from many years back. He greeted me warmly and congratulated me on my safe return.

"I'm putting Charles in the picture," said the Old Man. "Correct me if I go wrong, Taverner. Leonides came to London in 1884. He started up a little restaurant in Soho. It paid. He started up another. Soon he owned seven or eight of them. They all paid hand over fist."

"Never made any mistakes in anything he handled," said Chief Inspector Taverner.

"He'd got a natural flair," said my father. "In the end he was behind most of the well known restaurants in London. Then he went into the catering business in a big way."

"He was behind a lot of other businesses as well," said Taverner. "Second hand clothes trade, cheap jewellery stores, lots of things. Of course," he added thoughtfully, "he was always a twister."

"You mean he was a crook?" I asked.

Taverner shook his head.

"No, I don't mean that. Crooked, yes—but not a crook. Never anything outside the law. But he was the sort of chap that thought up all the ways you can get round the law. He's cleaned up a packet that way even in this last war, and old as he was. Nothing he did was ever illegal—but as soon as he'd got on to it, you had to have a law about it, if you know what I mean. But by that time he'd gone on to the next thing."

"He doesn't sound a very attractive character," I said.

"Funnily enough, he was attractive. He'd got personality, you know. You could feel it. Nothing much to look at. Just a gnome —ugly little fellow—but magnetic—women always fell for him."

"He made a rather astonishing marriage," said my father. "Married the daughter of a country squire—an M.F.H."

I raised my eyebrows. "Money?"

The Old Man shook his head.

"No, it was a love match. She met him over some catering arrangements for a friend's wedding—and she fell for him. Her parents cut up rough, but she was determined to have him. I tell you, the man had charm—there was something exotic and dynamic about him that appealed to her. She was bored stiff with her own kind."

"And the marriage was happy?"

"It was very happy, oddly enough. Of course their respective friends didn't mix (those were the days before money swept aside all class distinctions) but that didn't seem to worry them. They did without friends. He built a rather preposterous house at Swinly Dean and they lived there and had eight children."

"This is indeed a family chronicle."

"Old Leonides was rather clever to choose Swinly Dean. It was only beginning to be fashionable then. The second and third golf courses hadn't been made. There was a mixture there of Old Inhabitants who were passionately fond of their gardens and who

355

liked Mrs. Leonides, and rich City men who wanted to be in with Leonides, so they could take their choice of acquaintances. They were perfectly happy, I believe, until she died of pneumonia in 1905."

"Leaving him with eight children?"

"One died in infancy. Two of the sons were killed in the last war. One daughter married and went to Australia and died there. An unmarried daughter was killed in a motor accident. Another died a year or two ago. There are two still living—the eldest son, Roger, who is married but has no children, and Philip who married a well known actress and has three children, Your Sophia, Eustace and Josephine."

"And they are all living at—what is it?—Three Gables?"

"Yes. The Roger Leonides were bombed out early in the war. Philip and his family have lived there since 1938. And there's an elderly aunt, Miss de Haviland, sister of the first Mrs. Leonides. She always loathed her brother-in-law apparently, but when her sister died she considered it her duty to accept her brother-in-law's invitation to live with him and bring up the children."

"She's very hot on duty," said Inspector Taverner. "But she's not the kind that changes her mind about people. She always disapproved of Leonides and his methods—"

"Well," I said, "it seems a pretty good house full. Who do you think killed him?"

Taverner shook his head.

"Early days," he said, "early days to say that."

"Come on, Taverner," I said. "I bet you think you know who did it. We're not in court, man."

"No," said Taverner gloomily. "And we never may be."

"You mean he may not have been murdered?"

"Oh, he was murdered all right. Poisoned. But you know what these poisoning cases are like. It's very tricky getting the evidence. Very tricky. All the possibilities may point one way—"

"That's what I'm trying to get at. You've got it all taped out in your mind, haven't you?"

"It's a case of very strong probability. It's one of those obvious things. The perfect set-up. But I don't know, I'm sure. It's tricky."

I looked appealingly at the Old Man.

He said slowly:

"In murder cases, as you know, Charles, the obvious is usually the right solution. Old Leonides married again, ten years ago."

"When he was seventy five?"

"Yes, he married a young woman of twenty four."

I whistled.

"What sort of a young woman?"

"A young woman out of a tea shop. A perfectly respectable young woman—good looking in an anaemic, apathetic sort of way."

"And she's the strong probablility?"

"I ask you, sir," said Taverner. "She's only thirty four now—and that's a dangerous age. She likes living soft. And there's a young man in the house. Tutor to the grandchildren. Not been in the war—got a bad heart or something. They're as thick as thieves."

I looked at him thoughtfully. It was, certainly, an old and familiar pattern. The mixture as before. And the second Mrs. Leonides was, my father had emphasized, very respectable. In the name of respectability many murders have been committed.

"What was it?" I asked. "Arsenic?"

"No. We haven't got the analyst's report yet—but the doctor thinks it's eserine."

"That's a little unusual, isn't it? Surely easy to trace purchaser."

"Not this thing. It was his own stuff, you see. Eyedrops."

"Leonides suffered from diabetes," said my father. "He had regular injections of insulin. Insulin is given out in small bottles with a rubber cap. A hypodermic needle is pressed down through the rubber cap and the injection drawn up."

I guessed the next bit.

"And it wasn't insulin in the bottle, but eserine?"

"Exactly."

"And who gave him the injection?" I asked.

"His wife."

I understood now what Sophia had meant by the "right person."

I asked: "Does the family get on well with the second Mrs. Leonides?"

"No. I gather they are hardly on speaking terms."

357

It all seemed clearer and clearer. Nevertheless, Inspector Taverner was clearly not happy about it.

"What don't you like about it?" I asked him.

"If she did it, Mr. Charles, it would have been so easy for her to substitute a bona fide bottle of insulin afterwards. In fact, if she is guilty, I can't imagine why on earth she didn't do just that."

"Yes, it does seem indicated. Plenty of insulin about?"

"Oh yes, full bottles and empty ones. And if she'd done that, ten to one the doctor wouldn't have spotted it. Very little is known of the post mortem appearances in human poisoning by eserine. But as it was he checked up on the insulin (in case it was the wrong strength or something like that) and so, of course, he soon spotted that it wasn't insulin."

"So it seems," I said thoughtfully, "that Mrs. Leonides was either very stupid—or possibly very clever."

"You mean—"

"That she may be gambling on your coming to the conclusion that nobody could have been as stupid as she appears to have been. What are the alternatives? Any other—suspects?"

The Old Man said quietly:

"Practically anyone in the house could have done it. There was always a good store of insulin—at least a fortnight's supply. One of the phials could have been tampered with, and replaced in the knowledge that it would be used in due course."

"And anybody, more or less, had access to them?"

"They weren't locked away. They were kept on a special shelf in the medicine cupboard in the bathroom of his part of the house. Everybody in the house came and went freely."

"Any strong motive?"

My father sighed.

"My dear Charles, Aristide Leonides was enormously rich! He had made over a good deal of his money to his family, it is true, but it may be that somebody wanted more."

"But the one that wanted it most would be the present widow. Has her young man any money?"

"No. Poor as a Church mouse."

Something clicked in my brain. I remembered Sophia's quotation. I suddenly remembered the whole verse of the nursery rhyme:

There was a crooked man and he went a crooked mile
    He found a crooked sixpence beside a crooked stile
He had a crooked cat which caught a crooked mouse
    And they all lived together in a little crooked house.

I said to Taverner:

"How does she strike you—Mrs. Leonides? What do you think of her?"

He replied slowly:

"It's hard to say—very hard to say. She's not easy. Very quiet —so you don't know what she's thinking. But she likes living soft—that I'll swear I'm right about. Puts me in mind, you know, of a cat, a big purring lazy cat . . . Not that I've anything against cats. Cats are all right . . ."

He sighed.

"What we want," he said, "is evidence."

Yes, I thought, we all wanted evidence that Mrs. Leonides had poisoned her husband. Sophia wanted it, and I wanted it, and Chief Inspector Taverner wanted it.

Then everything in the garden would be lovely!

But Sophia wasn't sure, and I wasn't sure, and I didn't think Chief Inspector Taverner was sure either. . . .

CHAPTER 4

ON THE FOLLOWING DAY I went down to Three Gables with Taverner.

My position was a curious one. It was, to say the least of it, quite unorthodox. But the Old Man has never been highly orthodox.

I had a certain standing. I had worked with the Special Branch at the Yard during the early days of the war.

This, of course, was entirely different—but my earlier performances had given me, so to speak, a certain official standing.

My father said:

"If we're ever going to solve this case, we've got to get some inside dope. We've got to know all about the people in that house. We've got to know them from the inside—not the outside. You're the man who can get that for us."

I didn't like it. I threw my cigarette end into the grate as I said:

"I'm a police spy? Is that it? I'm to get the inside dope from Sophia whom I love and who both loves and trusts me, or so I believe."

The Old Man became quite irritable. He said sharply:

"For Heaven's sake don't take the commonplace view. To begin with, you don't believe, do you, that your young woman murdered her grandfather?"

"Of course not. The idea's absolutely absurd."

"Very well—we don't think so either. She's been away for some years, she has always been on perfectly amicable terms with him. She has a very generous income and he would have been, I should say, delighted to hear of her engagement to you and would probably have made a handsome marriage settlement on her. We don't suspect her. Why should we? But you can make quite sure of one thing. If this thing isn't cleared up, that girl won't marry you. From what you've told me I'm fairly sure of that. And mark this, it's the kind of crime that may never be cleared up. We may be reasonably sure that the wife and her young man were in cahoots over it—but proving it will be another matter. There's not even a case to put up to the D.P.P. so far. And unless we get definite evidence against her, there'll always be a nasty doubt. You see that, don't you?"

Yes, I saw that.

The Old Man then said quietly:

"Why not put it to her?"

"You mean—ask Sophia if I—" I stopped.

The Old Man was nodding his head vigorously.

"Yes, yes . . . I'm not asking you to worm your way in without telling the girl what you're up to. See what she has to say about it."

And so it came about that the following day I drove down

with Chief Inspector Taverner and Detective Sergeant Lamb to Swinly Dean.

A little way beyond the golf course, we turned in at a gateway where I imagined that before the war there had been an imposing pair of gates. Patriotism or ruthless requisitioning had swept these away. We drove up a long curving drive flanked with rhododendrons and came out on a gravelled sweep in front of the house.

It was incredible! I wondered why it had been called Three Gables. Eleven Gables would have been more apposite! The curious thing was that it had a strange air of being distorted—and I thought I knew why. It was the type, really, of a cottage, it was a cottage swollen out of all proportion. It was like looking at a country cottage through a gigantic magnifying glass. The slant-wise beams, the half-timbering, the gables—it was a little crooked house that had grown like a mushroom in the night!

Yet I got the idea. It was a Greek restauranteer's idea of something English. It was meant to be an Englishman's home—built the size of a castle! I wondered what the first Mrs. Leonides had thought of it. She had not, I fancied, been consulted or shown the plans. It was, most probably, her exotic husband's little surprise. I wondered if she had shuddered or smiled.

Apparently she had lived there quite happily.

"Bit overwhelming, isn't it?" said Inspector Taverner. "Of course, the old gentleman built on to it a good deal—making it into three separate houses, so to speak, with kitchens and everything. It's all tip top inside, fitted up like a luxury hotel."

Sophia came out of the front door. She was hatless and wore a green shirt and a tweed skirt.

She stopped dead when she saw me.

"You?" she exclaimed.

I said:

"Sophia, I've got to talk to you. Where can we go?"

For a moment I thought she was going to demur, then she turned and said: "This way."

We walked down across the lawn. There was a fine view across Swinly Dean's No 1 course—away to a clump of pine trees on a hill, and beyond it, to the dimness of hazy countryside.

Sophia led me to a rockgarden, now somewhat neglected,

where there was a rustic wooden seat of great discomfort, and we sat down.

"Well?" she said.

Her voice was not encouraging.

I said my piece—all of it.

She listened very attentively. Her face gave little indication of what she was thinking, but when I came at last to a full stop, she sighed. It was a deep sigh.

"Your father," she said, "is a very clever man."

"The Old Man has his points. I think it's a rotten idea myself —but—"

She interrupted me.

"Oh no," she said. "It isn't a rotten idea at all. It's the only thing that might be any good. Your father, Charles, knows exactly what's been going on in my mind. He knows better than you do."

With sudden almost despairing vehemence, she drove one clenched hand into the palm of the other.

"I've got to have the truth. I've got to know."

"Because of us? But, dearest—"

"Not only because of us, Charles. I've got to know for my own peace of mind. You see, Charles, I didn't tell you last night— but the truth is—I'm afraid."

"Afraid?"

"Yes—afraid—afraid—afraid. The police think, your father thinks, everybody thinks—that it was Brenda."

"The probabilities—"

"Oh yes, it's quite probable. It's possible. But when I say, 'Brenda probably did it' I'm quite conscious that it's only wishful thinking. Because, you see, I don't really think so."

"You don't think so?" I said slowly.

"I don't know. You've heard about it all from the outside as I wanted you to. Now I'll show it to you from the inside. I simply don't feel that Brenda is that kind of a person—she's not the sort of person, I feel, who would ever do anything that might involve her in any danger. She's far too careful of herself."

"How about this young man? Laurence Brown."

"Laurence is a complete rabbit. He wouldn't have the guts."

"I wonder."

"Yes, we don't really know, do we? I mean, people are capable

362

of surprising one frightfully. One gets an idea of them into one's head, and sometimes it's absolutely wrong. Not always—but sometimes. But all the same, Brenda—" she shook her head—"she's always acted so completely in character. She's what I call the harem type. Likes sitting about and eating sweets and having nice clothes and jewellery and reading cheap novels and going to the cinema. And it's a queer thing to say, when one remembers that he was eighty five, but I really think she was rather thrilled by grandfather. He had a power, you know. I should imagine he could make a woman feel—oh—rather like a queen—the Sultan's favourite! I think—I've always thought—that he made Brenda feel as though she were an exciting romantic person. He's been clever with women all his life—and that kind of thing is a sort of art—you don't lose the knack of it, however old you are."

I left the problem of Brenda for the moment and harked back to a phrase of Sophia's which had disturbed me.

"Why did you say," I asked, "that you were afraid?"

Sophia shivered a little and pressed her hands together.

"Because it's true," she said in a low voice. "It's very important, Charles, that I should make you understand this. You see, we're a very queer family . . . There's a lot of ruthlessness in us—and —different kinds of ruthlessness. That's what's so disturbing. The different kinds."

She must have seen incomprehension in my face. She went on, speaking energetically.

"I'll try and make what I mean clear. Grandfather, for instance. Once when he was telling us about his boyhood in Smyrna, he mentioned, quite casually, that he had stabbed two men. It was some kind of a brawl—there had been some unforgivable insult—I don't know—but it was just a thing that had happened quite naturally. He'd really practically forgotten about it. But it was, somehow, such a queer thing to hear about, quite casually, in England."

I nodded.

"That's one kind of ruthlessness," went on Sophia, "and then there was my grandmother. I only just remember her, but I've heard a good deal about her. I think she might have had the ruthlessness that comes from having no imagination whatever. All those foxhunting forbears—and the old Generals, the shoot 'em down type. Full of rectitude and arrogance, and not a bit afraid of taking responsibility in matters of life and death."

"Isn't that a bit far fetched?"

"Yes, I daresay—but I'm always rather afraid of that type. It's full of rectitude but it is ruthless. And then there's my own mother—she's an actress—she's a darling, but she's got absolutely no sense of proportion. She's one of those unconscious egoists who can only see things in relation as to how it affects them. That's rather frightening, sometimes, you know. And there's Clemency, Uncle Roger's wife. She's a scientist—she's doing some kind of very important research—she's ruthless too, in a kind of coldblooded impersonal way. Uncle Roger's the exact opposite —he's the kindest and most lovable person in the world, but he's got a really terrific temper. Things make his blood boil and then he hardly knows what he's doing. And there's father—"

She made a long pause.

"Father," she said slowly, "is almost too well controlled. You never know what he's thinking. He never shows any emotion at all. It's probably a kind of unconscious self defence against mother's absolute orgies of emotion, but sometimes—it worries me a little."

"My dear child," I said, "you're working yourself up unnecessarily. What it comes to in the end is that everybody, perhaps, is capable of murder."

"I suppose that's true. Even me."

"Not you!"

"Oh yes, Charles, you can't make me an exception. I suppose I could murder someone . . ." She was silent a moment or two, then added, "But if so, it would have to be for something really worth while!"

I laughed then. I couldn't help it. And Sophia smiled.

"Perhaps I'm a fool," she said, "but we've got to find out the truth about grandfather's death. We've got to. If only it was Brenda . . ."

I felt suddenly rather sorry for Brenda Leonides.

CHAPTER 5

ALONG THE PATH towards us came a tall figure walking briskly. It had on a battered old felt hat, a shapeless skirt, and a rather cumbersome jersey.

"Aunt Edith," said Sophia.

The figure paused once or twice, stooping to the flower borders, then it advanced upon us. I rose to my feet.

"This is Charles Hayward, Aunt Edith. My aunt, Miss de Haviland."

Edith de Haviland was a woman of about seventy. She had a mass of untidy grey hair, a weatherbeaten face and a shrewd and piercing glance.

"How d'ye do?" she said. "I've heard about you. Back from the East. How's your father?"

Rather surprised, I said he was very well.

"Knew him when he was a boy," said Miss de Haviland. "Knew his mother very well. You look rather like her. Have you come to help us—or the other thing?"

"I hope to help," I said rather uncomfortably.

She nodded.

"We could do with some help. Place swarming with policemen. Pop out at you all over the place. Don't like some of the types. A boy who's been to a decent school oughtn't to go into the police. Saw Moyra Kinoul's boy the other day holding up the traffic at Marble Arch. Makes you feel you don't know where you are!"

She turned to Sophia:

"Nannie's asking for you, Sophia. Fish."

"Bother," said Sophia. "I'll go and telephone about it."

She walked briskly towards the house. Miss de Haviland turned and walked slowly in the same direction. I fell into step beside her.

"Don't know what we'd all do without Nannies," said Miss de Haviland. "Nearly everybody's got an old Nannie. They come back and wash and iron and cook and do housework. Faithful. Chose this one myself—years ago."

She stooped and pulled viciously at an entangling twining bit of green.

"Hateful stuff—bindweed! Worst weed there is! Choking, entangling—and you can't get at it properly, runs along underground."

With her heel she ground the handful of greenstuff viciously underfoot.

"This is a bad business, Charles Hayward," she said. She was looking towards the house. "What do the police think about it? Suppose I mustn't ask you that. Seems odd to think of Aristide being poisoned. For that matter it seems odd to think of him being dead. I never liked him—never! But I can't get used to the idea of his being dead . . . Makes the house seem so—empty."

I said nothing. For all her curt way of speech, Edith de Haviland seemed in a reminiscent mood.

"Was thinking this morning—I've lived here a long time. Over forty years. Came here when my sister died. He asked me to. Seven children—and the youngest only a year old . . . Couldn't leave 'em to be brought up by a dago, could I? An impossible marriage, of course. I always felt Marcia must have been—well—bewitched. Ugly common little foreigner! He gave me a free hand —I will say that. Nurses, governesses, schools. And proper wholesome nursery food—not those queer spiced rice dishes he used to eat."

"And you've been here ever since?" I murmured.

"Yes. Queer in a way . . . I could have left, I suppose, when the children grew up and married . . . I suppose, really, I'd got interested in the garden. And then there was Philip. If a man marries an actress he can't expect to have any home life. Don't know why actresses have children. As soon as a baby's born they rush off and play in Repertory in Edinburgh or somewhere as remote as possible. Philip did the sensible thing—moved in here with his books."

"What does Philip Leonides do?"

"Writes books. Can't think why. Nobody wants to read them. All about obscure historical details. You've never even heard of them, have you?"

I admitted it.

"Too much money, that's what he's had," said Miss de Haviland. "Most people have to stop being cranks and earn a living."

"Don't his books pay?"

"Of course not. He's supposed to be a great authority on certain periods and all that. But he doesn't have to make his books pay —Aristide settled something like a hundred thousand pounds— something quite fantastic—on him! To avoid death duties! Aristide made them all financially independent. Roger runs Associated Catering—Sophia has a very handsome allowance. The children's money is in trust for them."

"So no one gains particularly by his death?"

She threw me a strange glance.

"Yes, they do. They all get more money. But they could probably have had it, if they asked for it, anyway."

"Have you any idea who poisoned him, Miss de Haviland?"

She replied characteristically:

"No, indeed I haven't. It's upset me very much! Not nice to think one has a Borgia sort of person loose about the house. I suppose the police will fasten on poor Brenda."

"You don't think they'll be right in doing so?"

"I simply can't tell. She's always seemed to me a singularly stupid and commonplace young woman—rather conventional. Not my idea of a poisoner. Still, after all, if a young woman of twenty four marries a man close on eighty, it's fairly obvious that she's marrying him for his money. In the normal course of events she could have expected to become a rich widow fairly soon. But Aristide was a singularly tough old man. His diabetes wasn't getting any worse. He really looked like living to be a hundred. I suppose she got tired of waiting . . ."

"In that case," I said, and stopped.

"In that case," said Miss de Haviland briskly, "it will be more or less all right. Annoying publicity, of course. But after all, she isn't one of the family."

"You've no other ideas?" I asked.

"What other ideas should I have?"

I wondered. I had a suspicion that there might be more going on under the battered felt hat than I knew.

Behind the jerky, almost disconnected utterance, there was, I thought, a very shrewd brain at work. Just for a moment I even wondered whether Miss de Haviland had poisoned Aristide Leonides herself. . . .

It did not seem an impossible idea. At the back of my mind was the way she had ground the bindweed into the soil with her heel with a kind of vindictive thoroughness.

I remembered the word Sophia had used. Ruthlessness.

I stole a sideways glance at Edith de Haviland.

Given good and sufficient reason. . . . But what exactly would seem to Edith de Haviland good and sufficient reason?

To answer that, I should have to know her better.

CHAPTER 6

THE FRONT DOOR was open. We passed through it into a rather surprisingly spacious hall. It was furnished with restraint—well-polished dark oak and gleaming brass. At the back, where the staircase would normally appear, was a white panelled wall with a door in it.

"My brother-in-law's part of the house," said Miss de Haviland. "The ground floor is Philip and Magda's."

We went through a doorway on the left into a large drawing room. It had pale blue panelled walls, furniture covered in heavy brocade, and on every available table and on the walls were hung photographs and pictures of actors, dancers and stage scenes and designs. A Degas of ballet dancers hung over the mantelpiece. There were masses of flowers, enormous brown chrysanthemums and great vases of carnations.

"I suppose," said Miss de Haviland, "that you want to see Philip?"

Did I want to see Philip? I had no idea. All I had wanted to do was to see Sophia. That I had done. She had given emphatic encouragement to the Old Man's plan—but she had now receded from the scene and was presumably somewhere telephoning about fish, having given me no indication of how to proceed. Was I to approach Philip Leonides as a young man anxious to marry his daughter, or as a casual friend who had dropped in (surely not at such a moment!) or as an associate of the police?

Miss de Haviland gave me no time to consider her question. It was, indeed, not a question at all, but more an assertion. Miss de Haviland, I judged, was more inclined to assert than to question.

"We'll go to the library," she said.

She led me out of the drawing room, along a corridor and in through another door.

It was a big room, full of books. The books did not confine themselves to the bookcases that reached up to the ceiling. They were on chairs and tables and even on the floor. And yet there was no sense of disarray about them.

The room was cold. There was some smell absent in it that I was conscious of having expected. It smelt of the mustiness of old books and just a little of beeswax. In a second or two I realised what I missed. It was the scent of tobacco. Philip Leonides was not a smoker.

He got up from behind his table as we entered—a tall man aged somewhere around fifty, an extraordinarily handsome man. Everyone had laid so much emphasis on the ugliness of Aristide Leonides, that for some reason I expected his son to be ugly too. Certainly I was not prepared for this perfection of feature—the straight nose, the flawless line of jaw, the fair hair touched with grey that swept back from a well shaped forehead.

"This is Charles Hayward, Philip," said Edith de Haviland.

"Ah, how do you do?"

I could not tell if he had ever heard of me. The hand he gave me was cold. His face was quite incurious. It made me rather nervous. He stood there, patient and uninterested.

"Where are those awful policemen?" demanded Miss de Haviland. "Have they been in here?"

"I believe Chief Inspector—" (he glanced down at a card on the desk) "er—Taverner is coming to talk to me presently."

"Where is he now?"

"I've no idea, Aunt Edith. Upstairs, I suppose."

"With Brenda?"

"I really don't know."

Looking at Philip Leonides, it seemed quite impossible that a murder could have been committed anywhere in his vicinity.

"Is Magda up yet?"

"I don't know. She's not usually up before eleven."

"That sounds like her," said Edith de Haviland.

What sounded like Mrs. Philip Leonides was a high voice talking very rapidly and approaching very fast. The door behind me burst open and a woman came in. I don't know how she managed to give the impression of its being three women rather than one who entered.

She was smoking a cigarette in a long holder and was wearing a peach satin négligée which she was holding up with one hand. A cascade of Titian hair rippled down her back. Her face had that almost shocking air of nudity that a woman's has nowadays when it is not made up at all. Her eyes were blue and enormous and she was talking very rapidly in a husky rather attractive voice with a very clear enunciation.

"Darling, I can't stand it—I simply can't stand it—just think of the notices—it isn't in the papers yet, but of course it will be —and I simply can't make up my mind what I ought to wear at the inquest—very very subdued?—not black though, perhaps dark purple—and I simply haven't got a coupon left—I've lost the address of that dreadful man who sells them to me—you know, the garage somewhere near Shaftesbury Avenue—and if I went up there in the car the police would follow me, and they might ask the most awkward questions, mightn't they? I mean, what could one say? How calm you are, Philip! How can you be so calm? Don't you realise we can leave this awful house now. Freedom— freedom! Oh, how unkind—the poor old Sweetie—of course we'd never have left him while he was alive. He really did dote on us, didn't he—in spite of all the trouble that woman upstairs tried to make between us. I'm quite sure that if we had gone away and left him to her, he'd have cut us right out of everything. Horrible creature! After all, poor old Sweetie Pie was just on ninety— all the family feeling in the world couldn't have stood up against a dreadful woman who was on the spot. You know, Philip, I really believe that this would be a wonderful opportunity to put on the Edith Thompson play. This murder would give us a lot of advance publicity. Bildenstein said he could get the Thespian—that dreary play in verse about miners is coming off any minute—It's a wonderful part—wonderful. I know they say I must always play comedy because of my nose—but you know there's quite a lot of comedy to be got out of Edith Thompson—I don't think the author realised that—comedy heightens the suspense. I know just how I'd play it—commonplace, silly, make-believe up to the last minute and then—"

She cast out an arm—the cigarette fell out of the holder onto the polished mahogany of Philip's desk and began to burn it. Impassively he reached for it and dropped it into the waste paper basket.

"And then," whispered Magda Leonides, her eyes suddenly widening, her face stiffening, "just terror. . . ."

The stark fear stayed on her face for about twenty seconds, then her face relaxed, crumpled, a bewildered child was about to burst into tears.

Suddenly all emotion was wiped away as though by a sponge and turning to me, she asked in a businesslike tone:

"Don't you think that would be the way to play Edith Thompson?"

I said I thought that would be exactly the way to play Edith Thompson. At the moment I could only remember very vaguely who Edith Thompson was, but I was anxious to start off well with Sophia's mother.

"Rather like Brenda, really, wasn't she?" said Magda. "D'you know, I never thought of that. It's very interesting. Shall I point that out to the Inspector?"

The man behind the desk frowned very slightly.

"There's really no need, Magda," he said, "for you to see him at all. I can tell him anything he wants to know."

"Not see him?" Her voice went up. "But of course I must see him! Darling, darling, you're so terribly unimaginative! You don't realise the importance of details. He'll want to know exactly how and when everything happened, all the little things one noticed and wondered about at the time—"

"Mother," said Sophia, coming through the open door, "you're not to tell the Inspector a lot of lies."

"Sophia—darling . . ."

"I know, precious, that you've got it all set and that you're ready to give a most beautiful performance. But you've got it wrong. Quite wrong."

"Nonsense. You don't know—"

"I do know. You've got to play it quite differently, darling. Subdued—saying very little—holding it all back—on your guard —protecting the family."

Magda Leonides' face showed the naive perplexity of a child.

"Darling," she said, "do you really think—"

"Yes, I do. Throw it away. That's the idea."

Sophia added, as a little pleased smile began to show on her mother's face:

"I've made you some chocolate. It's in the drawing room."

"Oh—good—I'm starving—"

She paused in the doorway.

"You don't know," she said, and the words appeared to be addressed either to me or to the bookshelf behind my head, "how lovely it is to have a daughter!"

On this exit line she went out.

"God knows," said Miss de Haviland, "what she will say to the police!"

"She'll be all right," said Sophia.

"She might say anything."

"Don't worry," said Sophia. "She'll play it the way the producer says. I'm the producer!"

She went out after her mother, then wheeled back to say:

"Here's Chief Inspector Taverner to see you, father. You don't mind if Charles stays, do you?"

I thought that a very faint air of bewilderment showed on Philip Leonides' face. It well might! But his incurious habit served me in good stead. He murmured:

"Oh certainly—certainly," in a rather vague voice.

Chief Inspector Taverner came in, solid, dependable, and with an air of businesslike promptitude that was somehow soothing.

"Just a little unpleasantness," his manner seemed to say, "and then we shall be out of the house for good—and nobody will be more pleased than I shall. We don't want to hang about, I can assure you . . ."

I don't know how he managed, without any words at all, but

merely by drawing up a chair to the desk, to convey what he did, but it worked. I sat down unobtrusively a little way off.

"Yes, Chief Inspector?" said Philip.

Miss de Haviland said abruptly:

"You don't want me, Chief Inspector?"

"Not just at the moment, Miss de Haviland. Later, if I might have a few words with you—"

"Of course. I shall be upstairs."

She went out, shutting the door behind her.

"Well, Chief Inspector?" Philip repeated.

"I know you're a very busy gentleman and I don't want to disturb you for long. But I may mention to you in confidence that our suspicions are confirmed. Your father did not die a natural death. His death was the result of an overdose of physostigmine —more usually known as eserine."

Philip bowed his head. He showed no particular emotion.

"I don't know whether that suggests anything to you?" Taverner went on.

"What should it suggest? My own view is that my father must have taken the poison by accident."

"You really think so, Mr. Leonides?"

"Yes, it seems to me perfectly possible. He was close on ninety, remember, and with very imperfect eyesight."

"So he emptied the contents of his eyedrop bottle into an insulin bottle. Does that really seem to you a credible suggestion, Mr. Leonides?"

Philip did not reply. His face became even more impassive.

Taverner went on:

"We have found the eyedrop bottle, empty—in the dustbin, with no fingerprints on it. That in itself is curious. In the normal way there should have been fingerprints. Certainly your father's, possibly his wife's or the valet's . . ."

Philip Leonides looked up.

"What about the valet?" he said. "What about Johnson?"

"You are suggesting Johnson as the possible criminal? He certainly had opportunity. But when we come to motive it is different. It was your father's custom to pay him a bonus every year —each year the bonus was increased. Your father made it clear to him that this was in lieu of any sum that he might otherwise have left him in his will. The bonus now, after seven years' service, has reached a very considerable sum every year and is still rising. It was obviously to Johnson's interest that your father should live as long as possible. Moreover they were on excellent terms, and Johnson's record of past service is unimpeachable—he is a thoroughly skilled and faithful valet attendant." He paused. "We do not suspect Johnson."

Philip replied tonelessly: "I see."

"Now, Mr. Leonides, perhaps you will give me a detailed account of your own movements on the day of your father's death?"

"Certainly, Chief Inspector. I was here, in this room, all that day—with the exception of meals, of course."

"Did you see your father at all?"

"I said good morning to him after breakfast as was my custom."

"Were you alone with him then?"

"My—er—stepmother was in the room."

"Did he seem quite as usual?"

With a slight hint of irony, Philip replied:

"He showed no foreknowledge that he was to be murdered that day."

"Is your father's portion of the house entirely separate from this?"

"Yes, the only access to it is through the door in the hall."

"Is that door kept locked?"

"No."

"Never?"

"I have never known it to be so."

"Anyone could go freely between that part of the house and this?"

"Certainly. It was only separate from the point of view of domestic convenience."

"How did you first hear of your father's death?"

"My brother Roger, who occupies the west wing of the floor above came rushing down to tell me that my father had had a sudden seizure. He had difficulty in breathing and seemed very ill."

"What did you do?"

"I telephoned through to the doctor, which nobody seemed to have thought of doing. The doctor was out—but I left a message for him to come as soon as possible. I then went upstairs."

"And then?"

374

"My father was clearly very ill. He died before the doctor came."

There was no emotion in Philip's voice. It was a simple statement of fact.

"Where was the rest of your family?"

"My wife was in London. She returned shortly afterwards. Sophia was also absent, I believe. The two younger ones, Eustace and Josephine, were at home.

"I hope you won't misunderstand me, Mr. Leonides, if I ask you exactly how your father's death will affect your financial position."

"I quite appreciate that you want to know all the facts. My father made us financially independent a great many years ago. My brother he made Chairman and principal shareholder of Associated Catering—his largest Company, and put the management of it entirely in his hands. He made over to me what he considered an equivalent sum—actually I think it was a hundred and fifty thousand pounds in various bonds and securities—so that I could use the capital as I chose. He also settled very generous amounts on my two sisters who have since died."

"But he left himself still a very rich man?"

"No, actually he only retained for himself a comparatively modest income. He said it would give him an interest in life. Since that time," for the first time a faint smile creased Philip's lips, "he has become, as a result of various undertakings, an even richer man than he was before."

"Your brother and yourself came here to live. That was not the result of any financial—difficulties?"

"Certainly not. It was a mere matter of convenience. My father always told us that we were welcome to make a home with him. For various domestic reasons this was a convenient thing for me to do.

"I was also," added Philip deliberately, "extremely fond of my father. I came here with my family in 1937. I pay no rent, but I pay my proportion of the rates."

"And your brother?"

"My brother came here as a result of the Blitz when his house in London was bombed in 1943."

"Now, Mr. Leonides, have you any idea what your father's testamentary dispositions are?"

"A very clear idea. He re-made his will shortly after peace was declared in 1945. My father was not a secretive man. He had a great sense of family. He held a family conclave at which his solicitor was also present and who, at his request, made clear to us the terms of the will. These terms I expect you already know. Mr. Gaitskill will doubtless have informed you. Roughly, a sum of a hundred thousand pounds free of duty was left to my stepmother in addition to her already very generous marriage settlement. The residue of his property was divided into three portions, one to myself, one to my brother, and a third in trust for the three grandchildren. The estate is a large one, but the death duties, of course, will be very heavy."

"Any bequests to servants or to charity?"

"No bequests of any kind. The wages paid to servants were increased annually if they remained in his service."

"You are not—you will excuse my asking—in actual need of money, Mr. Leonides?"

"Income tax, as you know, is somewhat heavy, Chief Inspector —but my income amply suffices for my needs—and for my wife's. Moreover my father frequently made us all very generous gifts, and had any emergency arisen, he would have come to the rescue immediately."

Philip added coldly and clearly:

"I can assure you that I had no financial reason for desiring my father's death, Chief Inspector."

"I am very sorry, Mr. Leonides, if you think I suggested anything of the kind. But we have to get at all the facts. Now I'm afraid I must ask you some rather delicate questions. They refer to the relations between your father and his wife. Were they on happy terms together?"

"As far as I know, perfectly."

"No quarrels?"

"I do not think so."

"There was a—great disparity in age?"

"There was."

"Did you—excuse me—approve of your father's second marriage?"

"My approval was not asked."

"That is not an answer, Mr. Leonides."

376

"Since you press the point, I will say that I considered the marriage—unwise."

"Did you remonstrate with your father about it?"

"When I heard of it, it was an accomplished fact."

"Rather a shock to you—eh?"

Philip did not reply.

"Was there any bad feeling about the matter?"

"My father was at perfect liberty to do as he pleased."

"Your relations with Mrs. Leonides have been amicable?"

"Perfectly."

"You were on friendly terms with her?"

"We very seldom meet."

Chief Inspector Taverner shifted his ground.

"Can you tell me something about Mr. Laurence Brown?"

"I'm afraid I can't. He was engaged by my father."

"But he was engaged to teach your children, Mr. Leonides."

"True. My son was a sufferer from infantile paralysis—fortunately a light case—and it was considered not advisable to send him to a public school. My father suggested that he and my young daughter Josephine should have a private tutor—the choice at the time was rather limited—since the tutor in question must be ineligible for military service. This young man's credentials were satisfactory, my father and my aunt (who has always looked after the children's welfare) were satisfied, and I acquiesced. I may add that I have no fault to find with his teaching which has been conscientious and adequate."

"His living quarters are in your father's part of the house, not here?"

"There was more room up there."

"Have you ever noticed—I am sorry to ask this—any signs of intimacy between Laurence Brown and your stepmother?"

"I have had no opportunity of observing anything of the kind."

"Have you heard any gossip or tittle tattle on the subject?"

"I don't listen to gossip or tittle tattle, Chief Inspector."

"Very creditable," said Inspector Taverner. "So you've seen no evil, heard no evil, and aren't speaking any evil?"

"If you like to put it that way, Chief Inspector."

Inspector Taverner got up.

"Well," he said, "thank you very much, Mr. Leonides."

377

I followed him unobtrusively out of the room.

"Whew," said Taverner, "he's a cold fish!"

CHAPTER 7

"AND NOW," said Taverner, "we'll go and have a word with Mrs. Philip. Magda West, her stage name is."

"Is she any good?" I asked. "I know her name, and I believe I've seen her in various shows, but I can't remember when and where."

"She's one of those Near Successes," said Taverner. "She's starred once or twice in the West End, she's made quite a name for herself in Repertory—she plays a lot for the little highbrow theatres and the Sunday clubs. The truth is, I think, she's been handicapped by not having to earn her living at it. She's been able to pick and choose, and to go where she likes and occasionally to put up the money to finance a show where she's fancied a certain part—usually the last part in the world to suit her. Result is, she's receded a bit into the amateur class rather than the professional. She's good, mind you, especially in comedy—but managers don't like her much—they say she's too independent, and she's a trouble maker—foments rows and enjoys a bit of mischief making. I don't know how much of it is true—but she's not too popular amongst her fellow artists."

Sophia came out of the drawing room and said, "My mother is in here, Chief Inspector."

I followed Taverner into the big drawing room. For a moment I hardly recognised the woman who sat on the brocaded settee.

The Titian hair was piled high on her head in an Edwardian coiffure, and she was dressed in a well cut dark grey coat and skirt with a delicately pleated pale mauve shirt fastened at the neck by a small cameo brooch. For the first time I was aware

378

of the charm of her delightfully tip tilted nose. I was faintly reminded of Athene Seyler—and it seemed quite impossible to believe that this was the tempestuous creature in the peach négligée.

"Inspector Taverner?" she said. "Do come in and sit down. Will you smoke? This is a most terrible business. I simply feel at the moment that I just can't take it in."

Her voice was low and emotionless, the voice of a person determined at all costs to display self control. She went on: "Please tell me if I can help you in any way."

"Thank you, Mrs. Leonides. Where were you at the time of the tragedy?"

"I suppose I must have been driving down from London. I'd lunched that day at the Ivy with a friend. Then we'd gone to a dress show. We had a drink with some other friends at the Berkeley. Then I started home. When I got here everything was in commotion. It seemed my father-in-law had had a sudden seizure. He was—dead." Her voice trembled just a little.

"You were fond of your father-in-law?"

"I was devoted—"

Her voice rose. Sophia adjusted, very slightly, the angle of the Degas picture. Magda's voice dropped to its former subdued tone.

"I was very fond of him," she said in a quiet voice. "We all were. He was—very good to us."

"Did you get on well with Mrs. Leonides?"

"We didn't see very much of Brenda."

"Why was that?"

"Well, we hadn't much in common. Poor dear Brenda. Life must have been hard for her sometimes."

Again Sophia fiddled with the Degas.

"Indeed? In what way?"

"Oh, I don't know." Magda shook her head, with a sad little smile.

"Was Mrs. Leonides happy with her husband?"

"Oh, I think so."

"No quarrels?"

Again the slight smiling shake of the head.

"I really don't know, Inspector. Their part of the house is quite separate."

"She and Mr. Laurence Brown were very friendly, were they not?"

Magda Leonides stiffened. Her eyes opened reproachfully at Taverner.

"I don't think," she said with dignity, "that you ought to ask me things like that. Brenda was quite friendly to everyone. She is really a very amiable sort of person."

"Do you like Mr. Laurence Brown?"

"He's very quiet. Quite nice, but you hardly know he's there. I haven't really seen very much of him."

"Is his teaching satisfactory?"

"I suppose so. I really wouldn't know. Philip seems quite satisfied."

Taverner essayed some shock tactics.

"I'm sorry to ask you this, but in your opinion was there anything in the nature of a love affair between Mr. Brown and Mrs. Brenda Leonides."

Magda got up. She was very much the grande dame.

"I have never seen any evidence of anything of that kind," she said. "I don't think really, Inspector, that that is a question you ought to ask me. She was my father-in-law's wife."

I almost applauded.

The Chief Inspector also rose.

"More a question for the servants?" he suggested.

Magda did not answer.

"Thank you, Mrs. Leonides," said the Inspector and went out.

"You did that beautifully, darling," said Sophia to her mother warmly.

Magda twisted up a curl reflectively behind her right ear and looked at herself in the glass.

"Ye-es," she said, "I think it was the right way to play it."

Sophia looked at me.

"Oughtn't you," she asked, "to go with the Inspector?"

"Look here, Sophia, what am I supposed—"

I stopped. I could not very well ask outright in front of Sophia's mother exactly what my rôle was supposed to be. Magda Leonides had so far evinced no interest in my presence at all, except as a useful recipient of an exit line on daughters. I might be a reporter, her daughter's fiancé, or an obscure hanger on of the police force, or even an undertaker—to Magda Leonides they would one and all come under the general heading of audience.

Looking down at her feet, Mrs. Leonides said with dissatisfaction:

"These shoes are wrong. Frivolous."

Obeying Sophia's imperious wave of the head I hurried after Taverner. I caught up with him in the outer hall just going through the door to the stairway.

"Just going up to see the older brother," he explained.

I put my problem to him without more ado.

"Look here, Taverner, who am I supposed to be?"

He looked surprised.

"Who are you supposed to be?"

"Yes, what am I doing here in this house? If anyone asks me, what do I say?"

"Oh I see." He considered a moment. Then he smiled. "Has anybody asked you?"

"Well—no."

"Then why not leave it at that. Never explain. That's a very good motto. Especially in a house upset like this house is. Everyone is far too full of their own private worries and fears to be in a questioning mood. They'll take you for granted so long as you just seem sure of yourself. It's a great mistake ever to say anything when you needn't. H'm, now we go through this door and up the stairs. Nothing locked. Of course you realise, I expect, that these questions I'm asking are all a lot of hooey! Doesn't matter a hoot who was in the house and who wasn't, or where they all were on that particular day—"

"Then why—"

He went on: "Because it at least gives me a chance to look at them all, and size them up, and hear what they've got to say, and to hope that, quite by chance, somebody might give me a useful pointer." He was silent a moment and then murmured: "I bet Mrs. Magda Leonides could spill a mouthful if she chose."

"Would it be reliable?" I asked.

"Oh, no," said Taverner, "it wouldn't be reliable. But it might start a possible line of enquiry. Everybody in the damned house had means and opportunity. What I want is a motive."

At the top of the stairs, a door barred off the right hand corridor. There was a brass knocker on it and Inspector Taverner duly knocked.

It was opened with startling suddenness by a man who must

have been standing just inside. He was a clumsy giant of a man with powerful shoulders, dark rumpled hair, and an exceedingly ugly but at the same time rather pleasant face. His eyes looked at us and then quickly away in that furtive embarrassed manner which shy but honest people often adopt.

"Oh, I say," he said. "Come in. Yes, do. I was going—but it doesn't matter. Come into the sitting room. I'll get Clemency—oh, you're there, darling. It's Chief Inspector Taverner. He—are there any cigarettes? Just wait a minute. If you don't mind—" He collided with a screen, said "I beg your pardon" to it in a flustered manner, and went out of the room.

It was rather like the exit of a bumble bee and left a noticeable silence behind it.

Mrs. Roger Leonides was standing up by the window. I was intrigued at once by her personality and by the atmosphere of the room in which we stood.

It was quite definitely her room. I was sure of that.

The walls were painted white—really white, not an ivory or a pale cream which is what one usually means when one says "white" in house decoration. They had no pictures on them except one over the mantelpiece, a geometrical fantasia in triangles of dark grey and battleship blue. There was hardly any furniture—only mere utilitarian necessities, three or four chairs, a glass topped table, one small bookshelf. There were no ornaments. There was light and space and air. It was as different from the big brocaded and flowered drawing room on the floor below as chalk from cheese. And Mrs. Roger Leonides was as different from Mrs. Philip Leonides as one woman could be from another. Whilst one felt that Magda Leonides could be, and often was, at least half a dozen different women, Clemency Leonides, I was sure, could never be anyone but herself. She was a woman of very sharp and definite personality.

She was about fifty, I suppose, her hair was grey, cut very short in what was almost an Eton crop but which grew so beautifully on her small well shaped head that it had none of the ugliness I have always associated with that particular cut. She had an intelligent, sensitive face, with light grey eyes of a peculiar and searching intensity. She had on a simple dark red woollen frock that fitted her slenderness perfectly.

She was, I felt at once, rather an alarming woman . . . I think because I judged that the standards by which she lived might not be those of an ordinary woman. I understood at once why Sophia had used the word ruthlessness in connection with her. The room was cold and I shivered a little.

Clemency Leonides said in a quiet well bred voice:

"Do sit down, Chief Inspector. Is there any further news?"

"Death was due to eserine, Mrs. Leonides."

She said thoughtfully:

"So that makes it murder. It couldn't have been an accident of any kind, could it?"

"No, Mrs. Leonides."

"Please be very gentle with my husband, Chief Inspector. This will affect him very much. He worshipped his father and he feels things very acutely. He is an emotional person."

"You were on good terms with your father-in-law, Mrs. Leonides?"

"Yes, on quite good terms." She added quietly, "I did not like him very much."

"Why was that?"

"I disliked his objectives in life—and his methods of attaining them."

"And Mrs. Brenda Leonides?"

"Brenda? I never saw very much of her."

"Do you think it is possible that there was anything between her and Mr. Laurence Brown?"

"You mean—some kind of a love affair? I shouldn't think so. But I really wouldn't know anything about it."

Her voice sounded completely uninterested.

Roger Leonides came back with a rush, and the same bumble bee effect.

"I got held up," he said. "Telephone. Well, Inspector? Well? Have you got any news? What caused my father's death?"

"Death was due to eserine poisoning."

"It was? My God! Then it was that woman! She couldn't wait! He took her more or less out of the gutter and this is his reward. She murdered him in cold blood! God, it makes my blood boil to think of it."

"Have you any particular reason for thinking that?" Taverner asked.

Roger was pacing up and down, tugging at his hair with both hands.

"Reason? Why, who else could it be? I've never trusted her—never liked her! We've none of us liked her. Philip and I were both appalled when Dad came home one day and told us what he had done! At his age! It was madness—madness. My father was an amazing man, Inspector. In intellect he was as young and fresh as a man of forty. Everything I have in the world I owe to him. He did everything for me—never failed me. It was I who failed him—when I think of it—"

He dropped heavily onto a chair. His wife came quietly to his side.

"Now, Roger, that's enough. Don't work yourself up."

"I know, dearest—I know," he took her hand. "But how can I keep calm—how can I help feeling—"

"But we must all keep calm, Roger. Chief Inspector Taverner wants our help."

"That is right, Mrs. Leonides."

Roger cried:

"Do you know what I'd like to do? I'd like to strangle that woman with my own hands. Grudging that dear old man a few extra years of life. If I had her here—" He sprang up. He was shaking with rage. He held out convulsive hands. "Yes, I'd wring her neck, wring her neck . . ."

"Roger!" said Clemency sharply.

He looked at her, abashed.

"Sorry, dearest." He turned to us. "I do apologise. My feelings get the better of me. I—excuse me—"

He went out of the room again. Clemency Leonides said with a very faint smile:

"Really, you know, he wouldn't hurt a fly."

Taverner accepted her remark politely.

Then he started on his so-called routine questions.

Clemency Leonides replied concisely and accurately.

Roger Leonides had been in London on the day of his father's death at Box House, the headquarters of the Associated Catering. He had returned early in the afternoon and had spent some time with his father as was his custom. She herself had been, as usual at the Lambert Institute on Gower Street where she worked. She had returned to the house just before six o'clock.

384

"Did you see your father-in-law?"

"No. The last time I saw him was on the day before. We had coffee with him after dinner."

"But you did not see him on the day of his death?"

"No. I actually went over to his part of the house because Roger thought he had left his pipe there—a very precious pipe, but as it happened he had left it on the hall table there, so I did not need to disturb the old man. He often dozed off about six."

"When did you hear of his illness?"

"Brenda came rushing over. That was just a minute or two after half past six."

These questions, as I knew, were unimportant, but I was aware how keen was Inspector Taverner's scrutiny of the woman who answered them. He asked her a few questions about the nature of her work in London. She said that it had to do with the radiation effects of atomic disintegration.

"You work on the atom bomb, in fact?"

"The work has nothing destructive about it. The Institute is carrying out experiments on the therapeutic effects."

When Taverner got up, he expressed a wish to look around their part of the house. She seemed a little surprised, but showed him its extent readily enough. The bedroom with its twin beds and white coverlets and its simplified toilet appliances reminded me again of a hospital or some monastic cell. The bathroom, too, was severely plain with no special luxury fitting and no array of cosmetics. The kitchen was bare, spotlessly clean, and well equipped with labour saving devices of a practical kind. Then we came to a door which Clemency opened saying: "This is my husband's special room."

"Come in," said Roger. "Come in."

I drew a faint breath of relief. Something in the spotless austerity elsewhere had been getting me down. This was an intensely personal room. There was a large roll top desk untidily covered with papers, old pipes and tobacco ash. There were big shabby easy chairs. Persian rugs covered the floor. On the walls were groups, their photography somewhat faded. School groups, cricket groups, military groups. Water colour sketches of deserts and minarets, and of sailing boats and sea effects and sunsets. It was, somehow, a pleasant room, the room of a lovable friendly companionable man.

Roger, clumsily, was pouring out drinks from a tantalus, sweeping books and papers off one of the chairs.

"Place is in a mess. I was turning out. Clearing up old papers. Say when." The Inspector declined a drink. I accepted. "You must forgive me just now," went on Roger. He brought my drink over to me, turning his head to speak to Taverner as he did so. "My feelings ran away with me."

He looked round almost guiltily, but Clemency Leonides had not accompanied us into the room.

"She's so wonderful," he said. "My wife, I mean. All through this, she's been splendid—splendid! I can't tell you how I admire that woman. And she's had such a hard time—a terrible time. I'd like to tell you about it. Before we were married, I mean. Her first husband was a fine chap—fine mind, I mean—but terribly delicate—tubercular as a matter of fact. He was doing some very valuable research work on crystallography, I believe. Poorly paid and very exacting, but he wouldn't give up. She slaved for him, practically kept him, knowing all the time that he was dying. And never a complaint—never a murmur of weariness. She always said she was happy. Then he died, and she was terribly cut up. At last she agreed to marry me. I was glad to be able to give her some rest, some happiness, I wished she would stop working, but of course she felt it her duty in war time, and she still seems to feel she should go on. She's been a wonderful wife—the most wonderful wife a man ever had. Gosh, I've been lucky! I'd do anything for her."

Taverner made a suitable rejoinder. Then he embarked once more on the familiar routine questions. When had he first heard of his father's illness?

"Brenda had rushed over to call me. My father was ill—she said he had had a seizure of some sort.

"I'd been sitting with the dear old boy only about half an hour earlier. He'd been perfectly all right then. I rushed over. He was blue in the face, gasping. I dashed down to Philip. He rang up the doctor. I—we couldn't do anything. Of course I never dreamed for a moment then that there had been any funny business. Funny? Did I say funny? God, what a word to use."

With a little difficulty, Taverner and I disentangled ourselves from the emotional atmosphere of Roger Leonides's room and found ourselves outside the door, once more at the top of the stairs.

"Whew!" said Taverner. "What a contrast from the other brother." He added, rather inconsequently "Curious things, rooms. Tell you quite a lot about the people who live in them."

I agreed and he went on.

"Curious the people who marry each other, too, isn't it?"

I was not quite sure if he was referring to Clemency and Roger, or to Philip and Magda. His words applied equally well to either. Yet it seemed to me that both the marriages might be classed as happy ones. Roger's and Clemency's certainly was.

"I shouldn't say he was a poisoner, would you?" asked Taverner. "Not off hand, I wouldn't. Of course, you never know. Now she's more the type. Remorseless sort of woman. Might be a bit mad."

Again I agreed. "But I don't suppose," I said, "that she'd murder anyone just because she didn't approve of their aims and mode of life. Perhaps, if she really hated the old man—but are any murders committed just out of pure hate?"

"Precious few," said Taverner. "I've never come across one myself. No, I think we're a good deal safer to stick to Mrs. Brenda. But God knows if we'll ever get any evidence."

CHAPTER 8

A PARLOURMAID opened the door of the opposite wing to us. She looked scared but slightly contemptuous when she saw Taverner.

"You want to see the mistress?"

"Yes, please."

She showed us into a big drawing room and went out.

Its proportions were the same as the drawing room on the ground floor below. There were coloured cretonnes, very gay in colour and striped silk curtains. Over the mantelpiece was a portrait that held my gaze riveted—not only because of the master hand that had painted it, but also because of the arresting face of the subject.

It was the portrait of a little old man with dark piercing eyes. He wore a black velvet skull cap and his head was sunk down in his shoulders, but the vitality and power of the man radiated forth from the canvas. The twinkling eyes seemed to hold mine.

"That's him," said Chief Inspector Taverner ungrammatically. "Painted by Augustus John. Got a personality, hasn't he?"

"Yes," I said and felt the monosyllable was inadequate.

I understood now just what Edith de Haviland had meant when she said the house seemed so empty without him. This was the Original Crooked Little Man who had built the Crooked Little House—and without him the Crooked Little House had lost its meaning.

"That's his first wife over there, painted by Sargent," said Taverner.

I examined the picture on the wall between the windows. It had a certain cruelty like many of Sargent's portraits. The length of the face was exaggerated, I thought—so was the faint suggestion of horsiness—the indisputable correctness— It was a portrait of a typical English Lady—in Country (not Smart) Society. Handsome, but rather lifeless. A most unlikely wife for the grinning powerful little despot over the mantelpiece.

The door opened and Sergeant Lamb stepped in.

"I've done what I could with the servants, sir," he said. "Didn't get anything."

Taverner sighed.

Sergeant Lamb took out his notebook and retreated to the far end of the room where he seated himself unobtrusively.

The door opened again and Aristide Leonides's second wife came into the room.

She wore black—very expensive black and a good deal of it. It swathed her up to the neck and down to the wrists. She moved easily and indolently, and black certainly suited her. Her face was mildly pretty and she had rather nice brown hair arranged in somewhat too elaborate a style. Her face was well powdered and she had on lipstick and rouge, but she had clearly been crying. She was wearing a string of very large pearls and she had a big emerald ring on one hand and an enormous ruby on the other.

There was one other thing I noticed about her. She looked frightened.

"Good morning, Mrs. Leonides," said Taverner easily. "I'm sorry to have to trouble you again."

She said in a flat voice:

"I suppose it can't be helped."

"You understand, don't you, Mrs. Leonides, that if you wish your solicitor to be present, that is perfectly in order."

I wondered if she did understand the significance of those words. Apparently not. She merely said rather sulkily:

"I don't like Mr. Gaitskill. I don't want him."

"You could have your own solicitor, Mrs. Leonides."

"Must I? I don't like solicitors. They confuse me."

"It's entirely for you to decide," said Taverner, producing an automatic smile. "Shall we go on, then?"

Sergeant Lamb licked his pencil. Brenda Leonides sat down on a sofa facing Taverner.

"Have you found out anything?" she asked.

I noticed her fingers nervously twisting and untwisting a pleat of the chiffon of her dress.

"We can state definitely now that your husband died as a result of eserine poisoning."

"You mean those eyedrops killed him?"

"It seems quite certain that when you gave Mr. Leonides that last injection, it was eserine that you injected and not insulin."

"But I didn't know that. I didn't have anything to do with it. Really I didn't, Inspector."

"Then somebody must have deliberately replaced the insulin by the eyedrops."

"What a wicked thing to do!"

"Yes, Mrs. Leonides."

"Do you think—someone did it on purpose? Or by accident? It couldn't have been a—a joke, could it?"

Taverner said smoothly:

"We don't think it was a joke, Mrs. Leonides."

"It must have been one of the servants."

Taverner did not answer.

"It must. I don't see who else could have done it."

"Are you sure? Think, Mrs. Leonides. Haven't you any ideas at all? There's been no ill feeling anywhere? No quarrel? No grudge?"

She still stared at him with large defiant eyes.

"I've no idea at all," she said.

"You had been at the cinema that afternoon, you said?"

"Yes—I came in at half past six—it was time for the insulin—I—I—gave him the injection just the same as usual and then he—he went all queer. I was terrified—I rushed over to Roger—I've told you all this before. Have I got to go over it again and again?" Her voice rose hysterically.

"I'm so sorry, Mrs. Leonides. Now can I speak to Mr. Brown?"

"To Laurence? Why? He doesn't know anything about it."

"I'd like to speak to him all the same."

She stared at him suspiciously.

"Eustace is doing Latin with him in the schoolroom. Do you want him to come here?"

"No—we'll go to him."

Taverner went quickly out of the room. The Sergeant and I followed.

"You've put the wind up her, sir," said Sergeant Lamb.

Taverner grunted. He led the way up a short flight of steps and along a passage into a big room looking over the garden. There a fair haired young man of about thirty and a handsome dark boy of sixteen were sitting at a table.

They looked up at our entrance. Sophia's brother Eustace looked at me, Laurence Brown fixed an agonised gaze on Chief Inspector Taverner.

I have never seen a man look so completely paralysed with fright. He stood up, then sat down again. He said, and his voice was almost a squeak,

"Oh—er—good morning, Inspector."

"Good morning," Taverner was curt. "Can I have a word with you?"

"Yes, of course. Only too pleased. At least—"

Eustace got up.

"Do you want me to go away, Chief Inspector?" His voice was pleasant with a faintly arrogant note.

"We—we can continue our studies later," said the tutor.

Eustace strolled negligently towards the door. He walked rather stiffly. Just as he went through the door, he caught my eye, drew a forefinger across the front of his throat and grinned. Then he shut the door behind him.

"Well, Mr. Brown," said Taverner. "The analysis is quite definite. It was eserine that caused Mr. Leonides's death."

"I—you mean—Mr. Leonides was really poisoned? I have been hoping—"

"He was poisoned," said Taverner curtly. "Someone substituted eserine eyedrops for insulin."

"I can't believe it. . . . It's incredible."

"The question is, who had a motive?"

"Nobody. Nobody at all!" The young man's voice rose excitedly.

"You wouldn't like to have your solicitor present, would you?" inquired Taverner.

"I haven't got a solicitor. I don't want one. I have nothing to hide—nothing . . ."

"And you quite understand that what you say is about to be taken down."

"I'm innocent—I assure you, I'm innocent."

"I have not suggested anything else." Taverner paused. "Mrs. Leonides was a good deal younger than her husband, was she not?"

"I—I suppose so—I mean, well, yes."

"She must have felt lonely sometimes?"

Laurence Brown did not answer. He passed his tongue over his dry lips.

"To have a companion of more or less her own age living here must have been agreeable to her?"

"I—no, not at all—I mean—I don't know."

"It seems to me quite natural that an attachment should have sprung up between you."

The young man protested vehemently.

"It didn't! It wasn't! Nothing of the kind! I know what you're thinking, but it wasn't so! Mrs. Leonides was very kind to me always and I had the greatest—the greatest respect for her—but nothing more—nothing more, I do assure you. It's monstrous to suggest things of that kind! Monstrous! I wouldn't kill anybody— or tamper with bottles—or anything like that. I'm very sensitive and highly strung. I—the very idea of killing is a nightmare to me —they quite understood that at the tribunal—I have religious objections to killing. I did hospital work instead—stoking boilers— terribly heavy work—I couldn't go on with it—but they let me take up educational work. I have done my best here with Eustace and with Josephine—a very intelligent child, but difficult. And everybody has been most kind to me—Mr. Leonides and Mrs. Leonides and Miss de Haviland. And now this awful thing happens. . . . And you suspect me—me—of murder!"

Inspector Taverner looked at him with a slow appraising interest.

"I haven't said so," he remarked.

"But you think so! I know you think so! They all think so! They look at me. I—I can't go on talking to you. I'm not well."

He hurried out of the room. Taverner turned his head slowly to look at me.

"Well, what do you think of him?"

"He's scared stiff."

"Yes, I know, but is he a murderer?"

"If you ask me," said Sergeant Lamb, "he'd never have had the nerve."

"He'd never have bashed anyone on the head, or shot off a pistol," agreed the Chief Inspector, "But in this particular crime what is there to do? Just monkey about with a couple of bottles. . . . Just help a very old man out of the world in a comparatively painless manner."

"Practically euthanasia," said the Sergeant.

"And then, perhaps, after a decent interval, marriage with a woman who inherits a hundred thousand pounds free of legacy duty, who already has about the same amount settled upon her, and who has in addition pearls and rubies and emeralds the size of what's-its-name eggs!

"Ah well—" Taverner sighed. "It's all theory and conjecture! I managed to scare him all right, but that doesn't prove anything. He's just as likely to be scared if he's innocent. And anyway, I rather doubt if he was the one actually to do it. More likely to have been the woman—only why on earth didn't she throw away the insulin bottle, or rinse it out?" He turned to the Sergeant. "No evidence from the servants about any goings on?"

"The parlourmaid says they're sweet on each other."

"What grounds?"

"The way he looks at her when she pours out his coffee."

"Fat lot of good that would be in a court of law! Definitely no carryings on?"

"Not that anybody's seen."

"I bet they would have seen, too, if there had been anything to see. You know I'm beginning to believe there really is nothing between them." He looked at me. "Go back and talk to her. I'd like your impression of her."

I went half reluctantly, yet I was interested.

CHAPTER 9

I FOUND Brenda Leonides sitting exactly where I had left her. She looked up sharply as I entered.

"Where's Inspector Taverner. Is he coming back?"

"Not just yet."

"Who are you?"

At last I had been asked the question that I had been expecting all the morning.

I answered it with reasonable truth.

"I'm connected with the police, but I'm also a friend of the family."

"The family! Beasts! I hate them all."

She looked at me, her mouth working. She looked sullen and frightened and angry.

"They've been beastly to me always—always. From the very first. Why shouldn't I marry their precious father? What did it matter to them? They'd all got loads of money. He gave it to them. They wouldn't have had the brains to make any for themselves!"

She went on:

"Why shouldn't a man marry again—even if he is a bit old? And he wasn't really old at all—not in himself. I was very fond of him. I was fond of him." She looked at me defiantly.

"I see," I said. "I see."

"I suppose you don't believe that—but it's true. I was sick of men. I wanted to have a home—I wanted someone to make a fuss of me and say nice things to me. Aristide said lovely things to me

393

—and he could make you laugh—and he was clever. He thought up all sorts of smart ways to get round all these silly regulations. He was very very clever. I'm not glad he's dead. I'm sorry."

She leaned back on the sofa. She had rather a wide mouth, it curled up sideways in a queer sleepy smile.

"I've been happy here. I've been safe. I went to all those posh dressmakers—the ones I'd read about. I was as good as anybody. And Aristide gave me lovely things." She stretched out a hand looking at the ruby on it.

Just for a moment I saw the hand and arm like an outstretched cat's claw, and heard her voice as a purr. She was still smiling to herself.

"What's wrong with that?" she demanded. "I was nice to him. I made him happy." She leaned forward. "Do you know how I met him?"

She went on without waiting for an answer.

"It was in the Gay Shamrock. He'd ordered scrambled eggs on toast and when I brought them to him I was crying. 'Sit down,' he said, 'and tell me what's the matter.' 'Oh, I couldn't,' I said. 'I'd get the sack if I did a thing like that.' 'No, you won't,' he said, 'I own this place.' I looked at him then. Such an odd little old man he was, I thought at first—but he'd got a sort of power. I told him all about it. . . . You'll have heard about it all from them, I expect—making out I was a regular bad lot—but I wasn't. I was brought up very carefully. We had a shop—a very high class shop —art needlework. I was never the sort of girl who had a lot of boy friends or made herself cheap. But Terry was different. He was Irish—and he was going overseas. . . . He never wrote or any- thing—I suppose I was a fool. So there it was, you see. I was in trouble—just like some dreadful little servant girl. . . ."

Her voice was disdainful in its snobbery.

"Aristide was wonderful. He said everything would be all right. He said he was lonely. We'd be married at once, he said. It was like a dream. And then I found out he was the great Mr. Leonides. He owned masses of shops and restaurants and night clubs. It was quite like a fairy tale, wasn't it?"

"One kind of a fairy tale," I said drily.

"We were married at a little church in the City—and then we went abroad."

"And the child?"

394

She looked at me with eyes that came back from a long distance.

"There wasn't a child after all. It was all a mistake."

She smiled, the curled up sideways crooked smile.

"I vowed to myself that I'd be a really good wife to him, and I was. I ordered all the kinds of food he liked, and wore the colours he fancied and I did all I could to please him. And he was happy. But we never got rid of that family of his. Always coming and sponging and living in his pocket. Old Miss de Haviland—I think she ought to have gone away when he got married. I said so. But Aristide said, 'She's been here so long. It's her home now.' The truth is he liked to have them all about and underfoot. They were beastly to me, but he never seemed to notice that or to mind about it. Roger hates me—have you seen Roger? He's always hated me. He's jealous. And Philip's so stuck up he never speaks to me. And now they're trying to pretend I murdered him—and I didn't—I didn't!" She leaned towards me. "Please believe I didn't?"

I found her very pathetic. The contemptuous way the Leonides family had spoken of her, their eagerness to believe that she had committed the crime—now, at this moment, it all seemed positively inhuman conduct. She was alone, defenceless, hunted down.

"And if it's not me, they think it's Laurence," she went on.

"What about Laurence?" I asked.

"I'm terribly sorry for Laurence. He's delicate and he couldn't go and fight. It's not because he was a coward. It's because he's sensitive. I've tried to cheer him up and to make him feel happy. He has to teach those horrible children. Eustace is always sneering at him, and Josephine—well, you've seen Josephine. You know what she's like."

I said I hadn't met Josephine yet.

"Sometimes I think that child isn't right in her head. She has horrible sneaky ways, and she looks queer . . . She gives me the shivers sometimes."

I didn't want to talk about Josephine. I harked back to Laurence Brown.

"Who is he?" I asked. "Where does he come from?"

I had phrased it clumsily. She flushed.

"He isn't anybody particular. He's just like me . . . What chance have we got against all of them?"

"Don't you think you're being a little hysterical?"

"No, I don't. They want to make out that Laurence did it—or that I did. They've got that policeman on their side. What chance have I got?"

"You mustn't work yourself up," I said.

"Why shouldn't it be one of them who killed him? Or someone from outside? Or one of the servants?"

"There's a certain lack of motive."

"Oh! motive. What motive had I got? Or Laurence?"

I felt rather uncomfortable as I said:

"They might think, I suppose, that you and—er—Laurence—are in love with each other—that you wanted to marry."

She sat bolt upright.

"That's a wicked thing to suggest! And it's not true! We've never said a word of that kind to each other. I've just been sorry for him and tried to cheer him up. We've been friends, that's all. You do believe me, don't you?"

I did believe her. That is, I believed that she and Laurence were, as she put it, only friends. But I also believed that, possibly unknown to herself, she was actually in love with the young man.

It was with that thought in my mind that I went downstairs in search of Sophia.

As I was about to go into the drawing room, Sophia poked her head out of a door further along the passage.

"Hullo," she said, "I'm helping Nannie with lunch."

I would have joined her, but she came out into the passage, shut the door behind her, and taking my arm led me into the drawing room which was empty.

"Well," she said, "did you see Brenda? What did you think of her?"

"Frankly," I said, "I was sorry for her."

Sophia looked amused.

"I see," she said. "So she got you."

I felt slightly irritated.

"The point is," I said, "that I can see her side of it. Apparently you can't."

"Her side of what?"

"Honestly, Sophia, have any of the family ever been nice to her, or even fairly decent to her, since she came here?"

"No, we haven't been nice to her. Why should we be?"

"Just ordinary Christian kindliness, if nothing else."

"What a very high moral tone you're taking, Charles. Brenda must have done her stuff pretty well."

"Really, Sophia, you seem— I don't know what's come over you."

"I'm just being honest and not pretending. You've seen Brenda's side of it, so you say. Now take a look at my side. I don't like the type of young woman who makes up a hard luck story and marries a very rich old man on the strength of it. I've a perfect right not to like that type of young woman, and there is no earthly reason why I should pretend I do. And if the facts were written down in cold blood on paper, you wouldn't like that young woman either."

"Was it a made up story?" I asked.

"About the child? I don't know. Personally, I think so."

"And you resent the fact that your grandfather was taken in by it?"

"Oh, grandfather wasn't taken in." Sophia laughed. "Grandfather was never taken in by anybody. He wanted Brenda. He wanted to play Cophetua to her beggarmaid. He knew just what he was doing and it worked out beautifully according to plan. From grandfather's point of view the marriage was a complete success —like all his other operations."

"Was engaging Laurence Brown as tutor another of your grandfather's successes?" I asked ironically.

Sophia frowned.

"Do you know, I'm not sure that it wasn't. He wanted to keep Brenda happy and amused. He may have thought that jewels and clothes weren't enough. He may have thought she wanted a mild romance in her life. He may have calculated that someone like Laurence Brown, somebody really tame, if you know what I mean, would just do the trick. A beautiful soulful friendship tinged with melancholy that would stop Brenda from having a real affair with someone outside. I wouldn't put it past grandfather to have worked out something on those lines. He was rather an old devil, you know."

"He must have been," I said.

"He couldn't, of course, have visualised that it would lead to murder. . . . And that," said Sophia, speaking with sudden vehemence, "is really why I don't, much as I would like to, really believe that she did it. If she'd planned to murder him—or if she and

397

Laurence had planned it together—grandfather would have known about it. I daresay that seems a bit far-fetched to you—"

"I must confess it does," I said.

"But then you didn't know grandfather. He certainly wouldn't have connived at his own murder! So there you are! Up against a blank wall."

"She's frightened, Sophia," I said. "She's very frightened."

"Chief Inspector Taverner and his merry merry men? Yes, I daresay they are rather alarming. Laurence, I suppose, is in hysterics?"

"Practically. He made, I thought, a disgusting exhibition of himself. I don't understand what a woman can see in a man like that."

"Don't you, Charles? Actually Laurence has a lot of sex appeal."

"A weakling like that," I said incredulously.

"Why do men always think that a caveman must necessarily be the only type of person attractive to the opposite sex? Laurence has got sex appeal all right—but I wouldn't expect you to be aware of it." She looked at me. "Brenda got her hooks into you all right."

"Don't be absurd. She's not even really good looking. And she certainly didn't—"

"Display allure? No, she just made you sorry for her. She's not actually beautiful, she's not in the least clever—but she's got one very outstanding characteristic. She can make trouble. She's made trouble, already, between you and me."

"Sophia," I cried aghast.

Sophia went to the door.

"Forget it, Charles. I must get on with lunch."

"I'll come and help."

"No, you stay here. It will rattle Nannie to have 'a gentleman in the kitchen'."

"Sophia," I called as she went out.

"Yes, what is it?"

"Just a servant problem. Why haven't you got any servants down here and upstairs something in an apron and a cap opened the door to us?"

"Grandfather had a cook, housemaid, parlourmaid and valet-attendant. He liked servants. He paid them the earth, of course, and he got them. Clemency and Roger just have a daily woman who comes in and cleans. They don't like servants—or rather

398

Clemency doesn't. If Roger didn't get a square meal in the City every day, he'd starve. Clemency's idea of a meal is lettuce, tomatoes and raw carrot. We sometimes have servants, and then mother throws one of her temperaments and they leave, and we have dailies for a bit and then start again. We're in the daily period. Nannie is the permanency and copes in emergencies. Now you know."

Sophia went out. I sank down in one of the large brocaded chairs and gave myself up to speculation.

Upstairs I had seen Brenda's side of it. Here and now I had been shown Sophia's side of it. I realised completely the justice of Sophia's point of view—what might be called the Leonides family's point of view. They resented a stranger within the gates who had obtained admission by what they regarded as ignoble means. They were entirely within their rights. As Sophia had said: On paper it wouldn't look well . . .

But there was the human side of it—the side that I saw and that they didn't. They were, they always had been, rich and well established. They had no conception of the temptations of the underdog. Brenda Leonides had wanted wealth, and pretty things and safety—and a home. She had claimed that in exchange she had made her old husband happy. I had sympathy with her. Certainly, while I was talking with her, I had had sympathy for her. . . . Had I got as much sympathy now?

Two sides to the question—different angles of vision—which was the true angle . . . the true angle . . .

I had slept very little the night before. I had been up early to accompany Taverner. Now, in the warm flower-scented atmosphere of Magda Leonides's drawing room, my body relaxed in the cushioned embrace of the big chair and my eyelids dropped. . . .

Thinking of Brenda, of Sophia, of an old man's picture, my thoughts slid together into a pleasant haze.

I slept. . . .

CHAPTER 10

I RETURNED to consciousness so gradually that I didn't at first realise that I had been asleep. The scent of flowers was in my nose.
In front of me a round white blob appeared to float in space. It
was some few seconds before I realised that it was a human face
I was looking at—a face suspended in the air about a foot or two
away from me. As my faculties returned, my vision became more
precise. The face still had its goblin suggestion—it was round
with a bulging brow, combed back hair and small rather beady,
black eyes. But it was definitely attached to a body—a small skinny
body. It was regarding me very earnestly.

"Hullo," it said.

"Hullo," I replied, blinking.

"I'm Josephine."

I had already deduced that. Sophia's sister, Josephine, was, I
judged, about eleven or twelve years of age. She was a fantastically ugly child with a very distinct likeness to her grandfather.
It seemed to me possible that she also had his brains.

"You're Sophia's young man," said Josephine.

I acknowledged the correctness of this remark.

"But you came down here with Chief Inspector Taverner. Why
did you come with Chief Inspector Taverner?"

"He's a friend of mine."

"Is he? I don't like him. I shan't tell him things."

"What sort of things?"

"The things that I know. I know a lot of things. I like knowing
things."

She say down on the arm of the chair and continued her
searching scrutiny of my face. I began to feel quite uncomfortable.

"Grandfather's been murdered. Did you know?"

"Yes," I said. "I knew."

400

"He was poisoned. With es-er-ine." She pronounced the word very carefully. "It's interesting, isn't it?"

"I suppose it is."

"Eustace and I are very interested. We like detective stories. I've always wanted to be a detective. I'm being one now. I'm collecting clues."

She was, I felt, rather a ghoulish child.

She returned to the charge.

"The man who came with Chief Inspector Taverner is a detective too, isn't he? In books it says you can always know plain clothes detectives by their boots. But this detective was wearing suede shoes."

"The old order changeth," I said.

Josephine interpreted this remark according to her own ideas.

"Yes," she said, "there will be a lot of changes here now, I expect. We shall go and live in a house in London on the embankment. Mother has wanted to for a long time. She'll be very pleased. I don't expect father will mind if his books go, too. He couldn't afford it before. He lost an awful lot of money over Jezebel."

"Jezebel?" I queried.

"Yes, didn't you see it?"

"Oh, was it a play? No, I didn't. I've been abroad."

"It didn't run very long. Actually, it was the most awful flop. I don't think mother's really the type to play Jezebel, do you?"

I balanced my impressions of Magda. Neither in the peach-coloured négligée nor in the tailored suit had she conveyed any suggestion of Jezebel, but I was willing to believe that there were other Magdas that I had not yet seen.

"Perhaps not," I said cautiously.

"Grandfather always said it would be a flop. He said he wouldn't put up any money for one of these historical religious plays. He said it would never be a box office success. But mother was frightfully keen. I didn't like it much myself. It wasn't really a bit like the story in the Bible. I mean, Jezebel wasn't wicked like she is in the Bible. She was all patriotic and really quite nice. That made it dull. Still, the end was all right. They threw her out of the window. Only no dogs came and ate her. I think that was a pity, don't you? I like the part about the dogs eating her best. Mother says you can't have dogs on the stage but I don't see why. You could have performing dogs." She quoted with gusto: " 'And they ate her all but the palms of her hands.' Why didn't they eat the palms of her hands?"

"I've really no idea," I said.

"You wouldn't think, would you, that dogs were so particular. Our dogs aren't. They eat simply anything."

Josephine brooded on this Biblical mystery for some seconds.

"I'm sorry the play was a flop," I said.

"Yes. Mother was terribly upset. The notices were simply frightful. When she read them, she burst into tears and cried all day and she threw her breakfast tray at Gladys, and Gladys gave notice. It was rather fun."

"I perceive that you like drama, Josephine," I said.

"They did a post mortem on grandfather," said Josephine. "To find out what he had died of. A P.M., they call it, but I think that's rather confusing, don't you? Because P.M. stands for Prime Minister too. And for afternoon," she added, thoughtfully.

"Are you sorry your grandfather is dead?" I asked.

"Not particularly. I didn't like him much. He stopped me learning to be a ballet dancer."

"Did you want to learn ballet dancing?"

"Yes, and mother was willing for me to learn, and father didn't mind, but grandfather said I'd be no good."

She slipped off the arm of the chair, kicked off her shoes and endeavoured to get onto what are called technically, I believe, her points.

"You have to have the proper shoes, of course," she explained, "and even then you get frightful abscesses sometimes on the ends of your toes." She resumed her shoes and inquired casually:

"Do you like this house?"

"I'm not quite sure," I said.

"I suppose it will be sold now. Unless Brenda goes on living in it. And I suppose Uncle Roger and Aunt Clemency won't be going away now."

"Were they going away?" I asked with a faint stirring of interest.

"Yes. They were going on Tuesday. Abroad, somewhere. They were going by air. Aunt Clemency bought one of those new featherweight cases."

"I hadn't heard they were going abroad," I said.

"No," said Josephine. "Nobody knew. It was a secret. They

weren't going to tell anyone until after they'd gone. They were going to leave a note behind for grandfather."

She added:

"Not pinned to the pincushion. That's only in very old-fashioned books and wives do it when they leave their husbands. But it would be silly now because nobody has pincushions any more."

"Of course they don't. Josephine, do you know why your Uncle Roger was—going away?"

She shot me a cunning sideways glance.

"I think I do. It was something to do with Uncle Roger's office in London. I rather think—but I'm not sure—that he'd embezzled something."

"What makes you think that?"

Josephine came nearer and breathed heavily in my face.

"The day that grandfather was poisoned Uncle Roger was shut up in his room with him ever so long. They were talking and talking. And Uncle Roger was saying that he'd never been any good, and that he'd let grandfather down—and that it wasn't the money so much—it was the feeling he'd been unworthy of trust. He was in an awful state."

I looked at Josephine with mixed feelings.

"Josephine," I said, "hasn't anybody ever told you that it's not nice to listen at doors?"

Josephine nodded her head vigorously.

"Of course they have. But if you want to find things out, you have to listen at doors. I bet Chief Inspector Taverner does, don't you?"

I considered the point. Josephine went on vehemently:

"And anyway if he doesn't, the other one does, the one with the suede shoes. And they look in people's desks and read all their letters, and find out all their secrets. Only they're stupid! They don't know where to look!"

Josephine spoke with cold superiority. I was stupid enough to let the inference escape me. The unpleasant child went on:

"Eustace and I know lots of things—but I know more than Eustace does. And I shan't tell him. He says women can't ever be great detectives. But I say they can. I'm going to write down everything in a notebook and then, when the police are completely baffled, I shall come forward and say, 'I can tell you who did it.' "

"Do you read a lot of detective stories, Josephine?"

"Masses."

"I suppose you think you know who killed your grandfather?"

"Well, I think so—but I shall have to find a few more clues." She paused and added, "Chief Inspector Taverner thinks that Brenda did it, doesn't he? Or Brenda and Laurence together because they're in love with each other."

"You shouldn't say things like that, Josephine."

"Why not? They are in love with each other."

"You can't possibly judge."

"Yes, I can. They write to each other. Love letters."

"Josephine! How do you know that?"

"Because I've read them. Awfully soppy letters. But Laurence is soppy. He was too frightened to fight in the war. He went into basements, and stoked boilers. When the flying bombs went over here, he used to turn green—really green. It made Eustace and me laugh a lot."

What I would have said next, I do not know, for at that moment a car drew up outside. In a flash Josephine was at the window, her snub nose pressed to the pane.

"Who is it?" I asked.

"It's Mr. Gaitskill, grandfather's lawyer. I expect he's come about the will."

Breathing excitedly, she hurried from the room, doubtless to resume her sleuthing activities.

Magda Leonides came in the room and to my surprise came across to me and took my hands in hers.

"My dear," she said, "thank goodness you're still here. One needs a man so badly."

She dropped my hands, crossed to a highbacked chair, altered its position a little, glanced at herself in a mirror, then picking up a small Battersea enamel box from a table she stood pensively opening and shutting it.

It was an attractive pose.

Sophia put her head in at the door and said in an admonitory whisper, "Gaitskill!"

"I know," said Magda.

A few moments later, Sophia entered the room accompanied

by a small elderly man, and Magda put down her enamel box and came forward to meet him.

"Good morning, Mrs. Philip. I'm on my way upstairs. It seems there's some misunderstanding about the will. Your husband wrote to me with the impression that the will was in my keeping. I understood from Mr. Leonides himself that it was at his vault. You don't know anything about it, I suppose?"

"About poor Sweetie's will?" Magda opened astonished eyes. "No, of course not. Don't tell me that wicked woman upstairs has destroyed it?"

"Now, Mrs. Philip," he shook an admonitory finger at her. "No wild surmises. It's just a question of where your father-in-law kept it."

"But he sent it to you—surely he did—after signing it. He actually told us he had."

"The police, I understand, have been through Mr. Leonides's private papers," said Mr. Gaitskill. "I'll just have a word with Chief Inspector Taverner."

He left the room.

"Darling," cried Magda. "She has destroyed it. I know I'm right."

"Nonsense, mother, she wouldn't do a stupid thing like that."

"It wouldn't be stupid at all. If there's no will she'll get everything."

"Sh—here's Gaitskill back again."

The lawyer re-entered the room. Chief Inspector Taverner was with him and behind Taverner came Philip.

"I understood from Mr. Leonides," Gaitskill was saying, "that he had placed his will with the Bank for safe keeping."

Taverner shook his head.

"I've been in communication with the Bank. They have no private papers belonging to Mr. Leonides beyond certain securities which they held for him."

Philip said:

"I wonder if Roger—or Aunt Edith— Perhaps, Sophia, you'd ask them to come down here."

But Roger Leonides, summoned with the others to the conclave, could give no assistance.

"But it's nonsense—absolute nonsense," he declared. "Father

signed the will and said distinctly that he was posting it to Mr. Gaitskill on the following day."

"If my memory serves me," said Mr. Gaitskill, leaning back and half-closing his eyes, "it was on November 24th of last year that I forwarded a draft drawn up according to Mr. Leonides's instructions. He approved the draft, returned it to me, and in due course I sent him the will for signature. After a lapse of a week, I ventured to remind him that I had not yet received the will duly signed and attested, and asking him if there was anything he wished altered. He replied that he was perfectly satisfied and added that after signing the will he had sent it to his Bank."

"That's quite right," said Roger eagerly. "It was about the end of November last year—you remember, Philip?— Father had us all up one evening and read the will to us."

Taverner turned towards Philip Leonides.

"That agrees with your recollection, Mr. Leonides?"

"Yes," said Philip.

"It was rather like the Voysey Inheritance," said Magda. She sighed pleasurably. "I always think there's something so dramatic about a will."

"Miss Sophia?"

"Yes," said Sophia. "I remember perfectly."

"And the provisions of that will?" asked Taverner.

Mr. Gaitskill was about to reply in his precise fashion, but Roger Leonides got ahead of him.

"It was a perfectly simple will. Electra and Joyce had died and their share of the settlements had returned to father. Joyce's son, William, had been killed in action in Burma, and the money he left went to his father. Philip and I and the children were the only relatives left. Father explained that. He left fifty thousand pounds free of duty to Aunt Edith, a hundred thousand pounds free of duty to Brenda, this house to Brenda or else a suitable house in London to be purchased for her, whichever she preferred. The residue to be divided into three portions, one to myself, one to Philip, the third to be divided between Sophia, Eustace and Josephine, the portions of the last two to be held in trust until they should come of age. I think that's right, isn't it, Mr. Gaitskill?"

"Those are—roughly stated—the provisions of the document I

406

drew up," agreed Mr. Gaitskill, displaying some slight acerbity at not having been allowed to speak for himself.

"Father read it out to us," said Roger. "He asked if there was any comment we might like to make. Of course there was none."

"Brenda made a comment," said Miss de Haviland.

"Yes," said Magda with zest. "She said she couldn't bear her darling old Aristide to talk about death. It 'gave her the creeps', she said. And after he was dead she didn't want any of the horrid money!"

"That," said Miss de Haviland, "was a conventional protest, typical of her class."

It was a cruel and biting little remark. I realised suddenly how much Edith de Haviland disliked Brenda.

"A very fair and reasonable disposal of his estate," said Mr. Gaitskill.

"And after reading it what happened?" asked Inspector Taverner.

"After reading it," said Roger, "he signed it."

Taverner leaned forward.

"Just how and when did he sign it?"

Roger looked round at his wife in an appealing way. Clemency spoke in answer to that look. The rest of the family seemed content for her to do so.

"You want to know exactly what took place?"

"If you please, Mrs. Roger."

"My father-in-law laid the will down on his desk and requested one of us—Roger, I think—to ring the bell. Roger did so. When Johnson came in answer to the bell, my father-in-law requested him to fetch Janet Woolmer, the parlourmaid. When they were both there, he signed the will and requested them to sign their own names beneath his signature."

"The correct procedure," said Mr. Gaitskill. "A will must be signed by the testator in the presence of two witnesses who must affix their own signatures at the same time and place."

"And after that?" asked Taverner.

"My father-in-law thanked them, and they went out. My father-in-law picked up the will, put it in a long envelope and mentioned that he would send it to Mr. Gaitskill on the following day."

"You all agree," said Inspector Taverner, looking round, "that that is an accurate account of what happened?"

There were murmurs of agreement.

"The will was on the desk, you said. How near were any of you to that desk?"

"Not very near. Five or six yards, perhaps, would be the nearest."

"When Mr. Leonides read you the will was he himself sitting at the desk?"

"Yes."

"Did he get up, or leave the desk, after reading the will and before signing it?"

"No."

"Could the servants read the document when they signed their names?"

"No," said Clemency. "My father-in-law placed a sheet of paper across the upper part of the document."

"Quite properly," said Philip. "The contents of the will were no business of the servants."

"I see," said Taverner. "At least—I don't see."

With a brisk movement he produced a long envelope and leaned forward to hand it to the lawyer.

"Have a look at that," he said. "And tell me what it is."

Mr. Gaitskill drew a folded document out of the envelope. He looked at it with lively astonishment, turning it round and round in his hands.

"This," he said, "is somewhat surprising. I do not understand it at all. Where was this, if I may ask?"

"In the safe, amongst Mr. Leonides's other papers."

"But what is it?" demanded Roger. "What's all the fuss about?"

"This is the will I prepared for your father's signature, Roger —but—I can't understand it after what you have all said—it is not signed."

"What? Well, I suppose it is just a draft."

"No," said the lawyer. "Mr. Leonides returned me the original draft. I then drew up the will—this will," he tapped it with his finger, "and sent it to him for signature. According to your evidence he signed the will in front of you all—and the two witnesses also appended their signatures—and yet this will is unsigned."

"But that's impossible," exclaimed Philip Leonides, speaking with more animation than I had yet heard from him.

Taverner asked: "How good was your father's eyesight?"

"He suffered from glaucoma. He used strong glasses, of course, for reading."

"He had those glasses on that evening?"

"Certainly. He didn't take his glasses off until after he had signed. I think I am right?"

"Quite right," said Clemency.

"And nobody—you are all sure of that—went near the desk before the signing of the will?"

"I wonder now," said Magda, screwing up her eyes. "If one could only visualise it all again."

"Nobody went near the desk," said Sophia. "And grandfather sat at it all the time."

"The desk was in the position it is now? It was not near a door, or a window, or any drapery?"

"It was where it is now."

"I am trying to see how a substitution of some kind could have been effected," said Taverner. "Some kind of substitution there must have been. Mr. Leonides was under the impression that he was signing the document he had just read aloud."

"Couldn't the signatures have been erased?" Roger demanded.

"No, Mr. Leonides. Not without leaving signs of erasion. There is one other possibility. That this is not the document sent to Mr. Leonides by Gaitskill and which he signed in your presence."

"On the contrary," said Mr. Gaitskill. "I could swear to this being the original document. There is a small flaw in the paper —at the top left hand corner—it resembles, by a stretch of fancy, an aeroplane. I noticed it at the time."

The family looked blankly at one another.

"A most curious set of circumstances," said Mr. Gaitskill. "Quite without precedent in my experience."

"The whole thing's impossible," said Roger. "We were all there. It simply couldn't have happened."

Miss de Haviland gave a dry cough.

"Never any good wasting breath saying something that has happened couldn't have happened," she remarked. "What's the position now? That's what I'd like to know?"

Gaitskill immediately became the cautious lawyer.

"The position will have to be examined very carefully," he said. "The document, of course, revokes all former wills and testaments. There are a large number of witnesses who saw Mr. Leonides sign what he certainly believed to be this will in perfectly good faith. Hum. Very interesting. Quite a little legal problem."

Taverner glanced at his watch.

"I'm afraid," he said, "I've been keeping you from your lunch."

"Won't you stay and lunch with us, Chief Inspector?" asked Philip.

"Thank you, Mr. Leonides, but I am meeting Dr. Gray in Swinly Dean."

Philip turned to the lawyer.

"You'll lunch with us, Gaitskill?"

"Thank you, Philip."

Everybody stood up. I edged unobtrusively towards Sophia.

"Do I go or stay?" I murmured. It sounded ridiculously like the title of a Victorian song.

"Go, I think," said Sophia.

I slipped quietly out of the room in pursuit of Taverner. Josephine was swinging to and fro on a baize door leading to the back quarters. She appeared to be highly amused about something.

"The police are stupid," she observed.

Sophia came out of the drawing room.

"What have you been doing, Josephine?"

"Helping Nannie."

"I believe you've been listening outside the door."

Josephine made a face at her and retreated.

"That child," said Sophia, "is a bit of a problem."

CHAPTER 11

I CAME into the A.C.'s room at the Yard to find Taverner finishing the recital of what had apparently been a tale of woe.

"And there you are," he was saying. "I've turned a lot of them inside out—and what do I get—nothing at all! No motives. None

of them hard up. And all that we've got against the wife and her
young man is that he made sheep's eyes at her when she poured
him out his coffee!"

"Come, come, Taverner," I said. "I can do a little better than that
for you."

"You can, can you? Well, Mr. Charles, what did you get?"

I sat down, lit a cigarette, leaned back and let them have it.

"Roger Leonides and his wife were planning a getaway abroad
next Tuesday. Roger and his father had a stormy interview on the
day of the old man's death. Old Leonides had found out something was wrong, and Roger was admitting culpability."

Taverner went purple in the face.

"Where the hell did you get all that from?" he demanded. "If
you got it from the servants—"

"I didn't get it from the servants, I got it," I said, "from a private inquiry agent."

"What do you mean?"

"And I must say that in accordance with the canons of the best
detective stories, he, or rather she—or perhaps I'd better say it—
has licked the police hollow!

"I also think," I went on, "that my private detective has a few
more things up his, her or its sleeve."

Taverner opened his mouth and shut it again. He wanted to ask
so many questions at once that he found it hard to begin.

"Roger!" he said. "So Roger's a wrong'un, is he?"

I felt a slight reluctance as I unburdened myself, I had liked
Roger Leonides. Remembering his comfortable friendly room, and
the man's own friendly charm, I disliked setting the hounds of
justice on his track. It was possible, of course, that all Josephine's
information would be unreliable, but I did not really think so.

"So the kid told you?" said Taverner. "She seems to be wise to
everything that goes on in that house."

"Children usually are," said my father drily.

This information, if true, altered the whole position. If Roger
had been, as Josephine had confidently suggested, "embezzling"
the funds of Associated Catering and if the old man had found it
out, it might have been vital to silence old Leonides and to leave
England before the truth came out. Possibly Roger had rendered
himself liable to criminal prosecution.

It was agreed that inquiries should be made without delay into the affairs of Associated Catering.

"It will be an almighty crash, if that goes," my father remarked. "It's a huge concern. There are millions involved."

"If it's really in Queer Street, it gives us what we want," said Taverner. "Father summons Roger. Roger breaks down and confesses. Brenda Leonides was out at a cinema. Roger has only got to leave his father's room, walk into the bathroom, empty out an insulin phial and replace it with the strong solution of eserine and there you are. Or his wife may have done it. She went over to the other wing after she came home that day—says she went over to fetch a pipe Roger had left there. But she could have gone over to switch the stuff before Brenda came home and gave him his injection. She'd be quite cool and capable about it."

I nodded. "Yes, I fancy her as the actual doer of the deed. She's cool enough for anything! And I don't think that Roger Leonides would think of poison as a means—that trick with the insulin has something feminine about it."

"Plenty of men poisoners," said my father drily.

"Oh, I know, sir," said Taverner. "Don't I know!" he added with feeling.

"All the same I shouldn't have said Roger was the type."

"Pritchard," the Old Man reminded him, "was a good mixer."

"Let's say they were in it together."

"With the accent on Lady Macbeth," said my father, as Taverner departed. "Is that how she strikes you, Charles?"

I visualised the slight graceful figure standing by the window in that austere room.

"Not quite," I said. "Lady Macbeth was essentially a greedy woman. I don't think Clemency Leonides is. I don't think she wants or cares for possessions."

"But she might care, desperately, about her husband's safety?"

"That, yes. And she could certainly be—well, ruthless."

"Different kinds of ruthlessness. . . ." That was what Sophia had said.

I looked up to see the Old Man watching me.

"What's on your mind, Charles?"

But I didn't tell him then.

I was summoned on the following day and found Taverner and my father together.

Taverner was looking pleased with himself and slightly excited.

"Associated Catering is on the rocks," said my father.

"Due to crash at any minute," said Taverner.

"I saw there had been a sharp fall in the shares last night," I said. "But they seem to have recovered this morning."

"We've had to go about it very cautiously," said Taverner. "No direct inquiries. Nothing to cause a panic—or to put the wind up our absconding gentleman. But we've got certain private sources of information and the information there is fairly definite. Associated Catering is on the verge of a crash. It can't possibly meet its commitments. The truth seems to be that it's been grossly mismanaged for years."

"By Roger Leonides?"

"Yes. He's had supreme power, you know."

"And he's helped himself to money—"

"No," said Taverner. "We don't think he has. To put it bluntly, he may be a murderer, but we don't think he's a swindler. Quite frankly he's just been—a fool. He doesn't seem to have had any kind of judgement. He's launched out where he should have held in—he's hesitated and retreated where he ought to have launched out. He's delegated power to the last sort of people he ought to have delegated it to. He's a trustful sort of chap, and he's trusted the wrong people. At every time, and on every occasion, he's done the wrong thing."

"There are people like that," said my father. "And they're not really stupid either. They're bad judges of men, that's all. And they're enthusiastic at the wrong time."

"A man like that oughtn't to be in business at all," said Taverner.

"He probably wouldn't be," said my father, "except for the accident of being Aristide Leonides's son."

"That show was absolutely booming when the old man handed it over to him. It ought to have been a gold mine! You'd think he could have just sat back and let the show run itself."

"No," my father shook his head. "No show runs itself. There are always decisions to be made—a man sacked here—a man appointed there—small questions of policy. And with Roger Leonides the answer seems to have been always wrong."

"That's right," said Taverner. "He's a loyal sort of chap, for one thing. He kept on the most frightful duds—just because he had an affection for them—or because they'd been there a long time.

413

And then he sometimes had wild impractical ideas and insisted on trying them out in spite of the enormous outlay involved."

"But nothing criminal?" my father insisted.

"No, nothing criminal."

"Then why murder?" I asked.

"He may have been a fool and not a knave," said Taverner. "But the result was the same—or nearly the same. The only thing that could save Associated Catering from the smash was a really co-lossal sum of money by next" (he consulted a notebook) "by next Wednesday at the latest."

"Such a sum as he would inherit, or thought he would have inherited, under his father's will?"

"Exactly."

"But he wouldn't be able to have got that sum in cash."

"No. But he'd have got credit. It's the same thing."

The Old Man nodded.

"Wouldn't it have been simpler to go to old Leonides and ask for help?" he suggested.

"I think he did," said Taverner. "I think that's what the kid overheard. The old boy refused point blank, I should imagine, to throw good money after bad. He would, you know."

I thought that Taverner was right there. Aristide Leonides had refused the backing for Magda's play—he had said that it would not be a Box Office success. Events had proved him correct. He was a generous man to his family, but he was not a man to waste money in unprofitable enterprises. And Associated Catering ran to thousands, or probably hundreds of thousands. He had refused point blank, and the only way for Roger to avoid financial ruin was for his father to die.

Yes, there was certainly a motive there all right.

My father looked at his watch

"I've asked him to come here," he said. "He'll be here any minute now."

"Roger?"

"Yes."

"Will you walk into my parlour said the spider to the fly?" I murmured.

Taverner looked at me in a shocked way.

"We shall give him all the proper cautions," he said severely. The stage was set, the shorthand writer established. Presently the buzzer sounded, and a few minutes later Roger Leonides entered the room.

He came in eagerly—and rather clumsily—he stumbled over a chair. I was reminded as before of a large friendly dog. At the same time I decided quite definitely that it was not he who had carried out the actual process of transferring eserine to an insulin bottle. He would have broken it, spilled it, or muffed the operation in some way or other. No, Clemency's, I decided, had been the actual hand, though Roger had been privy to the deed.

Words rushed from him:

"You wanted to see me? You've found out something? Hullo, Charles, I didn't see you. Nice of you to come along. But please tell me, Sir Arthur—"

Such a nice fellow—really such a nice fellow. But lots of murderers had been nice fellows—so their astonished friends had said afterwards. Feeling rather like Judas, I smiled a greeting.

My father was deliberate, coldly official. The glib phrases were uttered. Statement . . . taken down . . . no compulsion . . . solicitor . . .

Roger Leonides brushed them all aside with the same characteristic eager impatience.

I saw the faint sardonic smile on Chief Inspector Taverner's face, and read from it the thought in his mind.

"Always sure of themselves, these chaps. They can't make a mistake. They're far too clever!"

I sat down unobtrusively in a corner and listened.

"I have asked you to come here, Mr. Leonides," my father said, "not to give you fresh information, but to ask for some information from you—information that you have previously withheld."

Roger Leonides looked bewildered.

"Withheld? But I've told you everything—absolutely everything!"

"I think not. You had a conversation with the deceased on the afternoon of his death?"

"Yes, yes, I had tea with him. I told you so."

"You told us that, yes, but you did not tell us about your conversation."

"We—just—talked."

"What about?"

"Daily happenings, the house, Sophia—"

"What about Associated Catering? Was that mentioned?"

I think I had hoped up to then that Josephine had been inventing the whole story—but if so, that hope was quickly quenched.

Roger's face changed. It changed in a moment from eagerness to something that was recognisably close to despair.

"Oh my God," he said. He dropped into a chair and buried his face in his hands.

Taverner smiled like a contented cat.

"You admit, Mr. Leonides, that you have not been frank with us?"

"How did you get to know about that? I thought nobody knew —I don't see how anybody could know."

"We have means of finding out these things, Mr. Leonides." There was a majestic pause. "I think you will see now that you had better tell us the truth."

"Yes, yes, of course. I'll tell you. What do you want to know?"

"Is it true that Associated Catering is on the verge of collapse?"

"Yes. It can't be staved off now. The crash is bound to come. If only my father could have died without ever knowing. I feel so ashamed—so disgraced—"

"There is a possibility of criminal prosecution?"

Roger sat up sharply.

"No, indeed. It will be bankruptcy—but an honourable bankruptcy. Creditors will be paid twenty shillings in the pound if I throw in my personal assets which I shall do. No, the disgrace I feel is to have failed my father. He trusted me. He made over to me this, his largest concern—and his pet concern. He never interfered, he never asked what I was doing. He just—trusted me. . . . And I let him down."

My father said drily:

"You say there was no likelihood of criminal prosecution? Why then, had you and your wife planned to go abroad without telling anybody of your intention?"

"You know that, too?"

"Yes, Mr. Leonides."

"But don't you see?" He leaned forward eagerly. "I couldn't face him with the truth. It would have looked, you see, as if I was asking for money? As though I wanted him to set me on my feet again. He—he was very fond of me. He would have wanted to help. But I couldn't—I couldn't go on—it would have meant making a

416

mess of things all over again—I'm no good. I haven't got the ability. I'm not the man my father was. I've always known it. I've tried. But it's no good. I've been so miserable— God! you don't know how miserable I've been! Trying to get out of the muddle, hoping I'd just get square, hoping the dear old man would never need hear about it. And then it came—no more hope of avoiding the crash. Clemency—my wife—she understood, she agreed with me. We thought out this plan. Say nothing to anyone. Go away. And then let the storm break. I'd leave a letter for my father, telling him all about it—telling him how ashamed I was and begging him to forgive me. He's been so good to me always—you don't know! But it would be too late then for him to do anything. That's what I wanted. Not to ask him—or even to seem to ask him for help. Start again on my own somewhere. Live simply and humbly. Grow things. Coffee—fruit. Just have the bare necessities of life—hard on Clemency, but she swore she didn't mind. She's wonderful—absolutely wonderful."

"I see." My father's voice was dry. "And what made you change your mind?"

"Change my mind?"

"Yes. What made you decide to go to your father and ask for financial help after all?"

Roger stared at him.

"But I didn't!"

"Come now, Mr. Leonides."

"You've got it all wrong. I didn't go to him. He sent for me. He'd heard, somehow, in the City. A rumour, I suppose. But he always knew things. Someone had told him. He tackled me with it. Then, of course, I broke down . . . I told him everything. I said it wasn't so much the money—it was the feeling I'd let him down after he'd trusted me."

Roger swallowed convulsively.

"The dear old man," he said. "You can't imagine how good he was to me. No reproaches. Just kindness. I told him I didn't want help, that I preferred not to have it—that I'd rather go away as I'd planned to do. But he wouldn't listen. He insisted on coming to the rescue—on putting Associated Catering on its legs again."

Taverner said sharply:

"You are asking us to believe that your father intended to come to your assistance financially?"

"Certainly he did. He wrote to his brokers then and there, giving them instructions."

I suppose he saw the incredulity on the two men's faces. He flushed.

"Look here," he said, "I've still got the letter. I was to post it. But of course later—with—with the shock and confusion, I forgot. I've probably got it in my pocket now."

He drew out his wallet and started hunting through it. Finally he found what he wanted. It was a creased envelope with a stamp on it. It was addressed, as I saw by leaning forward, to Messrs. Greatorex and Hanbury.

"Read it for yourselves," he said. "If you don't believe me."

My father tore open the letter. Taverner went round behind him. I did not see the letter then, but I saw it later. It instructed Messrs. Greatorex and Hanbury to realise certain investments and asked for a member of the firm to be sent down on the following day to take certain instructions re the affairs of Associated Catering. Some of it was unintelligible to me but its purport was clear enough. Aristide Leonides was preparing to put Associated Catering on its feet again.

Taverner said:

"We will give you a receipt for this, Mr. Leonides."

Roger took the receipt. He got up and said:

"Is that all? You do see how it all was, don't you?"

Taverner said:

"Mr. Leonides gave you this letter and you then left him? What did you do next?"

"I rushed back to my own part of the house. My wife had just come in. I told her what my father proposed to do. How wonderful he had been! I—really, I hardly knew what I was doing."

"And your father was taken ill—how long after that?"

"Let me see—half an hour, perhaps, or an hour. Brenda came rushing in. She was frightened. She said he looked queer. I—I rushed over with her. But I've told you this before."

"During your former visit, did you go into the bathroom adjoining your father's room at all?"

"I don't think so. No—no, I am sure I didn't. Why, you can't possibly think that I—"

My father quelled the sudden indignation. He got up and shook hands.

"Thank you, Mr. Leonides," he said. "You have been very helpful. But you should have told us all this before."

The door closed behind Roger. I got up and came to look at the letter lying on my father's table.

"It could be forgery," said Taverner hopefully.

"It could be," said my father, "but I don't think it is. I think we'll have to accept it as it stands. Old Leonides was prepared to get his son out of this mess. It could have been done more efficiently by him alive than it could by Roger after his death—especially as it now transpires that no will is to be found and that in consequence Roger's actual amount of inheritance is open to question. That means delays—and difficulties. As things now stand, the crash is bound to come. No, Taverner, Roger Leonides and his wife had no motive for getting the old man out of the way. On the contrary—"

He stopped and repeated thoughtfully as though a sudden thought had occurred to him, "On the contrary . . ."

"What's on your mind, sir?" Taverner asked.

The Old Man said slowly:

"If Aristide Leonides had lived only another twenty-four hours, Roger would have been all right. But he didn't live twenty-four hours. He died suddenly and dramatically within little more than an hour."

"Hm," said Taverner. "Do you think somebody in the house wanted Roger to go broke? Someone who had an opposing financial interest? Doesn't seem likely."

"What's the position as regards the will?" my father asked. "Who actually gets old Leonides's money?"

"You know what lawyers are. Can't get a straight answer out of them. There's a former will. Made when he married the second Mrs. Leonides. That leaves the same sum to her, rather less to Miss de Haviland, and the remainder between Philip and Roger. I should have thought that if this will isn't signed, then the old one would operate, but it seems it isn't so simple as that. First the making of the new will revoked the former one and there are witnesses to the signing of it, and the 'testator's intention.' It seems to be a toss up if it turns out that he died intestate. Then the widow apparently gets the lot—or a life interest at any rate."

"So if the will's disappeared Brenda Leonides is the most likely person to profit by it?"

"Yes. If there's been any hocus pocus, it seems probable that she's at the bottom of it. And there obviously has been hocus pocus, but I'm dashed if I see how it was done."

I didn't see, either. I suppose we were really incredibly stupid. But we were looking at it, of course, from the wrong angle.

CHAPTER 12

THERE WAS a short silence after Taverner had gone out.

Then I said:

"Dad, what are murderers like?"

The Old Man looked up at me thoughtfully. We understand each other so well that he knew exactly what was in my mind when I put that question. And he answered it very seriously.

"Yes," he said. "That's important now—very important, for you. . . . Murder's come close to you. You can't go on looking at it from the outside."

I had always been interested, in an amateurish kind of way, in some of the more spectacular "cases" with which the CID had dealt, but, as my father said, I had been interested from the outside—looking in, as it were, through the shop window. But now, as Sophia had seen much more quickly than I did, murder had become a dominant factor in my life.

The Old Man went on:

"I don't know if I'm the right person to ask. I could put you on to a couple of the tame psychiatrists who do jobs for us. They've got it all cut and dried. Or Taverner could give you all the inside dope. But you want, I take it, to hear what I, personally, as the result of my experience of criminals, think about it?"

"That's what I want," I said gratefully.

My father traced a little circle with his finger on the desk top.

"What are murderers like? Some of them," a faint rather melancholy smile showed on his face, "have been thoroughly nice chaps."

I think I looked a little startled.

"Oh yes, they have," he said. "Nice ordinary fellows like you and me—or like that chap who went out just now—Roger Leonides. Murder, you see, is an amateur crime. I'm speaking of course of the kind of murder you have in mind—not gangster stuff. One feels, very often, as though these nice ordinary chaps, had been overtaken, as it were, by murder, almost accidentally. They've been in a tight place, or they've wanted something very badly, money or a woman—and they've killed to get it. The brake that operates with most of us doesn't operate with them. A child, you know, translates desire into action without compunction. A child is angry with its kitten, says 'I'll kill you,' and hits it on the head with a hammer—and then breaks its heart because the kitten doesn't come alive again! Lots of kids try to take a baby out of a pram and 'drown it,' because it usurps attention—or interferes with their pleasures. They get—very early—to a stage when they know that that is 'wrong'—that is, that it will be punished. Later, they get to feel that it is wrong. But some people, I suspect, remain morally immature. They continue to be aware that murder is wrong, but they do not feel it. I don't think, in my experience, that any murderer has really felt remorse. . . . And that, perhaps, is the mark of Cain. Murderers are set apart, they are 'different'—murder is wrong—but not for them—for them it is necessary—the victim has 'asked for it,' it was 'the only way.' "

"Do you think," I asked, "that if someone hated old Leonides, had hated him, say, for a very long time, that that would be a reason?"

"Pure hate? Very unlikely, I should say." My father looked at me curiously. "When you say hate, I presume you mean dislike carried to excess. A jealous hate is different—that rises out of affection and frustration. Constance Kent, everybody said, was very fond of the baby brother she killed. But she wanted, one supposes, the attention and the love that was bestowed on him. I think people more often kill those they love, than those they hate. Possibly because only the people you love can really make life unendurable to you.

"But all this doesn't help you much, does it?" he went on. "What you want, if I read you correctly, is some token, some uni-

421

versal sign that will help you to pick out a murderer from a household of apparently normal and pleasant people?"

"Yes, that's it."

"Is there a common denominator? I wonder. You know," he paused in thought, "if there is, I should be inclined to say it is vanity."

"Vanity?"

"Yes, I've never met a murderer who wasn't vain. . . . It's their vanity that leads to their undoing, nine times out of ten. They may be frightened of being caught, but they can't help strutting and boasting and usually they're sure they've been far too clever to be caught." He added: "And here's another thing, a murderer wants to talk."

"To talk?"

"Yes, you see, having committed a murder puts you in a position of great loneliness. You'd like to tell somebody all about it—and you never can. And that makes you want to all the more. And so— if you can't talk about how you did it, you can at least talk about the murder itself—discuss it, advance theories—go over it.

"If I were you, Charles, I should look out for that. Go down there again, mix with them all, get them to talk. Of course it won't be plain sailing. Guilty or innocent, they'll be glad of the chance to talk to a stranger, because they can say things to you that they couldn't say to each other. But it's possible, I think, that you might spot a difference. A person who has something to hide can't really afford to talk at all. The blokes knew that in Intelligence during the war. If you were captured, your name, rank and unit but nothing more. People who attempt to give false information nearly always slip up. Get that household talking, Charles, and watch out for a slip or for some flash of self revelation."

I told him then about what Sophia had said about the ruthlessness in the family—the different kinds of ruthlessness. He was interested.

"Yes," he said. "Your young woman has got something there. Most families have got a defect, a chink in the armour. Most people can deal with one weakness—but they mightn't be able to deal with two weaknesses of a different kind. Interesting thing, heredity. Take the de Haviland ruthlessness, and what we might call the Leonides's unscrupulousness—the de Havilands are all right because they're not unscrupulous, and the Leonides are all right

422

because, though unscrupulous, they are kindly—but get a descendant who inherited both of those traits—see what I mean?"

I had not thought of it quite in those terms. My father said:

"But I shouldn't worry your head about heredity. It's much too tricky and complicated a subject. No, my boy, go down there and let them talk to you. Your Sophia is quite right about one thing. Nothing but the truth is going to be any good to her or to you. You've got to know."

He added as I went out of the room:

"And be careful of the child."

"Josephine? You mean don't let on to her what I'm up to."

"No, I didn't mean that. I meant—look after her. We don't want anything to happen to her."

I stared at him.

"Come, come, Charles. There's a cold blooded killer somewhere in that household. The child Josephine appears to know most of what goes on."

"She certainly knew all about Roger—even if she did leap to the conclusion that he was a swindler. Her account of what she overheard seems to have been quite accurate."

"Yes, yes. Child's evidence is always the best evidence there is. I'd rely on it every time. No good in court, of course. Children can't stand being asked direct questions. They mumble or else look idiotic and say they don't know. They're at their best when they're showing off. That's what the child was doing to you. Showing off. You'll get more out of her in the same way. Don't go asking her questions. Pretend you think she doesn't know anything. That'll fetch her."

He added:

"But take care of her. She may know a little too much for somebody's safety."

CHAPTER 13

I WENT DOWN to the Crooked House (as I called it in my own mind) with a slightly guilty feeling. Though I had repeated to Taverner Josephine's confidences about Roger, I had said nothing about her statement that Brenda and Laurence Brown wrote love letters to each other.

I excused myself by pretending that it was mere romancing, and that there was no reason to believe that it was true. But actually I had felt a strange reluctance to pile up additional evidence against Brenda Leonides. I had been affected by the pathos of her position in the house—surrounded by a hostile family united solidly against her. If such letters existed doubtless Taverner and his myrmidons would find them. I disliked to be the means of bringing fresh suspicion on a woman in a difficult position. Moreover, she had assured me solemnly that there was nothing of that kind between her and Laurence and I felt more inclined to believe her than to believe that malicious gnome Josephine. Had not Brenda said herself that Josephine was "Not all there."

I stifled an uneasy certainty that Josephine was very much all there. I remembered the intelligence of her beady black eyes.

I had rung up Sophia and asked if I might come down again.

"Please do, Charles."

"How are things going?"

"I don't know. All right. They keep on searching the house. What are they looking for?"

"I've no idea."

"We're all getting very nervy. Come as soon as you can. I shall go crazy if I can't talk to someone."

I said I would come down straightaway.

There was no one in sight as I drove up to the front door. I

424

paid the taxi and it drove away. I felt uncertain whether to ring the bell or to walk in. The front door was open.

As I stood there, hesitating, I heard a slight sound behind me. I turned my head sharply. Josephine, her face partially obscured by a very large apple, was standing in the opening of the yew hedge looking at me.

As I turned my head, she turned away.

"Hullo, Josephine."

She did not answer, but disappeared behind the hedge. I crossed the drive and followed her. She was seated on the uncomfortable rustic bench by the goldfish pond swinging her legs to and fro and biting into her apple. Above its rosy circumference her eyes regarded me sombrely and with what I could not but feel was hostility.

"I've come down again, Josephine," I said.

It was a feeble opening, but I found Josephine's silence and her unblinking gaze, rather unnerving.

With excellent strategic sense, she still did not reply.

"Is that a good apple?" I asked.

This time Josephine did condescend to reply. Her reply consisted of one word.

"Woolly."

"A pity," I said. "I don't like woolly apples."

Josephine replied scornfully:

"Nobody does."

"Why wouldn't you speak to me when I said Hullo?"

"I didn't want to."

"Why not?"

Josephine removed the apple from her face to assist in the clearness of her denunciation.

"You went and sneaked to the police," she said.

"Oh," I was rather taken aback. "You mean—about—"

"About Uncle Roger."

"But it's all right, Josephine," I assured her. "Quite all right. They know he didn't do anything wrong—I mean, he hadn't embezzled any money or anything of that kind."

Josephine threw me an exasperated glance.

"How stupid you are."

"I'm sorry."

"I wasn't worrying about Uncle Roger. It's simply that that's

425

not the way to do detective work. Don't you know that you never tell the police until the very end?"

"Oh I see," I said. "I'm sorry, Josephine. I'm really very sorry."

"So you should be." She added reproachfully, "I trusted you."

I said I was sorry for the third time. Josephine appeared a little mollified. She took another couple of bites of apple.

"But the police would have been bound to find out about all this," I said. "You—I—we couldn't have kept it a secret."

"You mean because he's going bankrupt?"

As usual Josephine was well informed.

"I suppose it will come to that."

"They're going to talk about it tonight," said Josephine. "Father and Mother and Uncle Roger and Aunt Edith. Aunt Edith would give him her money—only she hasn't got it yet—but I don't think Father will. He says if Roger has got in a jam he's only got himself to blame and what's the good of throwing good money after bad, and Mother won't hear of giving him any because she wants Father to put up the money for Edith Thompson. Do you know Edith Thompson? She was married, but she didn't like her husband. She was in love with a young man called Bywaters who came off a ship and he went down a different street after the theatre and stabbed him in the back."

I marvelled once more at the range and completeness of Josephine's knowledge; and also at the dramatic sense which, only slightly obscured by hazy pronouns, had presented all the salient facts in a nutshell.

"It sounds all right," said Josephine, "but I don't suppose the play will be like that at all. It will be like Jezebel again." She sighed. "I wish I knew why the dogs wouldn't eat the palms of her hands."

"Josephine," I said. "You told me that you were almost sure who the murderer was?"

"Well?"

"Who is it?"

She gave me a look of scorn.

"I see," I said. "Not till the last chapter? Not even if I promise not to tell Inspector Taverner?"

"I want just a few more clues," said Josephine.

"Anyway," she added, throwing the core of the apple into the goldfish pool, "I wouldn't tell you. If you're anyone, you're Watson."

426

I stomached this insult.

"O.K." I said. "I'm Watson. But even Watson was given the data."

"The what?"

"The facts. And then he made the wrong deductions from them. Wouldn't it be a lot of fun for you to see me making the wrong deductions?"

For a moment Josephine was tempted. Then she shook her head.

"No," she said, and added: "Anyway, I'm not very keen on Sherlock Holmes. It's awfully old fashioned. They drive about in dog carts."

"What about those letters?" I asked.

"What letters?"

"The letters you said Laurence Brown and Brenda wrote to each other."

"I made that up," said Josephine.

"I don't believe you."

"Yes, I did. I often make things up. It amuses me."

I stared at her. She stared back.

"Look here, Josephine. I know a man at the British Museum who knows a lot about the Bible. If I find out from him why the dogs didn't eat the palms of Jezebel's hands, will you tell me about those letters?"

This time Josephine really hesitated.

Somewhere, not very far away, a twig snapped with a sharp cracking noise. Josephine said flatly:

"No, I won't."

I accepted defeat. Rather late in the day, I remembered my father's advice.

"Oh well," I said, "it's only a game. Of course you don't really know anything."

Josephine's eyes snapped, but she resisted the bait.

I got up. "I must go in now," I said, "and find Sophia. Come along."

"I shall stop here," said Josephine.

"No, you won't," I said. "You're coming in with me."

Unceremoniously I yanked her to her feet. She seemed surprised and inclined to protest, but yielded with a fairly good grace—

partly, no doubt, because she wished to observe the reactions of the household to my presence.

Why I was so anxious for her to accompany me I could not at the moment have said. It only came to me as we were passing through the front door.

It was because of the sudden snapping of a twig.

CHAPTER 14

THERE WAS a murmur of voices from the big drawing room. I hesitated but did not go in. I wandered on down the passage and led by some impulse, I pushed open a baize door. The passage beyond was dark but suddenly a door opened showing a big lighted kitchen. In the doorway stood an old woman—a rather bulky old woman. She had a very clean white apron tied round her ample waist and the moment I saw her I knew that everything was all right. It is the feeling that a good Nannie can always give you. I am thirty-five, but I felt just like a reassured little boy of four.

As far as I knew, Nannie had never seen me, but she said at once:

"It's Mr. Charles, isn't it? Come into the kitchen and let me give you a cup of tea."

It was a big happy feeling kitchen. I sat down by the centre table and Nannie brought me a cup of tea and two sweet biscuits on a plate. I felt more than ever that I was in the nursery again. Everything was all right—and the terrors of the dark room and the unknown were no more with me.

"Miss Sophia will be glad you've come," said Nannie. "She's been getting rather overexcited." She added disapprovingly: "They're all overexcited."

I looked over my shoulder.

"Where's Josephine? She came in with me."

Nannie made a disapproving clacking noise with her tongue.

"Listening at doors and writing down things in that silly little book she carries about with her," she said. "She ought to have gone to school and had children of her own age to play with. I've said so to Miss Edith and she agrees—but the master would have it that she was best here in her home."

"I suppose he's very fond of her," I said.

"He was, sir. He was fond of them all."

I looked slightly astonished, wondering why Philip's affection for his offspring was put so definitely in the past. Nannie saw my expression and flushing slightly, she said:

"When I said the master, it was old Mr. Leonides I meant."

Before I could respond to that, the door opened with a rush and Sophia came in.

"Oh Charles," she said, and then quickly: "Oh Nannie, I'm so glad he's come."

"I know you are, love."

Nannie gathered up a lot of pots and pans and went off into a scullery with them. She shut the door behind her.

I got up from the table and went over to Sophia. I put my arms round her and held her to me.

"Dearest," I said. "You're trembling. What is it?"

Sophia said:

"I'm frightened, Charles. I'm frightened."

"I love you," I said. "If I could take you away—"

She drew apart and shook her head.

"No, that's impossible. We've got to see this through. But you know, Charles, I don't like it. I don't like the feeling that someone —someone in this house—someone I see and speak to every day is a cold blooded calculating poisoner . . ."

And I didn't know how to answer that. To someone like Sophia one can give no easy meaningless reassurances.

She said: "If only one knew—"

"That must be the worst of it," I agreed.

"You know what really frightens me?" she whispered. "It's that we may never know. . . ."

I could visualise easily what a nightmare that would be. . . . And it seemed to me highly probable that it never might be known who had killed old Leonides.

But it also reminded me of a question I had meant to put to Sophia on a point that had interested me.

"Tell me, Sophia," I said. "How many people in this house knew about the eserine eyedrops—I mean (a) that your grandfather had them, and (b) that they were poisonous and what would be a fatal dose?"

"I see what you're getting at, Charles. But it won't work. You see, we all knew."

"Well, yes, vaguely, I suppose, but specifically—"

"We knew specifically. We were all up with grandfather one day for coffee after lunch. He liked all the family round him, you know. And his eyes had been giving him a lot of trouble. And Brenda got the eserine to put a drop in each eye and Josephine who always asks questions about everything, said 'Why does it say: *Eyedrops —not to be taken*' on the bottle? What would happen if you drank all the bottle?' And grandfather smiled and said: 'If Brenda were to make a mistake and inject eyedrops into me one day instead of insulin—I suspect I should give a big gasp, and go rather blue in the face and then die, because, you see, my heart isn't very strong.' And Josephine said: 'Oo,' and grandfather went on 'So we must be careful that Brenda does not give me an injection of eserine instead of insulin, mustn't we?'" Sophia paused and then said: "We were all there listening. You see? We all heard!"

I did see. I had had some faint idea in my mind that just a little specialized knowledge would have been needed. But now it was borne in upon me that old Leonides had actually supplied the blue print for his own murder. The murderer had not had to think out a scheme, or to plan or devise anything. A simple easy method of causing death had been supplied by the victim himself.

I drew a deep breath. Sophia, catching my thought, said: "Yes, it's rather horrible, isn't it?"

"You know, Sophia," I said slowly. "There's just one thing does strike me."

"Yes?"

"That you're right, and that it couldn't have been Brenda. She couldn't do it exactly that way—when you'd all listened—when you'd all remember."

"I don't know about that. She is rather dumb in some ways, you know."

"Not as dumb as all that," I said. "No, it couldn't have been Brenda."

Sophia moved away from me.

"You don't want it to be Brenda, do you?" she asked.

And what could I say? I couldn't—no, I couldn't—say flatly: "Yes, I hope it is Brenda."

Why couldn't I? Just the feeling that Brenda was all alone on one side, and the concentrated animosity of the powerful Leonides family was arrayed against her on the other side? Chivalry? A feeling for the weaker? For the defenceless? I remembered her sitting on the sofa in her expensive rich mourning, the hopelessness in her voice—the fear in her eyes.

Nannie came back rather opportunely from the scullery. I don't know whether she sensed a certain strain between myself and Sophia.

She said disapprovingly:

"Talking murders and such like. Forget about it, that's what I say. Leave it to the police. It's their nasty business, not yours."

"Oh Nannie—don't you realize that someone in this house is a murderer."

"Nonsense, Miss Sophia, I've no patience with you. Isn't the front door open all the time—all the doors open, nothing locked—asking for thieves and burglars."

"But it couldn't have been a burglar, nothing was stolen. Besides why should a burglar come in and poison somebody?"

"I didn't say it was a burglar, Miss Sophia. I only said all the doors were open. Anyone could have got in. If you ask me it was the Communists."

Nannie nodded her head in a satisfied way.

"Why on earth should Communists want to murder poor grandfather?"

"Well, everyone says that they're at the bottom of everything that goes on. But if it wasn't the Communists, mark my word, it was the Catholics. The Scarlet Woman of Babylon, that's what they are."

With the air of one saying the last word, Nannie disappeared again into the scullery.

Sophia and I laughed.

"A good old Black Protestant," I said.

"Yes, isn't she? Come on, Charles, come into the drawing room. There's a kind of family conclave going on. It was scheduled for this evening—but it's started prematurely."

"I'd better not butt in, Sophia."

431

"If you're ever going to marry into the family, you'd better see just what it's like when it has the gloves off."

"What's it all about?"

"Roger's affairs. You seem to have been mixed up in them already. But you're crazy to think that Roger would ever have killed grandfather. Why, Roger adored him."

"I didn't really think Roger had. I thought Clemency might have."

"Only because I put it into your head. But you're wrong there too. I don't think Clemency will mind a bit if Roger loses all his money. I think she'll actually be rather pleased. She's got a queer kind of passion for not having things. Come on."

When Sophia and I entered the drawing room, the voices that were speaking stopped abruptly. Everybody looked at us.

They were all there. Philip sitting in a big crimson brocaded armchair between the windows, his beautiful face set in a cold stern mask. He looked like a judge about to pronounce sentence. Roger was astride a big pouf by the fireplace. He had ruffled up his hair between his fingers until it stood up all over his head. His left trouser leg was rucked up and his tie was askew. He looked flushed and argumentative. Clemency sat beyond him, her slight form seemed too slender for the big stuffed chair. She was looking away from the others and seemed to be studying the wall panels with a dispassionate gaze. Edith sat in a grandfather chair, bolt upright. She was knitting with incredible energy, her lips pressed tightly together. The most beautiful thing in the room to look at was Magda and Eustace. They looked like a portrait by Gainsborough. They sat together on the sofa—the dark handsome boy with a sullen expression on his face, and beside him, one arm thrust out along the back of the sofa, sat Magda, the Duchess of Three Gables in a picture gown of taffeta with one small foot in a brocaded slipper thrust out in front of her.

Philip frowned.

"Sophia," he said, "I'm sorry, but we are discussing family matters which are of a private nature."

Miss de Haviland's needles clicked. I prepared to apologise and retreat. Sophia forestalled me. Her voice was clear and determined.

"Charles and I," she said, "hope to get married. I want Charles to be here."

"And why on earth not?" cried Roger, springing up from his

pouf with explosive energy. "I keep telling you, Philip, there's nothing private about this! The whole world is going to know tomorrow or the day after. Anyway, my dear boy," he came and put a friendly hand on my shoulder, "you know all about it. You were there this morning."

"Do tell me," cried Magda, leaning forward. "What is it like at Scotland Yard. One always wonders. A table. A desk? Chairs? What kind of curtains? No flowers, I suppose? A dictaphone?"

"Put a sock in it, mother," said Sophia. "And anyway, you told Vavasour Jones to cut that Scotland Yard scene. You said it was an anticlimax."

"It makes it too like a detective play," said Magda. "Edith Thompson is definitely a psychological drama—or psychological thriller—which do you think sounds best?"

"You were there this morning?" Philip asked me sharply. "Why? Oh, of course—your father—"

He frowned. I realised more clearly than ever that my presence was unwelcome, but Sophia's hand was clenched on my arm.

Clemency moved a chair forward.

"Do sit down," she said.

I gave her a grateful glance and accepted.

"You may say what you like," said Miss de Haviland apparently going on from where they had all left off, "but I do think we ought to respect Aristide's wishes. When this will business is straightened out, as far as I am concerned, my legacy is entirely at your disposal, Roger."

Roger tugged his hair in a frenzy.

"No, Aunt Edith. No!" he cried.

"I wish I could say the same," said Philip, "but one has to take every factor into consideration—"

"Dear old Phil, don't you understand? I'm not going to take a penny from anyone."

"Of course he can't!" snapped Clemency.

"Anyway, Edith," said Magda, "if the will is straightened out, he'll have his own legacy."

"But it can't possibly be straightened out in time, can it?" asked Eustace.

"You don't know anything about it, Eustace," said Philip.

"The boy's absolutely right," cried Roger. "He's put his finger on the spot. Nothing can avert the crash. Nothing."

He spoke with a kind of relish.

"There is really nothing to discuss," said Clemency.

"Anyway," said Roger, "what does it matter?"

"I should have thought it mattered a good deal," said Philip, pressing his lips together.

"No," said Roger. "No! Does anything matter compared with the fact that father is dead? Father is dead! And we sit here discussing mere money matters!"

A faint colour rose in Philip's pale cheeks.

"We are only trying to help," he said stiffly.

"I know, Phil, old boy, I know. But there's nothing anyone can do. So let's call it a day."

"I suppose," said Philip, "that I could raise a certain amount of money. Securities have gone down a good deal and some of my capital is tied up in such a way that I can't touch it: Magda's settlement and so on—but—"

Magda said quickly:

"Of course you can't raise the money, darling. It would be absurd to try—and not very fair on the children."

"I tell you I'm not asking anyone for anything!" shouted Roger. "I'm hoarse with telling you so. I'm quite content that things should take their course."

"It's a question of prestige," said Philip. "Father's. Ours."

"It wasn't a family business. It was solely my concern."

"Yes," said Philip, looking at him. "It was entirely your concern."

Edith de Haviland got up and said: "I think we've discussed this enough."

There was in her voice that authentic note of authority that never fails to produce its effect.

Philip and Magda got up. Eustace lounged out of the room and I noticed the stiffness of his gait. He was not exactly lame but his walk was a halting one.

Roger linked his arm in Philip's and said:

"You've been a brick, Phil, even to think of such a thing!" The brothers went out together.

Magda murmured, "Such a fuss!" as she followed them, and Sophia said that she must see about my room.

Edith de Haviland stood rolling up her knitting. She looked towards me and I thought she was going to speak to me. There was something almost like appeal in her glance. However, she changed her mind, sighed and went out after the others.

Clemency had moved over to the window and stood looking out into the garden. I went over and stood beside her. She turned her head slightly towards me.

"Thank goodness that's over," she said—and added with distaste: "What a preposterous room this is!"

"Don't you like it?"

"I can't breathe in it. There's always a smell of half dead flowers and dust."

I thought she was unjust to the room. But I knew what she meant. It was very definitely an interior.

It was a woman's room, exotic, soft, shut away from the rude blasts of outside weather. It was not a room that a man would be happy in for long. It was not a room where you could relax and read the newspaper and smoke a pipe and put up your feet. Nevertheless I preferred it to Clemency's own abstract expression of herself upstairs. On the whole I prefer a boudoir to an operating theatre.

She said, looking round:

"It's just a stage set. A background for Magda to play her scenes against." She looked at me. "You realise, don't you, what we've just been doing? Act II—the family conclave. Magda arranged it. It didn't mean a thing. There was nothing to talk about, nothing to discuss. It's all settled—finished."

There was no sadness in her voice. Rather there was satisfaction. She caught my glance.

"Oh, don't you understand?" she said impatiently. "We're free —at last! Don't you understand that Roger's been miserable—absolutely miserable—for years? He never had any aptitude for business. He likes things like horses and cows and pottering round in the country. But he adored his father—they all did. That's what's wrong with this house—too much family. I don't mean that the old man was a tyrant, or preyed upon them, or bullied them. He didn't. He gave them money and freedom. He was devoted to them. And they kept on being devoted to him."

"Is there anything wrong in that?"

"I think there is. I think, when your children have grown up, that you should cut away from them, efface yourself, slink away, force them to forget you."

"Force them? That's rather drastic, isn't it? Isn't coercion as bad one way as another?"

"If he hadn't made himself such a personality—"

"You can't make yourself a personality," I said. "He was a personality."

"He was too much of a personality for Roger. Roger worshipped him. He wanted to do everything his father wanted him to do, he wanted to be the kind of son his father wanted. And he couldn't. His father made over Associated Catering to him—it was the old man's particular joy and pride, and Roger tried hard to carry on in his father's footsteps. But he hadn't got that kind of ability. In business matters Roger is—yes, I'll say it plainly—a fool. And it nearly broke his heart. He's been miserable for years, struggling, seeing the whole thing go down the hill, having sudden wonderful 'ideas' and 'schemes' which always went wrong and made it worse than ever. It's a terrible thing to feel you're a failure year after year. You don't know how unhappy he's been. I do."

Again she turned and faced me.

"You thought, you actually suggested to the police, that Roger would have killed his father—for money! You don't know how—how absolutely ridiculous that is!"

"I do know it now," I said humbly.

"When Roger knew he couldn't stave it off any more—that the crash was bound to come, he was actually relieved. Yes, he was. He worried about his father's knowing—but not about anything else. He was looking forward to the new life we were going to live."

Her face quivered a little and her voice softened.

"Where were you going?" I asked.

"To Barbadoes. A distant cousin of mine died a short time ago and left me a tiny estate out there—oh, nothing much. But it was somewhere to go. We'd have been desperately poor, but we'd have scratched a living—it costs very little just to live. We'd have been together—unworried, away from them all."

She sighed.

"Roger is a ridiculous person. He would worry about me—about my being poor. I suppose he's got the Leonides attitude to money too firmly in his mind. When my first husband was alive, we were terribly poor—and Roger thinks it was so brave and wonderful of me! He doesn't realise that I was happy—really happy! I've never been so happy since. And yet—I never loved Richard as I love Roger."

Her eyes half-closed. I was aware of the intensity of her feeling. She opened her eyes, looked at me and said:

"So you see, I would never have killed anyone for money. I don't like money."

I was quite sure that she meant exactly what she said. Clemency Leonides was one of those rare people to whom money does not appeal. They dislike luxury, prefer austerity, and are suspicious of possessions.

Still, there are many to whom money has no personal appeal, but who can be tempted by the power it confers.

I said, "You mightn't want money for yourself—but wisely directed, money may do a lot of interesting things. It can endow research, for example."

I had suspected that Clemency might be a fanatic about her work, but she merely said:

"I doubt if endowments ever do much good. They're usually spent in the wrong way. The things that are worth while are usually accomplished by someone with enthusiasm and drive—and with natural vision. Expensive equipment and training and experiment never does what you'd imagine it might do. The spending of it usually gets into the wrong hands."

"Will you mind giving up your work when you go to Barbadoes?" I asked. "You're still going, I presume?"

"Oh yes, as soon as the police will let us. No, I shan't mind giving up my work at all. Why should I? I wouldn't like to be idle, but I shan't be idle in Barbadoes."

She added impatiently:

"Oh, if only this could all be cleared up quickly and we could get away."

"Clemency," I said, "have you any idea at all who did do this? Granting that you and Roger had no hand in it, (and really I can't see any reason to think you had) surely, with your intelligence, you must have some idea of who did?"

She gave me a rather peculiar look, a darting sideways glance. When she spoke her voice had lost its spontaneity. It was awkward, rather embarrassed.

"One can't make guesses, it's unscientific," she said. "One can only say that Brenda and Laurence are the obvious suspects."

"So you think they did it?"

Clemency shrugged her shoulders.

She stood for a moment as though listening, then she went out of the room, passing Edith de Haviland in the doorway.

Edith came straight over to me.

"I want to talk to you," she said.

My father's words leapt into my mind. Was this—

But Edith de Haviland was going on:

"I hope you didn't get the wrong impression," she said. "About Philip, I mean. Philip is rather difficult to understand. He may seem to you reserved and cold, but that is not so at all. It's just a manner. He can't help it."

"I really hadn't thought—" I began.

But she swept on.

"Just now—about Roger. It isn't really that he's grudging. He's never been mean about money. And he's really a dear— he's always been a dear—but he needs understanding."

I looked at her with the air, I hope, of one who was willing to understand. She went on:

"It's partly, I think, from having been the second of the family. There's often something about a second child—they start handicapped. He adored his father, you see. Of course, all the children adored Aristide and he adored them. But Roger was his especial pride and joy. Being the eldest—the first. And I think Philip felt it. He drew back right into himself. He began to like books and the past and things that were well divorced from everyday life. I think he suffered—children do suffer. . . ."

She paused and went on:

"What I really mean, I suppose, is that he's always been jealous of Roger. I think perhaps he doesn't know it himself. But I think the fact that Roger has come a cropper—oh, it seems an odious thing to say and really I'm sure he doesn't realise it himself—but I think perhaps Philip isn't as sorry about it as he ought to be."

"You mean really that he's rather pleased Roger has made a fool of himself."

"Yes," said Miss de Haviland. "I mean just exactly that."

She added, frowning a little:

"It distressed me, you know, that he didn't at once offer help to his brother."

"Why should he?" I said. "After all, Roger has made a muck of things. He's a grown man. There are no children to consider. If he were ill or in real want, of course his family would help—but I've no doubt Roger would really much prefer to start afresh entirely on his own."

"Oh! he would. It's only Clemency he minds about. And Clemency is an extraordinary creature. She really likes being uncomfortable and having only one utility teacup to drink out of. Modern, I suppose. She's no sense of the past, no sense of beauty."

I felt her shrewd eyes looking me up and down.

"This is a dreadful ordeal for Sophia," she said. "I am so sorry her youth should be dimmed by it. I love them all, you know. Roger and Philip, and now Sophia and Eustace and Josephine. All the dear children. Marcia's children. Yes, I love them dearly." She paused and then added sharply: "But, mind you, this side idolatry."

She turned abruptly and went. I had the feeling that she had meant something by her last remark that I did not quite understand.

CHAPTER 15

"Your room's ready," said Sophia.

She stood by my side looking out at the garden. It looked bleak and grey now with the half denuded trees swaying in the wind.

Sophia echoed my thought as she said:

"How desolate it looks. . . ."

As we watched, a figure, and then presently another came through the yew hedge from the rock garden. They both looked grey and unsubstantial in the fading light.

Brenda Leonides was the first. She was wrapped in a grey chinchilla coat and there was something catlike and stealthy in the way she moved. She slipped through the twilight with a kind of eerie grace.

I saw her face as she passed the window. There was a half smile on it, the curving crooked smile I had noticed upstairs. A few minutes later Laurence Brown, looking slender and shrunken, also slipped through the twilight. I can only put it that way. They did not seem like two people walking, two people who had been out for a stroll. There was something furtive and unsubstantial about them like two ghosts.

I wondered if it was under Brenda's or Laurence's foot that a twig had snapped.

By a natural association of ideas, I asked:

"Where's Josephine?"

"Probably with Eustace up in the schoolroom." She frowned. "I'm worried about Eustace, Charles."

"Why?"

"He's so moody and odd. He's been so different ever since that wretched paralysis. I can't make out what's going on in his mind. Sometimes he seems to hate us all."

"He'll probably grow out of all that. It's just a phase."

"Yes, I suppose so. But I do get worried, Charles."

"Why, dear heart?"

"Really, I suppose, because mother and father never worry. They're not like a mother and father."

"That may be all for the best. More children suffer from interference than from non-interference."

"That's true. You know, I never thought about it until I came back from abroad, but they really are a queer couple. Father living determinedly in a world of obscure historical bypaths and mother having a lovely time creating scenes. That tomfoolery this evening was all mother. There was no need for it. She just wanted to play a family conclave scene. She gets bored, you know, down here and has to try and work up a drama."

For the moment I had a fantastic vision of Sophia's mother poisoning her elderly father-in-law in a light-hearted manner in order to observe a murder drama at first hand with herself in the leading rôle.

An amusing thought! I dismissed it as such—but it left me a little uneasy.

"Mother," said Sophia, "has to be looked after the whole time. You never know what she's up to!"

"Forget your family, Sophia," I said firmly.

"I shall be only too delighted to, but it's a little difficult at the present moment. But I was happy out in Cairo when I had forgotten them all."

I remembered how Sophia had never mentioned her home or her people.

"Is that why you never talked about them?" I asked. "Because you wanted to forget them?"

"I think so. We've always, all of us, lived too much in each other's pockets. We're—we're all too fond of each other. We're not like some families where they all hate each other like poison. That must be pretty bad, but it's almost worse to live all tangled up in conflicting affections."

She added:

"I think that's what I meant when I said we all lived together in a little crooked house. I didn't mean that it was crooked in the dishonest sense. I think what I meant was that we hadn't been able to grow up independent, standing by ourselves, upright. We're all a bit twisted and twining."

I saw Edith de Haviland's heel grinding a weed into the path as Sophia added:

"Like bindweed . . ."

And then suddenly Magda was with us—flinging open the door —crying out:

"Darlings, why don't you have the lights on? It's almost dark."

And she pressed the switches and the lights sprang up on the walls and on the tables, and she and Sophia and I pulled the heavy rose curtains, and there we were in the flower-scented interior, and Magda, flinging herself on the sofa, cried:

"What an incredible scene it was, wasn't it? How cross Eustace was! He told me he thought it was all positively indecent. How funny boys are!"

She sighed.

"Roger's rather a pet. I love him when he rumples his hair and starts knocking things over. Wasn't it sweet of Edith to offer her legacy to him? She really meant it, you know, it wasn't just a gesture. But it was terribly stupid—it might have made Philip think he ought to do it, too! Of course Edith would do anything for the

441

family! There's something very pathetic in the love of a spinster for her sister's children. Someday I shall play one of those devoted spinster aunts. Inquisitive, and obstinate and devoted."

"It must have been hard for her after her sister died," I said, refusing to be sidetracked into discussion of another of Magda's rôles. "I mean if she disliked old Leonides so much."

Magda interrupted me.

"Disliked him? Who told you that? Nonsense. She was in love with him."

"Mother!" said Sophia.

"Now don't try and contradict me, Sophia. Naturally at your age, you think love is all two good looking young people in the moonlight."

"She told me," I said, "that she had always disliked him."

"Probably she did when she first came. She'd been angry with her sister for marrying him. I daresay there was always some antagonism—but she was in love with him all right! Darlings, I do know what I'm talking about! Of course, with deceased wife's sister and all that, he couldn't have married her, and I daresay he never thought of it—and quite probably she didn't either. She was quite happy mothering the children, and having fights with him. But she didn't like it when he married Brenda. She didn't like it a bit!"

"No more did you and father," said Sophia.

"No, of course we hated it! Naturally! But Edith hated it most. Darling, the way I've seen her look at Brenda!"

"Now, mother," said Sophia.

Magda threw her an affectionate and half guilty glance, the glance of a mischievous spoilt child.

She went on, with no apparent realization of any lack of continuity:

"I've decided Josephine really must go to school."

"Josephine? To school?"

"Yes. To Switzerland. I'm going to see about it tomorrow. I really think we might get her off at once. It's so bad for her to be mixed up in a horrid business like this. She's getting quite morbid about it. What she needs is other children of her own age. School life. I've always thought so."

"Grandfather didn't want her to go to school," said Sophia slowly. "He was very much against it."

"Darling old Sweetie Pie liked us all here under his eye. Very old people are often selfish in that way. A child ought to be amongst other children. And Switzerland is so healthy—all the winter sports, and the air, and such much, much better food than we get here!"

"It will be difficult to arrange for Switzerland now with all the currency regulations, won't it?" I asked.

"Nonsense, Charles. There's some kind of educational racket—or you exchange with a Swiss child—there are all sorts of ways. Rudolf Alstir's in Lausanne. I shall wire him tomorrow to arrange everything. We can get her off by the end of the week!"

Magda punched a cushion, smiled at us, went to the door, stood a moment looking back at us in a quite enchanting fashion.

"It's only the young who count," she said. As she said it, it was a lovely line. "They must always come first. And, darlings—think of the flowers—the blue gentians, the narcissus. . . ."

"In November?" asked Sophia, but Magda had gone.

Sophia heaved an exasperated sigh.

"Really," she said, "Mother is too trying! She gets these sudden ideas, and she sends thousands of telegrams and everything has to be arranged at a moment's notice. Why should Josephine be hustled off to Switzerland all in a flurry?"

"There's probably something in the idea of school. I think children of her own age would be a good thing for Josephine."

"Grandfather didn't think so," said Sophia obstinately.

I felt slightly irritated.

"My dear Sophia, do you really think an old gentleman of over eighty is the best judge of a child's welfare?"

"He was about the best judge of anybody in this house," said Sophia.

"Better than your Aunt Edith?"

"No, perhaps not. She did rather favour school. I admit Josephine's got into rather difficult ways—she's got a horrible habit of snooping. But I really think it's just because she's playing detectives."

Was it only the concern for Josephine's welfare which had occasioned Magda's sudden decision? I wondered. Josephine was remarkably well informed about all sorts of things that had happened prior to the murder and which had been certainly no business of hers. A healthy school life with plenty of games would

443

probably do her a world of good. But I did rather wonder at the suddenness and urgency of Magda's decision—Switzerland was a long way off.

CHAPTER 16

THE OLD MAN had said:

"Let them talk to you."

As I shaved the following morning, I considered just how far that had taken me.

Edith de Haviland had talked to me—she had sought me out for that especial purpose. Clemency had talked to me (or had I talked to her?). Magda had talked to me in a sense—that is I had formed part of the audience to one of her broadcasts. Sophia naturally had talked to me. Even Nannie had talked to me. Was I any the wiser for what I had learned from them all? Was there any significant word or phrase? More, was there any evidence of that abnormal vanity on which my father had laid stress? I couldn't see that there was.

The only person who had shown absolutely no desire to talk to me in any way, or on any subject, was Philip. Was not that, in a way, rather abnormal? He must know by now that I wanted to marry his daughter. Yet he continued to act as though I was not in the house at all. Presumably he resented my presence there. Edith de Haviland had apologised for him. She had said it was just "manner." She had shown herself concerned about Philip. Why?

I considered Sophia's father. He was in every sense a repressed individual. He had been an unhappy jealous child. He had been forced back into himself. He had taken refuge in the world of books —in the historical past. That studied coldness and reserve of his might conceal a good deal of passionate feeling. The inadequate motive of financial gain by his father's death was unconvincing—I did not think for a moment that Philip Leonides would kill his father because he himself had not quite as much money as he would like to have. But there might have been some deep psychological reason for his desiring his father's death. Philip had come back to his father's house to live, and later, as a result of the Blitz Roger had come—and Philip had been obliged to see day by day that Roger was his father's favourite. . . . Might things have come to such a pass in his tortured mind that the only relief possible was his father's death? And supposing that that death should incriminate his elder brother? Roger was short of money —on the verge of a crash. Knowing nothing of that last interview between Roger and his father and the latter's offer of assistance, might not Philip have believed that the motive would seem so powerful that Roger would be at once suspected? Was Philip's mental balance sufficiently disturbed to lead him to do murder?

I cut my chin with the razor and swore.

What the hell was I trying to do? Fasten murder on Sophia's father? That was a nice thing to try and do! That wasn't what Sophia had wanted me to come down here for.

Or—was it? There was something, had been something all along, behind Sophia's appeal. If there was any lingering suspicion in her mind that her father was the killer, then she would never consent to marry me—in case that suspicion might be true. And since she was Sophia, clear-eyed and brave, she wanted the truth, since uncertainty would be an eternal and perpetual barrier between us. Hadn't she been in effect saying to me, "Prove that this dreadful thing I am imagining is not true—but if it is true, then prove its truth to me—so that I can know the worst and face it!"

Did Edith de Haviland know, or suspect, that Philip was guilty. What had she meant by "this side idolatry"?

And what had Clemency meant by that peculiar look she had thrown at me when I asked her who she suspected and she had answered: "Laurence and Brenda are the obvious suspects, aren't they?"

The whole family wanted it to be Brenda and Laurence, hoped it might be Brenda and Laurence, but didn't really believe it was Brenda and Laurence. . . .

And of course, the whole family might be wrong, and it might really be Laurence and Brenda after all.

Or, it might be Laurence, and not Brenda. . . .

That would be a much better solution.

I finished dabbing at my cut chin and went down to breakfast filled with the determination to have an interview with Laurence Brown as soon as possible.

It was only as I drank my second cup of coffee that it occurred to me that the Crooked House was having its effect on me also. I, too, wanted to find, not the true solution, but the solution that suited me best.

After breakfast I went out through the hall and up the stairs. Sophia had told me that I should find Laurence giving instruction to Eustace and Josephine in the schoolroom.

I hesitated on the landing outside Brenda's front door. Did I ring and knock, or did I walk right in? I decided to treat the house as an integral Leonides home and not as Brenda's private residence.

I opened the door and passed inside. Everything was quiet, there seemed to be no one about. On my left the door into the big drawing room was closed. On my right two open doors showed a bedroom and adjoining bathroom. This I knew was the bathroom adjoining Aristide Leonides's bedroom where the eserine and the insulin had been kept. The police had finished with it now. I pushed the door open and slipped inside. I realised then how easy it would have been for anyone in the house (or from outside the house for the matter of that!) to come up here and into the bathroom unseen.

I stood in the bathroom looking round. It was sumptuously appointed with gleaming tiles and a sunk bath. At one side were various electric appliances; a hot plate and grill under, an electric kettle—a small electric saucepan, a toaster—everything that a valet attendant to an old gentleman might need. On the wall was a white enamelled cupboard. I opened it. Inside were medical appliances, two medicine glasses, eyebath, eye dropper and a few labelled bottles. Aspirin, Boracic powder, iodine. Elastoplast bandages, etc. On a separate shelf were the stacked supply of insulin, two hypodermic needles, and a bottle of surgical spirit. On a third shelf was a bottle marked The Tablets—one or two to be taken at night as ordered. On this shelf, no doubt, had stood the bottle of eyedrops. It was all clear, well arranged, easy for anyone to get at if needed, and equally easy to get at for murder.

I could do what I liked with the bottles and then go softly out

446

and downstairs again and nobody would ever know I had been there. All this was, of course, nothing new, but it brought home to me how difficult the task of the police was.

Only from the guilty party or parties could one find out what one needed.

"Rattle 'em," Taverner had said to me. "Get 'em on the run. Make 'em think we're on to something. Keep ourselves well in the limelight. Sooner or later, if we do, our criminal will stop leaving well alone and try to be smarter still—and then—we've got him."

Well, the criminal hadn't reacted to this treatment so far.

I came out of the bathroom. Still no one about. I went on along the corridor. I passed the dining room on the left, and Brenda's bedroom and bathroom on the right. In the latter, one of the maids was moving about. The dining room door was closed. From a room beyond that, I heard Edith de Haviland's voice telephoning to the inevitable fishmonger. A spiral flight of stairs led to the floor above. I went up them. Edith's bedroom and sitting room were here, I knew, and two more bathrooms and Laurence Brown's room. Beyond that again the short flight of steps down to the big room built out over the servant's quarters at the back which was used as a schoolroom.

Outside the door I paused. Laurence Brown's voice could be heard, slightly raised, from inside.

I think Josephine's habit of snooping must have been catching. Quite unashamedly I leaned against the door jamb and listened.

It was a history lesson that was in progress, and the period in question was the French *directoire*.

As I listened astonishment opened my eyes. It was a considerable surprise to me to discover that Laurence Brown was a magnificent teacher.

I don't know why it should have surprised me so much. After all, Aristide Leonides had always been a good picker of men. For all his mouselike exterior, Laurence had that supreme gift of being able to arouse enthusiasm and imagination in his pupils. The drama of Thermidor, the decree of Outlawry against the Robespierrists, the magnificence of Barras, the cunning of Fouché—Napoleon, the half starved young gunner lieutenant—all these were real and living.

Suddenly Laurence stopped, he asked Eustace and Josephine a question, he made them put themselves in the places of first one and then another figure in the drama. Though he did not get much result from Josephine whose voice sounded as though she had a cold in the head, Eustace sounded quite different from his usual moody self. He showed brains and intelligence and the keen historical sense which he had doubtless inherited from his father.

Then I heard the chairs being pushed back and scraped across the floor. I retreated up the steps and was apparently just coming down them when the door opened.

Eustace and Josephine came out.

"Hullo," I said.

Eustace looked surprised to see me.

"Do you want anything?" he asked politely.

Josephine, taking no interest in my presence, slipped past me.

"I just wanted to see the schoolroom," I said rather feebly.

"You saw it the other day, didn't you? It's just a kid's place really. Used to be the nursery. It's still got a lot of toys in it."

He held the door open for me and I went in.

Laurence Brown stood by the table. He looked up, flushed, murmured something in answer to my good morning and went hurriedly out.

"You've scared him," said Eustace. "He's very easily scared."

"Do you like him, Eustace?"

"Oh! he's all right. An awful ass, of course."

"But not a bad teacher?"

"No, as a matter of fact he's quite interesting. He knows an awful lot. He makes you see things from a different angle. I never knew that Henry the Eighth wrote poetry—to Anne Boleyn, of course—jolly decent poetry."

We talked for a few moments on such subjects as The Ancient Mariner, Chaucer, the political implications behind the Crusades, the Mediaeval approach to life, and the, to Eustace, surprising fact that Oliver Cromwell had prohibited the celebration of Christmas Day. Behind Eustace's scornful and rather ill-tempered manner there was, I perceived, an inquiring and able mind.

Very soon I began to realise the source of his ill humour. His illness had not only been a frightening ordeal, it had also been a frustration and a setback, just at a moment when he had been enjoying life.

"I was to have been in the eleven next term—and I'd got my house colours. It's pretty thick to have to stop at home and do lessons with a rotten kid like Josephine. Why, she's only twelve."

"Yes, but you don't have the same studies, do you?"

"No, of course she doesn't do advanced maths—or Latin. But you don't want to have to share a tutor with a girl."

I tried to soothe his injured male pride by remarking that Josephine was quite an intelligent girl for her age.

"D'you think so? I think she's awfully wet. She's mad keen on this detecting stuff—goes round poking her nose in everywhere and writing things down in a little black book and pretending that she's finding out a lot. Just a silly kid, that's all she is," said Eustace loftily.

"Anyway," he added, "girls can't be detectives. I told her so. I think mother's quite right and the sooner Jo's packed off to Switzerland the better."

"Wouldn't you miss her?"

"Miss a kid of that age?" said Eustace haughtily. "Of course not. My goodness, this house is the absolute limit! Mother always haring up and down to London and bullying tame dramatists to rewrite plays for her, and making frightful fusses about nothing at all. And father shut up with his books and sometimes not hearing you if you speak to him. I don't see why I should have to be burdened with such peculiar parents. Then there's Uncle Roger—always so hearty that it makes you shudder. Aunt Clemency's all right, she doesn't bother you, but I sometimes think she's a bit batty. Aunt Edith's not too bad, but she's old. Things have been a bit more cheerful since Sophia came back—though she can be pretty sharp sometimes. But it is a queer household, don't you think so? Having a stepgrandmother young enough to be your aunt or your older sister. I mean, it makes you feel an awful ass!"

I had some comprehension of his feelings. I remembered (very dimly) my own supersensitiveness at Eustace's age. My horror of appearing in any way unusual or of my near relatives departing from the normal.

"What about your grandfather?" I said. "Were you fond of him?"

A curious expression flitted across Eustace's face.

"Grandfather," he said, "was definitely antisocial!"

"In what way?"

"He thought of nothing but the profit motive. Laurence says that's completely wrong. And he was a great individualist. All that sort of thing has got to go, don't you think so?"

"Well," I said, rather brutally, "he has gone."

"A good thing, really," said Eustace. "I don't want to be callous, but you can't really enjoy life at that age!"

"Didn't he?"

"He couldn't have. Anyway, it was time he went. He—" Eustace broke off as Laurence Brown came back into the schoolroom.

Laurence began fussing about with some books, but I thought that he was watching me out of the corner of his eye.

He looked at his wrist-watch and said:

"Please be back here sharp at eleven, Eustace. We've wasted too much time the last few days."

"O.K., sir."

Eustace lounged towards the door and went out whistling.

Laurence Brown darted another sharp glance at me. He moistened his lips once or twice. I was convinced that he had come back into the schoolroom solely in order to talk to me.

Presently, after a little aimless stacking and unstacking of books and a pretence of looking for a book that was missing, he spoke:

"Er— How are they getting on?" he said.

"They?"

"The police."

His nose twitched. A mouse in a trap, I thought, a mouse in a trap.

"They don't take me into their confidence," I said.

"Oh. I thought your father was the Assistant Commissioner."

"He is," I said. "But naturally he would not betray official secrets."

I made my voice purposely pompous.

"Then you don't know how—what—if . . ." His voice trailed off. "They're not going to make an arrest, are they?"

"Not so far as I know. But then, as I say, I mightn't know."

Get 'em on the run, Inspector Taverner had said. Get 'em rattled. Well, Laurence Brown was rattled all right.

He began talking quickly and nervously.

"You don't know what it's like. . . . The strain. . . . Not knowing what— I mean, they just come and go— Asking questions. . . . Questions that don't seem to have anything to do with the case. . . ."

He broke off. I waited. He wanted to talk—well, then, let him talk.

"You were there when the Chief Inspector made that monstrous suggestion the other day? About Mrs. Leonides and myself. . . . It was monstrous. It makes one feel so helpless. One is powerless to prevent people thinking things! And it is all so wickedly untrue. Just because she is—was—so many years younger than her husband. People have dreadful minds—dreadful minds. . . . I feel —I can't help feeling, that it is all a plot."

"A plot? That's interesting."

It was interesting, though not quite in the way he took it.

"The family, you know; Mr. Leonides's family, have never been sympathetic to me. They were always aloof. I always felt that they despised me."

His hands began to shake.

"Just because they have always been rich—and powerful. They looked down on me. What was I to them? Only the tutor. Only a wretched conscientious objector. And my objections were conscientious. They were indeed!"

I said nothing.

"All right then," he burst out. "What if I was—afraid? Afraid I'd make a mess of it. Afraid that when I had to pull a trigger— I mightn't be able to bring myself to do it. How can you be sure it's a Nazi you're going to kill? It might be some decent lad—some village boy—with no political leanings, just called up for his country's service. I believe war is wrong, do you understand? I believe it is wrong."

I was still silent. I believed that my silence was achieving more than any arguments or agreements could do. Laurence Brown was arguing with himself, and in so doing was revealing a good deal of himself.

"Everyone's always laughed at me." His voice shook. "I seem to have a knack of making myself ridiculous. It isn't that I really lack courage—but I always do the thing wrong. I went into a burning house to rescue a woman they said was trapped there. But I lost the way at once, and the smoke made me unconscious, and it gave a lot of trouble to the firemen finding me. I heard them say, 'Why couldn't the silly chump leave it to us?' It's no good my trying, everyone's against me. Whoever killed Mr. Leonides arranged it so that I would be suspected. Someone killed him so as to ruin me."

"What about Mrs. Leonides?" I asked.

He flushed. He became less of a mouse and more like a man.

"Mrs. Leonides is an angel," he said, "an angel. Her sweetness, her kindness to her elderly husband were wonderful. To think of her in connection with poison is laughable—laughable! And that thick-headed Inspector can't see it!"

"He's prejudiced," I said, "by the number of cases on his files where elderly husbands have been poisoned by sweet young wives."

"The insufferable dolt," said Laurence Brown angrily.

He went over to a bookcase in the corner and began rummaging the books in it. I didn't think I should get anything more out of him. I went slowly out of the room.

As I was going along the passage, a door on my left opened and Josephine almost fell on top of me. Her appearance had the suddenness of a demon in an old-fashioned pantomine.

Her face and hands were filthy and a large cobweb floated from one ear.

"Where have you been, Josephine?"

I peered through the half open door. A couple of steps led up into the attic-like rectangular space in the gloom of which several large tanks could be seen.

"In the cistern room."

"Why in the cistern room?"

Josephine replied in a brief businesslike way:

"Detecting."

"What on earth is there to detect among the cisterns?"

To this, Josephine merely replied:

"I must wash."

"I should say most decidedly."

Josephine disappeared through the nearest bathroom door. She looked back to say:

"I should say it's about time for the next murder, wouldn't you?"

"What do you mean—the next murder?"

"Well, in books there's always a second murder about now. Someone who knows something is bumped off before they can tell what they know."

"You read too many detective stories, Josephine. Real life isn't like that. And if anybody in this house knows something the last thing they seem to want to do is to talk about it."

Josephine's reply came to me rather obscured by the gushing of water from a tap.

"Sometimes it's something that they don't know that they do know."

I blinked as I tried to think this out. Then, leaving Josephine to her ablutions, I went down to the floor below.

Just as I was going out through the front door to the staircase, Brenda came with a soft rush through the drawing room door.

She came close to me and laid her hand on my arm, looking up in my face.

"Well?" she asked.

It was the same demand for information that Laurence had made, only it was phrased differently. And her one word far more effective.

I shook my head.

"Nothing," I said.

She gave a long sigh.

"I'm so frightened," she said. "Charles, I'm so frightened. . . ."

Her fear was very real. It communicated itself to me there in that narrow space. I wanted to reassure her, to help her. I had once more that poignant sense of her as terribly alone in hostile surroundings.

She might well have cried out: "Who is on my side?"

And what would the answer have been? Laurence Brown? And what, after all, was Laurence Brown? No tower of strength in a time of trouble. One of the weaker vessels. I remembered the two of them drifting in from the garden the night before.

I wanted to help her. I badly wanted to help her. But there was nothing much I could say or do. And I had at the bottom of my mind an embarrassed guilty feeling, as though Sophia's scornful eyes were watching me. I remembered Sophia's voice saying: "So she got you."

And Sophia did not see, did not want to see, Brenda's side of it. Alone, suspected of murder, with no one to stand by her.

"The inquest's tomorrow," Brenda said. "What—what will happen?"

There I could reassure her.

"Nothing," I said. "You needn't worry about that. It will be adjourned for the police to make enquiries. It will probably set the Press loose, though. So far, there's been no indication in the papers that it wasn't a natural death. The Leonides have got a good deal of influence. But with an adjourned inquest—well, the fun will start."

(What extraordinary things one said! The fun! Why must I choose that particular word?)

"Will—will they be very dreadful?"

"I shouldn't give any interviews if I were you. You know, Brenda, you ought to have a lawyer—" She recoiled with a terrific gasp of dismay. "No—no—not the way you mean. But someone to look after your interests and advise you as to procedure, and what to say and do, and what not to say and do.

"You see," I added, "you're very much alone."

Her hand pressed my arm more closely.

"Yes," she said. "You do understand that. You've helped, Charles, you have helped. . . ."

I went down the stairs with a feeling of warmth, of satisfaction. . . . Then I saw Sophia standing by the front door. Her voice was cold and rather dry.

"What a long time you've been," she said. "They rang up for you from London. Your father wants you."

"At the Yard?"

"Yes."

"I wonder what they want me for. They didn't say?"

Sophia shook her head. Her eyes were anxious. I drew her to me.

"Don't worry, darling," I said, "I'll soon be back."

CHAPTER 17

THERE WAS something strained in the atmosphere of my father's room. The Old Man sat behind his table, Chief Inspector Taverner leaned against the window frame. In the visitor's chair, sat Mr. Gaitskill, looking ruffled.

"—extraordinary want of confidence," he was saying acidly.

"Of course, of course." My father spoke soothingly. "Ah hullo, Charles, you've made good time. Rather a surprising development has occurred."

"Unprecedented," Mr. Gaitskill said.

Something had clearly ruffled the little lawyer to the core. Behind him, Chief Inspector Taverner grinned at me.

"If I may recapitulate?" my father said. "Mr. Gaitskill received a somewhat surprising communication this morning, Charles. It was from a Mr. Agrodopolous, proprietor of the Delphos Restaurant. He is a very old man, a Greek by birth, and when he was a young man he was helped and befriended by Aristide Leonides. He has always remained deeply grateful to his friend and benefactor and it seems that Leonides placed great reliance and trust in him."

"I would never have believed Leonides was of such a suspicious and secretive nature," said Mr. Gaitskill. "Of course, he was of advanced years—practically in his dotage, one might say."

"Nationality tells," said my father gently. "You see, Gaitskill, when you are very old your mind dwells a good deal on the days of your youth and the friends of your youth."

"But Leonides's affairs had been in my hands for well over forty years," said Mr. Gaitskill. "Forty-three years and six months to be precise."

Taverner grinned again.

"What happened?" I asked.

Mr. Gaitskill opened his mouth, but my father forestalled him.

"Mr. Agrodopolous stated in his communication that he was obeying certain instructions given him by his friend Aristide Leonides. Briefly, about a year ago he had been entrusted by Mr. Leonides with a sealed envelope which Mr. Agrodopolous was to forward to Mr. Gaitskill immediately after Mr. Leonides's death. In the event of Mr. Agrodopolous dying first, his son, a godson of Mr. Leonides, was to carry out the same instructions. Mr. Agrodopolous apologises for the delay, but explains that he has been ill with pneumonia and only learned of his old friend's death yesterday afternoon."

"The whole business is most unprofessional," said Mr. Gaitskill.

"When Mr. Gaitskill had opened the sealed envelope and made himself acquainted with its contents, he decided that it was his duty—"

"Under the circumstances," said Mr. Gaitskill.

"To let us see the enclosures. They consist of a will, duly signed and attested, and a covering letter."

"So the will has turned up at last?" I said.

Mr. Gaitskill turned a bright purple.

"It is not the same will," he barked. "This is not the document I drew up at Mr. Leonides's request. This has been written out in his own hand, a most dangerous thing for any layman to do. It seems to have been Mr. Leonides's intention to make me look a complete fool."

Chief Inspector Taverner endeavoured to inject a little balm into the prevailing bitterness.

"He was a very old gentleman, Mr. Gaitskill," he said. "They're inclined to be cranky when they get old, you know—not balmy, of course, but just a little eccentric."

Mr. Gaitskill sniffed.

"Mr. Gaitskill rang us up," my father said, "and apprised us of the main contents of the will and I asked him to come round and bring the two documents with him. I also rang you up, Charles."

I did not see why I had been rung up. It seemed to me singularly unorthodox procedure on both my father's and Taverner's part. I should have learnt about the will in due course, and it was really not my business at all how old Leonides had left his money.

"Is it a different will?" I asked. "I mean, does it dispose of his estate in a different way?"

"It does indeed," said Mr. Gaitskill.

My father was looking at me. Chief Inspector Taverner was very carefully not looking at me. In some way, I felt vaguely uneasy. . . .

Something was going on in both their minds—and it was a something to which I had no clue.

I looked enquiringly at Gaitskill.

"It's none of my business," I said. "But—"

He responded.

"Mr. Leonides's testamentary dispositions are not, of course, a secret," he said. "I conceived it to be my duty to lay the facts before the police authorities first, and to be guided by them in my subsequent procedure. I understand," he paused, "that there is an —understanding, shall we say—between you and Miss Sophia Leonides?"

"I hope to marry her," I said, "but she will not consent to an engagement at the present time."

"Very proper," said Mr. Gaitskill.

I disagreed with him. But this was no time for argument.

"By this will," said Mr. Gaitskill, "dated November the 29th of last year Mr. Leonides, after a bequest to his wife of one hundred and fifty thousand pounds, leaves his entire estate, real and personal, to his granddaughter, Sophia Katherine Leonides absolutely."

I gasped. Whatever I had expected, it was not this.

"He left the whole caboodle to Sophia," I said. "What an extraordinary thing. Any reason?"

"He set out his reasons very clearly in the covering letter," said my father. He picked up a sheet of paper from the desk in front of him. "You have no objection to Charles reading this, Mr. Gaitskill?"

"I am in your hands," said Mr. Gaitskill coldly. "The letter does at least offer an explanation—and possibly (though I am doubtful as to this), an excuse for Mr. Leonides's extraordinary conduct."

The Old Man handed me the letter. It was written in a small crabbed handwriting in very black ink. The handwriting showed character and individuality. It was not at all like the handwriting of an old man—except perhaps for the careful forming of the letters, more characteristic of a bygone period, when literacy was something painstakingly acquired and correspondingly valued.

"Dear Gaitskill (it ran)

You will be astonished to get this, and probably offended. But I have my own reasons for behaving in what may seem to you an unnecessarily secretive manner. I have long been a believer in the individual. In a family (this I have observed in my boyhood and never forgotten) there is always one strong character and it usually falls to this one person to care for, and bear the burden, of the rest of the family. In my family I was that person. I came to London, established myself there, supported my mother and my aged grandparents in Smyrna, extricated one of my brothers from the grip of the law, secured the freedom of my sister from an unhappy marriage and so on. God has been pleased to grant me a long life, and I have been able to watch over and care for my children and their children. Many have been taken from me by death; the rest, I am happy to say, are under my roof. When I die, the burden I have carried must descend on someone else. I have debated whether to divide my fortune as equally as possible amongst my dear ones—but to do so would not eventually result in a proper equality. Men are not born equal—to offset the natural inequality of Nature one must redress the balance. In other words, someone must be my successor, must take upon him or herself the burden of responsibility for the rest of the family. After close observation I do not consider either of my sons fit for this responsibility. My dearly loved son Roger has no business sense, and though of a lovable nature is too impulsive to have good judgement. My son Philip is too unsure of himself to do anything but retreat from life. Eustace, my grandson, is very young and I do not think he has the qualities of sense and judgement necessary. He is indolent and very easily influenced by the ideas of anyone whom he meets. Only my granddaughter Sophia seems to me to have the positive qualities required. She has brains, judgement, courage, a fair and unbiased mind and, I think, generosity of spirit. To her I commit the family welfare—and the welfare of my kind sister-in-law Edith de Haviland for whose lifelong devotion to the family I am deeply grateful.

This explains the enclosed document. What will be harder to explain—or rather to explain to you, my old friend—is the deception that I have employed. I thought it wise not to raise speculation about the disposal of my money, and I have no intention of letting my family know that Sophia is to be my heir. Since my two sons have already had considerable fortunes settled upon them, I do not feel that my testamentary dispositions will place them in a humiliating position.

To stifle curiosity and surmise, I asked you to draw me up a will. This will I read aloud to my assembled family. I laid it on my desk, placed a sheet of blotting paper over it and asked for two servants to be summoned. When they came I slid the blotting paper up a little, exposing the bottom of a document, signed my name and caused them to sign theirs. I need hardly say that what I and they signed was the will which I now enclose and not the one drafted by you which I had read aloud.

I cannot hope that you will understand what prompted me to execute this trick. I will merely ask you to forgive me for keeping you in the dark. A very old man likes to keep his little secrets.

Thank you, my dear friend, for the assiduity with which you have always attended to my affairs. Give Sophia my dear love. Ask her to watch over the family well and shield them from harm.

Yours very sincerely,
Aristide Leonides."

I read this very remarkable document with intense interest. "Extraordinary," I said.

"Most extraordinary," said Mr. Gaitskill, rising. "I repeat, I think my old friend Mr. Leonides might have trusted me."

"No, Gaitskill," said my father. "He was a natural twister. He liked, if I may put it so, doing things the crooked way."

"That's right, sir," said Chief Inspector Taverner. "He was a twister if there ever was one!"

He spoke with feeling.

Gaitskill stalked out unmollified. He had been wounded to the depths of his professional nature.

"It's hit him hard," said Taverner. "Very respectable firm, Gaitskill, Callum & Gaitskill. No hanky panky with them. When old Leonides put through a doubtful deal, he never put it through with Gaitskill, Callum & Gaitskill. He had half a dozen different firms of solicitors who acted for him. Oh, he was a twister!"

"And never more so than when making his will," said my father.

"We were fools," said Taverner. "When you come to think of it, the only person who could have played tricks with that will was the old boy himself. It just never occurred to us that he could want to!"

I remembered Josephine's superior smile as she had said:

"Aren't the police stupid?"

But Josephine had not been present on the occasion of the will. And even if she had been listening outside the door (which I was fully prepared to believe!) she could hardly have guessed what her grandfather was doing. Why, then, the superior air? What did she know that made her say the police were stupid? Or was it, again, just showing off?

Struck by the silence in the room I looked up sharply—both my father and Taverner were watching me. I don't know what there was in their manner that compelled me to blurt out defiantly:

"Sophia knew nothing about this! Nothing at all."

"No?" said my father.

I didn't quite know whether it was an agreement or a question.

"She'll be absolutely astounded!"

"Yes?"

"Astounded!"

459

There was a pause. Then, with what seemed sudden harshness the telephone on my father's desk rang.

"Yes?" He lifted the receiver—listened and then said, "Put her through."

He looked at me.

"It's your young woman," he said. "She wants to speak to us. It's urgent."

I took the receiver from him.

"Sophia?"

"Charles? Is that you? It's—Josephine!" Her voice broke slightly.

"What about Josephine?"

"She's been hit on the head. Concussion. She's—she's pretty bad. . . . They say she may not recover. . . ."

I turned to the other two.

"Josephine's been knocked out," I said.

My father took the receiver from me. He said sharply as he did so:

"I told you to keep an eye on that child. . . ."

CHAPTER 18

In NEXT to no time Taverner and I were racing in a fast police car in the direction of Swinly Dean.

I remembered Josephine emerging, from among the cisterns, and her airy remark that it was "about time for the second murder." The poor child had had no idea that she herself was likely to be the victim of the "second murder."

I accepted fully the blame that my father had tacitly ascribed to me. Of course I ought to have kept an eye on Josephine. Though neither Taverner nor I had any real clue to the poisoner of old Leonides, it was highly possible that Josephine had. What I had taken for childish nonsense and "showing off" might very well have been something quite different. Josephine, in her fa-

vourite sports of snooping and prying, might have become aware
of some piece of information that she herself could not assess at
its proper value.

I remembered the twig that had cracked in the garden.

I had had an inkling then that danger was about. I had acted
upon it at the moment, and afterwards it had seemed to me that
my suspicions had been melodramatic and unreal. On the contrary. I should have realised that this was murder, that whoever
committed murder had endangered their neck, and that conse-
quently that same person would not hesitate to repeat the crime
if by that way safety could be assured.

Perhaps Magda, by some obscure maternal instinct, had recognised that Josephine was in peril, and that may have been what
occasioned her sudden feverish haste to get the child sent to
Switzerland.

Sophia came out to meet us as we arrived. Josephine, she said,
had been taken by ambulance to Market Basing General Hospital.
Dr. Gray would let them know as soon as possible the result of
the X-ray.

"How did it happen?" asked Taverner.

Sophia led the way round to the back of the house and through
a door into a small disused yard. In one corner a door stood ajar.

"It's a kind of wash house," Sophia explained. "There's a cat
hole cut in the bottom of the door, and Josephine used to stand
on it and swing to and fro."

I remembered swinging on doors in my own youth.

The wash house was small and rather dark. There were wooden
boxes in it, some old hose pipe, a few derelict garden implements
and some broken furniture. Just inside the door was a marble
lion door stop.

"It's the door stop from the front door," Sophia explained. "It
must have been balanced on the top of the door."

Taverner reached up a hand to the top of the door. It was a low
door, the top of it only about a foot above his head.

"A booby trap," he said.

He swung the door experimentally to and fro. Then he stooped
to the block of marble but he did not touch it.

"Has anyone handled this?"

"No," said Sophia. "I wouldn't let any one touch it."

"Quite right. Who found her?"

"I did. She didn't come in for her dinner at one o'clock. Nannie was calling her. She'd passed through the kitchen and out into the stable yard about a quarter of an hour before. Nannie said, 'She'll be bouncing her ball or swinging on that door again.' I said I'd fetch her in."

Sophia paused.

"She had a habit of playing in that way, you said? Who knew about that?"

Sophia shrugged her shoulders.

"Pretty well everybody in the house, I should think."

"Who else used the wash house? Gardeners?"

Sophia shook her head.

"Hardly anyone ever goes into it."

"And this little yard isn't overlooked from the house?" Taverner summed it up. "Anyone could have slipped out from the house or round the front and fixed up that trap ready. But it would be chancy . . ."

He broke off, looking at the door, and swinging it gently to and fro.

"Nothing certain about it. Hit or miss. And likelier miss than hit. But she was unlucky. With her it was hit."

Sophia shivered.

He peered at the floor. There were various dents on it.

"Looks as though someone experimented first . . . to see just how it would fall. . . . The sound wouldn't carry to the house."

"No, we didn't hear anything. We'd no idea anything was wrong until I came out and found her lying face down—all sprawled out." Sophia's voice broke a little. "There was blood on her hair."

"That her scarf?" Taverner pointed to a checked woollen muffler lying on the floor.

"Yes."

Using the scarf he picked up the block of marble carefully.

"There may be fingerprints," he said, but he spoke without much hope. "But I rather think whoever did it was—careful." He said to me: "What are you looking at?"

I was looking at a broken backed wooden kitchen chair which was among the derelicts. On the seat of it were a few fragments of earth.

"Curious," said Taverner. "Someone stood on that chair with muddy feet. Now why was that?"

He shook his head.

"What time was it when you found her, Miss Leonides?"

"It must have been five minutes past one."

"And your Nannie saw her going out about twenty minutes earlier. Who was the last person before that known to have been in the wash house?"

"I've no idea. Probably Josephine herself. Josephine was swinging on the door this morning after breakfast, I know."

Taverner nodded.

"So between then and a quarter to one someone set the trap. You say that bit of marble is the door stop you use for the front door? Any idea when that was missing?"

Sophia shook her head.

"The door hasn't been propped open at all to-day. It's been too cold."

"Any idea where everyone was all the morning?"

"I went out for a walk. Eustace and Josephine did lessons until half past twelve—with a break at half past ten. Father, I think, has been in the library all the morning."

"Your mother?"

"She was just coming out of her bedroom when I came in from my walk—that was about a quarter past twelve. She doesn't get up very early."

We re-entered the house. I followed Sophia to the library. Philip, looking white and haggard, sat in his usual chair. Magda crouched against his knees, crying quietly. Sophia asked:

"Have they telephoned yet from the hospital?"

Philip shook his head.

Magda sobbed:

"Why wouldn't they let me go with her? My baby—my funny ugly baby. And I used to call her a changeling and make her so angry. How could I be so cruel? And now she'll die. I know she'll die."

"Hush, my dear," said Philip. "Hush."

I felt that I had no place in this family scene of anxiety and grief. I withdrew quietly and went to find Nannie. She was sitting in the kitchen crying quietly.

"It's a judgement on me, Mr. Charles, for the hard things I've been thinking. A judgement, that's what it is."

I did not try and fathom her meaning.

463

"There's wickedness in this house. That's what there is. I didn't wish to see it or believe it. But seeing's believing. Somebody killed the master and the same somebody must have tried to kill Josephine."

"Why should they try and kill Josephine?"

Nannie removed a corner of her handkerchief from her eye and gave me a shrewd glance.

"You know well enough what she was like, Mr. Charles. She liked to know things. She was always like that, even as a tiny thing. Used to hide under the dinner table and listen to the maids talking and then she'd hold it over them. Made her feel important. You see, she was passed over, as it were, by the mistress. She wasn't a handsome child, like the other two. She was always a plain little thing. A changeling, the mistress used to call her. I blame the mistress for that, for it's my belief it turned the child sour. But in a funny sort of way she got her own back by finding out things about people and letting them know she knew them. But it isn't safe to do that when there's a poisoner about!"

No, it hadn't been safe. And that brought something else to my mind. I asked Nannie: "Do you know where she kept a little black book—a notebook of some kind where she used to write down things?"

"I know what you mean, Mr. Charles. Very sly about it, she was. I've seen her sucking her pencil and writing in the book and sucking her pencil again. And 'don't do that,' I'd say, 'you'll get lead poisoning' and 'oh no, I shan't,' she said, 'because it isn't really lead in a pencil. It's carbon,' though I don't see how that could be so, for if you call a thing a lead pencil it stands to reason that that's because there's lead in it."

"You'd think so," I agreed. "But as a matter of fact she was right." (Josephine was always right!) "What about this notebook? Do you know where she kept it?"

"I've no idea at all, sir. It was one of the things she was sly about."

"She hadn't got it with her when she was found?"

"Oh no, Mr. Charles, there was no notebook."

Had someone taken the notebook? Or had she hidden it in her own room? The idea came to me to look and see. I was not sure which Josephine's room was, but as I stood hesitating in the passage Taverner's voice called me:

464

"Come in here," he said. "I'm in the kid's room. Did you ever see such a sight?"

I stepped over the threshold and stopped dead.

The small room looked as though it had been visited by a tornado. The drawers of the chest of drawers were pulled out and their contents scattered on the floor. The mattress and bedding had been pulled from the small bed. The rugs were tossed into heaps. The chairs had been turned upside down, the pictures taken down from the wall, the photographs wrenched out of their frames.

"Good Lord," I exclaimed. "What was the big idea?"

"What do you think?"

"Someone was looking for something."

"Exactly."

I looked round and whistled.

"But who on earth— Surely nobody could come in here and do all this and not be heard—or seen?"

"Why not? Mrs. Leonides spends the morning in her bedroom doing her nails and ringing up her friends on the telephone and playing with her clothes. Philip sits in the library browsing over books. The nurse woman is in the kitchen peeling potatoes and stringing beans. In a family that knows each other's habits it would be easy enough. And I'll tell you this. Anyone in the house could have done our little job—could have set the trap for the child and wrecked her room. But it was someone in a hurry, someone who hadn't the time to search quietly."

"Anyone in the house, you say?"

"Yes, I've checked up. Everyone has some time or other unaccounted for. Philip, Magda, the nurse, your girl. The same upstairs. Brenda spent most of the morning alone. Laurence and Eustace had a half hour break—from ten thirty to eleven—you were with them part of that time—but not all of it. Miss de Haviland was in the garden alone. Roger was in his study."

"Only Clemency was in London at her job."

"No, even she isn't out of it. She stayed at home today with a headache—she was alone in her room having that headache. Any of them—any blinking one of them! And I don't know which! I've no idea. If I knew what they were looking for in here—"

His eyes went round the wrecked room.

"And if I knew whether they'd found it. . . ."

Something stirred in my brain—a memory . . .

Taverner clinched it by asking me:

"What was the kid doing when you last saw her?"

"Wait," I said.

I dashed out of the room and up the stairs. I passed through the left hand door and went up to the top floor. I pushed open the door of the cistern room, mounted the two steps and bending my head, since the ceiling was low and sloping, I looked round me.

Josephine had said when I asked her what she was doing there that she was "detecting."

I didn't see what there could be to detect in a cobwebby attic full of water tanks. But such an attic would make a good hiding place. I considered it probable that Josephine had been hiding something there, something that she knew quite well she had no business to have. If so, it oughtn't to take long to find it.

It took me just three minutes. Tucked away behind the largest tank, from the interior of which a sibilant hissing added an eerie note to the atmosphere, I found a packet of letters wrapped in a torn piece of brown paper.

I read the first letter.

Oh Laurence—my darling, my own dear love . . . It was wonderful last night when you quoted that verse of poetry. I knew it was meant for me, though you didn't look at me. Aristide said, "You read verse well." He didn't guess what we were both feeling. My darling, I feel convinced that soon everything will come right. We shall be glad that he never knew, that he died happy. He's been good to me. I don't want him to suffer. But I don't really think that it can be any pleasure to live after you're eighty. I shouldn't want to! Soon we shall be together for always. How wonderful it will be when I can say to you: My dear dear husband. . . . Dearest, we were made for each other. I love you, love you, love you—I can see no end to our love, I—

There was a good deal more, but I had no wish to go on.

Grimly I went downstairs and thrust my parcel into Taverner's hands.

"It's possible," I said, "that that's what our unknown friend was looking for."

Taverner read a few passages, whistled and shuffled through the various letters.

Then he looked at me with the expression of a cat who has been fed with the best cream.

"Well," he said softly. "This pretty well cooks Mrs. Brenda Leonides's goose. And Mr. Laurence Brown's. So it was them, all the time. . . ."

CHAPTER 19

IT SEEMS odd to me, looking back, how suddenly and completely my pity and sympathy for Brenda Leonides vanished with the discovery of her letters, the letters she had written to Laurence Brown. Was my vanity unable to stand up to the revelation that she loved Laurence Brown with a doting and sugarly infatuation and had deliberately lied to me? I don't know. I'm not a psychologist. I prefer to believe that it was the thought of the child Josephine, struck down in ruthless self preservation that dried up the springs of my sympathy.

"Brown fixed that booby trap, if you ask me," said Taverner, "and it explains what puzzled me about it."

"What did puzzle you?"

"Well, it was such a sappy thing to do. Look here, say the kid's got hold of these letters—letters that are absolutely damning! The first thing to do is to try and get them back—(after all, if the kid talks about them, but has got nothing to show, it can be put down as mere romancing) but you can't get them back because you can't find them. Then the only thing to do is to put the kid out of action for good. You've done one murder and you're not squeamish about doing another. You know she's fond of swinging on a door in a disused yard. The ideal thing to do is wait behind the door and lay her out as she comes through with a poker, or an iron bar, or a nice bit of hose-pipe. They're all there ready to hand. Why fiddle about with a marble lion perched on top of a door which is as likely as not to miss her altogether and which

467

even if it does fall on her may not do the job properly (which actually is how it turns out)? I ask you—why?"

"Well," I said, "what's the answer?"

"The only idea I got to begin with was that it was intended to tie in with someone's alibi. Somebody would have a nice fat alibi for the time when Josephine was being slugged. But that doesn't wash because, to begin with, nobody seems to have any kind of alibi, and secondly someone's bound to look for the child at lunch time, and they'll find the booby trap and the marble block, the whole modus operandi will be quite plain to see. Of course, if the murderer had removed the block before the child was found, then we might have been puzzled. But as it is the whole thing just doesn't make sense."

He stretched out his hands.

"And what's your present explanation?"

"The personal element. Personal idiosyncrasy. Laurence Brown's idiosyncrasy. He doesn't like violence—he can't force himself to do physical violence. He literally couldn't have stood behind the door and socked the kid on the head. He could rig up a booby trap and go away and not see it happen."

"Yes, I see," I said slowly. "It's the eserine in the insulin bottle all over again?"

"Exactly."

"Do you think he did that without Brenda's knowing?"

"It would explain why she didn't throw away the insulin bottle. Of course, they may have fixed it up between them—or she may have thought up the poison trick all by herself—a nice easy death for her tired old husband and all for the best in the best of possible worlds! But I bet she didn't fix the booby trap. Women never have any faith in mechanical things working properly. And are they right. I think myself the eserine was her idea, but that she made her besotted slave do the switch. She's the kind that usually manages to avoid doing anything equivocable themselves. Then they keep a nice happy conscience."

He paused then went on:

"With these letters I think the D.P.P. will say we have a case. They'll take a bit of explaining away! Then, if the kid gets through all right everything in the garden will be lovely." He gave me a sideways glance. "How does it feel to be engaged to about a million pounds sterling?"

I winced. In the excitement of the last few hours, I had forgotten the developments about the will.

"Sophia doesn't know yet," I said. "Do you want me to tell her?"

"I understand Gaitskill is going to break the sad (or glad) news after the inquest tomorrow." Taverner paused and looked at me thoughtfully.

"I wonder," he said, "what the reactions will be from the family?"

CHAPTER 20

THE INQUEST went off much as I had prophesied. It was adjourned at the request of the police.

We were in good spirits for news had come through the night before from the hospital that Josephine's injuries were much less serious than had been feared and that her recovery would be rapid. For the moment, Dr. Gray said, she was to be allowed no visitors—not even her mother.

"Particularly not her mother," Sophia murmured to me. "I made that quite clear to Dr. Gray. Anyway, he knows Mother."

I must have looked rather doubtful for Sophia said sharply:

"Why the disappoving look?"

"Well—surely a mother—"

"I'm glad you've got a few nice old fashioned ideas, Charles. But you don't quite know what my mother is capable of yet. The darling can't help it, but there would simply have to be a grand dramatic scene. And dramatic scenes aren't the best things for anyone recovering from head injuries."

"You do think of everything, don't you, my sweet."

"Well, somebody's got to do the thinking now that grandfather's gone."

I looked at her speculatively. I saw that old Leonides's acumen had not deserted him. The mantle of his responsibilities was already on Sophia's shoulders.

After the inquest, Gaitskill accompanied us back to Three Gables. He cleared his throat and said pontifically:

"There is an announcement it is my duty to make to you all."

For this purpose the family assembled in Magda's drawing room. I had on this occasion the rather pleasurable sensations of the man behind the scenes. I knew in advance what Gaitskill had to say.

I prepared myself to observe the reactions of everyone.

Gaitskill was brief and dry. Any signs of personal feeling and annoyance were well held in check. He read first Aristide Leonides's letter and then the will itself.

It was very interesting to watch. I only wished my eyes could be everywhere at once.

I did not pay much attention to Brenda and Laurence. The provision for Brenda in this will was the same. I watched primarily Roger and Philip, and after them Magda and Clemency.

My first impression was that they all behaved very well.

Philip's lips were pressed closely together, his handsome head was thrown back against the tall chair in which he was sitting. He did not speak.

Magda, on the contrary, burst into speech as soon as Mr. Gaitskill finished, her rich voice surging over his thin tones like an incoming tide drowning a rivulet.

"Darling Sophia—how extraordinary. . . . How romantic. . . . Fancy old Sweetie Pie being so cunning and deceitful—just like a dear old baby. Didn't he trust us? Did he think we'd be cross? He never seemed to be fonder of Sophia than of the rest of us. But really, it's most dramatic."

Suddenly Magda jumped lightly to her feet, danced over to Sophia and swept her a very grand court curtsey.

"Madame Sophia, your penniless and broken down old mother begs you for alms." Her voice took on a cockney whine. "Spare us a copper, old dear. Your Ma wants to go to the pictures."

Her hand, crooked into a claw, twitched urgently at Sophia.

Philip, without moving, said through stiff lips:

"Please Magda, there's no call for any unnecessary clowning."

"Oh, but, Roger," cried Magda, suddenly turning to Roger. "Poor darling Roger. Sweetie was going to come to the rescue and then, before he could do it, he died. And now Roger doesn't get anything. Sophia," she turned imperiously, "you simply must do something about Roger."

"No," said Clemency. She had moved forward a step. Her face was defiant. "Nothing. Nothing at all."

Roger came shambling over to Sophia like a large amiable bear. He took her hands affectionately.

"I don't want a penny, my dear girl. As soon as this business is cleared up—or has died down, which is more what it looks like —then Clemency and I are off to the West Indies and the simple life. If I'm ever in extremis I'll apply to the head of the family—" he grinned at her engagingly—"but until then I don't want a penny. I'm a very simple person really, my dear—you ask Clemency if I'm not."

An unexpected voice broke in. It was Edith de Haviland's.

"That's all very well," she said. "But you've to pay some attention to the look of the thing. If you go bankrupt, Roger, and then slink off to the ends of the earth without Sophia's holding out a helping hand, there will be a good deal of ill natured talk that will not be pleasant for Sophia."

"What does public opinion matter?" asked Clemency scornfully.

"We know it doesn't to you, Clemency," said Edith de Haviland sharply, "but Sophia lives in this world. She's a girl with good brains and a good heart, and I've no doubt that Aristide was quite right in his selection of her to hold the family fortunes —though to pass over your two sons in their lifetime seems odd to our English ideas—but I think it would be very unfortunate if it got about that she behaved greedily over this—and had let Roger crash without trying to help him."

Roger went over to his aunt. He put his arms round her and hugged her.

"Aunt Edith," he said. "You are a darling—and a stubborn fighter, but you don't begin to understand. Clemency and I know what we want—and what we don't want!"

Clemency, a sudden spot of colour showing in each thin cheek, stood defiantly facing them.

"None of you," she said, "understand Roger. You never have! I don't suppose you ever will! Come on, Roger."

They left the room as Mr. Gaitskill began clearing his throat and arranging his papers. His countenance was one of deep approbation. He disliked the foregoing scenes very much. That was clear.

My eyes came at last to Sophia herself. She stood straight and handsome by the fireplace, her chin up, her eyes steady. She had just been left an immense fortune, but my principal thought was how alone she had suddenly become. Between her and her family a barrier had been erected. Henceforth she was divided from them, and I fancied that she already knew and faced that fact. Old Leonides had laid a burden upon her shoulders—he had been aware of that and she knew it herself. He had believed that her shoulders were strong enough to bear it, but just at this moment I felt unutterably sorry for her.

So far she had not spoken—indeed she had been given no chance, but very soon now speech would be forced from her. Already, beneath the affection of her family, I could sense latent hostility. Even in Magda's graceful playacting there had been, I fancied, a subtle malice. And there were other darker undercurrents that had not yet come to the surface.

Mr. Gaitskill's throat clearings gave way to precise and measured speech.

"Allow me to congratulate you, Sophia," he said. "You are a very wealthy woman. I should not advise any—er—precipitate action. I can advance you what ready money is needed for current expenses. If you wish to discuss future arrangements I shall be happy to give you the best advice in my power. Make an appointment with me at Lincoln's Inn when you have had plenty of time to think things over."

"Roger," began Edith de Haviland obstinately.

Mr. Gaitskill snapped in quickly.

"Roger," he said, "must fend for himself. He's a grown man—er, fifty four, I believe. And Aristide Leonides was quite right, you know. He isn't a businessman. Never will be." He looked at Sophia. "If you put Associated Catering on its legs again, don't be under any illusions that Roger can run it successfully."

"I shouldn't dream of putting Associated Catering on its legs again," said Sophia.

It was the first time she had spoken. Her voice was crisp and businesslike.

"It would be an idiotic thing to do," she added.

472

Gaitskill shot a glance at her from under his brows, and smiled to himself. Then he wished everyone goodbye and went out.

There were a few moments of silence, a realisation that the family circle was alone with itself.

Then Philip got up stiffly.

"I must get back to the library," he said. "I have lost a lot of time."

"Father—" Sophia spoke uncertainly, almost pleadingly.

I felt her quiver and draw back as Philip turned cold hostile eyes on her.

"You must forgive me for not congratulating you," he said. "But this has been rather a shock to me. I would not have believed that my father would so have humiliated me—that he would have disregarded my lifetime's devotion—yes—devotion."

For the first time, the natural man broke through the crust of icy restraint.

"My God," he cried. "How could he do this to me? He was always unfair to me—always."

"Oh no, Philip, no, you mustn't think that," cried Edith de Haviland. "Don't regard this as another slight. It isn't. When people get old, they turn naturally to a younger generation. . . . I assure you it's only that. . . . And besides, Aristide had a very keen business sense. I've often heard him say that two lots of death duties—"

"He never cared for me," said Philip. His voice was low and hoarse. "It was always Roger—Roger. Well, at least—" an extraordinary expression of spite suddenly marred his handsome features, "father realised that Roger was a fool and a failure. He cut Roger out, too."

"What about me?" said Eustace.

I had hardly noticed Eustace until now, but I perceived that he was trembling with some violent emotion. His face was crimson, there were, I thought, tears in his eyes. His voice shook as it rose hysterically.

"It's a shame!" said Eustace. "It's a damned shame! How dare Grandfather do this to me? How dare he? I was his only grandson. How dare he pass me over for Sophia? It's not fair. I hate him. I hate him. I'll never forgive him as long as I live. Beastly tyrannical old man. I wanted him to die. I wanted to get out of this house. I wanted to be my own master. And now I've got

473

to be bullied and messed around by Sophia, and made to look a fool. I wish I was dead. . . ."

His voice broke and he rushed out of the room.

Edith de Haviland gave a sharp click of her tongue.

"No self control," she murmured.

"I know just how he feels," cried Magda.

"I'm sure you do," said Edith with acidity in her tone.

"The poor sweet! I must go after him."

"Now, Magda—" Edith hurried after her.

Their voices died away. Sophia remained looking at Philip. There was, I think, a certain pleading in her glance. If so, it got no response. He looked at her coldly, quite in control of himself once more.

"You played your cards very well, Sophia," he said and went out of the room.

"That was a cruel thing to say," I cried. "Sophia—"

She stretched out her hands to me. I took her in my arms.

"This is too much for you, my sweet."

"I know just how they feel," said Sophia.

"That old devil, your grandfather, shouldn't have let you in for this."

She straightened her shoulders.

"He believed I could take it. And so I can. I wish—I wish Eustace didn't mind so much."

"He'll get over it."

"Will he? I wonder. He's the kind that broods terribly. And I hate father being hurt."

"Your mother's all right."

"She minds a bit. It goes against the grain to have to come and ask your daughter for money to put on plays. She'll be after me to put on the Edith Thompson one before you can turn round."

"And what will you say? If it keeps her happy . . ."

Sophia pulled herself right out of my arms, her head went back.

"I shall say No! It's a rotten play and mother couldn't play the part. It would be throwing the money away."

I laughed softly. I couldn't help it.

"What is it?" Sophia demanded suspiciously.

"I'm beginning to understand why your grandfather left you his money. You're a chip off the old block, Sophia."

CHAPTER 21

MY ONE FEELING of regret at this time was that Josephine was out of it all. She would have enjoyed it all so much.

Her recovery was rapid and she was expected to be back any day now, but nevertheless she missed another event of importance.

I was in the rock garden one morning with Sophia and Brenda when a car drew up to the front door. Taverner and Sergeant Lamb got out of it. They went up the steps and into the house.

Brenda stood still, staring at the car.

"It's those men," she said. "They've come back, and I thought they'd given up—I thought it was all over."

I saw her shiver.

She had joined us about ten minutes before. Wrapped in her chinchilla coat, she had said, "If I don't get some air and exercise, I shall go mad. If I go outside the gate there's always a reporter waiting to pounce on me. It's like being besieged. Will it go on for ever?"

Sophia said that she supposed the reporters would soon get tired of it.

"You can go out in the car," she added.

"I tell you I want to get some exercise."

Then she said abruptly:

"You've given Laurence the sack, Sophia. Why?"

Sophia answered quietly:

"We're making other arrangements for Eustace. And Josephine is going to Switzerland."

"Well, you've upset Laurence very much. He feels you don't trust him."

Sophia did not reply and it was at that moment that Taverner's car had arrived.

Standing there, shivering in the moist autumn air, Brenda muttered, "What do they want? Why have they come?"

I thought I knew why they had come. I had said nothing to Sophia of the letters I had found by the cistern, but I knew that they had gone to the Director of Public Prosecutions.

Taverner came out of the house again. He walked across the drive and the lawn towards us. Brenda shivered more violently.

"What does he want?" she repeated nervously. "What does he want?"

Then Taverner was with us. He spoke curtly in his official voice using the official phrases.

"I have a warrant here for your arrest—you are charged with administering eserine to Aristide Leonides on September 19th last. I must warn you that anything you say may be used in evidence at your trial."

And then Brenda went to pieces. She screamed. She clung to me. She cried out, "No, no, no, it isn't true! Charles, tell them it isn't true! I didn't do it. I didn't know anything about it. It's all a plot. Don't let them take me away. It isn't true, I tell you. . . . It isn't true. . . . I haven't done anything. . . ."

It was horrible—unbelievably horrible. I tried to soothe her, I unfastened her fingers from my arm. I told her that I would arrange for a lawyer for her—that she was to keep calm—that a lawyer would arrange everything. . . .

Taverner took her gently under the elbow.

"Come along, Mrs. Leonides," he said. "You don't want a hat, do you? No? Then we'll go off right away."

She pulled back, staring at him with enormous cat's eyes.

"Laurence," she said. "What have you done to Laurence?"

"Mr. Laurence Brown is also under arrest," said Taverner.

She wilted then. Her body seemed to collapse and shrink. The tears poured down her face. She went away quietly with Taverner across the lawn to the car. I saw Laurence Brown and Sergeant Lamb come out of the house. They all got into the car. . . . The car drove away.

I drew a deep breath and turned to Sophia. She was very pale and there was a look of distress on her face.

"It's horrible, Charles," she said. "It's quite horrible."

"I know."

"You must get her a really first class solicitor—the best there is. She—she must have all the help possible."

"One doesn't realise," I said, "what these things are like. I've never seen anyone arrested before."

"I know. One has no idea."

We were both silent. I was thinking of the desperate terror on Brenda's face. It had seemed familiar to me and suddenly I realised why. It was the same expression that I had seen on Magda Leonides's face the first day I had come to the Crooked House when she had been talking about the Edith Thompson play.

"And then," she had said, "sheer terror, don't you think so?"

Sheer terror—that was what had been on Brenda's face. Brenda was not a fighter. I wondered that she had ever had the nerve to do murder. But possibly she had not. Possibly it had been Laurence Brown, with his persecution mania, his unstable personality who had put the contents of one little bottle into another little bottle—a simple easy act—to free the woman he loved.

"So it's over," said Sophia.

She sighed deeply, then asked:

"But why arrest them now? I thought there wasn't enough evidence."

"A certain amount of evidence has come to light. Letters."

"You mean love letters between them?"

"Yes."

"What fools people are to keep these things!"

Yes, indeed. Fools. The kind of folly which never seemed to profit by the experience of others. You couldn't open a daily newspaper without coming across some instance of that folly—the passion to keep the written word, the written assurance of love.

"It's quite beastly, Sophia," I said. "But it's no good minding about it. After all, it's what we've been hoping all along, isn't it? It's what you said that first night at Mario's. You said it would be all right if the right person had killed your grandfather. Brenda was the right person, wasn't she? Brenda or Laurence?"

"Don't, Charles, you make me feel awful."

"But we must be sensible. We can marry now, Sophia. You can't hold me off any longer. The Leonides family are out of it."

She stared at me. I had never realised before the vivid blue of her eyes.

"Yes," she said. "I suppose we're out of it now. We are out of it, aren't we? You're sure?"

"My dear girl, none of you really had a shadow of motive."

Her face went suddenly white.

"Except me, Charles. I had a motive."

"Yes, of course—" I was taken aback. "But not really. You didn't know, you see, about the will."

"But I did, Charles," she whispered.

"What?" I stared at her. I felt suddenly cold.

"I knew all the time that grandfather had left his money to me."

"But how?"

"He told me. About a fortnight before he was killed. He said to me quite suddenly, 'I've left all my money to you, Sophia. You must look after the family when I'm gone.'"

I stared.

"You never told me."

"No. You see, when they all explained about the will and his signing it, I thought perhaps he had made a mistake—that he was just imagining that he had left it to me. Or that if he had made a will leaving it to me, then it had got lost and would never turn up. I didn't want it to turn up—I was afraid."

"Afraid? Why?"

"I suppose—because of murder."

I remembered the look of terror on Brenda's face—the wild unreasoning panic. I remembered the sheer panic that Magda had conjured up at will when she considered playing the part of a murderess. There would be no panic in Sophia's mind, but she was a realist, and she could see clearly enough that Leonides's will made her a suspect. I understood better now (or thought I did) her refusal to become engaged to me and her insistence that I should find out the truth. Nothing but the truth, she had said, was any good to her. I remembered the passion, the earnestness with which she had said it.

We had turned to walk towards the house and suddenly, at a certain spot, I remembered something else she had said.

She had said that she supposed she could murder someone,

but if so, she had added, it must be for something really worth while.

CHAPTER 22

ROUND A TURN of the rock garden Roger and Clemency came walking briskly towards us. Roger's flapping tweeds suited him better than his City clothes. He looked eager and excited. Clemency was frowning.

"Hullo, you two," said Roger. "At last! I thought they were never going to arrest that foul woman. What they've been waiting for, I don't know. Well, they've pinched her now, and her miserable boy friend—and I hope they hang them both."

Clemency's frown increased. She said:

"Don't be so uncivilised, Roger."

"Uncivilised? Bosh! Deliberate cold-blooded poisoning of a helpless trusting old man—and when I'm glad the murderers are caught and will pay the penalty you say I'm uncivilised! I tell you I'd willingly strangle that woman myself."

He added:

"She was with you, wasn't she, when the police came for her? How did she take it?"

"It was horrible," said Sophia in a low voice. "She was scared out of her wits."

"Serves her right."

"Don't be vindictive," said Clemency.

"Oh I know, dearest, but you can't understand. It wasn't your father. I loved my father. Don't you understand? I loved him!"

"I should understand by now," said Clemency.

Roger said to her, half jokingly:

"You've no imagination, Clemency. Suppose it had been I who had been poisoned—?"

479

I saw the quick droop of her lids, her half-clenched hands. She said sharply: "Don't say things like that even in fun."

"Never mind, darling, we'll soon be away from all this."

We moved towards the house. Roger and Sophia walked ahead and Clemency and I brought up the rear. She said:

"I suppose now—they'll let us go?"

"Are you so anxious to get off?" I asked.

"It's wearing me out."

I looked at her in surprise. She met my glance with a faint desperate smile and a nod of the head.

"Haven't you seen, Charles, that I'm fighting all the time? Fighting for my happiness. For Roger's. I've been so afraid the family would persuade him to stop in England. That we'd go on tangled up in the midst of them, stifled with family ties. I was afraid Sophia would offer him an income and that he'd stay in England because it would mean greater comfort and amenities for me. The trouble with Roger is that he will not listen. He gets ideas in his head—and they're never the right ideas. He doesn't know anything. And he's enough of a Leonides to think that happiness for a woman is bound up with comfort and money. But I will fight for my happiness—I will. I will get Roger away and give him the life that suits him where he won't feel a failure. I want him to myself—away from them all—right away. . . ."

She had spoken in a low hurried voice with a kind of desperation that startled me. I had not realised how much on edge she was. I had not realised, either, quite how desperate and possessive was her feeling for Roger.

It brought back to my mind that odd quotation of Edith de Haviland's. She had quoted the line "this side of idolatry" with a peculiar intonation. I wondered if she had been thinking of Clemency.

Roger, I thought, had loved his father better than he would ever love anyone else, better even than his wife, devoted though he was to her. I realised for the first time how urgent was Clemency's desire to get her husband to herself. Love for Roger, I saw, made up her entire existence. He was her child, as well as her husband and her lover.

A car drove up to the front door.

"Hullo," I said. "Here's Josephine back."

Josephine and Magda got out of the car. Josephine had a bandage round her head but otherwise looked remarkably well.

She said at once:

"I want to see my goldfish," and started towards us and the pond.

"Darling," cried Magda, "you'd better come in first and lie down a little, and perhaps have a little nourishing soup."

"Don't fuss, mother," said Josephine. "I'm quite all right, and I hate nourishing soup."

Magda looked irresolute. I knew that Josephine had really been fit to depart from the hospital for some days, and that it was only a hint from Taverner that had kept her there. He was taking no chances on Josephine's safety until his suspects were safe under lock and key.

I said to Magda:

"I daresay fresh air will do her good. I'll go and keep an eye on her."

I caught Josephine up before she got to the pond.

"All sorts of things have been happening while you've been away," I said.

Josephine did not reply. She peered with her short-sighted eyes into the pond.

"I don't see Ferdinand," she said.

"Which is Ferdinand?"

"The one with four tails."

"That kind is rather amusing. I like that bright gold one."

"It's quite a common one."

"I don't much care for that motheaten white one."

Josephine cast me a scornful glance.

"That's a shebunkin. They cost a lot—far more than goldfish."

"Don't you want to hear what's been happening, Josephine?"

"I expect I know about it."

"Did you know that another will has been found and that your grandfather left all his money to Sophia?"

Josephine nodded in a bored kind of way.

"Mother told me. Anyway, I knew it already."

"Do you mean you heard it in the hospital?"

"No, I mean I knew that grandfather had left his money to Sophia. I heard him tell her so."

"Were you listening again?"

"Yes. I like listening."

"It's a disgraceful thing to do, and remember this, listeners hear no good of themselves."

Josephine gave me a peculiar glance.

"I heard what he said about me to her, if that's what you mean."

She added:

"Nannie gets wild if she catches me listening at doors. She says it's not the sort of thing a little lady does."

"She's quite right."

"Pooh," said Josephine. "Nobody's a lady nowadays. They say so on the Brains Trust. They said it was—ob-so-lete." She pronounced the word carefully.

I changed the subject.

"You've got home a bit late for the big event," I said. "Chief Inspector Taverner has arrested Brenda and Laurence."

I expected that Josephine, in her character of young detective, would be thrilled by this information, but she merely repeated in her maddening bored fashion:

"Yes, I know."

"You can't know. It's only just happened."

"The car passed us on the road. Inspector Taverner and the detective with the suede shoes were inside with Brenda and Laurence, so of course I knew they must have been arrested. I hope he gave them the proper caution. You have to, you know."

I assured her that Taverner had acted strictly according to etiquette.

"I had to tell him about the letters," I said apologetically. "I found them behind the cistern. I'd have let you tell him only you were knocked out."

Josephine's hand went gingerly to her head.

"I ought to have been killed," she said with complacency. "I told you it was about the time for the second murder. The cistern was a rotten place to hide those letters. I guessed at once when I saw Laurence coming out of there one day. I mean he's not a useful kind of man who does things with ball taps, or pipes or fuses, so I knew he must have been hiding something."

"But I thought—" I broke off as Edith de Haviland's voice called authoritatively:

"Josephine. Josephine, come here at once."

Josephine sighed.

"More fuss," she said. "But I'd better go. You have to, if it's Aunt Edith."

She ran across the lawn. I followed more slowly.

After a brief interchange of words Josephine went into the house. I joined Edith de Haviland on the terrace.

This morning she looked fully her age. I was startled by the lines of weariness and suffering on her face. She looked exhausted and defeated. She saw the concern in my face and tried to smile.

"That child seems none the worse for her adventure," she said. "We must look after her better in future. Still—I suppose now it won't be necessary?"

She sighed and said:

"I'm glad it's over. But what an exhibition. If you are arrested for murder, you might at least have some dignity. I've no patience with people like Brenda who go to pieces and squeal. No guts, these people. Laurence Brown looked like a cornered rabbit."

An obscure instinct of pity rose in me.

"Poor devils," I said.

"Yes—poor devils. She'll have the sense to look after herself, I suppose? I mean the right lawyers—all that sort of thing."

It was queer, I thought, the dislike they all had for Brenda, and their scrupulous care for her to have all the advantages for defence.

Edith de Haviland went on:

"How long will it be? How long will the whole thing take?"

I said I didn't know exactly. They would be charged at the police court and presumably sent for trial. Three or four months, I estimated—and if convicted, there would be the appeal.

"Do you think they will be convicted?" she asked.

"I don't know. I don't know exactly how much evidence the police have. There are letters."

"Love letters? They were lovers then?"

"They were in love with each other."

Her face grew grimmer.

"I'm not happy about this, Charles. I don't like Brenda. In the past, I've disliked her very much. I've said sharp things about her. But now—I do feel that I want her to have every chance— every possible chance. Aristide would have wished that. I feel it's up to me to see that—that Brenda gets a square deal."

"And Laurence?"

"Oh Laurence!" she shrugged her shoulders impatiently. "Men must look after themselves. But Aristide would never forgive us if—" She left the sentence unfinished.

Then she said:

"It must be almost lunch time. We'd better go in."

I explained that I was going up to London.

"In your car?"

"Yes."

"H'm. I wonder if you'd take me with you. I gather we're allowed off the lead now."

"Of course I will, but I believe Magda and Sophia are going up after lunch. You'll be more comfortable with them than in my two seater."

"I don't want to go with them. Take me with you, and don't say much about it."

I was surprised, but I did as she asked. We did not speak much on the way to town. I asked her where I should put her down.

"Harley Street."

I felt some faint apprehension, but I didn't like to say anything. She continued:

"No, it's too early. Drop me at Debenhams. I can have some lunch there and go to Harley Street afterwards."

"I hope—" I began and stopped.

"That's why I didn't want to go up with Magda. She dramatises things. Lot of fuss."

"I'm very sorry," I said.

"You needn't be. I've had a good life. A very good life." She gave a sudden grin. "And it's not over yet."

CHAPTER 23

I HAD NOT seen my father for some days. I found him busy with things other than the Leonides case, and I went in search of Taverner.

Taverner was enjoying a short spell of leisure and was willing to come out and have a drink with me. I congratulated him on having cleared up the case and he accepted my congratulations, but his manner remained far from jubilant.

"Well, that's over," he said. "We've got a case. Nobody can deny that we've got a case."

"Do you think you'll get a conviction?"

"Impossible to say. The evidence is circumstantial—it nearly always is in a murder case—bound to be. A lot depends on the impression they make on the jury."

"How far do the letters go?"

"At first sight, Charles, they're pretty damning. There are references to their life together when her husband's dead. Phrases like—'it won't be long now.' Mind you, defence counsel will try and twist it the other way—the husband was so old that of course they could reasonably expect him to die. There's no actual mention of poisoning—not down in black or white—but there are some passages that could mean that. It depends what judge we get. If it's old Carberry he'll be down on them all through. He's always very righteous about illicit love. I suppose they'll have Eagles or Humphrey Kerr for the defence—Humphrey is magnificent in these cases—but he likes a gallant war record or something of that kind to help him do his stuff. A conscientious objector is going to cramp his style. The question is going to be will the jury like them? You can never tell with juries. You know, Charles, those two are not really sympathetic characters. She's a good looking woman who married a very old man

485

for his money, and Brown is a neurotic conscientious objector. The crime is so familiar—so according to pattern that you can't really believe they didn't do it. Of course, they may decide that he did it and she knew nothing about it—or alternatively that she did it, and he didn't know about it—or they may decide that they were both in it together."

"And what do you yourself think?" I asked.

He looked at me with a wooden expressionless face.

"I don't think anything. I've turned in the facts and they went to the D.P.P. and it was decided that there was a case. That's all. I've done my duty and I'm out of it. So now you know, Charles."

But I didn't know. I saw that for some reason Taverner was unhappy.

It was not until three days later that I unburdened myself to my father. He himself had never mentioned the case to me. There had been a kind of restraint between us—and I thought I knew the reason for it. But I had to break down that barrier.

"We've got to have this out," I said. "Taverner's not satisfied that those two did it—and you're not satisfied either."

My father shook his head. He said what Taverner had said:

"It's out of our hands. There is a case to answer. No question about that."

"But you don't—Taverner doesn't—think that they're guilty?"

"That's for a jury to decide."

"For God's sake," I said, "don't put me off with technical terms. What do you think—both of you—personally?"

"My personal opinion is no better than yours, Charles."

"Yes, it is. You've more experience."

"Then I'll be honest with you. I just—don't know!"

"They could be guilty?"

"Oh yes."

"But you don't feel sure that they are?"

My father shrugged his shoulders.

"How can one be sure?"

"Don't fence with me, dad. You've been sure other times, haven't you? Dead sure? No doubt in your mind at all?"

"Sometimes, yes. Not always."

"I wish to God you were sure this time."

"So do I."

486

We were silent. I was thinking of those two figures drifting in from the garden in the dusk. Lonely and haunted and afraid. They had been afraid from the start. Didn't that show a guilty conscience?

But I answered myself: "Not necessarily." Both Brenda and Laurence were afraid of life—they had no confidence in themselves, in their ability to avoid danger and defeat, and they could see, only too clearly, the pattern of illicit love leading to murder which might involve them at any moment.

My father spoke, and his voice was grave and kind:

"Come, Charles," he said, "let's face it. You've still got it in your mind, haven't you, that one of the Leonides family is the real culprit?"

"Not really. I only wonder—"

"You do think so. You may be wrong, but you do think so."

"Yes," I said.

"Why?"

"Because—" I thought about it, trying to see clearly—to bring my wits to bear—"because" (yes, that was it) "because they think so themselves."

"They think so themselves? That's interesting. That's very interesting. Do you mean that they all suspect each other, or that they know, actually, who did do it."

"I'm not sure," I said. "It's all very nebulous and confused. I think—on the whole—that they try to cover up the knowledge from themselves."

My father nodded.

"Not Roger," I said. "Roger wholeheartedly believes it was Brenda and he wholeheartedly wants her hanged. It's—it's a relief to be with Roger because he's simple and positive, and hasn't any reservations in the back of his mind.

"But the others are apologetic, they're uneasy—they urge me to be sure that Brenda has the best defence—that every possible advantage is given her—why?"

My father answered:

"Because they don't really, in their hearts, believe she is guilty. . . . Yes, that's sound."

Then he asked quietly:

"Who could have done it? You've talked to them all? Who's the best bet?"

"I don't know," I said. "And it's driving me frantic. None of them fits your 'sketch of a murderer' and yet I feel—I do feel—that one of them is a murderer."

"Sophia?"

"No. Good God, no!"

"The possibility's in your mind, Charles—yes, it is, don't deny it. All the more potently because you won't acknowledge it. What about the others? Philip?"

"Only for the most fantastic motive."

"Motives can be fantastic—or they can be absurdly slight. What's his motive?"

"He is bitterly jealous of Roger—always has been all his life. His father's preference for Roger drove Philip in upon himself. Roger was about to crash, then the old man heard of it. He promised to put Roger on his feet again. Supposing Philip learnt that. If the old man died that night there would be no assistance for Roger. Roger would be down and out. Oh! I know it's absurd—"

"Oh no, it isn't. It's abnormal, but it happens. It's human. What about Magda?"

"She's rather childish. She—gets things out of proportion. But I would never have thought twice about her being involved if it hadn't been for the sudden way she wanted to pack Josephine off to Switzerland. I couldn't help feeling she was afraid of something that Josephine knew or might say . . ."

"And then Josephine was conked on the head?"

"Well, that couldn't be her mother!"

"Why not?"

"But, dad, a mother wouldn't—"

"Charles, Charles, don't you ever read the police news. Again and again a mother takes a dislike to one of her children. Only one—she may be devoted to the others. There's some association, some reason, but it's often hard to get at. But when it exists, it's an unreasoning aversion, and it's very strong."

"She called Josephine a changeling," I admitted unwillingly.

"Did the child mind?"

"I don't think so."

"Who else is there? Roger?"

"Roger didn't kill his father. I'm quite sure of that."

"Wash out Roger then. His wife—what's her name—Clemency?"

488

"Yes," I said. "If she killed old Leonides it was for a very odd reason."

I told him of my conversations with Clemency. I said I thought it possible that in her passion to get Roger away from England she might have deliberately poisoned the old man.

"She'd persuaded Roger to go without telling his father. Then the old man found out. He was going to back up Associated Catering. All Clemency's hopes and plans were frustrated. And she really does care desperately for Roger—beyond idolatry."

"You're repeating what Edith de Haviland said!"

"Yes. And Edith's another who I think—might have done it. But I don't know why. I can only believe that for what she considered good and sufficient reason she might take the law into her own hand. She's that kind of a person."

"And she also was very anxious that Brenda should be adequately defended?"

"Yes. That, I suppose, might be conscience. I don't think for a moment that if she did do it, she intended them to be accused of the crime."

"Probably not. But would she knock out the child Josephine?"

"No," I said slowly, "I can't believe that. Which reminds me that there's something that Josephine said to me that keeps nagging at my mind, and I can't remember what it is. It's slipped my memory. But it's something that doesn't fit in where it should. If only I could remember—"

"Never mind. It will come back. Anything or anyone else on your mind?"

"Yes," I said. "Very much so. How much do you know about infantile paralysis. Its after effects on character, I mean?"

"Eustace?"

"Yes. The more I think about it, the more it seems to me that Eustace might fit the bill. His dislikes and resentment against his grandfather. His queerness and moodiness. He's not normal."

"He's the only one of the family who I can see knocking out Josephine quite callously if she knew something about him—and she's quite likely to know. That child knows everything. She writes it down in a little book—"

I stopped.

"Good Lord," I said. "What a fool I am."

"What's the matter?"

"I know now what was wrong. We assumed, Taverner and I, that the wrecking of Josephine's room, the frantic search, was for those letters. I thought that she'd got hold of them and that she'd hidden them up in the cistern room. But when she was talking to me the other day she made it quite clear that it was Laurence who had hidden them there. She saw him coming out of the cistern room and went snooping around and found the letters. Then, of course she read them. She would! But she left them where they were."

"Well?"

"Don't you see? It couldn't have been the letters someone was looking for in Josephine's room. It must have been something else."

"And that something—"

"Was the little black book she writes down her 'detection' in. That's what someone was looking for! I think, too, that whoever it was didn't find it. I think Josephine has it. But if so—"

I half rose.

"If so," said my father, "she still isn't safe. Is that what you were going to say?"

"Yes. She won't be out of danger until she's actually started for Switzerland. They're planning to send her there, you know."

"Does she want to go?"

I considered.

"I don't think she does."

"Then she probably hasn't gone," said my father drily. "But I think you're right about the danger. You'd better go down there."

"Eustace?" I cried desperately. "Clemency?"

My father said gently:

"To my mind the facts point clearly in one direction. . . . I wonder you don't see it yourself. I . . ."

Glover opened the door.

"Beg pardon, Mr. Charles, the telephone. Miss Leonides speaking from Swinly. It's urgent."

It seemed like a horrible repetition. Had Josephine again fallen a victim. And had the murderer this time made no mistake? . . .

I hurried to the telephone.

"Sophia? It's Charles here."

Sophia's voice came with a kind of hard desperation in it.

"Charles, it isn't all over. The murderer is still here."

"What on earth do you mean? What's wrong? Is it—Josephine?"

"It's not Josephine. It's Nannie."

"Nannie?"

"Yes, there was some cocoa—Josephine's cocoa, she didn't drink it. She left it on the table. Nannie thought it was a pity to waste it. So she drank it."

"Poor Nannie. Is she very bad?"

Sophia's voice broke.

"Oh, Charles, she's dead."

CHAPTER 24

WE WERE back again in the nightmare.

That is what I thought as Taverner and I drove out of London. It was a repetition of our former journey.

At intervals, Taverner swore.

As for me, I repeated from time to time, stupidly, unprofitably:

"So it wasn't Brenda and Laurence. It wasn't Brenda and Laurence."

Had I ever really thought it was? I had been so glad to think it. So glad to escape from other, more sinister, possibilities . . .

They had fallen in love with each other. They had written silly sentimental romantic letters to each other. They had indulged in hopes that Brenda's old husband might soon die peacefully and happily—but I wondered really if they had even acutely desired his death. I had a feeling that the despairs and longings of an unhappy love affair suited them as well or better than commonplace married life together. I didn't think Brenda was really passionate. She was too anaemic, too apathetic. It was romance she craved for. And I thought Laurence, too, was the type to enjoy frustration and vague future dreams of bliss rather than the concrete satisfactions of the flesh.

They had been caught in a trap and, terrified, they had not had the wit to find their way out. Laurence with incredible stupidity, had not even destroyed Brenda's letters. Presumably Brenda had destroyed his, since they had not been found. And it was not Laurence who had balanced the marble door stop on the wash house door. It was someone else whose face was still hidden behind a mask.

We drove up to the door. Taverner got out and I followed him. There was a plain clothes man in the hall whom I didn't know. He saluted Taverner and Taverner drew him aside.

My attention was taken by a pile of luggage in the hall. It was labelled and ready for departure. As I looked at it Clemency came down the stairs and through the open door at the bottom. She was dressed in her same red dress with a tweed coat over it and a red felt hat.

"You're in time to say goodbye, Charles," she said.

"You're leaving?"

"We go to London tonight. Our plane goes early tomorrow morning."

She was quiet and smiling, but I thought her eyes were watchful.

"But surely you can't go now?"

"Why not?" Her voice was hard.

"With this death—"

"Nannie's death has nothing to do with us."

"Perhaps not. But all the same—"

"Why do you say 'perhaps not'? It has nothing to do with us. Roger and I have been upstairs, finishing packing up. We did not come down at all during the time that the cocoa was left on the hall table."

"Can you prove that?"

"I can answer for Roger. And Roger can answer for me."

"No more than that . . . You're man and wife, remember."

Her anger flamed out.

"You're impossible, Charles! Roger and I are going away—to lead our own life. Why on earth should we want to poison a nice stupid old woman who had never done us any harm?"

"It mightn't have been her you meant to poison."

"Still less are we likely to poison a child."

"It depends rather on the child, doesn't it?"

"What do you mean?"

"Josephine isn't quite the ordinary child. She knows a good deal about people. She—"

I broke off. Josephine had emerged from the door leading to the drawing room. She was eating the inevitable apple, and over its round rosiness her eyes sparkled with a kind of ghoulish enjoyment.

"Nannie's been poisoned," she said. "Just like grandfather. It's awfully exciting, isn't it?"

"Aren't you at all upset about it?" I demanded severely. "You were fond of her, weren't you?"

"Not particularly. She was always scolding me about something or other. She fussed."

"Are you fond of anybody, Josephine?" asked Clemency.

Josephine turned her ghoulish eyes towards Clemency.

"I love Aunt Edith," she said. "I love Aunt Edith very much. And I could love Eustace, only he's always such a beast to me and won't be interested in finding out who did all this."

"You'd better stop finding things out, Josephine," I said. "It isn't very safe."

"I don't need to find out any more," said Josephine. "I know."

There was a moment's silence. Josephine's eyes, solemn and unwinking, were fixed on Clemency. A sound like a long sigh, reached my ears. I swung sharply round. Edith de Haviland stood half way down the staircase—but I did not think it was she who had sighed. The sound had come from behind the door through which Josephine had just come.

I stepped sharply across to it and yanked it open. There was no one to be seen.

Nevertheless I was seriously disturbed. Someone had stood just within that door and had heard those words of Josephine's. I went back and took Josephine by the arm. She was eating her apple and staring stolidly at Clemency. Behind the solemnity there was, I thought, a certain malignant satisfaction.

"Come on, Josephine," I said. "We're going to have a little talk."

I think Josephine might have protested, but I was not standing any nonsense. I ran her along forcibly into her own part of the house. There was a small unused morning room where we could be reasonably sure of being undisturbed. I took her in there, closed the door firmly, and made her sit on a chair. I took another chair and drew it forward so that I faced her.

"Now, Josephine," I said, "we're going to have a show down. What exactly do you know?"

"Lots of things."

"That I have no doubt about. That noodle of yours is probably crammed to overflowing with relevant and irrelevant information. But you know perfectly what I mean. Don't you?"

"Of course I do. I'm not stupid."

I didn't know whether the disparagement was for me or the police, but I paid no attention to it and went on:

"You know who put something in your cocoa?"

Josephine nodded.

"You know who poisoned your grandfather?"

Josephine nodded again.

"And who knocked you on the head?"

Again Josephine nodded.

"Then you're going to come across with what you know. You're going to tell me all about it—now."

"Shan't."

"You've got to. Every bit of information you've got or ferret out has got to be given to the police."

"I won't tell the police anything. They're stupid. They thought Brenda had done it—or Laurence. I wasn't stupid like that. I knew jolly well they hadn't done it. I've had an idea who it was all along, and then I made a kind of test—and now I know I'm right."

She finished on a triumphant note.

I prayed to Heaven for patience and started again.

"Listen, Josephine, I daresay you're extremely clever—" Josephine looked gratified. "But it won't be much good to you to be clever if you're not alive to enjoy the fact. Don't you see, you little fool, that as long as you keep your secrets in this silly way you're in imminent danger?"

Josephine nodded approvingly.

"Of course I am."

"Already you've had two very narrow escapes. One attempt nearly did for you. The other has cost somebody else their life. Don't you see if you go on strutting about the house and proclaiming at the top of your voice you know who the killer is, there will be more attempts made—and that either you'll die or somebody else will?"

"In some books person after person is killed," Josephine informed

494

me with gusto. "You end by spotting the murderer because he or she is practically the only person left."

"This isn't a detective story. This is Three Gables, Swinly Dean, and you're a silly little girl who's read more than is good for her. I'll make you tell me what you know if I have to shake you till your teeth rattle."

"I could always tell you something that wasn't true."

"You could, but you won't. What are you waiting for, anyway?"

"You don't understand," said Josephine. "Perhaps I may never tell. You see, I might be—fond of the person."

She paused as though to let this sink in.

"And if I do tell," she went on, "I shall do it properly. I shall have everybody sitting round, and then I'll go over it all—with the clues, and then I shall say, quite suddenly:

"And it was you . . ."

She thrust out a dramatic forefinger just as Edith de Haviland entered the room.

"Put that core in the waste paper basket, Josephine," said Edith. "Have you got a handkerchief? Your fingers are sticky. I'm taking you out in the car." Her eyes met mine with significance as she said: "She'll be safer out of here for the next hour or so." As Josephine looked mutinous, Edith added: "We'll go into Longbridge and have an ice cream soda."

Josephine's eyes brightened and she said: "Two."

"Perhaps," said Edith. "Now go and get your hat and coat on and your dark blue scarf. It's cold out today. Charles, you had better go with her while she gets them. Don't leave her. I have just a couple of notes to write."

She sat down at the desk, and I escorted Josephine out of the room. Even without Edith's warning, I would have stuck to Josephine like a leech.

I was convinced that there was danger to the child very near at hand.

As I finished superintending Josephine's toilet, Sophia came into the room. She seemed astonished to see me.

"Why, Charles, have you turned nursemaid? I didn't know you were here."

"I'm going in to Longbridge with Aunt Edith," said Josephine importantly. "We're going to have icecreams."

"Brrrr, on a day like this?"

"Ice cream sodas are always lovely," said Josephine. "When you're cold inside, it makes you feel hotter outside."

Sophia frowned. She looked worried, and I was shocked by her pallor and the circles under her eyes.

We went back to the morning room. Edith was just blotting a couple of envelopes. She got up briskly.

"We'll start now," she said. "I told Evans to bring round the Ford."

She swept out to the hall. We followed her.

My eye was again caught by the suitcases and their blue labels. For some reason they aroused in me a vague disquietude.

"It's quite a nice day," said Edith de Haviland, pulling on her gloves and glancing up at the sky. The Ford 10 was waiting in front of the house. "Cold—but bracing. A real English autumn day. How beautiful trees look with their bare branches against the sky— and just a golden leaf or two still hanging . . ."

She was silent a moment or two, then she turned and kissed Sophia.

"Goodbye, dear," she said. "Don't worry too much. Certain things have to be faced and endured."

Then she said, "Come, Josephine," and got into the car. Josephine climbed in beside her.

They both waved as the car drove off.

"I suppose she's right, and it's better to keep Josephine out of this for a while. But we've got to make that child tell what she knows, Sophia."

"She probably doesn't know anything. She's just showing off. Josephine likes to make herself look important, you know."

"It's more than that. Do they know what poison it was in the cocoa?"

"They think it's digitalin. Aunt Edith takes digitalin for her heart. She has a whole bottle full of little tablets up in her room. Now the bottle's empty."

"She ought to keep things like that locked up."

"She did. I suppose it wouldn't be difficult for someone to find out where she hid the key."

"Someone? Who?" I looked again at the pile of luggage. I said suddenly and loudly:

"They can't go away. They mustn't be allowed to."

Sophia looked surprised.

496

"Roger and Clemency? Charles, you don't think—"

"Well, what do you think?"

Sophia stretched out her hands in a helpless gesture.

"I don't know, Charles," she whispered. "I only know that I'm back—back in the nightmare—"

"I know. Those were the very words I used to myself as I drove down with Taverner."

"Because this is just what a nightmare is. Walking about among people you know, looking in their faces—and suddenly the faces change—and it's not someone you know any longer—it's a stranger —a cruel stranger. . . ."

She cried:

"Come outside, Charles—come outside. It's safer outside . . . I'm afraid to stay in this house. . . ."

CHAPTER 25

WE STAYED in the garden a long time. By a kind of tacit consent, we did not discuss the horror that was weighing upon us. Instead Sophia talked affectionately of the dead woman, of things they had done, and games they had played as children with Nannie—and tales that the old woman used to tell them about Roger and their father and the other brothers and sisters.

"They were her real children, you see. She only came back to us to help during the war when Josephine was a baby and Eustace was a funny little boy."

There was a certain balm for Sophia in these memories and I encouraged her to talk.

I wondered what Taverner was doing. Questioning the household, I suppose. A car drove away with the police photographer and two other men, and presently an ambulance drove up.

Sophia shivered a little. Presently the ambulance left and we knew that Nannie's body had been taken away in preparation for an autopsy.

And still we sat or walked in the garden and talked—our words becoming more and more of a cloak for our real thoughts.

Finally, with a shiver, Sophia said:

"It must be very late—it's almost dark. We've got to go in. Aunt Edith and Josephine haven't come back . . . Surely they ought to be back by now?"

A vague uneasiness woke in me. What had happened? Was Edith deliberately keeping the child away from the Crooked House?

We went in. Sophia drew all the curtains. The fire was lit and the big drawing room looked harmonious with an unreal air of bygone luxury. Great bowls of bronze chrysanthemums stood on the tables.

Sophia rang and a maid who I recognised as having been formerly upstairs brought in tea. She had red eyes and sniffed continuously. Also I noticed that she had a frightened way of glancing quickly over her shoulder.

Magda joined us, but Philip's tea was sent in to him in the library. Magda's role was a stiff frozen image of grief. She spoke little or not at all. She said once:

"Where are Edith and Josephine? They're out very late."

But she said it in a preoccupied kind of way.

But I myself was becoming increasingly uneasy. I asked if Taverner were still in the house and Magda replied that she thought so. I went in search of him. I told him that I was worried about Miss de Haviland and the child.

He went immediately to the telephone and gave certain instructions.

"I'll let you know when I have news," he said.

I thanked him and went back to the drawing room. Sophia was there with Eustace. Magda had gone.

"He'll let us know if he hears anything," I said to Sophia.

She said in a low voice:

"Something's happened, Charles, something must have happened."

"My dear Sophia, it's not really late yet."

"What are you bothering about?" said Eustace. "They've probably gone to the cinema."

He lounged out of the room. I said to Sophia: "She may have

taken Josephine to a hotel—or up to London. I think she fully realised that the child was in danger—perhaps she realised it better
than we did."

Sophia replied with a sombre look that I could not quite fathom.
"She kissed me goodbye. . . ."

I did not see quite what she meant by that disconnected remark,
or what it was supposed to show. I asked if Magda was worried.

"Mother? No, she's all right. She's no sense of time. She's reading
a new play of Vavasour Jones called 'The Woman Disposes'. It's a
funny play about murder—a female Bluebeard—cribbed from 'Arsenic and Old Lace' if you ask me, but it's got a good woman's
part, a woman who's got a mania for being a widow."

I said no more. We sat, pretending to read.

It was half past six when Taverner opened the door and came
in. His face prepared us for what he had to say.

Sophia got up.

"Yes?" she said.

"I'm sorry. I've got bad news for you. I sent out a general alarm
for the car. A motorist reported having seen a Ford car with a
number something like that turning off the main road at Flackspur Heath—through the woods."

"Not—the track to the Flackspur Quarry?"

"Yes, Miss Leonides." He paused and went on: "The car's been
found in the quarry. Both the occupants were dead. You'll be glad
to know they were killed outright."

"Josephine!" It was Magda standing in the doorway. Her voice
rose in a wail. "Josephine . . . My baby."

Sophia went to her and put her arms round her. I said: "Wait
a minute."

I had remembered something! Edith de Haviland writing a
couple of letters at the desk, going out into the hall with them
in her hand.

But they had not been in her hand when she got into the car.

I dashed out into the hall and went to the long oak chest.
I found the letters—pushed inconspicuously to the back behind
a brass tea urn.

The uppermost was addressed to Chief Inspector Taverner.

Taverner had followed me. I handed the letter to him and he
tore it open. Standing beside him I read its brief contents.

499

My expectation is that this will be opened after my death. I wish to enter into no details, but I accept full responsibility for the deaths of my brother-in-law Aristide Leonides and Janet Rowe (Nannie). I hereby solemnly declare that Brenda Leonides and Laurence Brown are innocent of the murder of Aristide Leonides. Enquiry of Dr Michael Chavasse, 783 Harley Street will confirm that my life could only have been prolonged for a few months. I prefer to take this way out and to spare two innocent people the ordeal of being charged with a murder they did not commit. I am of sound mind and fully conscious of what I write.
            Edith Elfrida de Haviland.

As I finished the letter I was aware that Sophia, too, had read it—whether with Taverner's concurrence or not, I don't know.

"Aunt Edith . . ." murmured Sophia.

I remembered Edith de Haviland's ruthless foot grinding bindweed into the earth. I remembered my early, almost fanciful, suspicions of her. But why—

Sophia spoke the thought in my mind before I came to it.

"But why Josephine? Why did she take Josephine with her?"

"Why did she do it at all?" I demanded. "What was her motive?"

But even as I said that, I knew the truth. I saw the whole thing clearly. I realised that I was still holding her second letter in my hand. I looked down and saw my own name on it.

It was thicker and harder than the other one. I think I knew what was in it before I opened it. I tore the envelope along and Josephine's little black notebook fell out. I picked it up off the floor—it came open in my hand and I saw the entry on the first page . . .

Sounding from a long way away, I heard Sophia's voice, clear and self controlled.

"We've got it all wrong," she said. "Edith didn't do it."

"No," I said.

Sophia came closer to me—she whispered:

"It was—Josephine—wasn't it? That was it, Josephine."

Together we looked down on the first entry in the little black book, written in an unformed childish hand.

"Today I killed grandfather."

CHAPTER 26

I WAS to wonder afterwards that I could have been so blind. The truth had stuck out so clearly all along. Josephine and only Josephine fitted in with all the necessary qualifications. Her vanity, her persistent self importance, her delight in talking, her reiteration on how clever she was, and how stupid the police were.

I had never considered her because she was a child. But children have committed murders, and this particular murder had been well within a child's compass. Her grandfather himself had indicated the precise method—he had practically handed her a blue print. All she had to do was to avoid leaving fingerprints and the slightest knowledge of detective fiction would teach her that. And everything else had been a mere hotch potch, culled at random from stock mystery stories. The notebook—the sleuthing—her pretended suspicions, her insistence that she was not going to tell till she was sure. . . .

And finally the attack on herself. An almost incredible performance considering that she might easily have killed herself. But then, childlike, she never considered such a possibility. She was the heroine. The heroine isn't killed. Yet there had been a clue there—the traces of earth on the seat of the old chair in the wash house. Josephine was the only person who would have had to climb up on a chair to balance the block of marble on the top of the door. Obviously it had missed her more than once, (the dints in the floor) and patiently she had climbed up again and replaced it, handling it with her scarf to avoid fingerprints. And then it had fallen—and she had had a near escape from death.

It had been the perfect set up—the impression she was aiming for! She was in danger, she "knew something," she had been attacked!

I saw how that had deliberately drawn my attention to her

presence in the cylinder room. And she had completed the artistic disorder of her room before going out to the wash house.

But when she had returned from hospital, when she had found Brenda and Laurence arrested, she must have become dissatisfied. The case was over—and she—Josephine, was out of the lime light.

So she stole the digitalin from Edith's room and put it in her own cup of cocoa and left the cup untouched on the hall table.

Did she know that Nannie would drink it? Possibly. From her words that morning, she had resented Nannie's criticisms of her. Did Nannie, perhaps, wise from a lifetime of experience with children, suspect? I think that Nannie knew, had always known, that Josephine was not normal. With her precocious mental development had gone a retarded moral sense. Perhaps, too, the various factors of heredity—what Sophia had called the "ruthlessness" of the family had met together.

She had had an authoritarian ruthlessness of her grandmother's family, and the ruthless egoism of Magda, seeing only her own point of view. She had also presumably suffered, sensitive like Philip, from the stigma of being the unattractive—the changeling child—of the family. Finally, in her very marrow, had run the essential crooked strain of old Leonides. She had been Leonides's grandchild, she had resembled him in brain and in cunning—but his love had gone outwards to family and friends, hers had turned to herself.

I thought that old Leonides had realised what none of the rest of the family had realised, that Josephine might be a source of danger to others and to herself. He had kept her from school life because he was afraid of what she might do. He had shielded her, and guarded her in the home, and I understood now his urgency to Sophia to look after Josephine.

Magda's sudden decision to send Josephine abroad had that, too, been due to a fear for the child? Not, perhaps, a conscious fear, but some vague maternal instinct.

And Edith de Haviland? Had she first suspected, then feared—and finally known?

I looked down at the letter in my hand.

Dear Charles. This is in confidence for you—and for Sophia if you so decide. It is imperative that someone should know the truth. I found the enclosed in the disused dog kennel outside the back door. She kept it there. It confirms what I already suspected. The action I am about to take may be right or wrong—I do not know. But my life, in any case, is close to its end, and I do not want the child to suffer as I believe she would suffer if called to earthly account for what she has done.

There is often one of the litter who is "not quite right".

If I do wrong, God forgive me—but I do it out of love. God bless you both.

Edith de Haviland.

I hesitated for only a moment, then I handed the letter to Sophia. Together we again opened Josephine's little black book.

Today I killed grandfather.

We turned the pages. It was an amazing production. Interesting, I should imagine, to a psychologist. It set out, with such terrible clarity, the fury of thwarted egoism. The motive for the crime was set down, pitifully childish and inadequate.

Grandfather wouldn't let me do bally dancing so I made up my mind I would kill him. Then we would go to London and live and mother wouldn't mind me doing bally.

I give only a few entries. They are all significant.

I don't want to go to Switzerland—I won't go. If mother makes me I will kill her too—only I can't get any poison. Perhaps I could make it with youberries. They are poisonous, the book says so.
Eustace has made me very cross to day. He says I am only a girl and no use and that its silly my detecting. He wouldnt think me silly if he knew it was me did the murder.
I like Charles—but he is rather stupid. I have not decided yet who I shall make have done the crime. Perhaps Brenda and Laurence—Brenda is nasty to me—she says I am not all there but I like Laurence—he told me about Charlot Korday—she killed someone in his bath. She was not very clever about it.

The last entry was revealing.

I hate Nannie . . . I hate her . . . I hate her . . . She says I am only a little girl. She says I show off. She's making mother send me abroad . . . I'm going to kill her too—I think Aunt

Edith's medcine would do it. If there is another murder, then the police will come back and it will all be exciting again.

Nannie's dead. I am glad. I haven't decided yet where I'll hide the bottle with the little pill things. Perhaps in Aunt Clemency's room—or else Eustace. When I am dead as an old woman I shall leave this behind me addressed to the Chief of the Police and they will see what a really great criminal I was.

I closed the book. Sophia's tears were flowing fast.

"Oh Charles—oh Charles—it's so dreadful. She's such a little monster—and yet—and yet it's so terribly pathetic."

I had felt the same.

I had liked Josephine . . . I still felt a fondness for her . . . You do not like anyone less because they have tuberculosis or some other fatal disease. Josephine was, as Sophia had said, a little monster, but she was a pathetic little monster. She had been born with a kink—the crooked child of the little crooked house.

Sophia asked:

"If—she had lived—what would have happened?"

"I suppose she would have been sent to a reformatory or a special school. Later she would have been released—or possibly certified, I don't know."

Sophia shuddered.

"It's better the way it is. But Aunt Edith—I don't like to think of her taking the blame."

"She chose to do so. I don't suspose it will be made public. I imagine that when Brenda and Laurence come to trial, no case will be brought against them and they will be discharged.

"And you, Sophia," I said, this time on a different note and taking both her hands in mine, "will marry me. I've just heard I'm appointed to Persia. We will go out there together, and you will forget the little Crooked House. Your mother can put on plays and your father can buy more books and Eustace will soon go to a university. Don't worry about them any more. Think of me."

Sophia looked at me straight in the eyes.

"Aren't you afraid, Charles, to marry me?"

"Why should I be? In poor little Josephine all the worst of the family came together. In you, Sophia, I fully believe that all that is bravest and best in the Leonides family has been handed down to you. Your grandfather thought highly of you and he seems to have been a man who was usually right. Hold up your head, my darling. The future is ours."

"I will, Charles. I love you and I'll marry you and make you happy." She looked down at the notebook. "Poor Josephine."

"Poor Josephine," I said.

"What's the truth of it, Charles?" said my father.

I never lie to the Old Man.

"It wasn't Edith de Haviland, sir," I said. "It was Josephine."

My father nodded his head gently.

"Yes," he said. "I've thought so for some time. Poor child . . ."